ISBN: 9798631156395

Cover Artist: Cath Grace Designs

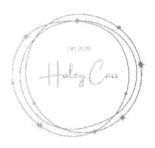

Other books by Haley Cass

When You Least Expect It

Better Than Expected

In the Long Run

Down to A Science

Dedication & Acknowledgements

This book would not exist (and most certainly not in the same form) without Kate, Elizabeth, Kuver, and Sam. Thank you for letting me scream about this for what seems like decades.

And a huge thank you to everyone who has read this, my first official novel, at any point in the making and thought it had the potential to be… this.

Chapter 1

"If you're waiting for a beautiful woman to come out of nowhere and sweep you off your feet, you're going to be waiting forever," Regan stated as factually as if she was reading it from a manual.

Sutton Spencer rolled her eyes. "I'm not waiting for *anyone* to sweep me off of my feet."

Maybe she had been, once upon a time. But that was a while – and several big romantic mistakes – ago.

With that, she slid off the stool at the breakfast bar in their shared apartment and went to sit on the couch, balancing the bowl of cereal she was having for dinner on her lap. She could still feel her best friend's incredulous stare from the other side of the room.

"Sutton, you haven't even been on a date in almost a year."

"I've been busy," she mumbled, even as she ducked her head.

Her friend flopped down onto the couch next to her with a sigh. "I'll give you time off after being with Joshua. He was nuts." The reference to Sutton's controlling, emotionally manipulative ex-boyfriend was an understatement to say the least. "But you haven't even gone out with *me* just to have fun in months – you refused to come out to the bar tonight! And you've been like this ever since you had your whole *revelation*."

Sutton could feel her cheeks burning annoyingly hotter and she knew they were as red as her hair as she shot Regan a glare. "I hate when you call it that. I just don't want to go out; it has nothing to do with my . . . self-discovery."

She also hated that she didn't have a better word to use.

"Yeah, well, you're becoming a hermit. You're sitting here on a Friday night, already in some pajama shorts, ready to – what, watch TV?" She fell back against the cushion with a groan. "You used to be slightly more fun."

"I'm not going to watch TV, I'll watch a movie."

Regan nailed her with a look. "You haven't gone out with a romantic intention since you came to terms with being into women. And if you think I don't know it's just because you're scared, then I'm honestly insulted that you think I don't know you at all."

Sutton supposed twenty years of friendship gave Regan an insight to her that was almost too good.

"What's the point of stepping out of the closet if you're too much of a chicken shit to go on a date with a woman?" Regan looked genuinely quizzical, which made the sarcastic remark die on Sutton's lips.

It was hard to describe, really.

Sutton *wasn't* in the closet. After a woman had danced – grinded, really – against her in a way that had surprisingly made arousal curl low in her stomach, and had then initiated a kiss in the club that Regan had dragged her to after her finals last spring, Sutton had spent the summer agonizing over her sexuality. She'd never thought of herself as anything other than straight, before. Because she'd always liked boys, and she liked to kiss boys, and she liked the way they felt. Then there had been the dancing and that kiss, and she'd liked that, too.

She'd *really* liked it.

As the summer had gone on, Sutton finally admitted to herself that she liked girls, too. After months of poring over websites and dipping her toe into some lesbian fiction, Sutton's sexuality clicked together like a puzzle she'd never even known wasn't solved.

As someone who had never had debilitating shyness when it came to talking to a woman, it turned out that approaching a woman when she knowingly attracted to her was very difficult.

She placed her bowl down on the table before she settled back and admitted, "Fine. I might be scared."

Might be, as in the idea of going out with a woman made her stomach flip-flop so intensely she thought she might vomit. It was both fear and excitement, but still.

Regan gave her a sympathetic look before she turned her attention to the phone in her lap and Sutton was grateful that the subject seemed to be dropped. Not that she thought it would be dropped for long, considering when Regan got her teeth into something, she held on tight.

Tonight, though, she was happy to relax and watch a movie before she had to start her outline for the first paper of the semester that she had to write for her Victorian Poetry class. All the while willfully ignoring the undeniably pitiful state of her love life.

"Done!" Regan announced a few minutes later.

"Done with what?" It was only as her question was ending that she realized Regan didn't have her own phone in her hand, but Sutton's. "What did you do?"

Her friend had a familiar bright-eyed devious look as she held Sutton's phone up and wiggled it – but not close enough for Sutton to swipe it out of her hand. "I'm helping you out."

"What in the world is that?"

Dread was already settling in her before Regan answered. "It's a dating app. You're welcome; you'll be getting messages from hot girls in no time."

For a moment, Sutton sat there, stunned into stillness. Only for a second, though, before she lunged forward, hands out and grasping. Regan eluded her, hopping off of the couch and running around the table as she started tapping at the screen.

Sutton jumped up. "Give it back."

Regan shook her head, not moving her eyes from the screen. "If I give it back, you'll never even browse."

She calculated the size of the coffee table. She had long legs; she could jump it.

Once more, Regan knew her too well, because she held her hands out in a peace offering gesture. "Look. I'll give you the phone. *If* you promise me you won't delete your profile, *and* you browse through some profiles. Maybe send a message or two."

She only hesitated for a moment, but it was enough for Regan to latch on to.

Regan crossed her arms, her hand still securely holding onto Sutton's cell phone, but her tone was considerably gentler than before. "Okay, since you didn't jump me, I know that there is at least a part of you that wants to try this out."

There was no argument against it even in her head because she *did*. There was that part of her that wanted to get over her nerves and at least see what was out there.

She found herself nodding through the anxiety and reaching for her phone. As she wrapped her fingers around it, she shot Regan a look and cautioned, "Just to look."

"Spoil sport," Regan muttered, letting out a long suffering sigh but releasing her phone anyway.

Sutton scoffed as she settled back onto the couch, cautiously looking at the app. She narrowed her eyes when she read the name: *SapphicSpark*. "You're kidding me."

"It's apparently a very reputable place!"

"How would you know?"

"You hear a lot of talk about people's dating lives when you work in a café!"

Turning away from her, Sutton shook her head, red hair falling over her shoulder and curtaining her from her friend's overly excited gaze from the other side of the couch. After a deep, calming breath, she looked over the profile her friend had created for her. She'd – thankfully – chosen photos that

Sutton might have even chosen for herself. The rest was fairly simple – her age, likes, and a message option.

Sutton, 25, New York City
Likes: literature, dogs, snow, knitting, running, and lemon cakes

She couldn't argue with any of that.

With trepidation, she pressed the button in the top right corner that was beckoning her to *Browse profiles!*

Not only had she never done this with women before, but she'd never done something like this with men, either. Men had always just . . . been there.

Finding a woman, who not only was she attracted to and liked but who also liked and was attracted to her was harder. And scarier.

It was somewhat comforting knowing that all of these women were out there and just as not straight as she was. And maybe some of them could be interested in her.

The thought of it made her heart beat a little faster.

Before it actually seemed to stop in her chest for a few beats upon her next swipe. Because the woman in the picture who was coyly smiling up at her from her phone made her stomach erupt in butterflies. Her light brown hair was perfectly tousled and even through a picture her piercing eyes were somehow flirty.

She was well aware that there were some people who simply took pictures really well or photoshopped them in ways to look better, but this woman was stunning any way she looked at it.

Charlotte, 28, New York City
Likes: puzzles, Indian food, rainy days, designer shoes, dancing, and gardening

"Oh, wow."

Regan's voice right next to her ear startled her, causing her to fumble her phone in her hands. She threw her friend a glare. "I thought you were going to give me time to look. *On my own.*"

"Well, I was. Then I noticed you were staring at someone and I wanted to see. And now that I checked, I have to say – you need to message her."

The *Message* button seemed to taunt her and her mind ran amuck with the idea of seeing that face in person. Or even going on a date with her. Just the thought was enough for her heart to race.

"Absolutely not."

"Why not? She's hot, you're hot. You need an introduction to the lady loving world and she looks like she'd be a really good one."

She glanced at Charlotte's picture again for a peek – yeah, she was that hot. "It's not that easy. She's – I'm not – I mean, just look at her. What am I going to say? *Hi, I'm a grad student who hasn't even dated a woman yet, do you want to go out even though you can clearly date anyone you want?*"

Regan was giving her the Sutton-is-being-unintentionally-amusing look that she was very familiar with but couldn't stand. "Well, I wouldn't exactly phrase it like that. Have some faith; it's not like you're chopped liver."

"I know that." She groaned fell back against the couch, phone in her lap. "But I'm not *that*."

That . . . confident, sexy-smile, flirty-eyed, my-picture-alone-can-seduce-you, was definitely not her.

When Regan *hmm*'d, Sutton should have known she was getting off the hook too easily. It was practically her own fault when her phone was snatched from her lap.

She jumped to grab for it, but Regan was already moving her thumbs quickly over the screen.

"Regan Marie Gallagher, give my phone back *now*." She knew in the momentary pause of Regan's typing that she did a pretty great job of channeling her mother's reproachful tone.

9

In a determined, calculated leap, she closed the distance between them, grappling for her phone.

It was fruitless. Because only a moment later, Regan cried out victoriously, "Sent!"

The sound that left the back of Sutton's mouth was nearly feral. "You *didn't*!"

"Of course I did." Regan's smile spoke of no regrets. "Now, have you changed your mind about coming out with me tonight?"

The glare Sutton sent her was answer enough.

"Suit yourself. Stay home and obsess about Stunning Charlotte." Regan slid the phone back to her.

Pointedly ignoring her, Sutton frantically navigated her own profile to see her sent messages. And then just about died.

> **Sutton, 7:43PM**
> *Hey there. I saw your profile and you look really interesting – and hot. Do you want to ~~hook up~~ meet up sometime?*

Horrified, she didn't acknowledge Regan at all as her friend all but ran out of the apartment. Sutton didn't think she could possibly blush more than she already was and, as panic started to build, she went back to Charlotte's profile to try to send another message.

Something where she would try to beg her to ignore Regan's message that made Sutton out to be pleading for a freaking hook up. Only to be informed: *For our users' well-being, SapphicSpark does not allow multiple messages to be sent to a user unless they allow it upon receiving your first message.*

What?!

Any other time, Sutton would have appreciated the step the app took to prevent forms of harassment. But not right now. Why couldn't there be this one little exception?

With a groan, she brought her hand up to rub at her temples.

Peering again at the picture of the woman, she bit her lip as a small sigh escaped. Charlotte was almost *too* hot.

Which was a good thing, she reasoned with herself. She probably wasn't even going to have to try to explain Regan and embarrass herself, because this woman – *Charlotte* – well, look at her. That woman was bound to have a ton of messages on here. She wouldn't look twice at Sutton.

With that in mind, she put her phone down on the table and tried to shake off the whole ordeal.

***

Two hours later, Sutton was very purposefully finishing Regan's favorite ice cream, rooted to the same spot on the couch. She wasn't a big fan of the coffee flavor, but it was a small strike back against her friend. She wasn't going to go far enough to exact Alex-level revenge – Sutton still shuddered to think about some of the pranks her sister had played on her as they'd grown up – but Regan should know there would be several small acts of justice coming her way.

When her phone vibrated on the table, she assumed it was either Regan, trying to get her to come meet her and some of their friends, or Emma, her fellow TA and closest friend from college. Maybe her mother or one of her siblings.

She wasn't expecting a notification from *SapphicSpark*.

The spoon she'd been holding clattered into the bowl as she hurriedly unlocked her phone and tapped on the notification. *New message from Charlotte!* Was displayed on the screen.

"What the fuck," she whispered.

She took a deep breath in an attempt to calm herself.

It didn't work and she clicked on the message anyway.

Charlotte, 10:02PM
My, that is one of the less subtle approaches
I've received on here, I must say.

Why would Regan do this to her?

Sutton, 10:04PM
God, I'm so sorry! I've been wanting to send
this for hours, but couldn't message you again
until you answered. That's not – I'm not the
person who sent that first message! My friend
created this account and sent that to you. I'm
sorry, again. And incredibly embarrassed.

Clasping her phone in her hand, she stared blankly at the movie on the television for a few moments. That was good, right? And now that Charlotte knew the truth, Sutton really shouldn't expect to hear from her again.

Which . . . was kind of disappointing.

She'd barely put her phone down when it vibrated again, sending a jolt of surprise – and excitement – through her.

Charlotte, 10:06PM
I never said lack of subtlety was a bad thing.
Perhaps in other matters, but not when it comes
to this. So, your friend arranged this? Are you
not looking for a sapphic spark, then?

Sutton, 10:06PM
Oh, I am. Yes. Well, kind of.

What in the hell was that? She berated herself, letting her head fall back against the couch. For a literature grad student, she could be the least coherent person ever.

Charlotte, 10:08PM
Kind of?

Sutton, 10:09PM
I meant to say, that I like both men and women.

Charlotte, 10:12PM
You haven't done this very much, have you?

Sutton, 10:13PM
No. Never, actually. Is it really obvious?

Sutton rolled her eyes at herself; of course it was obvious. She only had a second to wonder why this woman was even still talking to her before she got an answer.

Charlotte, 10:14PM
Only a little ;)

Charlotte, 10:16PM
Tell me, why did your friend deem it necessary to create this account and send messages from you that seem to be more suggestive than you would like?

Sutton, 10:17PM
She thinks I need to get out more, I guess. And she thinks that I should, um, go out and hook up with someone.

Charlotte, 10:20PM
And that's not what you want?

Sutton, 10:21PM
I – well, no. Not that I don't want to ever meet someone, it's just . . . I'm not wanting to go out and find a hook up just for the sake of hooking up. You know?

Charlotte, 10:23PM
Unfortunately, that is where you and I differ. Which is a shame, I might add.

Sutton's eyes widened as she triple-read that. Did Charlotte mean what Sutton thought she meant? She had to. After all, she realized with a pleasant swoop in her stomach, Charlotte *had* seen her profile and decided to write back.

For a moment, she thought about what that might mean. Entertained the idea that maybe this gorgeous woman had seriously been interested in hooking up with her – and to say it was a major rush was an understatement.

Then the thoughts dissipated, because what that also meant was that Charlotte was someone who – as Sutton was sure many women on this app were – only wanted a hook up. Which . . . Sutton really didn't think she could do, no matter how ridiculously hot the woman's picture was.

14

After a few moments of wondering whether or not she should just leave their interaction to end right then and there, because – well, she'd flat out said she didn't want a hook up, and Charlotte clearly did, so she couldn't imagine Charlotte wanting to keep wasting her time.

But . . .

Biting her lip, she was very grateful Regan wasn't here to witness this.

Sutton, 10:25PM
Do you? Do this very often, that is.

Charlotte, 10:28PM
Are you insinuating something?

Oh, God. This was why Sutton could never go out and meet a woman in real life; she couldn't even talk to one online without putting her foot in her mouth.

Sutton, 10:29PM
*No! No, no. I was asking because I was just,
well, curious about how this usually happens?*

Sutton, 10:30PM
*I mean, you seem . . . like you know what to do,
in situations like this. Unlike me, clearly.*

Sutton, 10:30PM
*God, that was probably a very silly thing to
ask. You can just ignore me.*

Charlotte, 10:32PM
*Oh, sweetheart. I don't typically make it a point
to reveal the inner-workings of my interactions on
here, you know. A true lady shouldn't reveal
her secrets.*

Charlotte, 10:33PM
*However, I could make an exception for a pretty
woman in need. I only need to know one thing . . .*

Sutton's heart beat just a bit faster at that, as she flushed and bit her lip. *A pretty woman in need.* She knew she'd been correct in wondering if Charlotte had done this before; she definitely knew what to say to make Sutton lap up every word.

Sutton, 10:34PM
Which is?

Charlotte, 10:40PM
*Just to be completely clear, there is no chance
of you being interested in – as your first message
said – a hook up? Because I absolutely will not
abide showing my hand in that case.*

Sutton hesitated. She thought of being that kind of person, who could go out and *hook up* with a gorgeous stranger and have that be it. No feelings involved. She was so very nervous about her first *everything* with a woman that maybe having sex with a stranger and getting it over with would be easier.

Then again, she'd already learned in life that easier was not always better.

16

Sutton, 10:42PM
I can confirm that I don't think I will be prepared
to hook up with anyone any time soon.

Charlotte, 10:45PM
Well, then, disappointed as I may be, I am now
willing to answer what you'd like to know. Do
you have specific questions in mind?

Sutton, 10:46PM
Do you only use this app for hooking up?

She regretted it as soon as she sent it. Why would she think it was all right to ask that to this random woman?

Charlotte, 10:48PM
Yes. Though in the name of honesty, I am
always upfront about my not-serious intentions.

Sutton, 10:49PM
Okay. But what happens then?

Charlotte, 10:52PM
I do hope you aren't asking me to explain the
proverbial birds and the bees, sweetheart. I was
under the impression you wanted this to be PG . . .

She rushed – by no means did she intend for this to become a makeshift first time foray into dirty messages. Well, first time for her. She had doubts about Charlotte.

17

Sutton, 10:53PM

*No! No, I know how . . . that . . . works. I meant,
like, how do you go about doing all of this? When
a woman messages you, what happens then?*

Charlotte, 10:56PM

*Well, it's all fairly straightforward, no pun
intended. We chat a bit here and make plans to
meet up. Typically at a bar or perhaps a club –
always somewhere public. We spend a bit of time
out to make sure we're . . . compatible. And from
there, I see if they'd like to go back to my place
for the night.*

Charlotte, 10:57PM

Not to boast, but they usually do.

Sutton, 10:57PM
Oh, I can imagine.

Her cheeks burned when she realized what she'd written.

Charlotte, 10:59PM

*That was smoother than I expected. Offense
entirely unintended.*

Sutton, 11:00PM
*None taken, as it was actually inadvertently
done.*

Charlotte, 11:03PM

You're an . . . interesting woman. Unfortunately,
however, it's getting late, and I have to get to
bed. I have an early morning tomorrow.

At least it wasn't a *complete* disaster; Charlotte seemed to be amused by her if nothing else.

She could do with getting to bed as well, she realized as she stifled a yawn. She had to grade the first assignments of the semester for her professor by Monday, plus her own paper to start working on, as well as going to see her sister.

Sutton, 11:05PM

I don't think I'm quite as interesting as you
are. But I should be going, too. Thank you, for
this. You know, not mocking me like you
undoubtedly could have.

Charlotte, 11:08PM

That's not really my style. But it was more
entertaining for me than I might have anticipated.
Goodnight, Sutton.

Sutton, 11:09PM
Goodnight, Charlotte.

Chapter 2

"As everyone here already knows, we're celebrating tonight that one of our very own will be announcing her campaign for the House of Representatives special election!" Dean Walker, mayor of New York City, proclaimed, holding up a glass of champagne, as he made eye contact with her from across the room.

Charlotte shook her head slightly, even as a pleased grin tugged at her lips. She'd halfheartedly asked Dean to refrain from making a toast, but she couldn't deny that she got a little thrill from it all.

"Though we will be inevitably sad to see her go, I can think of no one else who should be better suited to the position. Charlotte, I speak for myself and on behalf of the entire staff, when I say that we support you and believe in you unequivocally. So, though it means you'll be leaving us at the end of it all, here's to a successful election!"

He lifted his glass, cheerfully followed by the myriad of others who joined in with shouts and claps in her direction. She accepted them all with a nod and a smile, lifting her glass to them before taking a sip.

The entire mayoral staff was there, joined by a few of their fellow civil servants on the city council for the celebration. It wasn't often that they held a party in their actual office but Dean had deemed it a special occasion.

He made his way toward her, lightly brushing off the cuffs of his suit. Despite the fact that it was after-hours, he detested being seen as less than pristine.

She quirked an eyebrow toward him, a playful smile on her lips. "That was quite a touching speech."

"I believe the words you're looking for are *thank you.*"

She laid her hand that didn't have a light hold on her champagne flute on his arm. "Thank you."

Despite her banter, she meant it. Dean had been her boss for several years now and in those years, he had become someone she could trust.

Someone who managed to maintain her respect, even after she'd seen him come running out of her brother's apartment in nothing but striped boxers after sighting a mouse. That alone was a feat to be proud of.

Dean was a true friend, one of the only she'd made thus far in the game of politics.

It was why she'd been somewhat reluctant and even nervous to tell him about her plans to campaign for the recently empty House of Reps seat. She'd told him only a few days ago, because she could not stand that feeling of guilty nerves in her stomach; it wasn't something she was familiar with and she'd wanted to be rid of it as soon as possible.

"What? Did you think *I* thought you'd stay in our corner of the world forever? You should know better," he'd told her when she'd informed him that she thought he would have been a little more shocked at her wanting to leave.

Charlotte *did* love the work she was doing now; Dean was one of the most level-headed, progressive, and change-effecting mayors in the history of the city. And as the Deputy Mayor for health and human services working for him in the last few years, Charlotte had been able to implement programs and develop actual systems to help people. To actually make change.

Despite her love of her current position, however, it was only a footnote in the grand plan she had for her future. And Dean knew very well what her ambitions were.

She'd been in politics since she was old enough to be employed. She'd graduated from Yale with dual pre-law and political science degrees. She'd then completed her law degree at Columbia – just in case – as she obtained full time employment at the governor's office. From there, she'd then been appointed Deputy Mayor. Even before that, she'd had countless internships with various

21

departments in Congress throughout college. And she'd been *interested* in politics – the rise and fall and the rush and the adrenaline – since she was a child.

How could she not be, when her family was so deeply rooted in it all? She couldn't have grown up with the first female President of the United States as her grandmother without being dramatically influenced.

Charlotte planned to follow in her grandmother's footsteps since she truly understood what it was that her grandmother did. She intended to be voted as the President of the country, and she intended for it to happen at a younger age than it had happened for her grandmother. And regardless how much she enjoyed her life right now, there was no doubt that running for a notable elected office had to be her next step.

With a deep breath, she took another sip of champagne. She could feel a pleasant buzz from it, even as she nudged Dean with her shoulder to get his attention. "You'd better make an even better speech if I win the seat. I expect some tears to fall."

"*If?* Where is the confident Charlotte I know and tolerate?"

"The Charlotte you know and *love*, brat." She elbowed him, smiling despite herself. "And perhaps you should get your glasses, as I am right here. Confident in my abilities, yet realistic about the odds," she corrected mildly.

She *was* confident that she would put up a good fight for the suddenly vacant seat in the House of Representatives. Confident that she had a very real chance at winning the special election for it; she wouldn't go forward with the time and energy it was going to take to run a campaign, otherwise.

However, she also kept in mind that should she win this election, she would become one of the youngest people to ever do so, let alone the youngest woman. As it was still early, it was also unclear as to who she would be running against. Those were two variables that had the potential to either work in her favor or against her.

22

The seat had opened up unexpectedly a few weeks ago, upon the untimely death of John Kelvin, who had only just been re-elected. Charlotte's original plan, the one that she had outlined and kept close to her heart, had been to campaign for one of the open seats in either the next election or the one after that, even.

Yet, despite the fact that she was young and that she wasn't as prepared as she would have been for a campaign years from now, she couldn't deny that this move felt like it would be the best thing for her. She knew without a doubt that she would be able to hold her own against anyone who underestimated her.

"Well, in the chance that you do not win the seat, I'll try not to celebrate too much," Dean informed her as he reached down to the table next to them to pour himself a glass of wine.

Slightly confused, and more than slightly offended, she turned to face him. "Celebrating my loss? What happened to those pretty words of support from only minutes ago?"

He shot her a look of apology. "I *do* support you, of course. But when you leave, whether it be in a few months or in a few years, both myself and the local government will be losing a big asset."

She shook her head with a smirk. "You choose the most roundabout ways in order to tell me you'll miss me."

She lightly squeezed his forearm. Dean rolled his eyes at her but brought his hand up to squeeze her hand in return.

After a few moments, he tilted his head toward their coworkers, who were milling about. Some dancing, some just chatting. All seemed to be having a good time, though she supposed, of course they would be. Free food and drinks, supplied by their boss, who was letting loose at the office in a celebration that didn't have to do with anything unfortunate happening to precede it.

"Now, come and partake in the festivities. This party is in your honor, after all." Dean handed her another flute of champagne, before stepping slightly away to gallantly offer her his arm.

It was things like that, she knew, that had made rumors buzz about the two of them. Predominantly in her earlier years of working together, though there were still a few people who didn't entirely believe they were only platonic.

Charlotte knew that was one of the side-effects of keeping her sexuality a topic that she did not discuss at work. As a result, talk like that – about her love life and any male friendships she kept – would be speculated about the more she rose in the political ranks.

However, she also knew that a bit of speculation and wonder, as long as there truly was nothing salacious being hidden, was an angle that would prove to be beneficial in her burgeoning career. And she certainly had no scandalous tales involving men of any kind to be hidden.

With that in mind, she bit back a small sigh as she fixed a smile on and shook her head. "I have to grab something from my desk first. I'll be out there and asking you for a dance soon, though."

"We'll see if you can keep up." Dean started to unbutton his cuffs and crisply start to roll them up as he gave her a nod.

"Excuse you. Historically, only one of us ever needs assistance on the dance floor and it's not me."

He walked away with a wink that made her chuckle under her breath, before Charlotte made her way to her desk. It was far enough away from the center of the office that the festivities were not in her immediate area, which she was thankful for.

Brown eyes scanned for people as she took her phone out of her purse. She unlocked the device and scrolled until she got to the app that had been on her mind for days now.

SapphicSpark had served her very well in the past few years. She'd first made an account when she'd been fresh out of college and looking for a way to find

24

women who wouldn't know her on a personal level. Who didn't know Charlotte Thompson, politician. Looking for women who wanted the same thing she did: a short, casual, discreet hookup before moving on.

Charlotte knew that she already had a long road ahead of her if she was to accomplish her goals and that road had enough obstacles. She had no intention of adding the fact that she was a lesbian into the mix. At the very least, not for years to come. As far as she was concerned, it was unnecessary. Her sexuality had nothing to do with her ambitions.

Especially given that she had no intention of entertaining a so-called "love life" in the near future, regardless of the gender she was interested in. She prided herself on being able to read people, and it didn't take a genius to see that people could make foolish decisions when their hearts were involved. Charlotte intended to stay clear- and level-headed for her time in office, whether that office be a member of the House or the Senate or President, or even Deputy Mayor.

She'd found many a pleasurable night because of this app, and if she was being entirely honest, she didn't *want* to give it up. But it was in her own best interest. Now that she'd unofficially announced her intention to run for Congress, the ball was rolling. Within the next few weeks, she would officially begin her campaign, and her name would start to garner more public interest.

Depending on who would be opposing her, Charlotte had to be prepared for them to dig up anything, even her profile on a gay dating app. Though she would miss the hookups, they were not worth jeopardizing her dreams.

Last Friday, she had resolved to herself that she would run for the election and she'd decided then that she had to delete the profile. That was when she'd seen that she had a message from a woman whose profile she'd never come across before.

The woman with the red hair spilling over her shoulder in long waves, with startlingly blue eyes lit up with a candid smile that revealed straight white teeth. It was a picture that was clearly snapped while the redhead had been in

25

mid-laugh. Something genuine, where Charlotte could see the flush of laughter on pale cheeks, and she'd almost been able to *hear* laughter through her phone.

Charlotte had scrolled through what must have amounted to thousands of profiles over the years, had messaged and met up with a good amount of them. She'd seen stunning women, women who were gorgeous both in and out of their pictures. The woman – Sutton – was someone she would put into that gorgeous category, but mostly, she'd liked that she looked so . . . open.

So, even though she'd intended to delete her account that night, she'd been extremely pleasantly surprised to see the message proposing a hookup from Sutton. It couldn't hurt, she supposed to have one last *SapphicSpark* hurrah. It would be almost symbolic, in a way.

She hadn't been lying when she'd said that she'd been a bit disappointed about the fact that it hadn't actually been Sutton herself who'd proposed said hookup. But she *had* been surprised at the fact that she'd found herself a bit charmed by Sutton herself.

A bit awkward, a lot amusing, adorably naïve, almost alarmingly honest.

Shaking her head, she tapped her inbox. There were three new messages since she'd checked the app the previous afternoon, and as the first two popped up, she debated reading them for a few seconds, her thumb hesitating over them . . . before she hit delete, instead. Tonight was the night that she actually had to delete this little portion of her life.

However, the third message popped up, and she paused in surprise. Truthfully, the last thing she had expected was for there to be another message from Sutton in her inbox.

Despite the fact that she'd only opened the app in order to delete it . . . well, curiosity killed the cat.

Sutton, 4:24PM
Hi, it's just me, again. Obviously. I just wanted

to say thank you, again, for humoring me the
other night.

Quirking an eyebrow, Charlotte looked around her once more. When she was satisfied to see that no one was particularly interested in what she was doing, she turned her attention back to her phone. She had no idea what it was about Sutton's seemingly earnest thanks that made her endearing, but she found herself answering anyway.

Charlotte, 7:06PM
As I said, I'm always happy to talk to a pretty
woman in need. I'll admit, I'm a bit surprised
to see you still here.

She'd somewhat expected Sutton to have deleted her profile after having been so flustered about its existence.

Even though Sutton's message had been sent a few hours ago, Charlotte had a tiny kernel of hope that she'd answer back as quickly as she had on Friday. Especially because she had an inkling that Sutton hadn't messaged her *just* because she'd wanted to say thanks, again, four days later.

She nearly jumped – would have, if she hadn't had a lot of practice at maintaining her composure over the years – when she felt two hands land on her shoulders, and a familiar voice ask in her ear, "And who is that?"

Quickly, she locked her phone, as she grinned widely. "Caleb!"

She spun in her seat to face her brother, still dressed in his police uniform, a wide smile on his face. His thumbs were tucked into his belt, a knowing smirk on his face that she knew was very similar to her own, brown waves hanging over his forehead. He gestured to her phone. "Another one of your ladies?"

"Something like that. Tell me, officer, what are you doing here?"

"Well, you're breaking the law, you know. We *are* in an official government building, and I've heard a rumor that there is an obscene amount of alcohol on the premises," Caleb shifted back on his heels. "I don't want to make this into a big deal, but . . ."

Standing up, she shook her head in adoration as she tucked her arm through his. "I don't suppose an esteemed officer such as yourself can be swayed with the promise of indulging in said alcohol." She stood on her tiptoes and leaned in a bit to whisper in his ear, "Or with the promise to go home with a slightly inebriated mayor who is currently enjoying himself on the makeshift dance floor."

Her brother's eyes lit up and sought out Dean, who was indeed dancing. "I think I might be able to be persuaded."

"I thought so," she laughed quietly, and led him to the desk that was acting as a bar, "How did you find out about this little party?"

"I received a little message from the dancing queen," he informed her, and they shared a smile, as they reached the liquor, and he reached out for a bottle. He looked at her over the top, "I bet grandmother is thrilled that her little flower is following in her footsteps earlier than expected."

His tone was teasing, but with an underlying seriousness that she might have missed if she hadn't known him so well. He wasn't wrong, though. Their grandmother had praised her efforts and her plan to run now rather than later, especially given that she scorned half of the current Congress it seemed, and often gave thanks that she didn't regularly have to work with them anymore.

Still, she rolled her eyes at him. "Come on, you know she's proud of all of us."

The exasperated look Caleb gave her made her throw her head back in laughter.

"She called me a trained monkey with a gun last Christmas," he replied dourly, which only spurred on her laughter.

"That's just her way of showing love. You know that."

28

He continued to grumble for a moment, before he sobered, clinking his glass with hers. "Well, you already have my vote. I think you'll have it in the bag."

"We'll see," she murmured back, but couldn't deny the rush she got at the words. She'd had the feeling that her future was truly starting since the night she'd decided to run.

Caleb tipped his head back and finished his wine before placing his glass on the table, and he grinned down at her. "Now, lead me toward the dance floor."

***

A few hours later, Charlotte was still grinning as she let herself into her apartment. She wasn't drunk, but pleasantly buzzed and tired, and she had Caleb and Dean's goodnight calls still ringing in her ears. They'd walked her back to her apartment, all of them in fairly high spirits. And for a few moments, she'd stood back to watch the two of them walk down the sidewalk, walking close but careful to not be *too* close.

There were times when Charlotte felt that she was luckier than her brother and Dean. While Dean wasn't *as* secretive about his sexuality as she was when it came to work, he was still private enough to keep from dancing with Caleb in front of their coworkers. She was lucky, because unlike her brother and her boss, she didn't have the inclination to be in a relationship. She didn't have someone to make eyes at from across the room, while being unable to dance with them, to really *be* with them.

She dropped her purse on the counter, keys on the hook right next to it, before she started to take off her light jacket. As she made her way into her bedroom, she felt her pocket buzz. Blearily, she pulled out her phone, placing it on her dresser, as she pulled off her fitted dress pants. Once she was stripped down to her bra and underwear, she reached for her phone again.

Much of her grogginess disappeared when she saw that it wasn't a text from Caleb, as she'd expected, but instead a *SapphicSpark* notification.

29

She'd nearly forgotten that she'd messaged Sutton earlier, before the drinking and the dancing.

Sutton, 11:13PM
I'm actually a bit surprised that I'm still here,
too. I've told Regan I deleted it, out of spite.

Charlotte leaned back against the dresser, shaking her head at herself – because she'd meant to delete her own damn account *again* tonight, yet, here she was. And it didn't stop her from responding.

Charlotte, 11:17PM
Regan?

Sutton, 11:18PM
Yes. Regan is my roommate and friend, who
created this account for me. I want her to suffer.

She grinned, and wished – not for the first time, clearly – that Sutton would be interested in something casual. It wasn't like she was hurting for a hookup, but she enjoyed that thing about Sutton that rang . . . unique. Certainly unique to any of her other interactions on a dating app, because most of the women she encountered were more like herself.

Charlotte, 11:20PM
More devious than I might have expected of
you, sweet girl.

Sutton, 11:21PM
She created this profile and messaged girls –

30

well, girl, you know, you – asking to hook up,
on my behalf!

It was that picture, she decided. Sutton's picture with her mid-laugh and so animated, that made it so easy for Charlotte to imagine this righteous indignation. It was enough to make her chuckle.

Charlotte, 11:22PM
That's true. She got both of our hopes up; you
should make her suffer as much as possible.

Sutton, 11:23PM
Exactly. Um, I'm sorry for writing back to you so
late. I hope I didn't wake you up.

There was that feeling again. The feeling that Sutton had something to say beyond what she was actually saying, and Charlotte wanted to know what it was.

Charlotte, 11:25PM
Don't worry, I was out late doing something for
work. I'm usually up this late, anyway.

She didn't typically like to go in to even that much detail about her personal life with women on here, not even mentioning work at all. Though she'd never not been hooking up with one before, either, so she supposed it was okay.

Sutton, 11:28PM
I don't really stay up late, usually. I'm much more
of a morning person. But my sister is going away

31

soon, and she has horrible sleeping habits, so I was
with her tonight.

Sutton, 11:29PM
I realize that you didn't need or probably want
any details about my sister. I apologize for that.

                                     Charlotte, 11:31PM
You have nothing to apologize for. And while I
don't mind knowing your sleeping habits, or even
a few details about your sister, I have a sneaking
suspicion that you didn't message me to tell me
either of those things. Feel free to tell me whatever
it is. I don't bite.

                                     Charlotte, 11:32PM
Unless you've changed your mind about that
very first message, that is ;)

    She couldn't resist, and she put her phone back down before making her way into the bathroom. After doing an abbreviated version of her nightly routine – only cleaning off her makeup, washing her face, and brushing her teeth, because she was, actually, fairly tired – she made her way back to her room.

    Stripping off her bra and underwear now, she pulled on a tank top and a pair of shorts before reaching for her phone once more and crawling into bed. She was unsurprised to see that she had multiple messages from Sutton.

Sutton, 11:35PM
Oh. I haven't changed my mind about, um, you
know, hooking up. But – you are right.

Sutton, 11:35PM
The thing is, I really was going to delete my profile.
I keep telling myself that I should. I mean, you're
the only woman I've talked to on here, and you're –
well, you.

Charlotte, 11:38PM
Well, I'm certainly me, but I'm unsure of what
exactly you mean by that.

Sutton, 11:39PM
I just meant that – you are clearly gorgeous
and you can flirt without being weird, at all.
Even when I know I've said something stupid,
you make it seem like not a big deal.

So, it was a good thing, then. Charlotte knew she was attractive; she prided herself on self-awareness. She also knew that many other women found her good looking. But it was the casual, unassuming way Sutton just *said* it, without any expectations, that gave way to a pleased warmth.

Sutton knew how to make herself even more endearing without even trying, she decided. She had her own brand of charm that she didn't properly know how to use. And she knew that if it worked for her, it would work for others.

Charlotte, 11:41PM
Enough about me, charmer. Why do you think
that you should delete your profile?

Though, she was one to talk. As she *really* did need to delete this.

Sutton, 11:42M
Because I can't talk to women! You should already
know that better than anyone.

Once more, she imagined that pretty face flushing with indignation, and she could see it so clearly in her head that it made her smile. Even so, she yawned and shook her head as she wrote back.

Charlotte, 11:44PM
Don't underestimate yourself. You can hold your
own. Besides, the beginning of online dating can be
strange for everyone. Just settle into it.

Sutton, 11:46PM
That's the thing, though. It's not just . . . that.

Sutton, 11:47PM
It's not just online, I mean.

It took her sleepy mind a few seconds to connect the dots. But when she did, she sat up a bit, intrigued.

Charlotte, 11:48PM
Have you never been with a woman?

Sutton, 11:51PM
Well . . . no. I made out with one. Once. Or, she
made out with me. But I was a participant.

Charlotte dropped her head back into her pillow, groaning as she shut her eyes to curse . . . someone. Something. This whole situation. Because there was this beautiful woman who was clearly interested in exploring her sexuality, and Charlotte could be just the person Sutton needed. For one or two nights.

Which was the opposite of what Sutton actually wanted. Though they'd only spoken for such a short time, she knew that Sutton wanted the emotional connection that Charlotte had never been particularly wanting or missing.

Charlotte, 11:53PM
Do you want to know what I think?

Sutton, 11:54PM
I'm not sure.

Sutton, 11:54PM
But, yes.

Amusement settled in her stomach.

Charlotte, 11:58PM
I think that you not deleting this profile means that despite the fact that you're nervous and despite the fact that you're unhappy that your friend Regan forced you into this, you want to be here.

She reached over to her nightstand to plug in her phone, resting it on her chest as she leaned back once more. She did need to get to sleep – she did have work in the morning, after all – but she'd never had this sort of actual conversation with a woman on here. Which was her own doing, as she didn't want to complicate her sex life and turn anything personal.

But she was enjoying it, enjoying the fact that even though she wasn't going to be hooking up with Sutton, they could have a real conversation. She didn't actually have many honest conversations, at all, aside from with her family members and Dean.

Sutton, 12:00AM
I think you're probably right.

Charlotte, 12:01AM
I usually am, darling ;)

She put her phone down on her stomach and leaned back into her pillows with a comfortable sigh.

***

The alarm on her phone blared from where it rested on her stomach. Brown eyes blinked open as she groaned. Six in the morning came a lot faster than she ever cared for.

She brought up one hand to rub at her eyes, reaching down to shut off the alarm. When she noticed that she had five messages from *SapphicSpark*.

Sutton, 12:05AM
I just don't really know even what to say to start talking to someone. Or even what to look for, you know?

Sutton, 12:07AM
Because I'm sure that there are more woman

than not who are more or less only looking for
something casual, like you.

Sutton, 12:08AM
And it's not like I should just come out and ask
"hey, what are you looking for?"

Sutton, 12:08AM
Can I?

Sutton, 12:16AM
Oh, god. This is even more mortifying than our
first interaction, I think. Please ignore me, now.

Charlotte was instantly more awake now as she found herself chuckling. She didn't know how many other people she'd ever found so easily entertaining. She didn't know how many people sent four messages in a row in a ramble before realizing that the other person wasn't there. Certainly no one who texted her.

She gathered her hair over her shoulder and sat up.

Charlotte, 6:05AM
You shouldn't feel mortified; I fell asleep.

Tossing her phone onto the blankets next to her, she stretched. And then stared in amazement when her phone buzzed back.

Sutton, 6:06AM
That's a relief.

She wasn't sure whether to continue to be amused or to be actually concerned that this woman appeared to have been awake all night. Awake and . . . anxious about having sent Charlotte so many messages?

Charlotte, 6:09AM
Do you sleep?

Sutton, 6:11AM
Of course! I just woke up, actually. But I told you that I'm a morning person. Besides, I have a few things to do this morning.

With a disbelieving shake of her head, she wrote back quickly, pulling on her past experiences, before leaving her phone on her bed to decide what to wear for the day.

Charlotte, 6:14AM
Well, on the topic of the messages you sent while I was sleeping, I'll say that you can ask women what they are looking for. But there are other things you can look for, too. Little clues on their profiles that can indicate what they're after.

Sutton, 6:17AM
Can I ask you something that might be a bit odd?

Charlotte, 6:21AM
In all honesty, you've said several things that are a bit odd, and we're still talking. So, go ahead.

She smirked, and had a strange feeling of anticipation as she went to shower. It was quick, as she was feeling a little sluggish still, and she wrapped her towel around herself to make her way back into the bedroom.

After quickly getting dressed, she left her hair tied up in its towel to dry before reaching for her phone once more to see what "odd" thing Sutton wanted to ask.

Sutton, 6:24AM

You're right. Sorry, about all of that. But . . . maybe I could talk to you about profiles when I think perhaps I'll message the girl? Or if I'm in a small panic or have said something really dumb, maybe I could talk to you about it? Kind of like a mentor type thing. Only, not as weird as it sounds.

Sutton, 6:25AM

God, I know how weird it is. Believe me, I do. But, you said yourself that you have a lot of experience on here.

Sutton, 6:26AM

Actually, forget that I asked, please.

Charlotte had to read all of the messages over twice before it truly dawned on her what Sutton was asking. If she could help Sutton find her . . . princess charming on the app. The honest-to-god genuine laughter bubbled out of her. Not that she found Sutton herself laughable – no, she was adorable – but the idea that *Charlotte*, of all people, was being asked to help find someone romance.

She just had to take a moment to let it really sink in.

Charlotte, 6:50AM
*Darling, take a deep breath. I would be remiss
to say that I wasn't intrigued by your proposal.*

It surprised even herself how interested she was as to where that would lead, that much was true.

Charlotte, 6:51AM
*However, I would be even more remiss, if I didn't
inform you that I plan on deleting this account, for
personal reasons. Very soon, in fact.*

Sutton, 6:53AM
Oh. Okay.

Sutton, 6:57AM
*You're not deleting your account because I'm
coming off like a stalker or something, right?
Because I swear to you, I'm just a little awkward
sometimes.*

Oh, it was all too good. Charlotte was hard-pressed to remember the last time she'd been so amused. She quickly typed back.

Charlotte, 6:59AM
Someone certainly thinks highly of herself ;)

Charlotte, 7:01AM
But please don't worry. It's truly not you. I've
40

actually quite enjoyed our conversations.
Surprisingly so.

She made her way into the kitchen. As always, she was grateful for her timed coffee maker and she poured herself a large mug. She heard her phone go off as she stirred in her cream and sugar, giving herself a moment to arrange it just the way she liked before she checked her message and sat at her counter.

Sutton, 7:04AM
Good. I enjoy them, too. Rather, enjoyed them.
When are you deleting your account? If you don't
mind my asking.

Charlotte sighed, a strange feeling of regret settling in her stomach as she took a sip from her coffee. She, weirdly, enjoyed Sutton. She enjoyed her honesty and her naiveté when it came to this dating world she'd stepped in to, however unwillingly.

Charlotte, 7:07AM
Today, actually. I should have done it last night,
but I had a titillating conversation happening.

Sutton, 7:09AM
Oh. I'm sorry. I'm not sure if this is strange to
say, but you've already pointed out that I've said
quite a few strange things already, so: I've liked
talking to you, and I kind of wish you would be
around to give me advice.

41

Drumming her fingers on the countertop, she continued to drain her coffee, as the idea struck her. She wasn't fond of giving personal information out to women on here, but . . . it wasn't as though Sutton was a woman who she'd been meeting up with at a club and taking home, only to never see again after the next day. Besides, once she thought about it a bit more, she was a little concerned for Sutton.

She clearly trusted Charlotte. Luckily for Sutton, that trust wasn't misguided with her. But there were plenty of women on this app who would see a pretty little thing like Sutton and take advantage of those big blue eyes and romantic idealistic beliefs. Charlotte was straightforward with her purely casual intentions; not every other woman on here was so straightforward.

She never did something if she thought it would actually be a bad move, never acted on a thought without considering it carefully. So she thought on it for a few moments.

Giving her phone number to Sutton didn't really have many repercussions. At best, they could continue to talk the way they had been. At worst, Sutton turned out to use it *too* much and Charlotte blocked her. She didn't foresee that happening, but still.

With a deep breath, she wrote back.

Charlotte, 7:14AM
How about this: if you feel the need for my guidance, you can text me. I don't like the feeling that I've thrown you to the vultures.

Sutton, 7:15AM
Your guidance?

Smirking, Charlotte stood to place her cup in the sink. This was the right move, she decided. Sutton hadn't failed to entirely entertain her once yet.

Charlotte, 7:17AM
You did say that I'm your mentor, didn't you?

Sutton, 7:18AM
I told you to ignore that!

Charlotte, 7:19AM
You wrote it; I can't forget it after reading it.
Here's my number. You can use it or not; it's
your choice.

She hesitated before sending the message, because something like *that* really wasn't her style. Regardless, she sent it anyway, along with another message with her phone number, before she set her phone down on the counter, next to her purse.

It was only once she'd finished getting ready and was calling a car to take her to the office that she felt her phone vibrate again.

This time, it wasn't alerting her to a message from *SapphicSpark*, but a text, from an unrecognized number.

Unknown number – 7:25AM
Hi. It's Sutton. I've never had a mentor before.

Charlotte was fairly certain she was going to enjoy this.

Chapter 3

With her music playing in her earbuds keeping her grounded and focused, Sutton worked diligently at her desk in the cramped TA office that she shared with four other Literature TA's. It was nearing the end of the first month of the semester, which meant that she had to grade the first papers of the year for the Early American Lit class.

She'd been working for Dr. Martin for over a year now – having almost camped out in his office to persist in getting the coveted job. His classes were popular due to his wit and the way he engaged students into the material. He taught a wide range of courses, though he favored the Romantics. As did she.

It was nice to work with a professor who was well-respected for his intelligence, who didn't treat her as though she were merely an assistant, but somewhat of a colleague. Granted, a colleague who did work for him, but still.

On the flip side, Sutton had been given a very clipped speech upon getting this job that as he held himself to a high standard, he would also be holding her to one.

Which meant working on strict deadlines when it came to grading. These papers didn't technically have to be graded for a few more days, but Sutton liked to keep her deadlines slightly ahead of schedule. She knew that it was noticed and appreciated.

With only a few left to grade, she broke her concentration when the door opened and Emma stepped in. Emma gave her a nod and a quick smile, before dropping into her own seat as unobtrusively as possible.

Though they were both in their second year of grad school, Emma was a few years older than she was, and had supported herself through undergrad. Even though they'd been friends for over a year by now, there wasn't much else she'd learned about her past.

She stretched, sighing as she leaned back. "How was that test you took?"

The very non-content sigh Emma let out in response was enough of an answer. "Well. Your notes helped a bit but – gross. I have them if you want them back."

"No rush."

"And I'm gonna need a coffee if I'm going to make it through my class later. But, anyway, how did your grading go, Miss Popularity?"

She looked at Emma in question. All she received in response was a nod toward her phone. Strategically perched just out of her eye range for when she was grading to avoid distraction.

"I've only been in here for a few minutes and it's already gone off like ten times. Been buzzing like crazy." Emma informed her with a grunt as she dug into the depths of her perpetually messy backpack, emerging with a book.

She reached for her phone, eyes growing wide in concern when she saw that she had twenty-two unread messages. Sure, she'd been paying no attention to her phone for a few hours, but it was basically the middle of the day.

Her mind was already racing with worst-case scenarios when she saw that the majority of the messages were from the groupchat between herself and her siblings.

Alex – 11:13AM
brought to you practically live from london.
me kicking ass.
[3 attachments]

Sutton silenced her phone as she watched the clips her sister had attached. They were short videos of her, indeed, kicking ass. Alex had been interested in many sports over the years, and had played three – including football, much to their mother's chagrin – throughout her school years. However, even more to their mother's chagrin and blatant worry, the one that had stuck was mixed martial arts. It was really both of her older siblings, Lucas and Oliver's faults; when Alex had followed them around like they were gods, they'd been barely teenagers, and interested in learning to fight.

It made her flinch, not only when Alex got hit, but even when her sister landed a punch. Sutton had never been one for violence, which made the feeling of pride she got when Alex won these fights a strange, almost conflicting thing.

Alex had been training seriously for the last couple of years, since finishing high school, with some of the best coaches in the northeast, and was fighting in an amateur circuit that had competitions throughout the United States and Europe, on her way to being a professional.

She ran her eyes over her siblings' chat – her older brothers Oliver and Lucas congratulating her and taking joking credit for teaching her how to fight, their youngest brother, Ethan, who was still in high school, joining in to scream over how cool it was that Alex knocked out her opponents' teeth.

Even though she hadn't been *not* close with her siblings when she'd been younger, it wasn't until she'd moved away to New York for college seven years ago that she'd really realized how much she enjoyed them, how much she missed them when they were no longer around all of the time.

Still smiling from the feeling of home, she opened the next message.

Regan – 12:20PM
Been at the café since 6. Beth called out, so I'm working a double D: I could use an uplifting best friend visit! My break's at 1:30. There are freshly baked lemon cakes.

Sutton – 12:39PM
You know I'll go anywhere for those lemon cakes.

Regan – 12:41PM
Are you saying you wouldn't come just for me,
your best friend, who would do anything for you?

                                        Sutton – 12:44PM
                              . . . save me two lemon cakes :)

Regan – 12:45PM
Bitch. I'll see you soon.

Her excitement mounted as she opened the final message.

Charlotte – 12:25PM
Something to add to the list, darling: if a woman
ever asks you to go to The Echo – you know, that
hot club in midtown? Don't go, because she only
wants a hook up.

She brought up the note she'd kept saved on her phone since texting Charlotte like this two weeks ago.

True to her word, Charlotte had been acting in somewhat of a guide capacity. What was shocking about it, really, was that she hardly ever mocked Sutton for even asking in the first place. When she thought back on the moment, she could still feel her face burn in mortification.

Still, aside from moments where Charlotte teased her – and even via text, Sutton could tell that it was meant to be just as she took it, lightheartedly . . . if somewhat embarrassing – she was nothing but pleasant. Helpful. Friendly.

In her notes, she added *The Echo* at the bottom. With Charlotte's advice, she'd created a list of "red flags" to look for with women on the app. The list varied from key words found under interests – *I'm not saying to not talk to a woman based entirely on her interests . . . but sometimes there are things to look for. Like when a woman say she's interested in spontaneous fun – and there are several of them on here.*

To bios, which Sutton learned from Charlotte were an option that most people didn't use, as it cost an additional fee – *Trust me, sweetheart, there is no reason that someone would pay to use the additional bio when there is free messaging to get to know someone, unless they feel that their personality through messaging isn't enough to hold your interest.*

To the way women spoke in messages – *I know you're looking for someone long-term, or at least the option of long-term, so you know to avoid anyone who brings up casual flings, but you still need to look out for the women who will talk about marriage after talking to you for a few hours. You don't need that kind of craziness in your life.*

Those were only a few examples. Charlotte mostly had a great deal of colorful words to say about very many women on here who were looking to "dine and dash" – which had been a phrase Sutton had painfully and embarrassingly needed her to elaborate on – when a "pretty young thing" like Sutton was involved.

Sutton hadn't expected every woman that she might make conversation with to be interested in the exact same thing that she hoped for in the long term. But thinking about all of the potential traps that might befall her was daunting, to say the least.

Which was one of the reasons that she hadn't messaged anyone else from the app.

Sutton – 12:50PM
Done. Though I would like to ask why?

She placed her phone on her lap, unsure of whether or not she'd be getting an answer. On the occasion that Charlotte messaged her in the late morning or early afternoon, her responses were then typically sporadic until later that evening.

She organized her papers, shifting the graded ones to the top corner while clipping together the few she needed to complete before tucking them into her bag.

When her phone buzzed in an answer, she felt a surprised yet pleasant flip-flop at Charlotte's timely answer.

Charlotte – 12:55PM
I may have been there before, myself.

Sutton – 12:56PM
Oh, once or twice? :P

Charlotte always had extremely sensible explanations for her words of advice to Sutton, with a plethora of reasons, but it always came back to her own rather extensive experiences.

Charlotte – 12:57PM
Mmm, something like that . . .

Sutton – 12:58PM
What if I wouldn't mind going to a club?

With her phone back on the desk, she continued to meticulously place her items in her backpack. She had no more classes for the day, so when she left campus, she wasn't coming back.

Emma leaned back in her chair – consequently hitting it against the back of Sutton's, with a groan as she dropped the book in her hand to her desk. "God, I can't stand Tolstoy."

With a small drop of her shoulders, Sutton playfully nudged her chair against her friend's. "Want to take a break and come get a coffee with me?"

"Getting a coffee with you, or reading this shit book for Dr. Shepherd . . . let me think about that." She rolled her eyes. "Let me get a get to the end of this chapter and we can go?"

Sutton was already giving her a nod of assent before her attention was drawn back to her phone.

Charlotte – 1:01PM
Oh, "a club" is perfectly fine – depending on which
one you're wanting to go to. But not this one. This is
like a code. Trust me, any woman on SappicSpark who
suggests going to The Echo is only interested in one
thing.

Charlotte – 1:02PM
And it's not the sharp mind behind those baby blues.

She rolled her eyes. She made one inquiry about how exactly someone could dine and dash on a woman . . .

Sutton – 1:04PM
I got that!

Charlotte – 1:05PM
Just wanted to make sure ;)

She'd gotten used to things like that – the winking faces and the casual flirting that she'd started to learn was basically instinctive to Charlotte. So used to it that she didn't even respond to it anymore.

All right, almost. A slight flush had settled on her cheeks.

Sutton – 1:07PM

And what brought this comment on? Did you go there recently?

For a few moments after she sent it, she wondered if she'd asked too much. If it was too personal. Despite the knowledge Charlotte imparted to her with a few anecdotes on occasion, *and* the fact that they'd been talking every day, she was very sparse on the details she gave out about herself.

Which, admittedly, only made Sutton more curious about her. And she was so curious. Probably disproportionately so, given that Charlotte didn't seem to be overly interested in *her* life.

Curiosity was only a natural progression from this tentative friendship – if she could call it that – they'd cultivated, she reasoned with herself. After all, it had been weeks and she still had no idea why Charlotte suddenly deleted her profile. She couldn't be in a relationship, Sutton was sure of that. And she didn't seem like she wanted to be done with hooking up.

Charlotte – 1:12PM

No, no. I walked by it on the way home from a meeting over lunch. I can't believe I forgot to mention it before, actually. Have you ever been?

Sutton – 1:14PM

Are you kidding? You think I've been to a gay bar?

51

I've told you about my embarrassingly limited
experiences with women, remember?

Emma snapped her book closed. "Chapter finished! Coffee please."

They'd barely gotten out of the building before Emma looked up at her, curiosity written all over her face. Somehow, she managed it without looking nosy. "So, who's this person you've been texting all the time lately?"

Sutton stumbled, feeling her cheeks heat up. "I'm not texting anyone all of the time!"

"Yeah. That's the reaction of someone not hiding anything."

She hesitated. But the whole reason she'd told Emma so early on about her sexuality was because she was so laidback about everything and never tried to interfere with anything.

The only other person who knew about her sexuality aside from Regan and Emma was Alex, which was only because she'd eavesdropped on a conversation between herself and Regan last summer. Though she'd gotten closer to her sister in the last couple of years than she'd ever been in the past, Alex was still never particularly interested in her love life.

She took a deep breath. "Well, it all started because Regan created a dating profile for me, on *SapphicSpark* –"

Emma scoffed, loudly and with obvious scorn. "Of *course* she did."

"And she messaged this woman, Charlotte, on my behalf –"

"Of course she did!" Emma shook her head. "That woman never knows when to mind her own business."

Sutton sighed, though she was well-used to how much derision Emma had for Regan, and how much the feeling was mutual. Both were brash and opinionated, but in their own ways. Emma in her dour wit, Regan in her exuberance, and it apparently was like oil and water mixing.

It could be exhausting.

"Are you going to let me tell you or would you like to keep interrupting?"

Even though Emma made a show of rolling her eyes at her, she gestured for her to continue.

"So, Charlotte is this . . . gorgeous, smart, experienced woman, who really only does hookups. Which," she pulled a quick face. "You know, isn't exactly for me. And I told her that. But we got to talking a bit, and now she's been helping me with trying to figure out what actually might be. What might be what I'm looking for, that is," she added to clarify, hoping it would get rid of the incredulous look on Emma's face.

The look remained as she slowly asked, "You're telling me that there is a *gorgeous, smart, experienced* woman, who was interested in hooking up with you, and you . . . are talking to her about finding a date with someone else?"

"Why are you looking at me like that?"

Emma threw her head back and laughed. "You know you're doing this whole online dating thing wrong, right?"

"Shut up."

She acquiesced, even though she was still grinning as Sutton led them the rest of the short way to the café. Regan had worked here ever since moving here five years ago, becoming the manager last year.

Emma groaned. "You said we were having coffee. Not having coffee with Regan."

Regan shot her a look of haughty disdain in return. "You just willingly walked into my workplace; I wouldn't go to your TA office and not expect to find you there. But, by all means, you're welcome to leave. I didn't ask for *your* presence."

Sutton let out a long-suffering sigh. "Okay, children, that's enough. How about we just get our drinks and lemon cakes, and sit down?"

Regan quickly announced to her employees that she would be taking her break, before she deftly got them their drinks – coffee for the two of them, tea for Sutton. She set down a plate of lemon cakes that Sutton was already eyeing before the plate was already out of Regan's hands.

"I did see that they were gone from the case. Thanks for saving some for me."

"Of course. The least I could do as your *best friend*."

She threw in an exaggerated wink and Sutton knew it was to irritate Emma. Which worked.

"Seriously, though. Beth calling out could not have happened at a worst time. I barely got any sleep last night – there was a horror movie marathon on. And now I have to automatically stay until closing? I love the pay raise with being the manager –"

Sutton grinned, swallowing a bite from her lemon cake. "I know, you have the new shoes to prove it."

Regan jokingly tossed her hair over her shoulder. "Yeah, well. I just hate that now, this is my lot in life."

"Sucks to have responsibility, doesn't it?" Emma drawled, in a way that Sutton knew was supposed to agitate Regan.

Before she could say or do anything to diffuse the situation her phone chimed with a text. A quick glance told her that it was Alex sending another video. Quickly, she put her phone face down on the table, deciding to watch when she got back home.

As she reached for a piece of a lemon cake, Emma leaned in. "Is it the woman?"

"No," she answered quickly, hoping that her expression was enough for Emma to not mention it again. But it was too late and Regan's attention had already been caught.

Dark eyes were staring at her with avid interest. "What woman? There's a *woman*, and you told Emma of all people, but not *me*?"

Emma protested mildly, but was more amused than offended. Sutton merely raised an eyebrow at Regan. "I told you there would be consequences to your actions."

"I need to know these things!"

Before Sutton could even react, because she knew what was coming, Regan swiped up her phone. She took a sip of tea and just waited. . .

Regan's displeased gasp didn't disappoint. "You changed your password!"

"What did you expect?"

Regan stared at her as though she'd committed a treasonous crime; utterly betrayed. "I've known your password to get into your phone since – since you've first ever had a phone!"

"And you abused the privilege," Sutton plucked her phone out of her friend's hands, glad to have the upper hand.

She'd almost forgotten Emma was there, until she cleared her throat, and Sutton looked up to see her looking between the two of them. "Why is it such a big deal if Sutton wants to talk to this Charlotte chick? Even if she *is* doing it all wrong."

Sutton flushed, groaning as she didn't even have to look at Regan to know that the moment of realization was dawning on her. Even before she heard her gasp dramatically. "Charlotte? Stunning Charlotte?"

Regan was giving her a wide-eyed look when Sutton finally looked back at her. A wide-eyed look that she recognized the pride in – both pride in Sutton and in herself – before a smug smirk took over. "So my plan *worked*! You're chatting up Charlotte!"

Emma barked out a laugh, disregarding her typical distaste for Regan in order to correct, "No, Charlotte was only interested in a hookup. Sutton's chatting up Charlotte in order to learn from all of her lesbian expertise."

A disgruntled protest worked its way out of Sutton's throat. "Okay, that is how it . . . well, is. But it's not – it's not weird."

Not really.

Still, she'd expected Regan to be somewhat proud of her – once she would inevitably get over her betrayal at being kept in the dark. Instead, she was on the receiving end of a look of disbelief.

"You . . ." Regan trailed off, staring at her in something akin to wonder, before she pointed her finger at Sutton in accusation. "I gave you the *world*, Sutton Spencer! And *this* is what you're doing with it?"

"What the hell do you mean, *you gave me the world*? You put me in an awkward situation and I made the best of it!"

"Made the best of it?" Regan parroted. "Making the best of it would have been to have sex with this gorgeous woman who apparently told you that she wanted to fuck you! You were supposed to *sleep* with stunning Charlotte, not have her become your . . . your lesbian guru!"

"She's not my *lesbian guru*."

That just sounded stupid. They were . . . friends. Sort of.

Regan rolled her eyes. "Yeah, clearly not a very good one, considering you haven't gone on a date yet."

"You're way too invested in my love life."

Much to her surprise, it was Emma who jumped in. "I hate to agree with Regan, you really know that I do. But, like, you had a perfect window of opportunity to bang this apparently hot woman, and instead you made her your buddy?"

Regan pounded her fist on the table. "She *hates* to agree with Regan, but she is anyway! That's how you know Regan's right."

"All right, I'm going to take it back if you're going to start talking in third person."

Sutton pressed her fingers into her eyes to stave off the headache that was starting to form. "All right, that's enough! No more talk about my love life or else I'm going to bring *both* of your love lives into discussion, and I don't think that's something we want to discuss between the three of us."

***

It wasn't until late that night that Sutton heard from Charlotte again.

She was undeniably pleasantly surprised to see that Charlotte was messaging her at all this late. Though she did stay up fairly late the second time they'd spoken, that certainly wasn't the norm that they'd established in the past couple of weeks.

Charlotte – 11:22PM
You don't have to have slept with a woman
in order to gain entrance to a gay club, darling.

> **Sutton – 11:24PM**
> *Oh, really? Wow! Thank you very much for the info.*
> *But do I strike you as the type of person who has gone*
> *out to a gay club in the hopes of finding . . . anything?*

Charlotte – 11:25PM
You certainly have a point with that. Forget I ever
asked.

Charlotte – 11:28PM
Also, I apologize for not answering for so long.
I know that you're typically going to sleep by now,
but I had meetings all afternoon and just got home
from an evening with my brother.

A tired smile claimed her lips; it was always nice to know that Charlotte paid attention to the smaller details. It seemed like Charlotte rarely missed a detail or forgot anything.

> **Sutton – 11:30PM**
> *It's okay; I'm watching Casablanca for the*

hundredth time and I need to see the ending.

Charlotte – 11:32PM
Do you need an intervention?

Sutton – 11:33PM
From this? I'm offended you even asked.

As she sent the message, she went to rest her head back down, before Charlotte's message belatedly registered to her.

She reread, feeling re-energized. A brother! Charlotte had never texted about any family before. She was so private, about everything. There was no way her careful phrasing was incidental.

She had no idea what she did for a living, only that she pulled long hours wherever it was that she worked, seemed to have many meetings, and would often bring her work home with her.

Despite being curious, Sutton didn't ask. It went without speaking that Charlotte clearly wanted these boundaries.

Sutton – 11:35PM
How was your night out with your brother?

That was casual enough, right?

Charlotte – 11:40PM
It was good. We went out for drinks; we had a few things to discuss.

Sutton – 11:43PM
I've never actually gone out for drinks with my

58

brothers, but none of them live around here so
it's not as if it could be a common thing between
us, anyway.

Sutton – 11:44PM
I have three of them. Brothers, that is. Two older,
one younger.

She forced herself to drop the phone in her lap to refrain from sending any more word vomit. Even as she hoped that by offering information, Charlotte would feel more comfortable sharing her own.

Charlotte – 11:48PM
Three brothers and a sister. Quite a large family
you have. So you understand brothers, then.

Sutton – 11:50PM
More than most, I would say. I miss them, more
than I thought I would when I left home.

It was a perfect opening for Charlotte to ask her more. Ask her the obvious questions – about where "home" was, for example.

She didn't.

Charlotte – 12:01AM
I can imagine. I have a brother that I'm not as
close with, but the one I saw tonight doubles as
one of my best friends.

Charlotte – 12:01AM

*I have to get to sleep, though. I have early meetings
in the morning. And, if I'm not mistaken, this is
slightly past your bedtime on a weekday ;)*

Sutton – 12:03AM

*You're not mistaken, actually. I've been yawning
for over an hour. Goodnight and good luck with
your meetings.*

"Whatever meetings they are," she murmured.

Charlotte – 12:05AM

Goodnight, darling, and thank you.

Chapter 4

Charlotte didn't particularly believe in luck; she believed in creating her own opportunities, and typically she was damn good at taking advantage of whatever situation she found herself in.

She wasn't naïve. She was well aware that the family she'd been born into and the life she'd been given played a large role in who she was and what she had. The Thompson family had deep political, societal, and business connections back home in Virginia, and had for handfuls of generations.

On the rare occasion that something didn't go according to her anticipated plan, Charlotte typically took it in stride. Employed a back-up plan that she'd usually thought of concurrently with the original plan. She'd long ago learned that it was a requirement of a successful politician to plan for several roadblocks as well as being able to improvise.

She was skilled at thinking ahead, at creating doors for herself where there had previously been walls.

However, she couldn't deny that despite her belief that karma wasn't real, that good fortune didn't fall upon people for mere luck, she couldn't deny that there were times when everything in the universe simply seemed to align.

Today was one of those days, and she could not be more thankful.

Her heels clicked on the floor as she glided across the office, a satisfied smirk on her face as she tapped the folder in her hand against her palm. Without a knock, she entered Dean's office and swiftly shut the door behind her, striding up to the desk when he lifted his head from where he'd been focusing on the paperwork in front of him.

She placed the file on his desk, then tapped her fingertips on it decisively. "Jack Spencer is here."

The words came out in a conspiratorial whisper, tone undeniably excited.

Dean sat back in his chair. "Jack Spencer?"

"The one and only," Charlotte smirked as she leaned her hip against his desk. "He's having a meeting with my grandmother right now, and I presume he'll be staying for the charity fundraiser tomorrow evening."

In fact, she knew he would be staying for the fundraiser. Once she'd spoken to her grandmother the previous night and learned that he would be in New York – one of his very few work visits – she had made some inquiries about his plans and the duration of his trip.

She could see the dawning start in on her boss's face only seconds before he shot her an amused glance. "Ah. So you're planning to win over the illustrious Senator during the fundraiser?"

She scoffed. "Not *just* at the fundraiser tomorrow." She reached out to tap a finger against the file she'd brought in with her. "This is the follow-up on my meetings with the Mary from Children's Services, as well as the reviews you needed from me by the end of the day."

He nodded slowly. "Ah, so you've finished all of the work you were planning to do in the office this afternoon, because you don't plan on only sucking up to Spencer tomorrow night, but today, too."

She shot him a wink. "I love when you catch on quickly. A jump-start on winning someone over never hurt."

"Certainly not when you're dealing with Jack Spencer."

She let her mouth fall open in mock-offense. "Do you doubt my ability to charm?"

The look he gave her wasn't enough to make her drop her smirk, as she'd already steeled herself against potential worry. Charlotte knew that winning Jack Spencer over would be an uphill battle, especially in such a short amount of time. But she also knew that she *had* do it – or, at the very least, do as well as she could.

There were very few families in the nation who were as respected as the Spencer's. With even older societal and political ties than her own family, it would be pressing to think of a time when there was not a Spencer in some sort of public office in Massachusetts. With a continuously impressive approval rating, Jack Spencer seemed to be keeping up his family tradition.

Which meant that his approval of her running for the seat in the House would be quite a positive endorsement for her campaign. His support would be great in any election, but even more so for this particular seat. It was well-known that Jack Spencer and the deceased John Kelvin were very close, so whomever Spencer would endorse to take over John Kelvin's now-empty seat could make a difference to the election.

It was also well known that gaining Jack Spencer's respect was not a job easily accomplished, especially not in a short amount of time.

Plus Charlotte felt she was already at a disadvantage. It was yet to be made public who would be running for the seat as her opposition, not to mention the fact that she'd only ever met the Senator once before. Which had been over ten years ago, just after her grandmother had been elected as President for the first time. He'd only met her – briefly – as the granddaughter of a politician. Never as herself.

However, she took it in stride.

It was why she'd stayed up for hours later than she normally did to finish the work she'd needed to do today in the office. So she could be free to *conveniently* be close to her grandmother's office a few blocks away when her meeting with Spencer would be over. Free to just-so-happen to invite him for lunch.

Finally, Dean sighed. "I don't doubt your ability to charm; I doubt his ability to be charmed."

"Everyone can be charmed," she challenged. "There is always an angle," that, she murmured mostly to herself. The issue was finding the right angle.

She could see the amusement bright in his expression as he shook his head. "Well, you know the deal. During the campaign, your office hours are as flexible as you need, as long as you still get your work done, which I have no doubt you'll do."

Before she could thank him, the phone on the desk next to her rang. She shot him a smile before sliding off of her perch on the desk. "I'll see you later."

He gave her a nod as he reached for the receiver, and she closed the door behind her on the way out.

By her estimation, she had forty-five minutes before Jack Spencer's meeting with her grandmother would be finished. Well, technically it was an hour before his scheduled appointment would be over with, but she'd put together all of the information she knew about him and concluded that he would probably be as efficient as he could be in order to spend as little time in the meeting.

It was not a well-kept secret that the Jack Spencer would much rather keep to dealing with his own state and matters of interest that he was working on, rather than collude with the other politicians. He had some very close friends and politicians he worked with in Massachusetts and in a few other surrounding states, and would make the requisite trips to D.C. when necessary, but other than that . . .

He seemed to like her grandmother more now that she was no longer the President, and was instead the head of the Thompson Foundation. With a focus on poverty and homelessness, her grandmother had her home office here in New York, and, as it was also an issue of interest for Spencer, he made the trip to discuss initiatives every so often.

Just as she made it back to her seat, she felt her phone vibrate. She was fairly certain that even without looking, she knew who it was from.

Sutton – 11:47AM
Should I even ask why you answered my text at
three o'clock in the morning?

Charlotte – 11:49AM
You probably shouldn't. I will, however, tell you
that it was for a good cause.

While Charlotte would be drinking a bit more coffee than usual today in order to stay alert, this was one of the first days that could truly matter for her campaign.

Sutton – 11:51AM
I shouldn't judge how late you stayed up last night
anyhow. I was up later than usual, too. I only missed
your text by less than an hour.

Intrigued, Charlotte hummed under her breath. She'd been talking to Sutton through text for nearly a month now. In that time, it was impossible for her to not have learned her schedule by now. Even on weekends, Sutton didn't typically stay up later than one in the morning.

Charlotte – 11:53AM
And why were you up so late, darling? Hot date?
Hot date, and you never even told your lesbian guru?

She sent it with a smirk, before setting her phone down and combing her fingers back through her hair, reaching for a clip. Her hair was curled today, and she clipped it back, only taking a moment to double check that her curls were over her shoulders, not out of place.

Despite the fact that Sutton had still yet to delete her account on the app, she also hadn't actually gone out with anyone, either. Charlotte knew Sutton well enough to know that she certainly hadn't gone out to browse any profiles. But she knew women – especially many women who used *SapphicSpark* – and she was correct in thinking that she would have been eager to scoop a pretty little thing like Sutton right up, considering the amount of messages Sutton would tell her she'd received.

The only thing was that out of the women who had messaged Sutton, they fell into some category on the red flag list in some way, shape, or form. At least, that was as far as Sutton told her. Charlotte would never tell Sutton not to go out with someone, but Sutton never seemed terribly interested in anyone despite her warnings.

Sutton – 11:56AM
Ha ha. You're hilarious. Take your show on a comedy tour.

Sutton – 11:57AM
I never should have told you that my friends called you that.

Charlotte – 12:00PM
Probably not ;)

It amused her to almost no end.

Sutton – 12:02PM
Regardless, no, there was no hot date. Pretty much the opposite, actually.

Sutton – 12:05PM
*No date at all! I wanted to get everything done for
today and tomorrow, because I have plans with my
family. Well, my dad, really.*

Charlotte – 12:06PM
Your father is here? You must be happy.

She'd learned that Sutton was not from New York and that she missed her
family quite a bit. However, much like she'd not told Sutton the actual details
of her family, she didn't know the specifics.

It was strange, knowing someone the way she knew Sutton. She knew her
personality, at least through text message. She knew her sense of humor, that
she had a good heart. She knew facts about her, like that she loved *Casablanca*
and preferred tea to coffee, but not the big picture.

They'd formed . . . a friendship, in a sense of the word. A friendship in the
sense that she felt comfortable enough to discuss some things with Sutton that
she wouldn't have discussed with a woman she was hooking up with.

In hindsight, it truly was an arrangement that worked well for Charlotte.
While she had Caleb and Dean, she didn't have any female friends. No one
close who knew of her sexuality, who she could speak freely with about things
like that. No one who hadn't known her for years or knew the side of her that
she couldn't be at work.

This way, she had somewhat of a friendship with Sutton – where Sutton
knew her personality and she had someone to talk and joke with – but it didn't
get caught up in the very real, complicated matters of her plans, her goals, her
career.

Sutton – 12:09PM
I am. I didn't think I would be seeing him until
the holidays.

She received Sutton's text at the same time as her phone buzzed with the alarm she'd set, to make sure that she wouldn't be late to her plan of cornering Jack Spencer upon coming out of his meeting. Her stomach twisted in excited anticipation, the same feeling she got whenever she was proposing a new plan or especially when she'd been mapping out steps in her campaign in the last few weeks.

After taking a moment to make sure she was as composed and as well put-together as she always made a point to be, she grabbed her purse and her phone. She typed quickly as she walked.

Charlotte – 12:11PM
I'm sorry to cut this short, but I've got to meet
someone. I hope you'll have fun with your dad.

Sutton – 12:12PM
That's all right! I'm going to see him shortly,
anyway. Good luck with your meeting!

Charlotte walked with purpose out of the office, even as she couldn't resist tacking on another message.

Charlotte – 12:13PM
You always say that, you know. Every time that
I'm going into a meeting, you wish me luck.

Sutton – 12:14PM
Is that . . . a bad thing?

Charlotte – 12:16PM
No, not at all. It's just, I could be going to a meeting
of ill repute, and you are still wishing me luck.

Sutton – 12:18PM
I can't wish you luck in your meetings regarding
drug dealing or murdering or the like?

She grinned, even as she shook her head. Sweet, trusting Sutton. It was that aspect that made her feel this strange protective urge in the first place, and the joking wit of her first message that she'd discovered in the last few weeks that made Sutton even better to talk to.

Charlotte – 12:20PM
I've got to deal some drugs into my hitmen ring,
now. Have a good day, Sutton.

She tucked her phone away as she power-walked her way to the Thompson Foundation building, checking her watch to make sure she was on time just as she reached the double doors that would lead into her grandmother's office. With a deep breath, she squared her shoulders and nodded to the security team on either side of the entrance, before she pushed the door open and strolled in, right on time. On time as in fifteen minutes early.

Only to falter in her steps, when she saw through her grandmother's open door that she was on the phone, with no one else meeting with her in the office.

For a moment, she saw the plans she'd concocted start to fall away, before she closed her eyes and took a deep breath. Warding away the disappointment, she turned to face her grandmother's secretary. "Elinor, where is Mr. Spencer?"

The woman looked up at her from where she'd been typing at her computer, uncertainty on her features. "I'm not sure. His meeting with your grandmother was scheduled through twelve forty-five, but they seemed to have wrapped business up early."

"I can see that," she kept her voice light, measured, even though there was a potential headache brewing behind her eyes, "When did he leave?"

"Hmm." She checked her watch. "A little less than ten minutes ago, I would say."

Ten minutes . . . she could work with that. The wheels in her head were already turning. "Do you know where he went?"

Elinor grimaced – an answer even before she reluctantly shook her head. "I'm sorry. But I can pull up his schedule for tomorrow, if you'd like to see if there is an available meeting time?"

Charlotte was already shaking her head, but she gave her a quick, appreciative smile. "No, but thank you."

She hitched her purse over her shoulder, her pace hurried but not breaking into a run. Barring an emergency, never in public would she do that. A dignified composure was one of the best armors she could have.

She didn't want to have a *meeting* with Jack Spencer; that would clearly show her hand. A person didn't outwardly lobby for someone's respect – not a smart person, anyway. It had to be done naturally.

Or, appear to be done naturally, she thought with a grim amusement.

It was a friendly but terse conversation with one of the security guards outside of the foundation, a subway ride, and twenty minutes later that found Charlotte paused outside of Topped Off. It was a small, but brightly and neatly decorated café, rather close to an NYU campus.

She'd never been here and she took a moment to frown up at the sign. It was a cutely designed coffee cup, with the Topped Off logo splashed into a coffee mug. But she could not for the life of her imagine why Jack Spencer would be going here, out of all of the places to get a cup of coffee in the city.

The security guard had assured her that he'd just had a conversation with Mr. Spencer on his way out of the building, and that this was the place he was going . . . but he could have been wrong.

She took a deep breath and smoothed her hands down the sides of her skirt, wishing it would ward off the slight October chill in the air; she hadn't exactly been prepared for a prolonged period outside. Then she peered into the window of the café. It was decently empty, only a few of the tables taken up, with two young women working behind the counter. None of the patrons were the man in question.

Which had been the reason that she'd taken the subway in the first place. She'd wanted to beat him here, rather than make it appear as it truly was – that she was following him. After learning that he'd intended to walk, she went in the opposite direction to the closest subway stop.

But maybe she was in the wrong place entirely and this was all for nothing. Which would be such a frustrating waste of valuable time.

The only outward sign she allowed herself was a sharp, huffed out breath.

Which got cut off as when she looked up as someone turned the corner. The vexation that had been coiling inside of her melted away, her mouth shifting into an easy smile. Because perhaps this café was an unforeseen destination for Jack Spencer, notoriously serious Senator of Massachusetts, yet here he was.

Though she was curious about what the hell he was doing here, she couldn't care about anything other than the fact that she was in the right place.

Standing up straight, she turned to look at him fully. "Mr. Spencer! Coming for a cup of coffee?"

His footsteps faltered and he paused a few feet away, somber gray eyes scanning over her face in an obvious search for recognition. She knew he was coming up short, even before he spoke. "Uh, yes. I'm sorry, I don't recall . . ."

She offered her hand. "Charlotte Thompson. We've only met once, years ago, so no need for apologies."

He nodded and gave her hand a quick, firm shake. "Ah, right. We met at your grandmother's inauguration. How are you?"

"Quite well, thank you. I'm working as a Deputy Mayor for Dean Walker now, actually," she slipped in, as her hand fell back to her side. "Mostly focused on human services."

He gave her a considering look. "That's admirable work."

She felt slightly victorious already. She'd thought that he would appreciate her focus area, as it did often align with his own priorities when it came to social issues.

"Thank you. I'd actually read over several of the plans that you'd implemented when I was developing a deal between the homeless shelters and food banks. They were extremely helpful." It didn't really count as schmoozing when she was telling the truth, and her grin was genuine.

"I'm glad the plans could help."

His words were concise and final, his expression was still not engaged, though polite; he didn't want to discuss work, wasn't interested in jumping into a discussion on policy, as many other politicians she'd met were.

What was the way in?

His eyes wandered to the door of the shop behind her and she astutely stepped aside. "Would you like to perhaps get a cup of coffee with me?"

As he took a step forward toward the café, he shook his head. "Sorry, but I'm meeting my daughter here, very soon."

She appreciated that even though he wasn't actually regretful – that much was clear – he had the grace to apologize. But that wasn't enough to make her give up, especially not when she saw the way his gaze flit over the window, clearly looking for the daughter in question.

There was a triumphant feeling in her chest when she saw the slight changes in his expression, because that was it. His family could be the angle she'd been looking for. For a moment, she cursed at herself because of course she was well-read on his policies and the history of his leadership, even the history of his family.

However, she was unversed on the matter of his actual family, his children. It had been a naïve mistake of hers, she realized now, to assume that he wouldn't be a father first. Because of the fact that he was reputably somber, she'd assumed he would be all business. It had been a miscalculation.

But one that was easily remedied, and she reached for the door of the café. "Well, I certainly wouldn't want to get in the way of any father-daughter bonding time. Do you see her often?"

He beat her to it, opening the door for her, gesturing for her to go first. "Not nearly as much as I'd like. Neither of them, really."

Charlotte watched carefully as he spoke, even as she walked past him into the café. His expression didn't really change so much as slightly shift. Get a little softer at the mention of his children.

She could work with that. "You have two daughters, right?"

"Yes. My youngest, she's in England at the moment. But my oldest goes to grad school here," he explained and the location clicked. Knowing it was chosen by a college girl made much more sense.

She followed behind him toward the counter, thinking of what she knew of the Spencer children. Two daughters, yes. A few sons. The oldest, Oliver, was her age, already working toward becoming a partner at a prestigious law firm in Boston. He would most likely one day campaign for office, she assumed.

"And your wife, is she here, too? Meeting you and your daughter?" She hadn't been able to confirm whether or not Katherine Spencer had joined her husband when she'd done her limited research last night.

"She's working on a deadline of her own."

She, of course, was familiar with Katherine Spencer's writing, which was another avenue of conversation. But there was something about the succinct way he'd said it that told her he didn't like people questioning into his wife's business.

Before she could say anything, the woman behind the counter popped up from where she'd been behind the pastry counter, a bright smile on her face as she enthusiastically called out, "Mr. Spencer!"

A bigger smile than she'd been given crossed over his features and Charlotte turned to look at the woman. She was pretty, maybe a few years younger than herself. She had dark hair pulled into a ponytail, and she brushed her hands on the apron she was wearing.

He stepped forward. "Regan, how are you? Staying out of trouble?"

There was affection in his tone, but not *quite* warm enough to be the daughter who'd made him seem so soft in the eyes.

She winked. "You know me."

"That's why I asked."

She didn't even take his order before she called to the other woman working behind her, "Large, plain black coffee. Strong as we have. I got you, Mr. Spencer." The woman turned toward her. "And what can I get y – oh, my god!"

Both Charlotte and Mr. Spencer started. She looked around, searching for the cause of the outburst. But there was nothing amiss and the woman's – Regan, as Jack had referred to her – dark eyes were focused on her, uncomfortably alight.

Suspicious, she quirked an eyebrow and kept her expression firm in a way that she knew often cut through people's amusement. "I'll also take a plain black coffee. Large."

It didn't work with this woman, though, whose grin widened and she reached for a cup without taking her eyes off of Charlotte's face. She dug out a marker. "Can I get a name for that?"

74

There were alarm bells ringing in her head, and instead of answering, Charlotte peeked around at the few other patrons – many of whom didn't have names on their cups – before she deliberately stared at the cup the other girl was filling for Mr. Spencer, which was also blank.

She pointedly turned back to this Regan woman and she took a moment to scan over her face. There was no way she'd ever hooked up with her; there may have been many women and there may have been some alcohol involved in several hookups, but she didn't forget a face.

She didn't think this was someone she'd ever even met with in the past. The woman looked highly entertained, though, and the expression irritated her.

Regan-the-barista followed her gaze. "Oh, Beth never writes the names. She's new." She ignored the indignant "*Hey!*" called out from the woman behind her, as well as the dirty look.

Charlotte merely sighed; she had limited time with Jack Spencer and she didn't want to waste it. "Charlotte."

When Regan cackled, Charlotte narrowed her eyes.

"I'm not laughing at your name. Promise," she assured as Charlotte paid.

She knew to doubt the validity of this reassurance with such mirth dancing in her eyes. Still, she turned to face Jack, who didn't look nearly as concerned as she did by the behavior that could only be classified as weird.

He shrugged. "That's my daughter's friend; she's always been a high-energy girl."

It wasn't comforting because Charlotte still got the feeling that Regan knew something she didn't. Reading people was her skill and as far as she knew, it wasn't Jack Spencer's.

Limited time, she reminded herself. "So, if Katherine won't be joining you, are you still going to be attending the charity fundraiser while you're in town?"

She knew he had a plus one; she'd even called the event planner to double check and wheedled her way into getting their seating arrangement changed so that she could sit across from Jack and his plus one.

"Yes. I'll be there."

His face was almost comically the picture of displeasure at the prospect of spending the night rubbing elbows with the New York elite. It set her at ease, though, as this was all in his expected profile.

"So will I. The event is actually to raise money for a youth organization I've worked closely with; it's an extremely good cause," she slipped in, sincerely. The improvement of the free health clinic for homeless teens had been one of her greatest achievements in the last few years.

He gave her a considering look. "I've heard of some of the work done there."

His tone was as positive as she would have expected, but not very open to conversation. She worked around it. "Will anyone be joining you at the function?"

His eyes warmed notably and she knew she'd hit her target. "Yes, actually. My daughter agreed to come."

"That's wonderful. I'm sure she won't find it too boring. You said she's in grad school right now?"

"Yes. And far better at upholding her social graces than I am; she gets that from her mother." He turned to accept his coffee from the second girl – Beth – with a small smile, and a generous tip in the jar.

"Order up, *Charlotte*!" Regan called, placing the cup at the other end of the counter, but not letting it go.

Charlotte kept her expression congenial. "Did you make it special?"

She was met with a wide smile. "Of course. From the heart, with lots of . . . experience."

That tone sounded the warning bells even louder in her mind, as she reached out to accept her cup, eyes now narrowing the slightest bit. "Sounds perfect, thank you."

She dropped a tip in the jar, hoping by some nature that her money was going to Beth at the end of the day.

She walked to the station with the sugar, feeling Regan's eyes on her back. When the bell over the door rang to signal someone coming in, she was stirring in her sugar, and the only mind she paid to it was that she heard Regan call out, "Welcome, my beautiful, bright ray of redheaded sunshine!"

"Hello to you, too, weirdo," an appealingly husky, feminine voice said back, in a much quieter, calmer tone. Though, Charlotte noted, not a surprised tone. Perhaps Jack was right in saying that Regan was just a strange woman.

Shaking her head, Charlotte turned, first skimming her eyes over Regan dismissively, before turning farther. The woman who'd walked in had her back to Charlotte, as she faced Jack. His daughter, she decided in a moment, even before she threw her arms around his neck.

She could see his face over her shoulder, melting into a warm smile, and for a moment, she saw the man he must be around his family. A loving father, clearly. That was a nice surprise; it was rare for her to see such genuine affection in this world. Her own parents included.

She took a sip of her coffee as she turned her attention to the daughter. She was barely on her tiptoes as she had her arms wrapped around his neck in a hug – she was tall. A few inches taller than herself, without a doubt.

And no wonder, as she took in legs encased in tight jeans. Long, clearly lithely muscled legs that went on for miles, apparently. Charlotte took a deep breath in through her nose even though she didn't stop herself from continuing her gaze up and over her ass.

Which was just as phenomenal to look at as her legs were – or better.

Her eyebrow quirked slightly in interest before she shook her head at herself. She was thankful that she knew that she was discrete, because checking out the daughter of the man she wanted to win over – who always appeared to have somewhat traditional ideals – that was not a smart plan, no matter how subtle the checking out was.

But still. *Damn.*

With a deep breath, she pushed herself away from the counter, ignoring Regan whose gaze she could still feel. Slowly, she walked closer. Close enough to hear the daughter with the fantastic ass say, "I'm so happy you're here," as they pulled back from their hug.

Regan pointedly cleared her throat from behind everyone. "I'm happy we're *all* here."

"What are you on today?" The exasperation was clear in Jack Spencer's daughter's tone as she turned.

And it was only as she turned that Charlotte's eyes caught on the long braid pulled over her shoulder. The long braid of soft-looking, smooth, shiny *gorgeous* red hair. A shade that not many people had, but a one that seemed familiar to Charlotte.

Even if she'd only seen it in a picture.

Her heart started to pound uncomfortable as her gaze darted up at the woman's face, and – oh, yeah. There was no mistaking it, even from the few pictures she'd seen.

A well-defined jaw, skin that was just as flawless at it had been in the picture, with full pink lips, and a softly sloping nose. But it was the eyes that made her breath catch. The picture hadn't been able to do them justice, the brilliant blue that they were.

Eyes that landed right on her, staring wide in shock.

A shock that Charlotte refused to mirror on her own face, keeping her features schooled, even as her mind felt like it was absolutely screaming.

Charlotte always had a backup plan or managed to figure one out quickly. Jack Spencer goes missing? She finds out how to track him down. Jack Spencer's daughter turns out to be Sutton, the woman who not only knew about the sexuality that she kept very private around other politicians, but knew the ins and outs of Charlotte's sexual experiences . . .

It was enough to make her head spin and for the first time, she felt a small jolt of panic dart through her. This was so far from her realm of what to expect,

78

that she found herself speechless for a few seconds. Which, alone, was enough to startle her into action.

Shaking her head, she made sure her smile was kept in place.

Thankfully, though, Jack stepped in. "This is my oldest daughter, Sutton."

"Sutton *Spencer*," she murmured, the name flowing smoothly from her lips.

She didn't take her eyes from Sutton's face. Sutton, who was still staring at her, eyes wide, cheeks blushing a profuse red. God, of course Sutton blushed like that. In another situation, Charlotte might have found it cute.

Actually, she did find it cute.

But this was certainly not the time or place. She wished she could mentally communicate with Sutton to just . . . get through the next few minutes, without outing Charlotte or saying anything that implicated *anything*.

"Charlotte?" Her name fell from Sutton's lips in a soft, mystified question.

She wanted to squeeze her eyes closed for a few moments, just to gather her thoughts at whatever train wreck this was turning into. But she didn't – couldn't – and instead, she finally dragged her eyes away from Sutton, and looked at her father.

Who looked between the two of them. "You two know one another?"

He settled the question on Sutton, who coughed as her cheeks were still stained red. "I – um – yes. Kind of. I mean, we . . ."

Sweet Sutton, she realized at that moment, had not only not been with a woman, but was either not out to her family or was not comfortable enough with them to talk about her endeavors on a dating app.

Either way, Charlotte could work with that and she cleared her throat to get their attention. "We met here, once. Regan mixed up our orders and gave me Sutton's tea by mistake."

She threw the barista a look, who was watching the exchange with an enthralled smile. It was no wonder that she'd been so excited by Charlotte's arrival in the coffee shop – as far as she knew by Sutton's own description, Regan loved this kind of thing.

Regan shrugged, unabashedly. "Yeah, I stepped right into the middle of their meeting, Mr. Spencer. You wouldn't believe it."

Finally, at that comment, Sutton's wide eyes left Charlotte and she threw a glare at Regan. Who, though she clearly pushed boundaries, didn't say anything farther.

"That's Regan, always making a mess of situations that she has no business being involved in," Sutton bit out. Those startlingly blue eyes flickered back to Charlotte. "I . . . what are you doing here?"

It was strange being addressed by Sutton in person. She offered a small smile. "I was getting a cup of coffee."

"Charlotte works at the mayor's office. Her grandmother works at the Thompson Foundation," Jack explained, and Charlotte couldn't be happier that he seemed rather oblivious to the atmosphere. When she looked back in retrospect, she would also find it amusing that he'd referred to her grandmother as holding her current job running the Foundation as opposed to her presidency title. "She'll be attending the dinner tomorrow."

Realization dawned on Sutton's face, Charlotte watched it happen, and she could see the wheels turning. All of the times she'd talked about meetings, all of the hours she'd kept, it was snapping into place.

She prayed to god that in that realization, Sutton was also seeing why she'd been so pointedly private.

"Oh," Sutton muttered, staring at her for a moment, before another blush crept up her neck.

Charlotte had hit on this woman, this tall, gorgeous woman standing in front of her. The woman who knew her as a lesbian – who was somewhat of a friend to her. Who was also the daughter of a very important politician, whose favor Charlotte wanted to win. It was a strange, and unpredictable clashing of her worlds. Worlds that she'd never intended to or wanted to bring together.

Her façade didn't fade at all, her expression still unchanged even as her thoughts ran a mile a minute. What was clear, though, was that she needed to leave before anything was said or done to clue Jack Spencer in to the atmosphere around him.

She stepped forward to offer her hand to him. "It was nice to see you again, Mr. Spencer."

He shook her hand briefly, returning her sentiment.

Then she turned to Sutton, who met her eyes, looking down at her as long lashes fluttered. "It was nice to meet you, Charlotte."

Sutton's voice was soft, almost as soft as the hand she offered. She let herself take a moment to enjoy the warm softness of her palm against her own, long fingers clasping around hers for a brief moment. Only a moment, though.

She cleared her throat and pulled back, composing herself, as she shot Sutton a small smirk. "Don't you mean nice to meet you again?"

Sutton's eyes darted to her father. "Um, yes. That."

"I should be going. I've a meeting soon." It was an easy lie. "Have a good afternoon."

"Good luck," Sutton murmured, and Charlotte's gaze snapped to her. Sutton, for her part, didn't even realize she'd said it, until her eyes went wide, then closed tightly. "I just – in your meeting. Good luck."

Charlotte felt her lips tick up into an inevitable smirk, one she often wore when texting Sutton. "Thank you."

"Bye, Charlotte! It was a pleasure seeing you!" Regan's voice followed her as she started to walk.

With a measured expression, she turned to face her. "A pleasure," she echoed, and decided resolutely that everything Sutton had told her about Regan was definitely true.

She shook her head as she left the café, and she only allowed herself to look back once the door closed behind her. Sutton was staring at her, still looking shocked – as much, if not more, than Charlotte felt.

Lifting her eyebrow, Charlotte took a deep breath and shook out her shoulders as she walked away.

Out of every scenario she could have thought of, running into *Sutton*, who happened to be Sutton *Spencer*, the daughter of Jack *Spencer*, Massachusetts Senator . . . hadn't been on any list of possibilities.

Now she had to figure out how in the hell to handle it. Though she fancied herself to have a plan for everything, she truly hadn't thought to have a plan for this.

Chapter 5

Sutton kept her promise to attend the charity event with her father the evening after the disastrously awkward meeting with Charlotte for a small handful of reasons.

First, she'd promised her mother she would take her place for the event after her mom had to cancel in order to make a deadline for her next novel.

Second, she rarely got to spend one on one time with her father and she didn't want to pass up the opportunity.

Third, Regan had pushed her into it by threatening to go in her place if she canceled on her father.

It had nothing to do with the fact that Regan had excitedly stated that Charlotte had been checking her out at Topped Off. Nothing to do with wanting to see Charlotte again . . .

Okay, so even if she did want to see her again, she was still mortified at her reaction to seeing Charlotte in person. The last thing she needed was to spend time with Charlotte, a lesbian who knew about her sexuality and could so easily make her blush, while with her *father*.

They hadn't texted one another since the interaction, though, which left Sutton feeling more uncertain than ever. Clearly, Charlotte kept her political life far separate from her personal life and Sutton – she just hadn't been prepared for her in real life. At all.

As she arrived at the lavish function hall, she took a second to take it all in.

Once upon a time – when she'd been barely a teenager – lavish events like this, filled with wealthy, important people, had been something she dreamed about. She'd been the only one of her siblings who actually liked to attend parties and formal dinners and fundraisers.

The glamor had faded, though, when she'd gotten a bit older and seen that the wealthy, important people weren't the people she'd idolized them to be. It had become especially evident when she'd dated Joshua, whose parents had more money than God and had lived in New York, and thus attended and hosted more parties and dinners with these *glamorous* people in a couple of months than Sutton's parents did in a year.

Even after her disillusionment, Sutton remained the Spencer sibling that enjoyed these events the most, who did the best at remembering who was who, and what she should say.

Hopefully she could do that tonight, even when she saw Charlotte.

With a deep breath to try to calm her nerves, she held her hands against her stomach, pressing into the soft material as if it would help relax her. The dress she'd ended up in was chosen after a debate with Regan, and was a compromise. Sutton refused to wear one of her dresses that wrapped tightly around her hips, cleavage, or butt, nor would she wear one that only reached mid-thigh.

But she'd conceded that she also wouldn't wear one of her more conservative choices, either.

So, she'd ended up in what was actually one of her favorites. A royal blue color, with soft fabric that was snug over her abdomen and had a modest neckline, but that left her shoulders and arms bare. It belted at the waist, and the skirt fell loosely to just above her knees. She'd flat out refused to wear the shoes Regan wanted her to wear – fucking *stilettos*, yeah, right – and instead went with flats.

She'd run a straightener through her hair quickly, leaving it down and over her shoulders. Even if she'd wanted to do something with it, she'd had no time. As it was, she'd called her dad and told him that she would meet him at the fundraiser, rather than him picking her up, because it would give her a little more time to get ready.

She was cutting it close, as they were supposed to be inside and seated within the next few minutes. There were only a few people still milling around out on the front terrace, and it was easy to spot her father among them.

Seeing him outside of the large double doors that were open enough to let echoes of conversation spill out, looking vaguely uncomfortable with his hands in his suit pockets, waiting for her made her smile. It didn't make her apprehension disappear, but it did comfort her, just a bit.

"I'm sorry I'm a little late."

"Don't worry about that." He gave her an appraising look. "Are you feeling all right?"

No, actually, I feel as though I might be sick because you don't know it, but I'm bisexual, and the woman who has been acting as my secretive online lesbian guru is basically your coworker who is here tonight, and she's so gorgeous it's almost painful.

"I'm fine," she choked out, eyes closing briefly to push her thoughts to the back of her mind. Clearing her throat, she reiterated. "Really, I'm feeling okay. I was just running behind schedule and I didn't want to have to make you come all of the way to get me."

He accepted her words with a nod but she didn't miss the fact that his concerned look didn't fade completely. "I don't like the idea of you walking around the city, alone, though."

Now as she rolled her eyes, she felt more at-ease than she had in over a day. A familiar argument. "You *do* know that I live here in this city, right? I walk alone here every day."

"As if that makes me feel any less worried."

She was a prime candidate for her parents' worry, even more so than Alex, in their dad's mind. Sutton would never be able to forget the many, many lectures she'd received upon choosing to attend NYU.

Jack had tried hard to convince her to go to school somewhere more centrally in the northeast, even if it was just a smaller city. Her mother hadn't been as concerned about her being in a big city alone, so much as just not wanting her to be far from home at all.

As it was, there was Lucas who was a park ranger in Maine. Oliver was – and always would be – situated and happy to work close to home, not even really moving away to go to college. He'd chosen to go to Northeastern and lived within a ten minute drive to their parent's house in Newton. And Ethan, at age fourteen, still lived at home.

Alex had moved away, but hadn't truly settled – she went where her career would take her. All over the US or overseas to a multitude of European cities. Sutton was the only one who'd *settled* out of her family's comfort zone.

However, she didn't want to hear anymore lectures on the matter and she linked her arm through his. "Don't worry about me, dad." She spared a look through the doors, only for a second, eyes dancing over everyone she could see for a few moments. But no one stuck out. Charlotte wasn't among them, which gave her the courage she needed. "Should we go in before we're late?"

"I guess so. Let's go." He straightened his back and squared his shoulders in a way that she'd seen him do many times. Always when it came to business and political events, and she'd always thought that him dreading a party or a dinner more than important meetings that he took fairly frequently was so odd.

But she felt herself squaring her own shoulders now in a mirroring move, and for once, she understood.

With that feeling of nerves settling in the pit of her stomach again, they walked in. She moved the way her mother had always taught her to in times such as this, with poise and purpose. Nodding and smiling as they passed people that she'd met in passing over the years, as they did the same to her.

True to form, her dad didn't stop to talk to them. It was something her mother might have chastised him for, but Sutton was perfectly fine with it. Plus, they truly were cutting it close to when they were supposed to be formally seated.

As they arrived at the entrance of the ballroom, they were directed to their seating arrangement.

Unable to stop herself, Sutton searched through the crowd of people as her dad lead her to their table. Most of the guests were already sitting, engaging in conversation.

She saw several people she knew, but no Charlotte. Which was as relieving as it was disappointing, and she rolled her eyes at herself. Here she'd been, nerves wracked all day long at the prospect of running into Charlotte, but – damn Regan for being right – she had been thrilled by the prospect, too.

With a deep breath, she pulled herself together as best as she could. Because spending the night stressing about and thinking about Charlotte was silly. She was here with her dad to keep him company.

It was just in time, too, as they arrived at their designated table, which was already half filled. Half filled with people she knew, for that matter, though there would still be two empty seats after she and her father sat down.

Melissa Royce, the daughter of the current governor of Rhode Island, was out of her chair in a second, bounding over to her with exuberance. "Sutton!"

The small, practiced smile she'd worn as soon as they'd entered the building became genuine seconds before she was engulfed in a hug. "Mel, how are you?"

Melissa's considerable . . . assets were, as always, fairly on display, and, as always, she exuded confidence as she pulled back. "I'm fabulous, of course. I didn't know you'd be here!"

"My mother was supposed to come, but she was busy at home," she offered as an explanation, which was relatively true, just without detail. "I didn't know you'd be here, either."

She waved her hand back and forth lightly. "Oh, of course. I've been visiting the city for a few weeks and dad's a big supporter of the center, so, here we are."

Mel was shorter than she was, so it was no issue for Sutton to see beyond her to the rest of the group they were to be sitting with, even before she started to move back to her chair. Sutton followed, nodding first in the direction of Melissa's father. "Mr. Royce, it's nice to see you."

He gave her a smile. "Sutton! We were expecting your mother, but what better substitute is there?"

"Thank you," she accepted it as the compliment he intended, and really, there were fewer things Sutton felt could be said that made her feel more flattered than comparisons to her mom. Her eyes darted to the other occupants, landing first on an older woman, with graying hair. A former Connecticut Senator, Sutton placed her easily. "Mrs. Wilson, you look very nice."

Anna Wilson, who she was more or less just as familiar with as she was with the Royce family, gave her a warm grin. "You're as beautiful as ever, Sutton. Are you well?"

"Quite, yes. Thank you," she answered, distracted slightly as Melissa drew out the chair next to her, patting it for Sutton to sit down.

She did, catching her dad's eye with a grin as she could see him breathe a sigh of relief. There were fewer people her father would have been more comfortable sitting with at one of these functions.

She wondered if that had been an accident or if these seating arrangements were made with deliberate, thoughtful, precise accuracy. She couldn't imagine the event planner going to so much trouble, but it seemed like it was a big coincidence.

Her dad was already starting to talk to Mr. Royce and Anna when Sutton realized that the man sitting next to Anna wasn't one of her sons, as she'd assumed when she couldn't see his face, as it had been downturned and looking at his phone.

No, it was Kyle Summers and Sutton caught her cringe before it could truly show itself on her face, even as her stomach churned uncomfortably. She bit back her sigh and fixed on as polite of a smile as she could. "Kyle, it's . . . nice to see you here."

The smirk that quirked up his lips was smug and irritating. "Aren't you looking good?"

It was his wink that made her grit her teeth, annoyance welling up inside of her.

There were fewer people she'd rather *not* be sitting with. She'd had a hopeless crush on Kyle when she'd been a teenager, which she could excuse herself for. He was slightly older and extremely handsome, with his chiseled face and blue eyes and muscular body. It was everything that happened beyond her crush that she'd forgiven herself for, but would never forgive him.

Of course, her teenage-self hadn't been the most subtle of people, and he'd taken great pleasure in taking advantage of her crush during the summer that he'd spent interning in Boston. Pleasures that included but were not limited to pushing her at a fast pace to go further than she'd wanted to go physically, and convincing her that while they couldn't be in a legitimate relationship because he was going to be returning to Connecticut for school, it didn't mean they weren't *together*. Secretly.

It had gone on like that for quite a bit of time, until she'd finally ended it just before graduating from high school, because she'd heard that he'd gotten a girl at school pregnant. Another girl who he was *secretly* dating, no doubt.

She'd still never told her family about anything between them, as it would have been useless and awkward. Only Regan had known, and had been ready to kill him. Literally. In the years since, she'd only seen him a handful of times. Each one being extremely unpleasant and brief.

Instead of thanking him, as her manners told her that she should, she narrowed her eyes. "And what are you doing here?"

Sutton knew for a fact that he didn't give a care for any youth center.

His smirk remained firmly in place as he answered, "Mrs. Wilson needed someone to accompany her."

"And there was no one else?" she asked the question lightly, almost jokingly, but not quite.

Luckily, the only person who caught it aside from Kyle was Melissa, who turned to look at her suddenly, a questioning, mirthful look in her eyes. It made her feel somewhat satisfied when the smirk fell from Kyle's face, and he turned back to his phone.

It should have been a dead giveaway, anyway; none of Mrs. Wilson's sons would have had the bad manners to use their phone while they were sitting here like this.

Melissa slid her glass of champagne closer to Sutton. "Here, drink a bit to get that scowl off of your face. After we sit through the inevitably dull speeches, the bar will be open game and then we can really have some fun."

"Awesome," was all she managed before she took a sip.

"Ah, and here are our final companions!" Mel called out loud enough to garner the rest of the table's attention, and Sutton looked along with them to just beyond the empty chairs opposite her and her father.

Where Charlotte was walking – no, not walking. *Striding* – toward them.

She wore a green dress that was tight at her chest and her hips, stopping mid-thigh, and leaving the rest of her legs bare. Long and soft-looking, and she was wearing the kind of heels that made her legs look like they didn't even belong in this world.

Sutton skimmed her gaze up, feeling slightly dazed as she took in her bare shoulders, up her slender neck, taking in her deceptively simple looking done-up hair that allowed a few curly tendrils to fall around her face. Before she landed on her face, taking in the subtle makeup, small smile, and honeyed brown eyes.

That landed right on her.

The champagne she'd been about to swallow abruptly went down the wrong tube, and she felt herself choke on it, spluttering out a cough that drew the attention to her instead.

God, somehow in the time that she'd been stewing in her dislike for Kyle, she'd forgotten that she'd needed to be on the lookout for Charlotte! Even if she had been still looking for her, she doubted she could have been prepared.

She was certain that no one could be prepared for *that*.

"Sutton! Are you okay?" Melissa's voice was loud, and her hand was insistent as it hit her on the back.

It only made her cough more, eyes watering, as her heart pounded against her ribs. And it wasn't doing that for lack of oxygen, either.

How did someone manage to look classy and dignified, yet sexy at the same time? She wondered as she stared up at Charlotte, and as soon as the thought hit her, blue eyes widened in shock.

Damn it all, *this* was the whole reason she hadn't wanted to come tonight in the first place! Because Charlotte had only been in her presence for three seconds, and Sutton was already a mess.

It was only when she felt her dad's gentle hand on her shoulder that she realized she hadn't said anything, and she weakly managed, "I'm fine." She took in as deep of a breath as she could with her stomach twisting into knots. "It went down the wrong way."

Everyone seemed appeased with her answer, save for her dad, who kept his worried eyes on her for a few more seconds. She couldn't have thought of any other time that she would have wanted him to give her less attention ever in her life.

But when she was choking because the woman who she'd met on a gay dating app, who had explained euphemisms to her about eating out other women, among other things, was approaching the table in order to *sit right across from them* . . . yeah, this was the most apt time for her to hope he would focus on something – anything – else.

He seemed convinced enough by her words, and he, like everyone else, redirected his gaze back to the two people who were apparently supposed to complete their table.

She could hear pleasantries being exchanged, but she couldn't bring herself to look back up. Not yet. Not when she still felt as winded as that time Alex had "accidentally" roundhouse kicked her right in the stomach.

Her hands shook slightly as she reached for her glass of water, and the few careful sips she took did very little to make her cheeks feel less hot. The only thing she hoped was that she didn't look *as* red as her hair.

The shock and anxiety that wound through her nerves, laced with that bit of excited anticipation, steadily climbed through her, and she took a deep breath just in time to hear her dad greet, "Dean, it's been a few years. How are you?"

Her gaze flew up to the man in question, because she'd been so distracted and unnerved by the fact that she not only was seeing Charlotte, but was apparently sitting with her too, that she hadn't even noticed the man with her. The man who was Dean Walker, someone she'd met several times in the past, but fleetingly. He was just on the cusp of being friendly but not quite friends with her parents. He'd always seemed nice enough.

Dean nodded at her dad. "Jack, good to see you. I'm doing quite well, and yourself?"

Her dad answered, but Sutton didn't hear it – couldn't hear it, really – because all of her attention was on the way Dean's arm was wrapped around Charlotte's waist. It wasn't a tight or possessive grip, but it was one that screamed of familiarity. Something that had been done many times in the past.

When he pulled out her chair for her, resulting in the way she touched his hand afterward in thanks, suspicion itched at the back of her neck.

She had no time to dwell on the matter, though, not when she was being addressed by Dean, "Ms. Spencer, you're looking more and more like your mother every time I see you. Beautiful, as always."

She cleared her throat and hoped to God that everything that was racing through her thoughts couldn't be seen on her face. "I – thank you, Mr. Walker."

It was all she could say, and she was just grateful that her voice didn't waver.

"Sutton, it's nice to see you again," Charlotte's voice was smooth and sure, and Sutton was unable to not look at her again. In all of the times they'd spoken through message, she'd never imagined that elegant whisper of a Southern accent on her words.

Thankfully this time she didn't choke as she met bright, engaging brown eyes. Unlike yesterday, there was no sly and alluring smirk on her lips, and unlike herself there was no blush. Sutton's mind scrambled to wonder how she did it. She was giving her a smile, a polite one.

How Charlotte could manage to look at her with the same look that she'd given Melissa and her father, as though she was just giving another greeting? Like Sutton didn't meet her on *SapphicSpark* and like Charlotte hadn't flirted with her several times via text for a month?

Sutton was baffled by it – by her – as she gave her a nod and a small smile. "Yes, it's nice to see you, too."

And honestly, she was proud of herself for getting that out as effortlessly as she did.

She had no problem switching gears and glaring, though, when Kyle turned and leaned a little past Dean in order to look at Charlotte. "You are looking absolutely *exquisite* this evening."

It was then that Sutton realized that Charlotte's grins extended beyond coquettish smirks and polite smiles. In a move that was so slight Sutton hardly saw it, the polite smile turned cool as she turned to Kyle. "I'm surprised you noticed, having been on your phone since we arrived."

A surprised chuckle came out of the back of Sutton's throat before she even realized it. Kyle's charming smile soured a bit, and he leaned back in his chair, as Dean then joined in with a laugh.

With a deep breath, Sutton turned to look at Charlotte again. She was sitting directly in front of Sutton, but she wasn't looking at her. Which made sense, clearly, because Charlotte wasn't here for her, but . . .

It was all just so strange.

"So, Sutton, the last I knew, you were studying literature at NYU. What are you doing these days?" Dean asked, startling Sutton out of staring at the side of Charlotte's face.

Charlotte, who she saw give Dean a quirked eyebrow out of the corner of her eyes. Okay, so apparently she'd not told Dean that she and Sutton texted one another, and that only added to the feeling in the pit of her stomach.

Still, she resolutely kept her gaze on Dean; there was far less of a chance that she would make a fool of herself. "I'm actually still a student. In the graduate program, now, though."

"Still for literature?" He asked as he reached out for a glass of champagne.

"Um, yes. I'll be graduating this year," she mentioned, slightly distractedly, watching as he grabbed a second glass, and casually handed it to Charlotte. Who took it without even needing to look. As though this was just another song and dance for them.

He shot her a warm smile. "That's nice. Always a relief to see the light at the end of the tunnel, right?"

"Exactly," she answered, though she didn't necessarily agree. Sutton enjoyed her time at school, and she was rather nervous that it would be coming to an end.

She was also rather distracted with the way Charlotte handed Dean his cloth napkin, right at the time that he had been about to reach for it. The way that she'd anticipated what he was going to do – and she gasped.

Once again, attention was on her and she tried to think of something to say, even as she was bombarded by the absolute *shock* racing through her system.

"I – um, I apologize, I just thought about an assignment that I forgot about," she offered with a feeble smile. A pathetic smile for a pathetic excuse.

But it was the best she could come up with upon the realization that Mayor Dean Walker was Charlotte's boyfriend – or, even worse, her *beard*! It all made perfect sense, didn't it? That was why Charlotte had been so secretive about her life when they'd been texting. Why she didn't let on that she knew Sutton in any way. Why she'd been so adamant about never having more than a one night stand with a woman.

She was so effortless at lying because she apparently was lying to her boyfriend every day!

Sutton reached up to rub at her temple, feeling suddenly overwhelmed. She'd already been nervous about seeing Charlotte tonight, and this was just making it even worse. And now she felt guilty! Because she knew about Charlotte's apparent secret, and Sutton had been *ogling* Dean Walker's girlfriend right in front of him.

His lesbian girlfriend, who had flirted with Sutton and basically offered to hook up with her, before giving her tips about dating women!

If she thought she could get away with it, she would have buried her face in her hands like she wanted to. Instead, she only reached for her water glass to down the remainder of it, trying to calm herself.

She hoped that the conversation had turned elsewhere, but it was apparently still on her, as Dean asked, "So, what are your plans after graduation?"

Feeling herself flush, she shrugged, and she knew it was shaky. "Oh, well, I'm still figuring things out."

Her dad placed his hand on her shoulder. "We've been trying to convince her to move back home for years," he joked, but-not-really.

She could see his concerned look out of the corner of her eye, and if her cover wasn't doing enough to fool her dad, then she was hardly going to fool anyone else. So she took a deep breath to quell the myriad of emotions in her stomach and questions in her head, and fixed on a smile. "But that's probably not going to happen."

"Do you work, as well?"

The question snagged all of her attention, because this time it wasn't Dean, but Charlotte. *Charlotte* was addressing her, in a gracious but inquisitive tone, with a simple lift of a perfect eyebrow.

It was a tone and a question she'd used to address everyone else; nothing out of the ordinary.

But Sutton had to take a moment for it to register. Because Charlotte *knew* she worked, or at least that she did something other than school. Because Sutton had alluded to it during their texting in the last month!

And she was just sitting there, waiting for an answer, with a look on her face that made her look like she was the most innocent person who ever lived.

The contradiction of it all – of the stunning woman she'd been texting, who had a devious, flirtatious streak, and an air of knowing everything, and of *this* woman sitting across from her, who was still ridiculously gorgeous but was civil and soft spoken yet still with a sharp tongue – made Sutton's head spin.

When Melissa turned to look at her, waiting for an answer as well, Sutton realized that she'd been staring questioningly at Charlotte. Her eyes widened, and she coughed before she answered, "I – kind of, yes. I'm a TA."

"That sounds like it would be quite entertaining," Charlotte commented, in that well-mannered tone that gave nothing away.

Melissa scrunched up her nose, "Does it? I feel it would be the opposite."

Sutton found herself smiling at Mel's response, "No, it's actually great a lot of the time."

"Do you get to teach anything good?" Melissa asked, as she picked up her champagne and finished it.

Sutton knew she would be sticking to water for the remainder of the night. She shook her head, "Um, well I don't think I've had a bad class. This semester, it's Early American Literature, but next semester I think it'll be Romanticism through the Ages," which she was actually very excited for. "And I think Dr. Martin is going to include a tie-in to modern romantic classics."

"Like, *The Notebook*? Or *Fifty Shades*?" Mel asked, and actually sounded fairly interested.

Sutton couldn't control the way her nose wrinkled, "Um, well not that modern, probably."

"*Gone with the Wind*?" Charlotte added in, which stole Sutton's attention again.

Blue eyes stared at the woman across from her, who stared right back, but was so nonchalant about it all. Except – she *knew* Sutton loved that. They'd discussed it only last week, her love for older movies and books that highlighted the sweeping romanticism of it all.

Before she could even think of what else to say, there was a woman at the dais at the front of the room, the woman who was in charge of the fundraiser, and everyone's attention was turning to her. Sutton could think of very few times that she'd ever been more grateful for an interruption.

As she turned to face the front of the room, she caught Charlotte's eye, and was unable to look away. Especially when Charlotte winked at her.

It was a blink-and-you-miss-it moment, and Sutton was left gaping long after everyone else's attention had diverted to the front of the room.

The subsequent speeches passed by for over an hour, but Sutton didn't hear a word of them, because the blood was roaring too loudly in her ears, and she felt a bit lightheaded.

She tried to keep her attention on the speakers at the front of the room, at the very least she tried to keep her eyes on them. But she kept finding herself glancing across the table at Charlotte. Who looked cool and composed, and like she was giving her utmost attention to the people talking about the charity and the orphanage.

Sutton hadn't imagined that, right? Charlotte really did *wink* at her, when her . . . bearding boyfriend – bearded beard? – was sitting right there next to her?

She gave Charlotte another look, taking advantage of the fact that no one was truly paying attention to her, because she couldn't not stare, for just a few seconds. Because now, the two Charlotte's were mingling together as one, and it was like the Charlotte she'd known for the last month – flirty, all-knowing, surprisingly thoughtful Charlotte – was there, hidden under Charlotte-the-politician.

It was honestly damning for her to not have figured that out beforehand; she'd been around politicians all of her life. She knew they wore masks. And now, she was less nervous about Charlotte's and more intrigued.

She'd barely collected all of her thoughts by the time the speeches ended. She knew that this was the time for mingling, people would get up to chat, drink, and donate. This was truly her father's least favorite thing to do.

Sutton hadn't been looking forward to it, either. But now, she kind of wanted a chance to be able to talk to Charlotte face-to-face. An actual conversation, unlike the strange dancing around conversations they'd had in the last day and a half since meeting one another.

"This is my favorite part," Melissa half-whispered into her ear, making her jump from surprise. "All of the eligible men . . ."

"Mel! You're here with your *dad*."

"Exactly." Her lips quirked into a mischievous smile. "My dad, not a date. All of the men here are ripe for the picking."

The imagery made Sutton crinkle her nose. "I meant more along the lines of, how can you pick someone up when you're here with one of your parents. But okay."

Melissa laughed and shook her head. "Do you want to come with me?"

Sutton could think of many things she would rather be doing than help her pick up men at this fundraiser, and she quickly shook her head.

"Your loss." Mel shrugged, then shot her a wink before she stood to go on her hunt.

Sutton watched her go for a moment. Two winks. But only one of them had made her hands shake, and with that, she turned back to where Charlotte was sitting. Or, where Charlotte had been sitting.

It was empty now, along with Dean's seat.

Sutton had turned away for only a minute and she was gone!

"Sutton, I'm going to speak to the woman – that last speaker," her dad informed her, and she knew that this was where he would donate, rather than go through all of the steps of intermingling with the other guests.

"Okay," she murmured, and she didn't even think for a moment that she should have gone with him, until he got up and was joined by Mrs. Wilson and Mr. Royce.

Which left her at the table with Kyle, and the nervous anticipation and excitement that had crawled back to life inside of her started to rapidly fade as he leaned forward, a lewd smile on his face, "Just you and I, now. What do you say –"

"No," she cut off, quickly, before standing up. "Whatever you're going to say, it's a no."

With that, she walked away, with no direction in mind. She still couldn't decide if she was glad Regan forced her to come or if she should have stayed home. On the one hand, she hated seeing Kyle Summers for any reason, she was more interested in Charlotte than she was before, and she'd had to live through several embarrassing moments.

On the other hand, she'd liked to see her dad and Melissa, Charlotte had winked at her, and she was more interested in Charlotte than she was before.

She only left the main hall with the intention of going out to get some fresh air, because she didn't intend to ditch her father when he was done talking to the fundraiser organizer. Unlike earlier, when they'd gone into the ballroom and there had been several people milling about the grand hall, there was now no one.

It was rather eerie, and Sutton brought her hands up, rubbing them slight up and down her arms.

And then small but strong hands gripped her arm and pulled her into a small alcove, causing Sutton to stumble over her feet. She was pressed against a wall, and panic came swiftly and easily. Ready to scream, she felt fingertips land over her bottom lip, before a becoming-familiar voice whispered, "Shhh."

"*Charlotte?*" Her name came out in an unintentional whisper and as she spoke, Charlotte's fingertips gently brushed over her moving lips.

The feeling made something inside of her spark, the shock it racing through her causing her to pull her head back. Enough that she hit it against the wall, and she grimaced in pain.

"Were you looking for me?" Charlotte's voice was quiet, both curious and amused. She lowered her hand slowly, rubbing her fingertips with her thumb.

Baffled and still a little dazed, Sutton shook her head slowly, as her eyes adjusted to the relative darkness of the alcove. She hadn't *been* this close to Charlotte before. Close enough to smell her perfume – which was something subtle and floral and kind of enchanting – and see that her skin was literally perfect.

Finally, she breathed out, "No, I – I just wanted to get some fresh air."

Charlotte quirked an eyebrow. "I see. Then I apologize for dragging you in here and scaring a few days off your life," she added, in a teasing tone that made Sutton flush, and her stomach jump.

"More like a few months, but, um, you don't have to apologize," she told her, and slouched back against the wall, her palms brushing down the sides of the skirt of her dress.

That smirk – the same one from her picture on the app, the one she'd given Sutton on the sly at the café – returned to her face. Sutton wondered if Charlotte knew how much power there was in that smirk. "No?"

Oh. Oh boy, she definitely did know. Her heart skipped a beat, "I – I don't . . ."

Then Charlotte laughed. It was a quiet chuckle and it sounded genuine, as she took a step back from Sutton. She couldn't feel her body heat anymore, and a breath of relief left Sutton because she could *breathe* now.

"I'm glad you're like that in real life. The blushing, and all. But you don't have to worry, Sutton. I'm not going to jump you."

She gave her another wink and *there it was*, that feeling that Sutton had just narrowly avoided a life-threatening accident, and she felt heat creep up her cheeks. "Um, about that. I wanted you to know, that I'm not going to say anything. To your boyfriend," she added, rushing the words out and cringing at herself because she hadn't meant to bring this topic up like that.

Instead of looking relieved, like she thought she would, Charlotte's eyebrows came together in confusion. "My . . . boyfriend?"

"Or –" She couldn't bring herself to actually label him as her beard out loud, so she shrugged her shoulders, exasperated, "*Dean.*"

Whatever she'd thought Charlotte might say or do – and she truly had no idea at this point – she hadn't expected her to give her look with those big, doe eyes. Before throwing her head back and laughing. Actually laughing, little giggles escaping in a way that Sutton hadn't imagined, and she didn't know Charlotte could be *cute*, but here she was.

Still, she felt herself blush, and words kept falling out of her mouth, "So, you don't have to worry about – that. I'm not going to say anything. To him. Or my dad. Or anyone. Except for Regan, because, well, she already knows everything, basically."

Charlotte's quiet laughter died out, and Sutton was given a look that was borne of pure amusement and . . . well, it reminded her of the way someone might look at a baby kitten, "Sutton, darling, you know that I'm a lesbian, don't you?"

The term of endearment did not go unnoticed by her, and instead it served to make her blush even more, settling heavily into her stomach. Still, she rolled her eyes and pushed out a heavy breath, "No, what a revelation. But, I meant, if you weren't *out*, and he is your – your beard or something. I won't say anything."

"That's very sweet of you, but –"

A door that Sutton hadn't even known was there opened next to the alcove and Charlotte cut herself off, eyes lighting up.

It was only then that Sutton realized that she hadn't even asked what the hell Charlotte had even been doing *here*. "Why were y–"

The rest of her question was killed the second Charlotte reached up and pressed her soft hand gently but firmly against Sutton's mouth. She stepped even closer to Sutton, the fronts of their bodies *this close* to touching, and Sutton's heartbeat was positively thundering in her ears as she stared at Charlotte with wide, questioning eyes. Her hands shook slightly, but, well, forget the fact that she'd obviously never been this close to Charlotte; she'd never been this close to any woman who she'd been consciously attracted to. Aside from that one, tipsy kiss.

Charlotte had a determined glint in her eyes and she held her other hand up, index finger in front of her lips. As if the hand over her mouth didn't indicate that enough.

It was confusing and exhilarating and Sutton wondered what the hell was happening, but her eyes didn't leave Charlotte, who was listening intently to the conversation happening merely feet away.

"I thank you for your support, Mr. Verbeck," a female voice said, a voice that sounded familiar, but Sutton was too focused on the fact that Charlotte was *right there* and not moving and wondering what in the world was going on to try to connect any dots.

She did, however, easily recognize the voice that answered her, "Of course. This is an opportunity that shouldn't be passed up, and we both know that she already has some strong supporters in her corner."

David Verbeck – who she, thankfully, couldn't see and who, even more thankfully, couldn't see her.

The woman laughed in a cold, humorless way. "Yes, she does indeed. I must get back, but I trust you'll work on my behalf in the meantime?"

"I never pegged you as one who cares much about the dirty youth of the city."

"Perhaps you shouldn't presume," the woman told him, her tone giving way to the truth that she didn't care about *the dirty youth of the city*, and it was clearly a dismissal.

She heard his footsteps fade, and she tried to wrap her mind around whatever conversation they'd been listening to. Because Charlotte backed away from her, her eyes distant, as she clearly knew what they'd been talking about.

"Shit," Charlotte murmured under her breath, and Sutton's eyebrows drew together in confusion.

Tapping her fingers twice against the cool wall behind her, she asked, "What was that?"

Instead of getting an answer, though, what she got was the sound of the door closing, and she watched as Charlotte froze. Sutton did too, because they weren't alone anymore.

Instead, the saw Naomi Young-Carmichael poke her head around the corner, eyes narrowed. *Shit*, if Sutton hadn't been so distracted – and confused and a bit nervous – she would have placed that voice immediately.

As it was, she felt herself flush at the idea of being found hidden in this dark alcove, with Charlotte, secluded away from the party. Nerves jumped from her stomach, but rather than focus on her, Naomi's eyes landed on Charlotte. Who wasn't as shock-still as she'd been before, but was composed, standing with her arms folded against her chest.

And Sutton wondered how she could possibly do that? Because after the last few minutes, Sutton felt like she'd had so much happen, that she was going to pass out.

A slow, calculated smile slid across Naomi's face, but the hard, mean look in her eyes was just as Sutton remembered it from all of the times it had been directed at her when she'd dated her son, Joshua. Who, Sutton had figured out at the end of their relationship, had learned how to be cruel from his mother. "Well, well. What do we have going on here, Miss Thompson?" her tone was a masterclass in mockery.

But Sutton stared at the side of Charlotte's face, eyes widening, as she felt the bottom of her stomach drop to the floor. Thompson? Charlotte *Thompson*? And it only took her a split-second to connect that dot to Elizabeth Thompson, the former President, who had one granddaughter.

She braced her hand against the wall, closing her eyes for a moment, as her thoughts raced, because what the fuck had she gotten herself into?

Chapter 6

Charlotte had always loved puzzles. Not just actual board game type puzzles – though she enjoyed those, too – but real-world puzzles. The puzzle pieces that made people tick. What made someone do what they did? Why did someone act the way they did? What did they want? Were they genuine?

It was a big factor that had driven her into politics. Figuring out the game of it all was a big part of the draw.

Politics was a puzzle; a game. For someone like her – someone who had specific goals and aspirations – one wrong move could make the game a nightmare. Then again, navigating that tightrope was all a part of the draw, too.

Something she'd learned far before she'd even started her professional career was that there was a long game and a short game, and, if you were a good politician, you were playing both games constantly.

Charlotte's long game was already planned, mapped, and in the beginning stages of execution. Her short game was constantly in the balance. It was the decisions made at a moment's notice that determined what the result of the short game was.

The series of events that had happened in the last ten minutes involved making split-second decisions that seemed inevitable; almost like there hadn't been a choice at all, really.

She'd first spotted Naomi Young-Carmichael when the mingling was about to commence. And she'd been shocked, which was certainly an unwelcome feeling for her.

Charlotte wouldn't typically say she was ever *glad* about someone's death. Especially not a fellow politician. But when Robert Carmichael had died three years ago, she knew she wasn't the only person who hadn't felt particularly sorrowful.

Robert had held his New York Senate seat for many years, being re-elected usually on the basis of the fact that he was something of a war hero who had a good rapport with the public. The people loved that about him, regardless of the fact that he was fairly bawdy and somewhat obnoxious. To have him out of Congress was a relief to many, even if it had come through death.

Charlotte had only known Robert Carmichael sparingly, and their introduction had been the same night that she'd met Jack Spencer – her grandmother's inauguration ball. Unlike Jack Spencer though, Robert had hit on her, despite the fact that she'd been barely seventeen.

In spite of all of that, Charlotte had preferred Robert to his wife. Naomi Young-Carmichael might not have held a seat in Congress, but she was conniving, controlling, and had more influence than someone who didn't actually hold public office had the right to have. Without a doubt, it had to do with the fact that her father had been President before Charlotte's grandmother. And the fact that they came from a richer-than-God family who had hit it big in oil, decades ago, in Texas.

If conflict was, as Charlotte liked to theorize, a politician's bread and butter, Naomi provided enough of it to fill Charlotte's entire meal ticket.

There had been several people over the course of the years who underestimated Charlotte. Because of her family name, because of her age, because of her looks. Those people had tried Charlotte's patience, but she always proved her worth.

She'd quickly learned that Naomi was not one of the people who would overlook her causeless disdain for her once they could see what she was capable of achieving. From her very first position working with the governor, they'd butted heads every time they'd run into one another, with Naomi seeming to be opposing every single one of Charlotte's initiatives. And with her opposition, came the actual opposition from her significant handful of followers.

So when Robert had died, it wasn't that Charlotte was necessarily glad he was dead; it was more that she was glad his death somewhat forced Naomi to retreat back to her childhood home in Houston.

Charlotte relished a challenge, but she was more than happy to have the woman who acted as her nonstop opposition out of the way.

She'd hoped that the next time she would have to see Naomi, it would be from her podium as she was sworn in as President, if at all.

She most definitely hadn't hoped or planned to see her at a charity function that Charlotte had been using as a mingling platform at the start of her campaign for a Congressional seat.

If that alone wasn't enough to throw her slightly off of her game – because *how* had Charlotte not even known that Naomi was back in New York? That was the sort of news that typically spread quickly through their circles, yet there'd been not a word of it – seeing Naomi lead David Verbeck, a prominent business owner who was notoriously untrustworthy, out of the ballroom and into the main hall was *more* than enough to sound the warning bells in her head.

In that moment, Charlotte felt there was really no other choice but to follow her instincts that told her to follow the pair. Because Naomi resurfacing now, and choosing Verbeck for a private audience had given a home to deep-set suspicion in her stomach. She'd barely had a second to whisper to Dean where she was going.

That suspicion was only exacerbated when she trailed them – smartly, from a distance – and she could only hear snippets of conversation. She knew she'd heard the words *House of Representatives*, though, and that was enough.

She'd ducked into the alcove next to the room they'd gone into – which turned out to be futile, because she couldn't hear a word they were saying. But as she'd been waiting and thinking, the sound of another set of footsteps coming down the hallway had alarmed her. Perhaps there was someone else who would be meeting Naomi and Verbeck.

Charlotte's mind had already been compiling a list as to who it could be that was in cahoots with the most underhanded pair in the city, before she'd peeked out from her hiding spot. And she hadn't known whether she was relieved or not to see that it was Sutton wandering down the hall.

She'd made another split-second decision to pull her into the alcove with her. It hadn't really seemed like a choice, given that it was either that, or chance that Sutton would unintentionally happen upon whatever was happening only a few feet away, in the next room down.

And with Sutton in the alcove with her came the third choice that she questioned in hindsight. Because she'd pressed herself against her – which *had*, in fairness, been an entirely innocent act on her part – and she was close enough to feel how warm Sutton was, close enough to *feel* the fact that as soon as Charlotte was close enough, Sutton's heartrate went through the roof.

It was distracting, to say the least, in a situation where Charlotte truly didn't have the time to have any distractions.

But once she'd heard what was being said, it was easier to concentrate. Being able to focus on the situation at hand was what had made anger burn up inside of her, strong and fast, and laced with dread.

Because *of course* Naomi was showing up back in New York just in time to run for John Kelvin's seat. *Of course* David Verbeck was going to use his sneaky, conniving methods to assist her campaign.

And of course she would forget herself – and forget that Sutton truly had no idea what was going on – just in time to see Naomi popping around the corner.

Charlotte had nearly forgotten that look Naomi managed to adopt when she said the Thompson name. As though she was respecting Charlotte at the same time that she was actually insulting her.

Still reeling, she only had that split-second to gather herself. To recover from being caught in what could be construed as a compromising position with not only a beautiful woman, but one who happened to be the daughter of a notable politician.

108

It was, thankfully, second nature to slip into a congenial tone of voice. One that lacked the bitter bite that Naomi's had to it but was no less a slight. "Mrs. Carmichael, it's such a surprise to see you tonight."

She fixed on a smile as she resolutely did not offer her hand in a greeting, instead, keeping her arms crossed.

It was in the way that Naomi's eyes narrowed that she knew she hit the right spot. Even when her deceased husband had been alive, Naomi hadn't been too fond of being referred to by his name, and it was no secret. No secret to many who knew where to look that she'd maintained her extramarital affairs for years. At least, not to Charlotte, who paid attention to the barely perceivable changes.

"A surprise? How odd. I thought you would have known that I'd be here." Naomi's lips were pulled back into a mocking smile.

She kept her own butter-wouldn't-melt-in-my-mouth smile in place. "How odd indeed, given that I don't believe you were on the original guest list."

Which was actually something Charlotte knew for a fact.

"Yes, well, originally, I wasn't in New York," Naomi stated, but what she was *not* saying was even louder: *I'm back now.*

Despite the fact that Charlotte desperately wanted to groan in frustration, she only tilted her head in acknowledgement. "It's lovely to have you back." In a deliberately slow movement, she ran her eyes down Naomi's dress and then back up, "You're looking . . . well. Your return to Houston seemed to suit you, Mrs. Carmichael."

She took pleasure in the way the older woman's eyes narrowed again, nostrils flaring. Just slightly, but it was enough.

Naomi cocked an eyebrow. "It's actually just Young, again."

Charlotte didn't even have to fake the smile that tugged at the corners of her lips as she murmured, "Is it? An interesting thing, a widow going back to her maiden name. I suppose being referred to by your beloved's name might be a little difficult, though."

It was only in the minor tic of a muscle in Naomi's jaw that Charlotte knew she'd hit her target right where she'd intended.

Instead of responding to the dig, calculating eyes narrowed the slightest at her before they purposefully scanned her face and then deliberately at the alcove where she and Sutton were still shaded in from the hall. "An interesting thing as well, to be hiding out here in the middle of a fundraiser. Together."

The innuendo in her voice was anything but subtle, and the cold feeling that struck through the pit of Charlotte's stomach was unsettling. But, she reminded herself, it wasn't as though Naomi *saw* anything unsavory – there wasn't anything to see.

Still, she kept her smile in place. "Interesting? It seems you might understand a thing or two about disappearing from an event." She inclined her head in the direction of where she and Verbeck had been.

Rather than react, Naomi changed her course. Instead of keeping her focus on Charlotte, she turned to Sutton.

She couldn't put her finger on what it was exactly that made her stomach churn uncomfortably at that. It was a combination, she thought. A combination starting with the fact that Sutton might be Sutton *Spencer*, but she was also Sutton – the woman Charlotte had been talking to for a month.

Sutton, who wasn't deceptive. Who was anxious about the idea of messaging a woman on a dating app. The woman who literally choked on a sip of water earlier in the evening, just from a *look* Charlotte had given her. Sutton was clearly very intelligent, but there was still that thing about her.

That thing that had made Charlotte give Sutton her number a month ago, that had prompted her into giving all of those dating tips; it was this strange protective urge she had for the younger woman.

So there was that protectiveness inside of her, mixed with the fact that this needed to play out smoothly. She *needed* this to end smoothly – and quickly – because this was really just the beginning of what was to come.

For all that Sutton was adorable and had eventually managed to hold her own in the conversation earlier, it didn't necessarily mean anything. Because Sutton wasn't even in this game of politics, not really, and Naomi Young loved to play with her prey.

Especially prey like Sutton.

She gave Sutton a look out of the corner of her eye, the first time she'd allowed herself to do so since the interaction began, and she took in the way Sutton's hand was pressed against the wall, how she looked a little confused, blue eyes wide as she looked at Charlotte.

Charlotte hardly realized she'd taken a slight step forward, putting herself between Sutton and Naomi until she'd already done it. She truly did not like that somewhat predatory glint in Naomi's eye as she smiled at Sutton.

"Hello, honey. I had no idea that you were *friends* with Ms. Thompson, here," her insinuation hit right on target.

It was enough to make her clench her jaw, Charlotte's hackles rising. Trading barbs with Charlotte was one thing, and even though she knew Naomi wasn't above dragging someone else into a mess, it didn't sit well with her to have Sutton in the middle of anything. To know that she might have, inadvertently, brought her there.

Before she could even open her mouth, though, it was Sutton who spoke.

"Yes, we're friends. Good friends, actually," she asserted, in a voice that was low, calm, and even.

Surprise surged through her and she couldn't stop herself from turning to look at Sutton, full on. Who was now staring at Naomi, all big blue eyes and innocence – none of that blushing, flushing, heavy breathing kind of business that had been happening in this alcove only minutes ago.

Which was good, of course, but her mind was racing with the fact that Sutton was all adorably awkward with her, but then when Naomi Young appeared, she was collected? *That* was inconceivably unprecedented.

As amazed as she was, she didn't let it show. Instead, she ran her eyes over Sutton's face before turning back to Naomi.

"Really, now? Is that a recent development?"

"Fairly recent, yes," Sutton hedged.

"Hmm. A recent development that takes place in dark alcoves?" She let the question hang in the air, with a smug smirk on her face that Charlotte hated – had always hated.

The question gave pause to Sutton, whose face flushed and Charlotte could tell even from where they stood shaded from the light in the hallway.

Charlotte's eyes narrowed in derision as she took the shot for the opening she'd been given. "I know it must be difficult for you to imagine having an actual friendship, but yes. And now, we must get back to the fundraiser. Perhaps you'd like to show some actual support as well, considering I can't for the life of me remember the last time I've ever seen you volunteering there."

Check and mate, she thought in triumph as Naomi grit her teeth.

But before she could get a word in, Charlotte cleared her throat, "Come on, Sutton."

She quirked an eyebrow in challenge as she deliberately reached out to link her arm through Sutton's. She'd learned long ago that such innocuous touches between women garnered no attention at all, and she took advantage of the casual gesture.

Charlotte was already tugging her gently down the hall as Sutton's arm tightened around hers.

Absently, she reached up to lightly run her fingers over the backs of Sutton's in a calming move, still knowing that Naomi was watching them as they walked away.

Even in her heels, compared to Sutton's flats, she was just shorter than Sutton, her eyes an inch below those baby blues. Instead of looking back at her, though, Sutton's head was turned to look behind them as they turned to enter back into the event hall.

Her soft, thick red hair that had been left down for the night brushed over Charlotte's shoulder as she turned back so that they faced one another. Sutton was wearing an exuberant grin, something that made her eyes spark, and the excitement Charlotte could *feel* rolling off of her made her feel inexplicably lighter, despite the situation.

She hadn't been able to see this side of Sutton at all in their interactions yesterday at the coffee shop or earlier this evening, but she thought that she could imagine Sutton looking like this quite a bit. Mischievous.

But she didn't quite understand the excitement, not when a confrontation with Naomi generally made her feel . . . well, not excited. She lifted her eyebrow in question.

"It's just – I've never heard someone talk to her like that before."

The wonder in her tone made Charlotte feel a little mischievous herself. She lightly nudged Sutton with her shoulder as she murmured, "Well, stick around."

The teasing words made Sutton blush. But she couldn't focus on that sort of cuteness, because there was a grim truth to her words; there would be a lot more to deal with when it came to Naomi in the coming months.

Even now, she could feel the back of her neck prickling, feeling eyes on them. She smoothly led them through the doors of the ballroom, into the loud sounds of members of the wealthy and elite society of New York mingling amidst the music performed by the live band who were now performing at the dais in the front of the room.

As soon as they entered the room, she felt the change in Sutton. When she turned her head to look at her again, she could see the excitement start to fade into a speculative look.

"So . . . you're a Thompson."

For a few seconds, she stared back, slowly taking in the way Sutton looked at her. Serious, pensive, and curious. Both familiar and tentative at the same time.

She wondered if she looked at Sutton the same way.

"And you know Naomi Young well enough to talk back." Her question went unasked. *How? Just who are you, Sutton Spencer?*

It was an unfamiliar sensation, wanting to know more about a woman, and not for any gain other than her own personal curiosity. But she'd already been feeling that with Sutton for a month now, so she supposed that it continuing in person wasn't that odd.

Those intense eyes stared into her own for a few seconds as she could see the color creep up on pale cheeks, Sutton opening her mouth to answer. Whatever the answer was, a little frown line appeared in between her eyebrows, and Charlotte wanted to know *more* – a puzzle was her favorite thing, after all.

But over Sutton's shoulder she could see Jack Spencer striding in their direction. He didn't overtly look worried, but she could read someone like Jack – practically an open book – from a mile away. There was concern in the way his eyes slightly narrowed and in the determined stride he took toward them.

It was probably for the best. Despite the fact that she didn't have the chance to have a real conversation with Sutton, she still needed to process everything. And in a room full of people like this, it wasn't the best location for an open discussion.

She didn't realize their arms were still interlocked until she went to lean back, and she looked down at the point of contact in surprise.

Which Sutton must have interpreted some other way, because she cleared her throat, "I – uh – sorry." She pulled her arm back, before smoothing her hand down her dress in the same manner that she'd done at the café yesterday, over her jeans. She gathered that it was a show of Sutton's nerves. "Can we . . . I just –"

Charlotte shook her head, fixing her eyes directly above Sutton's shoulder at her incoming father. "Not now."

And then Jack was there, drawing a startled look from Sutton, who hadn't even known he'd been approaching. He darted his eyes between them curiously slowly, like he wasn't sure as though he should have a look of accusation before he settled his gaze on his daughter. "Sutton, I've been looking for you. You disappeared."

She expected there to be a blush that broke out on Sutton's ridiculously flawless cheekbones, but there was only a slightly sheepish smile. "Yeah, sorry, dad. I just wanted to go get some fresh air."

"Well, you know I understand that feeling." He gave a small smile back.

Charlotte stepped back from the Spencer's. "I had stepped out for a moment as well, and Sutton was kind enough to keep me company."

Jack nodded slowly, though she could see the query in his eyes as he looked between them once again. It didn't help that Sutton bit at her bottom lip before she looked at Charlotte through her lashes as she murmured, "You're welcome."

A puzzle, Charlotte thought again and she looked at her for just a moment longer than she told herself she should.

"Yes, well, I apologize for monopolizing Sutton's company. If you'll excuse me, I should go check in with Dean." With that, she gave a quick smile and turned away.

It wasn't difficult to find Dean, who tended to gravitate toward the bar at these sort of events. As Charlotte mingled, generally, Dean would skillfully evade the dance floor and any women wanting to dance with him, while simultaneously making enough small talk over drinks as to not be thought of as rude.

As she walked through the throngs of people, it was the first time at a charity event that she didn't stop to meet and greet handfuls of people as she walked by. At any event, really. After all, that was their purpose.

Well, networking was *her* purpose for attending.

But now that she had a bit of space, she was just replaying the last half hour in her head, and it all left her with such a sour taste in the back of her mouth.

Rather than the smile she typically fixed on, even in a bad mood, she was scowling by the time she reached Dean.

"You look like you're in a delightful mood." He took a sip of the drink in his hand, pausing for a moment before he wondered aloud, "Here I thought you were on some sort of urgent covert mission, yet instead I find you slinking back in here looking all flushed with Sutton Spencer."

She didn't need to see him to know that he was winking; his tone said it all.

She shoved his shoulder. Harder than she'd originally intended, but she couldn't control the frustration that was still bottled up. "Like I would do that *here*." She didn't say anything about whether or not she would do it with Sutton, because Dean might have been gay, but he was her friend; he knew her, and he had eyes.

Out of the corner of her eye, she could see the woman in question – not Sutton, but Naomi – come sweeping back into the room as well with practiced ease. God. Charlotte had known that the race for the House seat would be trying, no matter who she was running against.

But she'd really been hoping that she wouldn't be running against someone that would be a nightmare to campaign against. Not that she'd ever competed against Naomi Young for anything before, but the woman was a nightmare in general, so Charlotte already had the sinking knowledge that this was going to be a battle.

With that thought in mind, she leaned back against the bar and sighed as she held out her hand. "Give me your drink."

Dean let out an exaggeratedly scandalized gasp. "You want my whiskey? Where is Miss One-Glass-of-Champagne-per-Function?"

Charlotte scoffed as he mocked her rule. But it was a good rule of thumb; she'd seen enough people publicly humiliate themselves at parties like these, where the liquor was high quality and free, to know to never even possibly get buzzed at an event. However, being seen turning down a single glass of champagne or wine, whichever was primarily offered, could make her appear to be too uptight.

It was a balancing act. One that she'd mastered.

116

But right now, she grimaced as she informed him, "Naomi fucking Young is running for the seat."

Dean handed her his drink.

Charlotte wasn't typically someone who was anxious to leave a function early. They were a necessity. Socializing, mingling, schmoozing – all of it was in her wheelhouse.

However, it was less than two hours later – with the fundraiser still going fairly strong – that found her shrugging on her light jacket. Dean had given her a questioning look when she'd told him that she was leaving already, but Charlotte had had enough of this night.

It was intended to be some light socialization, rubbing elbows with people that she would be reliant on voting for her. Including Jack Spencer, who had been the focal point in this plan of hers. She'd had a vague plan of *playing it cool* when it came to Sutton, because though she knew they should talk, this wasn't really the time or place.

But nothing really went according to plan. Given the arrival of Naomi, Charlotte knew that the older woman would be the memorable event of the evening for the attendees.

Both Sutton and Jack had left the fundraiser an hour ago, slipping out without Charlotte's knowledge, which meant she'd lost her chance to win over Jack on his visit, because she knew that his trip wasn't going to last into the next work week.

And keeping distance between herself and Sutton had been completely thrown out the window in that alcove.

She was ready to go home, get a good night's sleep, and spend the weekend re-strategizing.

The fresh air actually *did* feel nice, especially after a long night.

She took her time as she started her walk home. Dean had driven her and had offered to leave with her. But she only lived a short distance away, and she needed some time with her thoughts.

In an effort to try to not think about strategizing – she really wanted to regroup tomorrow and just clear her head – she reached into her pocket for her phone, where it had been stashed away all night.

Caleb – 8:47PM
My day off from the night shift, and you've claimed rights to my boyfriend's time. Not fair. You owe me.

                               Charlotte – 10:58PM
                               I don't owe you anything. Dean is a grown man, he just clearly prefers my superior company.

It was when she saw the other texts that she had that gave her pause.

Sutton – 10:01PM
Hey, so I was just wondering . . . did you mean what you said to Naomi earlier?

Sutton – 10:02PM
I mean, about us being friends. Because you told her we were, but I understand that might just be something you said in the moment, because of . . . whatever was going on back there.

Sutton – 10:04PM
This is probably, like, weird. I don't mean for it to be. It's just that I have, you know, come to think of you as a friend. Even though there's clearly a lot we don't know about each other.

Sutton – 10:05PM
Like that you're the President's granddaughter!
Okay, well she isn't President anymore, but still.

Sutton – 10:15PM
I just realized you probably don't have your phone
on you right now. I don't even know where you would
be carrying it in that dress.

Sutton – 10:18PM
You can ignore that last part. Actually, you can ignore
all of these.

Charlotte bit her lip even as it curled into an unstoppable smile. She might not have chosen for their circumstances to have turned out the way they had, but it wasn't terrible.

She enjoyed that she could see the laughing woman in the picture on the app melding easily with the gorgeous woman with the expressive eyes.

Though she'd come into the evening unsure as to exactly how to approach Sutton, she found herself hitting the call button rather than typing out a reply. It just seemed easier and somehow more appropriate now.

It only rang twice before Sutton picked up. "Charlotte?"

"Who else would you expect to be calling you from my phone number?"

She heard Sutton moving around in the background for a moment before Sutton answered, "I don't know," she waited a beat. "Maybe your boyfriend, Dean."

Charlotte found herself chuckling, an actual, full-on laugh. "I can't believe you actually thought that."

"Well, I didn't know! I was just . . . telling you what I thought."

"You thought I troll for hookups with women online to cheat behind my boyfriend Mayor of New York Dean Walker's back, and the first thing you do is promise that you won't tell anyone," Charlotte summed up, teasingly, primarily for her own benefit. Their situation earlier hadn't truly afforded her the time she'd needed to really appreciate the fact that Sutton was earnestly honest in that respect.

Unlike the majority of people Charlotte knew and associated with on a daily basis.

Sutton was quiet for a few moments – Charlotte actually pulled the phone away from her ear to check that Sutton was still on the line – before she could hear her sigh quietly.

"So . . . you got my texts."

Charlotte turned the corner onto her street, wondering what exactly was going through Sutton's head. It was surprisingly hard to tell what Sutton was thinking sometimes for someone who was so transparent.

She answered truthfully, "Well, I'll admit that meeting you caught me off guard."

"It wasn't intentional."

Which made Charlotte huff out a laugh, picturing Sutton's open shock. "Clearly." When it became clear that Sutton didn't have anything to say to that, she added, "You being Jack Spencer's daughter was certainly unexpected, to say the least. And, as you are aware, I'm a very private person, so . . ." she trailed off, tipping her head back to look at the sky as she reached into her pocket to find her keys.

It was difficult to verbalize exactly what you were thinking about a situation such as this, when Charlotte hadn't imagined it was one she would be in.

Sutton sounded disappointed, "I understand. It's – it's not . . . I didn't imagine that you'd be *you*, either. Obviously. Um, I didn't think that my stepping out of the closet meant that I was coming out to the granddaughter of the most powerful woman in the country."

"Believe me, I didn't know that by answering your message, I would be coming out to anyone who would connect to my real world." She nodded at the doorman who worked at her building, giving him a small smile as she continued into the lobby. "But whether or not we planned it, you are in my real world already. So, it's already done."

She wanted to say that the puff of breath she heard Sutton exhale was through a smile. Like the excited one she'd worn earlier. "So, we *are* friends, then. For real."

She smirked. "Do you think I slink around in dark alcoves with people who aren't my friend, darling?"

It took her a few moments to realize that Sutton's silence this time was entirely deliberate, as she waited a determined amount of time before saying, "Well . . . I *do* have it on good authority that you had somewhat of an experienced past with women in all manner of places."

Charlotte's mouth fell open. "Excuse you!"

Sutton laughed, loudly, and she could picture the flush on her face. It was a nice image and despite so many of her plans for the night having fallen flat, she found herself grinning as she walked through her apartment door.

Though entirely unforeseen, maybe she could use a friend like Sutton.

"Now that we're friends, maybe we should get together sometime, for a planned meeting? Rather than a surprise run-in?" She proposed. The cat was out of the bag, so to speak, and there was no going back.

"Yeah, we could get a coffee. Or, well, tea for me. It's kind of our thing."

That pulled her up short. "We have a thing?"

Sutton laughed again, this time just a quiet little chuckle that almost sounded nervous as she explained, "Well, you told my dad that we met accidentally over coffee. And then we *did* actually meet at Topped Off. So, uh, maybe it's not like a *thing*, but it could be."

Her eyes rolled, even as a small smile played on her mouth and she shook her head. "Sure. We'll meet for coffee and tea. Our thing."

Chapter 7

Sutton pulled open the door to Topped Off, already scanning the tables as her stomach fluttered with excited nerves. Only to be a little let down when there was no familiar face already there.

She was supposed to meet Charlotte for their coffee date – uh, meeting – in only five minutes, and she'd run from campus to the café, as the class she'd been in ran a bit over time. For the first time in the semester so far, the students in her class had been engaged enough to want to talk *more* about the topic – well, a few of them. Which was exciting, and it made Sutton feel proud, like she was actually doing a good job.

But of all days for it to happen, of course it was when she had plans with Charlotte. Not that it appeared to have mattered all that much, anyway.

With a deep breath, she rolled her eyes at herself; she should be *glad* that she had arrived before Charlotte. She figured that out of the two of them, she was the one who needed the extra minute to gather herself.

Despite the fact that they'd started texting again in the last few days like they had before their unexpected meeting, and that their conversations weren't stilted or awkward, Sutton was still a little nervous.

It certainly didn't help when Regan called to her from behind the counter across the room, "Don't worry, your date isn't here yet!"

Sutton let the door close behind her, shutting out the chill, before she hurried across the café as she shot back, "It's *not* a date!"

She'd been saying the same thing for days, ever since Regan learned about the coffee . . . meeting. Regan had that jovial, mischievous look in her eyes though, and for the life of her, Sutton truly didn't know what she was thinking when she suggested Charlotte meet her at Topped Off. It was just her go-to place, and it had been a thoughtless action to suggest they meet there.

At the very least, she should have chosen to meet there *after* Regan's shift ended in an hour.

"Maybe it's not a *date* date, but it is a coffee date. And do you know who coffee dates are for? People who want to go on a date but think asking for one is too *forward*," she adopted mockingly helpless tone, fluttering her eyelashes for effect.

Sutton wanted to be exasperated, but was mostly amused. Throwing a look over her shoulder at the door – no sign of Charlotte, still, even though it was officially their agreed upon time – she worried at her bottom lip before giving in. "What gives you the authority to say that?"

Regan quickly restocked cookies in the display case without even needing to look, which was good for her because she was busy giving her the Sutton-is-oblivious-and-I'm-going-to-teach-her-something-new look that she'd perfected when they'd been eleven and she'd told Sutton about French kissing and that people don't only have sex with the person they're married to. "Because, babe, I work in a coffee shop. I see all the coffee dates."

An unattractive snort escaped from the back of her throat. "Maybe you should write a book with your omniscient knowledge."

Regan rolled her eyes. "You can mock me all you want, but I know what I'm talking about. Just like I know that *you* want it to be a date, because you've wanted her since you first saw her picture, and now you have a little crush –"

"Regan!" Sutton quickly looked around to make sure no one was listening and that Charlotte hadn't walked in at some point. Her cheeks burned with embarrassment, and she wished that the counter wasn't there to separate them so she could put her hand over Regan's mouth to stop her.

"I know she totally wants to bang you. And I know that it's a minute after she's supposed to have met you here, and if she doesn't get here soon, you're going to be a nervous wreck."

She finished by reaching over to tap her finger against Sutton's nose before it was slapped away only a second later as Sutton glared.

"I *told* you that I don't have a crush. We're friends."

"And I told you that you can't lie to me. Sutton, you can barely lie in general, but you can't lie to *me* at all," she informed her smartly, before she clucked her tongue in disappointment.

She crossed her arms defensively. "We're *friends*."

Of course, she was attracted to Charlotte; Sutton honestly doubted that there was a person who was attracted to women who wouldn't be. But there was nothing between them beyond Sutton's attraction, Charlotte's playful occasional flirtation, and the foundation of a friendship.

Regan only gave her a dubious look.

Sutton sighed. "Can I just have a tea please."

After a moment, she glanced at the clock. Charlotte was now three minutes late, and Sutton *knew* that was weird, because the Charlotte she'd been talking to for over a month seemed to run on a perfectly timed schedule. "And a coffee."

The way Regan's smile shifted into a saccharine-sweet grin tipped Sutton off to what she was going to be saying even before she sighed out in an exaggeratedly dreamy tone, "A coffee for *Charlotte*."

When her phone rang a second later, she jumped as she felt a little jangle of her nerves. Charlotte could be canceling, because maybe she didn't want to really be friends like this, or –

Or, it was just her mother, and Sutton was being paranoid. Calming herself, Sutton bit her lip for a moment as she debated whether or not to answer. She *was* waiting for Charlotte, the lesbian to whom Sutton was attracted, and her mother always had a knack for being able to read her, even when she couldn't actually see her face.

Still, she hadn't spoken to her mom in almost a week. Plus, if there was one thing she *didn't* need, it was Regan asking her why she wasn't going to answer, if this wasn't a date.

With a deep breath, her gaze flitted over to the door before she answered the call, "Hi, mom. What's – wait, you had your meeting with your publisher today, didn't you?" Just like that, the slight anxiety she'd had upon answering the call melted away into excitement. "How did it go?"

Her mother didn't keep her waiting, and even though her voice was typically reserved, Sutton could hear her enthusiasm as she told her, "The general public will have the next book available to them in six months – with three more to follow in the series." Then her tone dropped into the warm affection that was reserved for her kids, "And *someone* has the final chapters waiting in her email already."

Sutton couldn't help the squeal of excitement from escaping her. "Mom! I can't wait to read them."

"I know, hon. And *I* can't wait until you're home for the holidays, and we can brainstorm about the new series together. None of your siblings has the same gift as you do." Katherine sighed, full of affection and indulgence.

"I know. It's going to be great!"

Sutton looked forward to the holidays for a handful of reasons, and she did enjoy spending time at home more now, after she'd moved away. But there were fewer places she liked more than her mother's office.

Katherine Spencer hadn't really planned on being an author; she'd planned on being a best-selling historical fantasy sensation even less. In her childhood memories, her mother was a stay-at-home mom with no side profession. The best stay-at-home mother that there could possibly be, but still. She was dedicated to her family, and her kids were her primary focus.

When she would put them to bed or sit with them by the fire or take care of them while they were sick, her mom would tell them stories she'd made up. Tales of a woman – a heroic knight named Aurora. Sutton's childhood was full of these stories.

Sutton had always loved the tales, and unlike her siblings, she never really grew out of them. Also unlike her siblings, she never hit the phase where she was "too cool" to hang out with their mom. She'd loved to be her little helper, especially when Ethan had been born just after her eleventh birthday.

And throughout his baby and toddler years, Sutton had enjoyed sitting with her mother and her youngest brother. She grew more enamored with the stories her mom would tell, and started to help tell them. It wasn't until she'd been thirteen that her parents had sat with the owners of a publishing company when they'd been at the same event, and they'd heard some of Aurora's tales over dinner.

It all seemed to happen so fast from there; Katherine wasn't planning on having any more children, her eldest was going to be leaving for college in less than two years, and her youngest was no longer a baby. Jack had encouraged her to focus on something to make herself happy, and Sutton herself had begged her mom to really write about Aurora.

As Sutton had entered high school, Aurora's origin story hit the shelves, and sold out faster than anyone had anticipated. Her favorite thing was to curl up in her chair in her mom's office and talk about what was next for Aurora, giving her input on her mom's ideas.

"Let me know when you read it, I want to know what you think. You know I talk about it with your father and Oliver, but they aren't terribly creative."

"I will! I'll read it tonight when I get home," she promised.

"Are you still on campus?"

It was like a flick of a switch, the way Sutton zoned back in to exactly where she was; she found herself sucking in a quick breath, trying to be mindful of the way her words left her mouth, her broad smile slowly fading. "Um, nope, not on campus. I'm just at Topped Off for a bit."

"Order up for Sutton and her date!" Regan grinned.

Her eyes narrowed in annoyance. *I will kill you*, she mouthed to her, but Regan just kept grinning anyway because the damage was done.

She *knew* the look in her mother's eyes, even without having to see her. The look she wore when any of her kids "had their eye" on somebody new. It was both interested and cautious at the same time, and she could hear exactly that reflected in her tone, "A date? You didn't tell me that you were interested in someone."

Even though Sutton disliked tardiness, she sincerely hoped that Charlotte would continue to run just a little bit late. At least late enough for the blush that she was sure was darker than her hair to fade along with her embarrassment as she denied, "It's *not* a date; Regan's just being a jerk."

Her mother only *hmm*'d, and then sat quietly for a few moments.

Sutton knew what she was doing, because that was a trick that her mom had done so many times. . . .but it worked so well, and the words were already leaving her before she could think about it. "Really, mom, it's not a date. I'm meeting a – a friend."

She hated that she sounded so unconvincing, despite the fact that she was *telling the truth*.

"A new friend?" Katherine questioned, and still had *that* tone. The tone that said she knew that Sutton was hiding something.

"Yes," she dragged out the word. "Just, someone I met recently."

God. Oh, god. Her mother was going to *hear* it in her tone. She knew it was completely illogical and technically impossible. Because there was no way her mom could know that she met said girl on a lesbian dating app, just from her voice.

But what if she could?

"All right. Does this new friend have a name?"

"I – well, of course, everyone has a name. But this is a new friendship, and I don't want . . ." she trailed off, realizing as she spoke that she was only making it worse for herself.

She closed her eyes and tipped her head back, holding in a groan of frustration at herself.

Even if she didn't come to that conclusion on her own, the wildly entertained expression on Regan's face said it all. She was bracing her elbow on the counter, chin in her hand, with a shit eating grin on her face.

Sutton brought her middle finger up, trailing it over her neck in a threat before she turned around to avoid having to deal with Regan's face.

"So, in summary, you don't want me to know your new friend's name . . . in case it'll jinx your friendship?" Her mom sounded both confused and amused.

It sounded idiotic to her own ears, but she for the life of her couldn't find the words to tell her mother that it was Charlotte she was meeting. Not when her mother could so easily read her.

"Yes?" She offered, weakly.

"Okay. But I'll be here to listen about your date when you feel like sharing," She was clearly teasing, but Sutton's breath caught in her throat.

She coughed, twice. "Ha. Yeah. Okay, I've got to go. I love you."

"I love you too. Be safe."

As soon as she hung up the phone, Sutton brought it up to rest her forehead against, closing her eyes and shaking her head slightly. When she heard Regan cackling behind her, she spun around with a glare. "I hope you know that I'm not leaving you a tip."

"Why aren't you leaving Regan a tip?" Came the interested voice from behind her and Sutton froze, even as she felt a little tingle move up her spine at the somehow already familiar tone.

"Uh – no reason."

Sutton turned to face her and immediately was aware that Charlotte had a special skill – in that everything she wore looked like she was modeling it. She didn't believe that it mattered *what* she was wearing, really, but more of the way she carried herself.

With grace and elegance, and Sutton honestly believed that she could be wearing *anything* and still look like that. As it was, she stood in front of Sutton with a tight, fitted pencil skirt and blouse, with a light jacket over it.

It was such standard business attire, but Sutton couldn't help but think that Charlotte wore it like she was walking down a runway, and that, combined with Charlotte's small, side-tipped inquisitive smile just made her stomach twist –

She cleared her throat and reached for the coffee on the counter behind her. "Um, here. This is for you."

The small smile on Charlotte's face grew into one that was fully-fledged, and it made Sutton's chest go all warm with it directed at her. "Thank you so much. You have *no* idea how much I needed this today. *Need* this."

Sutton might have missed the slight frown – or, frown line between Charlotte's eyebrows, rather – that quickly smoothed out again had she looked away for only a few seconds if she hadn't been watching her so intently.

"I'm just going to get some sugar," Charlotte gestured to the station a few feet away.

She spun around to see Regan, practically bursting at the seams, and she whispered as menacingly as she could, "*Don't –*"

It was already too late. "Why don't you give her some sugar?"

Sutton's hand tightened around her cup, and her tea nearly spilled out as she felt her cheeks flame hot in mortification. With a quick glance over her shoulder, she saw that Charlotte appeared to be too far away to have heard the comment. Thankfully.

"One more comment, and I'm changing the locks," she threatened. Rather than wait around, she turned to look at where Charlotte was approaching, stirring her coffee and giving a questioning look between Regan and Sutton. "So, I was wondering, if you maybe want to . . . take a walk?"

And leave Topped Off before Regan undoubtedly says something so embarrassing that I'll never be able to look you in the eye again, she added silently.

Charlotte's caramel colored eyes seemed to brighten in amusement as she dragged her gaze one last time from Regan to Sutton. She ran them over Sutton's face in a slow perusal before she agreed, "Sure."

"Great. Good. Okay, let's go."

"I'll see you at home, my tall drink of water. Take care of her, Stunning Charlotte!" Regan called out to them, and Sutton threw an exasperated glare over her shoulder.

Which melted as soon as she felt Charlotte's steady, sure hand rest on the small of her back and heard her quiet chuckle in her ear as she led them out of the café. "I've come to realize that you didn't exaggerate about her when you told me stories."

Sutton hardly felt the crisp air hit her as she stepped out of the door. Despite the fact that she had a great tolerance for the cold, she was pretty sure it had something to do with the way she felt a bit warm all over with Charlotte's proximity.

Which, really, didn't *mean* anything, she assured herself.

The laugh that escaped her was shaky but genuine. "Yeah, there's no way to exaggerate about Regan."

She wasn't sure if she was disappointed or relieved when Charlotte dropped her hand as she started leading them down the sidewalk. She tried not to think about it, and instead took a sip of her tea, wondering what to say. Conversation flowed so well between them through text, and she hoped it would carry over –

"I'm so sorry I was late. Today was . . . well, it's been insanely busy all day long," Charlotte sighed.

"It's okay." Biting her lip in uncertainty, she hesitated for a second before offering, "Do you want to talk about it?"

"Don't worry, I wouldn't want to bore you with the details."

"I wouldn't be bored," the words left her quickly before she could even think about them, and she felt herself flush and hoped that Charlotte thought it was the wind. "That is – only if you want."

At that moment, she very much wished she could read minds, especially what was going on in Charlotte's as her look turned speculative, like she was trying to figure something about Sutton out. Which was so strange, because Sutton knew that she was no mystery.

Whatever Charlotte must have deciphered, it made her sigh and close her eyes for a moment. Sutton suddenly thought back to the times that they'd texted where she worried that she'd asked for too much personal information, and she thought about what Charlotte had said to her before. About how she wasn't used to different parts of her life coming together and colliding.

But then Charlotte spoke, "You know how there's a special election coming up for the House of Representatives?"

Sutton nodded. "John Kelvin's."

"Right. Well, I'm running for it, and campaigns were announced today. Which meant that everything at the office was . . ." she trailed off, using her hands to wave around in front of her for a second, before landing on, "Crazy. Even *crazier* because Naomi Young is also running, which just meant everything was doubly hectic. I have so much paperwork to do, I actually need to go *back* to work again, after this."

Sutton's mouth hung open before she managed to get out, "*Naomi Young* is running for a Congressional seat? And you are, too?"

Charlotte chuckled darkly before drinking her coffee. "That tone in your voice is basically what I heard all day long."

Sutton shook herself out of the slight stupor she'd fallen into at all of this information, hair shaking over her shoulders, before she took a moment to *look* at Charlotte. Beyond the general gorgeousness that she would probably always have, she thought she could see the dredges of exhaustion on her face.

"Do you . . . want to cancel, um, *this*?" She gestured between them before she quickly explained, "I just mean, if you're so busy. I don't want to – to make you more stressed, or anything."

Charlotte quirked her eyebrow in a perfect arch at Sutton for a moment, before turning to lead them across the street toward the High Line. And she took a deep breath before she looked up at Sutton and murmured, "No, darling, it's okay. I've actually been looking forward to this."

The words could have been meant casually, Sutton knew that. She knew, logically, that they shouldn't have made her heart speed up just a bit, or make her smile in the silly way that was threatening to take over. But she couldn't help it, because Charlotte said the words like they were a confession.

They walked up a set of stairs, and Charlotte tossed out her empty cup of coffee before sliding her hands into her pockets.

"Do you really think that Naomi could beat you in an election?"

Charlotte gave her a sidelong look, her eyes alone questioning and searching. "You apparently know her fairly well. Speaking of, exactly how *do* you know her? I assume you didn't meet her on a dating app." She bumped her shoulder into Sutton's, smirking.

Sutton's mouth fell open, equal parts scandalized and horrified. "No!" she practically shouted, garnering a few strange looks from people they walked by, before she blushed and lowered her voice to repeat, "No." She bit her lip and lowered her eyes in hesitation, because she didn't want Charlotte to judge her. She took a deep breath, "I dated her son – Joshua."

Charlotte's eyes widened in surprise as she took the information in, and Sutton waited for the inevitable *look* she got whenever someone who knew about Joshua gave her. Charlotte just gave her one of soft sympathy. "That's traumatic."

The blunt way she said it made Sutton choke out a surprised laugh, "Tell me about it."

"And because I don't want to make you think about *that* for any longer, I'll go back to your original question – Naomi is dangerous in her own way. Let alone the fact that she has so many ties with powerful people." She paused for a moment, considering her words. "Your own family, for instance. She was married to one of your father's oldest acquaintances. He and Robert went to school together."

132

Sutton almost tripped over her own feet before she came to a quick stop. She stared at Charlotte incredulously. "You – you actually think *my* father – anyone in my family, really – would support Naomi Young?"

Charlotte shrugged, before she took on a teasing tone, "For a supposedly straightforward group of people, the Spencers can be an unpredictable people when it comes to some things."

Sutton felt that playful spark in those honey eyes all the way to her toes, and it made her stomach flip-flop pleasantly for a few moments even as she ducked her head. "That's – that's not true."

"Can I ask you a question?"

"If you want." It's not really like Sutton had much to hide.

"Are you out? To your family?" Charlotte peered up through long lashes at Sutton.

"Um, no. Not really. I mean, my sister knows. But that's only because Alex eavesdropped on a conversation between me and Regan." She rolled her eyes fondly.

Charlotte lifted her eyebrows and Sutton could see that there was more she wanted to know even before she asked, "Why haven't you told them? You seem to be close."

"I don't know. They wouldn't be mad," she was quick to say, because she didn't want anyone thinking that about her family, let alone someone who *knew* them – or at least, knew them in a professional capacity. "They'd love me, no matter what. I know that," she murmured, though she thought it might take her dad a little while to wrap his mind around it. "But it's – I've barely figured myself out. I mean, I – well, you know."

"I *do* know." She gave her an amused smile. "And how is that going? The app," she elaborated.

She felt her cheeks heat, as she reached down to fiddle with the hem of her sweater. "I don't . . . it's *not* going, really. I mean – I'm not . . ."

133

She didn't know how to fully describe her ineptitude with dealing with women aloud.

Charlotte chuckled in a way that was more affectionate than anything else, before she reached out to loop her arm around Sutton's. "Okay, we won't talk about that." Charlotte tilted her head up to look at her in surprise. "How are you so warm? You only have a sweater on, not even a jacket!"

"My family spent every winter break at our cabin in Canada, Charlotte. This is nothing," she took a moment to take in the fact that Charlotte shivered slightly despite the fact that she *was* wearing a jacket, and she frowned. "Are you cold?"

"I'll be fine. Besides, you're next to me, and practically a human furnace apparently," she joked.

Sutton scoffed before biting her lip. "So . . . what about you?" Rolling her eyes at herself, she added on, "I mean, are you? Out?"

Charlotte hmm'd. "To my family, yes. To the general public, no."

"What about to your friends?"

Charlotte laughed. "To Dean and you? Yes."

Surprised – both at such a short list, and having herself included, despite the fact that it made her happy – she looked down at Charlotte. Who was looking ahead of them, looking unperturbed.

"So that's why you don't like to date? Or – or have a relationship? Because of your job?"

Charlotte turned to look at her sharply but didn't appear to be upset. She almost seemed more amused than anything. "I suppose you could think of it that way, but . . . it's not exactly the whole picture."

She let out a thoughtful sigh and disentangled their arms to step away and run her hand along the railing they were passing.

Charlotte shrugged before glancing over her shoulder at Sutton. Who looked back at her in confusion. "What *is* the whole picture, then?"

She sighed, a thoughtful look on her face. "It's not that I *want* to be alone. It's just that, I don't think that love is necessarily as important as people make it out to be. Or, maybe it is to some people, but not to me. Some people grow up, dreaming about falling in love or getting married. I grew up, dreaming about becoming a Senator. The President."

Her eyes narrowed contemplatively as she measured Charlotte's words, and she walked slowly alongside her. But she found herself frowning. "But – why does it have to be one or the other?"

Charlotte gave Sutton a fond look, "I'm not saying it has to be, for everyone. And maybe I'll find someone. One day. But I prefer to focus on my career, which is already difficult enough with my being so young and a woman, without adding sexuality into the mix. In that way, I suppose I'm lucky that I don't have the inclination for dating; nothing is at odds."

She spoke of it so lightly, as if it didn't affect her at all.

"It seems lonely."

She cringed at herself for letting the words escape her before she could really think about them. Even if it seemed like the truth to her.

Charlotte shrugged, not looking particularly upset – not nearly as upset as the idea of Charlotte being alone forever made Sutton feel. "It . . . has its moments. But doesn't everyone feel lonely sometimes, no matter what?"

Sutton shrugged, begrudging, "I guess so." She nudged Charlotte's shoulder with her own, trying to alleviate this uncomfortably heavy feeling in her stomach. "Your grand plans are safe with me."

Charlotte quirked an eyebrow playfully. "If I believed I couldn't trust you, Sutton Spencer, I wouldn't have told you anything."

She didn't wonder until much later if it was odd to feel so proud of herself, and practically elated, at the fact that someone like Charlotte – someone who was so very private and had all of those little compartments of her life tucked neatly away from one another – put her faith in her.

"I make an excellent friend," she promised, and her tone was light and joking, but she hoped Charlotte could see that she was being serious.

Charlotte gave her a thoughtful look, one that made the tips of Sutton's ears burn in a blush, but then her face melted into something of a self-deprecating smile. "That's good, because I could probably use one."

Sutton felt herself smiling back, before Charlotte led them through a clearing in the path, looking somewhat longingly at the shrubbery that was just starting to die with the chilly weather.

"Do you actually like gardening?" She asked, then wondered if it was weird that she remembered that. "I mean. It was on your profile."

"Yes, I do love to garden. That is all true. And what about you? Was yours all true?" She tipped her head to the side, narrowing her eyes in thought, "Lemon cakes, dogs, knitting, snow, literature, and . . ."

"Running," she supplied, feeling ridiculously flattered that Charlotte remembered all of that. "And yes, all of that is true."

Charlotte's smile was sharp and bright, "Well, literature definitely makes perfect sense, now that I know who you are." Sutton was surprised when she felt her soft, slightly cold hand reach out and snag her own, tugging a bit. "Now, come. I'll teach you something about flowers before I have to get back to work."

***

Over an hour and a walk down to the end of the High Line later, they were drawing up to Sutton's apartment building. Even though she had chapters of her mom's latest book to read waiting for her in her email – which she usually read *immediately* – she found that she didn't really want to say goodbye.

It had been even better than she was expecting, and she didn't know where along the way it had happened, but all of those nerves had faded long ago. She hadn't really made any new friends in a while – she had Regan, who she'd known forever. Emma. A few other girls at home that she kept in contact with, a few from undergrad that she caught up with on campus.

There was no one quite like Charlotte, though. And now she knew that it wasn't just the novelty of her being new in her life, but rather just *who* she was that made her so . . . cool.

"This was a very good distraction for the mess of paperwork I have waiting for me. Even better than I expected, actually," she added with an affectionate smile.

"We'll do this again, right?" She blurted out, hearing the eager inquiry in her own tone and mentally rolling her eyes at herself. Because she truly had, as Regan loved to tell her, no chill.

Charlotte chuckled softly. "Well, we *are* the most trusted of friends now." She shot her a wink. "Text me."

"I will," she assured, before she bit her lip, unsure of exactly how to say goodbye. Should she hug her? Like she did with her other friends?

She didn't realize it was happening until it was *happening* but Charlotte was leaning up, and her eyes widened in anticipation as her stomach dropped out. Her eyes snapped shut and she felt herself get warm all over.

Before she felt soft, cool lips against her cheek.

Her breath left her in a startled *whoosh*, and when she breathed back in, she felt immersed in that amazing perfume Charlotte wore, as the wind blew a few strands of light brown hair against Sutton's other cheek in a light caress.

She wondered if Charlotte could actually *feel* her blush, because she could surely feel her own hands shaking.

Sutton didn't realize she was holding her breath until Charlotte ended the lingering kiss, leaning back with an easy smile that Sutton could in no way replicate. Not when her heart was beating erratically in her chest the way it was.

"This was really fun, Sutton. I'll see you later." Charlotte squeezed Sutton's arm quickly, before she waved – how did she manage to still look cool while *waving?* – and she turned to go. She did it all in a more casual manner than Sutton could ever hope for.

The words, "I – yeah. I'll text you," croaked out of her somewhat dazedly, as she watched Charlotte slip her hands into her pockets and strut down the street.

It took her a few more moments to get a hold of herself, because her cheek was still burning and tinging. Her hands had the slightest tremor as she reached into her pocket to retrieve her keys.

God, if Charlotte could kiss her on the *cheek* and make her feel like she was about to faint, she could only imagine what it would be like if Charlotte were to ever kiss her, for real.

And just like that, she groaned, her stomach sinking. Because Regan was right, and she had a crush. A big, gay crush on Charlotte.

Chapter 8

The race for the late John Kelvin's House of Representatives seat is on. Kelvin, whose political career amassed over forty years, spent the last six years of said career in the House of Representatives. His untimely and unforeseen passing has left his seat open, calling for a special election to take place in the forthcoming month of March.

With campaigns announced only two weeks ago, two candidates have emerged in the running: Naomi Young and Charlotte Thompson.

Young, 52, is the eldest child and only daughter of former President Charles Young, in office 2004-2008, as well as the widow of the late Senator Robert Carmichael (1963-2016). She attended Baylor University, graduating with a degree in anthropology, and has been on the boards of multiple organizations over the years. Most notably, she worked as a liaison for the Committee of Consumer Affairs and Business Licensing for several years.

Thompson, 28, is the grandchild of former President Elizabeth Thompson, in office 2008-2016. She graduated at the top of her class from Yale University, with a degree in political science as well as a law degree from Columbia. She worked in the policy unit for Governor Mark Ford upon graduation, before her current job working as First Deputy Mayor to Mayor Dean Walker.

Imani Diop has the first official interview with candidate Charlotte Thompson:

Diop: *Naomi has already gone on record to question your experience as a politician.*

Thompson: *[laughs lightly] Yes, so I've heard.*

Diop: *What do you have to say to address her concerns regarding your age and experience?*

Thompson: First and foremost, I would like to state that Naomi Young can disparage my political career all she would like to, but it remains to be said that she herself has no formal experience in a professional setting. Political or otherwise.

Diop: So, you're saying that she has no right to criticize based on her own political record.

Thompson: Essentially, yes. That is to say, she has no political record to speak of.

Diop: Duly noted. Now, in a typical campaign for a Congressional seat, candidates have more time to prepare and plan. Given the circumstances of this race, you'll have just shy of six months. Do you believe that you are prepared?

Thompson: Yes, I believe so. Of course, there are always events that one cannot plan for, but that is all part of being a politician. However, I've spent my life preparing for this; I've spent over six years working in politics professionally, and even more time than that prior, ten years, if we're counting Congressional internships.

Diop: People often say first-time runners for elected positions don't know what they are getting in to. But you don't think that applies to you?

Thompson: Not to criticize anyone who has said that, or to imply that I know everything because that is a feat no one can claim. But I do know that I've been in politics and around politicians enough to know with a clear head of what I was getting into.

Diop: Your grandmother beat Naomi Young's father in the 2008 Presidential election. Would you say there is a bit of rivalry between your two families?

Thompson: I wouldn't exactly say there is a rivalry, no. In fact, the circumstances of this campaign were a complete surprise. I wasn't aware Naomi was in the running until after I'd already filed my campaign forms. [coy smile] Would I deny that our family dynamic is completely irrelevant to the race? Probably not.

Diop: Do you believe that having your grandmother – who has gone on record already to state her support for your campaign – will give you the upper hand?

Thompson: I can't speak as to what is on voters' minds so early in the campaign. I can say that I greatly respect and admire my grandmother and all of the work she has done for the country. And that while anyone who shares my thoughts on my *grandmother certainly wouldn't be led astray by voting for me, I am not running on my grandmother's platform. I am running as my own person.*

Diop: And who exactly are you? What is the platform you are running on, as your own person?

Thompson: My platform is very much rooted in the work that I am already doing and that I will continue to do. My work is to further address the plight of the people of this city. My role in the Mayor's office has been to work closely with homeless shelters, food banks, hospitals, and youth organizations in order to provide more stable environments for those in need. I think that it can be easily forgotten, in this game of politics, that the reason we are here is to serve the people. I'm running for the House to take the work I've been doing and magnify it to a greater scale.

Diop: All right. Thank you for your time, Charlotte. It's been nice to catch up with you.

Thompson: It has been lovely to talk with you, Imani.

An informal debate between Thompson and Young will take place in just under two months, on December 22nd, on C-SPAN.

Charlotte sighed lightly as she dropped the news article down onto the living room table, a small smirk pulling at her mouth. Her first official interview.

It had been three weeks, since she'd announced her plans to run for the seat, and she had already hit the ground running.

As she'd said in her interview, she wasn't at all surprised by the magnitude of what she'd gotten herself into. She'd known how much work this was going to be, and not just in a theoretical sense; maybe she had never run for office before, but she'd seen campaigns like her grandmother's and worked on enough of them through college that it would be impossible for her to be going in blind.

But knowing what would be expected of her and experiencing it all firsthand were two different things.

The workload alone was exhausting. Her role as the Deputy Mayor was already a full-time job; more than that, actually, if she ever wanted to get anything done. Now, she was at the forefront of her campaign, going head-to-head with Naomi Young, working to secure votes and strengthen relationships both in and out of the mayor's office, working to schedule interviews, and when she wasn't actively working, her mind was strategizing.

She'd been getting less than seven hours of sleep a night before campaigning; she was getting even less now.

But something must really be wrong with her – or very right, given her chosen life – because in spite of the pressure and the stress and the lack of sleep . . . she felt like she was thriving.

She got a rush of adrenaline whenever something new happened in the campaign, even when she'd seen that Naomi had gone on the record a few days ago, discussing her "youthful lack of experience." It was maddening, but thrilling in a way that fewer things were.

It was good to have that confirmation that she was in the right profession.

She sighed again, this time with some slight agitation, when her phone buzzed with a text. The only downside she could think of was that the publishing of the interview had also meant that her phone had been ridiculously busy all day. And not with actually relevant political matters either, but just people she knew who had seen it.

It was good, of course, the interest she was already gaining, and she was grateful and flattered by the support she was being shown. However, it also was irritating when she'd been trying to actually get work done at the office.

Her agitation faded, though, when she looked down to see that it was from Sutton. And it was entirely unrelated to her interview.

Sutton – 6:13PM
Okay, I've picked up the food, and I'm on my way.

Charlotte – 6:15PM
The door will be open, darling.

She quickly wrote back, a pleased smile working its way over her face. In the last few weeks, she'd seen Sutton four more times for coffee, and each of those times was simultaneously like an entirely new experience but simultaneously like spending time with someone she knew very well.

It was an interesting paradox, and Charlotte felt it mirrored the same one that Sutton herself presented. She was beautiful – clearly – yet, she was so easily flustered. And flirting could make her blush darker than her hair, yet she had those sassy, sarcastic moments that caught Charlotte off-guard every time.

She was both intelligent and naïve, awkward and bold, and Charlotte was very, very much enjoying it.

Tonight, for the first time, Sutton was coming to her apartment for dinner and a movie. It had been Sutton's idea; one of those bold moments, where she seemed to speak before she could let herself think it through – Charlotte very much enjoyed those moments. They both amused her and made Sutton that much more endearing, because those blue eyes would get so big, like Sutton couldn't believe she said what she'd said.

They'd been leaving the café down the street from City Hall, where they'd taken to meeting as Sutton was keen to avoid Regan whenever they hung out – which was also entertaining in and of itself – and Charlotte had finished commenting that she was feeling a bit of the stress of everything she had to do. Which had prompted Sutton to suggest this movie night as a way to "de-stress."

Even now, Charlotte shook her head, with a light laugh at the memory. Adorable Sutton Spencer, offering to help Charlotte de-stress . . . with dinner and a movie.

If anyone would have told her a few months ago that she would be having a beautiful woman over to her apartment, for dinner and a movie and nothing else, and that she would be *looking forward to it*, she would have laughed.

143

Yet, here she was.

She spun on her heel, smile still on her face, when she heard the door to her apartment open and then close rapidly. Eyebrows wrinkling in confusion, she looked down to see that Sutton had only texted her minutes ago, before she called out, "You got here quickly."

And honestly, she was a little surprised that Sutton had let herself in so confidently.

But rather than see Sutton walk around the corner and into the living room, she was greeted with the quizzical smile of her brother. "Did Dean text you that I was coming over?"

"No. What are you doing here?" She folded her arms, lifting her eyebrows at him in the same way she'd always done when she was displeased with him.

Not that she usually minded a drop-in visit from Caleb but he knew she preferred at least a phone call beforehand.

Her brother opened his mouth in mock offense. "You sound so cold! To me, your closest brother." When she rolled her eyes, he dropped the act, "Well, I was hoping that you wouldn't be home yet. Don't you usually have dinner with the old battleax on Mondays?"

She let out an exasperated laugh. "Caleb, I swear. You and grandmother are the worst. Besides, if you didn't know that she was back in Virginia for the next month, working on the Foundation's business in its home state – as her schedule has always been – then all hope is truly lost for you."

Caleb only shrugged, though he gave her a cheeky grin.

"I'm surprised I haven't heard about her calling you after your interview today," he commented, as he walked closer to bend down and pick up the paper she'd put on the table.

Charlotte scoffed, "I received a phone call from her first thing after the article was released, of course."

"I imagine she's pleased?" Caleb murmured, as he skimmed his eyes over the article.

She found herself grinning, thinking about the phone call in question. It had started out with her grandmother complaining about the fact that all of her meetings could be shorter, if they could all sit down and focus on what was important, how they all had important things to do.

And it had quickly escalated into her grandmother telling her that she was counting on Charlotte to win, because the day Naomi Young was a Congresswoman, would be the day she went into early retirement.

Charlotte had joked, "That'll be the day," because her grandmother was well past a respectable retirement age, but she didn't let that stop her. She never let *anything* stop her, and Charlotte respected that so much.

She nodded, "Well, grandmother says that she doesn't worry that I'll let her down."

Which Charlotte loved, because she loved knowing that her grandmother had so much faith in her. That she didn't doubt Charlotte's abilities or knowledge, despite her youth or anything else. But it also did make her feel the pressure more.

Caleb placed the article down on the side table next to her couch before he sat on the arm with an exaggerated sigh, "Yes, she never worries that you will let her down, unlike her grandsons."

He said it with the same agitated affection that their grandmother used when talking about Charlotte's brothers. Others might miss it, or mistake it for the impatience it often sounded like, but Charlotte knew them all well enough to know better.

It was no secret that Charlotte was their grandmother's favorite – something she'd reveled in during her youth, though as she'd gotten older, she also recognized that there could be potential downsides. There was a heavy expectation for her to uphold everything Elizabeth was and what she wanted for Charlotte. She supposed it was kismet that she held herself to those same standards.

Or perhaps it was a self-fulfilling prophecy.

145

Regardless, Charlotte knew that her grandmother had wanted all of her grandchildren to uphold her legacy in some matter. She'd had high hopes, at first, that William would grow more ambitious, as he had the intelligence and an affable demeanor for politics. But as he'd gotten older, it was clear that he didn't have the absolute ambition and motivation he would need for the game, and by the time he was going to university, he'd declared his major as veterinary science. Not to mention his aversion to big cities; he'd moved to a smaller city in Virginia than where they'd grown up and rarely ventured out.

Caleb, did, obviously, move away from Virginia and was happy to build a life here in New York. But much to their grandmother's chagrin, while Caleb had the looks and charming personality that would make a good politician, he was much more concerned with right and wrong in black and white.

Charlotte, as her grandmother had told her since her youth, was everything Elizabeth thought good about the Thompson name. It was both a bit heavy, yet something she was extremely proud of.

Charlotte reached up to scoop her hair up, twisting it into a ponytail even as brown eyes rolled. "You know she loves both of you."

"Oh, yes, grandmother is always thrilled enough to call Will *and* me whenever something happens in our careers," Caleb snarked back. "But I did get a great phone call about how none of us are doing our job carrying on the Thompson name. At least that is something where you fail in grandmother's eyes."

Well. Caleb was right about that. She'd heard it a thousand times before, how she, Caleb, and William were disappointments on the personal life fronts. Mostly Will, as he was now in his mid-thirties.

"Shut up," she told him, succinctly. "Now, what exactly are you here for?"

Finally, he sighed a long-suffering sound before he fell backwards gracefully to land on her cushions, "Dean wants to watch some mini-series about the Hundred Years' War," Caleb looked pained. It easily pulled a smirk from her.

"I was pretty sure you'd have it. You and Dean both, sadly, have similar taste in that respect. Boring documentaries."

"As Dean's luck and your distress will have it, I *do* have that," she walked over to the shelf filled with her movies, eyes skimming over the titles. Quickly, she picked out the one she knew Dean was talking about – they'd discussed it last week.

When she turned back around, Caleb wasn't laying on her couch anymore, and was instead looking at her coffee table. He had the DVD case of the movie she and Sutton were going to watch in his hands, and he groaned.

"Fuck, another documentary on Elizabeth I? Charlotte, there are only so many times someone can watch the life and death of one person before they just need an intervention."

She bopped him lightly on the top of his head with the DVD set, grinning in satisfaction when he yelped lightly and reached up to take the DVD from her with one hand, then rub over the spot with the other. "I'll have you know that I have a friend coming over who wanted to watch with me, smartass."

Though the life of Elizabeth I, and in general strong historical females, was a focus topic for her that she often indulged in alone, she was being truthful. Sutton had admitted that she'd never watched anything about her, because much of history depressed her.

But she'd easily agreed to watch tonight when Charlotte suggested it the day before.

She only raised an eyebrow to him in response to his confused expression. Which shortly melted into a lascivious grin that she already did not like the look of, even before he nodded. "Ahh, that's why you're so anxious for me to get out of here. You have a *movie* to *watch* with a *friend*."

The truth of the fact that she was ready for him to leave, and had been since he walked in, made her stomach twist uncomfortably when paired with his insinuation. Before she brushed it off with a laugh. "I *do*, and she *is*. A friend."

The knowing look he gave her was enough to immediately have her hackles raised, "Charlotte, you haven't had a woman over to your apartment who wasn't, like, a cousin or a miscellaneous friend that was visiting from our youth for 'just a movie' in . . . ever." When she merely crossed her arms and gave him a serious look, he lost the smirk. "What – who do you even know who is just a friend?"

The fact that she gained the upper hand so easily made her feel triumphant. And even slightly amused that all it took was the idea that she truly did have a female friend to throw him off base. Still, she rolled her eyes at him, her tone dry, "Caleb, you know that I've been spending time with Sutton Spencer lately."

He stared at her, flabbergasted, for a few moments before he threw his hands in the air, exasperated. "I thought that *getting coffee* with her was a euphemism!"

Charlotte couldn't quite stop the chuckle that left her, unable to stop herself from teasing him, "And whose fault is that?"

Though, she did realize with somewhat of a grudging acceptance, that she *could* see why he thought that. He wasn't exaggerating when he brought up the fact that she didn't really have many people that she'd let in and opened up to as a friend since living in New York.

Caleb gave her a scrutinizing look, that she faced head-on, and he folded quickly. "So, you *really* haven't slept with her?"

A disbelieving snort of laughter left her before she shook her head at him – at the both of them, really. "No!"

When he gave her a roguish smile, she was ready to start pushing him out the door, even before he asked, "But you want to, right?"

Her mouth opened, but no words found their way out. She wasn't in the habit of denying simple truths like that – especially not to Caleb, and especially when there was absolutely nothing wrong with finding someone attractive and wanting to act on that attraction.

And, she *did* find Sutton attractive and had wanted to act on said attraction since the first time she'd seen her picture.

Her attraction had really only grown in the past few weeks. As she'd become accustomed to Sutton's style, with her preppy tops and tight jeans and array of cute dresses that she liked to wear. As she'd realized exactly how easy it was to make her blush – and god, was it easy.

Still, she only shrugged, "That's neither here nor there; friends can be attracted to one another."

She didn't have many friends, but she knew that there weren't specific guidelines. They could be attracted to one another. Friends could enjoy making friends blush, and enjoy the slight tremor that went through the other friend when she was kissing her cheek –

Feeling the pleasant and familiar churning in the pit of her stomach at the thought, she blinked herself out of it. It had definitely been far longer than she usually went without having sex.

The look he was giving her was incredulous. "Charlotte, who *are* you? Who is this celibate woman standing in front of me? Since when do you have a not-straight woman that you are attracted to and you don't find a way to seduce?"

Only mildly offended, she scoffed, "I don't *seduce* people." Generally. Usually, a seduction wasn't really required. "Besides, Sutton isn't . . . like that."

He gave her a look that made her know he was simultaneously curious and humoring her. "Like what, exactly?"

She shrugged, twirling her hand in the air lightly like it would aid her explanation. "She isn't interested in things that are short term, or purely physical." She aimed a wry look at him, "She believes in love."

The laugh that he barked out made her cringe. "Just your type," he teased, before adding speculatively, "It's unlike you to seek out other . . . companionship."

"You make it sound like I'm a hooker or something. Hanging out with Sutton is fun," she settled on after going blank for a moment as to how to

149

describe it. She wasn't even sure fun was the right word; it wasn't the *wrong* word, but she enjoyed spending time with Sutton for a multitude of reasons, and she wasn't about to start waxing poetic about the virtues of friendship to her brother, "It's nice to have a friend who isn't a family member, which Dean practically is."

"Look at you – making *friends*." Caleb gave her a look of exaggerated pride. "Well, friend. I'm so proud of you for looking beyond your urges." He winked at her. "Especially when there is a woman as good-looking as Sutton Spencer involved. I've heard very flattering things about her."

Before Caleb could say anything that led her down that particular road again – because it was a road Charlotte actively tried not to stroll down in regards to Sutton – she grabbed his sleeve and started to tug him back down the hall.

"Now, you are going to leave, because she's going to be here any moment now. And you'll take advantage of her easily-blushing nature."

He wiggled his eyebrows in a way that made her laugh. "Like you don't."

She acknowledged him with a shrug and a coquettish smile. "Well, she's *my* friend."

"You're no fun," he sighed at her, even as he willingly walked along.

Charlotte had a retort on the tip of her tongue, before the tentative knock that sounded on her door grabbed both of their attention. Anticipation slid through her, though she was careful not to look *too* eager because she was very much aware that Caleb was watching her.

"Apparently I stayed until the perfect time." He grinned.

It just made her shake her head as she warned, "Behave."

The door slowly opened without her stepping toward it, as Sutton hesitantly started to walk through, a large bag of food in her arms. She was picking lightly at the corner of the bag as she muttered to herself, "She said to just come in. So, it's not weird."

Charlotte really didn't know how Sutton did it – managed to be charming even when she wasn't aware she was being watched – but she was grinning, lifting an eyebrow in Sutton's direction.

Just as she looked up, and froze upon seeing them. Blue eyes locked first on Charlotte, where they stayed for a few moments, holding her gaze before dropping slightly to take in Charlotte in the tank top and yoga pants that she'd changed into after getting out of her work clothes. It vaguely occurred to her that Sutton hadn't seen her not dressed either for the office or for a function before.

The flush on Sutton's cheeks was unmistakable as her gaze popped back up and then dodged to look at Caleb. The hot feeling that settled in her at Sutton checking her out, and the way her eyes widened and mouth opened slightly, was both satisfying and disappointing.

It was a familiar feeling, especially over the last few weeks with Sutton. The girl had no control over her automatic responses to her attraction, and Charlotte loved it. Even when it reminded her that she was living in celibacy for the first time in over ten years.

Sutton adjusted the hold she had with one of her arms around the bag of Thai food that she'd picked up, so she could offer an awkward wave to Caleb. "Um, hi."

"You must be Sutton." He gave her a pleasant, genial smile. It was amiable and charismatic, much like her brother himself was, and he reached out to offer his hand. "Charlotte's told me about you."

Sutton's eyes darted between them for a second, and she knew she wasn't imagining the pleased smile that tugged at the corners of her lips. "Really?"

Shaking her head, she stepped forward to take the food from Sutton. "This is my brother, Caleb."

Those big blue eyes blinked once, then twice, in recognition, "Oh! You and Dean."

Caleb only grinned wider. "I see you've heard of me, too. Well, I have some movie-night business of my own to attend to, so I'll be getting out of your way."

As he stepped around Sutton, he flashed Charlotte a knowing smile over Sutton's shoulder.

"Goodbye, Caleb. Don't fret over the Hundred Years' War too much."

His smile shifted into an innocuous one quickly, easily, as Sutton turned to face him. "It was nice to meet you."

"A pleasure," he assured her and didn't even seem like he was being insincere, which he was half of the time. "See you later, Charlie."

She grimaced at the nickname before ushering him out of the apartment and shutting the door behind him. When she turned back to Sutton, she was watching her with interest. "Do both of your brothers look like you? Caleb does, very much."

With a teasing smile, she asked, "Devastatingly good-looking?"

Sutton rolled her eyes, but the flush on her cheeks remained. "Are they both as modest as you are, too?"

Laughing lowly, she shifted the food in her grasp and nodded. "Oh, Caleb and I missed the mark on the humility gene far more than William," she admitted, unabashedly. "But while there is a resemblance between myself and Will, Caleb is the closer of the two, I think."

Using her elbow, she nudged Sutton lightly and nodded down the hall. "The movie is set up in the living room. I'll just grab us some plates and meet you in there?"

She enjoyed the way Sutton slowly dragged her eyes over the pictures and artwork on the walls, clearly trying to observe everything, as she nodded. "Okay."

As soon as she set the food down on the counter, she didn't even have a moment to grab for plates before her phone buzzed in her pocket. She debated looking at it; she already knew who it was.

Caleb – 6:41PM
*So . . . you might have mentioned that a seduction
wouldn't even be necessary.*

Caleb – 6:42PM
*Because that girl – very pretty, just your type –
definitely has a crush on you. You do know that
right?*

Charlotte lightly tapped her thumbs against the sides of her phone as she
blew out a low breath, debating what to say back.

Charlotte – 6:44PM
*Mind your own business, dear brother, and enjoy
your movie night. Be careful or I'll suggest this Queen
Elizabeth doc to Dean! :)*

Simple and effective, she decided, as she moved to start putting the food
onto plates.

Of course she knew that Sutton had a little infatuation with her; even if she
didn't have a finely tuned radar for reading people, she would have been able
to know that. She'd seen Sutton be checked out by several people during their
times out together, let alone the comments Regan liked to throw to her –
which she'd noted could range from exaggeratedly complimentary or nearly
lewd – and none of those things resulted in the same reaction Charlotte could
elicit with even a wink.

Which, honestly, was delightful and . . . stirring. Even if it wasn't a crush,
exactly, she knew that Sutton was attracted to her.

But it wasn't as though she was entirely unaffected by Sutton, either, so she figured they were even on that front. Even if she was far better at disguising it.

She opened the fridge and pulled out a couple of bottles of water, before carefully picking up the plates and walking into the living room.

She'd expected Sutton to be sitting on the couch, waiting for her. Instead, her back was to Charlotte, as she looked over her bookshelf. A smirk worked its way onto her mouth, and she shook her head. Of course .

As she placed everything in her arms down onto the coffee table, she took the moment to look Sutton over. A fond exasperation washed over her when she realized Sutton was only wearing a knitted gray sweater and no jacket; it was cold out. It was nearly November! They'd had this talk multiple times, though, and Sutton always only gave her a playful smile and insisted that she wasn't cold.

Which was honestly true, because Charlotte would often find that she was much colder than Sutton was as she would grab onto her arm as they walked.

Cold-blooded, warm-hearted Sutton, with her red hair contrasting with her sweater as it was done in a low ponytail, falling like straight silk down her back. She'd taken off the boots she'd worn over, neatly placing them next to the couch, Charlotte noticed, before she walked up next to her.

Sutton glanced at her, surprise coloring her features, as she sounded impressed, "You really are a fan of my mother's."

Charlotte looked at the shelf that had all of Katherine Spencer's novels lined up in order, taking in the slow, reverent way Sutton was running her hand over the spines of the books. She watched for a moment and wondered if Sutton realized that she instinctively traced over the *S* in Spencer on all of the spines with her index finger.

Then she turned back to Sutton, tilting her head up slightly to look her in the eye. "You thought I was lying?" She arched a purposefully incredulous eyebrow at her.

"No! Not . . .. really. But a lot of people say things that they think I want to hear, when they realize who my mother is. Especially at school, seeing as how, you know, I'm in literature." She shrugged, twice, embarrassed, and Charlotte watched in amusement.

When she turned again to see the book that Sutton's hand had paused on, she nodded at it, "That one is actually my favorite."

A large, glowing smile quickly stole over Sutton's face, and she simply beamed down at her. "Mine, too."

For a moment, Charlotte wondered how Sutton had so much warmth – from her smile to her actual temperature – before she cleared her throat and looked back at the book – *The Princess in Disguise*. The novel followed knightly Aurora going on what should have been a simple mission but had then turned into her stumbling into a much greater plot when she discovered that the girl acting as a castellan's daughter was truly the princess Clara that had been on the run and missing for years.

"While I do love Aurora, and I think she's a model heroine, there is something about Clara that I found so intriguing. I can't wait for the next one, when they're on the road together."

All right, perhaps she was actually a pretty big fan of Katherine Spencer's books. But the first one had come out when she was really coming into her sexuality and her stance on feminism, and Aurora was a great character to delve into for that.

But Sutton's smile only got even softer, impossibly so, before she took on a mischievous look. "It's *really* good."

Her eyes narrowed. "You've read it already?"

"You know I'm her daughter right? And her number one fan."

She found that stupidly endearing, and she shook her head lightly before she paused. "Wait, is the dedication in that book to you?"

Charlotte reached out to slide the book out from the shelf, flipping open the cover, and pointing to the inscription, *As always, thankful to my husband and my*

155

children. This book is particularly beholden to my own young princess; this book wouldn't have been nearly the same without your strength and creativity.

Sutton leaned in, and Charlotte felt her shoulder brush against her own, the fabric of her sweater soft against her skin. When she turned her head slightly to look at her, Sutton had a bashful smile on her lips.

"Yes." She seemed to hesitate for a moment, before saying, "She's mine. I mean, Clara Reiner, the princess? I created her. Originally, in the first draft that my mother had for the novel, Clara wasn't going to be an actual character, it was just going to be about Aurora, exposing the castellan while on her journey. But I had created the idea of Clara as a princess in disguise for my Fiction Writing class, and when I was talking about it with my mom, she evolved."

Sutton looked both proud and self-conscious, her hand coming down to fidget lightly with the bottom of her shirt. But Charlotte could only give her a surprised look that melted into a soft smile.

It wasn't as though she hadn't known Sutton was bright, but this – her creativity, and knowing that she was behind creating one of Charlotte's favorite characters – made an unfamiliar warmth settle in her chest.

"That's actually very impressive, Sutton. So, you *do* write."

There was a light blush on her cheeks, but the brightness in her eyes was unmistakable as she looked up at Charlotte. "Not *really*. Just with my mom."

She filed it away for later, because she'd learned that sometimes with Sutton it was better to let things be than to continue.

"Come on, the food is getting cold. And it's time for *you* to get acquainted with one of my favorites."

She walked back toward the couch and knew Sutton was following her, even before she sat down with a sigh. "I don't know why I agreed to watch this with you. It's just going to be miserable."

"Because life isn't all about *Casablanca*, darling," she teased. "Come, watch, and then you can have those lemon cakes that I saw in another bag for dessert."

Three hours, a meal of Thai food, with lemon cakes for dessert, and the rise and fall of one of her historic heroes later, Charlotte muted the credits as they played on the TV. Then she turned, pulling her legs up to curl under her on the couch, and looked at Sutton.

Who, she'd learned, was very serious about not making comments during movies – which Charlotte was very much the same about, and she was very grateful for it. Caleb and Dean both loved to talk throughout movies they watched, and it drove her crazy.

She took in the way Sutton had her arms crossed as she was leaning back against the couch. Then the way she sighed, soft and gloomy.

She propped her head up with her fist, as she drew out, "So . . . what did you think?"

The way Sutton swiveled her head to nail her with a *look* made Charlotte snort in laughter. She then indignantly crossed her arms and swung those long legs up to gracefully curl under her, in a position mirroring Charlotte's.

"I can't believe that this is one of your favorite topics. What is wrong with you?"

The chuckle that escaped her was surprisingly loud. "I love it. I love her."

Sutton blew out a long breath, before she began to rant, "It just makes me so *sad* –",

"She was one of the most prosperous monarchs in history!" She interjected, unable to help herself.

Sutton just glared. "It's *sad*, because her sister had her locked up, then she ruled while determined to be alone and never get married because it could have undermined her authority. And in the end, she was just depressed and lonely. It's not a happy ending, regardless of the middle!" Sutton spoke with her hands, moving them in a distinct *what the fuck* kind of gesture.

The agitated cadence in Sutton's tone was unfamiliar to her, and it sparked something in her that made her sit up a little straighter, a smirk taking over instinctively. Which Sutton noticed and it made her mock-glare.

"You don't agree? You don't think this is sad?" Sutton asked in disbelief.

Charlotte tipped her head, taking in a thoughtful breath as she felt Sutton's wondering eyes trace over her face from a few feet away. After a long moment, she admitted, "Well, it *is* a bit sad when you think of it like that, of course. But I don't feel sad after watching it." She shrugged as she brought her hand up to rest on the space of the cushion between them.

Sutton leaned in and Charlotte watched as those fire-touched strands brushed against the blanket she had folded at the top of her sofa. Sutton looked at her, interested and questioning. "What does it make you feel, then? Apparently, your human emotions don't function the way others do."

"I'm not *happy*, per-se, just not sad. But . . . empowered, in a way. Look at all she could accomplish, and that was centuries ago."

She wondered what Sutton thought of in the few moments where she couldn't quite control the way her expression scrunched up in thought, before smoothing out into a teasing grin. "Well, I don't think there is any way for your siblings to lock you up in a tower in today's world anyway."

She shifted forward so that she could reach out to push at Sutton's shoulder. Gently, though, not even really enough so that her hand was displaced, and she lightly traced her fingers over the knitted fabric for a moment, before dropping.

"When will I stop being surprised at your snark?"

Sutton laughed, but there was a slight catch in her breath. "Hopefully never, so I won't become boring."

Her expression leveled out. "Sutton, I can honestly say you've surprised me more than anything since the first time I got your message."

Sutton accepted her words with a pleased look crossing her features as she absently toyed with the blanket on the back of the couch again. It was only a

158

few inches away from where Charlotte's head was resting, and she ran her eyes over the gentle way Sutton's long fingers pulled at a loose thread.

Her thoughts were cut off when Sutton abruptly sat up, leaning farther in with her agency. The movement startled her, and she looked at her in surprise, eyes wide.

"Oh! Speaking of your convictions! I read your interview in the Times today. I meant to text you, but it was just before I had a meeting with my professor, and I forgot," Sutton explained.

Charlotte quirked an eyebrow. "I didn't think that you really enjoyed the political section of the Times."

In fact, she knew that to be true. Over their last few coffee hangouts, one of the things they'd discussed was that while Sutton and her oldest brother Oliver were the Spencer children who did the best in a political setting, and were up-to-date on important matters, she largely preferred to keep out of the intricacies of it all.

It had been amusing to listen to Sutton describe the fact that she voted in every election because she'd been raised to believe it was her duty to do so. And that if she couldn't fall back on prior knowledge about a candidate, she would spend a quick half hour to look up the important topics and where each candidate stood on them.

She enjoyed the way Sutton rolled her eyes. "I *don't*, typically. But usually my friends aren't featured there. I think I'll be paying closer attention during this race than I have during most others."

"Aw, you'll do it just for me?" she teased, but the pleased feeling she had was real.

"Shut up." After a few seconds, she took in a breath and looked back at Charlotte, looking her in the eye. "Your interview was really good, though. I don't know how, but I feel like you effortlessly managed to condemn Naomi and talk yourself up without being super obvious about it. And you were clear about your respect for your grandmother, but firm that you are your own person," Sutton lifted her eyebrows, her lips coming to a slight pout as she thought for a moment before she settled on, "It was very impressive."

Charlotte felt a pleasant warmth coursing through her, settling thick and smooth as honey through her veins. "Sutton Spencer, you flatter me."

"I'm being serious!" she insisted, with a laugh, before she settled back against the couch once more.

She was closer now. Close enough that Charlotte felt her warm breath lightly brush over her cheek, smelling faintly sweet, of the lemon cakes Sutton had brought as dessert. She'd been this close in passing over the past few weeks – moments where she would kiss Sutton's cheek gently in a goodbye.

Which *was*, in part, to actually say goodbye, of course. But then she'd realized it had given her a trill of excitement the way Sutton so obviously reacted to them. She reacted like Charlotte had kissed her for real. So, in turn, it became like a tease for Charlotte herself.

Because . . . it would be *so* easy to just turn her head in those moments, or lean in right now.

After a few moments beat by, Sutton licked her lips, and her eyes followed the motion closely.

Sutton took in a quick breath and asked, with her voice shaking slightly, "How are you feeling, about all of that? The, uh, the campaign. Do you feel less stressed?"

The words broke her out of her reverie, and Charlotte shook her head, drawing back and collecting herself. Taking in a deep breath, she released it with a soft laugh. "Though a movie isn't my typical method of de-stressing, I do feel oddly better."

She tossed Sutton a wink even though she wasn't really joking in the slightest.

"What have you done in the past?"

"Oh, Sutton . . ." Charlotte closed her eyes for a moment, taking a deep breath. "You can't possibly be asking me that."

160

"Why not?" she asked softly, and just – how was she so innocent but not, at the same time?

She moved without thinking, really, shifting in enough so that she could feel the warmth from Sutton's body, trailing her fingertips over Sutton's hand that was resting on the back of the couch. "Darling, the biggest issue for me so far in the election has been deleting my profile on *SapphicSpark*."

It was truly the biggest downside that had arisen in the past couple of weeks.

The fact of the matter was that whenever work and life in general got stressful, the best stress relief that she'd found for herself was through a physical release. While going through a hard time at work, Charlotte had often found that it was the best time to log in to the app and find someone to . . . work through her release with her.

Sutton's eyes widened as realization dawned, and her cheeks blushed in the way Charlotte loved.

"Oh. So. That was your . . . system."

She couldn't help but laugh, tracing her fingertip down Sutton's wrist, feeling the way her pulse sped up. She both heard and felt the way her breath hitched, and when she responded, her voice was unintentionally low, "My *system*, yes. It worked very well. What is it that *you* do, to de-stress?"

Fuck her, she honestly shouldn't have phrased it that way, and she scolded herself inwardly. Because any images she had of Sutton *de-stressing* were not at all innocent. A buzz of arousal shot through her, trying to push away images of Sutton *de-stressing* herself.

She cleared her throat, and swayed closer to Charlotte, and blue eyes darkened into a stormy gaze. "I, um . . . write. Or go for a run. Or I sometimes do yoga, if I don't feel like going out."

Her voice, which was normally so clear, dropped just rough enough to send a shudder up Charlotte's spine.

"Yoga?"

She didn't realize that she'd inched in, until she was close enough to see the way Sutton's eyelashes fluttered, casting light shadows over her cheeks. She had freckles this close, Charlotte realized, and god, it would be so *easy* to lean in.

"Um . . . yes. It really – um," she broke off to lick her lips. Charlotte's eyes ate up the motion hungrily. "Loosens you up. And . . . relaxes you."

Charlotte knew for certain that de-stressing with Sutton would be amazing. The idea of fucking Sutton, of being the first woman to have the honor of it . . . the desire settled low in her stomach.

Even just kissing her, with those full lips so inviting and only inches away from her own, was unimaginably appealing.

She felt Sutton's tentative fingertips brush over her own, curling lightly around hers. Her other hand started to crawl from where it rested between them to land on Sutton's thigh, thumb stroking her through her leggings. Her own eyes fell closed as her head tilted.

"I'm – Charlotte?" Sutton's barely-there whisper made her stop.

Because this was *Sutton*. Sutton who trembled at a kiss on her cheek. Whose blush Charlotte reveled in from a simple touch. Who Charlotte very much wanted to kiss, but . . .

She bit off a deep breath, and anticipation that had built up in her stomach died down as she leaned back a bit, sliding her hand off of Sutton's thigh. Because regardless of the fact of attraction and wanting, they were *not* on the same page when it came to anything involving romance.

Sutton had been very clear, the entirety of their friendship, that she'd longed for something deep. Something lasting. Something that Charlotte herself didn't even want, and was unable to provide even if she did want it.

Sutton was her friend, one who was turning into a good friend, at that. She was determined to be a good one, back. Even if that meant calling back her own urges when she felt them to preserve this friendship.

Sighing at herself, she lightly rubbed her fingers along the back of Sutton's hand as she pulled all of the way back, taking in Sutton's flushed cheeks and confused, widely-blinking eyes.

"Maybe we should do yoga, some day. Even though the movie was good, too," she spoke softly, trying to use a light tone. It normally wasn't difficult for her, masking over any emotion.

She could feel Sutton's deep breath as she breathed out and sat back, looking as dazed as Charlotte felt inside.

"Maybe."

Charlotte took a moment to close her eyes, taking in as much of a calming breath as she could, before she asked, "Do you want to watch another movie?"

"Sure," Sutton whispered back.

Despite the fact that Charlotte could see that her hands were still slightly shaking, she gave Charlotte a slight smile.

Which Charlotte returned, even as she tried to keep her mind off of yoga with Sutton. Friends. She might not have many – any – female friends, but regardless of what Caleb thought, she could control herself.

Chapter 9

Sutton was *nervous*.

She wasn't even sure how she'd gotten herself into this situation; okay, that was a lie, she definitely knew *exactly* how she'd gotten into this situation.

She was in this situation because of the women in her life.

Foremost, because Charlotte Thompson was ridiculously beautiful and sexy, even when she wasn't trying to be. Which meant that Sutton was alarmingly, palms-sweating-ly attracted to her.

Which would have been fine, except for the fact that her crush had only grown in the last few weeks. It shouldn't have been fair, she'd lamented – to herself – that Charlotte looked the way she looked, but she was also ridiculously smart, funny, ambitious . . .

And if *all of that* hadn't sealed the deal on her feelings, there was the fact that Charlotte had those sparing moments of vulnerability with Sutton. Which made her feel special, in a way. In the way that she knew Charlotte didn't have those moments often with other people.

Sutton could have managed all of that, maybe. If not for their movie night where Charlotte had been about to kiss her. Even though she was certainly no connoisseur of being with women, she'd known without a doubt that it was going to happen. It had been written into the way in which Charlotte had moved, the way her fingers had slid over Sutton's thigh, in a slow, smooth, warm, *knowing* gesture. How those big, brown eyes had glinted before dipping to look at Sutton's lips . . .

Anyway.

That led her to the second woman in her life that threw her life off balance, albeit in an entirely different way.

When Sutton had returned home from that movie date, she'd laid on the couch next to Regan and lamented about the kiss. Regan had brushed her hand over Sutton's hair in a comforting gesture, which had made her feel better.

She'd even found herself agreeing when Regan had asserted that it was time to 'put herself out there' for women other than Charlotte. That she had to "take control of her feelings" or whatever that meant.

Only, she never should have agreed to anything Regan said, especially when her friend had declared that she found the perfect thing. But how was she to know that Regan would find a lesbian speed dating event for queer women happening at a posh bar over in the East Village.

Apparently Regan signed up for the email subscription on *SapphicSpark* when she'd created Sutton's profile.

At the *very* least, she'd managed to stop her best friend from joining her on this speed dating experience. Apparently, for every *SapphicSpark* user that attended, they were allowed to bring two guests to boost attendance. Regan had taken the liberty to invite herself and Emma.

She'd never appreciated Emma's ability to quell Regan's over-exuberance more than she had earlier when Emma had realized what was happening and put a stop to it.

She bit her lip, hard, as she stared up at the restaurant hosting the event. Was she really going to do this?

It was her phone's buzzing that drew her out of her thoughts and she was grateful for the distraction. Maybe there was an emergency that would give her an excuse to bow out.

Alex – 6:42PM
hey so my tournament in London is over soon

She rolled her eyes. Her hope was for nothing.

Sutton – 6:44PM

I know. Not only did mom tell me, but did you
forget that you texted the group the video of you
practically killing that boy during your semi-finals?

Alex – 6:47PM

jesus christ the text wasn't finished. it was
actually supposed to be this:

Alex – 6:48PM

hey so my tournament in London is over soon
AND i'm going to be in NY for some training for
a little bit

Alex – 6:49PM

. . .

Sutton shook her head, huffing out a breath as she quickly replied, remembering the last time her sister had asked to stay with her for the month that her training company was going to be in New York for a tournament.

Sutton – 6:50PM

No.

Sutton – 6:51PM

No, you may NOT stay at my apartment. No, you
may NOT "crash on the couch" and no, you may
certainly not commandeer MY bed to sleep in because
"your back hurts" after training.

166

Alex – 6:54PM

sutton!! come the fuck on, i'm not THAT bad! i
have nowhere else to go. you're going to throw
your only sister out on the street just like that?

She hated that a snort of laughter left her at Alex's words.

Sutton – 6:56PM

On the street? The apartments that your company
buys out for you all are pre-paid for! You used to
love staying in them, what happened to that?

Alex – 6:59PM

uh yah i liked the apartments they had us living
in before the fucking crazy bitch was sharing my
apartment with me! now i have to live with her all of
the time whenever we're away at competition and she's
THE WORST.

Alex – 7:00PM

i think she's gonna murder me in my sleep one day!!
do you want that on your conscience?

Sutton – 7:02PM

And I'm the one who has always been called
dramatic?

With that – because she knew her sister would be indignant at the jab – she put her phone down again and turned to face the entrance. This night might end up being a mess; in fact, she was sure it would, but it was happening.

With a deep breath, she nodded to herself.

Before her phone started ringing and she rolled her eyes at her sister, answering without needing to look.

"Look, you could even stay with Chris if you wanted. You know I'm not going to tell Mom and Dad that you're staying with your little boyfriend."

"I don't believe I would like to take you up on your offer to stay with this man, darling."

She groaned. "Charlotte! Hi. Um. I thought you were Alex."

"I'm sorry to disappoint," she murmured, mirth clear in her tone.

"You're not," she was quick to assure, even as she cringed at herself, because – could she ever be any more obvious?

"Well, I was just calling to ask if you were busy tonight? I know you said earlier that you were just going to be grading papers and that everything was okay, but you sounded a little off yesterday."

Honestly, Sutton couldn't think of something she'd rather be doing than hanging out with Charlotte tonight. There was no question that she'd certainly rather be there than speed dating. Which was probably why she had to go.

Disappointed with the whole situation, she tugged lightly at the bottom of her jacket as a slight bump of panic set through her. "I thought you were working late tonight?"

It was easier to hedge around answering, because she hadn't actually told Charlotte what she was doing. Not that she thought Charlotte would really *care*, because she was the one who didn't believe in dating. But for her own dignity; Charlotte was the woman who walked into a room and turned every head. If she wanted to date, she would never need to resort to speed dating.

Charlotte sighed, and Sutton felt like she could hear the stress in the simple sound. "Yes, well, I *do* have work to do, but a lot of it is easily done from home.

I've already been at the office for a few hours later than any sane person could handle. Besides, I was worried about you, after you seemed skittish yesterday."

She thought back to their coffee date, where Charlotte had been her regular self – she'd gotten Sutton's tea before she'd even arrived and then had threaded her arm through Sutton's. She'd felt warm from both of those things. Which made her start to feel in her head about the crush, then about her speed dating plans, and – it went downhill from there.

"Um, no. I'm not – I'm good."

"Sutton." The way Charlotte said her name was demanding and yielding at the same time. Like she only had to say that one thing, and Sutton was compelled to answer her.

It was kind of like a weapon, Sutton decided, and she knew that Charlotte knew exactly what she was doing.

She only hesitated for only a moment before she admitted, "I'm not grading papers tonight. There's, well, there's this, um, *thing* that I'm going to. And I don't really want to go, and I'm not sure about it, but . . ."

"Okay, then, Ms. Vague. Are you going to tell me more, or am I going to be worrying all night that you're being held at knifepoint?" She let out a chuckle that only sounded half-kidding.

Sutton rubbed her hand against her stomach as if that would work to calm the tumultuous churning happening in there. And she knew she was just being stupid.

Because honestly, the one person who she could probably even ask for advice about this whole thing was Charlotte. Because even though Sutton liked her, and this just made her feel more pathetic, if any woman knew her enough to know that she would be freaking out about this, it was Charlotte.

Which was what prompted the words to spill out in a rush. "I'm going, like, dating tonight? Speed dating." She cringed at herself. "Regan found out about it. And I didn't want to tell you because I–" she snapped her mouth shut, flushing, because she was *not about to reveal her crush* on this phone call. "Because I'm me, and I'm *nervous*."

Then, there was silence.

She waited for a few moments, thinking that maybe Charlotte was amused by it all or didn't know what to say – even though Charlotte seemed to always have something to say. But when more seconds ticked by, she frowned.

After checking to see if the line had somehow disconnected – and finding that it hadn't – she cleared her throat. "Um, Charlotte?"

"I'm here, sorry. I'm just surprised. I thought you weren't interested in meeting women right now?"

Sutton shrugged to herself, wondering how to answer something that wasn't *I've already met one – you!*

"I am interested. I just don't . . . I don't think it's going to go well. I have no idea what to do or say, and there are going to be so many women there, who are pretty, and probably know a lot more than I do." She blew out a deep breath and fiddled with her sleeve.

Charlotte hummed under her breath before she spoke in a firm reassuring voice, "Sutton, darling, you are *gorgeous* and you have a lot to offer. Those women would be fools not to be interested."

She desperately tried not to take heart at the words. And tried to ignore the way they made her heart flutter in her chest. "Thank you."

"Now. When is this whole thing starting?" Charlotte asked, and Sutton listened to the sound of her heels pounding on the sidewalk as she walked – probably out of City Hall.

"Um, soon. I'm supposed to be inside, like . . ." She pulled her phone down to glimpse at the clock. "A few minutes ago, actually."

Charlotte let out a light laugh, that might have been the slightest bit strained. "Perhaps you should go then." The laughter trailed off. "And be careful tonight. Remember everything I've told you about women, okay?"

She blew out a breath. "I'll try."

She nervously gave her name to the man at the door, who directed her up a set of stairs. Sutton followed his direction, her hands tugging lightly at the hem of her dress as she tried to hide the fact that she was so nervous, she might throw up.

The music from the restaurant downstairs was playing when she walked in, and dimmed more and more as she made her way up the side stairwell, fading into a quieter, somewhat calming jazz that became clearer as she opened the door into the event room.

And then froze where she stood as she tried to take it all in, eyes wide.

There were women everywhere. Which, she knew would happen, on the fundamental level of the fact that this was an event for queer women. But . . . Sutton had never been to a place that had so many women who were all gathered for the shared purpose of finding another woman.

There were more than Sutton had been expecting. Granted, *what* exactly she'd been expecting, she didn't even truly know.

It was exciting, in a way. She wasn't alone.

"I don't mean to rush you. But we're going to begin soon."

Embarrassed, she turned to see a pretty woman with jet black hair that was pulled back into a braid and dark eyes that matched. The best way she could think to describe them was striking, as they glinted in amusement at her. She had a darker complexion than Sutton did, perfectly smooth olive-toned skin. There was the hint of a smile playing at her mouth as she looked up at Sutton from where she stood, several inches shorter.

Clearing her throat, Sutton forced herself to concentrate on *not* blushing. "I – sorry. But . . . what do I, um, do?" her voice unintentionally dropped to a whisper as her hand vaguely gestured out to the room.

Christ. She should have just walked out the door then.

The woman's features shifted into a full smile. "Definitely a first-timer, then. I thought so," she tilted her head as she ran her eyes down Sutton's body in a quick yet obvious way, before working back up to her eyes. "Well, for starters, I'm Alia Haddad. My mother created *SapphicSpark*."

She gestured over her shoulder to where an older, attractive woman stood, surveying the area and talking to another couple of people dressed in professional attire.

"So, you're here for work. Not for . . ." she trailed off, eyes darting to where the plethora of women mingled.

Alia's grin was immediate and devious. "Work now, play later." She shot her a wink. "Now, tell me, Red, what's your name?"

"Spencer. Sutton Spencer," she added on, inwardly rolling her eyes at herself because who did she think she was? An action movie hero? Maybe she *should* have allowed Regan to come. Regan would have no problem with any of this.

But Alia didn't seem to mind, and she just reached out to pick up a nametag off of the table to their left that read her name in large letters. "One of our last few to arrive. Are your two guests also coming?"

Shit. She froze, her hand in the air still reaching for her name tag, and suddenly felt guilty. She felt like she'd RSVP'd to an event with a lie even though it wasn't really her fault. She had to clear her throat again. "Um, no. They were . . . sick."

"No problem." Alia waved her excuse off, appearing unconcerned. "Nervous people are no-shows all of the time at these. It's the brave ones who come out."

She quickly shook her head. "No, I'm not – I'm just, I mean. I'm not *brave*, I'm just bisexual."

Yeah. She should just leave now before she could experience more humiliation.

Alia tossed her head back, though, and laughed. Her hand came out to land softly on Sutton's forearm. "You kind of make me wish I wasn't here for work."

Sutton had no idea why that made her feel a little bit better – still like her stomach had frogs leaping around, but it didn't seem like that was going to go away – and she straightened her nametag.

"Well, from your mouth to the lesbian's ears."

She froze when she realized that she'd actually said the words aloud, even as Alia chuckled again, amusement written all over her face.

Alia's smile deepened, laughing as she spoke, "All right, so this is what to expect: based on profiles, you've all been given a number for predicted compatibility. Either a one or a two. All of the ones will be sitting on the side against the wall, and they'll stay there –" she gestured at the long row of two-person tables, where one chair, indeed, was against the wall. Many people were already sitting in those seats. Then she pointed at the chairs across from them, " – And twos will sit across from the ones, and will switch tables."

She glanced down to a clipboard that was situated on the corner of the table. "You're a one; you'll sit there," she pointed to the table on the end, the closest to the door. "And every five minutes, there's going to be a bell, which is the signal for the twos to switch to the table to their right. It goes on for an hour – with a five-minute break in the middle. You'll meet between ten to twelve women, depending on how smoothly it all goes."

Sutton took it all in, unable to stop fidgeting with her nametag, as she looked around. She felt stupid but had to ask, "What then?"

She got a small, amused smile in response, as Alia handed her a small, blank white card and a pen. "*Then*, you write the names of all of the women who you'd like to talk to a bit more, and at the end you'll give us the cards, and we'll contact you with the names and numbers of the women who you've matched with. Or," her grin turned mischievous, "You can go to the club down the street after and *get to know* anyone who strikes your fancy."

"Um, probably not."

"Your prerogative." Alia's expression turned more professionally reserved, as she gestured over to the table she'd pointed to a few moments before. "Now, if you wouldn't mind taking your seat, we'll get started."

Sutton took a deep breath, pressing her hand to her stomach to calm herself, before she felt a soft touch of fingertips against her arm. It was gone within a moment, though, and she turned in confusion just as Alia leaned in to whisper, "Don't worry. It'll go better than you're imagining."

She didn't believe it for a second, but she appreciated her effort.

As she walked to her seat, she slid her jacket off of her shoulders, letting it fall down over her arms before folding it over the back of her chair. The woman who was already seated at the table next to her was giving her an appraising look, and she was already giving her a small smile in response before she even realized with a jolt that she was *checking her out.*

She barely had any time to really process it before it was announced that they would begin. Ready or not, it didn't matter. Within the first few moments, with her stomach tied up into tight knots, a woman slid into the chair across from her.

The woman seemed a little older, maybe early thirties. Blonde hair chicly bobbed, she was already wearing a sly grin as she placed the glass she'd clearly gotten from the bar at the far end of the room on the table.

"Well, hello." She gave Sutton a quick-and-obvious roaming of the eyes that didn't feel particularly flattering, but she felt her hands start to shake nonetheless.

"Um. Hi," Sutton eloquently offered her mind suddenly blank at what exactly she was supposed to say next.

Thankfully, the woman offered her hand. "Meredith." Spoken in a practiced low tone, and Sutton couldn't help but feel like it was like a B-list version of Charlotte's flawlessly effortless murmur –

Stop.

"Sutton," she supplied, and reached over to shake her hand.

Just as she made contact, Meredith shifted so that her foot stroked along her calf. Shocked, Sutton jerked her hand back, her wrist bumping into the half full martini glass. Which fell easily, but she watched with dread, almost seeming like it was in slow motion as the contents spilled into Meredith's lap.

Wide-eyed, and feeling her cheeks burning as a low-key panic set in, Sutton looked frantically around for a napkin, "I – I'm sorry! I can go get –"

Her spluttering apology was cut short by a tight smile, and Sutton tried desperately to convince herself that in spite of a sinking feeling that the tone for the evening wasn't set in stone.

The second date went a little bit better. Kind of. As in, no liquids were spilled.

They managed introductions, this time a short girl who seemed to be around her own age, who gave her a pleasant smile. Laura was her name, and she had brown hair that was a little duller than Charlotte's –

Nope.

"What is it that you do, Sutton?" she asked, leaning in on her elbow, lifting an inquisitive brow.

She let out an audible breath of relief – this much, she could do. She found herself smiling slightly as she kept her hands safely and firmly folded in her lap. "I'm getting my graduate degree at NYU right now, in literature. I graduate in May."

By the time she was done, Laura's smile dropped. Her own felt plastered to her face as she wondered what in the world she could have possibly said wrong.

She didn't have to wait long to find out.

"A degree in literature? What can you actually do with that?" She didn't give Sutton a chance to answer, though, before she continued, "I mean, if you're going to get a degree in literature, you might as well just throw your money away."

The third went . . . a little better. Candace, her nametag read, and she sat down with a slightly reserved smile that Sutton thought might match her own.

After the first two horror speed dates, though, she figured it just had to get better.

They sat in a slightly awkward silence for a few moments before Candace let out a self-deprecating, "You'd think after doing so many of these kinds of things, I'd be used to them by now."

Sutton found her smile growing, relaxing her shoulders, because *finally*, this sounded like something she could relate to. "I know. I mean, kind of. I've never actually been to one of these kinds of events before."

"New to *SapphicSpark*? What did you use before?" she asked, looking genuinely curious.

"Um, nothing? I've never really done the online dating thing."

Candace's eyes widened. "How did you find women before? You found them all in real life?"

A quick, harsh laugh escaped her before she could help it and she quickly shook her head. "No, no. That's not – I've never . . . I mean, I'm new to all of this. Dating women."

The most awkward way to explain it, really, but it seemed that Candace understood when her smile dimmed remarkably. Sutton's only experience with any queer woman so far was really limited – only Charlotte. But Charlotte had never judged her for not having been with a woman before.

It took less than a minute for Candace to launch into an aggrieved story about her ex-girlfriend – a bisexual, something Candace was *not* interested in, because she'd had left her to go back to a previous boyfriend.

The entire rest of the three and a half minutes they had together left Sutton with her stomach churning uncomfortably, and a bad taste in her mouth. Biphobia was clearly alive and kicking, and Sutton hadn't experienced it firsthand before this.

By the time the fourth woman sat down, Sutton had already lost all hope; it wasn't as though she'd really had much of it to begin with.

"I'm Sutton, I'm a graduate literature student, and I'm a newly-out bisexual," she blurted out, as soon as their five minutes began.

Her eyes widened when she realized that she'd actually said that *out loud*. Christ. All she wanted was to just lay her head on the table as she could feel her cheeks burn. She honestly expected the woman to hear all of that and decide to walk away of her own accord.

Shoulders slumped slightly in defeat now, she took in a deep breath as she closed her eyes. She'd known there was a reason she shouldn't have come tonight.

The woman, who was nearly as tall as Sutton herself, with shortly cropped brown hair, only smiled with what appeared to be sincere amusement. "I'm Allison, I'm a nurse, and I'm a lifelong lesbian. Would you like to know my sign, too?"

Her smile made some of the tension that had set in her shoulders loosen just a little as she managed one back. "I suppose it couldn't *hurt*."

"Well, I'm a Gemini." She propped her elbow on the table to lean in and whisper, "And, to be entirely honest, I'm thrilled that you were made a one while I was a two; as soon as you walked in, I noticed you. And, if I'm not mistaken, I thought you might have been looking at me, too."

Flattered, embarrassed, Sutton shrugged. "Honestly, I was just trying to take it all in," she was about to dive into the fact that she'd never been somewhere where they were so many queer women, when she saw Allison's face fall, smile dimming.

It took Sutton a moment to realize what she possibly could have said wrong. But when she did, it was too late to salvage, and she honestly wouldn't know how, anyway.

The fifth woman who approached her table had big brown doe eyes, and long light brown hair, with a knowing smile. The combination made Sutton's stomach swoop for a moment, causing her to sit up in her chair, defeated posture deserting her in a second.

Her nametag read Bella, and she gave Sutton a sympathetic look. "Rough time of it tonight? I know, some of the women can come off a little . . . strong. Sometimes I can be one of them," she threw in with a light laugh.

She found herself smiling back without much effort. "I'm just not used to it, I suppose. I've barely even used the app, let alone something like this."

Bella tossed her curls over her shoulder as she shrugged easily. "I don't often come to these events myself. But work has been crazy busy lately, and I haven't really had a moment to be able to try to find a date on the app, so I thought why not?"

It was in that moment that the spark of attraction she'd had fizzled out.

Because Sutton realized with a disturbed startle, that the only reason she was feeling it was because Bella reminded her a bit of Charlotte.

Abruptly, she stood. "I'm sorry. I'm just – I can't really do this. You're very beautiful." Obviously, because she reminded her of the object of her affections. "And you seem nice, but this isn't really for me. I'm sorry," she apologized again in a rush, before reaching back to grab her jacket.

Ducking her head, she crossed her arms as she made her way back to the check-in table, and handed her blank piece of paper back to Alia.

"Leaving so soon?"

Sutton fumbled slightly with her jacket before managing to slip it on, the nervous knots in her stomach finally loosening with the prospect of leaving. "I'm not . . . good at this," she settled on, "I'm sorry."

"You don't have to apologize, we're not holding you captive," Alia joked, before she placed the paper and pen back on the table. She gave Sutton a contemplative look. "I hope you don't take offense to this, but you don't seem like your heart is really in this."

She opened her mouth to automatically refute, but caught herself. "It's not. I'm not really – I'm not very good with talking to women."

Alia gave her a shrewd look. "While I don't entirely doubt that, I'm feeling there's something else there." She quirked an eyebrow, "Come on. Let me get you a drink."

Sutton flushed before she shook her head. "I'm not really . . . I mean. I *do* find you attractive and the few minutes I spent talking to you went better than the time I spent talking to anyone else. So, maybe in another universe where I'm not a disaster at this –"

Alia cut her off with a laugh and a hand at the small of her back, leading her to the bar. "Don't worry, this isn't me picking you up. Though in another universe where you weren't a disaster –" she winked, "– and I wasn't working, I would be trying. Think of this as a little advice session from an expert."

Sutton allowed herself to be guided as she gave Alia a skeptical look. "An expert?"

"I *do* work for a company that helps create dating matches. Basically an expert. Expert enough to know that there's something going on in your cute head besides nerves," she said smartly.

Instead of answering, she looked around the room, "Shouldn't you be . . . doing whatever it is you're supposed to be doing?"

Alia only shrugged as they got to the bar, and she gestured for Sutton to take the seat next to hers. "I was only helping out with check-in tonight because my mom was shorthanded. Besides, I was just watching everyone on their dates. You know, people getting drinks spilled in their laps and all." A wide shit-eating grin slid over her face.

"You were watching me?"

"I had a feeling you would be a good person to pay attention to, and I was clearly right."

Sutton wasn't sure how to feel about that, but the bartender came to fix their drinks before she could think too much about it.

He gave them an encouraging smile, before leaving their drinks on the bar. Sutton took a sip of her daiquiri and looked down at the bar, worried that in this momentary silence the awkwardness she'd felt all evening would come back.

At least, until Alia tapped her fingers on the bar. "So, tell me about her."

Surprised, and a bit embarrassed, because was she *really* that easily read? She played dumb. "Um, who?"

"Come on." Alia rolled her eyes, "The *woman* that you're hung up on. Look, I've been doing this long enough to know she exists. So, tell me about her. Is she an ex?"

Sutton quickly shook her head. "No, she's . . . a friend." The evening was already shot, so why not own it?

"Straight?"

"No, she's *definitely* gay," she murmured, her mind easily imagining all of Charlotte's flirting looks and light touches and suggestive comments.

Alia gave her an incredulous look. "And this *definitely* gay woman who you're friends with, doesn't want you?"

"I don't . . . well, I don't know." She frowned and lightly drew her fingertip around the edge of her glass. Her heart pounded in her chest as she recalled the memory for what had to be the thousandth time. "I think she might be attracted to me. I mean – she almost kissed me. We almost kissed," she rushed to add, because it seemed important for some reason. "But then . . ."

She trailed off, thinking of the memory. Thinking about how, when Charlotte had leaned in to her, she'd felt – felt like she was out of control somehow. Like her body was *wanting* in a way she'd never felt before, and that alone was enough to alarm her.

"Ah, that's more like it." Alia tilted her head slightly, drawing up a dark eyebrow as she guessed, "And you . . . didn't want her to?"

Embarrassingly vigorously, Sutton shook her head. "I did! That was what was so . . . daunting," she confessed.

The truth of the matter was that Sutton *had* wanted to kiss Charlotte that night on her couch. They weren't dating, they weren't even in the "pre-stages" of dating that Sutton had been in with men before, and she knew that Charlotte wasn't even interested in relationships at all. All of those factors should have meant that Sutton shouldn't have been so drawn in; it *should* have all boiled down to the fact that even though she liked Charlotte – despite the fact that she liked her, even – she normally wouldn't be so tempted.

But she was.

Even though she knew everything about Charlotte's experiences with women and the fact that she definitely didn't want to be anything more than Sutton's friend in terms of relationship status . . . she *wanted* her, still.

It had been that realization that night, as Charlotte's thumb had stroked over her inner thigh and she'd felt how warm her hand was through her leggings and she'd immediately been ridiculously turned on, that had made her squeak out Charlotte's name.

Which had, in turn, ruined everything, as Charlotte had pulled away and shut everything down, and hadn't brought it up since. She'd easily pretended it hadn't happened, which confused Sutton more than anything.

Rolling her eyes at herself, she bit her lip and tried to avoid Alia's confused stare. "She was going to kiss you and you wanted her to! What was the problem?"

It was strange to talk about this with someone who wasn't Regan, or even Emma. Someone who had been legitimately checking her out, who was interested in women. But, she found that she kind of liked it – an outside perspective – and she debated exactly how to answer, or what exactly she should say, before settling on, "It's complicated. She's not – she doesn't want to be in a relationship, and we're friends. She's very . . . experienced. And I'm not. And she was the one who pulled away from the almost-kiss, so."

She ended with a simultaneous sigh and shrug, because she truly didn't *know* where Charlotte stood in this. Even as she felt like she knew her pretty well, she also couldn't read her.

It was confusing and obviously she spent too much time thinking about it – about *her* – but she couldn't stop.

Alia was giving her a sympathetic look. "You really do have it bad for her, don't you?"

Sutton worried at her bottom lip. "It doesn't matter. *She* doesn't have it bad for me."

"But she was going to kiss you! You just said so yourself," Alia sounded exasperated.

"Except, she didn't," she reminded her, "She's recently made the choice to be celibate, after many years of being very, uh, active. So maybe the almost-kiss was because of that?"

Alia sat back. "So, she used to sleep around but now she's celibate. And she doesn't want a relationship, anyway. And *you* want a relationship, usually, but you want to fuck her even if it doesn't mean being in love?"

Blushing furiously Sutton took a surreptitious glance around to make sure they had privacy, which of course they did since everyone else was still on their dates. She slowly nodded, "I guess so, yes."

"And you're seeing this as a problem?" Alia asked, her voice raising slightly. Enough that if they had people actually around them, they would have garnered some attention. Sutton refrained from glancing around again, and instead took in the slightly excited look on her face.

"Isn't it?"

She knew she was right to not trust the look on Alia's face the moment she asked, "Haven't you ever heard of a little thing called friends with benefits?"

Flustered, Sutton's mouth fell open, "I'm – of course. But that's – I'm not – it's not me."

"Who says it's not? Have you ever been in a situation like this before?" Alia challenged, arching an eyebrow with damning precision.

Sutton paused for a moment before she slowly answered, "Well, no."

There had never been anyone before who made her want like this. She'd wanted Kyle back when she was a teenager, yes, but there had been no proof that he'd ever cared for her the way she knew Charlotte did already.

Alia nodded. "You know what you have to do, don't you?"

Sutton was almost afraid to ask. "What?"

"You just have to tell her! Look. This woman was going to kiss you – maybe she's celibate and misses sex or maybe she wants you just as badly as you want her," she smirked at Sutton, and she flushed even as she shook her head; she couldn't imagine Charlotte Thompson wanting her as acutely. Actually, she knew she didn't, because, well, there hadn't been a kiss! Still, Alia continued, "Either way, it needs to be done."

Astonished, eyes wide, Sutton managed to splutter out, "I can't do that!"

God, even imagining it . . . she swallowed thickly and took a shaky breath. She'd probably pass out.

"You've never, in your life, just told someone that you wanted them?" Alia stared at her, forehead crinkled.

"No!" She could hardly even manage the thought. "That's – people don't *do* that."

People *didn't* do that, usually, right? Unless you were Charlotte or Regan or, she guessed, Alia and – wow, maybe people *did* do that.

She received an indulgent smile. "You came here tonight. What did you think most of the women were going to want?"

Sutton shrugged both of her shoulders, before she slid her hands into her lap, grasping at each other. "I'm not sure. I thought maybe to find someone to date?" she offered with an exasperated huff of breath.

It was called speed *dating*, after all. Surely she couldn't be the only person who thought this was about *dating*!

A sly smile adorned Alia's face, "I love that you think that. Some, sure, some people are here for that, too. Regardless . . . look, Sutton. You're, by your own words, inexperienced and a disaster at talking to women. Which would all

183

improve with time, but just consider this: would you rather be here tonight, or are you only here to try to not think about your friend?"

Sutton flushed, but remained quiet, because the answer was evident.

"That's what I thought." A knowing glint reflected in her eyes. "Honestly, the only thing you should apologize for tonight is that you aren't going after what you really want. Or should I say, *who* you really want."

Sutton groaned. "How am I supposed to do that, then? I can't just . . . I can't just go to her apartment and say, hey, let's sleep together."

Alia gave a thoughtful hum, "Well, I wouldn't say you *can't* do that. Trust me, Sutton Spencer, you'd be surprised with the results you can get by being direct." She finished her drink, before leaning forward to tap Sutton lightly on her knee, "Look. She clearly already finds you attractive, but there's something holding her back. So it's up to *you* to go for it, and I think you'll regret it if you don't." She gave it a moment to sink in before hopping off of her seat. "Now, I've got to call for a break for the women who haven't got a *friend* on their minds."

Sutton sat back, the words echoing over in her mind, as Alia slipped a card onto the bar. "Now, this is me. If you ever want to talk or . . . anything else, let me know."

"I – thanks," she managed to get out, unsure of what exactly she was thanking her for.

She left before she finished her drink.

Rather than take the subway, she felt the chill from the early November air on her bare legs, and tucked her hands deep into her pockets as she decided to walk home. Her mind felt heavy, and she had too much to process before she could truly go home and share her evening with her friends.

The cold comforted her a little and it made it easy for her head to clear a bit as the wind blew around her. Still, the uncertainty that was weighing on her was heavy. Because . . . she wanted to laugh off what Alia had said, but what if she was *right*?

Without questioning herself enough to stop what she was doing, she turned around to go in the opposite direction of her apartment.

Because she had never been in a situation like she was in with Charlotte before. She wanted her, even if she could only just have her physically. And it wasn't like it was easy for Sutton to talk to other women, either.

Charlotte put her at ease even when she felt like her heart was beating out of her chest. She was kind and attentive, a good friend, despite the fact that she adamantly told Sutton that she wasn't really used to being a friend.

She was the most stunning woman Sutton had ever seen, on top of all of that. A stunning woman that had a wealth of experience – Sutton imagined that Charlotte was probably exceptionally talented in bed. Dangerously good, even.

Just thinking about it made heat steal over her and she felt like she couldn't breathe for a second, her mind taken over with images of Charlotte's smirk and the way she dexterously moved her fingers even in everyday life.

Despite everything else – the fact that a relationship wasn't going to happen, that Charlotte had pulled back from the kiss, that Sutton had no idea where Charlotte stood in terms of how much she wanted her – Sutton *wanted her*.

She gave a distracted smile to the doorman as her nerves banded together like a lead weight in her stomach, before getting on the elevator and mumbling under her breath. As she walked out and into the hallway she clenched her hands together in the pockets of her coat, because they were trembling.

They were still shaking as she got to Charlotte's door. She closed her eyes tightly, taking in as deep a breath as she could and trying to quiet the many thoughts that were running rampant through her mind.

She knocked before she could turn around and stop herself.

It was now or never.

This night was supposed to be about *putting herself out there*, and that's exactly what Sutton was going to do. If Charlotte answered the door before the rational side of her brain could catch up with what she'd done and make her turn around and run away, that is.

God.

What was she even *doing*? Was she really showing up at Charlotte's doorstep in order to tell her that she was attracted to her? That she –

When the door swung open, all of Sutton's thoughts cleared from her brain, and she was left staring at Charlotte.

Who was wearing one of those light and airy tank tops that she favored changing into when she went home after work. Her eyes roamed, taking in the tiny yoga shorts she was wearing, leaving ridiculously toned legs bare.

Her heart started to pound even faster in her chest, as she looked up to meet Charlotte's eyes. Which were alight with amusement and a genuine happiness, Sutton thought, as a small, surprised smile tugged at her lips. "Sutton? I thought you were out for the night?"

She wondered why her brain went into hyper focus on things like the way Charlotte's curls were messily piled onto her head in an unfairly attractive bun, and the way those doe eyes shone up at her.

Then she cleared her throat. "I – um – I *was*. Clearly," she uselessly gestured at herself, her dress, and shoes.

She foolishly didn't even think about the way Charlotte's eyes would follow her gesture, raking down her body and taking in what she was wearing in a gaze so heavy it felt like it could be a caress. She felt herself shudder and her breath caught in her throat, and despite the fact that she was feeling a little lightheaded from the way everything was weighing on her, that was enough to propel her forward.

She'd never felt that before. And she wanted more of it.

"Clearly," Charlotte agreed, her voice dropping low and appreciative, before she looked up at Sutton, her eyes dark, as she quirked an eyebrow. "Who in their right mind let you walk out of there?"

186

The pounding of her heart was all she could hear as she shivered. God, she hoped that Charlotte wasn't just being supportive or something when she said that. "Well, I wasn't . . . quite a catch tonight."

Damn. She'd wanted to say something smooth or something flirty – something that could hint at what she wanted to say but couldn't find the words for.

Charlotte stepped back and opened her door, the warmth from her apartment enticing Sutton in, as if she needed more enticement. "That's not true. But their loss is my gain."

Apparently Charlotte found the flirty remark Sutton had been looking for.

"Yeah, well . . ." she trailed off, hoping that her trembling hands weren't noticeable as she took off her jacket.

Dark eyes roved over the top of her dress and she knew that her shiver was obvious. She knew Charlotte couldn't possibly miss it and still, she merely deftly took Sutton's jacket and hung it up. "I was just finishing up some of the paperwork I brought home, so you came at the perfect time."

Before Charlotte could take a step too far, Sutton swallowed hard and reached out to place her hand on her shoulder. Her fingertips skimmed lightly over the soft skin there, and it would be so *easy* to chicken out.

Instead, she steeled herself and didn't let her hand fall away from Charlotte. "Wait. I – I didn't do very well tonight, because I . . ." *because I like you* wanted to roll off of her tongue, but she bit it back. "Because I'm too – too nervous, because I don't always know what to do or what to say. And some of the women weren't that great, either." The thought of the dates made her grimace.

Charlotte looked at her inquisitively as she reached up to take Sutton's hand with her own. She was so warm, Sutton thought, dimly, as she spoke softly, "Darling, take a deep breath and tell me whatever it is that you're trying to say."

Taking her advice, she took a deep breath. She released it slowly, thinking about Alia's words, and closed her eyes to gather her strength. "I think . . .

maybe, I'll be less nervous about dating women if I have sex with a woman that I trust, first," was what came out of her mouth.

There. Okay. That should work, right?

As she blinked her eyes open, she expected at least *some sort* of reaction from Charlotte. Hopefully one of desire or interest.

There was a bit of interest, she thought, as Charlotte's gaze dipped to her mouth briefly before coming back up to skim over her features. But other than that, she didn't appear moved. "Oh? Will you be sleeping with Regan?"

"No." Sutton fluttered her eyelashes, but refused to close her eyes this time and instead stared into Charlotte's. It took her a moment to gather every bit of courage she possibly could as nerves ate away any potential other feeling she might have experienced. "I was thinking, if you were open to it . . . I could sleep with you."

Chapter 10

Charlotte had never done any sort of hallucinogenic before. She'd even mostly avoided weed during her college years. She'd had her plans for her future in politics for so long, there was no way she was willing to even have that one indiscretion dredged up against her.

The closest she'd ever come to any such experience was when she'd been twelve, and she and Caleb were racing through their mom's rose garden outside of her childhood home in Virginia. She'd tripped – though she maintained that Caleb had tripped her, even to this very day – and hit her head on one of the marble benches.

She'd come to quickly, and had been disoriented, like the world was spinning off-axis a little.

This felt a bit like that.

I could sleep with you, echoed between them, and even though Sutton's voice had been low, the words rang in Charlotte's ears.

Closing her eyes, she shook her head slightly, dimly registering the hair that had fallen out of her bun brushing against the back of her neck. It was – she must have misheard. Even though that was something that had never happened to her before, and frankly, if someone else ever suggested that she was *hearing things*, her reaction would not be pleasant.

Charlotte had no clue what Sutton could have possibly said that she misheard or was misunderstanding, but she was quite sure that their wires had gotten crossed somewhere.

Because this was Sutton, who was standing in her apartment in one of the shortest, most well-fitted black dresses Charlotte had ever seen. As in, the second she'd looked at Sutton when she'd opened the door it had taken a fair amount of her considerable self-control to keep her gaze as respectful as she could. And her heels only further highlighted those deliciously long legs.

This was Sutton, whose red hair only seemed even more vibrant than usual against the pale expanse of her revealed shoulders and then the deep black of that dress. Whose cheeks were flushing like crazy, as though she'd actually really just suggested they should have sex.

But. This was *Sutton*, who – since their very first interaction – had insisted that she so didn't want any sort of casual sex.

Tilting her head, she looked up at Sutton, who was staring at her with imploring deep blue eyes. Eyes that searched her face even as she felt Sutton's hand – the one that held onto hers, still – trembled slightly in her grasp

Feeling Sutton's tremble somehow made these rushing thoughts calm down, and her lips quirked into a smile as she shook her head a bit as if to clear it.

"I'm sorry, darling. I think I've spent far too long working today; I mistakenly heard you propose having sex with me."

Sutton's blush only intensified and her eyelashes fluttered before she took in a deep breath as her hand flexed in a way that Charlotte recognized as her gathering her strength. "I did. I'm not – I'm not asking you to be my girlfriend, or anything."

Charlotte was at a loss for words, and for the first time in her memory just found herself blinking speechlessly up at Sutton.

She'd already been surprised by the times where Sutton could render her without something to say – because of all of the people in her life, who would have ever have known that it was the woman who wasn't calculating or manipulative who could stun her?

Just when she thought she had her pegged, Sutton would do something like walk into her apartment, looking like a fucking wet dream, and say that she wanted to have sex with her.

Even though her throat was running a bit dry, Charlotte managed to take in a deep breath through her nose before releasing it slowly through her mouth.

190

She pushed through all of the muddled thoughts and feelings she had and instead focused on the kernel of concern she'd had as soon as Sutton had shown up as fidgety as she was.

She stroked her thumb over the soft skin of Sutton's hand. "Are you drunk?"

Sutton shook her head, looking offended. "No! I had one drink the whole night. And I didn't even finish it. I'm sober and serious: do you want to – to have sex? With me."

As if Charlotte could mistake her intent. As if she wouldn't want to have sex with her! If *any* lesbian wasn't ready to show Sutton Spencer the wonders of sex with women, Charlotte wouldn't believe they were sane.

Charlotte *wanted* Sutton. She'd wanted her since she'd first messaged her, and even more since they'd spent actual time together. She was more than ready to pull Sutton into her apartment and show her exactly what she could do.

But it was because of that very strong urge to not question Sutton any further – to just pull her down the hall and into her bedroom, peel off her dress, and do what she'd wanted to do *with* and *to* Sutton since she'd seen her picture – that made Charlotte disentangle their hands. She did not need to feel Sutton's long and elegant fingers anywhere on her body right now.

Charlotte hadn't been a friend to someone who wasn't a family member or Dean in several years but she was well-versed in her social skills. And her etiquette, despite the damning voice yelling at her to ignore etiquette, was telling her that she shouldn't take advantage of Sutton like that.

Maybe, if Sutton was a woman at a club or one she'd just met online, then there would be no issue in letting her forget whatever was troubling her by fucking it out of her head.

But, she wasn't.

Taking a step back, Charlotte closed her eyes for a moment before she crossed her arms slightly in front of herself. And she asked the question she hadn't exactly wanted to know the answer to, "What *happened* tonight?"

Because she was sure that whatever had gotten into Sutton that had caused *this*, stemmed from something the vultures that had gone to that speed dating night had done or said.

As soon as Sutton had mentioned earlier that she was going to a lesbian speed dating night, Charlotte had gotten the most unfamiliar and unwelcome feeling in the pit of her stomach. Something that made her steps falter and felt foreboding in and of itself.

It had given her pause for longer than she would have liked, before she decided that it was sheer concern for Sutton. The whole reason Charlotte had even started talking to Sutton was to take her under her wing – so to speak – and protect her from the kind of women that would go to those dating nights, looking for a tall drink of water exactly like Sutton.

Someone with dreamy ideals and an even dreamier body, with a face to match.

Focusing on that, the idea that something – some*one* – had gotten into Sutton's head so much tonight helped dim the immediate fire that shot through her with the images of having sex with Sutton.

"Nothing, really." Her shoulders slumped dejectedly. "I met a few women, and I was a disaster with them. I was too nervous to even think around some of them, and the others were, well, awful."

She waited for a beat to see if more was forthcoming, but nodded in satisfaction. Because she could work with that; she could take that and steer this back into a direction that Sutton likely wouldn't regret in the morning.

"Sutton, I know that's... unfortunate. But one bad night of *speed dating*," she couldn't even keep her incredulous chuckle in, even though she did find it such an oddly charming Sutton-thing to have done. "Doesn't mean that you're a disaster."

The way Sutton had been lightly twisting her fingers around one another stopped as she blew out a breath and squared her shoulders. It was actually a very admirable show of the strength that Charlotte was positive it was taking Sutton to say all of this.

"I know you think I'm naïve, and – and maybe I can be, sometimes. But that doesn't mean that I'm some sort of child or that I don't know anything. That I don't have wants and desires, too," she asserted, voice strong.

And damn if it didn't turn her on. Sutton had *wants* and *desires*, and apparently, they included having sex with Charlotte. Which wasn't surprising. But she'd never fathomed that Sutton would ever have the nerve to suggest this.

She had to stifle a little groan that wanted to escape – a groan at herself for not just doing this, a groan at Sutton for instigating it, and mostly a groan because she *wanted* so badly – before she assured her, "I don't think of you as a child."

It didn't appear that Sutton heard her, or perhaps she was just ignoring her. "I was thinking that it could be like a deal."

Sutton's hands were starting to shake again, she noticed, but her mind was trying to make sense of it all. Because . . . where did Sutton's mind even go? What in the world had she concocted? And why couldn't she let this go, before Charlotte broke? She only had so much self-control when a beautiful woman was willfully asking to sleep with her.

"A deal?" Damn it, she couldn't help but be curious.

It seemed that somehow that was the wrong thing to say, as the strong façade Sutton had been wearing disappeared.

She didn't even get another word out before Sutton side stepped and sunk down onto the edge of one of Charlotte's chairs, long legs folding as she dropped low in the seat. She looked so defeated that it was heartbreaking. "God, I am *so* dumb. That was *so stupid*."

Charlotte was quick to shake her head now. "Sutton, no –"

She dropped her head into her hands. "Tonight *was* awful, okay? It was awful, and I was awful, but I really think – I think that everything I said is true.

I thought that experiencing it with *you* first would be easier. Because, no we're not in a relationship or anything, but you care about me."

"I do," she interjected.

Not only was she at a loss for words, but she was also at a loss for actions. She felt like she was in largely unexplored territory, and she wasn't sure of where to go from here. In fact, she was only sure of one thing, and it was the thing she was pretty sure was a bad idea.

Because she'd been doing her best to help steer Sutton away from women who would only want to sleep with her and not want anything else. And, romantically speaking, that was exactly who Charlotte was.

But . . . Sutton seemed to want that?

The whole night seemed absolutely surreal, and she wasn't certain which direction it was going to head in.

She hated that it kind of thrilled her.

Sutton tossed her head back, and Charlotte very much wanted to run her hands through the thick strands. "I just... I'm *really* attracted to you."

Blue eyes glittered up at her from where Sutton was sitting, Charlotte's breath quickened, and a little piece of her resolve broke off.

Sutton shrugged, before rubbing her hands up and down her thighs. Thighs that were only slightly covered by that dress, and Charlotte's fingers were *itching* to slide it up even more.

"Because you're, like, gorgeous. I mean, I'm not sure it should be legal for you to look like you do!"

Her cheeks were only stained in the slightest blush, and Charlotte faintly wondered if Sutton was just too deeply entrenched in *everything* that had happened so far, that her body had simply decided it couldn't blush anymore on this topic.

On a much more pressing level, Charlotte wondered if it really would be *taking advantage*, because Sutton wanted her. She knew Sutton was attracted to her, and not only that, but she was sitting here in her apartment *asking* for Charlotte to show her the wonders of sex! Without being in a relationship!

If that wasn't her own agency, she didn't know what was.

"Sutton –"

"And sleeping with you would probably be, like, really, *really* good," Sutton's voice dipped into a timbre that made Charlotte shiver, her spine tingling, heat settling low in her stomach.

Charlotte considered herself a relatively good person. She cared about those less fortunate than herself, she had worked hard to make a change in the world, and her goals in politics would only further those efforts.

That being said.

She was by no means a saint. Especially not when it came to having women in her bed and making them come so hard they forgot their names.

Actually, she was very much *not* a saint in that regard, and the idea of turning Sutton's active and creative mind to nonsense with her fingers and tongue was enough to make Charlotte's body react without her permission.

"But, if *you* don't want *me*, then –"

Charlotte ducked down. Because how did Sutton not realize that was exactly the opposite of the problem?

One of her hands cupped Sutton's jaw, her thumb stroking the soft skin of her cheek, as she used the other to brace herself on the chair right next to Sutton. Close enough that the inside of her wrist was brushing against the bare warmth of Sutton's leg.

She felt Sutton's breath hitch as she moved in close enough that there were only millimeters between them. And there was no hesitation as she pressed forward, her lips brushing against the soft, pink, plump ones that she'd thought about more than once.

A sigh left her at the contact, because *yes*, they were as soft as they looked. She reveled in it, as she tilted her head to slide her mouth along Sutton's enough to capture her bottom lip within her own.

Sutton responded immediately, her mouth opening to pull Charlotte's top lip between her own, and sucking on it softly. Those long fingers slid into Charlotte's hair, loosening her bun, her hair spilling down her back.

It had been months since Charlotte had kissed anyone. Even longer than that since she'd well and truly *desired* the woman she'd had like this. Not that she'd had sex with a woman that she wasn't attracted to on some level, really. But, there had been nothing like this.

Nothing like Sutton's hands flexing in her hair. Nothing like having the taste and feel of someone's lips that she'd thought about for months. Nothing even quite like the electric feeling she got from the way Sutton's thigh brushed against her as she crossed her legs, and then uncrossed them.

Charlotte had never desired a woman for so long without being able to have her, and the idea of *having* Sutton was making her lightheaded.

But as good as it felt, she couldn't... couldn't lose herself in it. Even if it would be *so* easy to.

With a gentle nip at the bottom lip she had captured, she felt Sutton's whimper more than heard it. It was more than enough to send the spikes of pleasure even lower, and she closed her eyes tightly as she pulled away.

Only far enough, though, so that she could see the brightness in those blue eyes so close to her own, and feel the erratic exhales of Sutton's breath hitting her cheek. She tried to search Sutton's gaze for what she was expecting to see – fear or regret or embarrassment or *something*.

All she saw was a heavily lidded gaze, eyelashes so long they cast light shadows over her cheeks. Sutton leaned in a little bit to follow her, before she seemed to catch herself. It made a smile ghost at Charlotte's lips.

"Sutton..." she had to break off, swallowing hard, "You're *sure* that you want this?"

She leaned another inch back, tilting her head to look at Sutton more clearly. She took in her flushed cheeks before her gaze wandered to look at Sutton's mouth as she slowly licked her lips, and… fuck. Charlotte looked back to her eyes, which seemed less dazed than a moment ago.

Sutton slowly nodded, twice, before she cleared her throat, "I'm nervous. But I think I will be with my – my first woman, no matter what," she confessed in a low voice, and Charlotte felt Sutton slowly slide her hands down, fingers disentangling themselves from her hair, before her hands fell back into her lap.

There it was. Charlotte had never had *any* qualms about being someone's first woman. She didn't care if she was a woman's first woman or her only woman or, really, what happened in the other woman's personal life after their encounter.

But this wasn't just any woman, it was Sutton.

Bowing her head slightly, she squeezed her eyes closed and tried to keep her mind as clear as she could, despite the electricity charging between them. Despite that she could still feel that slight tingling on her mouth from contact with Sutton's.

Only to open them again when she remembered what Sutton had said before, that she'd never gotten clarification on. "What did you mean when you said a deal?"

Sutton blinked up at her in momentary confusion as her hands twisted together, eyebrows furrowing in a look that was absurdly cute. Before her expression smoothed back out, and Sutton sighed softly, looking unsure as she explained, "I meant, well – I *thought*, that maybe we'd be getting different things out of it. You could, um, be my first woman experience, and… show me what it's like," she broke off, her blush catching up with her now, as she shook her head at herself.

"And, well, you said that you… liked to have sex whenever you'd been stressed out about things like work in the past. But because of the election and everything, you took down your profile, so you haven't been having sex. Even though you've been ridiculously stressed," she rambled on, her hands flexing against her knees, and she focused her gaze just beyond Charlotte's head as she spoke.

Before she slid her eyes to fix on Charlotte's, and her heart pounded in her chest at the heat in them, before Sutton took in another one of those strength gathering breaths. "So, you know everything. And you kissed me."

"I did," she murmured, and the fact of the matter was that she truthfully had no resolve left.

Sutton was an adult, she had her own reasons for wanting this. For coming to Charlotte's apartment and wanting to have sex. Who was Charlotte to turn her down, when she so clearly was into this?

She breathed in deeply through her nose, holding it in as she turned her head slightly. Just enough to try to breathe any bit of fresh air. So that she wasn't surrounded by Sutton's perfume and she could try to gather herself.

But what else was there to gather? She was ridiculously stressed out, she had an interview coming up, and she'd had this whole worry about Sutton on her mind for the last few hours.

Taking Sutton and being able to forget real life – because *Sutton* had been the one to suggest it! – seemed like the best possible scenario, honestly.

The only thing was that... she couldn't help but feel like she was somehow taking advantage in a way. She truly didn't want to be one of those women she'd warned Sutton about. There was a loose plan forming in her mind about how she could do this, without it being blurry.

She could make it a night for *Sutton*, though. For Sutton to experience being with a woman, as she'd said. If she was the only one doing the touching, then it wasn't anything like she was using her. If anything, it would purely be *Sutton* using *Charlotte* for sex, and – God – Charlotte was *so* okay with that.

Because saying she'd be getting nothing by having the pleasure of making Sutton Spencer come would be such an understatement.

She took a deep breath, and wondered if her plan was as solid as she thought it was or if she was only thinking that through the haze of lust in her mind.

Only for it to come rushing out of her in a light whimper when she felt Sutton lean in and press a light, tentative kiss under her ear. And then another under that. *Fuck*.

Turning her head, she captured Sutton's lips with hers, more forcefully this time than before. Especially because now her mind was already set.

If Sutton wanted Charlotte to *show her what it was like*, then Charlotte was going to give her exactly what she wanted.

This time, she didn't suckle softly at her lips. Instead, her tongue slid over before licking into Sutton's mouth, and she surged forward from where she was still crouched in front of Sutton.

Swallowing Sutton's gasp, she felt her eagerly respond. Her tongue stroked against Charlotte's as one of her hands came up and landed on her shoulder, before her fingers dug in slightly.

She slid her own hand from where it rested on the cushion to glide her fingertips over Sutton's bare thigh, reveling in the smoothness. As she nipped her teeth lightly at Sutton's tongue, her hand scratched up to just under the hem of that dress.

And she could feel Sutton's shiver, just as she heard her moan softly in the back of her throat. Charlotte couldn't control the smirk on her lips as she pulled back – simultaneously scratching her nails back down Sutton's leg – because this was going to be *so fun*.

Rapidly darkening eyes took in the way Sutton's eyes didn't flutter back open, and her mouth remained parted.

She couldn't resist leaning in to place another kiss against the corner of her mouth before she reached for the hand Sutton had on her shoulder. Easily entangling their fingers, she stood up. "Come on, darling."

Now Sutton's eyes fluttered open, dazed a bit still, before she followed Charlotte's lead. She frowned, and had to clear her throat twice before she adopted a wondering look. "Where –"

"If we're doing this, we're doing it properly," she murmured, because she was getting this one night, and she was not going to miss the opportunity to see the way that red hair contrasted with the stark white of her pillows. She wanted to see the way Sutton's long, lean body spread over her bed.

She wanted Sutton to clutch her sheets as Charlotte made her come. Repeatedly.

She was going to fuck Sutton the way she'd wanted to since the first time she'd seen her message on that app. Anticipation rushed through her, pulsing into her core as she led the way down the hallway toward her bedroom.

With a glance over her shoulder, she saw the way Sutton was taking in everything in her bedroom for the first time. Despite the fact that Sutton had been to her apartment several times now, the tour had never extended into her bedroom.

She felt Sutton's hand shake slightly in her own, as she took in a trembling breath and offered in a whisper, "I like your picture."

Charlotte quirked an eyebrow at that, unable to stop herself from grinning and shaking her head, because of course she would be taking Sutton into her bedroom for sex, and Sutton *would* immediately see the family picture she had on her dresser.

"Thank you," she offered back. No teasing because she knew Sutton was ridiculously nervous. It had taken her so much courage to get this far. Like, she never would have imagined this would be something Sutton would even *want*, let alone actually say she wanted.

Sutton had come to her – at least in part – because she *knew* what to do; she didn't want Sutton to feel like she was, in her own words, an awkward disaster even when she was here with her. So she stroked the back of Sutton's hand and offered her a comforting smile. As comforting as she could manage with how much she wanted to peel off Sutton's dress and kiss down her body, anyway.

It might have been a bit predatory.

Still, the trembling she felt in Sutton's hand lessened just a bit at it.

"We're friends," she whispered, and she saw the way Sutton shuddered as her breath hit her collarbones. She very narrowly resisted biting them. For now.

Sutton nodded, and she could see her swallow before she said back, "Friends," in a low tone.

"And this isn't going to change anything," she asserted, this time not just for Sutton, but for her own peace of mind as well. She arched an eyebrow up at Sutton, stomach dipping low from want, even as she waited for a response.

Which came quickly, Sutton squeezing her hand lightly as she affirmed, "I don't want it to."

Relieved, Charlotte took that as the only confirmation she needed, and she dipped her head enough to trail her lips up Sutton's neck. It was a light touch; just enough for her to feel the soft skin of her throat, for her to feel the way Sutton's pulse jumped.

She was almost ridiculously pleased that Sutton's body was so sensitive to her touch, but then she didn't know why she was surprised. Sutton reacted to even a light touch, never mind when she was trailing kisses up and down the column of her neck.

She moved to her tip toes, whispering, "Take off your shoes," before she pulled back. And with an indecent amount of satisfaction took in the way Sutton stared at her with wide eyes for a moment before complying.

As soon as Sutton's heels hit the floor with a thud, bringing her to a more manageable height – because as ridiculously sexy as they were, Sutton was already tall enough to move Charlotte onto her tip toes – she reached out to tug Sutton forward. She pushed up on her tip toes once more, pulling her into a searing kiss.

Sutton whimpered as Charlotte flicked her tongue up to stroke the roof of her mouth, and she slid her hands down her sides. The dress was so tight that she could feel the curves of Sutton's body and the fans of heat flamed even hotter inside of her.

There was a voice in the back of her mind that wondered exactly how Sutton was going to react, but she didn't stop as she traced her hands even lower, cupping her toned ass. She knew that Sutton liked to run – she knew that she'd done track in high school and throughout undergrad – so it was no surprise at all that she was all so defined under all of her soft skin.

But surprise or no, she loved it. She pulled Sutton even closer to her, the fronts of their bodies melding together easily, and a groan worked its way out of the back of her throat, because she'd *missed* this. Having a woman in her arms, trying to shift even closer, like she couldn't be close enough. Missed the jagged thrill of anticipation slash through her, and know she was making the woman she was with feel that, too.

And the fact that it was Sutton… just made it remarkably better.

She slid one of her hands up, sucking on Sutton's tongue as she did, and found the zipper at the top of her dress. The urge to undo it without a second thought had her flipping the zipper up and tugging it only slightly between her fingertips.

Easing back, she asked, "Can I –?"

She couldn't remember the last time she'd actually asked that – typically, both parties knew that was where this would be leading to, and she wouldn't hesitate.

Sutton squeezed her eyes closed and released a low breath as she nodded. "Yes. Yeah. I'm just –" breaking off, she fidgeted her hands at her sides, and admitted, "I – I've only ever even been with two men. And neither of them, um. It was never…" she trailed off, and even in the dimmed lighting of her room, she could see the color in her cheeks.

Leaning in, she pressed her lips to one of them, feeling how warm it was under her lips, as she whispered, "Okay, what I need you to do for me, is relax. Because this is about *you*. So, just let me," she tugged slightly on the zipper, enough that it gave and started to slide down, "Make you feel good."

She felt the shuddering breath Sutton released brush her shoulder, and she continued pulling down the zipper until the dress loosened and fell at her feet. Sutton stood in front of her, with only a tiny sheer lace thong on.

Brown eyes darkened, taking in the sight. Fuck, she'd known Sutton had an amazing body, but knowing it and seeing it were two different things. And as she took in all of that creamy skin, and the way her hair had fallen just over her shoulders so that the tips of red were brushing over already hard nipples, she licked her lips.

She was going to devour this woman.

Charlotte shifted on her feet slightly, pressing her thighs together because she could already feel how wet she was just by some light touching and looking. But she gathered herself within a few seconds, because she could see in the way Sutton fidgeted that she was close to covering herself up.

Reaching out, she quickly caught Sutton's hands in her own, keeping them at her sides. "Don't," her voice was low but firm.

She felt a quake run through Sutton as she dipped her head to make eye contact with her; she ran her hands up her sides, gliding her fingers over such soft skin, before stroking back down. She purposefully wasn't touching Sutton's breasts – even though she *really* wanted to – or even her ass again – even though, she also wanted to.

Charlotte was trying to be . . . good right now. Despite her spotless professional record, though, she'd never not played a little dirty when it came to her personal affairs.

That thought kind of disappeared when Sutton ducked down and attached their mouths again, wrapping her own arms around Charlotte's waist. She met the kiss with fervor, and without conscious thought, her hands started to roam again.

They mapped Sutton's back, slowly sliding up her spine, delighting in the shivers that she felt that made Sutton arch her back toward her, and pressed them entirely together. She could feel the hard press of Sutton's nipples against her chest, and she groaned in appreciation.

She slid her mouth to suckle on Sutton's bottom lip, pulling it within her own, trapping it as she laved attention upon it with her tongue. Charlotte scratched her hands down Sutton's back and over her ass again, feeling the flimsy lace under her fingers, before she turned them around easily and walked so that Sutton's knees hit the bed.

A breathless chuckle left her at Sutton's squeak when she was falling backwards, only to be cut off when her breath hitched in her throat. Sutton fucking Spencer in her bed, with red hair spread wildly over her sheets and her legs spread enough to allow Charlotte to kneel between them was the view of a lifetime.

Darkened blue eyes blinked up at her, and Charlotte pounced. Bracing her hands on either side of Sutton's hips, she bent down to press her lips right above the waistband of her underwear. The touch was light and made Sutton's hips jerk up at her.

Closing her eyes to ward off her own arousal – as if she could – Charlotte planted open-mouthed kisses up Sutton's stomach, feeling the muscles under her soft skin tremble in each place she touched. God, she had no idea how in the world *any* woman at that crazy speed dating event would have left without trying to take Sutton home.

But she'd meant it when she'd said that their loss was her gain; she just hadn't known at the time how much of a gain it was.

She pressed her lips to the curve of Sutton's breast as she slid her hand up to cup the other one, feeling the full weight in her hand. When she licked her tongue in a circle around her dusky pink nipple, she felt Sutton's hands slide into her hair once more, making her close her eyes as those long fingers twisted into her locks. And then when Sutton tugged her down slightly, urging her to move faster, Charlotte groaned as she complied, sucking on her as she ran her fingertips over the tip of her other breast before pinching it.

Sutton's moans above her were like music to her ears as she laved attention on her chest. When Sutton's hips started thrusting up against hers, Charlotte ground back down against her, moaning herself at the pressure.

She gave Sutton's nipple another broad lick, feeling her shiver, before she ducked to place kisses along the lightly freckled skin of her chest. And it took her a moment before she registered that Sutton's hands weren't pulling her closer, but were instead pushing.

Confused, and feeling more than a little hazy from her own desire, she pulled back and searched Sutton's face. "What? What is it?"

In the small corner of her mind that was still thinking logically, she thought that this would be the moment that it was done. Sutton had decided they'd gone far enough, and this was it.

She thought she'd see some sort of fear or uncertainty in her eyes, but was instead met with a look so heated it stole her breath. Sutton groaned – this time in frustration – as she tugged at the strap of Charlotte's tank top, "I, um, I want this off," her voice was somehow both assertive and questioning.

"Is that all?" she teased. Pushing herself up to bring her hands to the bottom of her tank top, she quickly pulled it over her head.

Her bra was still on, though, and she hesitated for a moment because she desperately wanted to feel all of Sutton's body on her own. But she shook her head slightly at herself; this was not about *her*. She was not going to make this in any way about her orgasming from Sutton or her long fingers that Charlotte were sure could – no. Just, no.

She felt a shiver run down her spine at the way Sutton pushed herself up onto her elbows to get a better look at her. And there was a lustful look in her eyes, but also one akin to wonder that was so utterly flattering in a way that was uniquely *Sutton*.

She found it strangely charming, especially in a moment like this where she didn't know how often she'd been "charmed" by someone in this state.

205

"You're so gorgeous," Sutton breathed out, before blushing – and the fact that she was doing that even as she was in Charlotte's bed was truly like a bonus – as though she couldn't believe she'd let those words fall out.

"Thank you, darling," she whispered back, as she slid her hands to rest on either side of Sutton's head and leaned down. Their stomachs pressed together in a smooth slide, especially as she felt Sutton's shake slightly as she inhaled.

She moved so that she was kneeling on either side of Sutton's thigh, before she pressed her leg slowly up between Sutton's. The wet lace brushed against her, and heat pooled in her center as Sutton gasped.

Grinding her leg slowly against her, she bent down so that she could press a series of kisses down Sutton's jaw, before she reached her lips. And she leaned in enough to brush their mouths together, breathing the same heavy air, as Sutton's hips started working in a slow matching rhythm with her, murmuring, "You're very beautiful, Sutton."

She dipped down enough so that she could place a deep but brief kiss, getting Sutton's taste on her lips again, before she drew back enough to look at her face. Wide blue eyes stared up at her as her mouth remained open with gasping breaths, and God, Charlotte could not have fathomed this would be how her night would have ended up.

Bringing her hand down, she guided it up Sutton's abdomen before settling on her breast, kneading there for a moment. Reveled in the way Sutton arched her back toward her.

She shuddered when Sutton's hips jerked up against her pelvic bone and ground down as her hands moved to tentatively stroke down her back. Fuck, Charlotte wanted Sutton's touch *too* much. It would be so, so simple to lose herself in it – in this easy chemistry that was only building by the second – and forget herself.

Forget that this wasn't a hookup or a night of fun or just a night of wild sex. This was a night to make Sutton come so hard she didn't have to think about trying to be with other women or about whatever shitty experiences she'd had with men.

So, she handled it by reaching back to take Sutton's hands. Even though she very much missed them on her, she pulled them away. Instead she brought them above Sutton's head, pressing them into the pillows. She pulled back to look at the confused look in Sutton's eyes, before she demanded, "Keep them there. And lift your hips for me."

She brought her hands back down, sliding her leg back even as a whimper left Sutton at the loss of contact. Charlotte tucked her fingers into the waistband of her underwear and tugged them down. Sutton was soaked and Charlotte couldn't even be surprised; she was still wearing her shorts and underwear, and she was just as wet.

She had short, trimmed red curls and those long legs tried to close as Charlotte licked her lips and took her time looking at her. Rather than tell her not to, Charlotte scratched her nails lightly over Sutton's inner-thigh, remembering the way she'd jerked and shuddered earlier from it. She felt victorious when this had an even better reaction, a whimper tearing from the back of Sutton's throat as her legs jerked even farther open.

This time, though, she didn't have the dress to stop her from moving up, brushing her fingers over Sutton's slit. A groan worked its way up and out of her throat as Sutton's wetness coated her fingers easily. She slid up to circle her clit, making Sutton buck up at her before she moved back down and slid two fingers into her.

Curling them, she ducked back down and started to move slowly, deeply, loving the way Sutton's walls pulled at her as uneven breaths broke over Sutton's lips.

"You're so wet for me, darling," she breathed out, unable to stop herself, because *fuck*, she loved it. She loved the way Sutton's body reacted to her, the way she squeezed tightly around her fingers, the way her hands clutched tightly at Charlotte's bed.

She *especially* loved the moans that were making their way out of Sutton's throat, and Charlotte pressed open-mouthed kisses there, lightly sucking on her skin. Not enough to bruise, but enough that she was sure Sutton could really feel her. God, even her smooth, warm neck tasted good under her lips, and she sighed against her, pumping her fingers in and curling up every so often. Every time, Sutton's hips thrusted hard up at her, and this delicious groaning whine sounded in the back of her throat. She couldn't get enough.

As soon as she brushed her thumb over Sutton's clit, she knew that it wasn't going to be long for her first orgasm to hit. She could feel her walls clamping tighter around her, and so she rubbed her thumb faster in circles, moving her mouth up to right behind Sutton's ear.

She licked there and heard Sutton cry out, as she whispered, "Come for me, darling. I want to feel you."

And as if her words were the magic touch, Sutton was clamping down around Charlotte's fingers tightly, a cry that she muffled by biting her lip leaving her that left Charlotte shaken to the core with desire. She'd honestly had no idea *how* unfathomably turned on she would get just from this.

From the sounds of Sutton under her and around her, feeling her wetness and hearing the gasps for breath she was making as she quaked from light aftershocks. It wasn't the most powerful orgasm, Charlotte knew. No, that was the orgasm she'd had because she hadn't had sex in a long while, and even before, she'd said it hadn't been very good.

Still, she pulled back enough to look down at Sutton, taking in her disheveled hair and completely debauched look under her. And the small spark of mischief inside of her was only fanned when Sutton opened wide, dazed blue eyes, as she bit her lip, "I – um, I. You're still in me," her whisper was a little hoarse, and the sound of it shot straight into Charlotte's core.

She sounded so mystified, and Charlotte both wanted to laugh and to fuck Sutton within an inch of her life.

A chuckle left her as she flexed her fingers that were, indeed, still inside of her. The blue eyes that had been watching her clouded over as her head fell back onto the pillow. Charlotte moved so that her face was right above Sutton's so she could nuzzle her nose into Sutton's cheek, pressing a kiss against her skin, as she answered, "I am, yes. That's the beauty of what it's like to be with a woman."

She slid her fingers out before pushing a third one in, reveling in the way Sutton stared up at her as she started to thrust. This time, she moved faster than before, loving how wet she was and the sound it made as she pumped her fingers, moaning under her breath at how damn *good* Sutton felt.

And she couldn't help herself. When Sutton flexed her leg as Charlotte's fingers curled and hit the right spot inside of her, she pressed down and ground against her thigh. Even the friction through her shorts felt amazing, because she wanted almost nothing more than to work herself into orgasm at the same time that she pushed Sutton into another one.

Her breath was coming shorter as her arousal spiked and she debated whether or not she should go down on Sutton this time or save it for the next time – because she *would* have a taste of her before this opportunity was gone. Sutton smelled so good, and she had no doubt that she would taste amazing. God, she wanted to have those thighs wrapped around her head as she made Sutton come in her mouth.

The decision that she was going to have to wait for that was made without her when she felt one of Sutton's long legs wrap around her waist. Because there was no way she was going to remove that long, toned leg from where it wrapped around her and held her close, not when that was also something she'd imagined several times. Her fingers worked into Sutton even deeper, into all of that heat, as she was pulled almost impossibly closer.

She was almost as shocked by Sutton's boldness as she was even more turned on by it.

Her mouth fell open in painfully undisguised arousal when Sutton whimpered out, "H-harder," as she dug her head back into Charlotte's pillow, sucking on her bottom lip, as if that made any of the sounds she couldn't stop any quieter.

"Shit," she murmured, because was Sutton trying to kill her? Pressing her hips down against her thigh, she used her other leg to back up her hand as she worked it into Sutton even harder. She pounded into her now, sliding Sutton up just a bit in her sheets, and she thought she might have gone too hard for a moment.

Before Sutton responded, with her back arching up toward Charlotte, cries in the back of her throat mingling with Charlotte's name echoing off of her bedroom walls. She nipped her teeth into Sutton's neck, moaning herself, and this time she might have left a mark; she wasn't entirely sure. She made her way down, sucking and licking and pressing kisses, far enough so that she could wrap her lips around her nipple.

Sutton swore loudly just as Charlotte could feel the leg that was wrapped around her waist start to shake. She knew Sutton was about to come again, even harder than before, even before her walls clamped down and started to pulse around her.

Charlotte slowed just a bit, gentling her thrusts as Sutton's peak hit, working Sutton through her orgasm. The sounds Sutton made softened to whimpers and her eyes closed tightly, wrapped up in the sounds and the feeling and the smell of Sutton all around her.

It would be so easy, she thought as she slowed the grinding of her hips. As soon as Sutton would give her a few well-directed strokes, Charlotte would easily come for her. It had been months since she'd had an orgasm given by anyone else, and even aside from that – she was so damn wet right now, so turned on from touching Sutton and making her shake and moan and come, she would orgasm within a few minutes.

She stroked her thumb lightly over Sutton's clit, and felt her entire body twitch as she slowly pulled out her fingers. They glistened with Sutton's wetness, and she didn't think twice before she brought them to her mouth. The taste of Sutton on her fingers only made her hunger for a taste of her even more, as well as make Charlotte feel the need to come even more, her center tightening on nothing, soaking her underwear.

It was truly a Herculean effort for her to stop herself from continuing to grind down into her, and to swing her leg back over Sutton's so that she removed the temptation from herself. Which, actually, wasn't even entirely true, because Charlotte was seriously tempted to touch her damn self. Right there and then, with a freshly fucked Sutton right next to her.

All right, so that might have been a part of the appeal.

Biting her lip to muffle a groan, Charlotte looked at Sutton. Who was still breathing heavily, with one arm strewn over her head and the other resting lax over where she'd been clutching at the sheets. Her chest was heaving, breasts moving with each inhale and Charlotte licked her lips.

"Are you okay?"

She had no idea when the last time was that she'd asked that to any woman she slept with. Then again, she'd never been *friends* with anyone she'd slept with, either, so perhaps she'd been a bit more callous in her regard for their emotional well-being.

Sutton hummed in the back of her throat, and Charlotte's lips quirked into a smirk. She couldn't help but feel self-satisfied, the feeling rolling through her warm and thick. Which seemed crazy, even as she was feeling ridiculously, physically *unsatisfied* at the same time.

Releasing a slow breath between her teeth – because she was *so* tempted to do something like guide Sutton's hand that was resting on the bed between them – she scooted a bit farther, toward the edge of the bed.

Self-control was something she prided herself on. And if she wanted to touch Sutton even more tonight, which she did, she was going to need every ounce of it that she had.

She'd never held back like this during sex before, and she wondered if – she frowned, turning her head a bit toward her bedroom door. Eyebrows coming together in confusion, she sat up a bit, hair tumbling over her shoulder.

That was definitely the sound of her apartment door opening.

Frowning, she flicked her gaze back to Sutton, who hadn't seemed to hear anything just yet. Which was probably good. She lowered her voice into a whisper, reaching out to stroke back a lock of soft red hair from Sutton's warm cheek, smoothing it onto the pillow, "I'll be right back."

She could already hear the muffled voices slightly through her door as she climbed out of her bed and tugged on the robe she had hanging on the closet. Resolutely, she didn't look back at Sutton, because... Sutton Spencer was spread out naked on her bed, and she was *leaving* her room.

On top of – or maybe because of – the fact that she was ridiculously turned on, Charlotte was very easily frustrated as she stepped out of her room and promptly closed the door. She crossed her arms and walked swiftly down the hall.

Only to find Dean and Caleb peeking in her kitchen, just starting to pull off their jackets. Dean spotted her first.

"Hey! We figured we'd stop by on our way back from the theater, especially since you were all grumpy about Sutton being busy."

"I *wasn't* grumpy." She'd been *concerned*. "And you two need to leave."

Before they realized what exactly was going on, and definitely before Sutton did.

Dean looked her up and down, narrowing his eyes. "We thought we'd be saving you from slaving over your paperwork all night. But apparently you've already finished?"

Caleb chuckled, reaching out to tug at the collar of her robe. "What, did you finish your paperwork and then go straight to bed? It's barely eleven. What are you, eighty? Speaking of eighty-year-olds, Grandmother released another statement today about your campaign."

She rolled her eyes so hard it nearly hurt as she pushed her elbow into his stomach, just hard enough to make him *oof*, and step back. "Of *course* I saw it, Caleb."

It had been a sly, snide dig at Naomi's campaign, which Charlotte had appreciated. And normally, she would love to talk politics with her brother and Dean. In fact, it was something she did nearly every day, and never got bored.

But it was *not* something she was going to do when she had Sutton, naked, in her bed, and she'd yet to get a taste of her. In fact, the *only* good thing about this impromptu visit, that she could see, was that she was rapidly losing that sharp edge of arousal that had nearly taken her over.

"I'm being serious, you two need to go. And you don't have keys to let yourselves in *when I'm home*." Her voice was sharper than it typically ever was on the topic.

They definitely took notice, and for a moment, Caleb looked confused. Before his face lit up into a mischievous grin. "Wait a second. It's too early for you to be in bed . . . unless, you're in bed with someone else."

"Ah, it all makes sense." Dean snapped his fingers. "This *is* the most stressful time of your life so far, really, with the campaign, and your usual stress relief management has been off the table – so to speak – for a while. Sutton has been your distraction –"

"And tonight she was busy, so..." Caleb finished for him. "You could have just told us."

Christ. She tugged the robe tighter around her body, narrowing her eyes at him. This was dangerously approaching what Charlotte would think of as the damage control stage, and she very much wanted to keep it in the preventative measures stage.

So she sighed and nodded – because it wasn't as though she was ashamed of her sexual history, which both Caleb and Dean knew all about, or at all ashamed of Sutton. Perhaps she was a bit wary of the men in her life finding out that she'd slept with Sutton, especially because of Caleb's dogged insistence that she couldn't manage to keep her as only a friend, but still.

She didn't need these boundaries to cross, not when this was a one-time thing. Certainly not when she was positive that Sutton wouldn't want them to know.

"Yes, fine, I do have someone here. You're right; I have been stressed and I needed a release." Okay, so she *still* needed a release, but that was neither here nor there. "So, goodbye and good night. I'll see you tomorrow, Dean."

Despite their teasing grins, she knew she had them both ready to leave, and she let out a sigh of relief as she brought her hand up to run through her hair.

Until she heard her bedroom door open behind her, and she closed her eyes tightly. This was definitely damage control time and she straightened her spine as she opened her eyes again. Just in time to see Caleb's kid-on-Christmas-morning smile – damn him – and the wide-eyed surprise on Dean's face.

She turned to face Sutton as well. Who had put on her dress again, the tiniest bit off-center, and her heels had been thrown back on with the straps haphazardly done up. All of that gorgeous red hair was so clearly mussed and Sutton had thrown it into a quick ponytail.

Seeing her made it very easy for Charlotte to want to make her turn around and go back into her room – into her bed – and make her come all over again. Which had been the plan, but now . . .

Sutton stared back at the three of them, first freezing upon seeing Dean and Caleb, before blushing the deepest red Charlotte had ever seen. "I – I, um. I was just leaving."

Baffled, Charlotte vehemently shook her head.

"No, *they're* going." She was careful to keep her voice low and controlled; she didn't want Sutton to read the annoyance in her tone that she had for the men in her life and think it was directed at her.

But Sutton either didn't hear her or was ignoring her. She walked right by the group of them, averting her eyes to the floor, heading right for the door. Charlotte shot both Caleb and Dean a warning look, because if they said or did anything else that made Sutton panic, she swore there would be hell to pay.

She quickly followed. "Sutton, wait –"

The look on Sutton's face wasn't one she could place exactly, but she knew in the way that Sutton wouldn't meet her gaze and the way stormy blue eyes watered slightly that there was *a lot* going on. She was somewhat gifted at reading expressions, especially on Sutton's face because she was so unguarded. But all she could see was distress that she *knew* hadn't been there earlier.

The concern she felt well up inside of her superseded everything else. "What happened?"

Something had to have happened between when she'd taken her last look at Sutton in her bed and now, right? Or maybe it was everything, all catching up to her. Damn it, Charlotte hated not knowing.

But Sutton looked at her, up and down her body, before her blush only intensified and she shook her head quickly. "I'm – I have to go, Charlotte. I'm *sorry.*"

Only, she didn't sound like she was apologizing strictly for leaving, and the feeling in Charlotte's stomach intensified into one of foreboding. Fuck it all, she'd known she shouldn't have done this. She'd *known* it, and still she'd done it, anyway.

Sutton reached for the doorknob and jerked the door open, mumbling, "I just... need to go home."

"Just stay here until you're less upset. It's late." She spoke softly, in the most calming tone she possessed.

Because maybe if she could get Sutton to *stop* and calm down, the anxiety she was sure Sutton was feeling would go away enough that they could handle it.

But Sutton already pulled the door closed behind her.

Chapter 11

Saturdays were typically a very productive day for Sutton. She'd always been an early riser by nature, so she usually made a nice breakfast. Went for a run, if the weather was nice. Got through all of her homework, including assignments that she needed to grade for Professor Martin. Did all of the shopping that needed to be done for the apartment, and the cleaning. Hung out with Regan, sometimes Emma, or Alex, when her sister was here.

Today . . . today, Sutton didn't think she was going to leave her bed at all. How could she?

With a groan, Sutton wiggled slightly deeper into the swaddle of blankets she'd wrapped around her through the night to try to comfort herself. She'd hardly slept a wink – two hours total, if that – and had spent the remainder of her time doing exactly what she was doing right now.

Staring up at her ceiling and wondering what in the hell was wrong with her?

Even just thinking about the night before made her want to crawl into a hole and die, because how could she have done that? How could she have practically begged Charlotte into agreeing to sleeping with her?

Sutton hadn't thought of it like that at the time. She hadn't connected the dots until after Charlotte had gotten out of the bed after . . . everything.

But there she'd been, completely naked in Charlotte's bed. Naked and feeling better than almost any time ever in her entire life, because Sutton had *never* experienced sex like that before. She was completely satisfied and sated, her body had felt like she could melt right into the mattress below. Supine and lax, with a fire still burning inside of her. Like, she wanted more; like she would always want more.

Sex had never been like that for her before. Even though it sometimes wasn't a necessarily *bad* experience, it had never been mind-blowing. She'd never before felt so thoroughly out of control before. She'd never lost herself so much in pleasure that she'd asked for *more*. *Harder*.

She'd thought that Charlotte would be amazing in bed, and she was. Sutton had been stripped bare, laid out, and thoroughly debauched. For the first few minutes after Charlotte had left the room, all she could do was revel in the feeling of it all.

It was after that, when she'd been in the room alone long enough to gather her thoughts, that she'd been able to see beyond *her* side of things and see what the night had really been.

Which was, for lack of a better word, pathetic.

Rather, *she* was pathetic.

Because in retrospect, it was all very clear: Charlotte hadn't responded favorably to her suggestion that they sleep together, at all. In fact, she'd tried to talk Sutton out of it, more than once. She'd only kissed her when Sutton had been on the verge of a total panic.

And then she had made Sutton feel so, so good, just like she'd promised to her in that whisper that had made Sutton's pulse go through the roof. But she'd done so while being fully clothed. Okay so, she'd taken off her shirt – Sutton had to ask! – but even then, she had still been wearing her bra.

Then there was that whole moving Sutton's hands off of her and placing them on the pillow thing. She'd only just managed to muster up enough courage and clarity of mind that Charlotte had been right *there* and on top of her and shirtless, and was hers to touch for the night when she'd tentatively stroked her hands up the older woman's smooth, lithely muscled back. And then Charlotte's hands had tugged hers away, off of her.

Which had made Sutton unhappy, but she'd forgotten it quickly, because then Charlotte was touching her and building her up and making her come, amazingly, twice. As soon as possible, though, Charlotte had climbed off of her and then had scooted away to the other side of the bed.

She knew Charlotte cared about her – it had been clear in everything that had happened between them last night. The way she'd touched her, the way she'd taken care of her – and that was why she'd done what Sutton had asked at all. Probably because she was worried she'd hurt Sutton's feelings if she'd continued to say no.

And, well, it *would* have hurt. But Sutton didn't think it would be as humiliating as realizing that the woman who had given you the best orgasms of your life didn't want you back.

The facts had stared right at Sutton when she'd managed to think clearly at all. The fact that she was in Charlotte's bed, and Charlotte, by her own proclamation, liked to use sex as stress relief, but she hadn't wanted to do it with *Sutton*.

Because if she had wanted to, Sutton didn't know how much clearer she could have been. She *threw* herself at Charlotte and had been very clear about her – her proposition.

How was she supposed to ever look Charlotte in the eye again? Knowing that she'd had to talk Charlotte into sleeping with her, and that Charlotte in turn had sex with her because she was trying to be kind, not out of any sort of desire? She didn't want to feel her naked body against Sutton's, the way Sutton had wanted to feel hers. She certainly hadn't wanted Sutton to touch her, which she'd *so* wanted to do.

It was without a doubt the most mortifying sexual experience in her life. Even if her previous experiences had never left her breathless and exhilarated and wanting more, there was at least the very baseline point that her partner wanted her in return.

That she hadn't had to coerce them into sex.

When she heard her phone buzz against her bedside table, she closed her eyes as she took in a deep breath and held it for a few seconds to try to calm the thoughts whirling through her head. She'd plugged her phone into the charger when she'd arrived home last night without looking at it, and had kept it turned face down throughout the night.

Honestly, she'd been avoiding it since leaving Charlotte's because she *knew* that Charlotte would reach out to her. She'd been able to see the worry written all over her face when Sutton had gone into full panic mode. If *she'd* had a friend who showed up at her doorstep, wanting to sleep together, who then ran out the way she had, she'd be worried, too.

Then again, Sutton didn't think she would be able to bring herself to have sex with someone she didn't really desire. Regardless.

What was she supposed to say to her? *Sorry I practically forced myself on you?* Or *great, thanks for the orgasms, I'll be sure to keep my hands to myself at all times in the future?* Or, even better, the question that had echoed in her mind for hours, *why don't you want me?*

No. She wasn't going to look at her phone; she was already in a low enough place.

But when it alerted her to a handful of texts, one after another, over the next twenty minutes, she couldn't ignore it anymore. Rolling over, Sutton reluctantly unwrapped herself from her comforter enough to reach her arm out and grab her phone from her bedside table. Her eyes widened in surprise when she saw how many messages she had waiting for her, as her hands started to shake slightly from nerves.

There was no way those could all be from Charlotte, right?

The breath that left her when she saw that not nearly *all* of the messages were from her was one of relief. With a deep breath, she started from the top.

Charlotte – 1 missed call, 12:44AM

Charlotte – 12:48AM
I think I might have an idea of what's wrong, but
I would really like to hear that you're okay.

Sutton's cheeks burned just from reading the message. Was she *okay*? How could Charlotte wonder if she was okay, if she knew what was wrong? Then again, Charlotte likely had no clue what it felt like to be undesired; anyone with eyes wanted her. Sutton had seen it every time that they'd hung out.

Charlotte – 7:53AM
Good morning early bird. Are you already
awake? Can we talk before I go into my
meetings?

"Oh, God," she whined under her breath.

Because not only had she completely thrown her own day – and self-esteem – into the garbage last night, but she hadn't even taken into account that today was when Charlotte was meeting with her campaign advisors.

She'd been anticipating her day full of meetings today for over a week, excited to meet with her whole team for hours without interruption. And Sutton had probably soured a part of her day because of all of this. Entirely unintentionally, but still.

With trepidation, she scrolled to the final message that Charlotte had sent her.

Charlotte – 9:36AM
We really need to talk soon, Sutton.

Clutching her phone tightly, she dropped her fist down onto the bed with a sigh, shaking her head at herself. Guilt, hurt, and anxiety welled up, twisting together tightly in her stomach as she debated whether or not to answer.

Because on the one hand, Charlotte was clearly concerned, and maybe even angry with her. Which she probably had every right to be, considering the way Sutton had left and then ignored her. And she *should* message her; Charlotte hadn't been anything but a good friend to her, regardless of how wrong last night had been.

But on the other hand.

She brought her phone back up and bit her lip as she read over the messages again. She didn't know what to say, other than maybe an apology. And she very, very much wanted to put off any sort of conversation where Charlotte would explain to Sutton about not wanting her the same way. She really couldn't handle that, not right now.

Not when she'd spent half of the night agonizing over it already.

Instead, she tapped the button to send her back to look at her other new messages. And the fact that they were all from the group chat set up with her siblings went further than anything else she'd tried to use to comfort her.

She dropped her head back after skimming her eyes over the the messages between Alex, Oliver, Lucas, and Ethan.

In all honesty, with everything that had happened last night, Sutton had forgotten that they all had plans with their parents to video chat while Alex's finals were on live feed. Her competitions in Europe were usually the only ones where no one in the family attended her finals. Many of her competitions were in New England, and Sutton always attended her finals, in addition to several others if she was free, despite the fact that she sometimes got a bit squeamish.

In spite of the fact that she'd forgotten, she wouldn't mind video chatting with her family. Their particular brand of craziness always made her feel loved. Comforted. Plus, she could do it from the comfort of her own bed, so, her plan for the day of not leaving was still intact.

She frowned a bit as she reached up to rub at her eyes, which burned a little because she'd had her contacts in a little too long last night, both during and after crying. Glasses were going to be necessary, then.

As she moved to put her phone back down, it chimed again, and she froze. Hoping that it would be someone in her family – because despite the fact that there was the traitorous little part of her that wanted to hear from Charlotte again, she had *no* idea what to even say to her, still – she took a deep breath and peered at the message.

And found that it was no one that she'd expected it to be, and an email no less, which was somehow both a relief and a disappointment.

From: Nicholas Martin
To: Sutton Spencer
Subject: Great news for your weekend
Date: November 6, 11:25AM

Sutton,

I hope the weekend has been treating you well so far. There are two pressing matters that have come to my attention. The first is that you're graduating in the spring, which means you'll be out of the comforts of school and into the harsh realities of the "real world." So, good luck with that endeavor. I know I'm not your advisor, but if you'd like to schedule a meeting with me about your plans for after graduation, I'd be interested in discussing some options with you.

The second concern is that the assignments you were going to grade for me by Wednesday now need to be completed on Monday.

Sincerest apologies,
Dr. Martin

She barely managed to stop herself from snorting out loud, because *sincerest apologies* her ass. The day Dr. Martin genuinely meant an apology for a sudden change in grading due dates was the day he stopped relating the stories they were going over in class to stories of his "misspent youth" – Sutton's words, not his – of traveling and drinking.

But then she pushed her head back into her pillow and groaned in frustration. Because those papers were situated firmly in her desk in the TA office. There was no way she could hide out in the safety of her own bed all day now.

It was with great reluctance that Sutton walked out of her room a half hour later, backpack slung over her shoulder as she quietly closed the door. Her stomach was still tied up in knots, and she still longed to be wrapped up in her blankets, but she had to keep up with her work in spite of whatever mortifying and upsetting rejections she was facing in her personal life.

She'd had a small hope that Regan wouldn't be home, despite the fact that she knew she didn't have work this morning and unlike her, Regan wasn't an early riser. So unless she had a reason to be up and about, she typically liked to lounge around on the weekends.

Regan was exactly where Sutton thought she would find her late morning on a Saturday – cuddled on their living room couch in a blanket, with a cup of coffee cradled in her hands. Her eyebrows scrunched up in confusion as she paused a rerun of *Grey's Anatomy.* "Sutton? I didn't think you were home; it's almost noon. Did you just get out of bed?"

She tried to keep her voice light, "I – yeah. I, um . . ." she trailed off, cursing herself for not preparing something to tell Regan beforehand.

It was very difficult to lie to Regan about most things. Regan was the one who knew everything about her experiences; something that no one else could claim, because even as close as she was with her mother, there were things she couldn't discuss with her.

She turned to look at her completely, dark eyes questioning, and Sutton knew within seconds that any semblance of trying to maintain a front was useless. Because Regan quickly sat up, that mischievous gleam in her eyes.

"Wait a second. You had sex last night!"

She threw her arms above her head. "How do you know that?"

Regan grinned victoriously. "Because I don't like to read books, but I can read Sutton Spencer fluently. Look at you, stumbling out of your bedroom late morning, all sleep deprived. Plus, the dead giveaway – you're wearing your glasses in the middle of the day! Which you usually only do when you're sick or when you've had a late night. And since you weren't home until after I fell asleep, which was, like, midnight, I *know* you had a late night."

Burying her face in her hands, Sutton groaned. "God, we *do* know each other too well."

"Oh my god, tell me *everything*! I assumed that you maybe met someone at speed dating and had some drinks; I didn't think you would actually go home with anyone!" Regan rubbed her hands together in glee as she leaned forward, waiting for the details that she always inevitably dragged out of her. "I love when you surprise me like this."

"You act like I'm giving you a present."

"Come on! Tell me, what was she like?"

It didn't hit Sutton until that moment that Regan truly thought she'd slept with a woman she'd met last night. Someone who wasn't Charlotte. Which, honestly, maybe it would have been better if she had. Because she didn't think it would be as *amazing* as she'd felt with Charlotte. But at least in the aftermath, she wouldn't have had these problems.

She wouldn't be feeling so conflicted, like she'd done irreparable damage to a friendship that she'd really come to love. She wouldn't have to face the fact that the first woman she had a major crush on truly didn't want her the same way.

But Regan was looking at her so intently, and she cleared her throat as she crossed her arms. "Um. She was... older," she had to clear her throat. "Pretty."

Then Regan narrowed her eyes, before she stood to step in a little closer, giving Sutton a look of utter suspicion. "What aren't you telling me?"

Damn, that was it; that was all of the lying Sutton had in her. She closed her eyes as she blurted out, "Okay! Okay, fine. It was Charlotte."

Her confession was met with silence, until she willed her eyes open and Regan stared at her wide-eyed. Then she shouted, "You *had sex* with *Charlotte Thompson*? Stunning Charlotte?!"

That was all it took for her to crumble, and she covered her face with her hands, muffling her voice, "Yeah. Kind of," because, had she? When she hadn't even touched Charlotte? Or did that just mean Charlotte had sex with her?

Ugh.

Regan reached up and dragged her hands away from her face. "You *are* aware that was the *opposite* of the point of last night, right? You were supposed to get over Charlotte."

"I got under her instead," she lamented, her voice weak, before she even realized the words that came out of her mouth.

"Sutton!" Regan crowed, laughing. "Well . . . was she stunning, as the name states, at least?"

Sutton turned to sit on the arm of the couch, blowing out a long breath as her stomach churned.

"Yes. She was – she felt – amazing." Because Charlotte had been better than Sutton had thought someone could make her feel. Her body *still* felt it.

She'd been both gentle and a little rough, had known just where and how to touch and kiss and scratch and bite. God, she felt herself flush, her stomach bottoming out at the thought of it. Her breath caught in her throat, eyed widening as she tried to think of anything else.

Like, for instance, about how that hadn't done anything for Charlotte.

But Regan wasn't mollified, as she crossed her arms and her voice became serious. Serious and somber in the way that it had whenever Sutton had told her about every time her Joshua had done something particularly awful.

"Shit. I don't know how I missed it; you've been crying! Look at your eyes!" Which made Sutton frown, because she *had* looked at her eyes, and she'd only seen very faint traces of her sleeplessness. "How did this even happen? Was she – did she ask you to have sex with her? When you told her that you were going speed dating?!"

"No! No, that's not – no," she stumbled over her words, shaking her head and pushing herself back up to stand in front of Regan. "She definitely *wasn't* jealous, and – and she wasn't the one to propose we sleep together," she finished in an embarrassed mumble.

Which only made Regan stare at her. For so long Sutton couldn't handle it, because it just reminded her about the fact that *she'd had to talk Charlotte into having sex*. "I'm going to go. I have to go to campus and pick up some papers."

But Regan reached out to grab her wrist before she could move, and she turned to look down into dark, concerned eyes, that had a touch of wonder in them. "Did you really ask her to have sex with you?"

Sutton bit her lip and nodded, holding her gaze.

"And . . . did she hurt you?" Regan asked, her forehead scrunching up, before her features shifted. "That's it. You know what? I'm going to have a talk with so-called Stunning Charlotte, and –"

Sutton tightened her hand around Regan's. "No! Regan, seriously," the urgency in her voice didn't even measure up to what had quickly seized up into her throat. Because Regan *would*. "She didn't do anything wrong. She didn't do anything I didn't ask for."

She felt her cheeks burning at that, because, damn, had she asked for it.

"Then why are you so upset?"

Sutton's face crumpled. "She doesn't want me back."

"Wait a second. That's – that's not even possible!"

227

But Regan hadn't been there, and she *so* didn't want to discuss the details aloud, so she quickly added on, pleading, "Please let it go. I have to get to campus."

Regan gave her an unwavering stare for a few long moments, confusion and incredulity written all over her face. But, despite all of the tendencies she had to overstep boundaries and to force issues, she was a friend first. And Sutton figured her desperation to try to forget about the previous night was fairly obvious when Regan bit her lip, undoubtedly holding back a litany of comments.

"Fine. But I have a lot of questions." Bingo.

"I'm sure you do."

Sutton had her own questions. Like, *why would she ever do that?*

With a sigh, she flicked her eyes to the clock above the TV. "But I really do have to go." As it was, she was going to have to video chat with her family from the TA office, and she really didn't want to be late.

Regan sighed, "All right," her eyes narrowed in thought. "But... am I really not allowed to have some words with her?"

God, Sutton could only imagine how terribly that would go over. Charlotte could tell Regan about how she was just being a good friend, and – no. Sutton couldn't even handle thinking about it, and she shook her head. "Don't. Please don't mention it at all, ever, actually."

Reaching up, she scrubbed her free hand over her face, knocking her glasses askew momentarily as she rubbed her thumb over her tired eyes. She heard Regan sigh, and then found herself pulled forward into a hug, Regan's arms wrapping around her waist.

Sutton allowed herself a moment to sink into her best friend's comfort for a few seconds, before she took a deep breath and pulled back, fixing on a forced smile. Which was more for her own benefit rather than Regan's, seeing as how she knew that Regan knew she wasn't okay.

With a quick wave, which was met with Regan's considering look, she left the apartment before Regan could say anything else.

The subway ride and subsequent walk to campus was brisk in the November air, and really didn't help Sutton clear her head at all. In fact, it only reminded her that she'd left her favorite jacket at Charlotte's last night.

She'd been in such a rush to *get out* so she wouldn't have to face Charlotte again, that it had completely slipped her mind that she'd left it there.

She tried to shake herself out of those thoughts, even though she was certain that it was close to impossible, as she let herself into the quiet office. There was rarely anyone else here on weekends, thankfully, and only a handful of people even in the building at all.

Pulling off the light scarf she had on, she draped it over the back of her chair as she pulled out her laptop to turn it on and pull up the video chat window. As it loaded, she sank into her chair with a tired sigh and pulled open the top drawer to find the assignments that needed to be graded sitting right on top of the pile, all in order with a paper clip holding them together.

That at the very least was going right today, she supposed.

Blowing out a breath through her teeth, Sutton reached out to click on the call button for her mother's account, which was the one that was always logged in at home. Her dad didn't typically make video calls, and Ethan's account had been deleted after staying up until three in the morning, playing video games while online with his friends.

The picture that her mom used as her icon gave her a little bit of comfort right away. It was one that Sutton had snapped herself, at Christmas last year, where her parents were exchanging soft smiles.

Her phone buzzed from where it sat on the desk next to her, and her gaze was drawn to it as her laptop started to ring with the call waiting to be picked up.

Charlotte – 12:57PM
If you don't respond to me soon, I'm going to
have to assume you are in a ditch somewhere.

Sutton stared at the text, her thumbs over the screen as another stab of guilt hit her right in the chest. It wasn't like Charlotte *deserved* to be ignored. She hadn't been lying to Regan earlier – Charlotte had only done what Sutton had asked her to. Repeatedly.

It wasn't her fault that she didn't feel the same desire Sutton had felt for her.

But, *god*, why couldn't she have just said it outright instead of taking Sutton into her bedroom? To her bed?

And – fuck – Sutton was only just remembering how she'd told Charlotte that she'd *liked the picture of her family* right after Charlotte had taken her into the room to strip her bare. Like that was what she needed to think about, on top of everything else!

Her phone dropped from her hand back to the desk when her call was picked up, and she heard her dad asking, "Sutton? Hello?"

Taking in a deep breath through her nose to try to take her mind out of her fixation, Sutton shook her head before she quirked an eyebrow at the call screen on her laptop. Which *should* have had the video of her father and whoever else was at the computer already, but instead it was just black.

Confused, she narrowed her eyes. "Dad?"

The relief in his voice was evident, "Oh, good. You're here. But I can't see you. The screen is black."

"I think you need to go into your settings, because I can't see you either." Her father's perpetual inability to deal with technology gave her some much needed levity.

"Settings? How do I . . ." he trailed off, muttering to himself, and Sutton breathed out a small laugh.

She was prepared to instruct him on how to turn camera settings on, before she heard Oliver's laughter in the background, "Did you try to get a jumpstart on the video chat, Dad? I'm impressed!"

Sutton shook her head, despite the fact that they couldn't see her yet. "Don't be *too* impressed; the camera isn't even on."

"Sutton?" His voice came even clearer, and within seconds, the camera was flicked on to reveal Oliver and her dad, leaning in toward the computer side-by-side. Her older brother's expression was jovial, cheerful in a way that was infectious, as he gave her a warm smile, "Hey, you!"

"Hey back. How did Jane's fitting go, for her dress?"

As always, her brother's face lit up at the mention of his fiancée and talk of his wedding, "It went well. She's looking forward to you coming back for the holidays to get you fitted for your bridesmaid dress."

Both of their attention was grabbed by Ethan, who shouldered his way in, rolling his eyes up at Oliver in a way that made her laugh. "God, Oliver, *enough* about your wedding. It's not happening for months." He sent her a bright grin, "Sutton! Did you hear the new song I can play on the drums?"

She nodded, thinking of the video he'd sent her last week. It wasn't very good, really, but then, not many of his songs were. She loved that he sent her the videos, anyway.

Before she could say anything, Ethan's attention diverted. "Wait! Lucas is calling!"

Within moments, Sutton's screen was filled with the main call of Ethan, Oliver, and her dad in the center video, and an additional smaller video call box in the top corner with a blurry Lucas.

She already felt more settled, finding herself smiling at them, before her mom walked into the room. Her smile melted into an even more genuine one, especially at the way her dad and brothers stepped aside slightly, letting her mom gracefully slip into the chair.

As always when they were all in one space, even if it was virtual, several conversations all started at once. Sutton easily tuned them out, just taking comfort in their voices for a few seconds, before she caught her mom's gaze, "Hi, Mom."

Her mom's smile was like home itself. "Hi, honey." She opened her mouth to say something else, before blue eyes – so like her own – narrowed in speculation and she leaned in closer to the camera. "What's wrong?"

Oh no. Sutton felt herself flush, because of *course* her mom noticed. Even if it was through a webcam. And suddenly, Sutton wasn't only subjected to her mom's thoughtful look, but her question also gained the attention of all of her brothers and her father.

Vehemently, she shook her head, mildly panicked.

The breath that she'd taken in caught in her throat and she had to cough a few times before she could manage to get out, "Nothing! Nothing's wrong, I'm just, uh, thinking about Alex's tournament."

It was convincing enough to pull her brothers back into the whole reason of why they were even video chatting, and they started talking again. All she had to do was avoid her mother's knowing gaze, which was easy enough to do, as Alex's first match out of three was set to begin in only a few minutes.

They all pulled up the website that streamed her mixed martial arts matches, and Sutton reached behind her to grab at her scarf, twisting it between her hands as her stomach jumped the moment she recognized her sister.

They all cheered for Alex at the very end, when she knocked her final opponent clear out. Even as Sutton cringed – because she was pretty sure her sister just knocked out that other girl's teeth in addition to her mouthguard in her final blow – she was smiling victoriously.

Winning this tournament in London was leading her sister one step closer from her amateur status to professional, and despite the fact that Sutton couldn't relate to this exact passion, she admired it. She used to tease her sister for her interest in mixed martial arts, especially because she was so small. But

232

she had so much fight inside of her, Sutton really wasn't that surprised at all that she was *making it*.

Despite Sutton's distaste for the actual blood in the sport, she was proud of Alex.

It was the same feeling she saw on all of her brothers' faces, too, as they all spoke excitedly over one another. Lucas's typically serious face had one of the biggest smiles of all, even as his connection crackled and he informed them, "I have to go. I'll talk to you later."

They echoed various goodbyes as his blurry video showed a little, awkward Lucas wave, before he exited the screen. And again, Sutton was left with only one screen.

Ethan and Oliver stood behind her parents on the camera, her little brother now taking swings at her older brother's hands as he held them out for makeshift target practice, as Oliver narrated, "And a right hook! Then a jab!"

Ethan landed a final punch, before Oliver dodged and captured him in a headlock, despite the fact that Ethan was in the midst of a major growth spurt, and Sutton laughed. She yearned for that feeling right now. For Oliver and Ethan's playfulness, for the feeling and smell of home.

"We're going to play catch!" Ethan informed them, before maneuvering his way out of Oliver's hold and over to the camera, his face large in front of Sutton as he gave her a large grin. "Want to read my paper for me this week? Please?"

His voice was earnest, and despite the fact that he had three intelligent and beyond capable adults in the same room as him, Sutton loved that he asked her for homework help. It was just like he did when he was so little and just starting school.

"Of course," she promised.

He gave her an even brighter smile as he backed up. "Thanks, Sutton!" Before he turned his attention back to their older brother, "Come on."

Oliver shook his head with affection, "I'll call you later in the week, okay?"

She nodded, as though Oliver didn't call her once every week or two just to check in. "I'll answer."

Sutton smiled as they walked out of the room, her heart lurching just a bit at the thought of being *home*. She'd gotten homesick a lot when she'd first moved to the city for college, especially because she hadn't even had Regan with her at the time. No, Regan had remained in Massachusetts, and Sutton had lived in a dorm. And despite how excited she'd been, there were many nights where she longed for home.

Those nights were far fewer now. Now that she'd made a true life for herself here, now that she considered this her home. Massachusetts, her family, would always be *home*, but in a different way.

But with the way she was feeling today? With her mind perpetually flashing back to the night before and making her hands shake with anxiety, as her head was trying to sort through everything all at once?

Yeah, she would like to be wrapped up in a blanket there, in her mom's office.

A small sigh escaped her, as she was brought back to the present just as her dad excused himself. And she was left with her mom, who was giving her the same look she'd given her the night that she'd snuck out past curfew when she'd been sixteen. Even though she hadn't actively gotten caught, her mom had *known*, and had just waited for Sutton to confess.

But this was not the same thing.

Her mom waited until she was alone in the den, and Sutton knew it was coming even before her mom lifted an eyebrow. "Okay, sweetheart, we're alone. What's wrong?"

Sutton was surprised by how much she *wanted* to tell her. at least a little bit. If only to receive some sort of comfort.

How could she get that comfort, though, without telling her the whole story? And how in the *world* could she ever verbalize to her *mother* that she'd gone to

234

a woman's – anyone's, actually – apartment and ask to have sex? Let alone . . . everything that came after.

She couldn't.

The words were stuck in her throat.

I like women.

I like a woman.

I don't know what to do.

She deflated on a sigh, as she picked lightly at the end of her scarf and looked down from the camera with a shrug. "I don't . . . know how to say it."

"You're a surprisingly hard woman to track down on a Saturday afternoon," Charlotte's voice came from her doorway, startling her.

Sutton's eyes widened, and she jerked uncontrollably in her chair as she quickly turned to face her, banging her knee painfully on the underside of the desk in the process. Her cheeks flooded with color, while her heart thudded quickly in her chest. "Charlotte?"

She could hear the shock in her own voice, but it wasn't as though she was seeing something that wasn't there. There was no way she could mistake Charlotte, standing there in the doorway of her TA office, wearing a fitted charcoal pencil skirt that was barely peeking out from a buttoned up black peacoat. Her hair was as perfect as always, even when it was lightly tousled from the wind outside.

It had even looked good last night, after Sutton's hands had run through it, tugging –

She gulped, blinking her eyes quickly to try to push that thought away.

"What are you doing here?"

Charlotte only arched an eyebrow at her incredulously as she took a step into the room.

Her tone was low and firm as she came closer, "Sutton, we need to talk about last night."

The way her voice dipped slightly made Sutton a little short of breath. Before she stopped breathing entirely, panicked, as she whipped back around to face her laptop, eyes wide. She sincerely hoped that her mother missed the implication in Charlotte's tone, but well, she didn't really have much faith in that hope.

There was a questioning lift to her mother's eyes. Though she wasn't sitting at attention, Sutton knew she was watching them like a hawk, as she cleared her throat, "Last night?"

Oh, *God*. She only narrowly resisted the urge to bury her face back in her hands, as she caught the momentary look of surprise on Charlotte's face. It was quickly covered, though, as she came even closer – her proximity setting Sutton on edge.

She hadn't even noticed the fact that Charlotte had her hands occupied with two cups until she placed them on the edge of Sutton's desk, before she leaned down. Tendrils of that soft, light brown hair brushed Sutton's cheek slightly as Charlotte ducked low enough to be seen next to Sutton in the video chat screen.

Sutton was at a loss for words as she stared at their webcam reflection. She was sitting here, with the woman who'd seen her naked only just last night, the woman who had brought her to orgasm only just last night, the woman who had been running all over her mind and causing her such turmoil all night... and her *mother* was staring at them with a knowing look that made Sutton's stomach clench.

Charlotte unsurprisingly recovered faster than Sutton's thoughts could catch up to her, and she gave Sutton a warm smile that – surely must have been only for show given that she'd run away from her last night and then hadn't answered any messages. But it *felt* real. And it was enough to zip through Sutton and warm her to her toes.

"Yes, last night. Sutton was supposed to stay at my place for dinner, but something came up, and she had to leave rather suddenly."

236

Dinner? Sutton tried to keep her confusion off of her face, before it quickly fell into simple amazement at the fact that Charlotte was able to come up with a lie so quickly.

Thankfully, Charlotte didn't seem to even need her to speak, though. She slipped on an easy smile. "You must be Sutton's mother; the resemblance is unmistakable. Not to mention I'm a big fan. I'm Charlotte Thompson," she offered, her voice fresh and light and effortlessly charming.

Apparently not to her mother, though, who merely offered a small, polite smile back. Sutton recognized it as the smile she gave to people that she wasn't sure about yet; her reserving judgment smile. "Yes, I'm Katherine Spencer. Charlotte? Are you a new friend of Sutton's?"

Sutton could feel Charlotte's slight pause against her back, and the feeling of it – of her – made Sutton shiver. Which then made her blush all over again, because *her mom was watching*.

Coughing, Sutton quickly sat up, because what she didn't need right now was for her mother to question her and Charlotte's friendship. She was already going to have to explain why she hadn't told her mother about Charlotte, and she hadn't the slightest clue what to say.

Because we met on a dating app for gay women?

Because I have a ridiculous crush on her?

"I – sorry, Mom, but I have to go."

Her mom's considering look that she'd been giving Charlotte changed into a warm, albeit concerned look as she focused on Sutton. "Okay, honey. I love you."

Was she being paranoid or did it sound more emphatic than usual?

"I love you, too."

She lifted her hand in a wave as she leaned forward to hit the button and end the call. And as she leaned back, she was relieved that Charlotte had shifted back to stand next to her desk again.

Suddenly, irrationally, she missed her mother's presence; because now it was uncomfortable. Now, she bit her lip before she remembered that she was wearing her glasses. She hastily reached up to take them off and put them down on the desk.

Not that it even mattered, really, because Charlotte hadn't even wanted her when she was stark naked in her bed. It didn't matter if she saw Sutton sitting in her glasses, with her hair still slightly damp from the shower in a braid over her shoulder.

Damn, she so wished she hadn't thought of that. She *so* wished she could take back the last entire twenty-four hours, so she could avoid this entire step in her relationship with Charlotte.

"So you *aren't* lying in a ditch somewhere, then." Charlotte crossed her arms.

Sutton's breath caught as she felt that guilt from earlier return at having not answered Charlotte's messages. She squeezed her eyes closed for a moment, running her hands over her face, as she shook her head. "Well. No. Obviously."

"Obviously," Charlotte echoed.

And Sutton took that as a moment to look at her. If she could ignore the many of the details of last night, she would be able to marvel at the fact that it had been *this woman* who she'd had sex with.

"How did you find me here?"

After all, it wasn't as though she spent many Saturdays here in the TA office.

"It wasn't all that difficult. I'm a resourceful woman." She gazed at Sutton for another moment longer, before releasing a sigh.

Sutton wished she knew what the sigh was about. She didn't *seem* angry, but . . ."I'm sorry," the words slipped out of her without much thought. But she meant them.

Charlotte looked genuinely surprised, forehead crinkling in confusion. "*You're* sorry?"

God, she couldn't say this while she looked at her, and Sutton's gaze fell to her lap, as she ran her palms up and down her jean covered thighs. She couldn't even sort out the myriad of feelings that were storming through her right now, but she settled on regret.

"I'm sorry for asking you to sleep with me."

Charlotte was quiet and Sutton dared to look back up at her. Her eyes were closed for a few moments, and when they opened again Charlotte's face was unreadable as she nodded. "I thought that might be the case."

"I know that . . ." she trailed off, swallowing hard, but she knew she had to say it, "I know that you were reluctant to do it in the first place."

Charlotte breathed in deeply, before she gave Sutton an intense look. "I didn't hurt you, did I?"

Surprised, Sutton's mouth fell open. Hurt her? Only her pride. Did Charlotte not remember anything about her crying out for *more*? The thought made her throat go dry, and she quickly shook her head. "No! No, you – I – no."

She cringed at herself. Truly eloquent.

Charlotte watched her intently, and she wondered how deeply they were going to delve into this discussion. God, she hoped not too much more. After a few seconds, Charlotte gestured to the chair next to Sutton's. "Do you mind if I sit?"

Flicking her gaze to the chair in question, she bit her lip, "Uh, well, that's actually Emma's chair."

Charlotte's lips quirked into that perfect teasing smile. "Do you think Emma would mind, then?"

"Probably not," Sutton conceded and tilted her head, indicating that Charlotte should sit. Inwardly, she tried to brace herself for whatever discussion could be coming her way.

Charlotte nodded toward the cup closest to her. "It's a tea, for you. You look like you might need it," her voice was impossibly gentle.

It made Sutton's treacherous stomach flutter more, even as heavy anticipation hung over it. Still. She *did* need it, and she reached out to take the to-go mug between both of her hands. "Thank you," she murmured.

It was her favorite, made exactly the way she liked it, and she felt a little surge of affection for Charlotte. Her chest felt a little warm, even as she waited for Charlotte to start to bring up hard truths.

When she didn't, and merely watched Sutton take another sip of tea with a speculative look, Sutton felt herself blush. Because it was apparently going to be up to her to start. So she took a deep breath, before she set the cup back on the desk, her hand still wrapped around it lightly.

"So. Why are you… here?"

"You're avoiding me after running out of my apartment nearly in tears, and then ask why I've come to see you?"

Sutton tensed, her thumb shifting up on her cup to toy with the lid as she tried to think of something – anything – to explain herself. "I wasn't avoiding you."

All Charlotte had to do was tilt her head and give Sutton a *look* – the same one that Sutton imagined she used at work in order to get answers from people. *Real* answers, the ones that politicians weren't always eager to discuss.

It worked, though, and it made Sutton fidget, though she didn't say anything as she averted her eyes back to her desk.

Rather than sound angry or annoyed, as Sutton thought she might, Charlotte only let out a small, quiet sigh. It got her to look back up, and she wished – not for the first time – that she knew exactly what was going on in Charlotte's mind.

"So, you can look me in the eye and tell me that you haven't been avoiding me because we had sex?" Her voice was light when she spoke, as if she was talking to an animal that might dart away from her at the slightest provocation. Sutton supposed that she wasn't entirely incorrect.

This time, her denial wasn't weak or questioning, and the word slipped out before she could stop it, "No."

It was the sex that *hadn't* happened that had been all wrong. It was the fact that Sutton wasn't only curious about what it was like to be touched by a woman, but that Sutton had also wanted to touch one. To touch Charlotte. It was how Sutton hadn't only wanted to experience what it was like to come for a woman, but to make one – to make Charlotte – come for her.

She'd imagined *casual sex* going very, very wrong in the past for a lot of reasons. But they all involved her not being able to reconcile the very idea of casual sex itself. Not with a stranger and not with someone she liked. Instead, it had been a completely unforeseen curveball that had been thrown into the mix to mess everything up.

She couldn't say that, though. She couldn't say any of that. Because it didn't *matter*. What mattered was that Charlotte was right, and her shoulders slumped slightly, defeated. Tired.

"Okay. I – well, I *did* have an appointment to video chat with my family and to watch Alex's finals tournament. And I do have papers to grade. But I might have been avoiding you."

"Sutton," Charlotte's interjection came swiftly and Sutton didn't know why exactly, but her tone managed to calm the churning in her stomach. It was soothing, and strangely, so was the way she lightly tapped her fingers against her cup of coffee, before she placed it on the desk next to Sutton's as she stated, "We're friends."

"Friends," Sutton echoed softly, but her own tone was disheartening as she leaned back in her chair, pulling her hand away from her tea as she reached for her glasses again, sliding them on.

She just… she didn't know *how* to deal with being friends with Charlotte after she'd humiliated herself like that. After Charlotte had seen her naked, had been inside of her, had heard Sutton cry out her name.

She didn't know how Charlotte was looking at her, big brown eyes full of concern that touched Sutton, when Sutton would have fully understood being upset with her for putting their friendship in a tenuous place. As her hand fell from pushing up her glasses into place, she toyed with the ends of her braid.

Charlotte's lips curved into a smile, before she dropped her hand from her coffee cup and reached out. Sutton's breath hitched slightly, before she felt Charlotte's soft fingertips lightly brush over the backs of Sutton's. Her hands stilled, and she felt herself blush at the light contact, but she couldn't help it. Even the gentle stroking like that over her own fingers, allowing Sutton to feel the softness of her touch made her heart pound a little faster, and a hot, heavy feeling slide through her.

"We're friends," Charlotte repeated, tone unyielding but questioning slightly as she asserted, "And I really want us to continue our friendship. I've really come to value it, you know."

Even though Sutton had known that Charlotte really did care for her, it was surprising to hear a note of vulnerability in her confession.

Her fingers twitched against Charlotte's as she fought off the urge to flip her hand around and hold on. Which probably wasn't a good idea at this particular moment in time. Not with everything from last night still freshly between them.

But for the first time since she'd left Charlotte's in that anxiety-ridden rush, she felt somewhat okay again. Apparently she hadn't irreparably damaged their friendship, and at that a small smile tugged at her lips.

"I value it, too."

"Good." Charlotte shifted to slide her fingers around Sutton's and give a quick squeeze, her warm, soft palm curving over the back of her hand. Then she shifted back in her seat and out of Sutton's space as she dropped her hand.

Charlotte's expression was more serious now as she fixed her gaze on Sutton's. "We said that sex wouldn't change anything between us, and I really want that. Nothing has to be strange if we don't let it."

Shaking her head, she cleared her throat and leaned back in her chair. Her uncertainty was back again as she ventured, "I know that's what we said. It's just... I've never..." she trailed off, her hands coming up in front of her, vaguely gesturing as if to reference their whole experience together.

But Charlotte didn't push for her to finish, and instead she shot Sutton a playful wink. "I know."

She knew she was too far gone when Charlotte's teasing wink made her feel comforted.

"How about you act the same as you always have, and I'll act the same as I always have, and we'll keep being friends, as we have been?" The playfulness of moments before had dropped, and sincerity shone through.

"And it's just that easy?"

"It will be that easy if we want it to be." She let that sink in for a moment, before she took her gaze from Sutton's face and shifted it around the room. "Now, tell me, how do you ever get work done in here when you have no space? I stole Emma's chair, and I'm practically on top of you."

Sutton had been feeling somewhat back to normal, before she choked on the air in her throat at Charlotte's choice of words. Her body tingled at the memory of Charlotte being quite literally *on top of her* and – God – it was going to take a little while for that image to go away.

Charlotte, for her part, seemed to be affected in a way by her own word choice, and Sutton wondered what was going on in that active mind of hers as brown eyes momentarily lost their focus as they gazed just above Sutton's shoulder.

Still. *Friends*. And she made herself stay on the task of their conversation; she had to get used to Charlotte's teasing comments again, she supposed, because she made them often enough.

"I tend to grade here when everyone else is busy. When I'm alone, it's actually kind of nice. I've got a view and everything."

She gestured to the small, shitty window that hardly even opened, that faced the brick wall of the building next to them. And she cracked a smile at the dismayed look on Charlotte's face as she took it in. For the first time in the afternoon, the tension disappeared from her shoulders, and she felt almost playful herself.

"And what a *charming* view it is." Before Sutton could say anything, Charlotte looked down at her wrist to her watch, before letting out a reluctant sigh, "I'm sorry to cut this a little short, but I have to get back to my meetings."

"You – you came here when you were supposed to be having your meetings?" She gaped at her. "They're not done?"

Charlotte only shot her a quick smile. "They indeed are *not* done, but I suppose that is the beauty of being in charge. I can call a small break to reconvene after lunch." She stood, tapping her fingers lightly against Sutton's desk. "I wanted to surprise visit you so you couldn't avoid me even longer. And I'm glad I did, even if I might have to stay at the office a little later."

Her words brought that heavy guilty feeling back, and Sutton remorsefully looked down in her lap for a moment, before tilting her head back to be able to look at Charlotte. "I'm sorry."

These meetings had been important to her, and Sutton had known that. She just hadn't known that she was that important, too.

"Don't be sorry at all. However, you do have to make it up to me. You owe me dinner." She nodded, as though it had been decided between them.

"I do?"

Charlotte pointed in the direction of her laptop, "Remember? You and I had . . . dinner plans, and you rushed out? A deal's a deal, Sutton. Don't make me a liar to your mother."

"I – um, I could pencil you in somewhere. When do you want to have dinner?"

Charlotte adjusted her purse over her shoulder. "Tonight, if you're not busy. I'll be having meetings straight through the early evening; maybe we could get something after."

"I – sure," she wondered if she should be excited about it, considering the fact that she'd been in such turmoil all morning. But she *was* happy that things could be normal between them. "Do you want to come over to my apartment? I can make something."

"I'd like that. I'm expecting a tour."

Which reminded her that Charlotte had never been to her apartment. She was going to need to get home and clean. And go to the grocery store.

"Bye, darling," Charlotte's voice brought her out of her thoughts, before she swooped down and pressed a kiss to Sutton's cheek.

It wasn't uncharacteristic of Charlotte at all. But it was clearly the first time it had happened since Sutton had felt Charlotte's lips on her own. Since she'd felt them trail down her body. Since she'd tasted them.

And she completely froze in her chair, hands tightening around her knees, as Charlotte stood back up. Sutton thought maybe she was a little more erratic than usual as she backed away, giving her trademark wave.

"Bye."

Sutton fell back into her chair, blowing out a long breath. God. She truly needed to get a hold of herself. But how could she when Charlotte was doing things like delaying her meetings to come and see her and giving her those soft cheek kisses?

Then again, those – at least, the cheek kisses – were things Charlotte had always done. And just because Sutton knew *for sure* that her crush was hopeless, it didn't mean it would just go away. It just meant that she had to deal with it, while also dealing with the fact that she knew, firsthand, what an absolute goddess Charlotte was in bed. And that she wasn't going to get to experience it again. Even though she wanted to.

Which . . . was fine. It was totally okay. As long as Charlotte apparently didn't think that Sutton shouldn't ever show her face in public again, then she could get over it. Her lingering embarrassment would go away in time.

Mom – 3:04PM
*Charlotte seemed... interesting. You know you
can talk to me about anything, don't you?*

Or, you know, maybe not.

Chapter 12

Charlotte leaned over the table in the room they'd taken over in City Hall for the day, her palm on the surface as she pored over the overview of the plans that had been determined today.

Though she'd had the general idea for her campaign over the last month – because never would it be said that Charlotte Thompson wasn't a planner – and even though she'd been in contact several times with the handful of people that she had on her team, it couldn't compare to what had happened today, with everyone in the same place and working in conjunction with each other.

It was like having a little taste of the future she'd envisioned for herself, and she couldn't wait to have it all.

In addition to Dean, who doubled as her campaign manager, she had cultivated a team of people she'd met, worked with, and professionally trusted in the last seven years to help run the financial, strategic, public relations, and technological aspects of her team.

Then there was Aaron Lark, who had been a gift, of sorts, from her grandmother. As someone who had worked closely on all of her grandmother's campaigns in the past two decades, Charlotte knew she could trust him in his official capacity as a strategist, as her grandmother called him.

Despite the fact that she'd been a little distracted in their earlier hours, given what had been going on with Sutton, Charlotte had spent the past few hours with what felt like electricity in her veins. By all accounts, she should have been exhausted; she'd only gotten a few hours of sleep last night after Sutton had left and then she'd worried over her not responding to phone calls or texts.

Not to mention the fact that her body had still been caught up in the rush of having Sutton in her bed, naked, coming for her. So, it had felt like the blink of an eye before she'd had to get up and get ready for her day of meetings.

And all of the planning and strategizing they'd accomplished had only made her buzz with anticipation, sending a thrill through her that was unique to this aspect to her life. It was in times like this that she *knew* this was her sense of purpose. That all of her careful plans and control were worth it.

Shaking her hair back, she scowled at the documentation of her meeting with Aaron. Though his official title was strategist, Charlotte knew that his job also pertained to matters that got hands a little dirty. It was during her time with him earlier that he'd discussed the fact that David Verbeck had been sticking his sticky little fingers into her history and into all relevant files on her. Not that he would find anything, Charlotte had assured Aaron.

Her professional record was *spotless*; Naomi and Verbeck could search in every nook and cranny that they could find, and they would still not be able to find anything on her. Charlotte had been extremely careful about every step she'd taken, academically, societally, and politically.

But it was simply the principle of the matter. Naomi and Verbeck together, despite the fact that they wouldn't be able to find any dirt on her, was enough to grate on anyone's nerves.

"Knock, knock," Dean's voice cut into her thoughts, and Charlotte looked up to see him pushing the door open. He'd left almost a half hour ago, along with everyone else, as shown by how he'd clearly already gone back to his office and packed up to leave as he was now standing there with his jacket buttoned up and ready. He nodded his head toward the laptop. "What are you looking at?"

She forced away her scowl. "Just the review from what Aaron said."

Besides, she couldn't be too upset about it. Not when she had never been more sure in her life that all she wanted for her future was well within her grasp. Naomi Young might want to fight dirty, but if she did, Charlotte was no woman she could easily take down.

"Ah." He lifted his eyebrows playfully as he stepped into the room. "The questions about your personal life?"

Slowly, she closed the laptop – the plans weren't going to change and they would be there for her to review all she wanted later – as she rolled her eyes, this time in actual exasperation.

"No."

After the brief discussion and assurance that her professional life was spot-free, Aaron hadn't even blinked before he'd asked about what Naomi would be able to find out about her personal life.

Which had given Charlotte momentary pause. Only just a moment, before she'd informed him, shortly, that *no*, there was also nothing that would be found on her personal life. No, she'd never had any affairs. No, she'd never even had a relationship. No, there would be no angry exes of any sort coming out of the woodwork and wanting to talk to her opposition.

No, she'd never broken someone's heart. No, she'd certainly never had hers broken. No, she'd never engaged in any rendezvous that resulted in any sort of lasting consequences. There was a reason she had always been upfront about her intentions and clear about discretion.

It was the fact that he was in the business of digging up dirt – as well as the fact that he was a longtime close employee who had her grandmother's trust – that Charlotte knew Aaron was also commenting on her sexual preferences.

But she'd been firm in her confidence that there was nothing to be found. Being a lesbian was no crime, of course, but Charlotte was under no delusions about what repercussions it would have for her future. About how her sexuality would make her political life and plans of success that much more difficult and she was already well aware that she would be fighting uphill battles in the case of her age and gender; there was no need to bring anything else into the mix.

Especially something that had such little bearing on her life as it did.

Dean grinned in the face of her derision about the questioning line of her personal life before he helped her pack up the remainder of her belongings and asked, "Care to join me for dinner? Caleb is working the night shift; we can surprise him with food and catch him up on all of your plans."

"As appealing as that is, I have plans," she informed him, before she paused to wonder if she actually did, indeed, still have plans.

When she'd returned for her afternoon meetings, she'd put her phone on silent and tucked it away. Finally able to focus clearly now that there were no niggling thoughts in the back of her mind.

She'd been so distracted this morning, despite being so in her element, because she hadn't known exactly how much her friendship with Sutton meant to her until she was worried about losing it.

Now, she knew that while things had been smoothed over somewhat, Sutton – sweet Sutton, who was clearly internalizing and blaming herself for last night – was still a little shaken and upset about having sex with her. Charlotte had purposefully pushed to have dinner together tonight in order to rid them of whatever awkwardness might be lingering.

As she pulled out her phone, she saw that she had a few messages from the woman on her mind. Perhaps she shouldn't have told Dean with confidence that she had plans, as she was half-sure that Sutton was going to cancel. She'd thought Sutton might do so once she had the time to actually think about the two of them spending time together.

Sutton – 5:46PM
You said that you were working past dinner time, but not when, so I'll just cook soon and have it ready for when you're done.

Sutton – 5:53PM
Not that there's any rush or anything, obviously. I mean, your meetings are important.

Sutton – 5:55PM
*Plus you already took time out of them to see me
earlier.*

Sutton – 6:31PM
*So, just, you know, let me know whenever you're
on your way and I'll make sure dinner is warm
when you're here.*

Charlotte couldn't help but smile, shaking her head slightly. Because she would take this awkward-rambling Sutton over an avoidant Sutton any day. Every day.

Charlotte – 7:47PM
*I'm leaving work shortly, and very much
looking forward to dinner.*

"Plans?" Dean questioned as he handed her purse to her from where it was perched on the chair next to him. Open curiosity was written all over his face.

She arranged her purse over her shoulder before reaching for her satchel – the designer bag Dean himself had given her last Christmas. Her voice was cool and calm in response, "I'm going to Sutton's for dinner, if you must know."

After Sutton had left, she'd given both her brother and Dean a piece of her mind. Because even if they hadn't caused Sutton to panic, it was still the world's *worst* timing.

"Oh, *plans*, with *Sutton*. And we were just talking about your personal life, weren't we?"

Charlotte gave him a *look*, one that meant no nonsense. Because if this was about her typical sex life, she would have laughed with him, but things with Sutton were still too tentative.

"I'm still not going to talk to you about what happened."

He held his hands up in surrender. "If you recall, it was your brother who wanted to know all of the details. While I'm surprised and vaguely interested, I'm still having trouble connecting the Sutton Spencer in my mind to the bisexual woman who you have apparently now slept with. But I mean... talk about what is going on in your *personal life*."

Charlotte couldn't quite believe that she'd slept with Sutton, either. Well, she *could* believe it, as the memory was quite vivid. Quickly, she blinked away the memories of Sutton under her, because that certainly was not going to help her get their friendship back on track.

Still, she couldn't help but feel a stone quickly sink in her stomach as she corrected, "Don't say *personal life* like that." The way Aaron had said it. "It's not like there is something sordid going on between Sutton and myself."

They were friends. Who had sex once. And were trying to breach a fallout from that.

"I didn't say there was anything sordid happening. I *am* saying that you had sex with her last night, went to see her over an extended lunch break, and are now apparently going to have *dinner* at her place." The speculative look he was giving her made an uncomfortable shiver work up her spine.

"We *aren't* having sex again. Sutton could hardly look me in the eye earlier as it is. This is just... dinner. With actual food," she added on, feeling it was necessary.

He held the exit door open for her and they walked out onto the front steps that were illuminated by the streetlights.

After a few moments, he relented, "Okay, while I do believe you aren't having sex again, because that's not quite your style, this is still new territory for you. Going to have dinner with the woman you slept with last night instead of, you know, having sex and planning on never seeing her again."

She shrugged. Yes, it was new, but, "It's not as though this is a date, Dean. Which means that anything that had happened beyond the realm of a . . .

typical friendship, doesn't qualify into any sort of category that Aaron need be concerned about."

She lifted an eyebrow at him, daring him to disagree with her on the matter.

He didn't and quirked his lips up in a small, wistful smile. "I was just saying. I suppose I'll go have dinner with Caleb by myself."

"Oh, what a hardship," she teased, backing up a few steps. "Thank you for today."

The Lyft ride to Sutton's was quick, and she spent it thinking about what Dean had implied. About her relationship with Sutton.

Charlotte was great at setting goals and attaining them.

Her current goal was simple: make Sutton relax into her typical self. As she'd told her earlier, their friendship could be as simple as they wanted it to be. All Charlotte had to do was take that direction, and she was positive that Sutton would follow suit.

Taking on a challenge she'd never faced before was always something she looked forward to and this wasn't so terribly different. It was a responsibility Charlotte had never had to shoulder before – trying to calm her partner after sex so they could maintain a relationship.

It was, in fact, the opposite of what she'd done in the past.

With that in mind, a different sort of thrill than the one that had thrummed inside her earlier was coursing through her as she walked down the hallway to Sutton's apartment. This determination combined with the gentle excitement she'd come to associate with hanging out with Sutton, as well as the anticipation that she knew was caused by her attraction. That much was unavoidable after last night, but she figured that it would fade to the background again in due time.

Her gaze slid over the warmly painted hallway, taking in the small personal touches that the apartment doors had on them. Though not in her own Tribeca neighborhood, Sutton's apartment building in Greenwich Village was secure, neat, and well-maintained. Not that she really expected anything less; Sutton was the daughter of affluent, respectable parents who were undoubtedly doting on their eldest daughter.

She'd been able to see it in the few interactions she'd seen between Jack Spencer and Sutton firsthand, and even in the brief exchange she'd unknowingly stepped into earlier between Sutton and her mother.

As she felt that new buzz shoot through her, she approached Sutton and Regan's door, taking in a deep breath. Before she knocked, she took in their entry with interest. They had a cheerful welcome mat as well as a small, bright yellow fabric bow up in the right-hand corner of the doorframe.

She'd walked Sutton to her apartment building several times in the past weeks, but it was always at the end of getting coffee or finishing taking a walk, and she'd never actually come inside. It just made sense to spend time at her apartment, as Sutton shared hers with Regan.

Just as she was about to knock, the door was quickly pulled open. Had Charlotte's reflexes not been as disciplined as they were, she would have jumped and possibly squeaked from surprise.

As it was, her eyes widened as her heart thumped in her chest. And rather than come face-to-face with Sutton, she found herself looking at Regan's scowling face.

Regan, who she'd met on several occasions, and who had always have a bright, jovial, almost scarily over-excited gleam in her eyes. Right now, however, those eyes were staring at her, narrowed, and clearly unhappy.

For all of Charlotte's ideas for how she and Sutton could slip back into their friendship, she'd failed to take Regan into account. It had been her own foolish miscalculation, because *of course* Regan knew about last night.

Despite the displeasure at the unforeseen potential complication of the evening, because Charlotte had never before had to deal with the protective friend before, she smiled as pleasantly as she could in the face of clear distrust.

"Regan, it's nice to see you."

She wondered how difficult Regan would make this when it became clear after several beats of silence that she wasn't going to get a congenial response. Then again, it wasn't as though Charlotte thought of Regan as the type to put on a façade, even for the sake of politeness.

"Charlotte. How stunning."

Her intonation of the descriptor suggested the very opposite of anything good, and Charlotte grimaced.

Still, she was nothing if not reliable in a social situation, and she gamely quirked her mouth into a smile. "And how are you?"

Regan crossed her arms, leaning against the doorjamb as she sighed and opened her mouth to answer. Charlotte braced for it – for whatever harsh words might come her way – because encountering an angry Regan hadn't even been in the realm of her thoughts. But people like Regan, as well as the assessing eyes of Katherine Spencer from earlier that day, came with the package of being Sutton's friend.

Especially being Sutton's friend who had slept with her. Just as Caleb and Dean, and her intense work schedule came along with being *her* friend.

But Regan snapped her mouth shut and rolled her eyes to send a look over her shoulder, somewhere into the apartment where Charlotte couldn't see from her vantage point. Then she lowered her voice, "Look, let's drop the pleasantries. Tell me this: what are your intentions with Sutton?"

A short, disbelieving laugh cut itself off in her throat as she shook her head. "Excuse me?"

Those were words she'd certainly never had aimed toward her. She was in somewhat of a state of disbelief that she was hearing them at all, but especially that she was hearing it from Regan Gallagher, who was somehow trying to stare her down.

"Your intentions. With Sutton."

Despite the fact that Charlotte had dealt with some of the most intimidating politicians many times – her own grandmother was known to be one of the most intimidating! – she found herself actually impressed with the stare down she was receiving. Impressed by the very serious show of loyalty. Impressed, but she refused to be cowed by it.

Yes, she knew that there might still be lingering ramifications to deal with when it came to this whole situation, but she was certainly not going to engage in a serious discussion about that with Regan. She and *Sutton* had barely even spoken about what happened last night, which, Charlotte actually thought that they should at some point but she didn't want to make Sutton panic even more.

So, no, she would definitely not be discussing it with Sutton's friend.

Besides, it wasn't as though there was anything to discuss with Regan. She wasn't there to pick Sutton up for a *date*.

"My intention is to have dinner. A *friendly* dinner," she stressed. She could feel the serious scrutiny Regan was giving her as eyes darker then her own raked up and down her face.

"I just want you to know that those who have mistreated Sutton in the past have experienced suffering at my hands. I might not look scary, but I have wrath," she threatened.

It was actually threatening, which Charlotte commended her for. She wondered about those in Sutton's past who had mistreated her, as she'd only heard small parts and put together a few vague conclusions of her own accord; she felt oddly satisfied that they'd suffered at the very least from Regan.

"I promise you that I have no intention of mistreating Sutton."

It was the truth.

She thought that there might have been a modicum of approval in her gaze, but she couldn't focus on it when she heard Sutton's voice call out from somewhere in the apartment, "Regan? What are you doing?"

She couldn't help the way her head perked up, peering over Regan's shoulder.

Sutton blushed furiously as she came into view and she quickly turned to face Regan. "What were you doing, waiting by the door?"

Charlotte took the opportunity to hold back a groan, teeth digging into her bottom lip as honeyed brown eyes briefly rolled to the ceiling. *Fuck. Me.*

It really wasn't a surprise, the hot and heavy slide of desire that rolled through her. Because she'd been attracted to Sutton for months, ever since they'd first met. The sheer magnitude of it wasn't even surprising. Because she'd been so turned on, so ridiculously aroused by Sutton only the night before and Charlotte hadn't been able to . . . *work out her stress* with Sutton the way she so wished she could have.

But god, Sutton wasn't making this easy on her. She was still wearing those thickly black framed glasses that she'd been wearing earlier – which had given Charlotte a shock when she'd first seen her in the TA office. There was something about studious Sutton wearing her glasses with that long, vividly red braid pulled over her shoulder, in jeans and a loose sweater that was nearly hanging off one shoulder that *really* was working for Charlotte.

Last night, Sutton had been sexy – like, mouth-wateringly, stomach tied in knots hot – and *that* had truly worked for her, too. Clearly.

There was just something about Sutton looking cozy and relaxed, that was an unexpected turn on for her. She'd managed to take it in and push it to the backburner a few hours ago, and there had been a small hope that maybe Sutton would at least have taken off her glasses before dinner.

Still, there was also a measure of excitement that shot through her that she hadn't. Charlotte was clearly masochistic, purposefully hanging out with Sutton the night after she *didn't* orgasm.

She hoped she schooled her features quickly enough, because God only knew that Sutton didn't need to see how much she wanted her. Talk about derailing the little bit of progress they'd made earlier.

"Well, maybe I was waiting by the door! Just a little?"

"I –" Sutton cut herself off with a huffed out sigh, before she turned from Regan to Charlotte, and she enjoyed the way she immediately flushed. "I'm sorry, I – do you want to come in?"

Charlotte nodded, shooting her a wink as she teased, "Well, unless we were going to have dinner in the hall."

"If Regan had any manners, she would have already invited you in." Sutton linked her hand under Regan's arm when her friend remained standing in the same place, prohibiting Sutton from opening the door wide enough to let Charlotte in, and tugged her backwards. She gestured down the short hallway in invitation, and Charlotte walked by the pair, just close enough that her shoulder brushed Sutton's.

She heard the soft intake of breath and refused to acknowledge the way her stomach flipped at it.

"Excuse you, I have manners," Regan interjected, though Charlotte noted she didn't look nearly as menacing when facing Sutton as she had moments ago.

Sutton shut the door and stared her friend down in a commanding way that Charlotte had yet to see from her, which was entirely too interesting. Before she lowered her voice to a murmur, "You *said* you weren't going to say anything."

Charlotte averted her gaze and instead focused on unbuttoning her jacket, sliding it off of her shoulders before folding it over her arm as she walked farther in enough to see more of the apartment. The walls were painted a pale, warm yellow, and the entire apartment smelled like spices that she couldn't quite name, but it was delicious either way.

It felt homey yet refined in a way that reminded her of Sutton.

"I wasn't – ugh, Sutton!" Regan complained, dark eyes narrowing in Charlotte's direction, but she didn't finish what she was going to say.

Sutton shook her head, lifting her eyebrows in a look that made her look very stern, especially with her glasses on, before she pointed in the direction over Charlotte's shoulder, farther down the hallway. "To your room."

The commanding tone she used made Charlotte shiver slightly, and she couldn't help but turn completely to face them again just to see this. Her amusement only amplified when she saw Regan roll her eyes. "Come on."

"We agreed that unless you could be friendly, you would hang out in your room during dinner," Sutton scolded, firmly, which made Regan groan and Charlotte grin.

She couldn't help it; commanding Sutton was simultaneously exciting and entertaining. And she was especially surprised when Regan sighed, then relented, "Fine. Yeah, I'll be in my room." She gave Sutton's arm a gentle squeeze, before she turned to face Charlotte, eyes narrowed once again. "But I'm going to be keeping my ear on things."

Charlotte's smile didn't falter in the face of her clearly serious threat – promise? – though she did manage to have a handle on the amusement in her voice, "You do that."

As Regan walked down the hall and into a doorway at the very end, Charlotte turned back to face Sutton, whose face was buried in her hands. She let out a muffled, "I'm sorry about her. I – she… she's really…just, protective," she finished with a deep breath and a shrug, as she lifted her head again to reveal brightly blushing cheeks.

Charlotte smirked as she shook her head. "There is no need to apologize. Though I can honestly say I hadn't been expecting it, I find her loyalty appealing."

Especially because the kind of person that inspired that kind of loyalty was more than deserving of it.

"Yeah," Sutton murmured, thoughtlessly, before she bit her lip and adjusted her glasses, silence coming between them.

Which Charlotte *had* been prepared for. For all that being friends with someone she had sex with was new for her, having casual sex at all was new for Sutton. Who could be – delightfully – awkward under less stressful circumstances. Between the two of them, it was up to her to make their relationship comfortable again.

"I can't believe you sent her to her room," the laughter in her voice wasn't false at all, "And that she listened."

"Well, I'd be lying if I said it hadn't happened before. That's actually the tone that my mom used to use when we were kids. It gets a lot done. The first time my mom scolded Regan, she was terrified," Sutton confided, her voice nearly a whisper.

Charlotte quirked a brow, because *yes*, she could imagine that. "How long have you and Regan been friends?"

It was something that she hadn't really thought about before, assuming it had been some sort of lifelong relationship. But it couldn't be, really, if Sutton remembered that.

"We met when we were seven," Sutton told her, a fond smile pulling at her mouth as she walked toward Charlotte. Standing beside her, she gestured at a cluster of pictures in a multi-layered frame a few feet away. She walked even closer, curious, and saw that all of the pictures were snapshots of Sutton and Regan, from childhood into teen years then adulthood. It was unexpectedly sweet.

Sutton had also apparently completely missed out on any awkward teenage years. There was not one picture where she wasn't absolutely precious. Charlotte herself had only experienced one – age twelve and thankfully before high school – but still.

Sutton came to stand beside her, and Charlotte could feel her warmth despite the fact that there were a few careful inches between them. "Regan moved to Newton when her dad got the job to be my dad's chief of staff, and during her second week of school, she saw me being teased by this boy –"

"You were teased?" Charlotte couldn't help but interrupt, but she couldn't suppress her surprise. And odd annoyance at whichever little shit had been teasing that adorable younger Sutton.

Sutton's eyes rolled, as she looked down at Charlotte, shuffling slightly on her feet. "Yeah. Just... I don't know, for being shy and because of who my dad was. It was only ever by a few people, like Matt. Regan came out of nowhere and shoved him. He tripped and when he fell, he slammed his face into the ground and broke his nose. We've been best friends ever since," she finished, an affectionate grin on her face.

Charlotte's appreciation for Regan grew. "I guess she wasn't kidding when she said that she had wrath for people who mistreated you."

As soon as Sutton registered what she said, her eyes widened. "She said – what?"

Charlotte shrugged it off, and was glad that the awkwardness that could have wedged in between them instead faded to only a minor, background feeling. She was confident and hopeful that it would soon be gone.

"It's not important. What *is* important is that I'm starving. What's for dinner?" she asked, as she turned toward what she thought was the direction of the kitchen.

"Oh!" Sutton's face lit up, "I made kind of a spread? It's all Indian food, because, um, well because it's your favorite. And you've had such a long day, which was super important to you. Plus you came to see me during your lunch break, so I thought you'd be really hungry," she cut her ramble off, gazing at Charlotte as she bit her lip.

An unfamiliar warmth settled in her stomach. "You made my favorite food? You didn't have to do that."

Sutton blushed, before she tangled her fingers together in front of her. "It was – I mean, today was a big day for you, so. Besides, I like to cook. And maybe you shouldn't thank me yet, because I haven't ever made it before."

Endeared, Charlotte shifted her jacket that was still draped over her arm, and before she could say anything, Sutton looked down at it. "Oh! Here, give me your jacket."

She reached out to take Charlotte's coat, before she quickly walked to a closet near the front door and hung it up with quick, deft movements. Then she slowed for a moment, smoothing her hands over the arm of it, her voice soft, "I – um, actually, I left my jacket at your apartment last night."

Charlotte's eyebrows lifted; she hadn't expected Sutton to make any mention of the previous evening. Still, she nodded, murmuring, "I know. I'm sorry, I didn't have it with me to bring back today."

Actually, while Charlotte *was* very much aware that Sutton had left her jacket, she had deliberately left it at her apartment this morning. She was a strategic thinker; she knew that it could have been a possibility that she would need to have a potential bargaining tool in order to get Sutton to talk to her.

Sutton just shrugged. "No, it's okay. I just, um. Never mind." She blew out a quick breath before she closed the coat closet. "Are you hungry?"

"Starved," she deadpanned, though she meant it. "And even though you've never made it before, I'm positive that it's going to be amazing. My cooking repertoire consists mostly of coffee, cereal, and salad," she admitted, and enjoyed the aghast look Sutton gave her.

The truth of the matter was that she'd never really learned how to make elaborate meals. She'd never spent much time in the kitchen with their maid who fixed dinner every night in her childhood; she'd been too busy keeping up with all of the extracurriculars that she took part in to care much for culinary exploits.

As it turned out, Charlotte was very much right about Sutton's cooking – which was delicious and impressive. And she was more than grateful their meal conversation didn't have any of those awkward lulls she'd worried about.

It was just *nice*. It was nice to have a meal with Sutton, who genuinely wanted to know about how her meetings went. Who listened intently as Charlotte told her all about her day. Talking about these matters with Dean wasn't the same, as he was there with her, in the thick of things.

And talking about these things with her brother was entertaining, but Caleb was less of the sit-back-and-listen-while-making-insightful-commentary type, and more of the come-right-out-and-say-whatever-he-thinks-in-that-moment type.

It only reinforced the fact that Sutton was a friend she very much wanted to keep around.

Even when their plates were empty they sat side by side, and Charlotte took a sip of the spiced wine Sutton had bought to complement their meal. "And what about your day? I believe you mentioned earlier about watching your sister's finals?"

An indulgent smile crossed her face, "She won. It was…" A slightly squeamish look took over, and Charlotte was fascinated. "Gross," she finished with a small laugh. Her hand came up to play with the ends of her braid in the same manner she'd done earlier. Like she was unsure of something, before she offered, "Do you want to see it? There's usually a highlight reel."

Surprised by how much she actually did want to, she nodded. "I'm intrigued."

She watched Sutton take out her phone and quickly shoot off a text, as she explained, "Alex always has her highlights saved on her phone." For a moment, she hesitated, before she handed her phone to Charlotte. "She'll send it to me, and then you can watch it. I, um, don't want to see it again so soon after dinner." A small shiver of disgust worked over her and she shook her shoulders slightly.

Her eyes lit up in amusement. "So, you'll see the fights in person and you'll watch them live, but it grosses you out that much?"

Sutton shrugged, a light blush coming back to dust her cheeks, before she defended indignantly, "I'm there for support."

Without thinking, Charlotte reached out to rest her hand on Sutton's, much like she had earlier. And much like she had earlier, she felt the light twitch of Sutton's fingers under hers and heard Sutton's soft exhale. God help her, but she still enjoyed her reactions. She couldn't resist stroking her fingertips over the back of Sutton's soft hand before she let her hand drop. "I think it's sweet."

Sutton's phone vibrated and she quickly stood, tugging her hands behind her back as they flexed. "Uh – that should be Alex. So, you watch the video, and I'll clean up."

Quickly, she shook her head. "Wait, you cooked everything. You shouldn't have to clean up on your own." ·

But Sutton was already stacking up their plates. "No, you watch," she insisted firmly, before she ducked her head and made her way into the attached kitchen.

Blowing out a quiet breath, Charlotte watched her through the doorway. Perhaps the touching had been a bad idea; she might have to keep a better watch on that for a little while. As much as she enjoyed Sutton's reactions, it wasn't as though she didn't get a reaction from it either. Then again, she'd clearly had a better time the evening before than Sutton had.

Shaking herself out of her thoughts, she reached for Sutton's phone and thoughtlessly tapped on the notification that popped up. Instead of a message containing a video, though, she was looking at a Facebook message that popped up along with a friend request.

Alia Haddad – 9:38PM
Okay, it's technically not advised for me to look
someone up from work events, but I figure that
since my mom owns it, I won't get into too much
trouble, right? Besides, I feel that you, Sutton Spencer,
are worth a little trouble ;) That, and I figured that you
might be too skittish to actually use my phone number.

The world came to a fast halt and there was a bizarre weight that was sinking in her stomach. Even as she didn't want to look, her eyes narrowed at the

264

accompanying picture with the message. This *Alia Haddad* had beautifully darker skin, and sleek long black hair with dark eyes to match. Pretty and playful-looking.

Exactly who was this woman? Why was she messaging Sutton about *last night*, and what was that about a phone number? The wheels in her mind were already starting to turn and she found that it took a lot in order to not click on her icon to find out more about who this woman was.

That uncomfortable heaviness that had set in only burned a little brighter inside of her, though, the more she thought about it. What exactly had happened at that event?

Had she done something that had brought on Sutton's wanting to sleep with Charlotte? The idea that another woman might have put that in motion, that another woman might have been the reason that Sutton had come to her, full of the desire that had broken Charlotte's previously perfect record of self-control, made her feel almost nauseous.

Okay, and the unmistakable jealousy that she was feeling was merely about sex. Because regardless of her romantic design, if she had any woman in her bed, *she* should be the only woman on her mind.

She hadn't even realized Sutton had come back until she could smell her subtle perfume as she came to stand next to her. Her eyes roamed up Sutton's body, until they met baby blues, which were alight with teasing as she sat back down in her chair. "I told you that it could be disturbing to watch."

"Yes," she murmured in agreement, before she realized that Sutton thought the expression on her face was because she was fazed by whatever mixed martial arts video Alex was supposed to send. Frowning, she shook her head slightly, flipping her hair over her shoulder as she sat up straight and schooled her features back to a nonchalant expression. Her voice was deliberately light as she handed the phone back to Sutton. "It actually wasn't your sister."

Sutton's forehead crinkled, her eyebrows coming together in clear confusion as she turned her attention toward the message Charlotte had just read.

And she kept her gaze trained on Sutton's face, because that pretty face didn't hide a thing. Her eyes widened as she read the message, her face flushing as even the tips of her ears turned red. She was flustered, Charlotte realized, and embarrassed. Sutton narrowed her eyes as she huffed out a breath, and her fingers hesitated over the screen, as though she was unsure of whether or not to answer, and even whether or not to accept the friend request.

Charlotte was usually a patient person. Not that she *enjoyed* having to wait for things that she wanted, but her chosen lifestyle was one in which she must play the long game. But her curiosity couldn't wait now.

Turning in her chair to face Sutton completely, her legs crossed at the knee and brushed against Sutton's. She couldn't help but ask, "I thought you said last night was a disaster?"

Because it clearly couldn't have been that bad, when there was this admittedly beautiful woman going out of her way to seek Sutton out the following day, after having apparently given Sutton her number.

Sutton's blush remained even as she vehemently shook her head, before haphazardly tossing her phone back to the table. "It *was* a disaster!"

Charlotte knew that she wasn't lying; that just wasn't who Sutton was. But there was so much *more* there that she hadn't gotten the answers to. And she had thought that maybe it wasn't that important to know all of the details, but it was. Because last night was still weighing between them, and it wasn't as though Charlotte was going to be able to forget about it no matter what.

She took in the frustration that was mixed in with the myriad of other emotions moving over Sutton's face, and that was all it took for her to take on an intense distaste for Alia Haddad. Given Sutton's reaction to her, Charlotte had no doubt that Alia was directly involved in the *disaster* of last night.

It wasn't difficult to imagine that the woman who was now seeking Sutton out was one of the vultures Charlotte had imagined would be there. Sure, she was pretty, and young, and apparently had been working at the event instead of looking for a date.

266

But that didn't mean she wasn't still a vulture.

"But, you got her number?" She couldn't help but push for an answer, despite the fact that Sutton clearly didn't intend on using said number.

Sutton used the back of her hand to push up her glasses as she groaned. "It's not – she... we weren't... she worked there!" She looked up at the ceiling as if she wished it would open and would suck her right out of the room.

A few beats of silence hit them and Charlotte took a deep breath, hoping it would loosen the knots that had settled in her stomach. She ran her eyes over Sutton's face, before she gently reached out to place her hand on the one Sutton had curled into a fist in her lap. "We are going to have to talk about what happened, Sutton."

The hand under hers flexed and Charlotte could feel it shake slightly. Sutton sucked in a sharp breath then, and insisted, "No. No, we really don't have to."

Charlotte narrowed her eyes, because there was *something* more here, and now she couldn't let it go. "We do, because we're friends, and this is what friends do." Well, it was what she and Sutton were going to do, anyway. "Now, tell me about... Alia Haddad," she couldn't help the grimace that her name came out on or the dark tone.

But there was something about this woman that she already didn't like.

Sutton's eyes searched hers and she wondered what it was that she was looking for, what she was thinking as she let out a defeated sigh. Elegantly sloped shoulders slumped before she shrugged. "I don't know what you want me to say. She... works for the app, so that's why she was there last night."

How unprofessional. Charlotte silently urged her to carry on by lifting an eyebrow.

"Before I left, she stopped me to buy me a drink." Sutton rubbed her palms along her thighs as she trailed off.

She bit her cheek; what, was this woman trying to get Sutton drunk?! She'd been right. Vulture. "Why did she stop you?"

Though, she had a guess that she figured was very accurate.

Sutton pulled her braid back over her shoulder as she gave Charlotte an unsure look. "I… well, she watched me on my dates."

Obviously a stalker.

Oblivious to Charlotte's inner judgement and rapidly growing dislike for this woman, Sutton continued, "And she could tell that I was having… a difficult time. So she – I mean, we – I don't know. Talked," she finished, her tone weak as she brought her hand down to tap against the table.

"You just talked? She didn't… try anything with you?" She was having difficulty finding the connection there about what must have happened to cause Sutton to come to her apartment proposing sex.

Sutton's light blush made her feel like she had her answer, even before she shook her head. "No? Not really. She – I mean, she flirted. I think." Sutton frowned thoughtfully, and it was ridiculously cute. "But it didn't matter. Like I told you, I was a disaster, and she knew it."

"So, she had nothing to do with you coming to my apartment?" She didn't like how much she needed to get the clarification.

Sutton opened her mouth, then closed it on a hum, before finally giving in and letting out a heavy exhale, "She might have talked with me about how having sex with, um, a friend could make me less nervous," she murmured, nervously.

There it was. That was all she needed to know in order to be sure that Alia Haddad was responsible. Even as she glared at Sutton's phone, though, she shook her head at herself. As much as she had heavy suspicions about the reason behind why this Alia was advising Sutton about being more comfortable in her sex life, she knew that *she* herself was responsible for things that happened the night before.

She drew her hand through her hair, catching Sutton's eyes with her own as she quietly told her, "I think that we should continue talking, about . . . everything else."

Sutton quickly shook her head, her voice higher than normal, "Ah, no. We really don't." Before Charlotte could gently insist that they *should*, Sutton was already rambling on, "I just – I get it, you know? I know that you were just trying to be a good friend, and I know that you don't want me back. And, and that's okay, because you can't control who you're attracted to, and I shouldn't have even put you in that situation in the first place. That was thoughtless and selfish, and I'm *sorry*. I really am. But I really don't want to talk about it," she finished, frenzied, and slightly out of breath.

But Charlotte couldn't – her brain had frozen, and she stared at Sutton as her mind processed what she'd just said. Her gaze was fixed on Sutton's plump lips, which were slightly parted as she took in quick breaths, a tingle starting in the pit of her stomach, even as she was convinced she must have heard wrong.

She was certain that she'd heard Sutton incorrectly, because... there was no way she'd just said what Charlotte had heard. How did Sutton do this? How did she manage to take a conversation and turn it on its head, rendering Charlotte speechless so easily?

"What did you just say?" She demanded to know, focusing all of her attention on Sutton because she had to be sure that she wasn't imagining things.

Sutton's blush intensified and she groaned, before she threw her hands in the air, the picture of exasperation. "I said that I know that you don't want me and that it's obviously not your fault, but I've spent all night thinking about it already and I would really rather just forget about it."

Charlotte sat straight up, an urgency racing through her despite all of her previous thoughts about nothing happening between them again. But she couldn't help it, because Sutton looked so distressed, and – how could they have been on such different pages?

How could Sutton even *think* that Charlotte didn't want her?

"Is that really what you thought?"

Sutton stared at her for a few seconds, as if *she* was the one who couldn't believe what Charlotte was saying. Her tone was colored in exasperated embarrassment, "Of course it is! And it's totally... fine. I understand," she grew quiet and small, her hands linking together. "But it's kind of mortifying. I'm sorry that I left the way I did, but I couldn't face you after realizing that."

There was a quiet pleading in her tone, as if begging Charlotte to understand. But she couldn't even wrap her mind around this. Sutton thought that when Charlotte was fucking her, she wasn't turned on.

"Is that why you left? You were upset because you thought I didn't want you? Not... any other reason?" The words left her slowly despite the need that was burning through her to know the answer.

And Sutton licked her lips which... Charlotte blew out a slow breath as she followed the action, before she sighed. "Yes. God, how much do I have to say it?"

Fuck. It was all she could think about, now. The fact that Sutton had only left the night before because she thought *Charlotte didn't want her*. She had no idea how aroused she'd been, how close she'd been to sliding off her shorts and having Sutton touch her – or touching herself right there next to her.

Or how much she wanted her right now, staring at her all wide-eyed with her glasses, breathing slightly erratically. How Charlotte knew how easy it would be to dip her hands under the sweater she was wearing, stroking her fingertips over the soft skin of her back. Her hands tingled with the want of it.

Sutton heaved a deep breath. "I honestly just really want to move on from it. I mean, you said earlier that we could –"

Yes, Charlotte had said earlier that they could! But it was far easier to say that and to try to forget all of the details of Sutton crying out her name when she was positive that Sutton had been so upset by it.

"– and of course I don't blame you for it, like I said, it's my fault for even proposing it in the first place, but –"

And she thought maybe she would regret this, but she just couldn't help it.

She leaned in, capturing Sutton's mouth with her own. She caught the widening of Sutton's eyes and her sharp intake of breath as her lips melded to those soft pink ones, mid-sentence. There was no stopping herself from nipping her teeth into Sutton's bottom lip, then swallowing the gasp Sutton let out into her mouth.

Sutton tasted slightly like the wine they'd shared and just like... *Sutton*. Like she had last night. Charlotte could feel her body positively vibrating with tension before she melted with a whimper into Charlotte's mouth, which she felt zing through her entire body.

How could they have been on such different pages? She couldn't even understand it; she couldn't understand how Sutton could have felt Charlotte's mouth on her own like this, felt the way she sucked on her bottom lip, the way her hands came to brush up her sides lightly, and think that she had no desire for her?

Releasing the hold she had on Sutton's lip, and then licking her own, she pulled away slowly to face Sutton's stare. The stare where those blue eyes were reflecting so brightly at her, shocked and amazed. Meanwhile, her hands lightly stroked back down Sutton's sides and fell into her lap.

The breathy, mystified way Sutton asked, "Why?"

Charlotte shook her head slightly, baffled. "I should be asking you that! Why would you *possibly* think I don't want you?" She slid her hands over Sutton's thighs, only taking a moment to appreciate the length and warmth of them, before she shook her head from a mixture of sexual frustration – if only she'd known that last night – and bewilderment. "God, I answered the first ever message I got from you – despite the fact that it was from Regan – about *hooking up*." It just made no sense to her. "We had sex!"

She'd literally been inside of Sutton, had ground down against her last night.

But Sutton was shaking her head. "But – not really!" she flushed, before pushing on, "I mean – you... touched me, and I liked it. But you didn't let me

271

touch you," her voice dropped to an embarrassed hush, "You didn't even take off your clothes, and then after, you rolled away."

Charlotte dropped her head back on a groan at the misunderstanding, curls falling down her back. "I was *trying* to be a gentlewoman! I didn't want to be a vulture who took advantage of you!"

"But I wanted you to take advantage of me!" The words burst from Sutton's mouth and hung between them, clearly shocking her for even saying it. It certainly shocked Charlotte, and the words sent even more licks of arousal through her. Sutton made a valiant effort to recover, clearing her throat, "I went to *you* because I trust you, and I wanted to . . . well, to *learn* about being with a woman. But I didn't even get to touch you back."

Jesus. Charlotte took back everything she'd thought about her self-control in the last day. Because she so wanted to take Sutton again right here and now, just so she could feel how much she wanted her back. The thought that it was all reciprocal – that Sutton wanted to touch her in return – was enough to bring back almost exactly how turned on she'd been the night before.

She could picture it so easily: straddling Sutton right there in that chair, guiding her hand to where she apparently wanted to touch . . . She took in a breath and shook her head, trying to clear it.

It wouldn't even take much, really.

Rather than a *complete* lapse of control, Charlotte leaned forward again. But paused when she felt Sutton eagerly lean in as well. She could feel Sutton's breath against her cheek, and she closed her eyes, as she whispered, "You are such a smart woman, Sutton, but *so* wrong."

This time when she made contact with Sutton's lips again, it was soft. Just a brush, really, and it was so fascinating to her that the simple contact made her mouth tingle, the warm spread of *want* sliding through her easily.

She really, truly wanted Sutton to feel that she wanted her, too. In the back of her mind, she wondered how bad Sutton's sexual experiences had been in the past if her self-esteem immediately jumped to *that* conclusion.

It was wrong that someone as beautiful as Sutton thought that Charlotte didn't want her, especially after all of the flirting – God, all of the comments she'd made that were jokes-but-not-quite-only-jokes – and her desperation of last night, too.

This kiss was a gentle apology, because she could only imagine what Sutton had been feeling earlier.

But it was Sutton who broke the contact this time, though she didn't go far. She was close enough that her mouth brushed against Charlotte's, making her breath catch at the accidental touch, as she whispered, "I thought we were just going to forget about last night and keep going on with the same friendship as before?"

She sounded painfully confused and Charlotte squeezed her eyes closed. It was mostly just annoyance with herself, because – yes, perhaps this was not the right route to go. "We… are, yes." She let out a low, slow breath, attempting to calm her raging libido, before she pulled back to take a few breaths of fresh air. Air that didn't smell enticingly of Sutton's perfume, which could easily seduce Charlotte into, well, seducing Sutton back into bed.

With another deep breath, she re-crossed her legs and smoothed her hands over the skirt she was wearing. And couldn't pretend she didn't enjoy the thrill she got when she saw Sutton's eyes slowly track over the length of her legs.

"That is – we *are* friends. And we will continue to be," she clarified, "But, just so you know: you have *nothing* to apologize for about last night. You didn't put me into any sort of situation that I didn't want to be in. That kiss was so that you know that I find you incredibly attractive." An understatement, but a dignified one. "And I don't want you to doubt that, despite the fact that last night was that one-time only sort of thing."

There. Okay. Misunderstanding completely cleared up. Charlotte could go on without thinking that she'd taken advantage of Sutton. Sutton could go on without the ridiculous notion that she'd taken advantage of an un-wanting Charlotte. Everything could go back to normal.

Well, normal for Charlotte now meaning that she knew that Sutton Spencer wanted to touch her and wanted Charlotte to *teach her* how to make a woman come. Fuck.

As she attempted to get herself back under control, she made the mistake of looking back at Sutton. Who she'd expected to maybe look more relaxed or less embarrassed or something that wasn't staring at Charlotte, especially with a very concentrated, thoughtful look in her eyes.

"What if . . . maybe friendship is determined by what you want it to be? We could, um, be friends, still. Without making last night a one-time only kind of thing."

She sincerely wondered if there would ever be a time where Sutton gave her a full day without shocking her. And she kind of hoped that she didn't.

"Are you suggesting a friends with benefits situation?" She asked, because after all of their miscommunications of the last day, she felt it was necessary. And she tried to tamp down the excitement that shot through her veins at the very idea of it.

Sutton gave a firm nod, meeting Charlotte's eyes even as that pink blush spread over her cheeks. "Yes. I mean, it would work for both of us, for all of the reasons that I said last night. And I mean. . . you didn't even get to – to, uh, release your tension."

Charlotte was very much clear on *that*. "To make sure that we are on the exact same page . . . you are proposing that we have casual sex?"

Sutton rolled her eyes. "Even though I've never done it, I know what friends with benefits is."

An agreement was already playing on her lips because in an ideal world that would be the perfect situation. There was no way she would be hooking up with another woman in the foreseeable future, not during this election at the *very* least. So, casual, discreet sex with a woman who was not only gorgeous but her actual friend for the time being . . . it looked like a Christmas present, tied together with a beautiful red bow.

But there was a wariness in her that kept her from agreeing right away. She didn't want to jeopardize this friendship, because after last night and this morning, she knew that this could be a monumental backfire. And it felt surprisingly shitty to have Sutton avoiding her.

Sutton apparently took her hesitance as a bad indication as she started explaining, "I mean. It could work well, right? Because I could, I mean, *you* could teach me about sex with women, while at the same time, you could get some stress relief."

Oh, Charlotte definitely didn't have to be *sold* any more than she already was and she breathed in through her nose to hold it for a moment, before slowly releasing. As much as she would love to say yes right now, she knew that letting that base instinct take over was not exactly the best idea.

She reached out to take both of Sutton's hands in hers to still them from where they were lightly tapping at her knees.

"I'm not saying *no* – and don't you dare think that I don't want you again. But I do think that before we do anything, we *both* need to think this through. The last thing I want is for our friendship to implode."

Sutton bit her lip as she nodded, her hands briefly moving to tighten around Charlotte's. "Okay. Yes. That's probably a good idea. I've never – you know, I've never even wanted to suggest something like that before."

Oh, Charlotte could imagine. And if Sutton thought that made her want her even less, she was dead wrong. "I know, darling. And I've also never been friends with someone I've had sex with before, so you see we're both new."

"I should probably go." After all, it was getting late, and she'd had a long day, but she was surprised by how much she didn't want to go, even as she leaned back. "But I don't want to give Regan another reason to want to kill me."

"That's *probably* a good idea."

Charlotte was careful to keep a slight distance between them as Sutton walked her to the door, because her body was still buzzing with the high of all

275

that had happened. She refrained from giving Sutton her usual kiss on the cheek before saying goodbye, though.

She wondered if that might be happening a lot now. If they were actually going to do this casual sex friendship, she wondered about how much else would change?

And she wondered if she should be afraid by how very much she *wanted* it.

Chapter 13

Despite the fact that it was only just past six o'clock on a Friday night, Sutton was sitting comfortably in her bed, already wearing pajama shorts and her favorite sweatshirt that she'd gotten from NYU her first year. Her laptop was set out on the bed in front of her, with her mother on the receiving end of her Skype call.

"Okay, everything is all set. Alex and I have roundtrip Amtrak tickets, set to leave in three weeks."

Kate smiled, slightly distractedly, as she picked up a pen to write something down on her to-do list that Sutton just knew she had laid out in front of her, "Thanks, hon," she murmured.

She'd initially been slightly wary to video chat with her mom when she'd asked. It'd been only last weekend, after all, that her mom had overheard part of her and Charlotte's conversation the night after . . . everything. Torn between knowing she didn't owe it to anyone to come out to them, but also knowing that her mother would be there for her no matter what – she'd avoided more conversations with her mother in the last week than she ever had.

Which seemed to be futile, as things between them right now seemed to be totally normal.

Her mother checked her watch as she finished scrawling down the travel plans they'd arranged. In all honesty, she could not wait to go back home for winter break in a few weeks.

"My editor is calling at six thirty, sweetheart. I wish we could talk a little longer; we've barely been able to catch up this week."

The words sounded innocent enough, but Sutton swore that there was a little something *knowing* in her mom's tone. Then again, she could just as well have been paranoid.

Still, it easily brought that guilt back to gnaw lightly at her, and she cleared her throat, "I – yeah. I'm sorry, I've just been really busy with school, with finals coming up soon. We can talk again this weekend."

Her mom merely lifted an eyebrow, a small glint in her eye that Sutton didn't want to think too much about – God, she *knew*, and suddenly Sutton wasn't looking forward to going home as much if she was going to be subjected to these constant knowing looks that were putting her back on edge – as she hummed for a moment. "Of course, don't worry about it."

The unease was still in Sutton's stomach, but she did her best to just breathe through it, only smiling at her mom.

"I nearly forgot – before we hang up, there is something I want to ask you. I know it's probably not something you want to discuss, given the private nature, but I've been meaning to bring it up." She paused for just a moment, and it was all Sutton needed for her breath to catch in her throat as her thoughts started to race.

Oh no. Oh, God.

She'd gotten too comfortable too fast, because this was *it*.

While she had no doubts that her mom was the best mother in the entire world, she *always* knew when something was going on with one of her children. It was a frightening uncanny ability as much as it was an impressive one. And part of what made her a good mother was that she acted on those instincts.

So, obviously, when she thought that something major was happening in Sutton's life, she was going to bring it up. She'd been naïve, frankly, to believe otherwise.

Sutton's stomach churned uneasily and she pressed her hand against it as if that would help, even as she tightly squeezed her eyes closed.

278

Taking in a deep breath and as much courage as she could muster, she blurted out, "Okay. Yes. I mean, I was kind of expecting this, but I didn't, um, I mean, I wasn't..." Cutting herself off, she shook her head slightly. "I'm bisexual – I mean, that's – I'm attracted to women? Not a lesbian though, I'm fairly positive. So, both men and women," the words tumbled from her and she cringed at herself.

Because *what even*?

But now that she started, she couldn't stop. "It's just . . . I haven't always known, you know? I only started figuring it out in the last six months or so, so I didn't want to – to tell you without *knowing* for sure." The words somehow made her feel like a weight was both lifted off of her shoulders but like there was also an added one of uncertainty being blanketed on, and she finally managed to open her eyes. "But I know, for sure."

Her voice was stronger than she'd expected, and even though her heart was thumping erratically in her chest and her nerves felt like they were tangling together, it felt good to say it aloud to her mother.

Sutton bit her bottom lip again as the rest of her breath left her in a fast exhale, and she looked up at her screen to see her mother's reaction.

Her mother, who was sitting back in her chair with an expression that Sutton couldn't quite read on her face. Even though it wasn't a *bad* expression – it looked more like a bit of surprise, if anything – it didn't feel reassuring, and her stomach twisted uncomfortably as her throat grew a little dry.

Her mom wasn't homophobic – neither of her parents were – and she'd heard so many discussions about fair and equal treatment of everyone throughout the years and had actually *seen* her parents lead by example. She knew it wasn't all just meaningless words to them.

Then again, none of her siblings were anything other than straight. Well, none of them had come out as anything other than straight, anyway, so it wasn't like she knew how her parents would feel knowing it was one of *their* kids.

Her teeth worried at her bottom lip some more as her thoughts raced.

But before she could say anything – only, what *could* she say, now? There was no taking back what she'd just revealed – her mom spoke, her voice soft and comforting, "I was going to ask you whether or not you thought it would be apt to invite Chris for the holidays, given his tumultuous family situation, because you know that Alex refuses to talk to me about their relationship."

And Sutton could only stare back at her as her cheeks burned in a furious, mortified blush, and the humiliation set in. Feeling like she swallowed a rock, her voice came out rough and low, "Oh." Staring wide-eyed at her mom, she forced herself to speak, "I – I think that would be nice."

Her voice sounded faint even to herself.

Even though she was tempted, so tempted, to hang up this disaster of a video call right then, she felt frozen, and they sat through a few beats of silence that felt like torture. And she tore her eyes away, instead looking down and focusing on a wrinkle in her comforter. Her hand went to it, picking at the fabric and tugging on it for a second as she cursed herself.

She couldn't handle it anymore, though, and words started spilling from her lips again, trying somehow to explain herself. Feeling like she *had* to. "I – I thought you were going to ask… because you sent me that text last week. I know you've been able to tell that I've been – well, that something has been going on."

There was an edge of desperation she felt rising inside of her, the backs of her eyes burning with tears that she knew would be coming quickly, because *why hadn't she said anything yet?*

But before any other words left her, she heard her mom speak again, this time in a comforting tone that reminded her of warm nights and soft hugs, "Sutton, please look at me."

Katherine's voice was warm and nearly pleading in a way that Sutton was not overly familiar with. And even though she was reluctant, she had no reason to doubt that warmth in her mom's voice; she never had.

This time when she dragged her gaze back to look at her, her eyes meeting such a similar hue through the computer screen, she was presented with a small smile, and – God – the same look full of love that she'd seen many times, as her mom leaned forward toward the camera. "Thank you for telling me."

"You already knew," she mumbled, unable to stop herself.

The grin that was on her mom's face grew a bit, as she shrugged lightly. "I suspected. But even so." Her expression grew more serious, though, as she seemed to try to search Sutton's face through the webcam, "You know that this doesn't change the way I love you. Or the way your father loves you. You're still our Sutton, no matter who you love."

And even though she had known that – she *did* – it didn't mean that hearing the words didn't make her feel so much relief that she could have melted right then and there into her bed. "Yeah?"

Those tears pricked at her eyes still, and she quickly reached up to wipe at them with her sleeve.

"Did you doubt it, honey?" Katherine's voice was so full of concern it could have made Sutton cry even more if she let it.

Feeling silly because of this overwhelming relief, she blew out a breath. "Not... really." And that wasn't necessarily a lie but it hadn't changed the fact that she'd been so nervous to change the way they thought of her. "It's just, I was scared. I don't... I'm just figuring it all out now." She shook her head at herself, because it didn't even matter, really. What mattered was that she felt *lighter* already, and her voice was small as she asked, just to make sure, "So, you're – we're okay?"

"Of course we are," her mom's voice was emphatic and pushed any remaining doubts away from her, before she asked, "Are *you* okay? I don't like to think that you've been so far from us, worrying about this all alone."

Sutton pulled her laptop up onto her legs as she leaned back against her headboard, all of the tension leaving her and making her feel like she was made of Jell-O, as she gave her mom a small, teasing smile. It was almost alarming how easy it was to smile now, when only moments ago she'd felt like her world was on a precipice. "Well, I've had Regan. I'm okay," she promised.

And it was true, she was – okay with herself, okay with her sexuality. And she was more than okay now that she knew for sure that her mom knew.

That lightness came trickling in, and with it a crazy sense of peace. It kept her smile in place, even as her phone buzzed with a new text.

She opened it automatically, even though her attention was still focused on her mom, who was giving her that warm look that said *I love you* even more than actual words did.

"I'm glad you haven't felt alone. And I'm so, so happy you told me, even if it happened because of a slight miscommunication."

A laugh worked its way out of her throat, her cheeks flushing, as she shook her head lightly.

Her mom continued, "Hon, you should know that the most important thing to me about anyone you date isn't about what gender they are, but about how they treat you."

But she only half heard the words, as her attention diverted to the text she'd opened.

Charlotte – 6:19PM
Sweet Jesus, this week has been insane. Are
you busy tonight? I was thinking we could
hang out.

Sutton felt like everything froze, except for her heart, which only skipped a beat before it started to pound rapidly in her chest.

She'd suggested being friends with benefits – she couldn't even believe she'd managed to get the words out – with Charlotte only a week ago. In all honesty, she was still in a state of disbelief at her own boldness.

She had no regrets about the suggestion. It had been a week. And in that week, Sutton had reflected and thought it over, and fantasized more than she would like to admit.

She *wanted* Charlotte, which was no secret or surprise. And she wanted her friendship, because Charlotte was a pretty great person. So if Charlotte didn't want to have the benefits part of the equation, then it would be okay with Sutton. They would keep being friends.

She just thought that Charlotte would have, well, responded in the next few days about whether or not they were going to have those benefits. They hadn't hung out all week – because not only had Sutton been a bit busy, but Charlotte had been very busy with not only her regular job, but also having three campaign meetings, a photoshoot, and another interview.

But they'd texted and talked. At first, every time Charlotte had texted her, Sutton had expected her to have some sort of answer or indicate which way she was leaning regarding this whole proposal that Sutton hadn't stopped thinking about.

And every time they'd talked, Charlotte acted the same as she always had. As though they hadn't had sex only last week, as though Charlotte hadn't told Sutton that she'd wanted her, as though she hadn't kissed Sutton until her knees felt like jelly. As though Sutton hadn't suggested they embark on having casual sex.

It was like she'd never suggested anything, and there were times where she wondered if she'd somehow made it all up in her head – even though sometimes she swore she could still feel the way Charlotte's mouth had felt on hers. Definitely not made up.

But now there was this text.

Hang out? Was that some sort of metaphor? Was this her actually responding to Sutton's friends with benefits suggestion, after a week of acting like Sutton hadn't said anything at all?

Okay, no. She was probably just overreacting, right? Just because they hadn't hung out in person since last weekend when *the suggestion* was made, Charlotte didn't have to mean anything other than just... hanging out.

Sutton – 6:21PM
No!

Her eyes widened and she barely resisted bashing herself over her head with her phone because *why* had she sent that?!

Sutton – 6:21PM
That is, no, I'm not busy. And yes, we can
hang out. Where and when?

She hit send just in time to look back up to catch her mother's speculative look, and she felt her cheeks burn. Clearing her throat, she waved her phone slightly in front of the camera.

"I – sorry. My friend texted me," she explained quickly, rushing the words out, before dropping it to her bed and out of her hands, because there was a time and a place for thinking about having sex and it was so *not* while she was supposed to be having a conversation with her mother.

Who was giving her a contemplative look that Sutton knew enough not to trust even before she asked, "Right. Speaking of friends – why don't you tell me a little bit about Charlotte Thompson?"

For just a moment, Sutton panicked at the idea that somehow her mother could see her phone, see the texts. Which was dumb, because even if she *could*, that message had been truly innocent.

It was just her own thoughts that weren't.

"I – what? She's nice. Um, smart. We – we met at..." quickly, she wracked her brain for whatever Charlotte had told her father over a month ago at their

284

surprise meeting. "Topped Off. Getting coffee." She took a moment to clear her throat, hoping that her blush wasn't as visible through the webcam. "Why, uh, do you want to know about her?"

Her attempt at casual was the *least* casual response in existence, and she knew it. Christ, Sutton was not in the habit of lying to or keeping things from her mom, especially when asked outright like this.

But it wasn't as though she could tell her mom about whatever sexual stuff was going on between them. *If* anything was even going on between them.

Charlotte – 6:23PM
My apartment. It's been such a long week,
I'd rather not go out. I just need to relax.

Charlotte – 6:24PM
I'll be out of the office in about an hour, so
I'll see you around 8?

The small squeak that left Sutton's throat was completely involuntary, as heat flashed through her body because – this *was* affirmation about being friends with benefits!

Maybe?

Right? Because by Charlotte's own admission, she used sex as stress relief, and *it's been such a long week* that she *just needed to relax.*

Sutton – 6:25PM
Yes. Yeah, I'll see you then. And there.

Before she could run her mind around what this might possibly mean, or if it meant anything more than what was written, the way her mom cleared her throat was somehow *knowing*, and it made her freeze.

Katherine lifted an eyebrow. "Well, it's strange that you didn't tell me about when you met her. We usually talk about all of your friends."

It was unquestionably true, but she forced a shrug. "It, um, was more about . . . her career. And Dad. You know how he can be, about politicians and all." She tried to make the lie roll from her tongue seamlessly.

If the slight look of disbelief on her mother's face was any indication, she failed miserably. But, well, she couldn't really dwell on that at the moment.

Shifting slightly in her seat, feeling somewhat restless now, she glanced down at the clock at the bottom of her laptop screen. "Aren't you supposed to get that call from your editor in, like, two minutes?"

It was a saving grace against any more Charlotte-related questions.

"Yes, but I can miss that if you want to keep talking. Not necessarily about your new friend, but about anything. You're more important than that."

Despite the Charlotte-inspired anticipation that had cropped up in her stomach, Sutton paused to allow herself to feel the appreciation slide through her once again. "I know. But, we don't have to talk anymore about it. Not today."

"Okay. If you're sure, then, I should probably go to take my call. I love you," Kate stated, almost as emphatically as she had a bit earlier, and it was still just as comforting to hear.

"I love you, too."

She had a second to take in a deep breath, before her phone alerted her to another text.

Charlotte – 6:29PM
Great. I have something exciting to show
you, too.

That – what did *that* mean? She was already excited and flustered and confused – emotions that were not foreign to her especially where Charlotte

286

was concerned – and she quickly closed her laptop and tossed her phone to the side.

God, she had so much to get ready!

An hour had already passed by the time Sutton was back in her room. She'd taken a shower, shaved, and dried her hair, letting it fall straight over her shoulders and down the back of her robe as she deliberated what to wear.

More precisely, what underwear to wear.

Shaking out her hands slightly, she bit her lip as she contemplated her options. Should she go for something sexy? Not that she really had a *ton* of "sexy" things, but some things were more enticing than others.

Or should she just act like this was a normal day, where she wasn't spending too much time thinking about what underwear she should wear to hang out with a *friend*?

She jumped in surprise as her door swung open, spinning on her heels in time to see Regan – clad in the sweatpants that signaled that she was going to have a night in – take a few steps in, while focused on her phone. "Hey, I was thinking about ordering a pizza. You haven't eaten yet, right? I'm starving. Let's get two pizzas."

Sutton slammed her drawer shut, and she flushed, annoyed with herself for being so *obvious*. "I, um, no I haven't eaten. But…" She cleared her throat as Regan looked up, lifting an eyebrow when she realized that Sutton was still in her robe. "I'm actually going out."

It was useless to hide the truth, and Sutton knew it as Regan took a few steps closer. She was so well-versed in reading Regan's face that she swore she could see her thoughts processing. Dark eyes were first alight with curiosity, moving swiftly into intrigue, then excitement – all in a matter of moments – before her gaze darted to the drawer that Sutton had snapped shut.

And then she saw the dawning of understanding. "You're going to sleep with Charlotte."

Sutton only rolled her eyes back at her, then repeated the action more dramatically when Regan groaned and threw herself onto Sutton's bed.

"Is there any use in trying to talk you out of it?"

"You've already tried," she reminded her, exasperated. "Regan, you're the one who has always been telling me to *get out of my bubble* and *live a little*."

It was actually a major component of their friendship.

Regan gave her a look of utter disbelief. "But I didn't expect you to ever actually listen to me! Need I remind you that the last time you went along with one of my dumb ideas two years ago, we were stranded in bumfuck Maine for the whole weekend, without cell service?"

God, that weekend had been horrible; truly she should have known better than to not look over the travel plans Regan had come up with before leaving with her.

"You're obviously the logical thought of our operation here and it's served us very well for almost two decades." Regan flopped onto her back, gesturing without looking up at Sutton, "And if *you're* going out and making the irresponsible decisions, what am *I* supposed to be doing, hmm?"

With an incredulous laugh that Sutton couldn't help, she retorted, "Maintaining your composure, clearly. And you're doing such a good job already."

When they made eye contact, Regan stuck out her tongue and Sutton grinned back for a moment. Before she glanced back at her phone, and the thought of Charlotte and what might possibly be happening between them came rushing back.

She sighed before dropping onto her bed next to Regan. "Look," she bit her lip for a moment to try to search for the right words. Because no matter how ridiculous Regan was, Sutton knew that her friend was just trying to look out for her. "This isn't crazy." At least, she didn't think so. Even so, if this might not be the soundest decision she'd ever made, it was hers to make. "I've thought about it, and I want this. So, can you just . . . support me? Even if you don't think it's the right move?" She was quick to add on.

Regan gave her hand a comforting squeeze. "I *do* support you. At the very least, Stunning Charlotte must really be something in bed if *Sutton Spencer* wants to engage in a sexual affair."

"Shut up. And it's not an affair," she muttered, because it wasn't like they would be doing anything illicit. Her other hand came up to pull at the end of her robe, which had fallen onto her thighs when she'd sat down. "Besides, I don't even know if she wants to do it."

Even if attraction wasn't in question anymore, Charlotte had never done something like this before, either. The sex, yes, clearly. But not sex with a friend or even the same person multiple times.

Regan gave her a look of disbelief, before she very obviously trailed her eyes over Sutton's robe, then also tugged at the hem. She ended by flicking at her knee. "Oh, she wants it, dummy. You can put the Charlotte into the Sutton, but you can't take out the obliviousness."

"You are the *worst*," she groaned.

Her friend ignored her, flicking her wrist over in the direction of Sutton's wardrobe. "Wear the matching black set you have. With the lace. Show off a little."

***

Less than a half hour later, Sutton's hands shook lightly with nervous excitement as she knocked lightly on Charlotte's apartment door. She could hear quiet music playing from inside and she focused on it as she took a deep, calming breath.

She knew what she wanted to happen tonight and she just hoped that Charlotte wanted the same thing. And she had already gotten her hopes up because of the whole *relaxing* aspect. Plus Charlotte had something to *show her*?

289

What was that supposed to mean?

And with Regan there to bolster her confidence – in addition to the very vivid memory of the way Charlotte had kissed her last weekend, with hunger on her lips, maybe her hopes weren't that far off from reality.

Charlotte opened the door already smiling and, as if part of a chain reaction, Sutton's stomach erupted in butterflies. She drank in the sight of her because a week was the longest they'd gone without spending any time together in months, and as always, Charlotte was a gorgeous sight.

She had already changed out of the form-fitting business clothes that Sutton knew she must have worn earlier, and was instead wearing her green tank top and yoga pants. Sutton made the conscious effort not to let her eyes wander to take her in.

Light brown hair that had clearly been in an up-do all day fell down around her shoulders, tousled and messy, and Sutton's fingers tingled with the memory of running her hands through the soft strands.

She felt herself grinning in response, taking in the wine glass in Charlotte's hand. Charlotte followed her gaze before elucidating, "Today was a long day."

Her eyes narrowed slightly as she took in Charlotte's smile, which didn't seem strained or tired, as it did on days where she'd had a taxing day. Instead it was soft and warm, and Sutton tilted her head as she took a guess, "But a good one?"

"You could say that." Charlotte winked, and Sutton swore that her heart stopped for a moment, only to pound harder than ever when Charlotte's gaze ran over her body. The glint in her eyes seemed to sharpen and those hopes she'd muted grew with leaps and bounds. Before Charlotte's eyebrows crinkled almost unnoticeably and smoothed out again in the blink of an eye. Sutton didn't have any time to reflect before their eyes locked again, and the smile on her face was inviting. "Come in, you look cold."

Shaking her head slightly, as if she could take herself out of the buzz that settled low in her stomach, she took the invitation in even as she refuted, "I've told you; you just don't have a cold tolerance." She'd especially giggled over it when Charlotte shared that her family had spent all of their winter breaks in their home in the Florida Keys.

She laughed at the way Charlotte exaggeratedly rolled her eyes. "Mhmm, so I hear."

Unzipping her coat, her fingers fumbled with the zipper slightly when Charlotte leaned over, her shoulder rubbing against Sutton's arm, so she could shut the door.

It took a few seconds for Sutton to gather herself, but she gamely tried to appear normal. Clearing her throat she asked, "So, what made today such a good day?"

When Charlotte straightened out, she reached out to help Sutton out of her jacket. Soft, nimble fingers brushed against her own and was it just her imagination or were they lingering? Then Charlotte leaned back, Sutton's jacket in hand as she shook her head. "We'll get to that in a minute. Now, tell me, how was your busy week?"

Her eyebrows crinkled slightly in confusion as she toed off her shoes. The thing was – Charlotte *knew* how her week was. She knew because even if they'd been avoiding the topic that was hanging between them even now, they'd still talked. And yet, Charlotte was still interested. It was in the way she quirked her head to the side slightly, her eyes alight and questioning. Like she wanted to know all of the little details that you didn't text because they were nearly insignificant.

Which – gave her that feeling. The one with her stomach dipping low as her chest seemed to warm. Biting her lip, she shrugged. "You already know most of it. Just... a lot of school stuff. Oh!" Feeling like an idiot, she gave Charlotte a small, sheepish smile, because there had been at least one decently sized development that she hadn't yet told her. "My mom knows. About me," she added, so that Charlotte didn't think her mother knew about *them*. Or the possibility of them, anyway. Even if she possibly… suspected. "That I'm bisexual," she clarified.

"When did that happen? We don't see each other for a few days, and I miss the big moments," Charlotte lightly teased, but her tone was sincere, "Is everything all right?"

Sutton took in a deep breath, shrugging even as she unstoppably smiled, thinking about her mom's face from a few hours ago. "She – well, she already knew, honestly. And then I blurted it out anyway."

"I'm shocked," Charlotte deadpanned.

The bright laughter in those eyes, shining right there along with something that Sutton thought was pride, made her feel a hundred feet tall. "But it was good. She was the best."

Charlotte gave her a warm look before quickly placing her wine glass on the small table next to the door. She whirled back around and before Sutton even realized it, strong bare arms wrapped around her tightly. Charlotte's hand stroked along her back, making her arch into the tingle from the sensation.

Charlotte spoke softly next to her ear, "I know you were nervous about it. I'm so glad for you, Sutton."

For a second, she wondered if her brain was short-circuiting, because she couldn't think of many times that they'd hugged before. Charlotte did a lot of touching. She flushed at the thought, flashing back easily to last weekend, but she meant in general.

Charlotte kissed her cheeks and held her hands and ran her fingertips through the ends of Sutton's hair. She'd learned early after meeting her in person that Charlotte was a fairly tactile person.

However, they hadn't really *hugged* like this. Where her whole body pressed against hers, able to feel her warmth through their clothes, feeling Charlotte's cheek rub against her own.

Her own arms wrapped around Charlotte after managing to shake herself out of her thoughts, and she took a moment to inhale. Her subtle perfume mixing with her shampoo was familiar and easily swept up her senses.

Before Charlotte pulled back and reached for her glass again, a pleasant flush apparent on her cheeks. Which, admittedly, made Sutton even more curious about what was going on in her mind.

"So," she started, "That was *my* good news of the day. What's got you all…" she trailed off, waving her hand toward the wine glass and then up at the smile on her face.

In response, Charlotte ghosted her fingertips over Sutton's wrist before she reached out to wrap her hand lightly around Sutton's. "It'll be better if I show you."

A pleasant rush swam through her from the contact as she more than willingly followed Charlotte down the hall, peering around as they went. She didn't know what to expect or where they were going to end up, but she was more than ready to find out.

Nothing appeared out of the ordinary. Not to her, anyway. The walls were still a calming green, the beautiful and undoubtedly expensive paintings and artworks strategically placed remained the same.

Charlotte slowed down as they turned into the kitchen and she walked over to her small table. She gave Sutton's hand a squeeze before dropping it as she came to a full stop, peering down at the tabletop before glancing back at Sutton with a quirked eyebrow, a smirk, and that gleam of excitement in her eyes.

Curious, she peered over Charlotte's shoulder as she walked closer to the edge of the table. And then came to a stumbling stop, crashing right into Charlotte when she was able to actually see what was there.

Her eyes widened when they landed on what amounted to what must have been over thirty different photographs of Charlotte. They were all professionally done, which meant that Charlotte was well-dressed – all beautiful, expensive clothing, with nothing that was really revealing, but was enough for someone with an active imagination like Sutton to imagine the possibilities.

In each picture that Sutton managed to take in, eyes darting from each one to the next, Charlotte could honest-to-God be an actual model. She vaguely thought of the pictures she'd first ever seen of the woman standing in front of her on SapphicSpark. Which had mostly been selfies, but Charlotte still managed to capture the camera completely with her presence.

It didn't matter if the pictures were professionally done or not, Sutton decided, because the way Charlotte looked coupled with the way she simply *was*, meant that anyone's attention was grabbed by her immediately.

"What do you think?" Charlotte asked in a tone that was somehow both self-assured and genuinely inquisitive.

Sutton could feel her gaze as she waited for her answer. It took a few moments, though she figured that her thoughts – which really could be summed up by *wow* – were probably visible on her face. She ran her fingertips above the pictures, not quite touching, as she murmured, "They're all really… amazing. You're so beautiful," she let slip out as she paused over one of the pictures where Charlotte was wearing a fitted suit, her hair up in an intricate bun.

Charlotte's smile was full-blown and smug, in an unduly attractive way, and Sutton tore her eyes off of the picture for a moment so she could roll her eyes. Even with her cheeks heating in a blush because she hadn't meant for the words to sound so… *reverent*, she tossed her hair over her shoulder. "Like you don't *know* that."

Her gaze found its way back to the pictures like a moth to a flame and she bit her lip. "I don't just mean, you know, your –" she cut herself off and gestured vaguely to Charlotte's face and body, "But I mean – you have this way of showing who you are just by… being. Like, you look here like you have all of the answers," she pointed at the picture she'd just gazed at, drawn to it again. "You look like you have all the answers. Like you're capable of doing *anything*."

294

She bit her lip, abruptly cutting herself off before she could ramble anymore about her thoughts on Charlotte and her many virtues.

Chancing a look at Charlotte, she took in the way those big brown eyes seemed incredibly soft, the grin pulling at her lips so different than the one she'd been wearing a minute ago. Then she cut her gaze to the photos on the table, a critical look coming across her features. "That's honestly exactly what I wanted to hear about these pictures. We have to make the final cuts as to which ones to use in the ad campaign by Monday."

Dawning came over her and she felt like a fool. "Oh! These are for the photoshoot you did."

"I know that there are still a few months of hard work ahead," Charlotte murmured, "But it's within reach. I know that it's *been* within reach, technically, this whole time. But, with having my team come together, putting together the ad campaign, knowing that the first debate is in less than a month – it's really happening."

Sutton turned away from the photos and instead turned to look at Charlotte. Who was looking at the photos with that pleased look on her face. She wasn't quite in disbelief at the campaign or at herself, Sutton knew, because Charlotte was more than sure about herself. She was just, for once, letting herself enjoy it.

It was something she'd noticed about Charlotte since they'd met in person, that she didn't even think Charlotte realized about herself. That she wasn't *unhappy* but that her mind was always working and always planning, and there were so very few times that she ever let herself just bask in the good things about the world around her in the moment.

Touched at being able to be one of the few people who got to exist with Charlotte in one of those rare moments, she couldn't contain a small smile. "I think it's *more* than within reach."

She wasn't one to underestimate Naomi Young. In fact, she would consider herself one of a small handful of people who saw her for all she was. Something that could be said about Naomi was that she would never deny that she would do almost anything to get what she wanted.

Yet, as she looked at Charlotte standing in the low light of her kitchen, wearing a form fitting tank top and yoga pants, bare feet with pink painted toenails, and a hopeful determination on her face... Sutton thought it would be the world's biggest crime to underestimate her.

"Thank you." Charlotte took herself out of whatever thoughts that had been churning in her mind to look at Sutton from the corner of her eye. Before she turned to face her, eyebrows furrowing slightly in confusion. "Wait, a second. What were you thinking at first?"

"What?"

"You said a minute ago *oh, these are for your photoshoot*. But you'd already looked at all of the pictures and said that I looked beautiful and capable," she explained, "So what did you think? That I called you over here just to look at pictures of myself to garner compliments?" her voice dipped into a teasing lilt, causing Sutton to blush.

"No," she denied, "That's not – I just, those were my first thoughts when I saw all of the pictures," she cut herself off when Charlotte tilted her head and chuckled. "Stop teasing me."

"In all seriousness, when I got these proofs before I left work, I texted you because I wanted you to let me know your opinion. So, in a way, you commenting on the photos without knowing what they were from makes your opinion on them even better. More unbiased. Thank you." Charlotte reached out and slid her hand down Sutton's in a caress.

She couldn't control the shiver but managed to stop the remark that had formed on her tongue. About the fact that she wasn't sure she was quite an unbiased source when it came to Charlotte, regardless of the circumstance.

Instead, she offered a weak shrug in return as her mind slipped back into that wondering loop. Charlotte called her here to look at her pictures; that's what she said. Which meant that the lacy underwear was for nothing, right? Because this was a *just friends* hangout and nothing else?

Then Charlotte's thumb swiped over the back of her hand before letting her go, and Sutton just – she just needed to know. Because what *was* this? Was this Charlotte being just normal charming flirty? Or was it – did she want more?

Taking in a deep breath through her nose, Sutton momentarily closed her eyes tightly to draw courage. And she willed the words to come out, "Have you thought about it?"

Charlotte paused, shifting slightly next to Sutton, and she opened her eyes in time to see Charlotte's eyebrow quirk up in question. "It?"

Even though she wanted to cringe at herself, she kept going, "I – yes. *It.* What I said last week." Refusing to give in to her inclined embarrassment, she continued, "Us. Sleeping together. Um, friends with benefits."

God, now that she'd actually said the words, she regretted them. Mostly because of this sudden silence they caused. But it was too late to turn back now.

"I mean, it's okay if you haven't thought of it." Even though it would kind of feel like somewhat of an insult when the topic had very much been on Sutton's mind all week. "And it's okay if you did think about it and you don't want to do it." Even though she would be disappointed. "But I need to know. Because I really don't like not knowing what you're thinking and if I just *knew*, I would know next time whether or not I would have to put special thought into every time you touch me or what kind of underwear I wear."

Charlotte's eyebrows rose dramatically at that and *damn it* Sutton was horrified at herself for letting those words come out. Why did she do this to herself? Why?

She tried very hard to control her heated blush even as she knew it was fruitless, as dark, interested eyes slid down her body for a moment.

Before Charlotte spoke, her voice quiet and controlled, "I truly did invite you over here tonight for a relaxing night as friends."

Sutton couldn't quite control the mortified groan that escaped her. Of course. Of course Charlotte hadn't had any other motives, and of course she *would* fall into word-vomit that made her want to crawl into a hole. She hardly managed to find her voice enough to croak out, "Oh. Okay. Can we just forget that I said anything?"

Charlotte's voice dipped impossibly lower as she swayed closer. Her curiosity was palpable as she asked, "Does that mean *you've* thought about it?"

Incredulous, Sutton rolled her eyes, "Of course I've thought about it! I don't – that's not really something I could not think about."

"And have you come to a conclusion about what you want?" Charlotte implored, and Sutton felt a little lightheaded, because she was even closer than before.

Her heart started beating erratically as her gaze flickered down to Charlotte's mouth. "I want you," she whispered, and for once she didn't mind the fact that she didn't seem to have control over what she was saying sometimes when Charlotte was around.

Not when her words made Charlotte's breath hitch and a pink tongue wet her lips, before she answered, "As long as you're sure..." Charlotte's eyes searched her own, and she wondered what she was searching for. "I've thought about it too," she admitted, "Probably more than I should have considering how much else has been on my mind this week."

She shouldn't be as gratified by that as she was. But considering she'd run herself to distraction thinking about all of the many ways she wanted to have sex with Charlotte throughout the week, it was only fair.

And she certainly wasn't expecting the power rush it gave her knowing that Charlotte Thompson, who was one of the most gorgeous, intelligent women she'd ever met who could probably sleep with most anyone she wanted, was thinking along the same lines about her all week.

Still, she shook her head lightly, pulling back an inch before she got sucked into this dizzying feeling. "Why didn't you say anything?"

298

A slim shoulder shrugged as Charlotte's gaze, serious and thoughtful, caught hers. "I figured that if you wanted to revisit the topic, you would bring it up again. I didn't want you to feel like I was… pressuring you."

"You wouldn't have been," she asserted. "I know that I'm inexperienced." She flushed and her mind quickly flashed through all of the possible ways Charlotte could expand her experiences. "But I'm still an adult. And if I don't want something, I won't be pressured by you just talking about it. That's really important, if we're going to do this."

And, God, she really wanted to do this. Her body was already humming in expectation. Excitement.

Charlotte lifted an eyebrow before she nodded. "You're right. And, believe me, I know that you don't have a problem saying something that is on your mind." The sudden flash of a grin she had made Sutton flush, before she continued, her voice lowering into a murmur, "You show up on my doorstep, wanting to sleep together. You propose us becoming friends with benefits. And once again, you bring it up tonight. I think that underestimating your boldness is a tragic mistake."

Her suggestive tone was enough to make Sutton's knees weak, coupled with the way her eyes had locked on to the way Charlotte's fingertips were skating along the edge of the table, coming to a stop just beside Sutton's thigh. She could feel Charlotte's thumb lightly stroke her there, and her breath left her in a quick exhale.

Before she gave in to the wickedly imploring look Charlotte was giving her, Sutton shook her head, and stepped back. She had to get to her jacket.

Ignoring Charlotte's confused – and disappointed? – look, she held up a finger to indicate that she would be back in just a minute. The whole walk here, she'd felt sort of foolish for letting Regan talk her into this, but now, as arousal was already settling low in her stomach and potentially going to cloud her head soon enough, she was grateful.

It took her only a few seconds to grab the folded piece of paper she'd put in there earlier before she hurried back to the kitchen to find Charlotte giving her a questioning look. In answer she unfolded the paper, her hands shaking just a bit from a combination of excitement and nerves and desire.

"I, um, came up with these rules." She grimaced. *Rules... sexy.* "Well, they're more like guidelines. Do you have a pen?"

Even though Charlotte was giving her an incredulous look now, she also looked intrigued. "Mhm, in my bedroom. Follow me." She turned, only to throw Sutton a heavily-lidded look over her shoulder that made her throat feel dry. "And what do you mean by guidelines?"

That embarrassment came back, just a bit now. Sutton's fingers toyed with the edge of the paper, folding it methodologically before unfolding it again. She followed Charlotte down the hall and explained, "Guidelines like... a few do's and don'ts that we might want to listen to before we start to do – this."

Charlotte opened the door to her bedroom and walked to the lamp to flick it on, before she grabbed a pen that was resting on her bedside table. She sauntered back to Sutton. "And what kind of *guidelines* do you already have on there?"

The question was pointless, though, as Sutton smoothed the paper out so that it was resting on the bureau for both of them to look.

1. *Strictly friend hangouts still happen*
2. *Kissing only happens during times of intimacy, not friend-hangouts*
3. *We listen to what each other wants and respect boundaries*
4. *Sleepovers can only happen after intimacy or only as friends, but not both (Charlotte can choose which)*

Leaning over slightly, she penned:

5. *Don't make assumptions about each other's wants or needs*

She suddenly felt sort of silly for this list, but... still. "I – well. Considering I've never done something like this before, and neither have you, having a solid foundation like this to fall back on seemed like a good idea."

When she looked at Charlotte, she noted the small smirk playing on her lips. Not her teasing one, but the one she wore when she thought Sutton was being endearing. "You... are certainly one of a kind. Of course you thought of this."

Sutton wondered for a moment if that was a bad thing, but Charlotte's gaze was so warm and affectionate, she couldn't help but enjoy it. When Charlotte took the pen from her she knew that the way she slid her fingers along Sutton's, stroking her index finger over her own, was deliberate.

Charlotte leaned down and started writing to amend the fourth point, and Sutton saw that she'd chosen for them to have sleepovers after friends-with-benefits times, not friend times. Which excited her, because she very much wanted to spend the night in Charlotte's bed as her lover.

"This way we can make sure that we're both on the same page about everything afterward. We don't want any repeats about our... misunderstanding from last week," her tone was more business-like than Sutton was used to, and it made her blink. Firm but agreeable, and she thought for a moment that this was probably how she got things done at work.

"That sounds like a good idea," she murmured, watching as she signed *Charlotte Thompson* at the bottom of the paper with an elegant flourish.

And when Charlotte started to smirk again as she tapped the pen once against the bureau before laying it down over the list, Sutton narrowed in on it. Glancing from the pen to Charlotte, she asked, "Did you really not have a pen anywhere but in your bedroom?"

That smirk grew and Charlotte shook her head. "Of course not. But you wanted this to be a learning experience, right?"

It was in the nearly predatory glint that was in Charlotte's eyes that had Sutton's breath catching in her throat, heart starting to speed up. She managed a small nod.

"Consider that the first lesson of tonight. There are many believable, easy ways to get the girl to come back to your bedroom and make everything a little bit easier," she finished, basically breathing out the words as she moved up onto her tiptoes, and Sutton felt her warm breath on her jaw.

She paused, just a breath away, and though Sutton's eyes had already fluttered closed, she didn't have to be able to see to know that Charlotte was waiting. Giving her this one last moment to be able to back out, to decide that this was not a good idea.

But she didn't want to back out, and she leaned down, her mouth finding Charlotte's in a second. As soft lips brushed against hers, she felt the answering tingle that she'd felt last weekend, and it was a comfort to know that she hadn't imagined it.

She felt Charlotte's tongue sweep across her bottom lip, and she responded, letting her in, as her hands came up to tentatively land on Charlotte's hips. When Charlotte whimpered softly into her mouth, pressing her body closer to Sutton's, it was as though all of the sparks that had been growing between them, in every change of tone and every small touch, turned into flame.

One of Charlotte's hands slid into her hair, her thumb rubbing behind Sutton's ear, while the other landed on her back, and scratched down. It tore a groan that she didn't even realize was coming from her own throat out of her, arching her back as the feeling shot desire through her body to land between her legs.

Charlotte moved her mouth to Sutton's neck and she gasped at the warmth on her sensitive skin. Teeth nipped at the spot just below her ear, making her eyes nearly roll back in her head as her hands squeezed tightly where they gripped slim hips. In the background of the blood roaring in her ears, she realized that she could feel Charlotte's smirk against her skin, just before she moved down to stroke her tongue over the hollow of Sutton's throat.

Tonight was even better than the first time, now that she knew that there was a highly likely chance that Charlotte kissing her, touching her, and feeling the way their bodies pressed against one another was making Charlotte just as wet as it was making her.

She managed a ragged breath, tilting her head back so that Charlotte's mouth could continue its skillful assault, and she slid one of her hands down and tugged at the hem of Charlotte's tank top. Then she dipped under, running her hand up the smooth skin of her back.

She could feel the way Charlotte's breath hitched against her neck. And when she scratched her fingers down, mirroring what Charlotte had just done to her, she reveled in the way Charlotte arched tightly against her and in the surprised scrape of her teeth against the base of Sutton's throat.

The hand that was still in her hair tightened and tugged her down, moving her mouth to meet Charlotte's again. She sucked on her bottom lip before she delved in, and Sutton whimpered.

As they kissed, she let her hands roam in a way they hadn't in the limited past moments that they'd had like this. Her fingertips explored soft skin and then slipped back out from Charlotte's tank top, to run up the fabric and touch her shoulders. Then back down, hesitating for only a moment before she slid down to cup a firmly muscled butt over her yoga pants.

Her explorative touch made Charlotte sigh into her mouth, and she pulled back slowly. Sutton blinked her eyes open to see darkened brown ones staring at her. The hunger in them was evident and made Sutton's blood pulse.

It was only when Charlotte licked her now swollen lips, eyes dipping, that Sutton even realized Charlotte had somehow unbuttoned her shirt without her even noticing. When her gaze flew back to Charlotte's, wondering, "When…?"

All she got in return was a mischievous smirk that somehow turned her on even more, because it should be illegal to be that attractive. Sutton was sure of it.

Then Charlotte shrugged, before she winked. "You'll learn."

And the flush that she already felt on her cheeks only intensified when Charlotte reached up, slowly, sliding her hands along Sutton's shoulders as she felt her shirt being slowly pushed off. She arched her back slightly to let her shirt fall down her arms more smoothly, feeling a little exposed, as she had last time, to be standing in front of Charlotte topless.

But then she thought of the desire that was evident on Charlotte's face as she took her in, murmuring, "So, you wore this –" She hooked her finger into the lacy cup of Sutton's bra. "For me?"

Though her brain felt like it was short-circuiting again and her breath left her in a rush, she nodded. "I wanted to look nice," she murmured, in place of the voice in her head that belonged to Regan telling her to *show off*.

"You do," Charlotte assured her, stepping closer so that her tank top rubbed against Sutton's bare stomach, and she felt goosebumps erupt from the contact. "But just so you know, you don't need to wear anything special when we do this."

Sutton was about to nod again even as she felt slightly dizzy with how hard her heart was pounding from Charlotte's proximity. Because – they were just friends. She wasn't Charlotte's girlfriend, trying to impress her with matching bra and underwear.

But then Charlotte's hands were on her waist, then scratching around to her back as she pushed onto her tiptoes again to bring her mouth to Sutton's ear. First she sucked on the lobe and she felt her knees weaken before Charlotte's words were roughly whispered, "Because it's just going to end up on my floor."

The choked sound that left Sutton as her words sunk in and her warm breath brushed over her skin was unstoppable.

Then Charlotte's mouth was on her jaw, making Sutton shudder. Only for her to realize, moments later, that Charlotte had unhooked her bra without her realizing, as well.

It was impressive, and she liked more than anything that Charlotte's fingertips stroked along her shoulders before sliding the fabric off. Because Sutton recognized it for what it was – the chance for her to slow things down.

Except slowing down was the opposite of what she wanted.

As Charlotte's *capable* hands slid slowly up her sides before cupping her breasts, Sutton shifted slightly from foot to foot as arousal ran through her. She remembered just what Charlotte could do to her, and how she could make her feel. The memory of the incredible feeling she got from Charlotte's hands and mouth on her body was more than enough for her to give herself over to it.

But what she wanted more than anything was to be able to make Charlotte feel like that.

Her hands came up to grab at Charlotte's wrists just as her thumbs brushed over her already hard nipples, and she moaned quietly before biting her lip. Charlotte paused instantly, though, her hands going slack in Sutton's. "Is everything –"

"I want to touch you, this time. I mean – first. I want to touch you, first," she got out, taking in the way her eyes widened and Charlotte licked her lips.

Charlotte's breath shuddered out. "You're sure?"

A flash of excitement bolted through her at the fact that she could *see* how much Charlotte wanted this too, and she hummed. "Yes. I'm positive." Her eyes tracked down Charlotte's body before moving back up – was she ever sure – before she released Charlotte's hands.

Which both came back up to pull Sutton's head down, capturing her mouth again. This kiss was more aggressive than before, and a thrill shot through her at the realization that Charlotte and all of her careful control was letting some of that façade crack. That she was showing Sutton the desire underneath as her mouth opened, more frenzied than before. Her tongue pushed into Sutton's mouth and she eagerly met it with her own.

She brought her hands back to Charlotte's hips, her thumbs brushing under her tank top, as she wondered what would be the best way to take it off. Because she didn't think she could be as smooth as Charlotte was – no, she knew it.

God, she *wanted* to touch Charlotte, to see her naked, finally, after having not been allowed to last week. But she also wanted to be good.

Her thoughts started to get the better of her, and she broke their kiss. Her cheeks colored with embarrassment as she had to clear her throat. "I – I want to make this good for you. I just don't... I'm not... I don't want to do anything wrong and you know I've never..." She closed her eyes tightly, hating herself.

Charlotte's hands slid to cup her jaw lightly, thumbs brushing her cheeks. "Darling, take a deep breath for me."

She complied, and slowly opened her eyes, to find Charlotte's smiling softly, if a bit strained, back at her as she continued, "Hear me when I tell you that I *know* you haven't touched another woman before, and I know it's nerve-wracking. But that's why we're doing this. You truly can't do anything wrong here, okay? And I'm not going to ask you to do anything that makes you uncomfortable."

She blew out the deep breath she'd taken, unsure of how to better convey that she trusted Charlotte. She just had doubts in herself.

Her inhale was sharp as Charlotte, almost as if she could read her mind, leaned in and flicked her tongue over the bow of her bottom lip. Before she whispered, "And let me tell you, that knowing you haven't done this before but that you want me enough to have started what's between us? Turns me on like you wouldn't believe."

The nerves that had arisen to break through the heavy desire that had settled inside of her quieted slightly. "I want to touch you," she repeated. "But, can you just – can you tell me what to do?"

"It just so happens –" Charlotte spun them, and started walking Sutton backwards until her knees hit her mattress, and she sat down. Charlotte ducked her head, brown curls curtaining the two of them, as she leaned in to nip at Sutton's earlobe. "That I *love* telling people what to do."

A strangled laugh started in the back of her throat, because *only Charlotte*. But it fell back down again when Charlotte pushed her back and then trailed her fingers down Sutton's stomach, leaving a tingling path in her wake, to hook her fingertips in the top of Sutton's leggings. "Take these off," she demanded.

Sutton complied, her heartbeat quickening at the husky tone of Charlotte's voice. Once again, there was that exposed feeling – because she was completely topless, her nipples hard and aching, only in her black underwear that was already wet – as Charlotte watched her for a few moments.

But that feeling went away marginally when Charlotte sighed low in her throat, before bending down again to press her lips to Sutton's as she ran her fingertips up Sutton's thighs. She pulled back to whisper, "You're sexy without even trying, darling. Let that be another lesson for you to keep, all right?"

She nodded… and then she nearly choked when Charlotte took a small step back and brought her hands to the bottom of her tank top before pulling it off in one swift motion. She hadn't been wearing a bra, Sutton realized dimly. And last week she hadn't taken off her bra, not to mention she hadn't really been in an ideal position for a good look.

Now, Sutton's eyes darkened as she took in the sight of Charlotte. The way her hips curved into her waist and then back out at her chest, revealing the epitome of perfect curves. And – *God*. Her breasts were bigger than Sutton's own, her nipples already tight, and Sutton's fingers itched to touch in a way she'd never felt before.

When she finally trailed her eyes up to look Charlotte in the face, she expected to be embarrassed about staring but was surprised when she wasn't.

Maybe it had something to do with the hungry way Charlotte was watching Sutton watch *her*, or the excitement that shone in her eyes.

Sutton's attention was drawn to Charlotte's hands, as they moved into the waist of her yoga pants. And apparently her underwear as well, because in another easy motion, Charlotte Thompson was standing only inches away from her – completely naked.

All of her skin looked so, so soft and smooth, naturally a few shades darker than Sutton's own, and she gulped as she took everything in, her throat dry. Then Charlotte's mouth descended on hers again, lips melding together hungrily.

This time, she hesitated less than earlier before she lifted her hands from where they rested on the mattress, and she brought them up to stroke along the outside of Charlotte's thighs. Her skin was as soft as she'd thought.

Before her curious hands explored any farther, Charlotte broke their kiss to nudge Sutton's nose with her own as she breathed, "Move back – sit against the headboard."

She didn't want to move away from Charlotte at all. She wanted to feel her body against her own, to feel those curves and her body heat. But from the look in Charlotte's eyes, she figured that would happen soon.

Anticipation crawled through her as she scooted back to sit where Charlotte directed. And she didn't have to wait before Charlotte followed, kneeling on the bed and following Sutton.

Who had never been more turned on in her entire life, excepting maybe the last time she'd been in this bed, than watching Charlotte crawl to her. Then up her legs, until she was nearly straddling Sutton's thigh.

Nearly, but not quite. Because Charlotte was hovering just over her leg, balanced on her knees still, but Sutton could feel her heat. She could *feel* Charlotte, and that alone stole her breath again as she tilted her head back to look into dark eyes.

Charlotte brought her hands up, balancing one on Sutton's shoulder and the other cupping her jaw, an imploring look in her eyes. There was an unspoken question there, and Sutton shook her head. "I'm good. I'm more than good. Can I..." She bit her lip and lowered her eyes to focus on Charlotte's clavicle, which was right in front of her, before gathering her courage. "Touch you?"

The smile she got in return was touched with desire and a little bit of exasperation. "Yes, Sutton. I want you to touch me."

It was all she needed to hear, and it made her feel a little awe because this ridiculously *hot* woman above her – wanted her. Wanted to be touched by her.

Sutton trailed her hands up Charlotte's legs, fingertips starting where her knees met the bed, before they trailed up her thighs again, feeling her muscles as Charlotte shifted slightly. Then she skimmed her hands up over Charlotte's stomach, before scratching lightly down, thinking about the reaction Charlotte had when she did it to her back.

This time Charlotte groaned, and Sutton marveled at the way she could see the way her stomach flexed. And when she moved her fingers upward, she paused for a moment before she got to the curve of Charlotte's breasts.

But only for a moment, because Charlotte was starting to breathe a little heavier, and the hand that had been on Sutton's shoulder slid down to Sutton's chest. Her head fell back on a groan when Charlotte lightly pinched her nipple, then tugged, and the feeling shot through her.

"Touch me," Charlotte urged, and Sutton's shaking hands listened.

She traced her finger over the curve that her knuckles had just brushed, and then moved her fingertips in circles, watching as she could *see* Charlotte's goosebumps in reaction to her touch. She could see the way dusky nipples tightened and she wanted – she wanted –

With a deep breath, she decided to just *do it* because that's what had gotten her this far, and Charlotte would probably like it. Sutton had loved when Charlotte had her mouth on her nipples.

Experimentally, she leaned in and ran her tongue on the same path her finger had taken. And Charlotte groaned, louder than Sutton would have thought, her hand tightening in Sutton's hair, and she'd never felt more emboldened in her entire life. Her mouth moved in a slow, smooth journey before she latched onto one of her nipples, pulling it between her lips.

The reaction was immediate, Charlotte's hips pushing down against her leg completely. Sutton pulled back on a gasp. "You're so wet," she breathed out, looking up at Charlotte's face.

Dark eyes had closed as curvy hips ground down into Sutton's thigh, and they fluttered open again a few seconds after Sutton had spoken. She arched an eyebrow at the same time that her hips moved in a slow circle, and Sutton's mouth fell open at how indescribably good it felt. To feel how turned on Charlotte was, to know that *she* caused it.

"I am," Charlotte agreed, her voice so low Sutton hardly heard it. "You know," she started, before pausing to take Sutton's hand in hers and guiding it back to her chest. She took Sutton's hand and mimicked the way she'd touched Sutton's chest. Sutton quickly did it herself, though, and she relished in the way Charlotte's head fell back on a moan, before she kept talking, "Last week, you thought I didn't want you. But I was so close –" she broke off and started a new rhythm with her hips.

Sutton could feel her clit dragging over her thigh and she experimentally shifted up into Charlotte. And was rewarded with Charlotte's breath hitching, and Sutton wasn't even sure she would remember how to talk because she knew for a fact now that she'd never been more turned on in her life than at this moment.

Charlotte let out a shuddering breath. "I was so close, and I was moving like this, against you, as I made you come. You have no idea how close I was to coming just like this." Her breath ghosted over Sutton's mouth as she finished, "It won't take me long tonight."

She leaned her head a fraction back from where she'd been watching the way Charlotte's hips rolled, and met her gaze. The look she was giving her was heavily lidded, and her hand threaded through Sutton's hair as she leaned in, tracing over Sutton's ear with her tongue and making her shiver, before murmuring, "Put your hand between my legs. I want to come with you inside me."

It was Sutton's turn to moan now as she slowly slid her hand down. She stroked her fingers over the top of Charlotte, just above her clit, and felt her shudder. Then she lifted her hips just a bit and Sutton hesitated, moving her head back to make eye contact with Charlotte again.

Who gave her a patient smile, despite the need that was evident on her features, before she reached down and met Sutton's hand with her own. Charlotte whispered, "Two fingers."

Sutton quickly obliged.

And Charlotte shifted again and Sutton's fingers were engulfed in wet heat. They both groaned, and held still for a beat.

Then Charlotte's hand held onto Sutton's shoulder as her forehead fell onto Sutton's, eyes staring intensely into hers. She moved her hand as best as she thought she should as Charlotte moved over her.

She never heard a better sound than the whimpers that left Charlotte's throat, and she felt conflicted because she wanted to kiss her, but she didn't want her to stop making those amazing sounds. It was solved for her when Charlotte's eyes went bleary and snapped shut, as she tilted her head and moved in for a kiss, speeding up her hips.

Working her tongue into Charlotte's mouth and her fingers into her heat, she felt wetness drip down her hand. Sutton didn't know if she'd ever felt better in her entire life.

Which, then she shifted her hand so that her palm bumped against Charlotte's clit and their kiss was broken because of the strangled cry working out of Charlotte's throat, so *yes*, that was even better.

311

"Fuck – *yes*, Sutton, keep doing that," Charlotte urged her breathlessly.

She maneuvered her hand so that she could rub Charlotte's clit every time she thrust her hips down. She was rewarded by the volume of the sounds that started to fall from her mouth, and how every breath Charlotte took in was more ragged than the last.

Around her fingers, she could feel Charlotte tightening and it was... she wanted to keep doing this. She wanted to feel this, to make Charlotte clench around her. It was with that thought that she used her thigh to push up her hand as Charlotte moved down.

Immediately, a choked cry broke from Charlotte and the hand she had braced on her shoulder tightened in a vice grip. She was coming, hard, even more wetness coating her fingers, now dripping down her wrist, and she rubbed her clit slowly, the way she would to herself.

Which seemed to be the right thing to do, as Charlotte let out a long, shuddering moan and slowly worked her hips with Sutton's hand as she came down, occasionally jerking against her.

Sutton's heart was thundering in her ears in tandem with the way she could feel Charlotte's beating as her body slumped against her chest. They stayed there for a few long moments, with Charlotte's forehead having fallen onto Sutton's shoulder. When Sutton got over her dazedness, she had the sense of mind to reach up with the hand that wasn't currently still between Charlotte's legs to gently rub at her back.

Which caused Charlotte to let out a weak chuckle that only lasted for a second before she husked out, "Mmm, scoot so we can lay down."

Sutton bit her lip before she slowly adjusted her thigh so that she could move her hand away from Charlotte, who let out a small groan at the feeling. Then she did as Charlotte wanted, scooting down on the bed enough so that she could lie back. Charlotte rolled off of her and onto her back.

Sutton missed the warmth but then moved up onto her side, leaning on her elbow so she could look down at Charlotte. Who was lying on the bed with one arm flung over her eyes and a pleased, calm look on her face, brown hair a tumble of curls all over her pillow, and Sutton felt a disbelieving giggle work its way out of her throat.

She didn't even try to stop when Charlotte dragged her arm from her face, her eyes opened – still a little hazy – and she asked, "What's so funny?"

"It's, um, nothing," she shook her head, the hair that had fallen over her shoulder moving over the sheets with the movement.

But . . . she'd realized as she took in Charlotte's dreamy, relaxed face and even the way her voice was just a little slower, a little more lethargic, that she did it. She'd not only found out how to make Charlotte's stunning brain shut off, but she'd caused it.

Sutton had never felt particularly confident in areas that involved sex; it just never felt quite right. But at that moment, as she was in Charlotte's luxuriously comfortable sheets, settled on her side, with one hand still resting on Charlotte's leanly-muscled thigh and wearing only a pair of lacy black underwear that were now ridiculously wet... she felt relaxed enough to smile and not even want to hide at the way Charlotte's eyes dipped to her chest as she laughed.

There really was a first time for everything, she supposed.

Her quiet laughter fell away when the cloudiness that had settled in Charlotte's eyes with her orgasm fell away and instead big, brown eyes flickered from her breasts to her eyes, darkened with arousal.

Her breath caught on an excited gasp when Charlotte's hand came up and her fingers scratched lightly over Sutton's hip, before settling there and pushing as she herself rolled. Her eyes widened as she found herself on her back, staring up at Charlotte in anticipation. Charlotte's gaze bore down on her as she rocked her hips, and Sutton's breath caught in her throat.

There were very exciting times for everything, she realized, and she was looking forward to all of them.

Chapter 14

Charlotte stared intently at her computer screen, eyes narrowed in thought, as she watched Naomi Young's interview from that morning for approximately the fifth time.

She'd figured that something like this was coming; her own ad campaign had started with a bang last week and she'd already done two interviews with reporters. Naomi Young was many things but she certainly wasn't going to sit back while Charlotte started to surge ahead. She'd *known* that, of course, so this wasn't shocking.

So, no, she hadn't been caught off guard, but Naomi had made her first strike. Which meant that it was important to be vigilant now even more than before. Even though her eyes were burning just a little bit from focusing so intently on the computer, she couldn't stop herself from watching the screen as she tapped her pen against a pad of paper.

She'd been writing down notes on everything she'd noticed. About what Naomi said, how she said it, the tone, which words were used – which words *weren't*. Notes about her body language, her clothes, how long her smiles lasted. Everything she could, so that when she went to the impromptu meeting she'd called with her staff tomorrow, they could talk about all of these details.

The day had started out normal. She'd come into work a little earlier than eight in the morning, and the interview hadn't aired until after nine. She'd already been entrenched in her work day and was in the middle of reading through a large proposal from a food bank when the surprise interview had aired.

She'd watched it, her mind torn between doing the work that she had to finish and wanting to inspect every detail of the interview.

Even as she'd gotten the rest of her work done throughout the day, it had inevitably been on her mind. Enough so that she'd re-watched it again at lunch, which was when she'd first started taking notes.

It wasn't like anything was explicitly or obviously out of place. Naomi was nicely dressed, her hair and makeup done well – typical. She smiled when she should smile; granted, Charlotte could see the butter-wouldn't-melt-in-my-mouth fakeness even through her computer. She looked. . . as sympathetic as Charlotte thought she was capable of looking when they spoke of her deceased husband. She was well-spoken, though not as well-spoken as Charlotte thought of herself.

She talked somewhat about her "platform" though the issues she was tackling were of less immediate value and importance than what Charlotte was taking a stance on.

All of the points lined up to where Charlotte could have predicted they would – except for one.

Her.

When it came to Charlotte herself, Naomi was much less heavy-handed in her insults than expected. Of course there were some barbed remarks concerning her youth relative to "inexperience," some comments about her grandmother, a remark about her photoshoot, and they were all decently innocent. Nothing especially nasty. And, beyond that there was nothing.

If it had been an interview done by someone else – nearly any other opponent, really – that wouldn't have been concerning. That would have aligned exactly where she might have expected.

However, if Charlotte knew anything about Naomi Young, it was that she most definitely was not in the business of pulling any punches when it came to getting what she wanted. And so, that wouldn't stop gnawing at the back of her mind; something else was happening or was in the works, she was sure of it.

But campaigns couldn't be run based on intuitive feelings, as her grandmother would tell her. And even though she knew it was getting a little late and that she *should* leave – try to rest and relax as much as she could – her brain just wouldn't stop.

Blowing out a sigh, Charlotte shook her head and brought her hands up, rubbing them over her face and then scooping them back through her hair. She knew she wasn't overlooking anything. Couldn't be. Still –

The multiple vibrations of her phone pulled her away from her thoughts, and quickly she reached for it. She'd contacted Aaron a few hours ago about her niggling feeling, and despite the fact that he'd answered only to say they would discuss it in person tomorrow, she couldn't help but think maybe he found something already.

It took her a moment in all of her anticipation of news about Naomi's campaign to realize that the texts weren't, in fact, from Aaron or anyone else on her staff, but Sutton.

Sutton – 8:13PM
Hey! I just had dinner and watched Naomi's
interview with a friend . . .

Sutton – 8:14PM
How are you feeling about it? I know you
said earlier that you needed to ruminate on it
before figuring out what you thought.

At that, a small smile tugged at her mouth because of course Sutton thought about that. Her phone had gone off like crazy right after her family and coworkers had gotten wind of the interview. And though she had only answered a select few, Sutton had been one of them.

Sutton who, unlike the texts that she'd received from everyone else, first and foremost asked how she was feeling. Because of course she did. But at the time, Charlotte hadn't had any time to process.

316

Sutton – 8:14PM
I was thinking you could come over when you
left the office and we could talk about it and
watch a movie.

Sutton – 8:15PM
Just, you know, because we haven't hung out
"as friends" as much lately. But it's okay if the
interview has you too busy!

Sutton was right; they hadn't hung out "as friends" very much since they'd agreed to be friends with benefits. Even though it was *Rule Number 1*, it had been somewhat neglected. Granted, with everything going on – not only with Charlotte's own schedule but with Sutton's end of semester coming up – they'd only seen each other three times in the last two weeks.

And every time had been about sex, or, at the very least, involving sex.

Charlotte wouldn't – couldn't – complain about that, either. It would be impossible to, because sex with Sutton every single time was enlightening.

She'd gotten to know the way Sutton's thighs trembled and tightened around her head when she was about to come. When she could *feel* that Sutton was trying to still hold on to control, but couldn't. She'd become intimately familiar with the breathy sounds that escaped from the back of Sutton's throat when she was *just* about to let go. She'd learned several of the spots that made Sutton go weak, the spots that made her hips jerk against Charlotte's with want.

She knew what it was to take Sutton slowly, to walk her through what she was doing. To tease – just a little. She'd ventured last time into fucking her faster and harder, and had been shocked when after Sutton had screamed for her, she'd immediately pulled her up to sit on her face.

317

She'd never had this wanting, this craving of having more sex and in all kinds of positions with the same person, especially after having already had sex with her. It was . . . heady.

And while all of that aspect was new for her, the entire sleeping with women aspect was new to Sutton. Who was more than eager and excited to try new things, to explore Charlotte's body. Her touches could be both hesitant and bold. Curious and intuitive. She was *so* open for Charlotte to tell her exactly what she wanted and what she needed. How and when and where she wanted Sutton's fingers and mouth; she was so ridiculously receptive.

Even though it had only been a few times that Sutton had touched her, she was quite the fast learner and somewhat of a perfectionist. They'd been charming traits when Sutton was just her friend, but introducing that into a sex life was –

Amazing.

And there was still so much Sutton had yet to experience, that the thought of it all made Charlotte's stomach dip in anticipation.

Blinking down at the messages before she leaned back in her chair, she realized that the heaviness weighing on her shoulders that had been there all day had somewhat melted away, replaced instead with thoughts of Sutton.

The fact that there was an actual *want* inside of her to go see Sutton and to give her mind a break from re-watching the interview yet again confirmed that having Sutton as a friend was something she'd never experienced before with anyone else.

Charlotte – 8:18PM
That sounds perfect. My head needs a break from watching this too much. Maybe a fresh point of view will give me a better focus.

318

She put her phone down on the desk before drumming her fingers for a moment, her eyes skipping back up to land once more on Naomi's face on the screen. They narrowed for a moment, her face pinching in annoyance once again because – *what was it?*

A few moments beat by before she hummed under her breath, slowly closing out of the internet browser and rolling her shoulders. What she thought bothered her the most about Naomi's interview, if she had to put it into words, was that there was something so obviously *not* going on, that it made her positive that Naomi was up to something.

And she knew that sounded ludicrous, but she just . . . knew that it was also the truth.

As she let out a deep breath, she forced herself to shut down her laptop and reached into her desk to get her purse before locking the drawer. It was pointless to let her mind run around in circles even more when she had no new information and no new eyes on the situation.

She stood, slipping into her jacket. First, the lighter one that she'd originally grabbed out of her coat closet – a dark blue one that went seamlessly over her dress, running just a bit longer than her others typically did, but it actually really worked for her. More for style than for weather protection. Then she reached for the heavier coat that she'd worn on top of the first when she'd realized exactly how cold it was.

It wasn't until the backs of her fingers brushed up against the lighter jacket as she zipped up the heavier one that she froze as the realization hit her: this was Sutton's jacket. The one that Sutton had left at her home in a hurry after they'd first had sex, a little over a month ago, now.

She'd had it in her mind to return it. Well, initially she'd had it in her mind to return it. But then they'd gotten distracted and this jacket had somehow seamlessly blended into her wardrobe with her own.

Which was actually a little strange, if she thought about the fact that for so long – her entire life – everything that was in her space was *hers*. There'd never been someone to have any mix-ups with.

And for a moment, she paused as she wondered about the possible implications about this. About wearing another woman's clothes, about another woman's clothes blending with her own.

But it only lasted for a moment, before she shook her head slightly, brown curls falling over her shoulders. Because all it meant was that Sutton was . . . Sutton. Her friend, the closest one she'd ever had, and that entailed things that Charlotte just wasn't used to.

Which apparently meant that one of said bonuses was stylish items unwittingly added to her wardrobe. She could get used to that part.

"No wonder I've only seen you twice in the last few weeks; you're apparently turning into a mole-woman who sleeps at work," Caleb's voice came from next to her and she turned sharply as her stomach jumped, eyes widened in surprise.

Her brother was dressed similarly in his own heavy winter jacket, though his was also joined with a hat that made her immediate smile grow even wider, fondness rushing through her. She *hadn't* seen her brother that much lately and texting wasn't the same.

Still, she rolled her eyes mockingly. "Sure, blame *me*, and not the fact that you've been working the night shift and sleeping during the day."

His eyes sparkled back at her in mirth as he walked closer, wrapping her in a quick, warm hug. "I've worked the night beat before and we've had time together. But suddenly my sister is becoming a bigshot, and I have to rely on my boyfriend for updates."

"Drama queen," she shot back as she shook her head, unable to wipe the smile from her face, as she reached for her purse that was still settled on her desk. "I hope you didn't come to try to kidnap me for drinks, though. I have plans tonight."

Caleb eyed her phone with interest, eyes still alight with amusement. "Oh, so you're *too busy* to spend a night out with your only brother –"

"I wonder how William would feel about being cut out from our family tree," she cut him off, tapping her finger to her chin, deadpanning.

He exaggeratedly waved her off, "You didn't let me finish – only brother who lives near you. I should have said closest brother in retrospect. Either way, you're working such long hours that you barely had enough time to have dinner with me the other night, but you're going to see Sutton tonight . . . interesting," he mused, his voice lofty.

Charlotte tilted her head, lifting her eyebrow in a challenge. "And your point is?"

He let out a dramatically aghast breath, pointing his finger at her in triumph. "I just want you to *admit* that she's your girlfriend! There's no shame, Charlie."

She narrowed her eyes at him, scoffing as she reached up to bat his accusing finger away. "Honestly, Caleb, you're acting like *you've* never had a friends with benefits situation before. There's no girlfriend to speak of."

From over his shoulder, she saw Dean approaching after locking the door to his office and she shot him a quick grin, colored in the exasperation she was feeling for her brother.

The appearance of his boyfriend didn't deter Caleb, however.

"No girlfriend? *No girlfriend?* But – about this tall." He held his hand up, waving it right under his own eye level. "Long red hair? Blue eyes? You've been having sex with her regularly, have an emotional attachment –"

Her mouth fell open in indignation. "*Friends* with *benefits*! Everything you just said is right there!"

"Yeah, friends with benefits is one thing. But one that's exclusive, with sleepovers . . . it's pushing the line," he kept his voice light and teasing but there was an underlying seriousness that she couldn't help but notice and it put her just the littlest bit on edge. "Sounds like a girlfriend to me. What do you think, Dean?"

Caleb turned teasing, interested eyes to his boyfriend, who shot him a look, even though there was adoration in it, too. Because he was all too used to Caleb's dramatics – and he loved them. Still, he looked at Charlotte, then back, lifting his hands palms up to both of them. "I abstain."

Before her brother could continue – because he would and Charlotte just . . . she didn't want to hear it. She loved her brother, more than almost anyone in the world, but sometimes he got the wrong idea and would run with it until it was six feet under. Which he was especially doing with Sutton, now. It was simply incorrect and not what she wanted to have on her mind when she was going to visit her *friend*.

Charlotte elbowed him in the ribs, triumphantly grinning when he yelped as she changed the subject, "What are you two doing here?"

Now it was Dean who answered, his eyebrow arching in question, "No, the correct question is what are *you* doing here? You told me when I left almost two hours ago that you were leaving soon!"

She'd told him that in order to gently break him off from the concerned speech he'd been giving her about devoting too much time to working, spending too much time at the office in the last few weeks.

She gestured to the coat she'd just zipped and the purse on her other arm. "And I'm leaving now. Just finishing some stuff up."

"Watching that interview again, more like it," Caleb interjected in a conspiratorial whisper.

She didn't have any shame in that, however, and acknowledged it with a nod and a shrug. "And taking copious notes. But what about you? I didn't disrupt some sort of afterhours office rendezvous, did I?" She gave them a wink.

"One time," Dean grumbled, shaking his head.

Caleb only grinned widely, wrapping an arm around Dean's shoulders as they all started walking out of the office. "Nah, not tonight. Dean here forgot his wallet in his office, though," he ribbed. "How is my sugar daddy supposed to buy me dinner without his wallet?"

Charlotte chuckled as Dean argued, "I think that someone here is forgetting who has a trust fund."

"Please, like you'd ever allow yourself to be a kept man," she added before she took a deep breath and burrowed slightly more into her warm jacket before she prepared for the cold weather outside that was about to hit when they opened the doors.

Dean turned his incredulous look to her. "Oh, and you would ever allow yourself to be a kept woman?"

The term alone made her grimace; so far from the future she'd planned for herself. "You have a point."

But Caleb *tsk*'d at both of them. "Oh, says the workaholic who's finally taking a break to go see her woman who has marriage and children written all over her homemade baked goods."

It was pointless to argue again, even as she sighed loudly to make her displeasure known. Then again, that description did fit Sutton, Charlotte could acknowledge. It simply didn't fit *them*.

Her brother, thankfully, let it drop for now. It might have had something to do with the fact that they were about to go in the opposite direction that she took to Sutton's in order to head to the parking garage and Caleb's car. "Speaking of homemade cooking though, can I get you to leave the office in time for dinner with me this week?"

A smile made its way onto her mouth as she nodded. "Even if I have to bring it to your squad car after I leave work." She didn't lift her hands from their buried position in her pockets for warmth to offer a wave, but gave quick kisses to their cheeks. "Have a nice dinner."

"You, too," Caleb shot back, wiggling his eyebrows and this time she couldn't help but huff out a laugh as she turned away, shaking her head.

She didn't bother correcting him – because tonight wasn't about *that* – but it was better to leave it on that note than his girlfriend assertions. His completely off-base assertions, which were laughable, when she thought about it. Which she did, as she walked briskly toward Sutton's apartment building.

However Caleb wanted to misrepresent what she had going with Sutton, Charlotte was enjoying this. Enjoying the time they spent together, that she had someone who cared about her, who she cared about, but who she wasn't beholden to beyond the bounds of friendship.

It was perhaps unfamiliar to her, but it only meant something if she had intentions to let it mean something. If she had intentions of letting her endearment of Sutton and appreciation of their friendship develop further, that would mean *something* more.

They were friends and they had literal rules written to protect that status. Charlotte liked that sort of order and had no intention of messing with it.

With that in mind, she stepped into the building Sutton lived in, in a better mood than she'd been in throughout most of the day despite Naomi's interview still clinging to the back of her mind.

She slipped her hands out of her pockets, ridiculously thankful to be out of the cold air again as she unzipped her heavier winter coat and made her way down the hallway and toward the elevator.

As the elevator doors opened she moved to step in, lifting her head to give a polite nod and smile to the woman walking out of them.

However, when she got the same polite-stranger smile back and made eye contact, she paused. Eyes narrowing slightly as they trained on the face smiling back at her. Because that face . . . it was picking at something in her mind. She *recognized* that face, from somewhere.

Charlotte rarely ever forgot a face; it was somewhat of a gift, given her chosen profession. It was entirely rare for Charlotte not to be able to recall someone she'd met, even if it had only been briefly.

And this woman – young, with olive-toned skin and rich dark eyes – was attractive; someone she was fairly certain she would remember meeting. So, she deduced, that maybe they hadn't actually met. But if they hadn't met in person, Charlotte knew she'd seen her somewhere. There was something about her . . .

Nagging enough in the back of her mind that she couldn't let it go and she let the elevator doors close without getting in.

Apparently, the feeling was mutual, given that the woman was tilting her head to the side in a speculative look that made Charlotte straighten her spine and set her jaw. It was a look that she didn't like at all; she couldn't place it immediately, but whatever it was about this woman made the faintest distaste run up the back of her throat.

That feeling only intensified when those dark eyes took on a glint, an accompanying smirk sliding over her face, as she looked Charlotte up and down. "*Oh.*"

It was that irritating smirk that gave her what she needed to place her face. This was the woman that she'd seen on Sutton's phone. The one who had sought Sutton out on social media, who had given Sutton her number at speed dating. The woman who Charlotte likened to somewhat of a vulture, seeking out pretty girls who seemed out of their element.

Alia Haddad. That name seemed burned into her brain for some reason.

Alia Haddad, who now ran her eyes over Charlotte's – Sutton's – jacket, and lifted a knowing eyebrow. Of course, because Sutton had been wearing this very jacket that night that she'd gone to that speed dating event. The thought of it made her clench her jaw for a moment, before she very deliberately released it.

"Coming to see our friend Sutton?" Alia positively drawled out, and Charlotte could not stand the excitement in her tone.

She allowed a slow smile to slide onto her face, knowing it was sharp and a bit feral, but not nearly as much as she could have let it be. Just enough, because the way she placed an emphasis on *our friend* gave Charlotte the worst feeling in her stomach. As if Sutton was her *friend* in the same way she was Charlotte's, which . . .

Sutton was a great friend. She'd seen that with Regan, and a bit with her friend Emma in the very limited time she'd met the other woman a couple weeks ago. But they didn't give her this feeling that – that she didn't want to name, but she didn't enjoy it.

Instead, she hummed in confirmation. "Yes, here to see my friend, Sutton," she found it necessary to repeat, before feigning ignorance. "I'm sorry, I didn't catch your name?"

"Alia. Haddad." She didn't offer her hand, for which Charlotte was grateful because etiquette demanded she would have to shake it, but she had no desire to do so. She tilted her head to the side, though, appraising Charlotte for a few moments before her smirk widened into a delighted smile. "I've seen your ads, Miss Thompson. Very impressive; I'll be voting for you."

Those were words that *should* have felt like a compliment. She *should* be flattered and thrilled that her name was getting out there, that she was gaining voters. It *should* have felt like an opening to discuss her campaign, or at the very least to thank her, sincerely.

Since she'd announced her campaign, that was exactly the response that comments like that she'd received so far had inspired.

Instead of the other times she'd heard similar words, this time they felt loaded. Loaded, because Alia must have been the friend Sutton had mentioned in her text that she'd watched Naomi's interview with, because apparently they'd been hanging out. And in a ludicrous feeling that Charlotte didn't enjoy in the least, she suddenly wished that she'd been the one to watch the interview with Sutton.

She quirked an eyebrow. "Thank you. Do you have an interest in politics, then?"

Alia shrugged, that damnably easygoing smile staying secure on her face. "Not really, actually. But I have a friend or two who are interested, so I keep current."

Yes, Charlotte would just bet that she had *a friend* who was interested in politics. A friend who lived in this very building, who had told Charlotte that the only reason she had such a vested interest in this current election was because *Charlotte* was running.

It was something that shouldn't matter at all but at this moment, faced with Alia Haddad, it did.

Because even if Sutton was wonderfully and beautifully naïve about some things, including her own charm, Charlotte certainly wasn't. And she'd pegged Alia's interest even before she'd had this face-to-face with her.

"I'm glad you have some *friends* who are so current, then – it's good for me and my business. I hope it makes you feel better knowing that you're giving your vote to a candidate who truly cares about invested constituents." She lifted her eyebrow and hoped that her meaning was clear. Her meaning that Sutton was her business, and that should any such vulture come sniffing around, Charlotte – who was likely more experienced and was even more protective than she'd thought she would be – would be there.

It didn't make Alia falter and that in and of itself set Charlotte on edge even more. "Oh, I do feel better about that, believe me. I also find myself invested in some of your constituents." She quirked her eyebrow. "Speaking of, Sutton's waiting for you upstairs, and I'm running a little late. Got a little caught up hanging out upstairs; you know how that can be. Lost track of time and all."

The heavy, dark feeling that sluiced through her and settled thickly in the pit of her stomach was unmistakable as jealousy. Despite the fact that her brushes with the feeling in terms of her personal life were very limited, she would be ignorant to let herself believe anything else.

She refused to focus on it as she made sure the smile remained on her face, as unstrained as it could possibly be. Silently, she thanked her ability to maintain composure in any situation. "Absolutely, I don't want to make you run late, nor do I want to keep Sutton waiting. Have a good night."

"Oh, you too," Alia shot back, before she glided by Charlotte, who watched her for a moment with narrowed eyes before jamming her finger at the elevator button again, unintentionally a little too hard.

The ride up and walk down Sutton's hallway was altogether too fast as her mind processed this uncomfortable, unfamiliar feeling. It wasn't as though she had the right to tell Sutton who to talk to or be friends with – or even that she wanted to! Sutton was a grown woman – a grown, intelligent woman who had her own agency and her own decisions to make, at that.

But – Alia. Charlotte couldn't shake that nagging feeling that Alia wanted Sutton the exact same way she did. And who wouldn't? Sutton was gorgeous, smart, and inspired feelings of endearment and affection effortlessly.

As she pursed her lips in thought, she gave a brisk knock on the door. Alia Haddad, regardless of how much Charlotte inherently didn't trust or like her, wasn't the problem here. Other people were always going to find Sutton attractive or want to be with her. That was fine; great.

The problem was that Charlotte didn't enjoy this feeling, not just the jealousy but the little part of her brain that wondered –

Her thoughts cut off as the door swung open and she was facing the woman in question. The woman who was wearing jeans with one of the long, comfortable sweaters Charlotte had come to learn Sutton favored in the winter.

She wore bright yellow socks and the sight of them made Charlotte's mood inexplicably brighten, just a bit, before she tracked her eyes back up Sutton's body. Her hair was tossed into a quick and messy bun, some strands falling out, but it was the smile that slid across Sutton's face – bright and instant – that warmed Charlotte right down to her toes.

"Hey! Come in." Sutton quickly stepped back, eyes sparkling in amusement that Charlotte couldn't overlook even despite that feeling in her stomach that was like a lead weight. "Two coats, lightweight?"

Still, the smile on her face wasn't forced like it had been earlier with Alia, because she couldn't resist the surge of genuine fondness that she felt with Sutton. "Funny," she allowed, teasingly.

Sutton's laugh was light as she turned on her socked heel and started walking down the hall, leading their way into the kitchen. "So, I made a pot roast for dinner a little while ago. I have some leftovers. Regan's working late tonight, so there's some for her, but there's more than enough for you. It's good to warm you up," she added earnestly.

She was just so . . . sweet. Charlotte registered that as she shut the door behind her and followed Sutton into the kitchen. She took in the slow sway of Sutton's hips as she made her way into the kitchen, her eyes watching just a moment too long for their *just friends* night.

Sutton had made dinner for herself and Alia, most likely. She pursed her lips at the idea. "Maybe in a little while; I'm not feeling too hungry right now, darling."

She had been hungry earlier, she realized with a bit of surprise. She'd been hungry even while she'd been entrenched in watching Naomi's interview. Even when she'd been in her earlier thoughtful and suspicious mood, she would have gratefully taken any of the delicious food she'd come to expect when Sutton cooked.

But that run-in with Alia was enough to take away her appetite.

Sutton's eyebrows drew together as she turned to give Charlotte a concerned look. "Really? I assumed you hadn't eaten since lunch. Are – the interview," she surmised, shaking her head at herself. "Such an idiot. I'm sorry."

Charlotte would have laughed if she felt like delving into detail about what was going on in her mind. If she thought she could – or *should* – explain to Sutton what she was feeling.

Then again, that was one of the things Sutton had said to her in the past. That she didn't want Charlotte to hide her thoughts, so with a deep breath, she started to speak slowly. Deliberately. "I ran into Alia in the lobby. I didn't know you two were . . . friends."

She didn't know that she'd ever have another reason beyond work to use her Politician Voice. The tone that she'd perfectly crafted over the years to sound perfectly normal and unaffected, where only her family could hear the subtle difference – if any – between it and her casual voice.

Yet, here she was. Glad to be able to disguise her . . . *damn it*, her ridiculous jealousy. That was the only word she could find for it at this point. That angrily hot and sinking feeling in her stomach and the matching gripping at the back of her throat at that stupid, knowing smirk on Alia's face. She was *jealous*.

Because Alia wanted Sutton – whether or not Sutton knew it, though Charlotte was fairly certain that Alia wasn't the type to keep her motives a secret.

Sutton's eyes widened, her words coming out in a rushed ramble, "Well, we're not really that good of friends yet, but we met for coffee a few days ago – remember, the day I texted you about the place near your work? And then we just started talking. She's nice, though. Funny, and –" Sutton abruptly cut herself off, her cheeks flushing deeply. "I guess, I mean. Yeah. We're friends."

It was in the way her cheeks flushed that made Charlotte's stomach clench tightly again, and with it an unmistakable and sudden urge to touch Sutton. Which was – it was illogical. It wasn't as though Charlotte couldn't control herself and her wants and needs.

But it was the fact that Sutton was blushing when she mentioned Alia almost in the way that she did when Charlotte flirted with her sometimes or when Charlotte winked at her or when Charlotte bit at the spot under her ear that gave her this *wanting*.

The need to push every thought of Alia Haddad out of Sutton's beautiful mind and replace it with herself. To put Sutton in the frame of mind where she was gasping out Charlotte's name the way she did right before she made her come.

"Um, why?" Sutton asked, her hands coming out in front of her and twisting together.

Charlotte didn't want to think too much about the fact that while Sutton was exploring sex, she wanted her to be just exploring with her. But it was absolutely the truth.

It hadn't occurred to her until that moment that her brother had used the word exclusive for them. And even though that had never been a word that Charlotte had applied to herself in terms of romantic or sexual liaisons, she realized that she hadn't even thought twice about it at the time. Because a part of her had assumed, when Sutton had been so adamant that *she* be the one to "show her the ropes," that she would be the only one.

She hadn't known until this moment how much she liked that idea. How much she'd been enjoying being the only one in Sutton's life in that capacity – for now – the way Sutton was the only one in hers.

She'd never been known to not go after what she wanted. Within proper parameters, naturally, which was what made her draw in a deep breath before releasing it slowly. She'd hoped it would give her a bit of clarity of mind, but instead all she was still thinking about was Sutton backed against the wall and melting under her hands.

It didn't work, and she felt the desire pool low in her stomach before she cleared her throat. "Sutton . . . do you still have that list of rules?"

Sutton gave her a confused look. "What –" before she cut herself off, blushing again as she nodded. "Uh, yeah. In my bedroom. Do you want it? Or to change something?" Her voice slowed and lowered as she asked. And she was so easy to read that Charlotte could essentially read the way doubts formed in her mind.

Instead of answering directly though, she stepped closer, slipping out of her heels as she did. She slipped the jackets off of her shoulders too and enjoyed the way Sutton's eyes watched the motion. "You could say that."

She lifted an eyebrow, before she reached up to her own hair, running her hand through the curls to shake them out. She then dragged her fingertips deliberately over her throat and collarbone before dropping them back to her side.

And Sutton watched her, taking in the motion as Charlotte could see her thickly swallow and a flush spread over her neck and cheeks. Satisfaction teamed up with the desire she felt striking through her.

She dropped her hands to Sutton's hips, and they walked a step back until Sutton was pressed against the wall. Deftly, she dipped her hands under the hem of Sutton's sweater, running them up so that her thumbs could swipe over the soft skin of Sutton's waist. She could feel Sutton's goosebumps; she smirked as she leaned in a little closer, moving her nose along Sutton's neck and taking a moment to enjoy the scent of her lotion.

Feeling Sutton shiver, she dropped her mouth in a light kiss against the soft, warm skin. "I think –" She placed another kiss, this time her mouth open and letting herself enjoy the taste of Sutton's skin for a few seconds. "– we should –" She moved up, nipping her teeth at Sutton's earlobe. "– add a rule."

It was in the easy way that Sutton melted back against the wall that sent another, deeper thrill through her. The need to take Sutton, to make sure that she was the only one to do this . . . it was all she could think of now.

But she wanted Sutton to think of this with a clear head, so she pulled back, scratching her nails down Sutton's sides for a moment before she made herself stop.

Big blue eyes were dark and they blinked at her slowly. A flush of arousal moved over her cheeks as Charlotte could feel her chest starting to heave with deep, heavy breaths, their chests brushing through their clothes. "Uh – I'm . . . um, what rule?"

"That for as long as we're sleeping together, we're the only ones. I won't sleep with anyone else, and neither will you," she clarified, her fingers itching to touch all of that soft, smooth skin again.

Sutton's eyebrows hitched in confusion as she licked her lips. Charlotte's throat felt dry as she watched it.

"I didn't . . . you were already the only one I wanted to – to have sex with," she murmured, eyes locked on Charlotte's, where she could read the raw honesty.

The groan in the back of Charlotte's throat surprised herself but it felt so damn satisfying to hear those words. One of her hands came to grip at curved hips under Sutton's shirt, while the other came up to slide into the soft hair that was still tied up in a bun. She used her grip to pull Sutton down as she surged up, her stomach twisting in anticipation.

Her mouth parted as soon as she made contact with Sutton's, licking into her mouth, as she scratched her hand up and down Sutton's side. Softly at first, the way she usually did, because she loved the way it made Sutton shudder lightly against her.

And then she let herself feel the still very present lingering jealousy in the pit of her stomach, and she scratched a little harder, her fingers leaving a mark on Sutton's body as she sucked at her tongue.

She *wanted*, she wanted to feel Sutton against her fast and hard and right here against her kitchen wall. Wanted to make her come around her fingers, to feel her clenching for her, hear her crying out for her. Right here, right now.

Before she could check with Sutton, though – because this wasn't what they'd done so far; she'd kept a leash on the more immediate needs like this with Sutton – she heard a low moan come from the back of Sutton's throat as her hips jumped against Charlotte's fingers, pushing against her own.

She quickly pushed back, pressing her hips to Sutton's and then forcing her back against the wall. She stayed there, slotting her thigh as well as she could between Sutton's, given that she was still wearing her dress and Sutton her jeans. For a moment, she regretted taking off her heels; she wanted to be taller now.

To be able to feel how hot she knew Sutton was for her already even between their clothes. To be able to give better friction for Sutton to grind against, not to mention how ridiculously hot the mental image was for her to imagine her fucking Sutton senseless while still in her dress and heels from work.

The thought alone made her groan into Sutton's mouth, and in return, she felt Sutton whimper before her hips ground down against Charlotte as best as she could but it wasn't enough. Not for either of them, and she pulled back, dragging her teeth over Sutton's bottom lip as she went, relishing in the shiver she got in response.

Sutton's hands moved, jumping to life, one digging into Charlotte's waist. The other sliding under her hair and onto her neck in a possessive way that might leave a bit of a mark, and it shot another spark down Charlotte's spine.

She ran her fingertips down over the soft skin of Sutton's stomach, feeling the muscles jump under her before she stroked just above Sutton's jeans. A mischievous smile tugged at her mouth when she heard the gasp Sutton let out and see the way Sutton's head fell back against the wall.

Charlotte leaned in again, this time using her tongue to run along Sutton's neck before she panted softly in her own need to *take*, "I want you," she dropped her hand lower, tracing up the tight jeans covering Sutton's inner thigh before pressing against the fabric covering her center. She rubbed, hard, her own breath coming out in quick, breathless pants along with Sutton's, even as she used her body to press against Sutton's, "Now. Not soft and slow, not stripped in your bed. I want to make you come right here, darling. Is that okay?"

She took her hand away, sliding up to hesitate over the button of the jeans, wanting nothing more than to slip inside but waiting . . .

Sutton nodded quickly; so fast that Charlotte might have been amused if she wasn't so – fuck – turned on herself. Her eyes were heavily lidded as they fluttered open and caught Charlotte's own, "I want – yes. Now."

∗∗∗

It was hours later, after they'd moved from the kitchen to the bedroom, after she'd made Sutton come again, and had the favor returned – twice, while also learning that Sutton not only enjoyed being taken *hard and fast* but she was also pretty amazing at giving it – that they laid in Sutton's bed.

She thought it was past midnight, but she couldn't be sure; from where she was lying on her side, she couldn't see any sort of clock. And her body felt too nice to move. Too *fucked*, really. But her brain was kicking back into high gear.

She was too well-fucked to do anything but wonder aloud, "So, you watched the interview?"

The chuckle that Sutton let out from next to her was indolent, red hair finally free and loose – a waterfall along the sheets behind her as she faced Charlotte. "Of course you think about that right now."

"Quite frankly, darling, I think it's a bit impressive that you managed to stop me from thinking about it for hours," she shot back, her own voice marginally more awake. Then again, sometimes that happened.

Sex was a stress relief for her, of course. And in this case, that had been so good she now felt somewhat wired. Like . . . she could take on the world. From the bed, anyway.

In an entirely amusing shy way, Sutton readjusted the blanket that rested over her torso, tucking her arm under it and against her chest. But Charlotte could tell in the way she did it that she was feeling pleased and proud, "That's true. But yeah, I watched the interview. She was good. You're better, though."

Her words weren't meant to be flattery; she could hear the honest, earnest tone that Sutton so often managed to have, and she didn't know when she came to enjoy that so much – to almost rely on it – but she had.

"Thanks," she whispered, before dark eyes narrowed, and she wondered for a moment if she should confide what she'd been thinking about Naomi earlier. Because it might be easier not to and to wait until tomorrow to talk about it

335

with her team first, but . . . she wanted to know what Sutton thought. "I got the feeling while I was watching it that there's something going on – behind the scenes. About me," she clarified. "She just . . . you *know* Naomi. You know her. She was fairly decent, almost, about me, all things considered."

And she hoped – God, she hoped – that it wasn't her reading too much into anything. That her instincts were on track.

"I think you're right," Sutton murmured, her voice getting sluggish and drowsy in a way that made Charlotte want to grin, soft and slow right back.

And she did, even though it was a little brighter than *soft and slow*, because, "Really? You agree?" dark eyes were fully alight with interest now, her mind – despite having slowed and calmed in the last few hours, the echoing of *Sutton* and her moans and whimpers drowning out the stress of Naomi and her interview – fully functioning and thinking back to the interview once again.

Those big blue eyes blinked up at her slowly, looking somehow both serious with the conversation and adorably lethargic, "Yes? I mean, Naomi is – she's not exactly someone who doesn't have tricks up her sleeve. You're smart to think something else might be going on; you're – well, you," she added with a quick uptick to soft, pink lips.

Charlotte smiled back at her, victoriously, with this inflating warmth in her chest at the knowledge that not only was she right to be worried, but that it was Sutton who agreed. She shifted a bit, her bare back pressing against a cool pillow as she looked up at the ceiling.

Her voice was quiet as it cut through the night air, "You have no idea how glad I am that you say that. I mean, I *knew* that there has to be something else going on, but without any way to prove it right now . . . it's just nice to know that you agree. I've been going over it all day, but –" she cut herself off with a small sigh, sinking down into the pillow, "And this isn't the best conversation to have right before bed, so maybe we can resume over coffee."

She turned her head to look at Sutton, and instead of seeing sleepy eyes looking back at her, she was met with soft, deep, even breaths as the younger

336

girl curled in on her side. It made Charlotte smile softly; this wasn't the first time that she'd seen Sutton sleeping.

Since they'd started this friends with benefits agreement, they'd stayed true to the rule where Sutton would spend the night at her place. Though she was sure now that Sutton wasn't going to leave in tears or worried about Charlotte not wanting her, because *that would be impossible*, they still stuck with the rule.

And it really wasn't bad when Sutton spent the night with her, despite having avoided any sleepovers with women at her apartment. She didn't steal blankets or sprawl over the bed, and she didn't really move all that much in her sleep or snore loudly. She generally fell asleep a little sooner than Charlotte did, but Charlotte was usually fairly soon after.

Plus, Sutton woke up even earlier than she did and slipped out of her bed seamlessly, made sure her coffeemaker was working, and went back to her own apartment before Charlotte was fully awake.

She was an unobtrusive morning guest and Charlotte appreciated that.

Dark eyes roamed soft and pretty sleeping features, the way Sutton's chest rose and fell under her blanket, the way her fingers rested on the pillow under her head. Like she'd tried to stay up and listen to Charlotte but couldn't stay awake.

Which was unbelievably sweet and very much *Sutton*, and that little rush of affection hit her again.

And even though they'd spent the night together, even though Charlotte had had "sleepovers" with Sutton now, this felt different somehow. It was different . . . because this was the first night that Charlotte was spending not in her own bed.

She'd had sex with women not in her bed – it was preferable that way, because then she could leave. She liked to leave after; their beds didn't feel as comfortable as her own did to actually sleep in, she liked her own space, and waking up around her own things.

But here she was. In Sutton's bed. Feeling warm and comfortable and like . . . she wouldn't mind falling asleep here and waking up in the morning, despite not having her own things around her.

That thought, however, wasn't warm and comfortable. In fact, it took the warmth right out of her, and instead, she sat farther up against the pillow. Her hand came up, running through her hair wincing as her fingers snagged on her curls, even as she shook her head at herself.

This was – it was normal. Despite the fact that she didn't have many close friends, she did have at the very least Dean. And she'd spent a few nights at his place. Had felt . . . comfortable there. This was essentially the same thing, enjoying the warmth of Sutton's bed and the subtle, enticing, now-familiar scent of her surrounding her in the blankets.

Her eyes narrowed as she looked down at Sutton, who was curled a little closer to Charlotte now. And – all she needed was some water. Just a glass of water, and then she would follow Rule 4, the sleepover rule, and leave in the morning, early and unobtrusive and happy to go back to her own bed. Alone.

Like usual.

Because sleeping in the soft, warm, comfortable, nice-smelling bed of your friends-with-benefits friend wasn't anything strange. It shouldn't make her feel freaked out at all.

She repeated that to herself as she slipped out of bed as quietly as she could. Her eyes adjusted enough in the dark room to find the sweater that Sutton had been wearing before she'd hurriedly tugged it off, and she pulled it over her head. Which, wearing her clothes also wasn't strange. No, it wasn't the same casual thing as wearing her jacket, but what was she supposed to do? Put her own dress back on just to go get some water?

No, she assured herself, because that wasn't how these things were done.

She left Sutton's door cracked as she made her way lightly down the hall and into the kitchen. Regan had gotten home a few hours ago; she'd knocked on Sutton's door and made a comment about being safe and keeping the volume down, which had made Sutton blush and also shout back for her friend to mind her own business.

Which gave Charlotte even more motivation to stay quiet as she turned into the doorway to the kitchen. Because the last thing she needed at this moment was to run into Sutton's best friend and roommate who disliked her enough already, while she was having slight internal worries about staying the night.

But this was one of the reasons Charlotte had been reluctant to do this in the first place. Because she was new at this, and Charlotte didn't do well with *new* things, like spending the night in the bed of the woman who had thoroughly fucked her, even if she was friends with her.

And when she did find herself in unfamiliar situations, she liked to master them. Quickly and subtly, so that it could appear as effortless as possible. Which certainly didn't entail leaving in the middle of –

"God!" the word left her in a shout, as loud as she could manage as her breath knocked out of her, when something – something small but solid – caught her in the stomach, so fast that she hadn't seen it coming, especially in the darkened rooms.

The pain wasn't blinding by any means, but she pressed her hand there instinctively, rubbing as she tried to blink enough to adjust when the light was thrown on. Her mind on high alert as she circled around to what the hell someone was supposed to do when this was happening, but she didn't have more than a few seconds before the next attack.

She only caught a glimpse of dark brown hair before her arm was grasped, and she was pressed against the wall. An uncommon jolt of worry shot through her, mixed with the bruising force of the hand gripping her.

The brunette wasn't Regan, she realized even before her vision had reacted enough for her to see clearly in the now brightly lit kitchen. No, it was someone several inches shorter, with hair cut short and a bit choppy, who was barefoot and wearing old sweatpants. She was shorter than Charlotte herself, but even when her other hand came up to push at her shoulder automatically

339

trying to distance herself and *get away*, the girl's slight frame didn't move more than an inch.

Bewildered and surprised and doing her best not to panic, Charlotte pushed again, though the grip holding her only tightened as a foot wrapped around her ankle in a move she recognized from a self-defense class Caleb had gotten her to take. A move that told her that her assailant was preparing to throw her to the ground.

It had only been seconds, but Charlotte was already cursing herself for how long it took her to respond, and regardless of how quiet she'd been for the last minute or so to get into the kitchen, she shouted, "Get *away* from me, you lunatic!"

And she wondered, with glaring gray eyes looking up at her, what the fuck this was. Was this some sort of botched robbery? Barefoot thief? Escaped mental patient? Was –

The hallway light was flipped on within seconds and hurried footsteps ran down the hallway, before Charlotte turned to see Sutton – with only a sheet wrapped around her while tired but shocked eyes were now alert as she took in whatever this ridiculous situation was that was going on between Charlotte and the small attacker.

But instead of . . . anything that she could have thought might happen, Sutton didn't look panicked as though she was being robbed or as though a mentally ill person had somehow broken in. Instead, she looked surprised and confused, recognition setting in on her face.

And the would-be robber, her aggressor, didn't waver in her grip even as she shot Sutton a sharp smile.

An easy smile that didn't look at all like she had just – was currently – assaulting Charlotte while she was only wearing Sutton's long sweater in the middle of the night in her kitchen. A smile that definitely didn't belong on someone's face while they held her in an unrelenting grip, after they'd been lurking around in the dark, "Sutton! You had an intruder."

340

Charlotte grit her teeth together in irritation now, all previous worry replaced with frustration, as she tried to pull her arm out of the tight hold. Because at least now she knew that this – this insane person *knew* Sutton somehow and that she wasn't about to be murdered.

Sutton shook her head at herself before she narrowed her eyes, and *that* was most definitely an angry look, aimed at the girl. "The only intruder right now is you; get off of her!"

The short girl shrugged like this was an everyday occurrence, dropping her hand and stepping back from her. And for all Charlotte knew, this wasn't the only time something like this had happened, because who in the world was that? Charlotte felt the urge to rub at her arm where the bruising grasp had been, but she resisted for now. At least until she was out of company with this . . . person. Not until she could be alone to show that it had actually been painful.

"What are you doing here, Alex?" Sutton's voice was puzzled, and she looked a little disgruntled, before she looked to Charlotte, and she could see the worry written all over her face, "Are you okay?"

She waved her off, even though her heart was still pounding a bit in her chest from all of the . . . action, "I'm – yes, I'm quite all right," she answered in a clipped tone, hoping that they both understood it was directed at the smaller girl.

Sutton seemed like she didn't quite know where to look, before her eyes focused on something on the floor behind Charlotte, "Did you throw my peanut butter on the ground and then assault my – my friend?" She stumbled a bit at the words, her cheeks flushing, even as she sent a *look* at the younger girl.

A look that Charlotte had never seen on her face, one of familiar exasperation. She placed it in the moment that she darted her eyes to see that her assailant had thrown a jar of *peanut butter*, hitting her in the stomach, before grabbing her.

She almost wanted to laugh at . . . everything, only she was still trying to process it all.

And the brunette just shrugged before she bent to pick it up, "I mean, I wouldn't have if it wasn't that extra chunky kind that I hate. I wouldn't have risked damaging a jar of smooth and creamy."

It was that moment that Charlotte realized – she knew that name. *Alex.* And that dark hair, those eyes – the fact that this small girl was made of muscle. The younger Spencer sister, and she hardly managed to hold in her groan and maintain her composure.

Apparently, the last thing Charlotte needed wasn't, in fact, running into Regan as she got a glass of water; it was being accosted by Sutton's little sister in the middle of the night while dressed only in Sutton's sweater.

Perfect.

Chapter 15

Alex had been the root of many embarrassing moments throughout Sutton's life. Her childhood and teenage memories were filled with those little moments.

However, her sister *attacking* her – her Charlotte in the middle of the night was beyond mortifying. She'd always been a light sleeper, and not only did she somewhat wake up when Charlotte slipped out of bed, but once she'd heard a thump and Charlotte's semi-shouted words, she'd been wide awake. And nervous enough about what she was going to find that she ran out as fast as she could. Not even grabbing something to wear beyond underwear other than her sheet.

And this, well, this had been one of the last things she could have expected to see.

Holding the sheet together at her chest, she pressed her hand to her cheek in an attempt to staunch the furious blush, before pressing it to her forehead and rubbing. Of *course* this would happen. Just – of course. Tonight, the first night she got to fall asleep with Charlotte in her own bed, of all nights.

She couldn't quite bite back a tired sigh, tinged with embarrassment and exasperation. An exasperation that only Alex could bring out in her, really. "Charlotte, this is my sister Alex. Alex, the woman that you attacked is my friend Charlotte. Who you owe an apology to," she quickly added, reprimanding in a tone that was almost too close to their mother's.

She hoped it would work enough to get Alex to do as she suggested.

It was sort of strange, introducing Charlotte to her sister. Strange and still mortifying, because even though Alex knew about her sexuality, she'd never imagined something like this. Not to mention, Alex had never exactly gotten along with anyone Sutton had been . . . romantic with.

Not that she and Charlotte were *romantic*, but – rolling her eyes slightly at herself, she shook her head and let her hand fall to her side.

She bit her bottom lip as she watched Alex turn to face Charlotte, her gray eyes alight with a suspicion and amusement that Sutton could recognize. Her eyebrow winged up in indecipherable question as she tilted her head. "Hey. Sorry, about the peanut butter. And throwing you against the wall." She shrugged affably, in a way that was natural and didn't surprise Sutton in the least because it was so *Alex*. But, it was an apology. That was all she could ask for.

"In my defense, though, you were skulking around my sister's apartment in the dark in the middle of the night," Alex added, decidedly unapologetically.

Sutton groaned this time, her head falling into her hands. "Really, Alex?"

Before she could make any excuses, though, she watched as Charlotte tugged the bottom of the sweater she was wearing in a quick, effortless movement to straighten it out and her shoulders drew back, tall and straight. Sutton felt her stomach drop in amazement tinged with attraction, because wearing only Sutton's wrinkled sweater, with brown curls tousled and falling down her back, Charlotte looked somehow more dignified than most people could when they were dressed in formalwear.

Despite the fact that she'd just been practically attacked in the middle of the night, Charlotte appeared effortless as she inclined her head. "It's a pleasure to meet you, regardless of the circumstances."

There was the smallest tick in her jaw though. Sutton's posture straightened in unconscious excitement and a bolt of surprise at the fact that she'd caught that small tell. A few months ago, she wasn't sure that she would have picked up on one of the cues of irritation Charlotte tried to hide; she was so good at concealing them.

"And I might add that it's an interesting addendum coming from someone who was standing in the room in the middle of the night after apparently giving no notice of impending arrival," Charlotte's voice was light and jabbing, with an underlying seriousness.

It made a slightly too excited feeling skitter down her spine, before she took note of the way Alex's eyes glinted back. Before she had to intervene a different voice rang out, and Sutton squeezed her eyes closed because *of course*.

"What in the hell is going on out here? It's after one in the morning, and –" Regan cut herself off as she rounded the corner, and Sutton was already shaking her head at the way Regan's eyes positively lit up in delight. "Oh, wow. It's never what I expect," she murmured, the last part mostly to herself.

Sutton grit her teeth. "Go back to bed."

Her words went entirely unheard. "Alex, I didn't know you were coming here tonight."

"No one did," Sutton interjected again, irritation clear in her tone as it sat heavily in her stomach. But her best friend and sister were *long* used to her exasperation.

Charlotte shook her head, expression placid, as she *hmm*'d softly but skillfully enough to draw everyone's attention. "Regardless of the lovely time we're all having, I do have work in the morning. It was quite the experience meeting you Alex, always a privilege to see you Regan. If you'll excuse me."

The look she shot both of the brunettes was enough to quell anything other than Regan's too chipper, "Goodnight!"

But she walked by Sutton, close enough to brush their shoulders together. Sutton's was still bare, but the sweater that Charlotte was wearing – *her* sweater, which shot a little thrill through her in spite of everything that had just happened – was soft and warm now. She shivered, her hand clenching briefly on the sheet she was holding to herself.

She couldn't help but let her eyes trail after Charlotte for a few seconds as she somehow managed to stride back down the hallway. But the snickering that came from Regan and Alex had her snapping her gaze back to them, older sibling annoyance returning easily as she demanded, "Alex, *what* are you doing here?"

Alex's laughter tapered off as she threw her hands in the air, as if she was the put-out party. "You knew I was coming back to New York!"

Sutton's other hand came up to tug through her hair, impatience cutting through everything else. Because she did know that Alex was coming back to New York; they'd talked about it a few weeks ago, not to mention that they were leaving to go home together in less than a week. However, that wasn't the point. "Yes, I knew you were coming back from London but what are you doing *here*, when I distinctly remember telling you that you couldn't stay here?"

She went to fold her arms in the stern way she'd taken to when scolding her sister over the years, then remembered her sheet and dropped her other arm back down while holding it in place.

Alex's eyes rolled at her, an exaggerated groan coming from the back of her throat. "Sutton, you know I just had to share a suite with my arch nemesis for *three months*, and I practically slept with my eyes open every night. I have nowhere else to go," she insisted before picking up the peanut butter with as close to a sheepish look as Alex could manage.

Sutton's own eyes rolled back before she squeezed them closed.

Even with a deep breath, her shoulders were still rigid with frustration as she reminded, "Your company *pays* for apartments for you to stay in when you're here for training. You literally have a home paid for to go to."

Sutton knew because when her sister had been recruited, she'd bragged for days about her "sweet setup." And she knew that the woman Alex referred to as her arch nemesis was legitimately awful.

But that didn't mean she should have to have her sister as a houseguest, either.

"And what about Chris? You know, your boyfr-"

Alex promptly cut her off, "*Not* my boyfriend," she grumbled, because for reasons beyond Sutton's comprehension, her sister would have an exclusive –

346

by all accounts – relationship with a good guy, introduce him to their parents, and routinely stay with him when she was in New York, yet still refuse to call him her boyfriend.

Sutton didn't think she would ever understand her sister completely.

"Besides, I was going to stay with him, but I was on a plane for over seven hours, I have to go to a training meeting in the morning, and I just finished a tournament; Chris is closing down the bar," she added on, shedding some light. Chris, who worked at a bar and lived above it, so even if he wasn't working late, it would have still probably been loud as fuck. "I'm tired," her tone softened, almost petulantly.

Which, oddly, was what made Sutton's resolve weaken. Because she knew that the three month tournament in London had taken a lot out of her sister, and for Alex to openly admit that she was so tired to her, in that vulnerable tone – well, it made her feel the distinct protective feeling she got only when she was dealing with one of her younger siblings.

Biting her lip, she let her shoulders slump in defeat. "You are *not* staying here for more than a single night. I mean it. Not after last time."

"Seconded!" Regan jumped in quickly, before shrugging unapologetically when Alex turned a betrayed look at her. "You made your bed, kid."

More aptly, Alex hadn't made her bed. *Hers*, as in Sutton's. Because last summer, Alex had dropped in on their doorstep, exhausted, and complaining about sharing her apartment with her arch nemesis, and Sutton had been unable to refuse her.

Which had been an awful mistake, because it seemed that five years of not living with Alex let her forget how much they'd wanted to *kill each other* when they did live together. It had been a week of living with her sister before both Sutton and Regan had gone crazy and worked as a team to kick her out.

Alex considered their words before humming and shrugging, placing the peanut butter back on the counter. "One night is all I ask."

Even though Sutton doubted it, she didn't have it in her to argue anymore. Especially when they both knew her well enough to know that she'd already lost. "And you're sleeping on the couch. No arguments."

Alex's mouth fell open but before she could dispute the charge, Sutton adjusted the sheet around her before spinning around and throwing over her shoulder, "Now, I'm going back to my room. I'll see you both in the morning."

She had to bundle up her sheet a bit so that it didn't get stuck awkwardly around her heels as she quickly walked into her room, shutting the door behind her. She'd expected the lights to be off, for Charlotte to have climbed back into bed – the prospect of it had her excited, despite everything.

Instead, her room was cast in a soft shadow as the lamp on her bedside table was on, and she had to blink for a few moments to adjust. When she did, she saw that instead of crawling back into bed, Charlotte was standing a few feet away. She was adjusting the hem of her dress even as her other hand was starting to tug on her heels.

It had only been the span of, what, two minutes, tops? But Charlotte was already dressed and there was no way Sutton could possibly believe that she was getting dressed in *that* to go to sleep. Which meant . . . "You're leaving?"

She bit her lip after she heard her own voice – nerves and insecurities and confusion that she could feel inside seeping into her tone. But she couldn't help it; everything had been fine, hadn't it?

Charlotte nodded, her hair glinting in the dimmed light as she finished slipping on her heels. "I'm just going to go, darling. Your sister is here and you haven't seen her in a while."

But Sutton quickly shook her head, refuting, "I mean, no I haven't seen her for a while. But I'm going to be seeing her all of the time when we go see our parents for Christmas. It's not like we're going to be catching up tonight." She didn't like the way Charlotte didn't meet her eyes as she secured her earring, her stomach dropping so low with unprecedented disappointment she thought it was going to fall to the floor.

Charlotte finally flicked her gaze to Sutton's, teasing smirk in place. "No more bonding beyond her throwing me against a wall after assaulting me with peanut butter?"

Playfulness or not, Sutton's eyebrows drew together in consternation without her able to stop it, and she waved her hand in the air dismissively. "That's . . . well, that's Alex. Which isn't an excuse! You know, she really is, um, she wouldn't have intentionally hurt you if she knew we were friends. She drops in and out as she pleases; I'm used to it."

If Alex had been what caused this – the fact that Charlotte wasn't going to spend the night in Sutton's bed for the first time when she'd thought about it more than a handful of times in the last few weeks – she was going to be royally pissed off with her sister.

What she'd said didn't change Charlotte's mind, apparently.

She moved to stand right in front of Sutton, standing perfectly at eye level thanks to Sutton's bare feet and Charlotte's heels. Her hair was still tumbled despite the fact that she'd clearly run her hands through it multiple times, but it looked unfairly sexy. And she smelled like an enticing combination of her own perfume mixed with Sutton's and just a bit like sex still.

Sutton very much wanted for both of them to climb back into bed and to cuddle. Just how Charlotte usually did in her sleep, as Sutton had learned the first night they'd spent together. Every time they slept in the same bed without fail, she woke up with Charlotte curled up against her, and Sutton always let herself enjoy it for just a couple of minutes before she left.

Her voice was doing that thing where it was soft but firm, leaving no room for argument, "Sutton, your sister is here. I'm going to go, and you can spend some time with her now or in the morning. I know you've missed her." The look Charlotte gave her dared Sutton to disagree.

She *had* missed her but Charlotte leaving in and of itself was so disappointing. Even beyond that, Sutton felt like something was off. Maybe she couldn't say exactly why she felt like that, but the truth of it was sitting heavy in her chest. The fast turnaround of the night, the way Charlotte was ready to go, the way she hadn't met her questioning gaze at first . . .

"It's almost two in the morning." Uncertainty laced through her veins easily, and she tangled her hands in front of her, eyes searching Charlotte's as she took a deep breath and asked, "Is everything okay?"

She watched closely in the dim lighting of her bedside lamp, for any sign that Charlotte wasn't telling her the whole truth. And for a moment, she thought maybe her expression shifted into something like a grimace, but then her face shifted into that beautifully quirked smile. "Of course."

Her hand came up and cupped Sutton's jaw, her thumb rubbing lightly over her skin and Sutton couldn't suppress her shiver. Charlotte leaned in and Sutton's mind jumped in excitement to *kiss*. Kiss goodbye, which wasn't necessarily something they did, because . . . well, the *rules*. Kisses were for sex. Not hellos and goodbyes, but at this very moment she wanted it. Badly.

Then, though, the hand cupping her jaw gently tilted Sutton's head to the side, and soft, warm lips pressed to her cheek and lingered. Lingered long enough that her eyes fluttered closed, and a sigh escaped her throat while her shoulders untensed a bit.

When Charlotte pulled back with another stroke of her thumb over Sutton's cheek, she was met with another soft grin. "I'll see you later this week? For a strictly friend hang out, since tonight's missed that mark."

"Okay," Sutton murmured back, managing a smile back. "I'll see you."

Charlotte, with her tumbled hair and clothes that were rumpled, managed to stride out of her room at two o'clock in the morning like the picture of class. Like she wasn't leaving after a night of sex that *she'd* initiated. Like she wasn't confusing the hell out of Sutton.

Still feeling that uncertainty, tinged with disappointment, Sutton heaved a deep sigh. She dropped her sheet before pulling on a pair of shorts and a T-shirt to sleep in. Charlotte had said everything was fine, that she had an early morning. And she had just gotten off to a strange start with Alex, so Sutton couldn't even really blame her for wanting to leave, she supposed.

Besides, it certainly wouldn't be the first time she read into things that weren't there with Charlotte. Thinking something was going on now just because of a few fleeting expressions on Charlotte's face and a *feeling*, well . . . that was basically meaningless, right?

She quickly grabbed one of her other sheets from her closet and used it to make her bed, tossing the one that she'd been wearing into her hamper. Slowly, she climbed back into bed, her teeth worrying at her bottom lip. If something was wrong with Charlotte, she probably wouldn't know what it was unless Charlotte told her.

A huffed breath left her throat as she pulled her blankets over herself before reaching up to shut off her lamp, the room falling into darkness. Everything had been going so well . . .

Despite her uneasiness, she turned onto her side, curled up in her covers, and closed her eyes to try to sleep. Everything was probably fine, she assured herself. Though she didn't convince her own mind, she tried to force her mind to stop working overtime.

She still had a final to take in the morning, not to mention her meeting with Dr. Martin afterward; Charlotte wasn't the only one of the two of them with an early day.

She'd only been settled back into bed for a minute – not even long enough to calm her mind enough to fall back to sleep – when she heard her door creak open. Her heart skipped a beat in excitement that maybe Charlotte *was* going to spend the night after all.

Before *that* was proven wrong, as she felt her bed dip and heard a too-familiar groan of her sister. "I'm so jealous of your comfy bed."

Rolling her eyes, annoyance curling through her, Sutton reached out to fruitlessly push Alex. "I know, which is why I'm sleeping in it and *you're* sleeping on the couch."

Her sister didn't move an inch – Sutton supposed that's what happened when your body was basically made of muscle – only to roll onto her side to face Sutton. From the limited view she had of Alex in the dark, she could see that her face was teasing. "Your *friend* sure left quickly."

"Well that's what happens when your little sister assaults her in the middle of the night," she retorted, pulling her hand back and rolling her eyes.

Alex shrugged before Sutton felt her slip under the blankets. "Yeah, well, as the only other Spencer in New York, isn't it my right to put the fear of God into your girlfriend?"

Cheeks burning, Sutton pulled her pillow over her head in an attempt to take herself out of this conversation. "She is *not* my girlfriend."

"That's what Regan said," Alex tossed back easily. "I have two eyes and I don't even need them both to have seen the way you look at her. Besides, *Sutton Spencer* having a fuck buddy? It's practically unheard of; you would never sleep with someone you didn't have feelings for."

She reached up to grab the pillow that she'd been using to cover her face and hit Alex with it. She gained some satisfaction in the surprised *oof* and the knowledge that she'd hit her sister right in the face. "Like *you're* one to give any sort of relationship advice?"

She groaned when her own face was hit with a pillow in retaliation. "Damn, I'm not judging you. I'm just saying . . . you like her. And she was out of here like someone lit a match under her. That's just because of me throwing a jar of peanut butter at her?"

Sutton wanted to laugh at the ridiculousness of it all; she truly did. Because how had the night that had started out so well turned out like this? Instead, Alex's words sat heavily on her shoulders. "Can we just not talk about this anymore? Ever? I'll forget the fact that you broke into my apartment, attacked my friend, and injured my peanut butter if you can forget the fact that you saw – everything that you saw," she quickly added on, blushing again at the memory of the state of undress Alex had walked in on.

352

Alex was quiet for a few moments, before she shrugged. "I guess," but her voice was more thoughtful than Sutton would have given her credit for. Alex was never overly concerned with Sutton's relationships, save for the few times she'd offered to beat up some past boyfriends.

More than anything, though, she didn't want to ruminate any longer over Charlotte or her leaving or her little sister seeing both of them in any stage of nudity.

"I'm not going to let go of the fact that you climbed into my bed when I *told* you, you have to sleep on the couch." But even with the irritation of Alex sneaking in unannounced, with her possibly having something to do with Charlotte leaving, and with her inevitably going to spend the night in Sutton's bed instead of the couch, she couldn't keep the affection out of her voice.

Alex didn't miss a beat, grumbling, "You know I hate your couch. And your bed is comfortable as fuck; I've been sleeping in the same room as my enemy for three months, do you think I've gotten a good night's sleep?"

Now, she couldn't help but let out a small chuckle, before she reached out to tap Alex lightly on the chin. When they were children, she'd done it to annoy her because it had been easy to get a rise out of her that way. And now, even though Alex would still sometimes bat her hand away, it was a sign of affection.

"Well, enjoy your one night of good sleep here then, because that's all you get," she repeated, her voice as firm as possible because she *meant it*, before she rolled over onto her side and closed her eyes. "You're lucky I've missed you."

"Yeah, yeah, no need to get all sappy," Alex's voice was gruff the way Sutton knew it got when she was sleepy and when she had emotional cues to meet that she didn't always want to say aloud. It was enough to make her smile a bit. A few seconds beat by in silence, a calming silence, as she felt Alex shuffle around a bit in bed the way she did when she tried to get comfortable. Her sister's voice was soft as she said, "And . . . I guess . . . I missed you, too."

Despite the tension she'd felt with Charlotte's departure, she couldn't help but let it melt away a bit as her smile became a little bit bigger. "Goodnight, Alex. I'm glad you're home."

Her sister hummed back and Sutton felt her settle under the covers a bit more. "G'night."

With a deep breath, she willed herself to relax, and cuddled under the blanket more. Before she heard Alex groan. "Jesus. You two were having sex *here*, right in your damn bed, weren't you?"

Embarrassed all over again, Sutton scoffed out a laugh. "Don't be such a drama queen . . . there's a different sheet on. But you are more than welcome to move to the couch."

Alex huffed and kicked out her legs – a move that made Sutton wince, because her sister would soon be kicking her legs out in her sleep and inevitably hitting Sutton and causing pain – before she hit her palms against the mattress. Her voice was defeated, "Meh. I'm in a mixed martial arts company with a bunch of dudes. I've been in grosser places."

An exasperated, tired chuckle slipped out of her and even though she still had that *feeling* of worry low in her stomach wondering about Charlotte, even though she knew Alex would inevitably make for an uncomfortable time once she fell asleep, having her sister there was a comforting presence.

Within the next few minutes, she fell asleep.

***

The next morning found Sutton knocking on Dr. Martin's office door, unconsciously fidgeting with the strap of her backpack as it was slung over her shoulder. She hadn't fallen asleep until after three, after everything that had happened, and her alarm had woken her up at six since she'd had one of her last finals to take at eight.

354

Despite the relief she felt at the fact that she was nearly done, she couldn't help but desperately wish for a tea and possibly a nap. The already sparing three hours of sleep she'd gotten had been even worse because, true to form, Alex had started kicking once she'd truly fallen asleep.

Sutton already had bruises forming on her legs.

The only good news she'd gotten this morning came when she'd been tiredly drinking her morning tea, and she'd seen that her jacket was gone. The one that Charlotte had stolen from her. Well, granted, she'd left it at Charlotte's that first night. But Charlotte had been keeping it from her, deliberately! Wearing it herself.

Wearing *Sutton's* jacket. And Sutton would be lying if it hadn't made a rush of excitement go through her, warming her chest and her cheeks the previous night when she'd realized that Charlotte was wearing her clothes.

It was nice, to have that. To share something easy like that. And while she was serious about the fact that it was her favorite jacket and she *did* want it back . . . she couldn't help but love that Charlotte had taken it with her when she'd left last night.

Maybe it was dumb, but it was a little thrill of that faux-battle of ownership of that jacket with Charlotte and she was looking forward to it. Especially if it brought about more times like last night.

"Miss Spencer, come in," Dr. Martin's voice called out, pulling her from her thoughts.

Shaking her head slightly, she pushed open the office door. It was an imposing space, but warmly filled with books and maps, and after working for Dr. Martin for a few years she was familiar with it.

She offered her professor a small smile and wave as she made her way to one of the chairs opposite the desk where he sat, putting her backpack and jacket down on the empty seat next to her.

Despite the fact that she *knew* she hadn't done anything wrong, she couldn't help but feel slightly nervous. It brought her back to the one time she'd been called to the principal's office in school to get in trouble.

With a deep breath to try to quell those nerves, she pressed her hands into her lap. "Hi, Dr. Martin. Did you get the email I sent you? With the potential essay questions for the final?"

"Ah, yes, expedient and intelligent work as always." He nodded at her somewhat distractedly as he started to flip through the files he had resting on his desk. "I trust your finals are going well?"

Her smile was a bit easier now as she relaxed a bit into her chair; in the past, the few times she'd done something Dr. Martin was unhappy with, his meetings were short and to the point. A bit sharp at moments, he didn't mince words when it came to his expectations and she appreciated that.

"They are; I actually took my last one just now." She tilted her head, trying to peer at whatever it seemed that he was looking for on his desk, her interest piqued. "Do you . . . I'm sorry, Dr. Martin, but is there something else that you need for me to do before the semester is over?"

His forehead wrinkled in thought before he snapped his fingers and opened the top drawer in his desk, pulling out another file. "Actually, yes. Sutton, you know that typically I've gone through TAs in my past fairly frequently, correct?"

More confused, especially because his voice took on a familiar, lofty I-know-things-you-don't-know tone, Sutton nodded. "Um, yes, I do."

She was well aware that Dr. Martin was known as a fairly demanding professor to work for. He asked a lot of those who worked for him, and when they made a mistake, he was quick to point it out. And, sometimes, continued to point it out, even if it was in a teasing manner. He'd had TAs who hadn't even lasted full semesters in the past.

It was somewhat of a point of pride that Sutton had with herself.

"In the time you've spent working with me, you've consistently surpassed my expectations – which is not an easy feat to accomplish. Your writing is thoughtful and engaging, your editing is impeccable, you're organized, timely, and adaptable." He tapped his fingers against the file, and gave her a sharp smile. "You've managed to make me a little disappointed to have to find a new idiot to replace you next year."

Surprised, she blinked back at him for a moment before a smile bloomed over her face. Still, though, she didn't quite understand . . . "Thank you? I mean, thank you, Dr. Martin, that is actually high praise coming from you. But I'm not quite sure what you – is this some sort of holiday present?"

It was the only thing she could think to guess. Dr. Martin wasn't often one to sing the praises of others without reason; even when he'd given her a compliment in the past, it was a quick one.

The incredulous look he shot her was almost comforting with how typical it was. "You must have very low standards for gifts if my stating facts about your abilities counts as a present." His mouth quirked in a smile, though, and he shook his head. "No, that's not a gift. It is however, me leading up to the question: what are your plans for post-graduation? You'll have an advanced degree from a great university, and I've yet to get a request from you for a recommendation for your next step. Which either means you don't have definite plans or you don't plan on asking me for one. If it's the latter, I assure you that for all of my many faults, my word in our field is still a good one."

Sutton flushed as she quickly shook her head in denial. "No, it's not – I'd be honored to have your recommendation, Dr. Martin. It's just, I haven't . . . I'm not sure what I'm going to do in May."

Her words came out more flustered than she usually was with her professors, and it made her flush even more in embarrassment. Because Sutton had always been a planner; she'd always known what her next step was. But she hadn't been able to plan her next move yet, not exactly. She wanted – many things. To teach, collegiately. Probably. As it was, though, school was all she'd really truly

357

known. How was she supposed to know for sure if this was what she wanted or if this was just what she was comfortable with?

It scared her, more than she wanted to admit.

Dr. Martin was watching her closely, perceptively, before he asked, "What is it that you plan to do for a career? I'm sure that regardless of how good you are at working as my assistant, that isn't the sort of life you've planned on."

"I – no, it's not. I want . . ." She trailed off, feeling her cheeks burn slightly and she curled her hands into fists, speaking slowly, "I'd like to write, I think, but I know that isn't just something you can fall into." Well, Sutton knew that she could potentially have certain connections to do so, but she didn't necessarily feel comfortable with that. "And doing this, working with you, has also made me think that maybe I'd like to be a professor? But I didn't want to jump right into a doctoral program next year. I want a little break from school, I think, so I'm not – I just don't know what the next step is," she admitted, uneasily.

Whenever this had been brought up with her family in the past few months, she was met with the simple reassurance that *you can do anything you put your mind to* – which was nice and comforting, because she knew her family members actually thought that. But it wasn't particularly helpful when determining if she should charge ahead into more schooling or try to figure out some internship that could fit with her degree and try to help her sort through her options.

She knew that her family would be there to help her and support her no matter what, and her mother's subtle intonations that she could always move home if she wanted to while she figured everything out reminded her that she did have somewhere to go should she truly need it.

School, though, had always been good for her, good to her; she liked the environment, she had the motivation to do well, studying and writing papers came naturally to her. She enjoyed it.

However, simply being smart, and being good in school weren't the biggest helpers when it seemed like everyone in her family had a calling.

Sutton . . . liked to read, she liked to write. She enjoyed working as a TA, the structure of a schooling environment. Grading, helping to create assignments, editing papers.

But it was also all she knew, right now. That had been the environment she'd built for herself, and she liked it. She just wanted to know for sure what would be the next best step, when nothing immediate came to mind.

The look on Dr. Martin's face when she bit her lip and looked over at him wasn't judging or even that lightly mocking one he sometimes wore. Instead, it was considering. "I'd say that writing or teaching would both be within your reach, if that's what you want. And, not to *brag*." The look he shot her *now* was somewhat mocking, but it worked to make the tension in her shoulders loosen a bit. "But that is somewhat along the lines of what I was thinking."

Surprised and flattered, she gave him a wide-eyed look. "Really?"

He picked up the file he'd retrieved earlier and tapped it once against the desk, before holding it out to her. "I think this is something you should consider."

Intrigued, she reached out and grasped the file, flipping it open. "The Roman Archives?" She skimmed over the top of the first page before glancing back at her professor, confused. "You think I should . . . visit the Roman Archives?"

Not that she would be opposed to doing so, it was somewhere she'd always been curious about, but – still.

The look he gave her was one of patented impatience. "You think I would recommend to you to visit the Archives? Not visit, Miss Spencer, but *intern*."

Almost with a mind of their own, her fingers flipped to the next page, and she drew her gaze back down. Indeed, there was the first page of an internship application, and she shook her head, murmuring, "I didn't even know there were internships there."

The Roman Archives were world-renowned and one of the biggest drawing points for one of the oldest cities in the world. Literature – dating further back than they could truly name, from all over the world – was kept there. Archived, put into displays. They were copied and edited for newer editions to be published and distributed. Artworks were there as well – some of the greatest and most memorable pieces of art that the known world had could be found there.

"They offer ten internships every year. It lasts for six months, with five interns of their choice staying on for an additional three. You'd get paid a stipend, small but fair. They provide housing. And you work with some of the masterpieces we know in our time; it's quite an opportunity. But, it's all there." He gestured back to the file in her hands, which seemed even bigger now with the realness of its meaning right there in her hands.

Both heavier and lighter somehow, and she looked back at it in wonder. "You think *I* should apply?" she asked, hearing the incredulity of her own tone but unable to help it.

Because she might be a good student, could be a fairly decent writer, and might even be a great TA, but . . . she wasn't necessarily special enough for a prestigious internship.

Dr. Martin merely lifted an eyebrow in derision. "I think you'd do very well there, actually, and it would certainly reflect well on you should you choose to become a doctoral candidate."

Sutton's mouth fell open in amazement as she flitted her eyes back down to the file, momentarily speechless as her mind tried to take it all in.

It didn't seem to matter to Dr. Martin, though, who pushed back from his desk. "Well, I've got a lunch date to attend to. The application is due by the end of the week; I apologize for the late notice, but . . . well, you have it now."

She slowly closed the file, stroking her fingertips over it thoughtfully even as her mind spun with possibilities. "I – thank you, Dr. Martin."

He shrugged. "If you *do* choose to apply, I have a recommendation already written."

The approving smile he gave her got one in return as she gathered her items and stood, holding the file tightly to her chest. "I'll see you in a few days for the final."

***

Two hours later, Sutton had commandeered her usual table at Topped Off. When Regan had started working at the coffee shop, Sutton had become one of the regulars, and the table in the corner at the front window was her favorite. It provided natural light and some seclusion, and not too much exposure to the windows to be a distraction. It was small enough that Sutton didn't feel like she was taking up too much space when she sat there by herself, but large enough for her to be able to spread her work out.

Currently, it was covered with the papers from the file Dr. Martin had provided for her. In the file there was the application, as well as all of the details about the program, not to mention testimonies about how wonderful the experience had been.

Luckily, Regan had worked until closing last night and wasn't working until later this afternoon. If she'd been working, Sutton didn't think she would have as much clarity of mind to be able to think about all of this the way she needed to.

By "it's due by the end of the week" her professor truly meant "it's due in four days." Which was far faster than Sutton had ever made such a big decision in her life.

She had to decide, like, today if she wanted to complete her application and edit her written piece on time. As it was, she was already going to have to workshop a piece she'd already written.

The indecision warred inside of her, exacerbated by the feeling of being *rushed*. Her parents would both worry about her being alone in another country. They already worried and she was only a four-hour drive away.

And there was a part of her that thought . . . maybe she didn't want to ask her family and friends for advice. That maybe she should just apply – or not – and do this on her own. Decide her future without the input of anyone else to figure out what she wanted.

She knew her siblings would have various ranges of excitement and worry. She knew that Regan would flip out – in both good and bad ways. She knew that Emma would tell her to go for it no matter what, with a combination of both envy and pride in her voice. She knew what everyone else would say, but not herself.

Biting her bottom lip and running her fingertip absently around the top of her mug of tea in thought, she leaned over the table and skimmed her eyes over another of the papers with the finite details, yet again. Then she tapped her pen against the column or pros and cons she'd written out so far.

Pros – travel, new experiences, amazing learning possibilities, Roman Archives!, looks great on resumé, improve skills

Cons – would be alone/no support system, Regan/apartment/rent? guilt for leaving, begins only days after graduation & would have to go almost immediately after, leaving Charlotte

The last one gave her pause, and she'd been reluctant to write it down at all, but it was . . . well, it was how she felt. She knew they weren't dating but she enjoyed them. Enjoyed what they were and their friendship, and that would certainly be coming to an end if she left. Maybe not their actual friendship but definitely the sex. There was no such thing as long distance friends with benefits, Sutton knew that much.

"What are you concentrating so hard on there?" the woman in question's voice came from right next to her, making her jump as her heart pounded in her chest.

Eyes wide, she scrambled quickly to pull all of her papers together and hoped that Charlotte didn't actually see her own name on the list. She didn't want her to take it the wrong way.

She moved so quickly she nearly knocked over her mug of tea, which wobbled slightly before Charlotte reached out and steadied it. And only then was Sutton able to take a deep breath and turn to look up at her, taking in the look of amusement she was receiving. And, as very nearly always, inhaled sharply as she took her in. Perfect brown curls cascaded over Charlotte's shoulder, contrasting with the white peacoat she wore over one of her form-fitting dresses.

Always perfectly put together and always enough to make Sutton's heart pound.

"Hey!" Too eager. "Uh, hey. What are you doing here? I thought you had a busy day today?" She *knew* Charlotte had a busy day today, given Naomi's interview from the day before.

An amused eyebrow arched up in response as Charlotte hummed in affirmation. "I've had two meetings with my team already, and I had just enough time to run out for a coffee break." She held out her to-go cup as if to tell Sutton, *see.* "And I saw you here, looking a little – frankly, a little distressed. So, I don't have much time but I wanted to know that you're all right?"

The subtle clench of Charlotte's jaw made her think that she hadn't quite covered up her list fast enough, and her stomach knotted in uncertainty. But if Charlotte didn't bring it up, neither would she.

She frowned and cleared her throat before sliding all of the papers back into the file as she explained, "I just – well, there's an opportunity," she settled on, tasting the words on her tongue. "Dr. Martin told me about it today. And I'm just . . . I'm wondering about whether or not I should apply for it."

Dark eyebrows came together and Sutton could tell from the expression on Charlotte's face that she was waiting for more.

With a deep breath, she drummed her fingers against the table. "It's an internship for the Roman Archives."

Charlotte's eyes searched her own before a small smile came over her face. "Sutton, that would be an amazing experience. Especially given how much you love literature."

Her words affirmed one of the things she'd already been thinking herself. Of course she *knew* it would be an amazing experience – she loved literature and there was no better option she could imagine for having access to classic arts.

Still . . .

"I'd be gone for at least six months – maybe even a little more," she spoke slowly, unable to stop her gaze from flickering from her file and up across the table to Charlotte, watching her as closely as she could.

Because maybe Sutton truly was reading into things between them; maybe she was the only one out of the two of them that would miss . . . *this*. This closeness they'd developed, faster than she ever had with anyone else in the past. This feeling that settled warmly and heavily in the pit of her stomach whenever she was with her or even spoke to her.

So she watched intently – maybe too intently – as Charlotte's eyes widened just a bit as they looked back at the file in Sutton's hands. And listened too intently to the seconds that drifted by between them in silence, her heart beating a little faster.

Because it was possible that she wasn't the only one who felt this way, despite the fact that they had their agreement. Maybe it wasn't just her who thought finding a similar internship or job *here in New York* while she took a year or two off before applying to doctoral programs would be a better idea. Maybe not for the overall experience but for proximity's sake.

Charlotte cleared her throat. "I understand being reluctant to leave for so long, but . . . if it's something you want, I absolutely think you should." There was a sincerity in her eyes as she met Sutton's gaze with her own. She thought something else flickered there, too, but it was gone quickly and could have just been her imagination.

She quirked her lips up, forcing a smile, as that little balloon inside of her that said maybe she wasn't the only one who anticipated seeing how far their friends with benefits could possibly take them deflated.

It wasn't anything to truly be disappointed about, she knew. Because they were *friends* and that was their deal, but there was still that small seed inside of her of *what if* that had been forming. The small seed that sank a little lower especially with Charlotte's encouragement. Their sex life would then have a deadline.

Shaking her head slightly, telling herself not to let herself read into anything, she sighed. "I don't know if I'd go, anyway. I mean, we both know the Archives are prestigious. And they only accept ten interns every year from across the world! I might not even be accepted."

Another one of her worries.

Charlotte frowned before she took a sip and watched Sutton over the rim of her coffee cup. She couldn't help but watch Charlotte's lips as she swallowed, rubbing her hands against her thighs.

Charlotte tilted her head to the side, as a genuine smile blossomed over her mouth for the first time in the café. "Sutton, that's absolutely ridiculous. I mean, not even mentioning who your parents are – which, I know you wouldn't take advantage of, but it would be foolish to think they wouldn't play a role. But Dr. Martin, if I'm not mistaken, is a huge benefactor to the Archives, so if he thinks you should apply, then I have no doubt how highly he thinks of you. Plus I've read some of your papers and they're brilliant. You shouldn't doubt yourself." Charlotte lightly chastised and that resolute tone she had made warmth well up inside of her.

Especially when Charlotte reached out to brush her fingertips over the backs of Sutton's. It was comforting but also made her shiver, and she couldn't help but smile herself. For real, this time.

"Thank you," she murmured back, resisting the urge to turn her hand and hold Charlotte's that still rested over hers. Barely.

Charlotte shrugged as if her praise was nothing. Then again, sometimes Charlotte said and did things like that – sweet things – and thought nothing of them. "It's just the truth."

She sat like that for a moment, and the thoughts that had been bombarding her before slipped away, giving her some clarity that she found she very much wanted. Needed. She breathed easier with Charlotte sitting with her, with a curious little head tilt that made Sutton wonder what was on her mind.

Even so, the lingering worry she still wondered about from last night melted away, and she only felt the slightest inclination to ask Charlotte about it. But for once she managed to keep her words to herself. And she was only the slightest bit disappointed when Charlotte gently squeezed her hand and pulled back to wrap it around her coffee cup.

With a quirk of an eyebrow she took another sip and long, elegant fingers tapped before Charlotte asked, "So, I see that Regan isn't working right now. Were you planning on . . . meeting someone?"

Confused, Sutton leaned back and looked around, before giving Charlotte a self-deprecating smile, "Like who?" She only had a handful of friends that she saw on a regular basis, including Alex, and by now Charlotte knew all of them.

The shrug Charlotte gave her was perfunctory and light, as was her voice, "Oh, I don't know. Emma . . . or Alia."

For the life of her, she didn't know why Charlotte seemed to be watching her intently now, but Sutton could only give her a wondering glance as she shook her head. "No . . . I was just having somewhat of a crisis over this," she sort-of joked as she gestured to the file. She leaned back in her chair. "Why?"

Charlotte only shrugged and easily waved her hand slightly in the air. "I was just wondering if I should expect someone to be wondering why I'm in their seat," she teased, and Sutton grinned, before Charlotte sighed and her eyes flickered up to the television in the corner, which – as usual – was airing the news. The anchor was currently discussing politics and it was so easy for her to see the way Charlotte's demeanor shifted and her shoulders straightened a bit. "I really should be getting back to the office though. My lunch hour is cut to this coffee break, and even then I really don't have that much time."

Sutton swallowed the bit of disappointment as she nodded, then paused as the thought occurred to her and she looked up in question. "If you didn't have that much time, why did you come all the way here for coffee?"

Adjusting her jacket, as if she looked anything other than completely put together at any moment that she'd been there, Charlotte's gaze was thoughtful as it roamed the shop for a moment, before landing back on Sutton. "To be entirely honest with you, there's something about this place that I really like." Was all she offered, but with an engaging grin. "I've been stopping here for coffee on my lunch breaks for a few weeks now. Regan didn't tell you?"

"She didn't," Sutton murmured, rolling her eyes slightly at Regan's reluctance to accept Charlotte as Sutton's friend. Then she frowned. "She's not . . . is she rude to you?"

Charlotte rolled her eyes briefly, playfully, before offering a small smile. "She makes comments, but I'm not entirely certain she doesn't make similar comments to half the people who come in here."

It didn't remove the frown on Sutton's face.

"If I can't handle a few comments from Regan that are at least coming from a good place, I'm in the wrong profession," Charlotte informed her, settling her hand on Sutton's shoulder and squeezing a bit. "Good luck on your application, darling. I hope you get in."

I hope you get in.

The words instigated a confusing mix of happiness and discontent which she pushed away as she gamely smiled in appreciation.

Charlotte hesitated for a moment, her gaze dropping ever-so-quickly to Sutton's mouth. Once again one of the things she could have easily missed a month ago, but not now, and Sutton's lips parted in surprise and *want*. The moment ended soon though, with a quick grin and the hand on her shoulder squeezing again before she turned to leave.

And Sutton watched until the door of the café closed behind her, unable to help herself. She wondered how Charlotte so easily made things feel so off-balanced but also so good.

Shaking herself out of it, she quickly finished her tea before packing away her papers; she had to do some more research at home before she committed to applying completely. Within minutes she stood and slung her bag over her shoulder, turning as she looked down and fished her phone out of her pocket.

Which caused her to walk right into someone, and she stumbled as she tightened her grip on her phone before it dropped to the floor. A hand came to her elbow and didn't let go even when she righted herself. She was already trying to politely shrug it off before she turned to see who it belonged to.

She was met with the smiling face of David Verbeck. Her shrugging became more insistent than polite until his hand dropped, but the small, knowing smile on his face didn't. She met the smiling look on his face with a small one of her own that was barely more than a grimace.

Despite the fact that she'd met him in several capacities throughout her life – as a businessman with many political ties, he'd been a fixture on the very perimeter of her parents' social circle since she'd been a teenager – she'd never been able to shake the uneasy feeling he gave her.

Especially when he readily disliked most of her siblings after Oliver and Lucas had come up with some unfortunate but funny nicknames for him, but he always went out of his way to be too-kind to her. Even though he'd lived in New York since she'd moved here, she'd very successfully avoided him and his lingering gaze.

"Sutton! Better watch where you're going." His tone was joking but held that undercurrent of something *more* that he too often had. It was somewhat reminiscent of Charlotte's knowing tone, but instead of being playful or enticing, it was unsettling.

368

"Right . . . sorry, Mr. Verbeck." She stepped backwards, before she remembered the manners her mother had drilled into her so much in her youth that they were irrevocably a part of her now, and she straightened her shoulders. "I don't typically see you here?"

He took his eyes off of her and ran them around the establishment. He lingered on the table she'd just been sitting at, and then back to her. "It's not the sort of shop that typically entices me. I found myself in this area today, though, and saw something that drew my interest."

There was that tone again, and Sutton had to work to school her features to not show her unsettled confusion.

Maybe he saw it anyway though, as he gestured to the *specials!* board behind the counter and added, "The blueberry coconut muffins."

She looked up at the board in question and then back to his face, thinking about the last time she'd seen him. Or, well, heard him. At the fundraiser she'd attended with her father, where he had met with Naomi for a conversation that she had been utterly confused about. Still was, kind of.

"Okay, well, I'll let you enjoy your snack. I should get going." She offered a cool, polite smile. Then got a much warmer one in return with the sensation that she was missing something.

He stepped back and nodded, smile still in place. "I'm sure it'll be delicious. Enjoy your day, Sutton."

Even though that uneasy feeling remained, she tried to shake it off as she zipped up her jacket. Mr. Verbeck had always been somewhat creepy; it was just who he was. Nothing new about today.

And at the moment, Sutton had other things to worry about. Like her potential internship on the other side of the world, removing her sister from her apartment, and texting her best friend to stop giving attitude to her – her Charlotte.

369

Chapter 16

"You look absolutely dreadful. I can't be the first person to tell you that," Charlotte's grandmother's voice jarred Charlotte into blinking her eyes open.

It took her a moment to register where she was: reclined on the chaise in her grandmother's office. Though it was still only the early afternoon and Charlotte had a whole day ahead of her, her head felt. . . foggy, and had since she'd woken up that morning.

It was only when she'd sluggishly made her way toward the shower that she fully *felt* the pounding inside of her head and the soreness in her joints. Despite the glaring signs of sickness, Charlotte didn't have the time or patience to be feeling ill. Not right now. Not ever, honestly, but not right now especially.

Though as the morning had gone on, it became increasingly apparent that maybe there was a *slight* chance she truly was getting sick. Because despite the fact that she'd chugged coffee, taken vitamins, and consumed a small array of medicine after choking down some toast. . . she'd only felt worse.

Her sinuses had gradually felt fuller and heavier throughout the day and she was utterly exhausted. She'd hardly been able to keep her eyes open during the meeting she'd had with her campaign team.

If she was honest with herself, it wasn't shocking; her debate with Naomi was right around the corner and Charlotte had been getting less and less sleep. But how was she supposed to sleep when there were questions and answers to practice, speeches to prepare, and debate strategies to perfect?

She'd had to wipe at watery eyes repeatedly – irritatingly – as she'd sat at her desk, which had prompted Dean to urge her to go home. And maybe she'd sniped at him a little more aggressively than she should have when she denied that she was feeling under the weather.

Which brought her back to the moment and she shook her head slightly at her grandmother in an attempt to clear it. And then she narrowed her eyes, as she sarcastically tossed back, "Wow, Grandmother, thank you. It's lovely to see you today too," even as her throat felt a bit scratchy.

Her rejoinder didn't faze her grandmother at all – not that she'd expected it to – and Elizabeth raised both of her eyebrows as she ran her eyes over Charlotte's face critically. "You've got circles dark as night under your eyes and you're paler than you should be; you've been early into work and late to leave, and I doubt your work stops when you go home. You shouldn't be surprised that I keep note of these things."

Charlotte's jaw set even as she sighed a bit. She wasn't surprised that her grandmother took note of her work habits; she was, proudly, her prodigy.

Still. "I'm *fine*," she stressed, sitting with her shoulders back.

Elizabeth shot her a *look,* one that had made many diplomats wither before her. It made Charlotte feel somewhat at home.

"If you are so *fine*, what are you doing napping in my office in the middle of a work day?" Elizabeth questioned, her eyebrow winged up in that probing manner she'd mastered so well.

And then Charlotte's hands tightened slightly on the envelope in her grasp; her focus relegated to the reason she'd sought out her grandmother in the first place. Her fingers tapped over the elegantly embossed writing on the front as she deliberated for a moment.

"I wanted to ask your advice. About this," she added on and held up the envelope for good measure.

As though they were working in sync, her grandmother was already holding out her hand for Charlotte to give her the envelope just as Charlotte was giving it to her. Muffling a yawn – damn, she was sick of those today – she felt her stomach twist slightly as her grandmother pulled the contents out.

The contents being an invitation.

An invitation that had arrived just after lunch, delivered with her other mail at work. Amidst all of her work-related mail that had been dropped to her desk, was a stylish envelope that had drawn her attention.

An envelope that held a formal invitation. To the annual Spencer Family New Year's Eve event – personally inviting Charlotte to spend the evening at their family estate.

She tracked her eyes over her grandmother's facial expression as she took in the invitation before meeting Charlotte's gaze. It was validating to know that they were of the same mindset. Because she'd first sought out Dean, given work place proximity. And he'd been more oblivious about it than she'd have liked, questioning why getting an invitation to a holiday party merited any extra thought.

But her grandmother's knowledgeable eyes met hers, that wise spark as evident as it was in her tone as she tapped the invitation against her leg, "Well. It would seem that you have been given quite the opportunity."

Quite the opportunity, indeed. Because as anyone in politics knew, the Spencer New Year's Eve event was really the *only* gathering of all prominent northeastern politicians and highly reputable business and society members. It was, in theory, a networking heaven, given that the group of people there were typically a group who were fairly unreachable to break into and gain the trust of.

"I know," she replied slowly, and was even more irritated that her head felt a little cloudy at the moment. She needed to be able to process this from all fronts.

"I haven't even been granted one of these, my dear girl." Elizabeth lifted an eyebrow, a slight mocking tone in her voice. Charlotte knew well enough that it was directed not to her but toward the Spencers, and that affiliated group in general, for having ranks so closed and "exclusive" that not even the President had been invited.

But it made her scoff out a laugh and hold her hand out for the invitation to be given back. "I know," she echoed herself.

Her grandmother shook her head before she spoke, voice questioning in that impatient way she had, "If you know what a rare opportunity you've been given, I'm afraid I fail to see why you've sought out my council."

Charlotte's stomach knotted – and not because she was feeling less than in perfect health. But because the way her name stared up at her from underneath *Jack and Katherine Spencer invite you*. Jack and Katherine Spencer. Invite her, Charlotte Thompson. To their *home*. To their holiday party that was so exclusive not even her grandmother – when she'd been the fucking President, and had known and worked cordially with Jack Spencer for years – had garnered an invitation.

The words were difficult to form on her tongue. More difficult than words usually were between herself and the woman she considered her personal hero. "I'm. . . wary of the reasoning behind why I was given the invitation."

"You must have made quite the impression on the honorable Jack Spencer during his visit a few months ago," Elizabeth shot back as she leaned back in the chair opposite Charlotte.

"I'm not entirely certain that's the reason I was given the invitation," she admitted, biting her lip thoughtfully, debating what to add on.

It wasn't as though she wanted to say *I think I've made far more of an impression on Katherine Spencer as her daughter's friend – friend who I'm sleeping with, not that she hopefully knows that – than I did on Jack Spencer as a politician*.

Though Charlotte knew Sutton hadn't told her mother about the true nature of their relationship, she also knew that Katherine was a smart woman. A smart woman who was very close to her daughter who was not a good liar, and who recently came out to her. She simply had been letting herself believe that nothing further had come from the inferences she could have made.

She was saved, though, from figuring out how to voice her thoughts as her grandmother sipped from her tea before nodding and waving her hand. "You were invited because of your . . . *friendship* with the Spencer woman."

It took a moment – just a moment – for the words to settle in Charlotte's cloudy mind, and she stared at her grandmother. "Well, yes." She wasn't sure why she was surprised by her grandmother knowing about her particular friendship with Sutton.

Her grandmother knew everything.

She knew everything and she had this little air of amusement with that revealing of her knowledge. It sparkled in her eyes right now and Charlotte huffed out a breath from her mouth – annoyingly, her nose was almost completely stuffed – falling back into the chaise once more, loathe to admit that it made her entire body feel relieved.

Honestly it was best that her grandmother had just come out and said it. Because, frankly, Charlotte wasn't in the business of trying to keep secrets from Elizabeth and even if she was, she certainly didn't have the energy for it right now.

"I didn't make quite the impact on Jack Spencer as I had hoped to make when he'd visited a few months ago," she reflected, rubbing her hand over her forehead and grimacing slightly.

No, she'd been a bit preoccupied with the whole Sutton-being-Jack-Spencer's-daughter aspect of it all.

Her gaze fell to the invitation and narrowed as she continued, "So, though I'm not in any sort of formal. . . relationship with Sutton, I think that I've garnered a bit of interest from some members of the Spencer family because of all this."

Even though her thought process hadn't been its best today, she'd had enough time to contemplate that. That even without the details laid out, Sutton's family, her parents – her *father*, a politician whose support she was hoping to gain – knew she was involved in his daughter's life.

The uncomfortable tightness in her stomach and difficulty swallowing at the knowledge that her biggest concealed secret could be public threatened to make her feel nauseous. And the only thing that calmed her, really, was the knowledge that Jack and Katherine Spencer likely wouldn't want to out their own daughter.

She admitted, "I'm reluctant to accept an invitation gained not through my own merit."

If her friendship with Sutton was nonexistent and she'd received this elusive invite, she would be thrilled and would have already confirmed her attendance. A perfect time to network, to build strong political ties in a setting that few people were granted, earned by her work ethic and policy ideas.

That would be a dream.

But that *wasn't* the case, and it was giving her a sour taste in her mouth. Charlotte was fortunate to have been born to her family. She was more than fortunate to be raised with and learn from her grandmother. But Charlotte had also worked tirelessly to make a name for herself.

This invitation was an opportunity that not many were afforded. But it also rankled and sat heavily on her shoulders with the almost certain knowledge that she'd been granted this opportunity not because of herself but because of her affiliation with someone else.

"I thought that might be the case." Elizabeth thoughtfully set down her cup with a sharp *clink*, before she shook her head. "And you know I'm not one to dance around stating my opinion."

"Certainly not something you've been known for," Charlotte interjected, unable to stop a small smile at the way her grandmother scoffed at her.

"So, I'll tell you that regardless of the reason you received this invitation, you would be an idiot to miss it. As it is, the Spencer's are far more likely to act as though they have no idea about their suspicions than to actually ask if you've corrupted their daughter in bed," she snorted derisively. "Given that, you've no reason to not attend and win them over."

Her words rang true, despite the fact that she was still left with an uncomfortable feeling in her stomach. Nerves, maybe, but she hated having them about an event that, in any other situation, should fall right into her wheelhouse.

She squared her shoulders and nodded. "Simply because *this* invitation isn't based on my own repute doesn't mean future ones won't be."

Not after she made a favorable impression on the people in attendance this year, anyway, and subsequently – hopefully – won this election. Now, it just had to be her mission to accept and gain favor.

Elizabeth grinned with a look of approval that Charlotte had basked in from an early age. "That's the idea." She was contemplative for a moment, aiming a look at Charlotte that set off an alarm bell before her grandmother even asked, "And what does your Spencer girl have to say about this invitation?"

Charlotte's eyebrows rose on her forehead as her stomach churned again at the term *your Spencer girl* – and it wasn't a feeling that was making her feel even more sick . . . but it was . . . unfamiliar and uncomfortable.

Many things with Sutton were like that. Unfamiliar and somewhat uncomfortable but in a way that wasn't necessarily that bad.

"She's not . . ." She cut off her denial, knowing that she didn't want to protest too much. "I haven't discussed it with Sutton."

She hadn't seen Sutton very much in the last few days, anyway. Not since running into her at Topped Off, when Sutton had been making her list about whether or not to apply for an internship.

The fact that Charlotte saw her own name on the list of cons . . . well, it gave her a jolt of unease. Not that she really should think overly into it, really, because in the brief moments she'd had to skim the list over Sutton's shoulder before alerting her to her presence, she'd also seen Regan's name on that list. It didn't have to mean something in a romantic sense.

And yet, it was a strong enough feeling that it had helped her to urge Sutton to apply. It *was* a good opportunity and Sutton *should* apply for it regardless of whoever was on the cons list - Charlotte truly did believe that.

At her very core, she believed that no one should give up any opportunity they wanted for anyone else; it was how she intended to live.

And if the thought of Sutton leaving for six months gave her a momentary pause, Charlotte couldn't let herself get caught up on that. Sutton was, in essence, her closest friend. Of course she didn't want her to be gone.

She would miss that. She would miss their physical relationship. It was all something she didn't want to look *too* closely at, especially not when she had so much else to focus on at the moment. If Sutton was accepted – and Charlotte was sure she would be, because Sutton was intelligent and charming, far more than she even gave herself credit for – and subsequently decided to go, she would deal with it as it happened.

Deal with it and be absolutely fine; friends were friends despite the distance. Even if, granted, Charlotte was very much used to having Sutton around. Frankly, it was an entire thing that Charlotte did not want to think about.

And because this debate was happening so soon and Charlotte felt this immense pressure sitting on her shoulders from it, she didn't really have time to think about it anyway.

Elizabeth stood up and walked to her desk, running a finger down her agenda, before she turned back to face Charlotte. "The fact of the matter is this: nothing was handed to me on my political rise. I was underestimated and overlooked far too often. Something I've learned is that when you're given an opportunity, typically there are two reasons: either someone wants something in return and you need to be cautious, or in rare moments, you've hit a spot of fortune. In those rare times that leave you beholden to no one . . ." She trailed off, tilting her head meaningfully.

Charlotte picked up on all that was unspoken and nodded. "Then you'd be an idiot not to take advantage of it. *I'd* be an idiot not to," she finished with a murmur, as she smoothed her fingers over the invitation before leaning down and slipping it into her purse.

"You know what else you'd be an idiot to do?" She posed the question harshly, but there was softness in her eyes as she walked close enough to press her hand to the top of Charlotte's head, "If you didn't go home to recuperate before you feel worse."

It took effort for Charlotte not to roll her eyes or pout, and that alone was enough to tell her that she truly *was* experiencing a cold; this exhaustion was getting to her.

Even so, she took a deep breath and shook her head in refusal. "I can't; I have a department meeting this afternoon with Dean and some paperwork to catch up on. This isn't the time to be taking things easy; my debate with Naomi is in less than a week."

Her mouth snapped shut as her grandmother tapped her smartly on the chin. "Your debate is in less than a week, and you need to be recovered enough so that you aren't looking like you crawled out of a sewer live on camera. Your debate is exactly my point; you're working yourself into exhaustion over it."

The sewer comparison made Charlotte frown; there was no way she looked *that* bad.

"Besides, dear, you have a big future ahead of you – do you know how many sick days you'll wish you could take? I was in the office –"

"Less than a week after you had surgery on your knee. I know," Charlotte finished with a small smile, tilting her head back to look at her. She'd been at her side as much as her grandmother would allow during that time, acting as a somewhat intern during her summer break in high school.

She aimed her a questioning look. "Doesn't that mean that I *should* be working through the pain, so to speak?"

"It means that I have the utmost faith that you will be in my position one day. So I'm telling you now to take a day off while you can afford to." Her tone offered no room for arguments.

Still, a part of her resisted. Even though her limbs felt heavy and her head felt too full. With a small sigh, she suppressed a yawn and forced herself to stand up. "Perhaps I will this afternoon. Maybe I'll leave a little early. After my department meeting."

That would work. She would do as much paperwork as she could manage after downing some more ibuprofen when she was back at her desk and make it through the meeting. But, for once, she wouldn't stay late.

Compromise.

Elizabeth gave her hand a small squeeze. "I'll see you on Sunday for afternoon tea; we'll review debate points together. Now, rest tonight," she directed.

Charlotte grinned back. As much as her schedule had been busy and as much as she'd had going on in her personal life . . . she'd missed her when she'd been dealing with the foundation headquarters in DC. She always did.

She walked a bit slower than usual back to City Hall. It admittedly was because when she walked at her typical brisk pace, the world seemed like it was spinning a little *too* fast.

She was seriously considering the advantages of sequestering herself away into Dean's office for a power nap to get her through the afternoon when she saw it. More aptly, saw *her*.

A copy of the *New York Times* that Charlotte had yet to see today had been left for her on her desk. She looked around at her coworkers but was only met with the familiar sight of people working and a few caught her eyes with small smiles of acknowledgement before they went back to their work. Nothing out of the ordinary.

But her lips were already pursed in agitation as she looked back down to the paper. A picture of Naomi Young – one of her few official campaign pictures – was printed at the top, slotted above the front page interview.

The political world has had all eyes on the campaign for the unoccupied seat in the House of Representatives, vacated by the late John Kelvin. Candidates Naomi Young

379

and Charlotte Thompson have been engaged in a hard-fought and spirited campaign for the past three months.

For those just joining us in this impassioned campaign, Young is the daughter of former President, Charles Young, who was unseated by Thompson's grandmother, Elizabeth Thompson. Given this family history, there was bound to be an embittered campaign from the start.

Given the call for a special election, Young and Thompson will have a total of six months to run a full campaign. With those six months halfway over, we are closing in on an informal debate between the candidates.

Imani Diop has the final interview with candidate Naomi Young before the debate:

Diop: It's been reported that you and Charlotte Thompson have yet to meet face-to-face during the official campaign. Is this correct?

Young: Yes, that is correct. I presume we're both waiting until the official debate to fully come to a head. Though we've all certainly seen her around, haven't we? [quiet laughter]

Diop: Yes, it's apparent that Charlotte has been very proactive in her campaign strategy. The amount of interviews she's arranged in print and live television nearly doubles the appearances you've made on your campaign run thus far; I'm to assume this was a calculated decision from your team?

Young: Your presumption is accurate. Ms. Thompson has seemingly made it her mission to pop up everywhere possible and as often as possible. While I'm sure a strategy like that seems "proactive" to someone of her age and inexperience, the fact of the matter is that elections aren't won because of how much time you spend parading yourself about, but on substance.

Diop: And naturally, you feel your campaign is more substantive than your competitor. But in the last couple of months, a few of your stances have been criticized, especially in comparison to Thompson's more hot topic issues. Would you care to speak about that?

Young: In comparison to Ms. Thompson's platform? Would you care to elaborate?

Diop: Of course. For example, Charlotte has spoken at length about topics such as homelessness – a rampant issue in this city as I'm sure you're aware, better programs for public schooling across the nation, and working in tandem with governments in Europe about climate change. Your platforms –

Young: Yet Thompson speaks very little about international business, an issue which I have discussed in detail. I was the liaison for the Committee of Consumer Affairs and Business Licensing for years, among several other boards. And I'm aware that my support of the arts as one of my main subjects has come under some criticism, but I will continue to challenge those who pass judgement to look into my previous statements.

Diop: Right, you bring up a good poi –

Young: Furthermore, I implore you to think about disparaging the arts as a platform when being a proponent for my competitor, who – I will remind readers – has become fairly well-known because of a photoshoot, of questionable taste I might add, in a magazine.

Diop: Ms. Young, the Times, and myself, in any official capacity as an interviewer and journalist – have made no official statement of support in this election as of yet.

Young: Mhmm, maybe there have been no "official" statements, but it's no secret as to which way this publication leans. Regardless. Let's continue.

Diop: As I was going to say before, you brought up a good point; you've been on the board of several organizations and worked with the Committee of Consumer Affairs and Business Licensing. That has been another matter of contention during this election – your lack of personal experience in politics.

Young: I have not only been involved in meetings and fundraisers for nearly the entire time that Charlotte Thompson has been alive, but I grew up with my father – an esteemed and brilliant politician – not to mention my marriage to my departed husband. I was the wife of a congressman for much of my adult life; I have personal experience in politics.

Diop: So, essentially you might say you feel that this election is also a matter of measuring what one might feel is more valuable: a shorter amount of time with direct hands-on experience or a longer time on the sideline.

Young: I suppose someone could think of it such as that, though I would dare anyone to compare working in the Mayor's Office for merely a few years to something such as learning from my father during his time in office. Inexperience will always reveal itself. Whether you're relying on nepotism or not.

Diop: Certainly a matter that I believe will come up during your debate with Charlotte Thompson, and I'm sure many are looking forward to it including myself; I do wish very much that we could discuss more, but we are currently out of time. Thank you for joining us today, Ms. Young.

Young: Yes, I look forward to viewing your column, Ms. Diop.

The first debate between Young and Thompson is next week – December 22nd on C-SPAN.

Charlotte's teeth clenched so hard it physically pained her, and her already slightly blurred vision was suddenly enough to leave her a little dizzy. She was going to beat that woman in this election if it was the *last* thing she did. Every single time she saw any of Naomi's interviews, this feeling that she managed to contain only just burned up inside of her.

It wasn't just the insults – truly, Charlotte had grown so sick of those weeks ago, especially given that they were typically on the same subjects. Her age, her grandmother, her campaign strategy, her "inexperience" – because she'd seen all of those coming.

But really, it was the fact that she still had yet to truly pinpoint where Naomi was in this election. Despite the fact that Charlotte was up in all of the pre-election polls, Naomi didn't seem to be very concerned. Which was concerning in and of itself.

It set her on edge, and that? Well, that made Charlotte all the more antsy for their debate in three days. With a deep breath – that she was forced to take in from her mouth given her stuffed nose – Charlotte did her best to release the tension in her shoulders. Right in the writing in front of her was the date of her first face-to-face debate with Naomi on live television.

And despite the fact that she was already ahead and that it was truly the second debate, which would be less than a month before the election itself, that mattered the most, Charlotte wanted to *win*. She wanted to win gracefully and elegantly, appearing effortless even when it wasn't.

As much as it pained her to admit it, that wouldn't happen if she was sick.

She pinched the bridge of her nose, helping alleviate some of the pressure in her sinuses for a moment, before she glanced toward Dean's office. For the first time in her damn *career*, Charlotte was taking the afternoon off for a sick day.

***

Despite reassuring Dean when she left work, much to his relief, that she would go home and rest, Charlotte found herself poring over all of Naomi's interviews – both from past and present. Her own file sat side by side with Naomi's, the contents spilled over her coffee table.

She'd intended to rest. Really, she had. She'd talked herself into resting as she'd gone home early. Telling herself that maybe she *was* working just a little too much lately.

Despite the fact that she was tired, that her eyes were a little sore and her head was hurting, she couldn't stop herself from reviewing all of the information she'd compiled. It was –

When her phone beeped, it took her a moment to register it through her slightly disoriented thoughts, already swamped with work.

Sutton – 6:32PM
Hey! I know you've been really busy this week,
preparing for the debate and all. I just wanted

*to know if I could drop something off at your
apartment?*

Sutton – 6:33PM
*I know you're probably still at work, and you've
been so busy the last few days. I just . . . well, I have
a little something for you and I'd like to make
sure you get it before I leave.*

She frowned.

Charlotte – 6:35PM
Where are you going?

Sutton – 6:36PM
*Home! For the holidays, remember? And in, you
know, the spirit of the holidays I have a little gift
to drop off for you. You don't think it would be –*

Sutton – 6:36PM
*I can leave it outside your apartment door,
right?*

Sutton – 6:37PM
*Not that I think your neighbors are untrustworthy
or anything like that; you live in a really nice place.*

Sutton – 6:37PM
. . . you know what I mean.

Despite the fact that Charlotte wasn't feeling well and was stressed – for a multitude of reasons – and that she hadn't felt well all day, she felt herself smiling. It was impossible not to, not with Sutton's rambling texts.

She'd missed her. It had only been a few days, and a part of that had been Charlotte processing everything that had happened in the coffee shop. Meaning partial avoidance of Sutton and then throwing herself headfirst into her work.

Not that the two had any sort of correlation. But still.

She'd missed her. And yes, Sutton had been busy herself. Finishing everything up for the semester, spending time with her sister, and getting ready to go home for the holidays. Not that she had any shopping to do, as Sutton had proudly texted her that she'd had all of her holiday gifts for her family and friends prepared over a month ago.

The nerd.

Charlotte shook her head a bit, trying to clear it as she narrowed her eyes to focus and reread the texts. It was only then that she realized . . .

Charlotte – 6:40PM
Are you outside my door now?

Without waiting for an answer, Charlotte set her phone and stood. Then immediately regretted her action, as the living room spun for a moment with how light her head felt before she gathered her bearings.

Sniffling slightly and clearing her throat because she was acutely aware of how awful her voice had sounded earlier, she walked to her apartment door and slowly opened it.

Sure enough, there Sutton stood. She had her phone in one hand and a small giftbag in the other, her jacket on but – Charlotte noted with a small eyeroll even as she wanted to grin just a little – unzipped. It revealed a sweater underneath, a deep blue that made her eyes look even bluer, as if that was

385

possible. Her hair was in a braid pulled over her shoulder, a scarf around her neck and her face was adorably flushed from the December cold.

Charlotte had missed the sight of her in the last few days and the way her stomach had felt uncomfortably knotted lessened slightly.

"You're a sight for sore eyes." She grinned as she said it, and managed a wink even as she leaned against the door to help steady her.

Normally, her flirting got a smiling blush and small headshake from Sutton, or even an eyeroll that Charlotte could tell was pleased. She could see the start of a smile on Sutton's face as her eyes flickered from her phone in hand up to Charlotte's face.

Any semblance of a smile completely disappeared, replaced in seconds by a deep frown, forehead crinkling as her eyes sparked in worry. "Oh my God, Charlotte! Are you okay?"

Charlotte was very rarely embarrassed. In fact, it was difficult to remember the last time she'd been genuinely, truly mortified. Sutton had seen her in professional clothes, her more casual clothes, skimpy underwear and tank tops that she'd thrown on to sleep in, and completely naked.

However, Charlotte realized, she hadn't seen her in the baggy sweatpants that were only reserved for times she was in desperate need of being comfortable, her thermal long-sleeved shirt that was years old, and her hair tossed up into a messy ponytail, mostly just to stay out of her way while she'd worked.

Not to mention the ringing of her grandmother's words in her head that she looked like she'd come crawling up out of a sewer. And she hadn't been wrong. Her eyes were glassy, with bags under them, and a sallow complexion that she'd seen in the mirror when she'd gotten home . . . she knew it didn't make for a pretty picture.

Which was fine when she'd sequestered herself on the couch by herself to recover all alone. It was less fine when the woman who had never seen her as anything but put-together saw her looking like a mess.

A *sick* mess, nonetheless.

Shaking her head slightly, she grabbed the door handle. "I forgot . . ." With a deep breath, she squared her shoulders and refused to look as sheepish as she might have felt. "I came home from work not feeling quite my best. I've been resting."

The look on Sutton's was adorably concerned, her eyes wide as she quickly tucked her phone in her pocket. "You're sick?"

Pink lips pursed and Sutton seemed to instinctively step forward, her hand coming to rest on Charlotte's forehead gently. Her touch was cool and comforting, and the tension that had been lodged in her shoulders loosened at the brush of her fingertips.

It was out of her control, the way her eyes slipped closed for a moment, as she murmured, "I'm just tired, that's all. I've been working a lot."

When Sutton's hand disappeared, Charlotte's eyes opened slowly as she leaned more of her weight against the door. The frown on Sutton's face was the deepest Charlotte had ever seen on her, and she found that she didn't like to be the cause of it.

"You've been working yourself sick," her voice was tinged with disapproval. "Have you taken any medicine today? Eaten anything? Did I wake you up?"

The rapid questioning made Charlotte's head spin a bit and she held up her hand. "I took some ibuprofen for my headache, the thought of eating makes me nauseous, and don't worry; I haven't been napping." Muffling a yawn, she inclined her head. "I was actually looking at my notes for the debate; you could take a look if you –"

She cut herself off as Sutton stepped inside, more commanding than she usually did, shaking her head at Charlotte as she walked by her. Charlotte's eyebrows furrowed low on her forehead in confusion, though she wasn't displeased by the fact that Sutton was staying.

Slowly she closed the door and followed Sutton into her living room, where she was met with a surprisingly stern gaze. "You're telling me that you feel awful because you've been killing yourself working all day and night with the campaign and even though you're clearly not well, you're pushing yourself to keep working?"

It was pride and defensiveness that she felt tying together inside of her, and an alarming amount of *shame* from Sutton's words. Which – Charlotte had never been cowed by anyone about how much she put into her work, considering either time or energy.

"I couldn't help it?" She offered, her voice soft and scratchy. Even though Charlotte was fully aware that she *did* push herself more than others would – a matter of pride – the closer the debate came, the more time she felt was being wasted when she could be preparing. What was an hour or two – or three – of sleep in comparison with winning this election?

Clearing her throat again, she caught Sutton's gaze. "You know that Naomi is an underhanded competitor; you also know me –" Sometimes Charlotte still found it weird. That she had a friend who wasn't Caleb or Dean who *knew* her that well in only a matter of months. "I can't go into this without both eyes open."

The words apparently worked to calm Sutton's worry and she sighed. She bit her lip as she looked Charlotte up and down. "You can barely keep your eyes open right now," she murmured with a small smile that Charlotte returned, before shaking her head. "Come here."

For a moment, she thought Sutton meant *here* as in, to her. Before she realized that Sutton was instead gesturing at the couch, where, earlier, Charlotte had brought out one of the quilts she had folded in her linen closet that she had then wrapped around herself.

She walked closer, watching as Sutton efficiently grabbed at the comforter and shook it out before patting it down. Her eyes met Sutton's as she lifted her eyebrows before turning to arrange the pillows she had at the top of the couch.

"Sutton, darling, I'm not particularly in the mood for my typical stress relaxant." The corners of her mouth lifted slightly even as she sighed in regret.

Being able to have another night of marathon sex with Sutton would have been an ideal way to burn off some of her stress.

Sutton rolled her eyes but there was that light in them of amusement that Charlotte could identify even right now. "No kidding. Climb in here," she demanded softly, lifting the blanket that she'd arranged so that when someone laid down in it, the blanket would fold down over them.

Charlotte baulked, however, folding her arms over her chest. Looking like a mess and being exhausted to the point of being sick or not – "I'm not an invalid, Sutton."

It just so *happened* that her body chose to betray her at that moment and – damn it – she couldn't control the fact that she sneezed. Repeatedly, and hard enough that her eyes were watering and her head felt so light after, the room seemed to spin for a moment.

Still, though, she remained upright despite the fact that she hated being seen like this. She hadn't felt this unwell for years, and the last time she had, the only person who'd seen her was Caleb. And that had only been after she'd accidentally slept for over twelve hours and he'd been worried enough about her for missing their dinner plans that he'd let himself in.

Showing this weakness in front of her brother was one thing; showing it in front of Sutton, who had always seen her as better than this, stronger than this – the way she wanted everyone to see her – was different.

Even if the fact that the light of concern in Sutton's eyes was so strong it made her resolve weaken just a bit.

"I know you're not an invalid but you need rest. I'll put on that documentary we started a few weeks ago about the Peloponnesian War." Sutton only flushed a little bit as she said the words, and Charlotte grinned lecherously at the memory.

"It's your fault we didn't finish it," she retorted, and was still pleasantly surprised with the fact that Sutton had initiated sex between them that night, on a night that was supposedly going to be a friend-night.

With a blush, Sutton shot Charlotte one of those put-upon looks. "I don't understand your fascination with history." And when her blush deepened slightly, she clasped her hands in front of her. "And I personally find you more appealing than all of that."

Charlotte's eyebrows came up on her forehead as she tilted her head, knowing that Sutton had these moments where she could surprise her with her words and her actions, but loving that she was still impressed with her.

When Sutton's hands slid to her hips in a rather take-charge manner, Charlotte's eyes were drawn to the action. Her throat, which had been feeling a little sore, a little raw, all day, dried a little with the idea of Sutton *taking control* at other times.

It was frustrating that she was positive that she wouldn't be able to summon enough energy to act on any sexual thoughts right now. She barely caught herself from groaning aloud in irritation; the ease that she typically had holding herself together left her when she was feeling like this, and she hated it.

She wondered if Sutton could tell – because Sutton could read her more than most people could at this point.

When her own tired and heavy eyes made contact with Sutton's imploring ones, she didn't put up a verbal hesitation before walking back to the couch and standing in front of Sutton for a moment.

Her hands balled on her hips for a moment as she looked up at Sutton, who gave her a look of questioning amusement back. "I'll lay down . . . if you'll go over my debate notes with me. It would be nice to be able to talk to you about them."

Blue eyes narrowed at her, before rolling as Sutton relented, "Fine. If you lay down, *and* eat something, I'll go over your notes."

Feeling victorious, despite the way her stomach rolled a bit at the idea of food, Charlotte smirked. "Deal."

As she climbed into the little blanket nest Sutton had created on the couch, resting her head on the pillows, she supposed that showing this bit of weakness in front of Sutton wasn't all that bad. It wasn't as though Sutton was one of the women she'd hooked up with in the past, who Charlotte would have outright refused to spend time with like this.

It was Sutton, who wasn't looking at her with any sort of disgust regardless of how unsightly Charlotte was sure she looked.

Sutton, who tucked the blanket in around her in a way that was snug but not too snug; it was comfortable enough that Charlotte felt like her body was melting into the couch in relaxation only moments after laying down.

"I'm going to make some tea and get something easy for your stomach," Sutton informed her quietly as she smoothed the blanket over Charlotte, and her touch over the blankets made a warm, solid, persistent *feeling* settle in Charlotte's chest. Different from the lust and attraction she typically felt with her.

It was that feeling that prompted Charlotte's words to come out in a slightly drowsy whisper, "You're good at this."

Sutton leaned in just enough to press her cool hand against Charlotte's forehead and smooth back some of her hair. "It's not hard."

She begged to differ but wasn't up to the argument at the moment.

The way Sutton's thumb stroked over her cheek and lingered was soothing in a way Charlotte hadn't felt in days, and her mind stopped feeling like it had to run a mile a minute. Instead, it was easy for her to slip her eyes closed as Sutton gently moved her hand and padded into the kitchen.

She would just rest her eyes a bit while Sutton figured out what she deigned would be easy on Charlotte's stomach. Then she would go back to her debate prep, and hopefully gain some new insight, because she trusted Sutton's opinion.

She even had a list of topics she'd thought to ask Sutton's opinion on that she'd compiled over the last few days. Yes, she would just rest her eyes for a few moments first.

***

When she opened her eyes again, she didn't have immediate access to a clock, but she *knew* that it had been more than "a few moments" that had passed.

She knew because while she was still tired – she could probably go back to sleep and sleep through the night – she didn't feel that same bone-deep sleepiness that she'd felt all day earlier. And, if she'd been honest, a little bit the day before, too. She knew because her eyes weren't burning as she blinked them open, as though they were begging to close again. She knew because everything she'd been feeling before – the small aches and pains – were still there, but dulled down a bit.

Dulled down enough for her to instinctively know that she had gotten some *rest* for the first time in days.

She also knew that some time had passed because instead of a pillow under her head, there was a thigh. Soft and warm and smelling nice. Like Sutton. She was facing the television, which was off, but she heard soft music coming from somewhere.

As her vision cleared from cloudy grogginess, she could see that all of the debate prep work she'd had laid out all over the coffee table was organized into piles in the corner, instead of the spread-out way she'd had it. And she registered that long, gentle fingers were combing through her hair.

It was intimate was her first thought and her heart beat a moment too fast at the realization that Sutton was here and Charlotte was sleeping in her lap like this. But, then again, Sutton was someone who took care of other people naturally. Something like this for her while Charlotte hadn't been feeling well was second nature.

Beyond that, they'd shared a bed to sleep, while both being naked. Granted, those were designated sleeping-together nights, whereas this clearly wasn't. But it was comfortable, Charlotte decided, and it would be entirely unnecessary for her to dig around it too much when it could just be simple.

With a sigh, she turned slightly. Sutton's fingers stilled in her hair as Charlotte rested the back of her head there and blinked up at Sutton, who was haloed slightly from the lamp next to the couch. Red hair was both muted and highlighted, and the effect was almost dizzying.

Sutton smiled down at her, placing her phone on the table. Charlotte realized that was where the soft music was coming from, and it continued to play even as Sutton tilted her head, eyes wide and imploring as she asked, "Are you feeling better? You look a little better."

"A little sleep apparently was what the doctor ordered," she replied, letting out a small sigh before her eyebrow wrinkled in question. "What time is it?"

Sutton bit her lip before she flickered her eyes to Charlotte's stacks of paperwork on the table. "Um, it's almost ten."

Charlotte almost wanted to lament about the time that she'd lost, but it was difficult to do when her body felt more relaxed than it had in days. Still, she frowned and made herself sit up, despite the fact that the voice in the back of her mind was telling her that she didn't really want to.

"You didn't have to stay for so long," she admonished, quirking an eyebrow at Sutton.

Who shifted slightly, just enough to face Charlotte, and their knees pressed together. Sutton gave her a look that she somewhat recognized as one Sutton would sometimes give Regan. "Don't be ridiculous; I wasn't just going to leave you here while you were passed out."

"I suppose you did make a comfortable pillow," she teased and enjoyed when Sutton flushed. She took a moment to enjoy that slightly red tint on her face before she trailed her eyes over Sutton, noting that the jacket she'd still been wearing when Charlotte had fallen asleep was gone, revealing the soft blue sweater that her cheek had been rubbing against. On the table next to Sutton was her promised cup of tea and a box of crackers, and Charlotte couldn't help but quirk a grin. "You found something for me to eat I suppose."

Sutton followed her gaze for a moment, turning her head to look at the table next to her before she smiled sheepishly. "Well, I drank the tea while you slept. I could make more! If you wanted. You also had some soup, but when I came in to ask you what kind you wanted, you were asleep. And –" She cut herself off, biting her lip as she played with the ends of her braid.

Curious, because Sutton did not have that great of a poker face and Charlotte could tell there was something else there, she pushed, "And . . .?"

Sutton shook her head quickly and her eyes dropped to her lap before she took a deep breath and murmured, "And, well, I know you enjoy coming off as perfect, but you're still human. So, I couldn't just leave you here like that."

There was more to it than that, she could tell. But she let it go, for now, and dropped her mouth in mock-offense. "You're saying I'm not perfect, then?"

"Pretty close," Sutton tossed back and even though she was nudging Charlotte's leg with her own in a teasing way, she could hear the sincerity in her voice.

It made her stomach twist in that way, that Sutton way that made Charlotte feel good but also *scared*. And it was that feeling that reminded her of the invitation from earlier.

With a deep breath, she trained her eyes on Sutton's face and kept her voice deliberately light as she asked, "Sutton . . . did you invite me to your family's New Year's Eve party?"

Charlotte knew her answer as soon as Sutton's hand that was playing lightly with her hair froze and her face scrunched into a confused frown. "No? Are – did you get an invitation?"

Charlotte hesitated for a moment before nodding. "Earlier today," she explained. And she wasn't sure if it made her feel better or worse that Sutton wasn't the one behind the invite. Better, she supposed, because it meant there were no . . . lines being blurred there. Worse, because it most definitely came from someone in her family, then.

Sutton's perfect teeth dug into her bottom lip and her eyes flickered around the room for a moment before those baby blues locked onto Charlotte's, imploring, "Are . . . well, you don't have to come, if you don't want to." She let out a quiet, flustered laugh. "I just mean – you know, a lot of politicians get invited. And you met my dad a few months ago and all."

She watched the way Sutton's fingers tugged at the hem of her sweater for a few moments, before she thought of her grandmother's words from earlier. "Exactly; I figured that I would go, make some connections. You don't mind?" She ran her eyes over Sutton's face, looking for a sign that Sutton might not want her to meet her family.

She clearly wasn't going there as someone *involved* with Sutton, but still. Sutton was only newly out to her family, and Charlotte wasn't even sure if it was her entire family yet or not. She might not want the friend she was sleeping with there.

But Sutton released her bottom lip and shrugged. "No, it's okay; you should come. It'll be good for your campaign . . . and for you to experience some true cold," she finished with another nudge to Charlotte's leg.

And even though there was still this unease inside of her, she couldn't not chuckle even as she rolled her eyes. "All right, brat, we'll see just how tough you are then, won't we? When do you leave?"

"Tomorrow morning," Sutton sighed slightly. "Driving back with Regan and Alex in the same car for hours is never fun." Charlotte could imagine. Sutton continued, "I was finishing up packing earlier and that's when I realized that I still had your Christmas gift. That's why I came over, actually."

Charlotte sat up a bit straighter, only now thinking about the giftbag Sutton had when she'd first arrived. "You got me a gift?"

Sutton swallowed visibly and shrugged. "It's nothing really big. I mean, I get them for all of my friends for the holidays," she was quick to add on. "I just – well, I thought you'd like it."

There was an excitement to her, though, and Charlotte saw it in the energy she had as she quickly hopped up from the couch. She tracked Sutton with her eyes, watching her walk into the kitchen to where, Charlotte supposed, she'd left the gift.

After a few moments of debating with herself, she pushed herself up too. Walking to the closet right off from the living room, where she stored all of her Christmas gifts, she pulled down a small box right in the front. It had been a split-second decision, buying Sutton a present. It wasn't as though she was averse to the idea of exchanging gifts; Sutton was her best friend. And when she'd been walking around the mall with Caleb a few weeks ago at her brother's insistence, Charlotte had seen something that just . . . reminded her of Sutton.

Her hesitation only came a bit once she'd gotten home and wrapped it. Because maybe there were some small lines blurring between herself and Sutton. It was just some small things, though, and nothing that she felt was done consciously. They mostly followed Sutton's written guidelines, even if things sometimes didn't seem so easily clear-cut.

And during the moments Charlotte let herself really think about it – which was not often – she realized she wasn't only worried about lines blurring for Sutton, but also for herself. Which was something she'd never had to worry about before with anyone else.

It was unsettling.

The small wrapped box was in her hand as she sat back on the couch, curling her legs under herself on that small nest of blankets. Her eyebrows were furrowed in thought when Sutton came back to the room.

Her eyes lit up, that irresistible blue brightening as she waved the giftbag back and forth a bit, and that unsettling feeling faded. It just . . . it was difficult to focus on when she had Sutton grinning at her so brightly, even though her fingers tightened a little on the box in her hand.

Sutton's eyes latched onto it, and her whole face lit up in a way that was impossible not to smile at. "You got me something too? Even though I didn't tell you I got you something?"

Uncharacteristically self-conscious, Charlotte resisted the want to rub at the back of her neck. "It's just something small. Here."

She offered it to Sutton who took the small box with reverence, a glow in her cheeks, and excitement in her eyes. She looked from Charlotte's face to the small box that she was now moving her fingers over once, then twice, before Charlotte sighed and urged, "Open it."

Open it before she could let herself feel strange about the gift again.

Sutton's nimble fingers shifted the box open, revealing the earrings inside. They'd caught her eye as she and Caleb had passed a jeweler, and she couldn't help but be drawn to them. Because the blue of the sapphires perfectly matched Sutton's eyes, uncannily so. The gems were tear-shaped and fell from a diamond-studded white gold twisting design. She imagined the way the white gold would reflect in that red hair, just knowing it would be enchanting. They were elegantly beautiful. Understated, and stylish.

They reminded her of Sutton.

Then the smile on Sutton's face disappeared into more of a slack-jawed expression, and it made Charlotte's stomach drop.

"Charlotte – I . . . you . . ." Sutton trailed off, her voice light and full of wonder, matching the look on her face as she held Charlotte's gaze, a question in her eyes. A disbelieving laugh left her throat as she shook her head. "I can't – these must have cost a fortune. I can't . . ."

But her fingers gently stroked over the earrings, and the fact that Sutton was marveling over them in such a way gave Charlotte a heavy feeling of satisfaction. "So you like them?"

A job well done always made Charlotte feel accomplished, and she was finding that the way Sutton's breath left her quickly with a breathless chuckle made her feel headily so.

"I – of course I *love* them. But I can't accept them." She tore her eyes from the jewelry and regretfully met Charlotte's gaze in a look that was a transparent melding of sadness and guilt.

Charlotte was having none of it, as she reached out and gently but firmly closed the lid on the box and put her hand over Sutton's to press it toward her. "You *can* and you will. They'll look perfect on you, darling, and it's a holiday gift. Frankly, *not* accepting it is the rudest thing you could do to me."

"But . . . the price – mine . . . I mean, you'll see in a minute, but it's not nearly as extravagant as these are," Sutton feebly resisted, but Charlotte could hear that her heart wasn't in it, even as her fingers tightened around the earrings.

She didn't know if she'd ever felt quite so proud of herself over a gift before. Though, granted, she always had been good at reading people.

Having to clear her throat, her voice just a little scratchy still, Charlotte stroked her fingers down over Sutton's knee for a moment and gave her a wink that worked far better than the one she'd tried a few hours ago. "A pretty girl like you deserves pretty jewelry."

Sutton rolled her eyes but couldn't stop a wide grin even as she carefully placed the earrings on the table, as if she was afraid to damage them by being too rough. "They're beautiful; thank you so much, I . . ." She trailed off again, this time with a sigh, and Charlotte didn't miss the way Sutton's gaze fell to her mouth for a moment, before she looked away.

Looked away just in time for Charlotte to feel herself shiver a bit and lick her lips. She knew that Sutton wanted to kiss her; she recognized that look. But – tonight was a friend time, not a benefit time.

The thought was gone a moment later when Sutton reached down to grab at the gift bag and presented Charlotte with it, a small frown on her face. "I wish I had given you mine first."

Charlotte rolled her eyes and scoffed, "Enough with that; I'm going to love it." And oddly, Charlotte had the feeling that she might like whatever it was that Sutton would give her, even if it wasn't a gift she necessarily wanted.

Sutton worried at her lip again before offering Charlotte the bag. "There are two things in there."

Accepting the words with a nod, she took out the tissue paper before clasping the first object. She pulled it out, finding a container of seeds. She was already pulling them closer, to identify them, as Sutton explained, "I – well, we were talking about flowers a little while back, and you told me about all of the ones you loved to grow when you were a kid. I, well, have never had these –"

"Gardenias," Charlotte finished for her, and she continued to examine the seeds. She remembered that conversation with Sutton, and it was a typical feeling for her to miss all of the gardens her parents had at their home. How she hadn't seen anything here that could compare. "My favorite."

Sutton beamed. "I remember." Clearing her throat, she shook her head and scooted closer. "Anyway, a few weeks ago, I got the number for my parents' groundskeeper, and she sent me what she said are the best seeds and some instructions on how to best make them grow here this winter."

Charlotte was already thinking about where she should put them. It had been a while, too long, since she'd really done any gardening. Even something small, like for these flowers.

Coming back to herself, she shook her head and aimed a look at Sutton. "How could you possibly think I wouldn't enjoy these?" Her smile was large enough that it made her cheeks hurt a bit, because Sutton was just so . . .

Sutton shrugged, her eyes falling back on the earrings on the table. "I mean, they're seeds. Compared to – you know." But before Charlotte could reassure her, and she actually would *mean* it, Sutton shook her head, and that excitement from earlier came back a bit. "But, look at the next thing. Please."

Curious and excited herself, Charlotte placed the seeds on the table and reached back in, this time pulling out –

"Oh my God!" She gasped, unable to stop it – and unwilling to care. Her hand was almost shaking as she gripped the gift tightly. "This isn't supposed to come out for another four months."

Because right in her very own hands was a copy of *The Danger of Illusion* – the next in the series of Katherine Spencer's novels about Aurora the Knight.

Sutton was watching her, a bright smile and her hands tightly clasped together. "I got my official advanced copy." Sutton gestured to the book in Charlotte's hands. "I've already read it, and I was thinking about how we talked about how you were excited about *The Danger of Illusion*, and I thought – well, obviously you can tell what I thought."

"I can't wait to read it. After the debate, obviously, but . . ." She shook her head in disbelief, looking down at the book again. "Thank you, Sutton. These are some of the *most* thoughtful presents I've ever gotten. I mean it. How lucky am I for you," the words left her without thinking, as she smoothed her fingers over the cover.

The blush on Sutton's face was clear and pronounced even as she shrugged and looked away. "I guess pretty lucky," she returned with a teasing smile.

Reluctant to put the novel down, Charlotte did anyway. "The next time that I see you, we can talk about it."

That excited Sutton even more, and Charlotte couldn't take her eyes away from how radiant she looked, even as a yawn escaped her. It was the yawn that had Sutton's smile fading a little.

Her expression was still warm as she reached out and tucked the blanket that Charlotte was sitting with more tightly around her. "You should get some more sleep; I should probably leave," her voice was regretful. "I wish I could stay a little longer."

Charlotte *did* settle back comfortably against the couch; she was still, admittedly, exhausted, even if she didn't feel as badly as she had earlier. "Oh? Because you had a great time sitting here while I slept and you cleaned and organized?"

Sutton rolled her eyes, busying herself with pulling the blanket around Charlotte in a way that made her feel like she was wrapped in a cocoon. It was odd, the way she felt relaxed and calmed so easily. No one had ever made her feel this cared for before.

Or maybe she hadn't let anyone make her feel cared for before, a voice that sounded annoyingly like Caleb inside of her head pointed out. Semantics.

Sutton's hands smoothed down over Charlotte's sides before she brushed back her hair again gently and gave a soft smile as she stood. "I actually *did* have a nice time. It's nice to know for sure that you got some rest. And it was nice to see you before I leave," she finished in a whisper, her fingers brushing against Charlotte's ear lightly before it dropped.

She missed it.

For a moment – for one, silly moment, Charlotte wanted to ask Sutton to stay. The words dried up in her throat. To ask her to curl up around her and cuddle and give her that easy comfort she so effortlessly gave off. On a night where they weren't having sex – which was not the way to maintain boundaries. Which was entirely out of "the rules." In a way that was so not the right way to do this, that they'd expressly decided *not* to do it.

Sutton leaned in, and she could feel her body warmth as she pressed her lips to Charlotte's forehead. "Goodnight."

Maybe this was some sort of fever-induced craving, Charlotte wondered, even as she blinked her eyes open, only to see that Sutton hadn't pulled away very far, and was only inches away from her face. "Have happy holidays with your family."

"I'll be watching your debate," Sutton told her, and Charlotte could feel her warm breath against her face.

"You better," she murmured seriously, holding that contact. She didn't know why, but she wanted Sutton to watch. It *mattered*.

A few seconds beat by and Sutton didn't properly stand yet. Instead, she bit her lip and sighed lightly, sweetly, and Charlotte looked up at her, questioning with a quirked brow. For only a moment, because then Sutton was leaning in and closing that gap between them.

Sutton's lips brushed a kiss over hers, sweet and gentle. It was soft and decidedly *not* leading to anything else. It was comforting and sweet and made that warmth in Charlotte's chest that she'd felt earlier not only return but feel like it was bursting, as Sutton's fingers lightly traced over her jaw.

It made Charlotte's breath catch, and a feeling twist in the pit of her stomach. A feeling she was not familiar with but she was reluctant, not a moron, and she understood what that feeling was.

Sutton pulled back, standing swiftly and slipping the earrings gently into her bag. Seemingly entirely fine while Charlotte's heart hammered in her chest and she felt dumb, somehow. In a way that she was decidedly not okay with.

Her eyes were wide and she knew it, as Sutton smiled at her completely normal. She reached for her jacket and her voice was not out of breath as Charlotte felt she was as she told her. "Feel better."

"Yes. Bye," she dimly replied, taking in Sutton's quick wave as the other woman slipped out of her apartment.

Leaving Charlotte sitting on her couch, now wide awake.

Damn.

Chapter 17

Sutton typically loved being back at her parents' home for the holidays. She loved the comfort and familiarity. She loved having homemade cooking by someone other than herself, because Regan *could* cook, but didn't like to. She loved the holiday music and baked goods and the chaos of family dinner.

This year her enjoyment level wasn't quite as high as it had been in the past. The week in which she'd been home had been somewhat stressful. Her family was as wonderful as always; her own ability to simply concentrate on them was the issue.

When Charlotte hadn't answered her calls or texts during the first couple of days, Sutton hadn't thought much of it. Charlotte hadn't been feeling well right before she'd left and she had her debate to plan for.

But after four days had gone by without word from her, Sutton had started to actually miss her. They'd texted daily for the last several months, even if it was something small. Now, though, she was getting radio silence. The *only* response she'd gotten from her messages had been short and perfunctory. Such as *feeling better, thank you* in response to asking how she'd been doing.

Sutton might not have been an expert on reading people, but she'd spent so much considerable time in the last months talking to Charlotte, both in and out of text, that she knew when something was out of the ordinary. And six days of no conversation was so out of the ordinary for them, it was worrying.

It confused her, a lot. And it hurt, probably more than it should.

She just didn't understand. Was it because she was back in Massachusetts – an out-of-sight, out-of-mind sort of situation? Something about that made her stomach twist painfully; she didn't want to believe she was that forgettable.

"I just don't get it," she murmured to Grace, the dog she'd gotten as a teenager who still lived with her parents. A Belgian Sheepdog, she was several feet tall, weighed over fifty pounds, and loved running around outdoors. Sutton's New York apartment certainly wouldn't be fit for her, no matter how much she often wished it was.

Her dog's bright eyes looked back at her, and she nudged her head gently back into Sutton's hand as if she understood what she'd said. Sutton liked to believe she did.

They slowed their run to a walk as the house came back into view from the trail they were on.

"I think she's avoiding me." Saying the words aloud made her stomach twist uncomfortably, but it was the truth. "I just don't understand *why*."

With another sigh, she used her sleeve to swipe her flyaway hairs back before absently landing her hand lightly between Grace's ears and scratching as they started their walk back, eyes narrowed in thought.

Things had been going so well between them.

Charlotte had given her those earrings – the most beautiful, thoughtful gift she'd ever gotten from anyone in her life. Sapphire earrings that, as Regan had pointed out, matched her eyes perfectly.

She knew Charlotte didn't have many friends. It was her own choice, but still. She knew Charlotte chose to not keep the company of many other people, and maybe that could factor into some of the why behind the gift. Because Charlotte only let a few people truly into her life and if Sutton was one of them, she'd wanted to give her something nice.

Sutton could reasonably accept that. She could accept that maybe the earrings were a friendly gift from Charlotte, even if they stirred Sutton's more-than-strictly-friendly feelings, even despite Regan's not-so-subtle screeching about how *friends* didn't give other *friends* jewelry that cost several hundred dollars, if not more.

But Sutton's favorite part of their last evening together hadn't even been the earrings. When she'd seen Charlotte sleeping on her couch, beautiful even while sick, she'd allowed herself to watch her for a few minutes. But had then

404

told herself to stop being creepy, softly stroked Charlotte's hair back behind her ear, and intended to go sit in the kitchen.

Until Charlotte had shifted slightly and whimpered when Sutton had pulled her hand away. Those big, doe eyes hadn't even opened as Charlotte had shifted again, and her voice had been heavy and rough with sleep as she'd mumbled, "Don't go."

She'd been utterly powerless to resist, her heart thudding in her chest pleasantly as she'd situated herself. And had only felt better and better when Charlotte had nuzzled into her leg, seeming only to be truly restful when Sutton had started stroking her fingers through Charlotte's soft hair.

All of it, combined with the way Charlotte had sleepily sighed out her name when she'd nuzzled against her in her sleep, had been the last boundary to break inside of Sutton. There was no denying to herself from that moment that while she adored everything she had with Charlotte now – their friendship and their sex life and every moment in between – that she wanted to see whatever more they could have.

Then, she'd been given those earrings and there was just no going back. It wasn't just the little crush she'd had in the beginning, but something bigger. Real feelings.

The crushing weight of these feelings wasn't shocking for her in the least and she didn't know what exactly to do with them, because she knew that Charlotte's focus was currently securely on her career. But Sutton was okay with that, and she didn't intend to change anything between them at the moment. Charlotte wasn't the type to fixate on her feelings like Sutton was and she didn't intend to push her on anything, no matter how much she hoped that Charlotte's subtle signals indicated something deeper.

This unsettled feeling only nestled deeper inside of her, though, as she tried to figure out what exactly had happened. What could possibly have happened to cause Charlotte to essentially avoid her?

Seeming to sense her mood, Grace's nose gently rubbed at the back of Sutton's hand, and it was enough to drag just the smallest smile out of her, despite this heaviness she was feeling.

"I know Charlotte and I aren't together," she spoke softly, "So maybe I'm just overreacting."

Grace huffed out a breath gently against her hand.

"I don't think so either," she agreed.

They were still friends, at the very least. And the one time *Sutton* had gone into avoidance mode – after the first night they'd had sex – Charlotte had tracked her down the very next day to get answers from her. To make known how much their friendship meant to her.

And even if Sutton wanted to do that to Charlotte, and if she had the courage to, she couldn't anyway because she was here and Charlotte was in New York.

The light snow crunched under her feet, the grips on her running shoes holding tight as her breath puffed out in front of her, her childhood home getting closer and closer. She didn't want to ask Charlotte what was going on, though. It sounded needy, even to herself. And she definitely couldn't bring it up today.

Charlotte's debate, her first public face-to-face with Naomi, was tonight, and Sutton wasn't going to cause her any undue stress.

She worried at her bottom lip and tried to remember if Charlotte had mentioned anything that night that could give her a clue. Their present exchange had seemed to genuinely make her happy, so it wasn't that. She'd seemed begrudgingly accepting of Sutton's overwhelming need to take care of her, so she didn't think that was a problem either.

They neared the house and her eyes skimmed over the van belonging to the catering company her mom always used. They'd stopped by to finalize the hors d'oeuvres menu an hour ago and seemed to be packing up –

Sutton drew up short, nearly stumbling over her own feet and bringing Grace to a halt at the same time.

What if the problem had been right in front of her the whole time? Her *family*.

Sutton hadn't really questioned Charlotte's invitation to her family's New Year's Eve party. Charlotte was a politician, her dad was a politician, and they'd met a few months ago. It was easy for her to not overthink at the time.

But now that she was thinking about it – she knew that being outed amongst politicians was one of the few things that could truly make Charlotte nervous. And if she thought that she was invited to Sutton's parents' house because of *their* . . . relationship – she wanted to slap herself on the forehead for being so stupid.

Charlotte had a world-class mask in place, but she'd gotten better and better at reading it. There had been something slightly off in the way she'd brought up her invitation, but she hadn't thought it was something she needed to dig into. Clearly, she'd been wrong.

Her dad never mentioned Charlotte to her and if he'd been interested in getting to know her more, even politically, he would have asked Sutton about her. He was straightforward like that. Which meant that it had to have come from her mom.

Her mom who was *not* always so straightforward. Christ. Her mom, who knew of her sexuality, had invited her sex-friend to a family party. And that invitation was likely the cause of Charlotte's anxiety-induced avoidance.

"Come on," she urged Grace back into a jogging pace, feeling the urgent need to talk to her mom, even if she didn't know quite what to say.

There was Christmas music coming from the den and she followed it knowing that her mom had intended to enlist Ethan and Alex in bringing down their Christmas decorations this afternoon from the attic.

She zeroed in on her sister, whose attention was focused on the television that had the volume muted but was tuned to an MMA fight, as she absently sorted through a box of decorations. Setting her jaw, it was all she could do to not groan in irritation as she thought of the disastrous night when Alex had slunk into her apartment and met Charlotte half-clothed . . .

God, if Alex had said something to their mom about herself and Charlotte, she would kill her.

Taking a deep breath to calm her nerves, she cast another look toward her mom and Ethan, who were arguing across the room about why he wasn't allowed to decorate the tree before Lucas arrived tomorrow.

Approaching Alex, she kept her voice low as she got right to the point, "Did you tell Mom?"

Alex didn't look away from the televised fight and her response was a distracted, "What?"

"About Charlotte," she hissed in a whisper. "What did you tell Mom about Charlotte?"

That got Alex's attention and finally she looked at Sutton with a familiar glint in her eye. Teasing and mischievous. "Oh, you mean, the girl who came stumbling out of your room half-naked a couple of weeks ago, that Charlotte?"

Irritation and embarrassment flashed through her and she had to bite hard onto her lip to contain herself. "*Yes*, that Charlotte."

That smirk didn't go away even as Alex shrugged. "Why would you think I said anything?"

Sutton crossed her arms, holding tight to herself. "Because all of a sudden, Charlotte got invited to the New Year's Eve party and it just so happened that it was *after* you saw . . . what you saw . . . in my apartment."

Alex looked like she was getting far too much enjoyment out of watching Sutton stumble over trying to find the right words. She quirked an eyebrow. "Oh, and you, the sister who's been meddling in *my* relationship with Chris for years – including talking to Mom about it – is now blaming me for Mom trying to meddle in your love life."

If *that* wasn't some sort of confirmation, Sutton didn't know what was. Indignation rose, burning up in her stomach. "I never told Mom anything about your *sex life* even when I had ample chance. What did you tell her?"

"Fuck, Sutton, I didn't tell Mom or Dad or anyone about your stupid girlfriend!" Alex snapped out loudly in lieu of the whispers and murmurs they'd been talking in previously.

Everything felt like it came to a halt, including Sutton's heart, as both Ethan and their mother sharply turned to look at them.

"Alex!" She barely resisted the urge to bury her face in her hands because *God* why did stuff like this always seem to happen to her?

"You have a girlfriend?!" Ethan shouted from across the room at the same time.

Her cheeks *burned*. "No!"

Her blood rushed in her ears; Sutton had barely had this sexuality conversation with anyone aside from her mother and sister. She loved her younger brother so much but he had a very, very large mouth, and he was far from the next person she would have chosen to tell.

He ignored her, blue eyes imploring excitedly as he dropped the ornament he was holding and came bounding over closer to her. "Is she pretty?"

Unable to stop herself, all she could picture was an image of Charlotte's grinning face. And her stomach dipped low, because this was *not* how she wanted this to go. "I don't have a girlfriend."

She turned back to face her sister. "I can't believe you! You can't just – just yell about that!"

Gray eyes turning stormy, Alex turned to square off against her, hands on hips. "You're the one who came in here, yelling at me for no reason."

"I didn't yell! I *asked*. Quietly," she said pointedly, trying to take a calming breath.

Which was somewhat difficult when her brother came up next to her to ask, "Is she nice?"

"Yes," the word fell from her mouth and – damn. "I mean – no! She, uh, we aren't . . ."

God, she couldn't stand herself. She groaned, burying her face in her hands and somehow wishing she could take back everything and just go back to suffering in silence about Charlotte.

"That's quite enough of all this," Katherine's voice cut through everything in that effective way she managed. Sutton didn't think she had ever been more grateful to hear it, especially when her mom's hand landed on her shoulder in quiet comfort. "Ethan, go to the kitchen and start cutting the vegetables for dinner. I'll be there in a minute."

"But –" He gestured widely toward Sutton and Alex, indignant. "I want to know!"

Their mom silenced him with a look, and he sent Sutton big, begging eyes. That had always worked well on her, admittedly. But she couldn't focus on them with the way her stomach was in knots so tightly.

Though, it did make her relieved to note that there was no sense of judgement in those eyes.

Ethan heaved a sigh. "I'm the only one who even lives here anymore and I *still* get kicked out when the good stuff happens."

"Ethan –"

He quickly held his hands up in surrender at their mom's tone. "I'm going! I was just saying."

She waited until he had shuffled out of the room before lifting her hands in front of both Sutton and Alex, pre-emptively cutting off anything they were going to say. "Sutton, I was the one who decided to invite Charlotte to the party, without any prompting from your sister."

"I told you," Alex huffed out, crossing her arms in annoyance.

Their mother gave Alex another look, before turning to face Sutton. Her gaze sought hers out, catching and holding it with a look of warmth and patience. "After Alex mentioned meeting her –"

That warm comfort so easily taken from her mom dissipated with a feeling of vindication welling up inside of her, as she narrowed her eyes. "I *knew* you said something."

"Oh, barely," Alex shot back. "I told Mom that I met her. Literally that's all I said; not that I met her pants-less in your apartment at two in the morning."

Sutton barely restrained herself from whacking her sister in the arm, mostly because her little sister was more muscle than anything else and it would hurt herself more. Instead, she settled on a glare even as she felt herself blush again. "Alex, God, can you just *stop?*"

Sutton could live with the fact that apparently now her little brother knew she wasn't straight. And she could even deal with the fact that he had a big mouth and that for all she knew, he'd already told their other brothers. She could not live with everyone knowing *that*.

Hell, she could barely stand to know that Alex had said it in front of their mother. This awful mortification might never really go away.

Kate turned to Alex. "Please bring the empty boxes back into the attic."

"I'm being punished even though I didn't do anything?"

"You aren't being punished, I just want to talk to your sister."

"Yeah, yeah." She sighed, dipping a bit to grab at the stack of boxes the decorations had come from.

Sutton fastidiously avoided her mom's gaze, because – ugh – all she could think about now was the fact that she knew that Charlotte walked around her apartment in varying states of undress.

"Sutton, please look at me," she urged, her voice a murmur, as she reached out and placed her hands lightly on Sutton's shoulders. It was enough to make Sutton pull her eyes away from the floor where she'd been focused and instead look up and meet her mother's. Her thumbs stroked in gentle, comforting circles against Sutton's shoulders as she said, "I didn't need Alex to tell me that your friendship with Charlotte is . . . special."

It was too easy to lean into the comforting touch. "You didn't?"

411

"Hon, you've talked about Charlotte Thompson with me only a handful of times but whenever you do, you get this smile." Her mom lifted one of her hands up to gently swipe her thumb over Sutton's chin in a gesture she'd done to make her smile since before she could remember.

Sutton dropped her head back in embarrassment, her stomach clenching even as she shook her head. "No, I don't."

Kate smiled slowly. "You do, and it's been quite some time since I've seen someone make you smile like that, if I ever have. So it occurred to me after your sister mentioned meeting Charlotte – in passing – that I, too, would like to meet this woman."

Worrying at her bottom lip, she pressed, "She – she really didn't tell you?"

"She really didn't," her mother assured. "So, you might want to apologize for that. All she told me was that she met her when she came to see you, but no details." A thoughtful look crossed over her, expression playful, as she tilted her head. "I didn't know about the no-pants aspect until moments ago."

"Mom!" Sutton jerked back so her mother's hands fell and a surprised, choked-off laugh escaped her. Bringing her hands up, she rubbed at her cheeks as if hoping to get rid of her blush – which she was almost entirely certain was going to stain her face at this point.

After a few moments, she managed to take in a deep breath and her sneaker kicked lightly at the ground as she peered back up at her mom. Who, for all of her credit, looked completely composed.

"Charlotte really isn't my girlfriend though," she informed her, keeping her voice level, but needing her mom to know. "She's just – we're friends." And because she knew her mom wouldn't easily believe her, she pushed, "Really, Mom. She's . . . Charlotte, she isn't *out* – like, in public – because of her career and I don't want to be the reason that anyone knows. I just mean, you know, that should be her own thing."

Her mom seemed to understand exactly what she wanted to say, and she nodded, giving Sutton one of those warm, proud looks that she'd always relished in. "I haven't even discussed it with your father, I promise you."

"Thank you," she murmured, taking a deep breath before letting her head drop back a bit. Her ponytail swung down her back and relief swept away the tension in her shoulders.

Katherine got a look on her face like she wanted to say something else, but before she did, Ethan poked his head back in. "Um, nothing's wrong or anything," he started with a winning smile. "But hypothetically, if I were to have knocked the flour onto the floor, what is the best way to pick it all up?"

Sutton couldn't help but smile, a chuckle working its way out of her. Especially when she saw, now, the light dusting of flour in her brother's hair that he'd obviously tried to dust away.

Kate let out a long-suffering sigh. "You were supposed to start the vegetables. What in the world were you doing with the flour?"

Some more of the tension drained from her shoulders. She had a possible reason as to why Charlotte was avoiding her. And she would figure out how to make it stop. Somehow. For now, she would just do her best to be present with her family and not fixate on Charlotte.

**

Not fixating on Charlotte didn't extend to not watching her debate against Naomi, of course. Sutton had watched the debate with Grace for company, watching Charlotte in all of her glory on the biggest television in the house.

She'd been unable to resist texting her minutes before the debate, wishing her luck. And had held her breath when her message had been opened and seen immediately . . . only to get no response.

Still, Charlotte had been gorgeous and poised and utterly brilliant. She'd easily taken the debate, had deliberate and concrete answers for every question

413

thrown her way, and firm, serious yet witty rejoinders for everything Naomi tossed her way.

It was exhilarating to watch Charlotte on that scale. She'd felt a kind of pride she'd never had before in another person. She'd never been bored by politics or debates, it was just that it had never been her own passion.

Tonight had felt different. Personal.

When she hadn't heard from Charlotte post-debate, she told herself not to take it personally and had tried to keep busy. Charlotte was surrounded by her family and people who wanted to celebrate with her. Just because Sutton very much wished she could be a part of that at the moment didn't mean she would begrudge Charlotte celebrating herself.

She'd only let herself scroll on a handful of news sites to make sure that the general consensus ruled Charlotte as the victor in the debate before forcing herself to put the phone down to get some sleep just after midnight.

Only to jerk up, her eyes opening a bit frantically as her heart pounded at the sound of an incoming call. Grace, who had been lying at her feet, popped her head up too.

Shaking her head as her heart calmed, Sutton tried to calm her dog with a slightly clumsy head rub.

"I know, I know," she murmured, squinting slightly in the dark as her eyes adjusted, and she narrowed her eyes trying to locate where she'd placed her phone on the edge of the bed.

All of her hard-won sleepiness completely scattered, though, when she saw that it was Charlotte calling. And not just a regular phone call, but a FaceTime call. Quickly drawing her hand through her hair but then giving up because it was a mess from tossing and turning, she answered.

Her excitement didn't even fade as she had to blink blearily as the video she was seeing shook and wavered, moving around and shifting so much that it might make her dizzy.

Charlotte's face wasn't actually visible and it looked like she was walking.

Blowing out a breath, Sutton cleared her throat, "Charlotte? Um . . . are you there?"

The motions on the phone stilled, and after a moment – and a muffled curse coming from Charlotte that made Sutton smile – she was face-to-face with her. Charlotte's hair was a bit mussed, as opposed to the perfectly styled look she'd had on television earlier, and her face was washed free of makeup.

Sutton's heart skipped a beat in her chest at the slow, wide smile that immediately appeared on Charlotte. "Sutton, you're here."

Okay, definitely not an accidental call, then. That much was more relieving than she could properly say – than she *should* properly say. But it had been a long week of herself initiating texts or calls, to almost no avail.

"I am," she answered slowly. "Where are you?" She asked as Charlotte continued to walk – she could see the slight blurring of the background behind her, this time keeping her face onscreen though.

"My apartment. I just got home for the night, actually. I was taking off my coat when I started the call, so I apologize for that." Charlotte sighed, humming softly under her breath, as she spun the camera so that Sutton could see for a fact that Charlotte had indeed just entered her bedroom.

The humming was abnormal and Sutton's eyebrows furrowed together slightly in a bit of confusion. Still, she shrugged. "It's all right. I'm – I'm glad to hear from you," she told Charlotte, truthfully, quietly. And she huffed out a light laugh as Grace sat up farther, nudging her face lightly to see the source of light, Sutton's phone.

As Charlotte turned her phone back to her face, her smile quickly disappeared. It was instead replaced with a wide-eyed look of what Sutton thought was shock; she'd never seen that before on Charlotte's face. "Sutton, what is that?"

Her tone was teasing but also carried an underlying tone of genuine alarm, as if she couldn't decide which one to use, and Sutton couldn't help but let out a loud laugh before she managed to cover her mouth – remembering that she was at her parents' house and it was after midnight. "This is my dog, Grace. I told you about her. You look big but you're just my baby, aren't you?" She cooed softly at Grace, who wagged her tail at the tone and rubbed her face against Sutton's.

Charlotte watched with a tentative smile, even though her eyebrows remained doubtfully raised just a bit. "If you say so," her teasing was more pronounced now, but even so a bit apprehensive.

"I do," she nodded, before she pointed at Charlotte and Grace followed her lead. "This is Charlotte. Charlotte, this is Grace. Aside from Regan, my best friend growing up."

And those large brown eyes narrowed ever so slightly as she leaned in closer to the camera and cleared her throat. "Nice to meet you, Grace."

Her tone that wavered somewhere between serious and playful as she greeted her dog made Sutton's heart flip-flop in her chest. It hadn't been long since they'd spoken, not really, but she had missed her. She looked down at her comforter, letting this feeling of utter relief wash through her.

When she dragged her gaze up to the camera, Charlotte was staring right back at her, eyes dark, and the corner of her mouth tugged up in her typical smirk.

Well, almost like her typical smirk – it was a bit deeper, almost lascivious, and . . . were her eyes a bit glassier than usual? Added in with the late-night FaceTime call that had started out so imbalanced as she'd walked, the previous quiet humming under her breath, and –

It dawned on her in that moment. "Are you drunk?"

Her mouth dropped open a bit in surprise. She'd known from months ago, back in the very beginning before they'd met, when Charlotte had given her tips and stories about picking up and hooking up with women, that it wasn't as though Charlotte never drank.

However, in the months that they'd been talking, Charlotte hadn't had more than one glass of any alcoholic drink at a time. Well, that was in public. She'd maybe have two when she'd had dinners and nights in with Sutton a few times, but not even enough to really be tipsy.

Charlotte shook her head, *tsk*ing for a moment. "Don't be ridiculous, darling, I'm not drunk." She grinned, mischievously. "Though, I might have imbibed a bit; Caleb and Dean were *awful* influences after the debate."

Her eyes narrowed in confusion. Not that she didn't think Charlotte deserved to celebrate and she'd assumed that she was, but Charlotte had been so staunchly against *imbibing*, against being anything but her top-functioning ability at all times, that Sutton wondered if this was related to Charlotte's other strange behavior.

She would make an awful detective.

Grace nudged her again before jumping off of her bed and leaving the room through the cracked-open door.

Charlotte chuckled softly. "I apologize, is Grace against alcohol?"

Sutton rolled her eyes playfully back. "No, but she's used to being asleep already."

"Did I call too late?" Charlotte asked as she stationed her phone on what Sutton thought was her bedside table.

"No, it's okay," she was quick to say. "I'm actually glad you called. I wanted to tell you how amazing you were tonight."

The smile she got in response was almost dazzling in its sincere joy. It wasn't a look Charlotte wore often, and it was beautiful.

"I'm glad you were watching. I wanted to call you when I got your text before the debate." Charlotte paused after speaking, her eyes widening at her own admission.

But warmth flowed through Sutton, helping to soothe all of the sadness she'd felt in the last few days. "You did?"

Charlotte huffed out a breath at herself, sounding frustrated, before she shook her head. A thoughtful frown pulled at her mouth as she stood from her bed, leaving her phone where it was, and walked to her dresser. "I felt – less

417

nervous than anxious, I suppose, and I wasn't a fan of that." Charlotte sighed, sounding a bit far away – and not because of the bit of distance between them, either. "Before I even realized it, really, I was thinking that I'd like to hear your voice."

She couldn't quite discern her tone, certainly not through this FaceTime call when Charlotte wasn't even facing her, but . . . it made that small glimmer of hope burn brighter in her stomach. "Yeah?"

"Mm." Charlotte confirmed, the short sound seeming pensive. In the way one's voice got when they'd been drinking. Not quite enough to be drunk, but enough to be noticeable.

"Maybe because we haven't spoken much lately," she hedged, trying to keep her voice light, but also just wanting so much to *know* if there had been anything behind it.

Charlotte reached up to take off her earrings, and it was sort of mesmerizing in a way. With the camera on her phone directed toward her back, her dress showed the way her shoulder blades moved with her now that the light, sleek blazer she'd been wearing earlier was gone.

Her silence in the next few moments was not comforting at all, and Sutton bit her lip as Charlotte turned back to face her. The look on her face was serious, and she tilted her head as she looked at Sutton.

"That's probably it," was all she said, though, before shaking back her hair and undoing it so that all of those luxurious curls fell down her back and shoulders. "I've gotten used to you being here, so it was a comfort to hear from you before I went out there."

It should be unfair to look so good doing *anything*. Instead, it just made her admire Charlotte more, and her throat went dry.

"I've . . . gotten used to having you here, too," she told her, thinking about all of the little stories she had, things that she had wanted to tell Charlotte about in the last week.

She stared at her in contemplation. She knew more about Charlotte than most people, and sometimes she was still a mystery to her. Like, if she'd wanted to talk to Sutton in the last few days, why hadn't she called? Or answer Sutton's calls with more than cursory responses?

How could Charlotte make it sound like she missed her when she'd been the one to create the distance?

So, even though she knew it sounded very girlfriend-esque, she couldn't help but ask, "Did I do anything wrong before I left?" She bit her lip, hating that she sounded needy but wanting answers. "Or did I do something to upset you?"

Charlotte gave her a puzzled look that seemed so genuine, it alleviated some of the weight that had been sitting on her shoulders. "Why would you say that?"

Okay, with Charlotte giving her that concerned, confused look as she walked closer to her phone, Sutton maybe felt a little stupid.

She blushed, shrugging, grateful that the only light in her room was from her phone. "It's just – you didn't really seem in the mood to talk to me. Texts or calls or anything, even though we've basically talked almost every day ever since we became friends, so . . . I thought; well, I already told you what I thought."

She decided not to mention the affectionate nicknames that she'd been missing, too.

Those big, brown eyes looked at her and even though they were miles away, in different regions, she swore she could *feel* the concern in them. And maybe what she thought was regret, before Charlotte shook her head and closed her eyes for a moment, as if gathering herself.

"You did nothing wrong, Sutton, you're honestly – perfect," Charlotte told her, and she sounded so sincere and looked so serious that Sutton couldn't not believe her.

Especially because Charlotte said the word *perfect* with this sense of exasperation, which Sutton didn't understand at all.

419

"The best friend I've ever had," Charlotte murmured. She gave her a small smile before shaking her head, a small crease appearing between her eyebrows. "There was simply something on my mind that I was dealing with, and I seem to have dealt with it in a manner that inadvertently hurt you. I promise, it's not about y–" Charlotte bit off her sentence, inhaling sharply, before she amended, "I promise that it's nothing you are going to have to know about."

That wasn't as reassuring as Sutton would have liked, and she knew that her doubt was showing on her face – because she could see her face in her little camera box.

"Do you want to talk about it?" She offered, and really hoped Charlotte would.

But Charlotte shook her head before saying, "I have it handled. It wasn't as big of a deal as I was making it. Thanks, though."

She was receiving that look Charlotte gave her, that affectionate warm one, so she supposed maybe it really wasn't that big of a deal after all. Besides, Charlotte was one of the most capable people Sutton had ever met – she imagined she could handle most anything.

"All right, but if you *did* need something, I'd be here to listen," Sutton couldn't help but add.

Apparently to Charlotte's amusement as she grinned, her eyes dipping to the floor before looking back up into the camera at Sutton. "And that is why you truly are the best friend I've ever had."

It was that comment that for some reason made her think about her own issue from earlier in the day; her mother – and siblings, now – knowing that Charlotte actually wasn't her girlfriend but was more than her friend.

Biting the inside of her lip, she debated telling her. It wasn't like she wanted Charlotte to know that anyone in her family *knew* about their . . . arrangement. Because Charlotte hadn't reacted that well to Alex's finding out, having fled her apartment immediately afterward.

Sutton's *mom* knowing? That was a whole other thing. And she had Charlotte here with her – in a manner of speaking – for the first time in basically a week. For the first time in a week, she felt like things were normal for them.

But she felt this guilt lodged low inside her stomach at the thought of not telling her when she knew that it was probably something Charlotte should know. Especially before Charlotte walked into the party.

It was common courtesy, right?

Groaning quietly at herself, Sutton rubbed her hand over her forehead, for once wishing that her brain would just be quiet.

"Not to, um, add to your stress or anything, but just so you know . . . my mom, well, she sort of knows that we're more than – that we've slept together."

She twisted her blanket in her hand as she quickly added on, "Not that I think she's going to say anything to you. Actually, she's said that she won't. But, she invited you to the party and I wanted you to . . . know," she finished lamely.

But instead of the look she was worried she would be met with, not that she'd ever seen Charlotte ever looked panicked, Charlotte was just giving her a quietly patient stare. Her eyebrow lifted slightly, with a small smile on her lips.

"I figured," was all she said, with an easy shrug. "It's all right."

"You *figured*?" she asked, incredulous. "It's okay?" She'd worked herself up over that for nothing?

Did that mean – something? Did it mean that it was okay that them being more-than-friends was more of an openly known thing?

Charlotte tilted her head, seeming a little amused, as she placed her phone back down on the bedside table. "Yes, I thought it was somewhat of an odd thing to get an invitation, especially given that you said you weren't responsible for it. And, well, she's your mother. It's not like she's going around discussing your sex life with people."

421

Sutton couldn't help but let out a short, disbelieving – at herself – laugh, as her head fell back onto her pillows. Her eyes closed slightly as she blew out a short breath. Of course Charlotte had already put it together; who did Sutton think she was talking to? And of course Charlotte had already pegged her mom as discreet.

Okay. Well, that solved that.

That really was a weight off of her shoulders. Because if it wasn't the party, then Sutton could truly not name a reason for anything pertaining to her that might have caused Charlotte to avoid her. She supposed it really was something that Charlotte was just dealing with.

"You know," Charlotte began, and Sutton picked her head up from where she'd dropped it back against the headboard. "I called earlier because I was thinking about you on my way back from celebrating with Dean and Caleb at their favorite bar, and I wished you would be here."

For a moment, Sutton's heart warmed at the words because: Charlotte wished she was there.

But then she registered the low tone Charlotte was using, one that she recognized from when they'd had sex. It was low like when Charlotte would say her name, when Charlotte would tell her what to do to her. *Harder, faster, more, God yes* – that voice.

She couldn't exactly see Charlotte's eyes clearly because she was standing a few feet away, but she knew the look on her face.

And she flushed, feeling the blush deep in her cheeks as her stomach clenched. "You – yeah?"

God, her throat was already dry and she had to clear it just to get that word out.

"I'm having this *energy* right now," Charlotte informed her, her tone still a little low, a little breathless as she reached her hands up behind herself. "And I've been feeling it ever since I won the debate. Just – this rush of adrenaline. Excitement. Then we were at this little private club the boys have gone to, and the drinks and the dancing . . . mm, well, that only made me feel even more wanting."

"Dancing, um, at a club?" Sutton's mouth went dry as she heard Charlotte pull down the zipper of her dress. Even though the thought of Charlotte out dancing, dancing with other women in a club, didn't sit evenly in her stomach. Not when she knew that was how Charlotte had previously found the women she'd had her hookups with.

"It was one of my interests listed on the app on which we met, Sutton," Charlotte's teasing tone had her gulping. Or maybe it was the way Charlotte moved her arms and let her dress fall in one, sleek motion to the floor.

They'd had more sex by now than she could individually recall. But with Charlotte standing there on display, unreachable, wearing only a matching strapless bra and a tiny, lacy thong . . . Seeing her never got old.

"Fuck," she breathed out, barely biting back a whimper, because Charlotte didn't even look like she was real. She looked – she looked like she was some sort of pinup, and Sutton squeezed her thighs together subconsciously, trying to get some friction.

Charlotte's hands slid up to rest on her own hips, and Sutton's eyes were glued to the motion as her own fingers twitched. Wishing *she* could touch those hips, the ghost of the feeling of that warm, soft skin under her hands.

Charlotte sighed, running one of her hands up her stomach and pausing at her throat, the other moving to hook her thumb into her panties, moving lightly against the skin of her hips. "I was there, dancing, and getting worked up, and I just kept thinking about how much I wanted to come home and have you make me come."

"You did?" Sutton was still breathless, her hand grabbing tightly at her blanket. "You wanted me? Even . . . while you were out?"

Charlotte's chuckle was low and skirted over Sutton's body in this way that shot right through her body. It shouldn't be possible for a single sound to make her wet, but she could feel herself.

423

Her eyes were glued to her phone screen as Charlotte reached behind her and fluidly undid her bra. Her nipples were already hard, and she slid her hand forward again, pinching at one.

Sutton knew by now just the way to suck and nip with her teeth to feel Charlotte's back arch, and the whimper that would escape her throat. The way her hands would slide into Sutton's hair and hold her there.

Charlotte hummed low in the back of her throat, scratching her own hand lower, down over her stomach. "God, Sutton . . . you say you've never fucked a woman, but you are such a fast learner. Delightfully fast."

It was so heady. Charlotte's words adding to the aching between her legs, the fact that not only had Charlotte been turned on for hours – but that she specifically wanted Sutton. Charlotte could have anyone she wanted.

And she chose to come back home, to her.

Her head fell back again, this time with a groan. "You're a really good teacher."

"Oh yeah?" Charlotte sauntered closer to where she had the camera resting on the bedside table.

Her breath caught in her throat, heat building in her stomach, moving down, her clit already starting to throb, with the sight of Charlotte's body right there. Right in front of her. She had a perfectly close view of those soft, firm breasts, and the light definition in Charlotte's stomach muscles as she leaned over to where Sutton couldn't see.

She bit her lip, hard, her hand not holding her phone slipping under the blankets and pressing hard against her thigh. "Charlotte, are . . . what are we doing?"

Finally, Charlotte shifted back enough so Sutton could see her face again, close enough now that she could see her eyes. Dark, so dark, and the way her lips were wet from having sucked on them in the way she did when she was turned on.

"I thought it was obvious by now what we were doing. I want to come," Charlotte practically purred, the sound skittering over Sutton, making her shiver. "And I want to see you while I do. I want us both to come, just like this."

Sutton groaned quietly, uncontrollably, even as her eyes widened. "You – you want us to touch ourselves together? Watching each other?"

Charlotte's laugh was low and quiet as she settled back into her bed. Her phone was still on her bedside table, now facing her though as she laid against the pillows, and Sutton had a perfect view of her from the chest up.

Once again, Charlotte's hand slid up, coming into view and cupping her own breast before pinching and pulling her nipple. And once again, Sutton's eyes were glued to the vision before her, and – God, she could hardly contain the moan that wanted to leave her throat.

"What did you think I was getting at when I stripped in front of you, darling?" Charlotte asked, before she sighed, switching to her other nipple, her second hand coming up to tangle into her hair.

Sutton's mouth was ready to water at the want to be *there*. To suck and lick and bite Charlotte's chest. "I, I wasn't really thinking clearly," she admitted.

"Tell me, do you want to do this?" Charlotte implored, slowing her motions.

Sutton found herself nodding, her heart thumping in her chest. "I've never done this before." She knew for a fact she'd never, ever wanted someone the way she wanted Charlotte. Would never have been this aroused, this wet, just from seeing someone else she'd slept with strip for her.

"Perfect," came the slightly breathless response, and Charlotte looked at her in the camera, "Now. Tell me," she rasped out.

Sutton's hand was digging hard into her thigh, and her thighs were still pressed together, even though she couldn't help but rock her hips slightly. "Tell you?"

"Touch yourself, beautiful girl, and *tell me*," Charlotte repeated.

Her eyes flew open and she knew her cheeks were dark red in a second from her blush. "I can't – I can't do that."

"You can't touch yourself?" Charlotte's tone dropped low and Sutton gulped, and she could feel herself dripping already.

It had been too long without Charlotte's touch, and she'd gotten accustomed to it. Gotten used to the way Charlotte could make her come so hard she couldn't think, could barely breathe from the intensity.

"Uh, no, that's not what I'm saying." She swallowed hard and felt almost dizzy with the intensity of Charlotte's stare. "I just – what . . . do you want me to tell you?"

Charlotte shifted even closer. "I want you to touch yourself and tell me how wet you are. Tell me what you want, what you wish I was doing to you. God, Sutton, I want you to just moan for me if that's what you want to do."

She – okay, she could do that. Slowly, she nodded, and bit her lip as she brought her hand up a bit to dip into the waist of her pajama shorts.

She shivered as she brushed against her own waist, her fingers pausing even as her breath came a little shorter. She was surprised at how much she actually wanted to do this – wanted to come for Charlotte, with Charlotte watching. But, it couldn't leave the back of her mind: what if she was bad at this . . . video sex?

Charlotte was watching, though, arousal heavy in her gaze, and she seemed to understand exactly what had Sutton pausing.

Luckily for both of them, Charlotte had no such hesitations.

"On top of your panties at first, darling. Slide your hand down, and rub yourself," Charlotte instructed, her voice coaxing.

And Sutton shuddered hard, her hand sliding just as Charlotte had directed.

Her mouth fell open as she pressed her fingers against her panties. She'd needed friction so badly, and she hadn't even realized just how much. Just *how* wet she'd gotten from watching the way Charlotte had stripped for her. From hearing Charlotte tell her what she wanted.

426

"I'm . . . I'm wet," she whispered, pressing harder against herself, her hips rocking into her hand.

Charlotte let out a quiet sound, and Sutton could see her hands still on her chest, tugging her nipples harder. "Yeah? You can feel how wet you are through your panties?"

Sutton nodded, biting her lip, but it didn't stop the half-moan that got caught in her throat. "I – yes." She groaned. "I'm, my panties are wet. I can feel myself through them."

She rocked down harder, rubbing at her clit through her panties and sending sparks through her body, exhaling on a groan when she saw the way her words made Charlotte shiver.

"That's . . . oh, that's good darling. Go under your panties, then. Go under and tell me just how wet you are." Charlotte's hands had stilled, but she was looking at Sutton so intensely, she thought she would explode from it.

She followed Charlotte's words, sliding her hand into her panties and pressing right against herself. The gasp that left her with the contact right against her clit was uncontrollable, as was the automatic continued rolling of her hips.

"I'm – really wet. Um, oh . . ." She trailed off, sliding her fingers lower, her head falling back a bit as she rubbed over her entrance, her fingers easily slipping through her lips, coated from her wetness. "S-so hot."

"Fuck. Keep touching, tell me what you're doing," Charlotte told her, her voice more urgent than before. Needier.

Sutton liked it.

She slipped her hand up again slightly, whimpering in the back of her throat as she tried to talk. "I'm touching my clit. In circles. Uh . . . oh, God, it's hard. Th-throbbing against my fingers," she managed as her head fell back into her pillows completely and she rubbed her clit faster.

Charlotte moaned in response. "Just like when I wrap my lips around it."

Sutton's hips jumped into her hand hard at her words. "Yes," she groaned out. "Just like that."

God, the thought of Charlotte's mouth on her already had her clenching and she slipped lower, fingers slipping inside of herself.

"I'm, t-two fingers inside," she whispered, moving her hand faster, pushing in deep and feeling herself squeezing. Moving even harder, rubbing at her clit with her thumb and – she didn't think she was going to be able to last much longer.

"I love fucking you just like that, darling. Pressing my fingers into you, feeling the way you squeeze around me, working yourself around my fingers. Fuck, you feel so good," Charlotte's voice seemed to float to her, sounding almost choked with how breathless she was.

Sutton's eyes were closed so tightly, her body drawing up even more tense as she moved into herself faster and faster, stroking her clit even as her body started to shake. "You feel better," she managed to say on a low moan.

She was so close. So close to coming, she could feel her hips already jerking into her hand, her clit starting to pulse.

"Charlotte – I'm," she breathed, her teeth clenching as the heat coiled tightly low in her stomach, fanning out slowly. "I need . . ."

"I need to see you come, Sutton," Charlotte told her, whimpering, and it was all she could do to not drop her phone as her orgasm hit her with Charlotte's words.

The feeling hurtled through her, a strangled moan caught in her throat as she managed to open her eyes just enough to see the way Charlotte was watching her. God, her body shuddered harder, heat sparking through her for long moments as the blood rushed in her ears.

She was breathless when she came down from her orgasm, the grasp on her phone so tight she thought it might hurt her hand later. And she thought she heard a muffled buzzing sound, but maybe it was still the blood rushing in her ears.

She felt somewhat boneless, melting into her bed, as she brought her phone closer. It took her a moment to see that Charlotte's eyes were no longer turned toward her, but instead her head was pressed hard into her pillow, and Sutton could see her neck straining.

Her mouth was open, breathless whimpers and groans escaping her as one of her hands grabbed tightly at the headboard above her and the other –

The other was out of her view, but she could see her arm moving quickly and – holy hell, she was the sexiest thing Sutton had ever seen. So stunning her throat felt too dry, even when she tried to swallow.

Charlotte's back arched a bit, a furrow in her brow. "Sutton," broke from her lips, and despite having just come hard, she felt herself shudder.

"You're incredible," escaped her in a murmur, and she wished viscerally to be able to *be* there, to feel Charlotte.

Charlotte's eyes fluttered open at that, brown eyes bleary and barely able to focus on her. And then Charlotte's back arched so hard, her chest was pushed up in the air, her head snapping back, and Sutton could see the way she shuddered so hard it wracked her entire body as she came.

With Sutton's name on her lips.

She watched, entirely too enthralled to look away as Charlotte came down from her peak. Her chest was heaving as her back fell into her pillows, and she had to blink a few times at Sutton before her eyes cleared.

The hand that had been out of her range of vision, came up, holding a –

Her eyes widened. "Is that a vibrator?"

Charlotte hummed in confirmation before switching it off, and that buzzing Sutton had been hearing disappeared. She placed it on the table, a sleepy yet satisfied smirk on her face. "If I don't have you here to touch me, that's the next best thing."

Her mouth was dry, assaulted with images of Charlotte using the vibrator on herself like she just had been. With images of using it *on* Charlotte.

"That's . . . smart," she said, her throat dry, still slumped into her own pillows.

Charlotte sighed, languidly, as she stretched. "We should use it one of these times together," she murmured as she pulled a blanket over herself.

"I – would like that," she agreed, and . . . she hadn't thought about it before, but now that she was, she very much wanted to.

Charlotte let out a large yawn. "Despite you telling me about not having many sexual adventures, I'm finding that I love how much you want to try out with me."

Sutton didn't know why she was still blushing at that, not after Charlotte had just touched herself while watching Sutton come on video, but it was happening. Still, she gave a small, sheepish smile. "You make me feel more confident. More . . . sexy," she confessed.

Charlotte's yawn was contagious though, and she reached out to balance her phone on her own bedside table so that she could cuddle back into her own blankets. Unlike earlier, she wasn't having any issue for her eyes to feel sleepily heavy.

Big brown eyes, despite clearly being exhausted, opened. "You're incredible sexy," there was no teasing tone, no playfulness. Just a serious informative tone and it made Sutton flush, even as a warmth spread in her chest.

"I like that you get me to try new things," she told Charlotte quietly in the dark, as they both settled into their beds.

"Mm, me too," Charlotte whispered, her eyes closing. "Coming with you, celebrating winning my debate. I count tonight as a win."

"I agree." Sutton watched her for another long moment, eyes taking in the soft vulnerability Charlotte seemed to only have when she was sleeping.

She had no energy to reach out and end the call, and she certainly wasn't going to if Charlotte wasn't going to.

So she settled into her blankets, letting her eyes close while her mind drifted, and felt completely relaxed for the first time in days.

She was half-asleep when she thought she heard a soft, "I still wish you were here."

But she wasn't sure if she dreamt it or not.

Chapter 18

The drive up to the Spencer family home for their New Year's Eve party – after turning up onto the long, gated driveway – had been just beautiful enough to distract Charlotte from the unsettled feeling in her stomach that she was loathe to refer to as nerves.

It was how she'd felt the last time she'd seen Sutton. Since she'd been hit with the realization that under her affection and endearment and attraction for the woman was also genuine *feelings*. Romantic feelings that made Charlotte want to do . . . things.

Like buy earrings because they perfectly matched Sutton's eyes and call her before she went to bed just to hear her voice. When she had women hitting on her in the club, she didn't even feel entirely right dancing with them because she'd wanted to be dancing with Sutton.

Feelings that were unplanned and unfamiliar, and she'd done her best to process them the week after Sutton had left by maintaining her distance and focusing as much as she could on her debate.

She silently berated herself that it took her a week to decide that nothing had to be done about these *feelings*. They didn't matter, they couldn't matter, and they wouldn't matter.

It was only what she *did* in regard to them that mattered.

If she never changed her actions toward Sutton, there would be no need to take a closer examination at anything she didn't want to scrutinize any further. As simple as that. She was still herself. Sutton was still Sutton. Their arrangement was the same one they'd always had, and they were still friends. Their conversations had gotten mostly back on track too.

Simple.

Only, she thought as she and Caleb stood outside the large home that seemed like a fairytale situated in a winter wonderland, it didn't *feel* simple right now.

"It's actually perfect foresight, for them to have arranged cars to and from all of the guests' hotels," Caleb commented, tugging at the collar of his jacket so it was closer to his ears. "Then again, I imagine they'd have to, unless they wanted all their drunk guests spending the night."

Charlotte only hmm'd in agreement, even though she *did* agree that it was perfect foresight. The Spencer's apparently made arrangements every year with a chauffeur service to and from the establishments where their party guests would be staying; Sutton had told her about it on the phone the other day to prepare a car for her and Caleb.

During the talk they'd had the day after Christmas, where she'd called Charlotte after breakfast, and they'd ended up talking for over an hour.

Charlotte shook her head slightly to clear it, feeling her hair bounce at her shoulders over her heavy jacket, as she mentally prepared her checklist. Tonight was going to be a night where she would hopefully make connections that would not only help her in this election, but also in her future life plans.

She'd even polished up her knowledge about the politicians and businesspeople who had typically been invited to the Spencer party in the past, just to be sure to be on her toes. There was no reason she should be feeling anything less than her usual partygoing best.

No real reason, and yet here she was with an irritating feeling lodged low in her stomach. Not a feeling of actual irritation, no. But one she would be forced to categorize as *anxiety*.

"You okay there?" Caleb asked as they drew closer to the wraparound porch.

"I'm great, thanks," she bit back, quirking her eyebrow at him and daring him to challenge it.

He rose to the challenge, amusement sparkling in his eyes. "You're not nervous about –"

"Don't," she cut him off, eyes narrowed dangerously before she glanced around to ensure that none of the other arriving guests – though it seemed they'd beat any crowds – were in close enough proximity to them.

"Don't?" Caleb echoed, shoving his hands deeper into his pockets as he muttered, "Fuck, it's freezing." He blew out a breath. "You mean, don't discuss your burgeoning feelings for –"

She grit her teeth so hard it hurt. "I deeply, deeply regret getting drinks with you after my debate."

And she meant it. Because if it hadn't been for those drinks, she never would have ended up telling her brother and Dean about these Sutton-feelings.

Glancing around again, she pulled him to a stop far back in the immaculately shoveled and prettily-lit walkway.

Despite being the only ones there, she kept her voice low, "I allowed you to be my plus one tonight because you wanted to see what the 'elite' Spencer New Year's Eve party was like –"

"And to be your wingman," Caleb cut in, looking indignant.

Charlotte set her jaw in annoyance. "Yes, as in, I don't want Sutton's family to think I'm here as anything other than a friend, and bringing my brother makes me seem far less like I've debauched their daughter," she hissed.

Which was true. Because she had no problem going to events alone; in fact, sometimes she even preferred it. But bringing her brother along as a buffer in this specific scenario had seemed like a good idea.

But right now? Standing outside Sutton's childhood home? The home in which Sutton's family resided, a family that knew of her . . . circumstances with Sutton. Or, at the very least, her mother and sister knew.

That was what was giving Charlotte this unpleasant feeling in her stomach that had been mounting the entire drive, and her brother's commentary was certainly not helping. She was so used to knowing what to do, what to say, having every step planned. But she couldn't necessarily plan for this.

Charlotte didn't *do* meeting the family for any woman in the past that she'd had a physical relationship with. Hell, Charlotte didn't even have many friends, let alone ones she was close enough with to meet their families.

Not to mention the fact that Sutton was a Spencer, and the Spencer family weren't just – people. They were in her world; what they thought of her could impact her life. Plus, well . . . Sutton loved her family so much, which made Charlotte feel like – like she wanted them to like her for that reason too.

That thought alone was chilling.

"Debauched their daughter?" Caleb repeated, bringing her back to the moment with his laughter. "Are we in the 1800s? You have feelings for the woman! That's –"

Charlotte rolled her eyes, even as her stomach sunk like a stone, and she quickly held up her hand to stop him from continuing. "If I have to tell you to cut it out with the comments one more time, you aren't even going to come to the party, you're going to spend the night outside freezing all of your extremities off."

He gave her an exasperated look. "I don't know why I'm more excited about you *finally* having feelings for someone than you are."

"Really, Caleb?" She almost drew blood with how hard she bit at the inside of her cheek.

Sometimes, despite how close Caleb was to her, his complete lack of knowledge about where she was coming from was both baffling and frustrating.

He rolled his eyes. "Uh, yeah, really, Charlotte."

Her frustration mounted, bubbling inside of her like it had been all week but she'd been biting her tongue. Because she could handle a comment here or there; if Charlotte couldn't take a well-intentioned, albeit teasing, comment from a family member, she was most certainly in the wrong career.

Tonight was different.

"You're acting like this is a good thing. Like my having romantic feelings is going to lead to anything but a more difficult situation if I let these feelings actually go anywhere beyond what I'm doing now."

Caleb scoffed. "And *you're* acting like your life is over because you're a fucking human who likes a woman –"

She pursed her lips hard as he spoke, feeling how tense her shoulders were, until she couldn't stop herself from interrupting him, "Do you really not know anything?"

Her hands balled into fists, so she could control herself from running them through her hair or shoving at her brother's chest like she would when they fought as children .

"You think that's what all this is about? Are you kidding me?" It was rare that her temper flared like this – and that she allowed it to – but she couldn't stop it. "I'm not in denial of my sexuality. I'm not hiding who I am to myself or my family. But it makes my entire life so complicated. It puts everything I've *ever* wanted at risk."

The truth of the words hung heavily in the air between them; it was the first time she had said it aloud. It wasn't like she didn't know that it was the truth – it wasn't like this hadn't been something she'd thought long and hard about in the past.

But the fact that it could be a reality now, with Sutton, *scared* her. She didn't deal well with fear; she never had.

"The risk . . ." Caleb rolled his eyes and it only infuriated her more.

"I've spent my entire life in politics. Planning to climb the ladder all the way to the top, planning every single step I've ever taken." God, she felt like her throat was on fire with the heat of the anger and the honest truth inside her as her eyes narrowed into a glare. "Like you don't know that I've spent every break from school since I was fifteen doing internships, sacrificing friendships and relationships and time I could have spent doing *anything* else."

436

She had to clear her throat to keep going as her throat tightened, and her spine straightened and tensed so tight she could feel the ache in her shoulders. "Like you don't know that I worked in congressional internships through college, that I've worked late nights and weekends for *years*, because I refuse to not do everything I possibly can to get where I want to be."

"Charlotte –" Caleb cut in, his voice quieter than it was before but it didn't slow her down.

"I'm the youngest woman to ever have my job, and my job before it." The fire was still there, crawling through her, even as her words were hushed.

"I know," his voice softened even more, eyes bearing into hers. So often, she felt connected to Caleb but right now she felt such a disconnect.

Because if he really *knew*, then he wouldn't be so obtuse.

She tilted her chin up to meet his eyes, determined, as she took in a deep, stabilizing breath. "If I win this election, I will be the youngest woman elected to Congress, ever, and one of the youngest people – period."

God, she so very much wished she could say *when I win*. *When*, because she couldn't let anything endanger this. She wouldn't.

"I know." He sighed, even as she could see his jaw working, clenching his teeth.

"And if I intend to be President, let alone to most likely only be the second woman, do you honestly think I'll be able to do that while being openly gay?" She challenged, arching her eyebrow and absolutely refusing to let any of the feelings she had about the matter show. Because her feelings about it couldn't matter. "Or do you know, just like I do, that my entire future would be in jeopardy?"

"I know!" Caleb's voice was strong and sure and very nearly snapping in anger. "You think *I*, of all people in your life, don't understand what it's like?"

"Then act like it," she threw back but refused to shout. Refused to lose her composure, especially here and now, even when she could feel her body nearly vibrating from it. "Because this isn't just about me and my feelings. This is about my entire future, my *life*."

Everything she'd ever wanted, everything she'd ever dreamed about. The goals she'd done everything in her power to make possible. And the thing was, she could attain it.

So, perhaps her life goals did mean she had to make some sacrifices along the way. But she'd refused to ever let anything come in the way of her dreams. It was *her* choice to make – and she'd long since made it.

Caleb was quiet, before he slowly nodded, clenching his jaw with clear force to hold back whatever else he wanted to say. "Yeah. You're right. It's your life, your choices."

"Thank you," she murmured. And because it was Caleb, she allowed her shoulders to slump a bit as they burrowed into her jacket and some of the tension slipped out of her. Only for a moment, though, before she quirked an eyebrow at him. "And this means no more choice commentary."

He rolled his eyes, but playfully, and bowed his head in compliance. "As you command."

It was only then, after some of that adrenaline wore off, that she could feel herself shivering again, and she could see her brother doing the same. As if easily jumping back onto the same page as her, at least about this topic, he tilted his head. "Ready to face the wolf's den?"

The small smile on his lips got her to smile back, if only a little bit. "I'll lead the way."

Truthfully, she still felt less ready than she did at grander events like charity galas and state dinners. Focus on the politics, she reminded herself, squaring her shoulders, and started mentally running through names and facts and policies as they approached the front door.

Do not focus on the fact that Katherine Spencer knows about your sexuality. And that you've slept with her daughter.

It was a task easier said than done.

She rolled her shoulders and only let herself hesitate for a moment before she rang the doorbell.

Then she caught her brother's eye as he was giving her an entirely too amused look, that instantly put her on guard. "What?"

"Just – a little nervous, are we?" He bumped her shoulder with his.

She kept her face impassive. "I have no idea what you're talking about. I'm going to keep tonight as professional as possible. You and I both know I don't have nerves when it comes to that."

"Oh, right," he scoffed back. But even as she narrowed her eyes in annoyance – did she have to bring up their previous conversation *already*? – he ran his thumb and index finger over his lips. "I'm not saying anything, though."

"Think you already did," she murmured back, taking a deep breath and straightening her shoulders.

Tonight would be fine; it would be more than fine, she assured herself. Because Charlotte didn't set her sights on being better than fine. Her grandmother was right – no matter the reason for her invitation, she would take advantage of the connections she could make.

What were the odds that she'd even be spending much time with the Spencer's, anyway? This party was going to be filled with –

Her thoughts cut themselves off as the door opened, and Charlotte had expected someone working this event or perhaps a maid to answer the door, much as one would at her own parents' home. She was instead faced with Katherine Spencer herself.

These damning and uncomfortable nerves in her stomach came back to life, even as she purposefully slid on a smile. "Mrs. Spencer, it's lovely to meet you in person. I'm –"

"Charlotte Thompson, of course. We met through that Skype call, a while ago," Kate acknowledged with a small smile and a nod. "It's nice to see you in person as well."

She was wearing a sleekly elegant blue dress, somehow looking both imposing and kind. There was that smile on her mouth but there was no mistaking the smart, measuring look in her eyes.

Charlotte had no doubt that Katherine Spencer was trying to get a read on her. There was a reason she'd invited her here tonight, after all.

She didn't let her shoulders tense. "Of course, I remember. Difficult to forget someone whose work I admire so much." At the very least there was no pretense in that statement; it wasn't sucking up or schmoozing, she assured herself, when it was the truth.

Katherine's smile remained unsettlingly unreadable. "Sutton mentioned that she gave you the pre-release of my latest novel. Have you gotten a chance to read it?"

"Actually, I brought it with me to read on the flight home; I was so busy with work and then the holidays that I couldn't give it the attention it deserved," she told her, bowing her head in a light apology.

Her excuse was semi-true. She had been busy, but she'd had downtime post-debate. Her parents spent the holidays in the south of France every year, and Caleb typically spent them with Dean's family. She'd taken a day to visit their other brother, William, in Virginia but that had been the extent of her holiday celebration.

But every time she'd gone to read, she'd been able to picture that adorable look Sutton had worn when she'd given Charlotte the gift. And then those thoughts quickly had tumbled into Sutton kissing her goodbye, unbidden during that very platonic gift exchange, and then – of course – came the thoughts about these feelings, and . . .

It had seemed like a better plan to keep busy.

Katherine waved her hand. "Whenever you get the chance; I hope you'll enjoy it. Sutton actually had a hand in creating some parts."

Her tone was so practiced yet casual as she mentioned Sutton that Charlotte knew she wasn't the only one here who was well-versed in veiled social interaction.

She couldn't help herself from speaking the words that came right to her mind. "Right, yes, she told me about the origin of Clara Reiner."

"She did?" Katherine arched an eyebrow at her. "Sutton very rarely discusses her accomplishments; I'm usually the one talking her up when it comes to her work with me."

Charlotte felt a far more sincere smile tug at her mouth. "Oh, I understand that; she's very reluctant to discuss her accomplishments." She thought of the blush Sutton had when she'd told Charlotte about her writing or even her success when it came to academia. "But she's remarkable. She told me the entire story of the creation of Clara, and I was riveted."

Katherine nodded slowly, thoughtfully, and Charlotte replayed what she'd just said. She could even *hear* how her tone had sounded – warm and reverent, in a way that it hadn't been in the previous minutes.

And it took all of her self-control not to take a moment to close her eyes and curse herself, thankful that at the very least she knew she wasn't blushing. Charlotte did *not* blush.

"Not to be rude, Mrs. Spencer, but is there anything I could offer you that might prompt an invitation inside?" Caleb interjected, his voice cheerful, and the calculating gaze that had been on her instead flickered to her brother.

She had never been so thankful for him.

Katherine quickly opened the door wider, stepping back. "Of course, that was extremely rude of me. Come in."

She turned to face away from them for a moment as she and Caleb moved to enter and she caught her brother's teasing expression as he mouthed, "*Professional*," at her with a wink.

Her eyes narrowed but she only allowed it for a moment before she schooled her features again and entered the Spencer home.

441

The entry hall had a high ceiling and still radiated an aura of warmth as they stepped inside.

"I can take your jackets," Katherine offered as she turned back around.

Charlotte was already unzipping hers, trying to not be as obvious as she felt when looking around as much as she could. There was music in the distance and she could see that the walls were lined with what she presumed to be pictures and paintings, before she tracked her gaze back to Katherine. "Your home is very beautiful, Mrs. Spencer."

"Thank you; it's always a pleasure to host friends of the family this time of year," she responded, and Charlotte wondered if she was being paranoid or if there was actually a different tone when she said *friends of the family*.

Still, she kept the fixed smile on her face. "Oh, well the Spencer New Year's party is renowned. I'm glad to have been invited."

"Any friend of Sutton's is always welcome," was the reply she got, with a smile of measured warmth, as Katherine seamlessly took their jackets. "How was it that you met Sutton, again? Given your career, I take it you're a few years older than she is."

The question was polite; amiable, even, and said without any sort of undertone. Still, Charlotte could so easily picture how they actually had met. Could so easily recall the night she'd opened the dating app, intending to delete it, and stumbling across Sutton's message. Or, she supposed, Regan's message, proposing to hook up. And her very active libido wanting to take her up on the proposal.

God.

How did people who partook in relationships manage this time after time? She wasn't even dating Sutton and she felt like she had to read into everything. Then again, she didn't think she'd feel this anxiety if she was anyone else. Someone who didn't have her career or her ambitions.

In spite of her whirling thoughts, she held Katherine's gaze steadily, even if she felt as though that sharp gaze could see through her as she answered, "Oh, we ran into one another one day in the coffee shop that Regan works in, and hit it off."

The words rolled off her tongue easily, thankfully, and it was no trouble to remember the fabrication she'd told upon meeting Jack Spencer.

At least she had her wits about her, and that was a somewhat calming thought. Still, she hoped Katherine wasn't going to continue down this line of questioning. Even if she *had* prepared herself for it, just as she'd prepared for the other guests. It could never hurt to be prepared.

But Katherine accepted her answer with a nod. "I've been there on my visits to see the girls; it's charming. And Sutton does love the pastries they sell." She shook her head a bit, a warm hint of a smile on her lips.

"Especially the lemon cakes," she agreed, as she brushed her hands along the fitted suit jacket she wore. It was a dark blue and she'd had the designer label sitting in her closet waiting for a perfect night.

She hadn't accounted for the appraising look she received and it caught her off guard.

What exactly had she said to prompt that look?

"Our Sutton does love a lemon cake." Katherine all but hummed out, before she turned her attention to Caleb. "And Mr. Thompson, what is it that you do? In the political world, like your sister and grandmother?"

Charlotte was incredibly relieved that no eyes were on her when she realized that she'd said *our Sutton*. Their Sutton? Theirs? Alarm bells rang in her head even as that unsettling feeling – both uncomfortable and warm – sat in her stomach.

Her brother merely bumped his shoulder with hers as he laughed. "Me and politics? Never, Mrs. Spencer; I don't have the stomach for it, unlike my family and my boyfriend. I'm a police officer."

All right, so maybe she and Caleb *were* cut from the same cloth, as she noticed his casual boyfriend-drop. Katherine didn't even bat an eye at the gay comment. "You and I have that in common. Not the profession, of course, but –" She waved her hand slightly. "Politics."

"I apologize for having to cut this a little short, but I should get your jackets to the coat room and check in with the caterers before the party truly starts to get under way." She turned and tilted her head to motion for Charlotte and Caleb to follow her a bit down the hall. "The main rooms for the party are just down at the end of the hall. Not many have arrived yet, but my kids are there already."

"Thank you, Mrs. Spencer." Charlotte fixed on her smile, though she was still hearing *our Sutton* in the back of her mind.

"Of course; enjoy your night. I'll see you later." With that, she swept down another hallway, adjusting the coats over her arm, and both Charlotte and Caleb watched her go.

Caleb turned to her. "So . . . not that I'm going to bring up that which we are not to be discussing, but is it just me or did she sound a bit ominous with that *I'll see you later* bit at the end there?"

She rolled her eyes, even though she'd been wondering the same thing. "Shut up and let's go."

Still, she blew out an even breath. That hadn't been so bad, and Katherine was the one she'd been worried about.

After a short walk, they found themselves in an immaculately decorated grand room, and – wow. Charlotte supposed rooms like these – spacious, with tall, ornate ceilings and arching doorways – would be common in homes like the semi-famed Spencer home. Which had been well modernized and renovated handfuls of times over the years, but much of it existed from when the original structure had been built several generations ago.

Katherine had been correct in that there were very few other guests thus far, and the ones that had arrived, she didn't recognize. Family friends, she presumed, quickly running through the information she'd compiled.

"Charlotte! You're here," Sutton's voice came from behind her, sounding a little breathless, and it sent a shiver down Charlotte's spine.

It wasn't as though she hadn't heard Sutton's voice several times in the last few weeks; they'd spoken on the phone more than once. But it wasn't the same.

It wasn't the same, she thought again as she turned around, her throat going dry at the sight of Sutton. The sky-blue dress she wore that clung to her – sleek, long-sleeved, and cutting off at mid-thigh – was . . . it made Charlotte feel absolutely parched.

She'd seen Sutton in all states of dress – and undress – by now. But she wasn't prepared for this feeling that hit her in the chest then melted through her veins until it landed heavily in her stomach. Just like it had felt the last time she'd seen her in person, sitting in her living room.

She'd been hoping that it had been somewhat of a fluke. That the feeling had hit her so hard at the time because she'd been under the weather and that it had been the first time she'd confronted these feelings.

She knew in this moment it hadn't been a one-time thing.

Still, despite the fact that her breath left her too quickly, she merely straightened her shoulders subtly. The smile that bloomed on her face was uncontrollable, unease or not. "Always early. Hello, darling."

Sutton's cheeks deepened in color as she eyed Charlotte up and down and the look in them thrilled her as Sutton cleared her throat. "I – you look – um," she coughed lightly, before casting her eyes back to meet Charlotte's amused ones. "Nice. You look nice."

They both pretended not to hear Caleb disguise a laugh into a cough, and she resolved to elbow him sharply for it later.

Drawing her spine straight, Sutton's hands tangled in front of her as she aimed a quick smile at Caleb. "You look very handsome tonight."

Her brother gave an easy grin back. "I do love a good suit."

Genuine warmth spread in Sutton's eyes, before she turned back to Charlotte. "Can I talk to you? In private?" She bit her lip and added, "It'll be quick, I promise, you won't miss the party."

Confused – and disliking that almost as much as the anxiety she was reading on Sutton – she nodded. "Of course."

The corner of Sutton's mouth ticked up. "Come on."

In a move Charlotte hadn't been expecting, Sutton reached out to take her hand and she hadn't realized how much she'd missed this feeling. The simple softness of Sutton's hand on hers.

She was led out of the room she'd entered through a side door and down a hallway lined with family photos. Not that she had much time to really look at them, but she took in everything she could before Sutton turned another corner and she found herself in a small alcove, with a window seat perch.

She took it in slowly, wondering – was Sutton going to kiss her again, like the last time, despite the fact that this was not a benefits night, but a friends night?

More pressingly, would Charlotte let her?

Damningly, she probably would. The knowledge made her stomach clench.

She shook her head slightly. That was not going to happen; the lines between them needed to remain, as blurred as they were becoming.

"I missed you but I'm not sure this seat affords much comfort or privacy," she teased.

It was like she couldn't help it; it was so easy to do with Sutton. Maybe she shouldn't but it was normal for them – for her to tease and for Sutton to blush – and *normal* between them was what she very much wanted.

Sutton did blush, charmingly, and delighted golden brown eyes took it in.

The deep breath that Sutton had taken in seemed to catch in her throat before she got one of those contemplative looks of hers. "You did?"

Confusion clouded in and she shook her head. "I'm sorry, I need you to elaborate a bit."

446

Those vivid blue eyes somehow seemed even deeper before Sutton ducked her head and murmured. "You missed me?"

It took that moment, with Sutton peering at her from under her lashes for the storm inside – her feelings, meeting Sutton's family, what this night could do for her career, the election – to come to a slower calm.

Because while these feelings were unfamiliar, this was Sutton. Sweet, smart, beautiful Sutton, who never put expectations on Charlotte. Sutton who was always there, and always thoughtful, and so different from anyone else in Charlotte's life.

"I did," the words left her quietly, surprising even herself, and she knew her eyes were wide when Sutton's searched them.

Way to act casual, she cursed herself. But it was also difficult to actually feel badly about it when Sutton was smiling like that.

"I missed you too."

The words landed in Charlotte's stomach with dual punches – good in the obvious way, and bad in that . . . she knew they were walking such a fine line.

Sutton took a deep breath, the look on her face becoming more serious as she squeezed the hand that was still clasping Charlotte's before she let it go. "But, no I didn't bring you here for – *that*. I wanted to check . . . First, my mom didn't say anything to you about, well, anything she shouldn't have, right?"

She thought of the measuring eyes, of the comments that shouldn't have had the intensity that they did. Of the unfamiliar nerves she'd felt.

"No, your mother was lovely."

The tension in Sutton's shoulders seemed to melt a bit, "Good." She twisted her fingers in front of her as she bit at her lip, "I just – well I want you to know that you don't have to worry. No one in my family is going to tell anyone about your sexuality or anything. I promise that."

The fact that Sutton looked so completely earnest made Charlotte want to do too many things. But it was so damn endearing and of course she'd fallen for this woman. "I appreciate that."

Which, she did. Even if somewhere along the line it had become less alarming that Sutton's family knew about her sexuality and more so about what they thought of her.

"*And* I wanted you to know that I can make up for it. For, you know, the whole you-being-invited-because-of-our . . . friendship. I can help you," Sutton finished, blowing out the rest of her breath before she bit her lip, looking expectantly at Charlotte.

With Sutton's low heeled pumps and Charlotte's five-inch stilettos, they were the same height. And she had a perfect view of the way Sutton was flushed and the bright look in her eyes. It was adorable but did nothing to allay Charlotte's building confusion.

"First of all, Sutton, there's nothing you need to make up for." She couldn't help but lean in a little closer into Sutton's gravity, feeling her warmth and smelling that subtle perfume as she searched her face. "Why do you think you need to make up for my being invited here for any reason?"

That look of uncertainty flashed over Sutton's face, and – Charlotte hadn't really planned on this. She'd been entirely too selfishly focused on what *she* was feeling that she felt lost realizing that something was bothering Sutton.

One of those slim shoulders shrugged as Sutton dropped her eyes. "Well, I figured maybe you didn't want anyone here to only associate you with me. As my friend. Especially since after you got the invitation you were a little . . . distant," she finished, her eyes dropping contact, large and a little sad.

She did not like that look in Sutton's eyes at all. And she definitely hated being the cause of it. But there was no way she would explain everything that had prompted her distance.

"What do you mean by help?" She asked instead.

"Not that you *need* help," Sutton rushed to say, as her eyes flew back to Charlotte's, re-energized. "It's just – I was thinking about how a lot of people here that you'll want to meet can be a little . . . reluctant to meeting and talking to people they think of as outsiders. My dad's one of them."

"Ah, yes, I can recall," she murmured, easily thinking to her first and only interaction with Jack. Granted, it had been torpedoed by her also meeting Sutton face-to-face, but still.

"But I figured that I could help a bit," Sutton stood proudly, a hint of excitement in her tone. "And give you some personal information that you might not have and maybe make some introductions for you." A deep blush spread over Sutton's cheeks as she was quick to add, "Not that you need my help, because I'm sure you could do it on your own. Because you're, well, you."

Her voice was soft and she was peering at Charlotte through her eyelashes in a way that she could feel down to her toes. She'd had people believe in her ambitions and ability to get where she wanted to be in life. But her grandmother's mentoring and her family's general encouragement didn't feel quite like this.

That feeling warred for a moment with her instinctive want to turn down the help. It was a fiercely independent streak she'd had for far longer than she could remember; it was one thing to cultivate a team to work with, because Charlotte wasn't stupid and she knew she could get virtually nowhere in politics alone.

It was another entirely to rely on someone who wasn't on your political campaign or a member of your family to work with. Especially someone you were trying your damndest to maintain a normal distance from.

"I want tonight to be worth your time. Not just . . . something you ended up coming to because of me, and not getting anything out of it," Sutton finished, brushing her hands over her stomach in the way Charlotte recognized as one of her little anxious habits.

More than anything though, she hated the uncertain look written all over Sutton's face. It was surprisingly easy to say, "It wouldn't be a waste, Sutton. At the very least, I'd see you on New Year's," she teased.

No, she didn't typically accept help from most people, nor did she think she needed to.

But this was *Sutton*.

"I'd be happy to have your help. At least until you believe I can charm some stubborn politicians and socialites on my own."

The smile that slid over Sutton's face made her heart skip a beat. She wanted to reach out and place her hand over Sutton's to stop her fidgeting and just to feel that *thing* between them.

Her hands remained at her sides.

"I think you probably really wouldn't have any issues with that," Sutton's voice was hardly more than a whisper, and the quiet tone had her unconsciously swaying a bit closer.

Okay, she couldn't help but let her eyes flicker to those full, pink lips. Subtle lipstick, Charlotte noted, most likely smudge resistant.

"I appreciate your vote of confidence," she murmured back, and she wondered when exactly Sutton moved even closer to her or if she was imagining that.

"It's hard to not be confident in your abilities," she sounded nearly breathless and Charlotte couldn't stop herself from flickering her eyes back down to her mouth.

"Sutton? What are you doing back here?" Jack's voice from behind her startled Charlotte enough that her heart started pounding in her chest, and she barely refrained from jumping back guiltily.

Not that she had anything to be guilty of, she reminded herself, taking a split-second to regain her composure. Because the last thing she needed was for Jack Spencer to stumble across her just as she was seconds away from giving in to kissing his daughter against the wall in a dark hallway in his home.

Especially when she shouldn't be doing it at all.

"Dad!" Sutton's eyes were wide and despite the fact that it was dimly lit, she could see the flush on her cheeks. She licked her lips before she asked, "What are *you* doing back here?"

450

Damn if the suspicious look on Jack Spencer's face as he looked between her and Sutton in this dimly-lit alcove off of a back hallway as they'd been *holding hands* didn't make her stomach knot up.

She slowly blew out her breath and fixed a small smile on her face as gray eyes slowly flickered from Sutton to her. "I was just finishing up some work in my office." He gestured vaguely down the opposite end of the hallway that they'd come from.

They were standing so close she could feel the deep breath Sutton took in. "Us, too! That is to say, um, Charlotte and I were talking about one of the initiatives she's been thinking about . . ."

Sutton trailed off, coughing a bit, and Charlotte almost wanted to smile at it – especially because, since when was Sutton so quick on thinking on her feet when put in such a situation? – but Jack was still giving them a clearly suspicious look.

She merely straightened her spine and resolutely did not inch away from Sutton, no matter what their proximity said about them. Charlotte did not flinch away from a situation, especially when *she hadn't been doing anything wrong*, she reminded herself. Another minute, and maybe she could have been –

Fixing on a smile, she nodded. "Yes, we were actually discussing the policy I've been planning to enact this winter season, providing more shelters and sustenance for the homeless population in the city. Very similar to the policy you have in assisting the low-income population in Boston."

The best lies, after all, came from a truth, and that initiative was a truth.

After a few long moments running his eyes over the both of them, he scratched at his chin and nodded. "Right." He drew his hand through his hair before blowing out a deep sigh. "Well, if you'd like I could send along some of my foundations for enacting that policy; they were somewhat difficult to get entirely approved and I imagine you will run into even more red tape in New York. Sutton can bring them back for you."

The smile that she'd kept plastered to her face nearly fell in genuine shock. "Really? That would be incredible. Thank you so much, Mr. Spencer."

"It's no trouble. And you can call me Jack," he offered quietly, before looking between them again with a look that was more perplexed than anything.

But for this once, she wasn't going to look a gift horse in the mouth.

"Then thank you, Jack," she corrected, her smile melting into one much more real.

He continued to study them even as he took a step backward out into the hall. "I should be checking in with your mother about the party."

Though he didn't leave.

Even when Sutton nodded. "You probably should."

He eyed the alcove. "Yes. And you two should get moving along as well. Everyone is starting to arrive."

His words weren't commanding so much as speculative. He was definitely dad-Jack instead of politician-Jack right now. Despite being a tough nut to crack when it came to politics, she would rather try to talk shop than engage dad-mode Jack Spencer, who may or may not know that she'd slept with his daughter.

So, she followed his lead and edged back out into the hallway. "You're absolutely right. It would be a terrible shame to miss even a moment."

That garnered her a thoughtful smile even as Sutton impatiently brushed by him. "Talk to you later, Dad."

She could sense his eyes on them as they walked down the hallway, and it took everything she had not to let herself think more about the interaction than taking it at face value. As they turned the corner, her spine relaxed a bit.

It was so easy – too easy – to sway into Sutton a bit, nudging her with her arm. "That went well."

The cute little furrow between Sutton's brows didn't disappear even when she did that thing where she shook her head as if to clear her thoughts. "Yeah," she agreed, slowly, "It's just – odd." Those blue eyes turned to her finally. "He just – he's never so forthright about politicians he's unfamiliar with calling him Jack. Or, most people in general when he doesn't really know them."

Sutton didn't move away, instead pressing their arms closer together, and the warmth was so alarmingly comforting.

"Maybe he likes me," she dared to tease.

Pink lips curled into a smile, even as Sutton shook her head slightly. "I guess so. Who wouldn't?"

Eyes narrowed as her stomach betrayed her and dipped with a pleasant warmth Charlotte nudged her again. "Smooth woman."

"Honest woman," Sutton corrected as they neared the grand room again, where Charlotte couldn't yet see inside but she could already hear that there were more people.

Now was not the time for distractions or feelings; it was showtime.

With a deep breath and a familiar feeling sliding through her at the prospect of networking – professional excitement, which was a rush she found headier than almost anything – she quirked an eyebrow. "Can you keep that good luck up with politicians who aren't your father?"

Her tone was light, deliberately so, and it was an unfamiliar look that lit up Sutton's eyes. Determination, she thought, filing it away, as Sutton nodded.

People Charlotte didn't recognize on immediate sight now filled the room, and she'd admit that she was glad to have Sutton for this part. The very beginning, she assured herself, and then she would let Sutton get on with her evening while she networked solitarily.

In a move that surprised her, Sutton's hand landed on her lower back to guide her as she murmured, "We should start over there," Sutton nodded to the far side of the room, and Charlotte saw a tall, hulking man. "Perry Bennett. If you don't get to him early, he'll be too drunk to remember anything important."

"He was in the military for years," Sutton murmured, warm breath washing over her ear and making her shiver as they approached him. "And his oldest son is a Marine now."

He'd greeted Sutton jovially, loudly – regarding her with barely more than a wary look after their introduction – before Sutton had segued into getting him to reminisce about the time he beat Jack while playing hockey, years ago. It was clearly something he'd loved to talk about, and Charlotte listened with a rapt look on her face, before Sutton cut in at the end, "Right! And Perry Jr. played too, right? How is he doing?"

The man was clearly proud of his son, boasting, "Fucking incredible!"

She hadn't expected the ease with which Sutton drew her in, "Charlotte, a friend of mine from New York, is actually quite invested in military spending."

"Yeah?" He was clearly weighing what he wanted to say to her – perfect time to cut in.

By the time they were done talking, she'd had an exchange of business cards and a rather jarring but exuberant pat on the shoulder. And so the night began.

Sutton led her from politicians to businessmen and businesswomen, all the while whispering information and providing seamless introductions – she provided personal and professional tidbits that there was no way Charlotte could have known even from her research:

"Kelly Kingston – even though she's probably going to be the next choice for the Supreme Court, don't bring it up. She loves skiing in Aspen, and her daughter just opened a winery – she loves talking about that."

"Martin Jones – yes, the environmentalist. Talk about the exhibit we saw at the Met; he loves art. He *wants* to talk shop but everything you discuss is a pointless test until you gain his trust."

"Sofia Rodriguez – talk up your work supporting immigration at the Youth Center and don't ask about her family; she'll think you're being fake."

They worked like a well-oiled machine, as if this routine had somehow, someway been rehearsed. When Sutton turned expectant, intelligent eyes onto her at a break in conversation, she was already extending her hand to introduce herself, and continued to walk away with genuine smiles and exchanged information.

They'd only bumped into one of Sutton's siblings, the youngest, young with the promise to become handsome, with unruly auburn curls and a winning smile. He hurried past them, adjusting his bowtie with a grin. "Sorry, Sutton!" He not-so-subtly told Sutton, "She *is* pretty!"

It went without saying that she relished in the blush high on Sutton's cheeks as she shoo'd her brother along, and in the way she'd toyed at the bottom of her sleeve as she'd quickly explained, "I, um, might have bribed my siblings to mind their own business tonight. Even Oliver. He'd rally for you over Naomi any day though."

Along the way, she forgot that Sutton was doing this because she felt she'd forced Charlotte into being somewhere or doing something she hadn't wanted to do tonight. She forgot that she'd expected Sutton to taper off and enjoy her evening with her friends and family.

It was so *easy* that she didn't even realize how close they were standing and how much she was enjoying that warmth until they were leaning into one another next to one of the refreshment tables.

"Over two hours, and I swear we've talked to half the room," Sutton spoke conspiratorially, as she handed Charlotte a glass of water.

She couldn't not grin back, feeling the same rush. "I know."

As Sutton's eyes roamed the room, hers were glued to Sutton, enjoying the flush of excitement on her cheeks.

"You're really good at this," the words slipped out softly, and she wanted to curse herself because she could *hear* the affection in them, but it was so true.

"What?" Sutton gestured for her to explain.

"This," Charlotte gestured around the room. "You know just what to say to who, you remember all of the details. My grandmother is having a party in a couple of weeks. Every year, on the anniversary of her inauguration, she throws this big thing – lots of people from Virginia and D.C., and from all over, really. A lot of who's who – that my grandmother wants to talk to or get support from, of course," she added with a wink. "You should come."

Sutton's eyes widened and that surprised smile lit up her face. "Really? To your grandmother's party?"

God, she could only imagine the look she was going to get from Caleb, but it was too late to take it back. "Yes, you should."

"I'd love that."

She opened her mouth to answer, but before anything came out, she noticed the commotion behind Sutton's back. And by commotion, she meant Regan, who was giving her a look she couldn't quite place. But like most looks Regan directed toward her, it wasn't extremely pleasant.

It was enough to make her draw back, realizing just exactly how close they were standing, that they were in public.

"Sutton, I haven't seen you in forever." Regan reached them, bumping her hip lightly against Sutton's. She wore a black dress that draped nicely over her body, as she slung her arm over Sutton's shoulder in an enviably casual way.

"I saw you this morning," Sutton tossed back, nudging Regan in return.

Regan rolled her eyes. "Yeah, but *usually* at this party, you're with me and the other girls. Do you have any idea how many times I've been grilled about what you're doing?" She fixed Charlotte with a speculative eye, that gleam still making her uneasy. "Might I say, I do love the complementary outfits tonight."

She didn't have to look to know that Sutton was blushing, because she thought even she might if blushing was something she *did*. Because, fuck her, they *were* complementing one another . . . Her dark blue suit, Sutton in her light blue dress –

And they'd been together all evening, giving one another those easy touches, and Charlotte had to take a deep breath to calm her stomach. It didn't mean anything, she told herself, to any outside observer they were just friends.

Which they were.

456

Sutton elbowed Regan in the ribs. "We are *not* . . . matching," she muttered even though her eyes fixated on Charlotte's suit.

Regan shrugged, tightening her arm around Sutton's shoulder. "Sure you aren't, babe. Now, hopefully I'm not pulling you away from anything too serious." Charlotte could swear there was a sharp dig in there somewhere, even if she couldn't pinpoint it. "But I would very much like to get our group picture and some dancing in before midnight strikes and you turn into a pumpkin."

"Regan, I told you –" Sutton paused, giving Charlotte a speculative look.

Sutton had thrown her whole night into helping Charlotte when this was a party she typically enjoyed with her friends and family. That, coupled with the fact that this was the complete opposite of managing her feelings, made her quickly shake her head.

"No, you should go enjoy the rest of the night. You've done more than enough for me," her voice gentled unintentionally as she finished, making eye contact with Sutton and holding it. "Really. I don't want to take up your whole night. You deserve to have some fun."

"I *was* having fun," she insisted, before biting her lip. "I guess, though, if you want to finish up alone, I could go . . ."

"Perfect. I'm sure Charlotte here is *talented* enough to finish making contacts all by herself," Regan piped in with the falsely cheery voice she always used with her. The one that sort of sounded like a serial killer, but Charlotte was fairly certain Regan liked it that way.

"Regan –" Sutton started again and there was something loaded in the look they exchanged that Charlotte wasn't privy to. It was galling how much she wanted to be privy.

That alone made her stomach clench uncomfortably. "You go have fun with your friends."

"You heard the woman." Regan nodded at her. "Come on, you've got a full dance card already. Me being the first on the list, of course."

Sutton rolled her eyes, hesitating as she looked back to Charlotte. "I guess . . . okay. If you don't . . . well. I'll be around."

"We'll just be across the dance floor. If Stunning Charlotte wants to dance with you," another unmistakably pointed look, "I'm sure you will make room."

It was an irrational – and unfair and ridiculous – thought that crossed her mind as to *who* exactly was on Sutton's dance card. She forced a smile onto her lips.

"Don't forget, the Whitman's," Sutton mouthed over her shoulder, tilting her head to the other side of the room, where their next "targets" so-to-speak stood.

She sent Sutton a smirk and a wink. "Got it."

She took a minute to gather herself. Working the room with Sutton had felt natural. She'd networked with Dean and sometimes with other co-workers, but they were always just peripheral fixtures. Sutton had been a main event. Her eyes flickered to where Sutton now stood with her friends, laughing easily with them.

She'd already admitted to herself that she was out of her depth here. But she only allowed this weakness for the few moments it took to finish her water. She made eye contact with Caleb, who seemed to be having the time of his life dancing, before she took a deep breath. Working the room by herself was what she'd expected and it was what she was used to.

It wasn't *lonely*.

Drawing her spine up straight, she fixed a smile on her face, and went to work.

***

Less than ten minutes to midnight, with the crowd increasingly inebriated, Charlotte let herself grab a glass of champagne.

It had been a successful evening, she thought, as she let out a deep breath. She had plans for future meetings with so many people she'd never have connected to without tonight.

It was difficult to hide her smirk.

She'd even managed quite well to resolutely not look at Sutton, for the most part, in the last few hours. And certainly to not feel any sort of jealousy as she had indeed looked like she'd been enjoying herself on the dance floor.

She was mid-sip when she saw out of the corner of her eye that she wasn't alone any longer. The moment she'd allowed herself to relax disappeared, even as she lowered her glass as normal.

Katherine held her own glass of champagne, but if Charlotte were a betting woman, she would gamble that she only drank the smallest bit. Much like herself.

There was a look in her eyes that made Charlotte's spine straighten. "Ms. Thompson, I was hoping we'd have another moment to chat this evening."

She gave a slightly apologetic grin. "I apologize; I've been somewhat on the move," she offered, even as she steeled herself and tried to clamp down on nerves.

Something told her this wasn't about politics.

"The party has been lovely. Thank you, again, for inviting me," she took a small sip of her champagne. Very small, because she couldn't afford to lose any of her guard in front of Katherine Spencer.

She angled her head slightly in acknowledgement. "Frankly, it's given me the opportunity to observe you a bit. And by all accounts, you seem to be an accomplished, charming, and intelligent woman. I can see why my daughter enjoys your company."

It was difficult, really, to school her features in the way that was usually second nature to her, with the rush of surprise she got – followed by the suspicion curling low in her stomach.

Words *should* sound like a compliment sounded like anything but.

"Ah, thank you?" The look in Katherine's eyes was making her increasingly uneasy.

Katherine's mouth drew into a firm line. "And while I told Sutton that I wasn't going to discuss this, I would be remiss if I neglected this opportunity to have an actual conversation with you. While you seem admirable, Ms. Thompson, I know that you have ambitions, and that those ambitions will lead you down certain paths with your personal life."

Charlotte swore her entire stomach dropped with dread. Her voice was even, though, as she tilted her head. "What exactly do you want to *discuss*, Mrs. Spencer?"

She supposed if there was something about Katherine that she liked, it was that she was direct. "Your sexuality and who you choose to share it with is private; I wouldn't dare take that from you. But I want you to know that you are not the only person your decisions affect. Sutton cares for you, very much, and she cares for your . . . friendship. And when my daughter cares for someone, she is extremely selfless. Which can often be taken advantage of – even inadvertently – by those who are more selfish."

The words pierced low in her stomach. "I can assure you, hurting Sutton is the last thing I want. There's nothing between us that she has misconceptions about."

Charlotte had been honest with Sutton about everything in their relationship, no matter what, from the beginning.

Katherine's eyebrows lifted as she *hmm*'d. "I'm not trying to imply that you're a bad person or that you shouldn't have your wants and ambitions. I'm merely saying that I know you're in a difficult position but I would very much advise you to be careful with your footing. I've seen my daughter be hurt far too many times."

Charlotte very deliberately took a sip of her champagne, even as her heart hammered, her thoughts moving a bit too fast for comfort. "I do care for

Sutton," she spoke slowly, her throat burning with the truth of it. "And I don't want to hurt her."

Was this that traditional parental warning when one was dating their child? *Dating*, the word wrapped tightly around Charlotte's throat and pulled painfully, blood rushing in her ears.

Katherine regarded her with a frighteningly knowing look. "I'm glad."

It was too much. It was all just too much, because she and Sutton *weren't* together. She didn't even plan to give a name to the feelings she had regarding Sutton.

Clearing her throat, she delicately placed her glass down. "If you'll excuse me, I need some fresh air." For the first time in her life, Charlotte fled a conversation.

She reached the double doors that led out to the well-lit balcony in what had to have been record timing, especially given that she hadn't let herself run.

The cold air was again like a slap without a jacket, but as she shut the door and leaned back against the siding of the house, it felt like clarity.

It helped her slow down and tell herself that Katherine hadn't said anything she didn't really know; it just confirmed that she knew she and Sutton were more than just friends. And that perhaps she was more in-tune to Charlotte's feelings than even her daughter was.

A frightening thought on its own, but not unbearable. She tilted her head back and took in a breath of icy air deep into her lungs, eyes closed.

Her eyes snapped open, her posture righting itself, when she heard the door open again.

It was Sutton.

The door stayed cracked open behind her, filtering out some sounds of music and chatter from inside, and illuminating Sutton's face.

That open concern and those wide eyes tracking over Charlotte's features. "I . . . I saw you talking to my mom." She worried at her bottom lip, drawing

461

Charlotte's gaze. "Did she – she told me she wasn't going to say anything. Did she say anything to upset you?"

The sheer concern in her voice was almost enough to bring Charlotte to her knees.

Anything to upset her? Like bring up Charlotte's feelings for Sutton? Like give her some version of the family-threat? Like make Charlotte really think about what a dangerous line she was walking, doing this with Sutton *Spencer*, whose family had so much influence in her professional world?

Like make her think all over again that these feelings alone were enough to jeopardize her entire world and she had no idea what to do with them?

She let out a slow deep breath that she hoped masked the shudder that *wanted* to escape, and she shook her head. "No. Your mother loves you very much. It's nice."

It *was* nice, abstractly, to think about that. To know how much Sutton loved her family and to see that it was mirrored right back at her. Charlotte never cared much that she wasn't close to her parents but it was . . . nice.

"Are you sure?" Sutton asked, dubiously. "Because you can tell me. I know my family can sometimes be intrusive, and I can blackmail my siblings into minding their own business, but my mom – well."

She shrugged, adorably, looking so nervous that there was something in her expression that worked to calm Charlotte somehow.

"I'm sure. Your mother is a formidable woman, but I just needed a moment to breathe," she told her, leaning back against the wall.

She could relax like this around Sutton. Sutton could see her without her perfect posture and professionalism.

"Okay, good." Sutton flickered her eyes back inside, where there was a hush that Charlotte only just noticed, before there was a startling collection of *ten!* Called out.

Sutton took a deep breath as she shut her eyes for a moment, her chest rising and falling as she seemed to collect herself. "That's not the only reason I came out here."

Nine. Oh. It was the countdown.

"No?" Her whisper was carried on the wind to Sutton, and she quirked an eyebrow.

Eight.

Sutton shook her head, her hands tangling in front of her, as she took a step away from the door and closer to Charlotte.

Seven.

Her heart hammered in anticipation even as her thoughts came to a halt. Sutton was going to do it again. On a non-benefits night, there was going to be a kiss. Against the rules. Charlotte's lips tingled already. Damn it.

Six.

"I know it's not – I know we aren't having a benefits night," Sutton began, taking another step closer and Charlotte's body already got goosebumps thinking about having Sutton's warmth close enough to feel.

Five.

"But it is a holiday tradition and all, so I thought . . ." Another step closer, and her hands pressed against her thighs.

Four.

"We could, um," her breath washed over Charlotte's jaw with how close they were.

Three.

"Because of . . ." Sutton trailed off, her eyes dipping to Charlotte's lips, and she licked them without thinking, enjoying the way Sutton's breath hitched. "Tradition."

Two.

"Tradition," Charlotte repeated, and her thoughts had landed on a resounding *no*. Every logical thought she had told her to let Sutton down and stick to the rules.

One.

Her hands didn't listen, though, and she reached out to stroke her hands along Sutton's waist, feeling her, as the cheers erupted from inside.

Their lips met slowly at first, Charlotte leaning up off the wall as she tasted Sutton for the first time in weeks. Their breaths mingled, so warm in the freezing air, enticing, with just the whisper of their lips touching.

Then Sutton pushed forward a bit more, pressing Charlotte back against the cold wall, making her mouth drop in a gasp as she felt Sutton's hands stroke down her sides. She tugged at Charlotte's suit as Sutton's soft lips encased her bottom one and sucked in a way that made Charlotte's toes curl.

Not to be outdone, she dug her nails in just a bit, enough to feel Sutton's quickening of breath against her, as she flicked her tongue up along Sutton's top lip, and –

"Charlotte," Sutton sighed so softly into her mouth that she *felt* it more than heard it, sending shivers down her spine.

God, she *wanted* this woman. There never seemed to be enough of her, and Charlotte didn't have any clue what to do with that. It was a sobering thought. Sobering enough to have her press a soft, chaste kiss to the corner of Sutton's mouth as she drew back.

Heavily lidded eyes blinked back at her, but didn't move away. Not yet.

Her conversation with her brother earlier seemed to echo in her ears. Her life goals meant she had to make sacrifices along the way, and she held Sutton's bright blue gaze with her own.

Charlotte had never minded having to make that sacrifice. She'd never let herself feel enough for anyone that it really felt like a sacrifice. Until now.

Chapter 19

By the time Sutton arrived at the Guggenheim for Elizabeth Thompson's inauguration anniversary gala, she was over half an hour late. Which was totally and completely out of character for her, but in all fairness, she felt like there was more at stake here than there had ever been at any other event she'd gone to.

No matter what their romantic non-relationship status was, it was extremely special to be invited to Charlotte's grandmother's annual party. After all, it was *Elizabeth Thompson* – not only was she one of the most influential women on the planet, but she was the grandmother and idol of the woman she had feelings for.

It didn't matter that family members of past dates and all of her friends liked her; this felt bigger. At the very least it meant Charlotte thought Sutton wouldn't be out of place and that she wanted her to meet the woman who shaped her life so much. Which was already a pretty big thing for Charlotte.

Plus, it hadn't helped that on her way out the door, Regan had given her a softly disapproving look. She'd given up on explicitly trying to warn Sutton away from Charlotte. Instead, all she'd said in the last few weeks since New Year's Eve was, *"Just, be careful. Charlotte has made it pretty clear that she isn't going to see beyond herself to notice how good you are and what an amazing girlfriend you would be."*

Regan's protectiveness was unstoppable, always had been, and Sutton, overall, loved that about her.

She just couldn't explain to Regan all of the little things about Charlotte that made her want to sigh while she was sure little hearts exploded over her eyes.

The way she would concentrate on Sutton when it was just the two of them as if nothing else existed. The look where she smiled so unguardedly, so differently than the one she gave to the rest of the world. The moments where she held onto Sutton, clutching even as she fell asleep. The moments that Sutton was sure Charlotte wasn't truly able to let herself accept – yet.

Like the way Charlotte had kissed the breath from her last week when she'd returned to New York and stroked her cheek so tenderly. How she'd stayed in bed five minutes later than her alarm – which she knew by now never happened – and when she *had* gotten up, she'd murmured to Sutton that she could stay if she wanted, despite the fact that Charlotte had to go to work.

No, Charlotte wasn't professing feelings, but . . . it was something. Something different than what it had been at first. And she was patient, very much willing to let Charlotte come to terms with these things on her own time.

The entrance was swarmed with photographers and journalists, and in combination with the sheer volume of guests, Sutton had to pause to take it all in.

She fumbled her phone out of her clutch and felt a rush of warmth when she read the messages from Charlotte that she hadn't had time to check in her rush to arrive.

Charlotte – 7:54PM
Your name is on the list at the door. You'll have no trouble getting in

Charlotte – 8:02PM
Let me know when you arrive? I'm excited to see you.

God, she barely held back the groan under her breath. These were the things Charlotte did that made her heart skip a beat.

Sutton – 8:25PM
Sorry! I didn't realize how crazy it was
going to be to get here.

Sutton – 8:26PM
But I'm here now.

She paused, looking at the building for a long moment. She was relatively familiar with the museum but she'd never seen it looking as glammed up as it did right now. But she supposed when you had the sort of power and influence that Elizabeth Thompson had, you could throw your party wherever you wanted.

Pushing through the crowd near the entrance, managing to slip behind the majority of the guests and out of the way of the media, she jumped when she felt a hand skim over the back of her jacket.

Then shivered at Charlotte's voice teasingly whispering, "You were taking so long I was worried you'd gotten lost."

She spun on the step to face her and felt her throat go dry instantly. Charlotte was wearing a white dress with an intricately embroidered snug body that then loosely fell at her hips. Her arms and shoulders were bare, save for the perfectly styled brown curls.

"I – hi! You came outside to get me?" She cringed as soon as the words were out of her mouth. Because clearly, that's what had happened.

Somehow, even after months, she could still make a fool of herself in front of Charlotte. Whose smirk widened into a genuine smile that . . . almost looked uncharacteristically sheepish, just for a few moments before that confident look was back.

"Well, it did take you a while to get here and you're not one to typically run late, so . . ." she trailed off, waving her hand and pursing her lips.

Sutton ran her eyes over Charlotte's face carefully, taking in those subtle nuances of her expression, before it dawned on her. "You were worried about me?"

It was so odd, seeing Charlotte look even a little bit flustered, but it was also so incredibly appealing and Sutton swore she could feel it all over.

A smile stole over her face. Charlotte was at a networking event, hosted by her cherished grandmother, and she was thinking about *her*.

Charlotte swayed a bit closer, her arm sliding around Sutton's waist as she leaned in close enough that her warm breath glided over Sutton's cheek. She shivered even before she felt Charlotte's warm breath wash over her. "Enough with that teasing smile, darling. *Perhaps* I was worried about you. *Perhaps* I just felt like coming outside."

There was just enough space between them for their eyes to meet and the grin Charlotte wore was meant just for her.

The moment shattered as a light flashed in their direction. A camera flash, she realized with a start, when it happened again. She started in surprise as she turned to face it.

She hadn't noticed anyone even near them, but only a step down was a photographer with a badge hanging around his neck.

By the time she blinked enough for her eyes to adjust a few seconds later, Charlotte's hand had slid up to her waist, the touch casual and light. The look on her face wasn't at all the same as the one they'd shared, but one of her easily disarming grins.

She was able to smile herself after the shock wore off. It wasn't her *first* time at an event with photographers, but she did think back to the many times her parents had done much throughout her childhood to shield their kids from this aspect of their relatively high-profile life.

It wasn't until another photographer called Charlotte's name that Sutton turned and realized – okay, well, she supposed it shouldn't be shocking that there were a few others now facing their direction.

After all, given who Charlotte was in terms of family status and her own political designs at the moment . . . it made sense.

But it was – weird. She froze again, even as she gamely tried to keep the uncertain smile on her face. The cameras flashing and the general *sounds* happening made everything feel a little jumbled.

Her body relaxed slightly when Charlotte squeezed at her waist. She could feel in the touch that it was there for comfort and it worked.

No, she wasn't used to this but it was sort of thrilling in a way. In a way that made her flush a bit in excitement, her smile easing. She was here with Charlotte Thompson, who was the most gorgeous woman she'd probably ever met, with her arm around her.

She was still grateful, though, when Charlotte started to guide them up the stairs, murmuring, "Sorry. I should have warned you it can be somewhat of a mad house."

Though she was still blinking away the last of the flashes still going off behind her eyes, Sutton shook her head. "No, it's okay. Yeah, I was surprised, but it was . . . sort of interesting."

Charlotte lifted an eyebrow at her and Sutton saw the small questioning smile on her face as they entered the ornate entryway. "Yeah?"

Sutton handed her jacket to an attendant, biting her lip in uncertainty as she looked at Charlotte. "As long as you don't mind, um, then it was kind of nice."

Especially when Charlotte's arm around her had felt *safe*.

The bit of nerves in her stomach buzzed as Charlotte's look seemed to minutely pause, all of the little tells Sutton had learned seeming to be closed off.

"No. I don't mind." Her voice was soft before she cleared her throat. "After all, you're a brilliant and beautiful woman. Anyone would be lucky to be associated with you."

She would give almost anything to be able to know exactly what was on Charlotte's mind in those moments. Still, she let it go as Charlotte's hand landed on her lower back, guiding her down toward the party. It was impossible to *not* feel a pleasant warmth at the touch.

Her eyes widened as they entered the main hall, taking in what she could only describe as splendor. "Wow. This looks – amazing. Even more amazing than it ever does during the day. Do you think the new exhibit on French Modernism is up?"

Charlotte murmured, "I have it on good authority that it will be open to the public next week."

As they approached the doorway she felt Charlotte's hand fall from her lower back, and she had to bite back her disappointment; it was just . . . colder.

Which, she told herself, was silly. Because it wasn't as if she could expect those touches throughout the night. Not like they'd done at her family's party. They didn't need to work as a team here, Charlotte didn't need her by her side in this crowd. She'd known going into this that Charlotte would probably go off to socialize on her own throughout the night.

And that was okay, even though Regan's words from earlier echoed, unbidden, in her head.

"Come on." Charlotte easily pulled her from her thoughts. "I'm going to introduce you to my grandmother before I get swept up in any business talk."

Her eyes widened – now *that* was an effective way to get Sutton to stop overthinking. "What? Now?"

Charlotte lifted an eyebrow at her, amusement written all over her face. "I thought you wanted to meet her?"

An anxious excitement settled heavily in her stomach. "I *do*," she was quick to reassure, because who wouldn't? "It's just, well, I'm sure she's probably busy, and has so many other people to talk to right now. I mean, the night's only just beginning; there must be tons of people here who are vying to talk to her."

Sutton wasn't one to typically be nervous around powerful people. But this was different.

470

"You're not wrong. But you have quite the advantage over everyone else here." Charlotte tossed a wink at her as they weaved through the crowd. "Me."

The words – *you have me* – delighted her even as she wondered how much of Charlotte she really had.

There was no time to ruminate on that when Charlotte was leading her over to where Elizabeth was standing, drink in hand, staring critically at the older man speaking to her.

He was someone Sutton didn't recognize and as if reading her mind, Charlotte leaned in to tell her, "Maxwell Tatro. He's an up-and-coming architect in the city." Her eyes met Sutton, twinkling with mischief. "Grandmother isn't exactly a fan."

Getting this seemingly inside scoop from Charlotte made her relax a bit more. It was a strange sort of pride; pride in how much Charlotte knew, who she knew, all of the ins and outs of this world that she was determined to figure out.

She took a deep breath as they approached one of the most powerful women in the world, keeping her amused expression in check as Charlotte swept in and interrupted Maxwell with a smile so disarmingly charming anyone would be enthralled by it.

As he walked away, Charlotte's smile went from calculatedly appealing to one of pure warmth. The admiration in her eyes was clear as day as she looked at her grandmother, with a rare expression free of pretense. And Charlotte in return received a look full of pride.

It was actually pretty heartwarming and Sutton found herself smiling, even as nerves skittered up her spine when Charlotte turned to her.

"And this is my friend, Sutton Spencer," she tilted her head a bit, inclining toward Elizabeth, and Sutton thought that Charlotte looked a little excited herself.

She shifted her gaze to Elizabeth and her stomach dipped again as they came face to face. She was giving her a critical look, questioning almost, the expression that had been there only moments before when she'd been looking at her granddaughter completely gone.

"Right. Your friend," Elizabeth muttered, cutting an indecipherable look to Charlotte. For only a moment, though, before she tilted her head and beckoned Sutton to come closer. "So, you're the Spencer girl."

Despite the butterflies in her stomach, her hand was steady when she offered it. "Yes, ma'am."

Elizabeth gave her hand a firm shake, still giving her that considering look. "The woman who likes my granddaughter so much, your parents invited her to that elusive party that I myself have never been invited to."

Her cheeks burned and before she could even stutter over her response, Charlotte shot a *look* at Elizabeth, hissing, "Grandmother!"

If anything, Elizabeth looked more satisfied than chastised, as she continued, "I don't know why you're blushing when it's my granddaughter who likes you enough to have attended."

Even though she could still feel that she was blushing, she had to bite her lip to attempt to stop her pleased smile. If Charlotte's grandmother thought she liked her all that much . . . well, the butterflies in her stomach seemed to bump up just a bit.

"Grandmother," Charlotte gritted out.

Looking at Charlotte killed some of those butterflies. Charlotte certainly wasn't smiling; in fact, if the tense, rigid way she had her jaw clenched was any indication as to how she was feeling, it was decidedly not good.

She kept her smile plastered on, though, because . . . what was she supposed to say to that?

She certainly didn't expect Elizabeth to narrow her eyes at Sutton, as if reading her inside and out, before turning to Charlotte. "The Lancaster girl, the socialite, arrived while you were outside. You may want to talk to her before she gets swept up by someone else."

Her tone was both firm and encouraging, and it was easy for Sutton to imagine the many years of mentorship. Easy to imagine a young Charlotte eagerly taking her grandmother's direction.

Charlotte shot her an unreadable look before she turned back to her grandmother. "I'm sure I'll manage later."

Elizabeth gave a placid smile that was deceptively sweet. "You don't want to squander your time at events like these. Give me a moment to get to know your friend."

Sutton was beginning to feel like she was witnessing something she wasn't supposed to see when the two women in front of her made and maintained eye contact. They didn't say a word but she swore there was an entire conversation in that look. It was a mastery of silent communication, and she would have marveled at it if it didn't make her anxious.

She wasn't so certain she wanted to be the sole focus of that look. Especially when she could see that Charlotte clearly didn't want her to be here alone with her grandmother, either.

She didn't know if she should be grateful that Charlotte was looking out for her or worried that Charlotte had planned on introducing her to her grandmother but didn't want her to actually talk with her.

Refusing the urge to shuffle her feet, she cleared her throat to get their attention. "I can make myself busy. It's clearly a busy night for you – the both of you. I don't want to take up your time when there are so many other people here hoping for the same opportunity."

She had no idea what to make of that considering gleam in Elizabeth's eyes. "Don't be ridiculous. You stay. *You*, go." She nodded pointedly across the room.

Charlotte took a deep breath and shook her head before searching out Sutton's gaze. "I'll find you, later."

The words were soft and imploring, despite being a statement rather than a question. That confusing but endearing Charlotte softness struck again.

Before she could say anything, Elizabeth sighed impatiently. "Christ – no one is going off to war."

Charlotte set her jaw. "Be nice."

As she walked by Sutton she squeezed her arm, and Sutton knew Elizabeth noticed. She could feel her face heat up and resolutely did not let herself turn to watch Charlotte go.

"For such a bright woman, my granddaughter has her moments of being slow on the uptake." Affection colored her abrasive tone.

Even so, Sutton couldn't help but shake her head. "I think she's brilliant."

Sharp eyes turned to focus entirely on her and she gulped. It was very easy to see the shrewd intelligence there. "I'm sure you do."

God, did Sutton have a sign on her forehead that announced her feelings for Charlotte?

She let out a small breath of relief when instead of asking her anything about Charlotte, she switched topics. "Given who your father is, and your family history, can I assume you've designs on politics yourself?"

A scoffing laugh shot out of her before she could stop it. "Oh, no. Definitely not."

"What is it that you do, then?" Elizabeth asked, and her straightforward manner reminded Sutton of the many speeches and interviews she'd watched this woman give.

"I'm in grad school, for literature," she hesitated to add on, mentally bracing herself. She was used to people in this setting – her father and brother's colleagues in particular – judging that.

Elizabeth pursed her lips in thought, before giving a small nod. Reserving judgment, Sutton supposed. "And what is it that you intend to do with that?"

She felt like an idiot for not preparing ahead of time something she could say to impress her. By this point in her own life, Elizabeth Thompson was already a trailblazer as a woman in politics. That same ambition was a part of Charlotte too.

Feeling a bit embarrassed, she shrugged. "I'm, um, leaning toward going into academia. Right now, I work for Dr. Nicholas Martin as his TA. Getting into writing in the future would be a dream, but I know it can be difficult."

She almost wanted to bring up the internship in Rome, but – well, she wouldn't hear back from that for another couple of weeks. And she *still* wasn't sure if she would go, if she even got in, regardless of how impressive it was.

"No doubt your mother would like to see that, then," she intoned, her voice almost bored, even as her eyes bore into Sutton.

Something about it made her hackles rise. "She . . . would want me to be happy, yes. Both of my parents would."

Elizabeth narrowed her eyes. And, God, it took so much for her to not fidget, but she channeled her mother as much as she could, and held still. She lifted her chin and wondered what this crazy powerful woman thought about her.

And if it would mean anything – either positively or negatively – to Charlotte.

Elizabeth shook her head slightly, chuckling in a manner that Sutton didn't quite think sounded like she found anything particularly funny. "I'm sure your parents would quite like for you to be happy, yes." The words already sounded like a patronizing dismissal even before she said, "Now, if you'll excuse me, young lady, I must make some rounds."

Her hand was given a firm squeeze before Elizabeth brushed by her, and Sutton found herself flabbergasted, turning to watch her go.

Was that . . . Had she failed some sort of test? They'd only spoken for two minutes! How could she have possibly done so badly in two minutes? And what had Elizabeth been searching for? She lamented silently, resisting the urge to bury her face in her hands as she walked to a refreshment table toward the back wall.

Letting out a sigh, Sutton arranged herself a small plate and uncertainly looked around the room. As if magnetized, she sought out Charlotte in the crowd. She found her easily, despite being all the way across the room from her.

It was almost painful how beautiful Charlotte was as she laughed with the woman she was talking to. She recognized her as Payton Lancaster, someone she'd only seen in magazines.

A young and gorgeous socialite, full of social causes, and despite never having seen her in person before this, that wasn't necessary to know how gorgeous she was. It was clear as day in the way she smiled back at Charlotte.

Charlotte laughed with her, and it wasn't really *jealousy* that burned low in her stomach at their exchange. Because she knew that the more people Charlotte talked to, the more connections she made, and it was a good thing for her. People with money and influence; Charlotte needed as many of those people in her corner as she could find.

And Charlotte was utterly captivating, and *should* use that to her advantage whenever possible. It made sense. Sutton couldn't expect anyone else to not fall for everything Charlotte projected the same way she had.

Worrying at her bottom lip, Sutton cut her gaze from the pair. Only to look back a few seconds later.

It wasn't jealousy . . . Only it was. Jealousy and something else, a little deeper.

It wasn't like Charlotte was sleeping with other women. It had been *Charlotte's* idea for them to be exclusive in the first place, and that thought gave her an alarming feeling of satisfaction still.

Besides, Charlotte wouldn't want to hook up with someone in this world, anyway.

Not that Sutton would have any right to care if she did.

That thought wasn't comforting in the least and she barely suppressed a groan. Because it was jealousy and this damning insecurity.

She isn't going to see beyond herself to see how good you are and what an amazing girlfriend you would be. She didn't realize how tightly she'd been holding onto her plate until she looked down and saw how white her knuckles had turned.

Patience, she reminded herself, with a deep breath, as she turned slightly so that she was facing the displayed art instead of the crowd. She just had to be a bit more patient with the whole situation.

Pushing someone into something they weren't ready for, when did that ever work out well? Sutton wasn't built for that.

Brow furrowed, she stared down at the food on her plate. She just needed to focus on something other than jealousy of the woman she was in love with –

Her eyes widened at the thought, the bite of a finger sandwich she'd just taken going down the entirely wrong way, making her cough.

Was she *in love* with Charlotte? She knew . . . God, she knew she had feelings for her, serious feelings, but, there was a difference between having feelings and being in love.

Right?

Still coughing, she rubbed her hand over her cheeks. She'd had feelings for men before, but she knew at this point in her life that she hadn't been in love with them. Even when she'd thought she'd been at the time.

Suddenly, she wished she wasn't here at all. She wished she stayed home tonight, wished she could have some time to herself to really think about everything the way she needed to.

She needed – she needed to write this out, or to lay in bed and let herself really think, or to talk it all out to decipher everything she was feeling, to pick apart all of the swarming feelings in her stomach.

"I don't mean to be rude, but you look the way I feel about all of this socialization tonight," a voice came from behind her, and she jumped.

"I'm sorry," she managed and turned to face him. She tried her best to slow her heart because this was not the time or the place to be having, um, those sort of thoughts. "Am I in your way?"

She awkwardly gestured to the food behind her, quickly stepping to the side.

"No! No, you can, uh, you don't have to – I was just saying that you don't seem like you're having a particularly good time tonight." He shook his head and grimaced. "Not that you don't look nice."

She closed her eyes tightly for a second, trying to rid the chorus in her head – *in love, in love, in love* – and made herself focus. This was so not the time and place for this.

She blew out a deep breath and looked at him. Tall, leanly muscular, with short but slightly curling light brown hair and golden brown eyes, it was easy enough to recognize him as a Thompson.

The picture in Charlotte's apartment told her that he was William.

"Oh." Forcing a small smile, she shrugged. "No, I'm all right. I've been to events like this before."

Perhaps not quite to this magnitude, but still. How did she explain that the reason she was looking like she was freaking out was because she *was* freaking out, about maybe, possibly, probably being in love with his sister?

"Runs in the family, then?" He asked, eyebrows lifting in what appeared to be genuine interest.

Sutton nodded, before huffing out a quick laugh. "Not to the same scale as yours, clearly." She gestured to the room.

He lifted his eyebrows in question, and it was only then that she realized he hadn't exactly told her who he was.

Feeling herself blush, she was seconds away from excusing herself, before he offered his hand. "Should I bother introducing myself as William Thompson? You don't *look* like a member of the press, with the lack of a notebook or a pass."

"No, no, I'm not. I'm just –" Cutting herself off, she started over. "I'm Sutton Spencer. It's nice to meet you."

She shook his hand as he gave her a considering look. Charlotte had only mentioned him offhandedly a few times in the last months. That he was a veterinarian, quieter than she and Caleb were, shyer. But with that thoughtful look, she recognized the resemblance.

A charming, crooked smile stole over his face. "Spencer, yeah, I see your family resemblance." He cleared his throat. "I met your mother once, at a book signing. She was amazing."

The *in love* chorus in her mind slowed with something real to focus on, and she returned the smile for real. "Yeah, she is pretty awesome."

William tilted his head. "So, you're Charlotte's . . . friend?"

The questioning tone made her freeze. He seemed genuinely inquisitive.

But Sutton paused, because she really didn't know what he knew. A large part of her wanted to make an intimation that they were more, and she held herself back.

It wasn't a bad thing to be known as Charlotte's friend, at any rate.

Her eyes found Charlotte again easily in the crowd, and this time Charlotte was in conversation with a politician Sutton vaguely recognized from around the mayor's office the few times she'd been there.

"Yes. She's a good friend." She mumbled, before she snapped her eyes back to William.

He watched her for a few seconds, an unassuming smile on his face. "Good. My sister could use more good friends."

Wanting to steer clear of conversation about Charlotte before she said *something* dumb, she changed the subject, "So, you're not a fan of all this? The parties and whatnot?"

He scratched at the back of his head. "No, it's not really . . ." He trailed off, shrugging sheepishly. "I prefer the company of animals to people, usually."

"I understand that, sometimes." She imagined curling up with Grace and talking out all of these feelings to her best listener. "I have a dog, who lives back with my parents. She's listened to many quandaries."

"Really? I have three dogs who have all listened to my own issues," he informed her with a conspiratorial tone. "What breed is she?"

479

"She – well, hold on." She put down her plate, before reaching into her clutch to pull up a picture on her phone. "Here she is."

William leaned in, brushing his shoulder against hers as he took a close look. "She's gorgeous. Belgian sheepdog?" His eyes were wide and excited as he turned to look at her.

She laughed a bit at his eagerness. "Yeah." She looked down at her phone fondly before tucking it away. "I got her when she was just a puppy, from the MSPCA."

"They're one of the few breeds I've never had brought into my clinic," he told her excitedly. "I'd love to see one in person. Their intelligence and loyalty is supposed to be incredible."

Sutton beamed. "It's . . . well, probably true." She couldn't resist agreeing. "What dogs do you have?"

"Oh, they're all a bit of this, a bit of that; I typically rehab dogs that come into the clinic who don't have homes. The three that stayed with me are a few who didn't end up finding a family," he told her, shrugging.

It was nice to get to know Charlotte's older brother, someone she'd mentioned in sparing stories but with affection in her eyes. It was like learning new pieces of the puzzle as to what really made Charlotte who she was.

William was easy for her to get along with, for his own merit, as well, as he drew out his phone and maneuvered a little closer, showing her the lock screen. "That's Duncan, Benji, and . . . well, Aurora."

A surprised laugh left her as she turned to look at him. "No! Did you really name your dog after –"

"Your mom's books, yes," he finished, rubbing a hand at his jaw, clearly embarrassed. "I'm, uh, a big fan."

Grinning up at him, she nodded. "I should have gotten that from when you said you went to a book signing and all."

"Someone had to step up and try to get Charlotte to enjoy reading." He rolled his eyes, full of warmth. "Never could get her into the romantics, though, not even when I would read them to her at bedtime."

The image of little Charlotte being read to like that was impossible to resist, and she leaned in a bit to whisper, "I think it might have worked the tiniest bit."

While, no, romantic tales weren't Charlotte's favorites the way they were Sutton's, she'd caught Charlotte with big, soft eyes a few times when it had been her turn to choose a movie.

He chuckled. "So, you're a fan too? I'll never get over the teasing I got from Charlotte and Caleb for how much I love Casablanca."

"That's one of my favorites!" She'd ruined the VHS tape when she'd been a child, and she was about to tell him so when she felt a warm hand press lightly at the small of her back.

Her body relaxed into the touch easily, even before she could smell Charlotte's faint, luxurious perfume. She swore she could feel the light touch all the way down to her toes – *did that go along with being in love? This electricity?*

Charlotte had purposefully dropped her hand from this same spot when they'd entered the room earlier. Now, she pressed close enough that Sutton could feel her body heat completely against her side. She shivered, giving Charlotte a curious look.

"Sorry to interrupt; I just need a bit of a break from talking about what to expect from the next debate with Naomi; as if I'll be revealing anything to these people." She smiled at her brother, and Sutton narrowed her eyes because . . . it looked like something was off.

She felt like she was onto something even as Charlotte stepped forward and gave him a kiss on the cheek. "William, it's always strange to see you north of the Mason-Dixon line. The one time a year that it happens," she teased, leaning back to stand next to Sutton, her hand now falling to her hip.

"And as always, I'm already ready to go home," he tossed back, a smile on his face.

Charlotte rolled her eyes. "What did I miss over here?"

It felt like Charlotte was studiously avoiding her gaze, and she stared at the side of her face.

William shrugged. "Nothing much. We were actually just talking about Casablanca, and how it's apparently a mutual favorite."

She could feel more than observe the deep breath Charlotte took, before she finally looked at Sutton. "Oh, really? I should have known the two of you and your commonalities would hit it off."

Sutton tilted her head at the smile that seemed a fraction too tight at the edges.

Still, she smiled back, her body far too relaxed and responsive at Charlotte's closeness. "It's actually a bit funny that you say that, because we were just talking about our dogs; you never told me William named a dog after Aurora?"

Charlotte's smile looked a little more strained even as William's was easygoing. "I have to say, I was eaten up with jealousy when I saw that Charlotte had an advanced copy of the newest book."

"Friends in high places," Charlotte deadpanned. "Speaking of which, you wouldn't mind if I borrowed Sutton, would you?"

He lifted an eyebrow to give them a curious look, before shrugging. "Not at all. It was great to meet you."

The hand Charlotte had slung around her hips was already applying a gentle pressure to lead her away. She looked at William over her shoulder. "It was nice to meet you too!"

Confused, she easily followed Charlotte, unable to look away from her profile, even as Charlotte gave seemingly light grins and nods to some people as they passed.

"Are you okay?" She couldn't resist asking, especially as Charlotte led them into a quiet hallway, away from the party. Her confusion kicked into high gear, nerves tangling in her stomach. "Don't you have a lot of people to talk to?"

"The night is young," Charlotte said, taking a deep breath and shaking her head. At what, Sutton couldn't tell. "And I need . . . some space."

"With me?" She couldn't stop the words before they escaped, cringing at herself.

Sutton accepted the way Charlotte's fingers intertwined with her own easily, naturally, as they slid from her back. "Of course with you, darling. Who else?"

Any number of people in the room, she didn't say. *The pretty socialite who was enjoying your company.*

She trailed her eyes over the art on the walls, taking it in as quickly as she could as Charlotte led her down into a closed-off area, their footsteps echoing in the empty hall.

She reeled back, her voice a hissing whisper, "Are we *allowed* to be here?"

"Darling, it's my grandmother's party. We can go wherever we want . . . as long as we're quiet." She threw a wink at Sutton.

Whose heart beat faster at the risk. "Right. Okay."

"And you did say you wanted to see the French Modernism exhibit. The last man who'd been talking to me happened to be on the board for the museum, and I may have slipped in a question about where it was . . ."

Sutton's jaw dropped, surprised excitement coursing through her as she squeezed Charlotte's hand. "Really?"

Charlotte didn't say anything, but she squeezed her hand back.

In love, in love, in love echoed in the back of her mind and made her heart stutter in her chest. But it was still not the time to think of it. Not yet.

They came to a pause outside of a door a moment later, and she found herself giggling quietly as Charlotte quickly dropped her hand to usher her through. "Shh."

Despite the fact that they didn't flip on the lights, and what she was seeing was only highlighted in the low lighting that reflected under the displays, she gaped at what was in front of her.

It was almost surreal. This entire past hour felt surreal. She wondered again if this was what being in love really felt like. Surreal.

They stood in companionable silence, the museum around them so quiet she was certain they could hear a pin drop, before Charlotte cleared her throat. "So . . . my brother seemed quite taken with you."

"William?" She questioned, incredulously, as she turned to face her.

Charlotte's expression was back to seeming almost strained, even as she tried to smile. "Well, Caleb is gay and you were only talking to the one."

"Well, even though *that* is true, I'm pretty sure he wasn't. We were just talking about our dogs."

Charlotte's mouth pursed. "Darling, I know my brother. He sought you out to talk; do you know how often he does that at these functions?"

"I'm going to guess not too often?" Her eyebrows drew together, thinking about the way William had asked about her friendship with Charlotte.

"Never." Charlotte stepped closer. Close enough that she could feel how warm she was in the still air, and she couldn't stop her shiver.

It took Sutton embarrassingly long to put it together: Charlotte coming to interrupt, the hand on Sutton's back, the stilted conversation and pinched smile . . .

Her mouth fell open with the realization. "You were jealous."

Charlotte's advances halted, the stilted pause probably the most uncoordinated thing Sutton had ever seen from her. Those big, doe eyes blinked once, then twice. "What? No."

She'd heard Charlotte reframe statements, refute points, swiftly step around what she didn't want to discuss. She'd never heard Charlotte say anything so unconvincingly.

Tilting her head to the side, she narrowed her eyes and felt nothing but sure. "You saw me talking to William, you knew we would get along. And you found this information out about the exhibit, because . . . you were jealous."

As it clicked into place, Sutton wondered if she should feel any certain way about this. In the past, she'd had boyfriends who had been jealous; it had been frustrating and sometimes frightening.

But here was Charlotte Thompson, standing in front of her and having these *feelings* for her – enough that she might not be jumping to tell Sutton she wanted them to be together but she didn't want Sutton to be interested in anyone else, either – and . . .

And it sent a heady rush through her. Giddy, but with this edge to it.

Charlotte wanted her. Not just her body, but *her*, and it settled heavily in Sutton's stomach. She could feel it spreading through her veins, and she bit at her bottom lip.

Charlotte huffed out a quick breath of impatience. "No." With a deep breath, she folded her arms. "I found out the information to show you the exhibit before seeing how good of a time you were having with William."

"I'm surprised you noticed anything with me when you were talking to Payton Lancaster," she muttered, the words surprising even herself, and she could feel her cheeks heat.

Embarrassing, perhaps, but it had an effect on Charlotte. Her posture relaxed and that languid easiness that made the way she moved seem almost sensual returned, her eyebrow quirking up.

"So, I'm not the only one of us who was . . . jealous," she murmured, taking a step closer to Sutton.

Her heart skipped a beat, and she swallowed hard, glad that Charlotte had admitted to it, first. It made it easier to say, knowing it was allowed.

"Well. She is very pretty," she whispered, "And, um, dedicated. Wealthy. Influential," she listed only the highlights of what she could remember from articles she'd read, but it was a bit difficult to think when Charlotte was so close to her now that she could feel her warmth through her dress.

"True," Charlotte agreed. She lifted her fingers and walked them over Sutton's hip, trailing her eyes down Sutton's body and then back up, her eyes hungry. "In all honesty, there's no one who could quite distract all of my attention from you."

Her heart jumped, heat sliding through her at the admission. How did Charlotte make her feel this *want* with just a look? She could feel the fingers on her hip grip tighter and she pushed into it.

"Yeah?" She could hear her own breathlessness, but she couldn't control that. Not when Charlotte pressed even closer, her breasts brushing against Sutton's, her breath hot against her jaw.

She reached out to Charlotte's waist, stroking over the curve there that was just barely highlighted in her dress.

Charlotte leaned up, stopping just a breath away from Sutton. Her warm breath washed over Sutton's mouth and she parted them, ducking her head to try to connect their lips.

But Charlotte pulled back. Just a hair, just enough to evade her kiss. Her body pressed against Sutton's, her hand tightening on her hip even more as her other stroked up Sutton's bare shoulder. The soft touch made Sutton shiver, swallowing hard.

She leaned in again, wanting so very much to feel Charlotte's mouth on hers. To be able to kiss her the way she'd wanted to when she'd first seen her tonight. The way she always wanted to.

To be able to taste Charlotte, to feel her panting into her mouth, making that damning insecurity about the what-ifs of this situation disappear. To remind herself that *this* was only between them, that she was the only one who got to know Charlotte in this way right now and that it had been Charlotte's idea to make this exclusive.

Their lips barely brushed, warm and soft and fleeting, before Charlotte pulled back just enough to evade her again, but pressing her body even closer.

She ached with wanting.

Her eyebrows furrowed in confusion when Charlotte pressed their foreheads together, tilting her head just enough that her bottom lip grazed Sutton's top one. Then she leaned back again when Sutton tried to connect them.

"Do you want me, darling?" Charlotte's voice dipped, to the timbre she had when telling Sutton what she wanted during sex, when she cried out her name as she came.

"Charlotte," she breathed, a whimper falling from her mouth. "Kiss me."

Instead of kissing her, Charlotte traced her fingertip up Sutton's neck, before she cupped her jaw. Charlotte's thumb, warm and soft, rubbed at her bottom lip. The feeling sent a shudder down her spine, landing between her legs, and she could feel already how wet she was.

Nail scratching lightly at her lip, Charlotte's eyes locked onto hers. "Do you want *me?*"

She wanted to tell Charlotte that she had nothing and no one to be jealous of. That Sutton would be with her, would be *hers*, if she only asked.

That she already was.

Her hands slid slowly around to meet at Charlotte's lower back, feeling the fabric of her dress bunch as she went, loving the feeling of her curves under her hands. And the way Charlotte's breath stuttered as she answered softly, "You know I do."

Charlotte dragged her thumb down over her chin, the touch guiding Sutton's open mouth to hers.

She'd expected the kiss to be soft, with the vulnerability in Charlotte's voice. Instead, it was hard and ravenous. Charlotte's tongue slid against hers, eliciting a full-body shudder so hard her hands fisted in the material of Charlotte's dress, pulling her completely against her.

Teeth nipped at her tongue then her lip, and she gasped, her hips jerking into Charlotte's. The hand on her hip slid down to her ass, gripping hard, and she couldn't stop the moan from falling from her mouth.

It only got louder when Charlotte walked, forcing Sutton backward until her back hit the wall. She *wanted* so badly everything Charlotte had to give and when Charlotte slid her hand between her legs, she widened them as much as she could in this dress without thinking.

Charlotte's hand was hot as she stroked Sutton's thighs, just under the hem of her dress, and her clit was pulsing already. Her head fell back against the wall on a gasp. "H-here?"

The hand on her jaw held her still, Charlotte's eyes on hers as she panted against Sutton's neck. "Here. Now." She lifted an eyebrow, her hands stilling, and she knew Charlotte was giving her the moment to say no.

Sutton had never had sex somewhere in public before. Fully clothed sex. She'd never even considered it. Certainly not when there were a couple hundred people nearby.

But she'd never wanted someone the way she wanted Charlotte. She'd never felt this satisfying feeling of knowing that behind these doors that separated them from everyone else, she had Charlotte like this.

"Yes," she breathed back, stroking her hands up Charlotte's back and feeling the lean muscle through her dress.

Charlotte didn't hesitate, the hand on Sutton's jaw tipping her head back as she dropped her mouth to Sutton's throat. Her lips sucked kisses down the expanse of her skin and everything in Sutton felt molten at the touch, her hips bucking into Charlotte's. Who merely slid her hand inches up Sutton's dress, pausing to stroke her skin.

Everywhere Charlotte touched *burned* and she wanted her to keep going, to slide up and touch her for real.

Then she gasped, ending on a groan, when she felt Charlotte bite at her neck.

It was hard, harder than Charlotte's typical small nips and light, teasing scrapes of her teeth. She shuddered, feeling herself soak through her underwear, arching her back against Charlotte.

And then crying out when Charlotte bit again, just a little lower, sucking on the skin there.

Charlotte groaned back and she could feel the vibration against her, could feel the way Charlotte scraped her teeth against her in tandem with scratching down the other side of her neck, and the dual sensations sent sparks of arousal shooting through her.

A moan left the back of her throat when she felt the backs of Charlotte's fingers brush against her underwear. She whined when Charlotte slid back down, gripping her thigh instead.

"Shh," Charlotte murmured into her neck. "We have to be quiet."

Sutton tried to grind her hips down against Charlotte's hand, needing to feel *more* than just that fleeting, light touch against her core. She felt desperate when Charlotte instead dragged her fingers slightly down, away from where she needed her.

"Please. I'll be quiet," she whispered, panting, eyes falling closed when she realized that seemed to be what Charlotte had been waiting for.

She traced her knuckles back up Sutton's thigh and stroked through her underwear, the touch light. "God, Sutton, you're so wet for me. I can feel you, already. You're fucking soaked."

Biting her lip to try to stop herself from making too much noise, she nodded. Her head fell back again, panting when Charlotte sucked hard again at the spot on her neck, the way her fingers stroked at her at that same pace through her underwear.

"Fuck, I love this dress," the words were said into her skin. The roughness in Charlotte's honey-smooth voice made her shudder and jerk her hips, and she was so fucking relieved when Charlotte stroked her firmly in response.

Only once, as she kissed a trail back up her throat. "I couldn't tell you the proper way when I first saw you outside, but . . . fuck, Sutton. Open your legs as much as you can for me."

Sutton broke out in goosebumps, her hips grinding down, clit throbbing hard, as she did what was asked of her. Which, frustratingly, wasn't as much as she would have liked, with the cling of her dress not being very giving.

It just made Charlotte chuckle darkly against her, though, "Don't worry, baby. I can make you come just like this."

Everything felt so *hot*, and she whined as she could feel herself starting to drip down her thigh.

Charlotte must have been able to feel how wet she was, as she moaned low in her throat, pressing her lips just under Sutton's jaw and slipping two fingers into her underwear. She stroked her entrance, and Sutton whimpered, because she was already *so* –

A guttural groan fell from her throat as Charlotte pressed her fingers inside of her. She felt like she could barely catch her breath as she dug her fingers into Charlotte's back to try to ground herself.

She didn't have a chance to feel *grounded*, though, not when Charlotte slid into her as deep as she could, pulling out and stroking over her clit, before pressing back inside. Her back arched so hard it almost hurt, and she saw sparks behind her eyelids as the fingers inside of her moved even faster.

Fast and hard, and she could dimly hear herself panting, then moaning when Charlotte rubbed at her nerves with her thumb.

"Ch-Char –" She cut herself off, biting her lip hard, as she forced herself to open her eyes. She found Charlotte's watching her, eyes big and dark and wanting and –

She could feel her legs shaking, her knees feeling weak while the feeling in her stomach built and built, and Charlotte fucked her faster.

Her mouth fell open on a cry as she came, Charlotte's hand quickly coming up and clamping over her mouth as her orgasm washed over her. She was

490

completely coming apart at the seams, hips jerking uncontrollably into Charlotte's hand, unable to catch her breath, the unbelievable heat finally taking her over.

Long moments later, she leaned back against the wall, blowing out a deep breath as Charlotte's hand fell from her mouth. She shuddered when Charlotte slowly slid her fingers out from between her legs.

"God," she panted out, regaining her breath. Then losing it again when Charlotte sucked her wet fingers into her mouth.

The hold she had around Charlotte's waist tightened, pulling her forward to press their lips together again to taste herself on Charlotte's mouth.

She'd had no idea how quickly and easily she could *want* before, how desire could eat her up so fast, how hard she could come . . . She hadn't known any of it, before Charlotte. She kissed her deeper, swallowing Charlotte's quiet moan.

Thinking about it, about all those small insecurities, thinking about Charlotte and someone else, about how *jealousy* had been the reason this was happening right now made her tighten her arms, and spin them.

She didn't realize how much pressure she'd used, how hard she'd pressed Charlotte into the wall, until she heard the thump of her back against the wall. Then felt Charlotte's breath rush out, and heard her surprised gasp as she pulled out of the kiss.

Panting, she was about to apologize when she saw how blown Charlotte's pupils were, and the arch of her eyebrow.

"You liked that?" She wondered aloud.

Charlotte's eyes absolutely gleamed up at her. "Dirty talk, Sutton Spencer? Tonight is full of new things," she whispered as she slid her hand to the back of Sutton's neck to pull her down.

Sutton slid her lips over Charlotte's, reveling in the damp softness as she dimly realized – Charlotte thought *you liked that* was dirty talk. And that she seemed to actually like it. Much like she'd possibly liked when Sutton had been – unintentionally – rough?

Almost experimentally, she slid her hands down, wrapping each one around Charlotte's wrists and tugging her hands away from her body. She held them above her head as she leaned in close enough to press Charlotte hard against the wall again, not giving her anywhere to go, grinding her hips down and into Charlotte's.

For a moment, she felt everything freeze, her heart stuttering, preparing to drop Charlotte's hands and –

Then Charlotte let out a choked, surprised groan. "*Yes.*"

"You *do* like this, huh?"

Charlotte flexed her hands, not trying to really move them, she realized. Just *moving*, feeling Sutton's hold on them. She nearly reflexively let go, then squeezed lightly instead and Charlotte sucked in a breath, shuddering against her.

"You like that I'm stronger than you," she realized aloud, vaguely remembering past times where Charlotte traced over her toned muscles.

"Fuck, Sutton." Charlotte arched as much as she could against her, cheeks flushed. "I want you to *take* me."

The words hit her, hard.

It felt like an entire new door had opened to her when it came to sex, and despite just having come, hard, she felt arousal slide through her all over again. She felt hungry for Charlotte, wanting to make Charlotte come as hard as she had.

Wanted to give Charlotte something that she wanted from Sutton.

Her eyes narrowed in determination – she could do this. She was shocked at how much she *wanted* to do this.

Sliding her hands from Charlotte's wrists to her hands, she tugged her from the wall and instead to the bit of the wall that had a waist-height bar attached to keep people from getting too close to the exhibit.

With a deep breath, she put Charlotte's hands behind her, having her hold onto the rail and squeezing her hands over Charlotte's. "Here," she whispered.

Sutton leaned down, sucking Charlotte's bottom lip into her mouth, before she could question herself.

Nipping with her teeth, she dipped down a couple of inches and brought her hands to the backs of Charlotte's thighs. She heard and felt Charlotte groan into her mouth when she dug her fingers harder than she typically would, confidence boosting.

Boosting even higher when Charlotte pressed her hips against her, jerking them unevenly, so obviously wanting.

Tightening her hold, she tugged her legs apart, then gripped and lifted. It was a thrill, holding Charlotte up like this, the way she gasped into her mouth and her thighs tensed.

Easing forward, she pressed Charlotte against the wall, balanced as much as she could on the railing, as Sutton pushed forward. Hard enough that Charlotte was forced completely against the wall again, her thighs on either side of Sutton's hips, and she slid her hands down under Charlotte's dress to stroke up her outer thighs.

God, her skin was so unbelievably soft and so warm under her hands. Biting her lip, she watched through heavily lidded eyes as Charlotte dropped her head back against the wall with a *thump* as Sutton reached below her knees and tugged her legs around her waist.

She pushed forward, rolling her hips into Charlotte's, hard, loving the way she bucked even more against her.

Scratching her nails up Charlotte's thighs, she reveled in her soft swearing and the goosebumps that followed her touch. She thanked God that unlike her dress, Charlotte's was loose enough to be pushed up all the way to her hips, bunching it there.

Sutton could see how wet Charlotte was, see the dampness on her panties and the little red lines from where she'd scratched forming on the outside of her thighs. *Her mark.* Her throat went dry.

493

She slid her hands around, cupping Charlotte's ass and lifting her off the bannister as she pressed back in, rolling her hips again.

She could hear and feel Charlotte's gasps and broken groans against her neck, her quietly hissed out, "*Yes. Fuck, yes, Sutton*." When she ground hard enough into her, she could feel Charlotte's clit throb against her, even through her underwear, her legs spread lewdly wide.

Charlotte placed disjointed, wet kisses to Sutton's neck, whimpering into them, rocking her hips faster. She could feel how uneven Charlotte's breath was coming out as it washed over her neck, and knew she was going to come soon.

When she felt Charlotte's hands reach for her, grabbing at her shoulders as her thighs started to tremble, Sutton reached up, taking her hands and forcing them back down. "I said to keep them here. You're going to come like *this*."

Her voice was rougher than she'd ever heard it, and she was shocked at herself – where did *that* come from? – even as she held Charlotte's hands down and ground down as hard and close as she could, keeping Charlotte pressed between herself and the wall, Charlotte's legs shaking around her hips.

Charlotte's hands flexed under hers, a strangled, "Fuck," falling from her mouth before she fell into her orgasm, her chest arching hard into Sutton's, breath panting out in choked off whimpers.

Her body shuddered hard, rhythmically jerking against Sutton, and she pressed close, keeping Charlotte held up against the wall with her body. She brought her hands to Charlotte's thighs again, this time stroking as she came down from her orgasm.

Eventually, Charlotte slouched back against the wall, still breathing so hard Sutton could feel how hard her heart was beating. Her hair was mussed, her eyelids heavy as she looked up at Sutton.

"That was . . . something else." Charlotte's voice was soft and throaty, an affectionate smile on her lips. "You are something else, Sutton Spencer."

It was teasing again, but also sounded almost *reverent*, which was probably somewhat silly to think. But all Sutton could imagine was how she was the only one Charlotte trusted like this. Who got to see this softness, got to see the difference between projection and truth, and how much more complex Charlotte truly was.

No one was lucky enough to see all of that, except for her.

The tough Charlotte, the enigmatic Charlotte, the sexy Charlotte, the vulnerable Charlotte, the needy Charlotte, the brilliant Charlotte.

Knowing that made her chest feel so warm – unlike anything she'd ever felt. Something completely overwhelming, but calming, in a way. A way that made her want to stroke back the tousled curls of Charlotte's hair and kiss her forehead and lean into her and just *know* that everything was good.

Oh.

Oh.

In love, in love, in love.

There was no maybe, possibly, probably about it, she realized. It was real, it was filling her up, and she inhaled sharply.

Charlotte watched her closely, lifting her eyebrows at her in question. "What is it?"

Sutton froze.

She shouldn't say anything. She should not say anything, at all, and she knew it. It was not the right time and entirely the wrong situation. They weren't really *together*, not girlfriends, and things were confusing.

"I . . ." *I love you.*

Charlotte tilted her head, the amused expression on her face quickly growing more concerned.

She took a deep breath, stalling to figure out what to say. Then she froze at a sound coming from the large, echoing hall outside of this particular exhibit.

Not just any sound but footsteps, walking quickly and getting louder. Coming toward them.

As if exploding into motion, Sutton let Charlotte's legs down, and she jumped back from her so fast she nearly tripped over her heels. She started tugging her dress into place as fast as she could, panic making her movements jerky, her hands shaking.

Charlotte had tugged her dress back down and was combing her fingers through her hair before they both came to a heart-stopping pause when the footsteps stopped right outside the door.

Charlotte moved in what must have been a flash, gripping Sutton's arm and pushing her back in front of one of the wall displays. Hastily she dropped her hand and stepped a good arm's length away, also staring up at the wall, feigning interest just in time for the door to swing open.

Sutton heart pounded – she nearly felt it absolutely stop at the idea of how this could look for Charlotte.

"Ah, have I finally found them?"

Of course, out of all people, it was David Verbeck. She hadn't seen him earlier, but there had been hundreds of people there and she supposed it wasn't necessarily shocking. He was involved in many big businesses in the city.

But what did he *mean* by that?

Despite knowing they'd been found she couldn't move from where she was, facing the wall, wide-eyed and nervous.

Thankfully, Charlotte was a miracle, and her posture wasn't jerky or panicked at all as she turned. She shot him a glance that seemed casual. "Oh, were you looking for the new exhibit too? Sutton and I were dying to see it."

How did she do it? Sutton felt like her heart was beating in her throat – just a minute ago, she'd had Charlotte pressed against the wall, and now . . .

Verbeck scoffed. "Of course I was looking for the exhibit. I just went on quite a little journey searching different halls for . . . it."

Swallowing hard, she forced herself to turn slowly. She tried to smile, even though it might have looked more like a nervous grimace. "Well, you've found it."

She couldn't even dare look at Charlotte for fear of blushing darker than her hair.

Verbeck gave her that *look* that he so often gave her, the one that made her skin crawl, with a slow smile. "Isn't that just lovely? Speaking of lovely, I was quite surprised to see you here tonight, Sutton." He flicked his gaze to Charlotte. "And you appear to be having quite the evening."

Oh, God.

"It's quite exciting to be able to see something like this in a private showing," he concluded, gesturing to the painting behind Sutton.

She was never prouder of herself than she was at that moment when she didn't stammer, "Right, yes. The art is incredible. And, you know, it's not every night you meet a former President."

He slid his eyes over her. "I would say so, indeed."

She was ridiculously relieved when Charlotte brushed by her, standing in front of her, with her eyes narrowed. "And are you enjoying your evening, Mr. Verbeck?"

Her voice was a masterful combination of seemingly genuine but also with a firm edge that Sutton adored.

Verbeck lifted his eyebrows, scratching at his chin. "Not as much as some, but yes, indeed. I wish I hadn't wasted so much time trying to find this hall. But at least I'm here now."

"Lovely. Well, Sutton and I will make our exit so that you can properly enjoy the exhibit you've taken such an interest in," Charlotte told him, that firm tone in place. She gave Sutton a look over her shoulder. "Come on, let's get back to the party. I have it on good authority that desserts will be put out soon."

She waited for a moment and Sutton realized she wanted her to walk in front of her. Heart still hammering, she quickly walked by Charlotte and then Verbeck, keeping as much distance as she could from him. She could feel how closely Charlotte was following her.

"Enjoy your evening," he called from behind them.

"Yes, you too," Charlotte's tone was purposefully insincere.

Sutton forced herself to walk slowly, breathing deeply, until she rounded the corner at the opposite end of the hallway.

Then she completely deflated, her limbs feeling like jelly with the residual nerves.

Charlotte threw another look down the hall, suspicion written all over her face, before she seemed satisfied that he wasn't behind them. Her hands came to her hips and she blew out her own deep breath, shaking her head in disgust.

"That man is absolutely vile. And the way he looked at you? I don't even feel comfortable leaving you alone in the same room with him for a second."

As the nerves started to subside, Sutton managed a little smile. "I appreciate that."

She pressed a hand to her stomach to calm her nerves. No one had walked in on their semi-public sex. Charlotte seemed to be okay, if intensely in thought. The awkwardness was over.

She tentatively reached out to draw her hand down Charlotte's arm to get her attention. Charlotte shook her head slightly but didn't pull back from her touch, and she counted it as a victory.

"Back to the party? Is there actually dessert?"

The side of Charlotte's mouth ticked up. "There is." She looked around them before she leaned in and whispered, "But the real *dessert* will commence at my place, later."

She shot her a wink, before leading the way down the hall.

Sutton watched her go.

That was the woman she was in love with.

God.

Chapter 20

From the moment she woke up on the day of her second, and more formal, debate with Naomi, Charlotte was *ready*.

Nerves were nearly nonexistent: she'd emerged from their first head-to-head as the clear winner, and all of the preliminary polling numbers put her ahead. This feeling had followed her all morning and into her afternoon meetings with her campaign staff.

The meeting was more perfunctory than anything else. Reviewing the overall campaign so far, as there was barely a month left until the election. Picking through all of the details as a team, making sure everyone was updated and on the same page.

On the negative side of being so well-prepared and anxiety-free about her debate came the fact that she struggled to give the meeting all of her attention. Which was *ludicrous* because focusing on this big of a meeting should have been no problem.

Yet she found herself growing distracted more than once, her thoughts always circling around to Sutton. It was disconcerting to say the least, but she could at least blame some of her distraction on the pictures.

The pictures that had been pinned up to a whiteboard on the wall, displayed about an hour ago. Her PR specialist, Isaiah DuPont, had revealed his display a couple of hours ago – every picture, he'd explained, that had been snapped of her by any media source since the last debate.

He was thorough, it was why she'd hired him. He kept track of every time her name and face appeared in any newspaper or magazine or media outlet, and – as he'd said when he'd set the display up in their meeting room – she was "really getting out there" among the public. Becoming more recognizable.

She just hadn't realized exactly how often she'd been "getting out there" with Sutton until it was here, staring her in the face. She'd known, clearly, about the amount of time they spent together, but they had no idea that it was so – public.

She'd known about the picture that was placed at the forefront of the display, glossy and professional, of the two of them from the night of her grandmother's party. That picture had been in the paper the very morning after.

But the others – the one with her and Sutton walking down the steps of City Hall together last week when Sutton had come to bring her dinner. The one from a couple of days ago, when they'd gotten a coffee together. The one that had to have been taken and released from someone at the Spencer party on New Year's Eve, of the two of them talking animatedly with someone who was off-camera –

There were just so many.

It wasn't as though they were ever doing anything inappropriate. Their official status of *friends* rang true in all of the photos.

She'd never seen her own face when she looked at Sutton. And to have it staring back at her from the eye of the media . . . God, but Sutton was such an unexpected variable.

Sutton, who she'd invited to spend the night at her place more often than not in the last couple of weeks since her grandmother's party. Who she'd found herself cuddling up to in the mornings before getting out of bed because it was *so* nice to have her there, smelling so good and feeling all warm.

Sutton, who had helped her prepare for her debate for hours, tirelessly, and had seemed to also enjoy doing it. Sutton, who wrote little reminders in her *campaign notes* and instead of feeling irritated, she couldn't help but smile whenever she saw the neat scrawl next to her own.

Sutton, who had slept at her apartment last night and they'd spent the morning drinking coffee and tea, respectively, while working on debate prep and a term paper, respectively. And when she'd had to leave to get to this meeting, it had been second nature for her to tell Sutton that she could stay at her apartment and finish her paper, telling her to lock up when she was done.

Charlotte had come *this close* to kissing her goodbye, too. She'd wanted to – badly. With the way Sutton was sitting at her kitchen table, hair done in a braid over her shoulder, looking cozy and at home, Charlotte had been unable to stop herself from stroking her fingers over Sutton's cheek, reveling in the softness and lingering more than she should have. Lingering even when she knew it was bad for her.

It was frustrating, challenging, scary, and, well, a whole host of other emotions that ate away at her in uncertainty when she was not with Sutton. Then . . . they melted into the back of her mind when they were together.

At the base of it all, Charlotte didn't like this version of herself. This version of herself that was unsure about all these feelings, who was wanting and needy. This version of herself that knew when something was a bad idea and still did it anyway. The one who knew that there was damage control to be done to end the sex part of her relationship with Sutton in order to preserve the friendship, but who was so unwilling to actually take a step back from her.

The version of herself that she'd had no idea existed before that always seemed to come out when Sutton was near.

It was more than unsettling; it was nerve-wracking. It was irritating. She should be better than that. She could never have predicted that this, of all things, would have been when her poker face would let her down.

The last thing she needed on the day of a debate with Naomi was to see that not only was her growing Sutton-distraction an internal problem, but also externally visible.

Keep it together, she commanded herself, straightening her spine. Perhaps she couldn't control everything – she could only fantasize about that – and not even her own thoughts at times, as of late. But she could control focusing as much as she could on the meeting.

On her debate, to be more exact. Because that did need her attention. This was her future at stake. Plus, a quick look at her watch told her that the meeting was nearly over, anyway.

Shaking her hair back, Charlotte let out a quiet sigh and looked across the table to Isaiah, who ticked his pen along the side of his paper as he reviewed, "So, in summation: after tonight, followed by your interview tomorrow – assuming all goes as expected, of course – we should see consistent polling numbers. If not a slight increase."

It worked to take a bit of the weight off her shoulders. A small smirk tugged at her lips, and she nodded at him before turning to Helena Langford, social media expert, who slid the page full of statistics about the online presence and trackers that she'd set up in Charlotte's name across the table to her.

"Your accounts, the searches on your name, and your websites are getting more traffic than typical House campaigns get. A significant uptick in searches in the last few weeks. Because of the light being shone on the debate tonight?" She mused, quirking an eyebrow over her laptop.

Charlotte pursed her lips in thought. More interest in this election, in her, was something they'd been hoping for and planning for; it was, after all, the foundation for her future career being built.

Her eyes flickered to the pictures of herself and Sutton; for as much as she wanted to take complete ownership of the reason behind this increased interest, she couldn't help but wonder.

Fuck, she hated any facet of *not knowing*.

Dean cleared his throat, calling their attention. "I think it stands to reason that given your family history, as well as Naomi's, there was already a relatively higher interest in the election from the beginning. Not to mention just *you* being a young, attractive, intelligent, and strong woman."

She grinned even as she rolled her eyes. "You're already my friend and will always have a place on my team, Dean. No need to flatter me."

It earned a small titter from her staff and the expected eyeroll from Dean.

"Political rivalry certainly has something to do with the increase in interest," Aaron spoke quietly from where he sat apart from the others at the table.

She trusted everyone on her team, of course. But Aaron was – for all intents and purposes – on loan from her grandmother's staff, someone who'd worked with her grandmother for nearly Charlotte's entire life.

Given how much of his job involved keeping an eye and ear right on the pulse of secrets, Charlotte knew how valuable he was. He was someone who had seen and foretold handfuls of political scandals days or weeks before anything happened publicly, and that was only the aspects that she knew about. And she would never delude herself into thinking that politics was not a dirty game at times.

He tapped his fingers on the table. "Political rivalry, family history. The fact that Thompson and Young are both names of public knowledge and interest. The fact that two younger, attractive people are running against each other; these are all factors. And, of course, the commentary that has been made by Naomi about you, particularly in the last few weeks."

Levity gone, Charlotte leaned back in her chair.

"Her remarks about my age, experience, and supposed nepotism have been par for the course," she asserted, and had to pause and resolutely *not* let her eyes flicker to the pictures of herself and Sutton. "Her comments about my love life, slightly less expected."

Her voice remained steady, even though the first time Naomi had made a veiled comment about her personal life last week in an interview had made Charlotte's heart race.

Isaiah, the last member of her team that she'd disclosed her sexuality to, scoffed. "She's tried to make an intimation about your love life, but it was pathetic. A reach. After all, the only photos you've been seen in – in any recent past – have been family members, coworkers, or Sutton Spencer."

Charlotte swallowed back any nerves that wanted to surface. "That is all . . . true."

"The searches on your name and hits on any of your social media went up after that interview, it's true," Helena hazarded, and Charlotte turned to make eye contact with her. "But realistically, your friendship with the daughter of a well-liked and well-respected politician – who also happens to be young, attractive, and smart – is only more good press."

She gave Charlotte a small, comforting smile. She wished it worked. "Thank you."

"It may be good press," Aaron agreed. "For now." Charlotte's gaze snapped to him. "But I would advise you to tread carefully. As of right now, there isn't much speculation about your lack of a romantic life. However, Naomi's comments have started a quiet buzz on the periphery. I'm sure it'll only get louder as you become more prominent . . . if there's anything to hang on to."

His gaze flicked to the pictures of her and Sutton.

Charlotte's throat seemed to seize for a moment as complete silence took over the conference room. She could feel the stares of her team but she only tilted her chin up and maintained eye contact with Aaron.

"I know," she admitted, and her voice was steady and firm.

She could see in the firm set of his jaw that he wasn't finished, even before he continued, "I'm not here as an advisor or to give any opinion on how to live your life. My capacity here is to make sure you're aware that this could cause a big reaction, and that however you plan to address your personal life in the future, we want to be ahead of anything, before it gets ahead of us."

It wasn't anything Charlotte hadn't already told herself. She knew that Aaron really wasn't voicing an opinion of any sort, but that he was someone who was all about facts.

"I'm well aware."

There was just the damning matter of her stomach revolting when she thought about ending things with Sutton.

"There have, in the past, been several failed careers that trace back to the root of personal matters –"

"I don't need a history lesson," she interrupted, more than knowledgeable of the very small pool of out – or outed – politicians, and the many careers that people led in the closet. "And there is nothing to get ahead of."

She used the tone that Caleb had in the past referred to as her "scary dictator voice," something she generally tried to stay away from. But it worked, as Aaron offered a nod. "As long as you have all of the sides."

Dean gave her a long imploring look. A look as though he knew just what she was feeling despite never discussing it. One that spoke of putting his own possible political aspirations on the backburner and instead focusing on the job he loved but was safe from higher scrutiny.

"I'm handling everything that needs to be handled."

***

It was a relief that her burning, eager, competitive edge sluiced through every possible doubt she could have during the debate. That in spite of anything else on her mind, she could do *this*.

The tightening of Naomi's jaw when she was asked about the motions and bills currently being worked through Congress and how her platform would work within existing systems showed that Naomi had clearly not been anticipating that question. Charlotte hadn't been either, but she was much more knowledgeable about the current motions than Naomi possibly could have been.

The way her eyes set in a near-permanent glare at Charlotte when the moderator asked one of the final questions to her, "Ms. Thompson, throughout the campaign so far, I believe one of the biggest concerns that has been raised about you is your age and experience. It's been something Ms. Young has mentioned several times. Is there an official comment you'd like to make about it?"

505

She met Naomi's eyes, maintaining her polite but firm semi-smile. "This isn't something I necessarily address directly, typically, as I do like for my work thus far to speak for itself, as well as the initiatives I've already detailed stand for themselves." She let a beat go by, before she could feel her smile turn a bit feral. "I admittedly may not have as extensive of a work history as some of my colleagues, but I daresay it's better than having none."

"Ms. Young, anything you'd like to say to that?"

The tightness in Naomi's smile was evident and Charlotte reveled in it "Yes, thank you. My *opponent* speaks of my lack of professional work history, but also forgets that I was married to a politician for nearly two decades. That my father was a politician my entire life; this is far from a new playing field for me. Beyond that, I have far more *life experience* at large. Of course, Ms. Thompson, your youthful ambition is . . . admirable," the tone of her voice dripped with disdain. "But you have much to experience in life to come."

There was a small tension in the room in the audience, and she felt it building as people turned their attention back to her.

Charlotte inhaled, that fire burning even brighter inside of her stomach. "I can say with absolute clarity that I've spent my entire adult life taking strides to make this country a better place, so your comments on my ambitions are entirely accurate. Yet, for all of your life experience, where has *your* ambition been?"

There was a smattering of applause and the muscle in Naomi's cheek twitched. "I've worn many hats over the years. As I'm sure so many can attest to, life experience is something that cannot be overlooked when it comes to political standing. I've been a wife, a mother, a widow."

She stayed attuned to Naomi's body language with every word she spoke, and she could tell something was coming even before Naomi stood just a bit straighter. There was the faintest bit of a gleam in her eyes as she continued, "There are universal experiences that you cannot even imagine relating to, as your own personal life has been a bit of a source of speculation in the past few weeks."

By you, Charlotte added silently, as she forcefully pushed aside the way her stomach dipped unpleasantly. This was a Naomi tactic. Nothing more.

"My personal life experiences, as a public figure, are open to public speculation. There is no one on my romantic horizons at the moment. I'm sure anyone who had any interest in such speculation could attest that there's very little to speculate on." She let the corners of her mouth tilt up into a smile. "I can assure you that I know how to prioritize."

Naomi lifted an eyebrow. "It could appear that way. Or it could appear as though one is working a little too hard to have any possible *scandal* overlooked. After all, the last time a politician had such a dry public image was Anthony Batista."

The sinking feeling in her stomach was back with the smug look on Naomi's face, like she knew she'd landed a punch. Mentioning a politician whose career was derailed by a sex scandal a handful of years ago, and drawing the parallel back to Charlotte.

Her hand tightened nearly imperceptibly against the podium for only a second before she caught herself. She took a deep breath against the lights that seemed glaringly bright all of a sudden to center herself.

Fucking Naomi Young.

She met her gaze head-on, merely quirking an eyebrow. Despite the digs Naomi had taken at her throughout the election, thus far she'd remained free from naming anything explicitly about Charlotte's romantic or sexual life. She had to believe it was due to the fact that Naomi wasn't without her own past *rumors* about her sex life and didn't want those dredged up.

With a decidedly friendly smile, she shook her head. "As I'm sure you're fully aware, I have no scandals to hide. Though, I'm not entirely sure bringing scandals into the conversation would make for a conversation you would want."

She'd be willing to bet that certain talk about multiple extra-marital affairs, including one with an underage gardener, would ring a lot of bells. Let alone the fact that the timeline of those affairs called into question the parentage of her children. And she'd thought it was somewhat of an unspoken agreement that they were purposefully not directly bringing these matters up in the election.

The bit of a teasing tone was purposeful, to make it light enough that the audience tittered in amusement. But she saw the way Naomi inhaled a sharp breath, feeling victorious when that haughty mask slipped.

It made her feel like she was back and steady. "To conclude my answer to the proposed question: I view my youth as an advantage in this current atmosphere, rather than a hindrance as my opponent seems to believe. The fact of the matter is that the amount of people in my generation who are politically knowledgeable and passionate about the future of this country is at an all-time high. Despite that, the amount of people from that demographic involved in politics is extremely low. I may be young, but youth also speaks to innovation and change, to progression. The voice of my generation is the voice of the future of this country, and it deserves to be heard."

She knew easily in the deafening applause that erupted that the feeling of victory coursing through her wasn't unfounded, and this time the smile on her face was wholly genuine.

The feeling thrummed through her through the remainder of the debate, into the short meet-and-greet afterwards, and followed her backstage.

It quieted from a roar to a buzz, but it was impossible to not be giddy from it. Because she had officially completed two out of the three debates of the first campaign she'd ever been in, and she'd won them both.

The big, celebratory message from Sutton with too many emojis – so ridiculous, but they made her want to sweep Sutton into her arms – made her only feel that much brighter.

Really the only thing that could be better would be if she could see Sutton tonight. Now. It could have happened, because before she'd gone to her meeting Sutton had eagerly offered to reschedule her plans to see a movie with Emma in order to celebrate with her. Charlotte had known that, assuming things went well, she'd very possibly be feeling this craving to be with Sutton and celebrate.

Which was precisely why she'd forced a smile and insisted Sutton go out with Emma and that she would see her later this week.

More distance between them right now, even when she damningly didn't want it, could only be a good thing. It helped her keep her focus.

The other messages from family and friends and acquaintances on her phone . . . were nice, too.

The grin only grew at the short knock on her door. Assuming it was Dean and Caleb, there to take her out for dinner, she opened it without thinking.

But her spirits and her smile dipped when it was Naomi standing there, a few inches taller than Charlotte, her immaculate blonde hair still done up perfectly.

She quirked an eyebrow. "Did you come to congratulate me? I have to say this is unexpected."

"Oh, please. As if congratulations are in order."

Okay, so this was what they were doing – no pretense. Then again, when was there much pretense with Naomi?

"You coming to congratulate me would be less unexpected than your, say, bringing up scandals at the end of the debate. You were making quite the reach." Charlotte purposefully kept her voice light.

"A reach?" Naomi frowned in faux-contemplation. "Not a reach in the least; quite the contrary, you placed that topic right in my lap."

Charlotte's eyes narrowed, all of the previous buzz disappearing dizzyingly quickly. "You can comb through my entire professional history, every public word I've spoken –"

509

Naomi waved her hand, imperiously cutting her off. "Oh, I'm sorry. I should have said this: you placed this topic right in my lap, in the shape of Sutton Spencer."

Her stomach clenched so hard, lurched so uncomfortably, that it took all of her self-control not to outwardly show it. Her face remained challengingly impassive and she lifted an eyebrow. "I wasn't aware that having a friend was a scandal."

Naomi's smile was slow and lethal, condescending and victorious at once. The combination was one of the most unsettling things Charlotte had ever seen. "I wasn't aware that adult friendships involved sleepovers and such familiar touches."

The words only built on the sickening foreboding lodged at the pit of her stomach. But she forced as patronizing a smile as she could onto her face, trying to calm any overzealous thoughts that were jumping to conclusions. Naomi Young was nothing if not a manipulator; this was a scare tactic.

"You're right. I'm quite sure *you* wouldn't realize anything that an actual friendship entails."

Scare tactic or no, it was disconcerting, right to the bone, the way Naomi was smiling easily at her. That her eyes hadn't sharpened in that agitated way. That her jaw hadn't set.

It was the way all of those little things mingled together that told Charlotte that Naomi was still playing a little game with her.

She hated it.

The smile on her face seemed to sharpen, as she tapped her fingers against her hip, "That picture, the one in the *Post* the morning after your grandmother's little party? With you two standing on the steps outside of the Guggenheim, your arm around her waist – painted quite the picture," she mused, tilting her head. "I'm sure there are very few friends who would look so off-guardedly . . . intimate."

Charlotte took as deep a breath as she could, as her thoughts seemed to be going in a circle of *fuck, fuck, fuck*. She did her best to look composed, and she shrugged. "A politician, good friends with the daughter of another politician. Not quite the scandal you're looking for there. I'm afraid you'll have to figure something else out."

The gleam in Naomi's eyes as she leaned forward made her teeth clench in anxiety and annoyance even before she spoke, "But the scandal that comes along with fucking that same-sex *good friend* is absolutely the kind of scandal that, I daresay, ruins campaigns . . . and careers."

It was as though all of the air had left her lungs and she *had* to look beyond Naomi to make sure there was no one else in the hall who could overhear.

It was more relieving than she would ever care to admit that there was no one else around, and she drew back to meet Naomi's gaze, drawing her back straight up. "And I daresay I have absolutely no idea what you're talking about."

Naomi's smile was positively glowing. "You don't?" She brought a hand up, glibly tapping at her chin for a moment, and Charlotte's hand tightened where it still remained on the doorknob. "I believe that French Modernism exhibit would dare to disagree."

For a long moment, all Charlotte could hear was the blood rushing in her ears as she felt like her heart dropped right out of her chest.

She knew.

It was one thing to know that there was quiet speculation, to know there were rumors whispering around on the far reaches of the sidelines. Things that were ultimately too quiet and removed to have real consequences. It was another to have it confronted right to her face.

Despite maintaining her composure, she could *feel* the blood drain from her cheeks. All of the tension inside her made her spine snap so straight it hurt. "You have no idea what you're talking about."

Her voice was as offhand as she could make it, but she was still painfully aware that it wasn't much. Because Naomi referencing a specific, public sexual interaction she'd had with Sutton . . . it was the closest Charlotte could ever remember to completely losing it.

"But I do." All smiles had fallen, eyes and voice were sharp. "You see, your grandmother might be a fucking trailblazer, and you may think that gives you all of the connections you need. But I also have friends, who know many, many things. Friends who see many things. Who *hear* many things."

It was the knowing tone that made Charlotte's stomach cramp, even as she outwardly only managed to clench her jaw when it clicked together.

David fucking Verbeck.

Not that she'd thought he had just been oh-so-curious about the exhibit at the museum that night; she wasn't naïve. But she . . . they'd *finished* before he had been close enough to them. She was sure of it.

She knew at this point that flat-out denial truly was pointless and Charlotte didn't play a fool's game. She blew out her breath as slowly as she could. She flexed the hand Naomi couldn't see that was still behind the door as an outlet for this overwhelming feeling that was threatening to make her dizzy.

Narrowing her eyes, she cut to the point as she asked, "What do you want?"

Inwardly, though, she also cursed herself. What had she been thinking that night? She'd never made such an unthinking, emotionally-steeped choice that could truly mess something up; in fact, she'd spent years deliberately avoiding situations like that.

She'd been jealous of her own brother for talking to Sutton and having so much in common with her, that it had been that easy for all of her carefully deliberated, *smart* plans to be shot to nothing.

For her to forget that one lapse in judgment could ruin her.

Naomi having that information was really a nightmare come true, and the utter dread that clawed at her made her feel sick.

"Just one little shred of proof to *any* reputable media outlet and it seems your chances at this election – and future ones – will depend on far more than a good debate," Naomi finished, and Charlotte could only describe the look on her face as gleefully hateful.

It was the closest to a panic she'd ever come, and she had to force herself to take a deep breath. Then another, and ignore the look on Naomi's face, as she steeled herself.

Panic was not an option for her. It just wasn't; the only option was to try to find a solution –

The realization hit her, and the relief with it was so fast she almost got a headrush. "Just one little shred of proof could be devastating," she acknowledged, finally able to take the breath that she needed. "But you don't have any evidence of my hypothetical affairs."

Naomi's eyes finally narrowed in that way, the one that spoke of losing an upper hand. "Quite fascinating that you're so sure."

Flexing her hand one last time on the doorknob, Charlotte let it go; it was no time for anything that could make her look weak, especially when she finally found proper footing in an ambush.

"The party happened nearly three weeks ago. If you had any evidence at all, it would have been to every news source the next day. You have nothing."

Because Naomi Young did not play a carefully calculated game, she was not playing this for the long-game. There was little subtlety in her tactics; there was no way any substantial *proof* of Charlotte's sexuality, of her relationship with Sutton, was in Naomi's hands, without her having already outed it.

She recognized this for what it was: a last resort.

She held onto that thought and let it breathe the life back into her.

Naomi, however, didn't look fazed or as disappointed as Charlotte would have thought she should. She shrugged before she crossed her arms. "Perhaps I don't."

"You don't. So, it appears this conversation is much like many endeavors you take on. Improperly planned with unreliable follow-through." She took pleasure in the way Naomi's eyes flashed in agitation.

"Perhaps I have no proof *yet*. From what I've put together, this little romance of yours is still young. It's only been a few months, and already you've jeopardized much more than I thought you would. I don't want to play my hand too much . . ." The flash of her smile made Charlotte's stomach cramp again. "But I feel more than comfortable knowing that I have intel on handfuls of mornings with young Ms. Spencer staying the night at your home. Pictures of her leaving in the early morning, in different clothes than ones she's arrived in, with quite the glow about her."

That steady footing she'd thought she'd gained slipped from under her.

"Dozens of moments where you've been far too close for merely *friends*, including a lovely photo of you trying her ice cream while wearing what I believe is her sweater, if my sources are correct. Somewhat blurry, as it's through that bay window of hers, but it's still quite the sweet image, if you ever want a copy."

Charlotte swallowed hard, and for a moment, she swore she wasn't breathing. She could feel bile burning the back of her throat at not only the fact that Naomi knew *everything*, but the fact that they'd undeniably been followed.

These weren't moments that had been in the public eye, ones she'd had up on the board at her meeting earlier. These were private, detailed, purposeful photos. Moments that she'd thought were only between herself and Sutton had been spied on and exploited. The photo with the ice cream had been in Sutton's apartment, for Christ's sake.

Naomi continued on, more joyful with every word, "If rumor is to be believed, you've even shared some moments at the Spencer party that you were so conspicuously invited to. Perhaps I have not found irrefutable proof that could sink a political career. Yet."

"And you won't," her voice was lower than she'd intended, rough with the way her throat felt too tight with all of this worry and anger and – and too much tangling together.

"It also makes you wonder about Sutton. I hope she's ready to take this on her shoulders as well; she's not quite as versed in masks as you are."

She snapped her eyes to Naomi's, anger flaring. "Leave Sutton out of this."

"Me? You brought her into it."

Her eyes narrowed, and she had to fold her arms to stop her hands from shaking as her nerves felt so jangled. "It must be so lonely to have so very little in your life that you find all of your focus on mine. So absolutely sad that the only way you know you would have any chance at winning an election against me is by trying to scare me. I have news for you, Naomi: it will be a cold day in hell before you democratically rise to any high governing position in this country. The fact that you had to resort to around-the-clock surveillance on me just for a scrap of blackmail to use to be able to win is incredibly telling, and pathetic, and very you."

She could tell her words affected her in the way Naomi swallowed, then glared, but Charlotte got no sense of enjoyment out of it this time. It was impossible, especially as Naomi hissed back, "Yes, I would feel threatened if I were you, too. After all, it's only a matter of time before everything inevitably *comes out.*"

Her heart skipped at a beat at the very deliberate phrasing. "If this is all you had to discuss with me, I think we're done."

"Mm," Naomi hummed, running her gaze up and down Charlotte. "Yes, you do have quite the victory to celebrate, don't you?"

She kept the door open, making sure to watch until Naomi was at the end of the hallway – just in case – before shutting it quietly. Barely restraining herself from slamming it like she wanted to. Her arms were shaking from the fear and anger and frustration and guilt and –

Gritting her teeth, she pressed her forehead against the door, coaching herself on taking deep breaths, in a manner which she hadn't had to utilize since she was a teenager. Clenching her hands into fists, she took in a breath and held it, trying to calm the racing of her heart. And repeated.

It took too long to get her strength back, because she'd never felt a fear like that before. A fear where she could *see* how it would all play out if Naomi really did have proof of her arrangement with Sutton. Where she could see the downfall of her career before it really even began, and the ripple effects of it through her life.

Everything in her wanted to rage, wanted to rave about the fact that Naomi had just gone too far – which, she had. That she was resorting to ugly, pathetic tactics – which, she was. That she was wrong, that she wouldn't end up finding evidence of herself and Sutton engaging in their relationship – and that was where she got tripped up.

Because she wasn't wrong.

And it chilled her to the bone.

***

She ducked out of the celebration dinner with Caleb and Dean, and instead went directly home. She couldn't celebrate when she kept hearing the conversation over and over in her head. Hearing the thinly-veiled threats, thinking about that abject fear that had never before felt so real.

She'd never been someone who dragged her feet on doing *anything*. Her nanny would always say she walked before she could crawl; there was a video to prove it. Yet, she'd been finding every reason to put off ending things with Sutton.

Those excuses had run out, officially. She *had* to break it off – soon – and her stomach was in knots.

For once, she let her shoulders slump as she walked down the hallway to her apartment. She needed a bath and maybe to watch highlights from her debate to pick herself up and keep her focused, and eventually figure out how she was going to go about this whole conversation with –

"Sutton?" The name left her in a whisper, far more reverent than she intended. "What are you doing here?"

It was so incredibly messed up, she realized, as she felt her heart thud in her chest. Because seeing Sutton usually, somehow, made her feel *soothed*. Like she forgot all of the reasons she shouldn't feel soothed.

But here, now, seeing Sutton standing there in front of her door, all that long, red hair falling over her black jacket, with her nose tinged adorably pink from the slight chill outside – it was all too much.

Sutton's face brightened, blossoming into one of her wide, gorgeous smiles. "Well, first of all, you were incredible tonight! Just like I knew you would be. And secondly." She bit her lip, smile dimming as she tilted her head and gave Charlotte a questioning look. "Um, Caleb messaged me? Which was sort of weird. He said that you canceled on all your plans, and he wanted to know if you were going out with me." She tangled her fingers together in front of her. "And, you know, I knew you weren't. So. I got a little concerned, too. Now that I can see you, I'm even more concerned," Sutton rambled, and it was something that normally made Charlotte smile.

But now, as Sutton stepped toward her, Charlotte shook her head and bit her lip. Damn Caleb.

"No, darli – Sutton. I'm . . ." She blew out a sigh. "It's just been a longer day than expected."

Sutton frowned, taking a step closer to follow her retreat; Charlotte both hated and loved that she knew that Sutton was seeing everything no one else could possibly read on her face.

"Do you want me to make you a cup of tea or something?"

She barely managed to hold back her scoff. What she wanted was for everything to be easier. What she wanted was to be able to live two lives. What she wanted was for her sexuality to not matter. What she wanted was for her past self to have *listened* to her first instinct, the night Sutton proposed having sex, that it would be a dangerous mistake.

"No, thanks." She held up her hand before Sutton could come any closer, and she quickly looked around, narrowing her eyes. Her stomach lurched again, feeling like she'd been invaded, as she thought about Naomi informing her about all of the moments she was aware of between her and Sutton.

"We should go inside." She knew her voice sounded as off to Sutton as it did to herself.

Perhaps she was now just being paranoid, but she couldn't help but feel more secure as she shut the door behind them. She hated that, too, and she had to take a deep breath to try to center herself.

She tore her gaze away because it *hurt* looking at her, as Sutton gave her a tentative smile.

"Well, if you are up for company, I have notes on the debate. I was going to type them up and offer to go over them with you the next time we hung out, so you could keep them in your file. But I have them saved on my phone if you want to just have some to read over."

She was so eager and sweet, and . . .

And Charlotte smiled at her, despite herself, her chest *aching*, because Sutton was so perfect. Of course she had notes and wanted to study them together. In an ideal world, they could curl up together and do just that.

This wasn't an ideal world though, and the smile on her face slipped. She looked down at her hands, walking farther into the kitchen, as if it would give her any new perspective.

Sutton followed closely behind. "Are you okay?" She asked, a concerned frown on her face. "I don't want to push you or anything but . . . last debate, you were acting a lot differently than this."

518

Last debate hadn't ended with Naomi coming *this close* to publicly being able to out her. Last debate hadn't ended with Naomi threatening to lie in wait until Charlotte's next miscalculation – one that would not only end in consequence for her, but also in Sutton's outing to the entire world, when she wasn't even out to her entire family.

The sincerity of Sutton's worry made Charlotte want to cry, and she – she didn't know what was wrong with her. This being one step away from tears, this aching in her chest, this wasn't normal.

You are just bringing an end to the sex, she reminded herself. She was *not* losing Sutton from her life. There was a difference. And she could live with that.

She took a deep breath and gathered all of the courage she had left. "Sutton, I think we need to talk. Not about the debate or anything like that, just –"

In every romance movie she'd ever seen, she'd always thought these emotional moments were exaggerated. She'd spent her whole life thinking that those moments were dramatized.

But finding these words, the words to end this, was killing her.

She didn't duck and run, though. That was not her, and with that, she resolutely kept her eyes on Sutton even as she wanted to look away. "I've been doing some thinking, and I think that it's getting to be the time that we . . . rethink this."

"This?" Sutton's hands fidgeted in front of her. There was a flash of *something* across her face that Charlotte couldn't quite recognize with how fast it disappeared, before Sutton rocked back and forth on her heels. "I – I've kind of been thinking about it, too. I think. Are we both talking, uh, about the same 'this'?"

Sutton had been thinking about it, too?

It hurt. Which was hypocritical and unfair.

Licking her lips, she caught Sutton's eyes with her own. "Our arrangement," she clarified, clearing her throat. Twice, because it felt like it was tightening too fast, too painfully. She remembered Sutton coming to stand here in this very

519

kitchen months ago, proposing *rules* to their friends with benefits situation, as if it was a business arrangement.

The memory made her almost made her smile. Almost.

At the very least it made it easier for her to rush out the words, "I think we should forgo the benefits part of our friendship."

There. She said it. She said it, and she – well, her hands were shaking, and the backs of her eyes burned, but it was out there. It was for the best, for everyone, she reminded herself, and forced herself to keep going, "After all, I'm only going to get busier and deeper into the political world and I don't think there's anything else I could possibly teach you about sex, at this point."

She tried to smirk, tried to make the words come out as playful, to lighten the moment.

But that was wrong, so wrong. There were so many things she wanted to do with Sutton, do to Sutton, and the thought of Sutton exploring that all with someone else threatened to make her sick.

Swallowing those feelings down, she watched Sutton's face.

From the furrowing of her eyebrows in confusion, to the realization, to the crestfallen look, and every step of it made her stomach sink even more.

"What . . . did I do wrong?" Came out in a strangled whisper.

Charlotte's stomach bottomed out, the change throwing her off balance as she shook her head. "Nothing. You didn't do anything wrong, Sutton. Ever, not between us."

There was a begging sound in her voice that she couldn't have gotten rid of even if she wanted to.

"Well, something must have gone wrong," Sutton insisted, her voice breaking and with it, the last shreds of Charlotte's strength.

Yes! Charlotte's brain screamed. *You kiss me hello and goodbye and you make me miss you and want to cuddle, and that wasn't supposed to happen!*

"No," was all that came out. She barely heard herself over the pounding of her heart in her ears.

"Then . . . why?" Sutton asked, her voice thick with tears that tore Charlotte apart, almost as much as seeing them shining in her eyes.

She didn't know what to say, her mouth opening and no words coming out. *Because we're one small step away from everything falling apart? Because I want you so much it's terrifying and life-changing? Because I want you but I also want my future and I can't have both?*

"It's just . . . time."

Sutton's face crumbled completely and the vice around Charlotte's heart tightened that much more. "What does that even mean? Are you – are you tired of having sex with me?"

"No!" God, that was the last thing she wanted her to think. She vehemently hated every single person in Sutton's past who ever played into her insecurities, and she was now terrified that she was one of them. "Absolutely not. You're so . . ." Beautiful. Sexy. Incredible. Brilliant.

There were so many words and none of them made it easier. She couldn't stop herself from reaching out and cupping Sutton's jaw in her hands, feeling the warm, soft skin under her fingertips. She stroked in circles with her thumbs trying to commit the feeling to memory, even as she promised, "That's not it, Sutton, I promise."

This was a mistake, she realized, touching her. Because she didn't want to move. The deep, shuddering breath she took in almost broke on a cry that she kept in with everything she had.

She was going to miss *touching* Sutton, so freely. She hadn't even realized it until now, and everything was moving too fast, far out of her control.

"Then, why?" Sutton repeated, her words a cracked whisper. Those tears fell down her cheeks, as she made no move to pull away from Charlotte's hold.

Which only made her heart thud even heavier, duller, in her chest. She felt like she was only a moment away from dissolving herself and she managed to let her hands fall.

Even as she tugged them through her hair they felt *empty*. "I think it should end before this gets any more serious." The truth came out, and she could barely speak in more than a whisper, one that scraped her throat on the way out. "I think we both know that we've been blurring our lines a bit." What an understatement. "And if we want our friendship to be intact, we need to end it now."

It's for the best, she reminded herself, as forcefully as she could. The pain is fleeting and it'll be over and things will be okay.

Her mantra could only work the slightest bit to loosen the tightness in her chest, but she had to believe in it. She had to.

Especially as Sutton was wiping at her eyes with her palms, giving an erratic nod. "I – yeah." A sob broke, even as Sutton pressed her lips together. "You're right."

It was a desperation that overtook her, because she . . . she *needed* Sutton. Maybe it wouldn't be romantic or sexual or intimate in that way, but, "Please, Sutton, I don't want to lose you. I can't –" She cut herself off, swallowing hard. "You are so important to me. More important to me than almost anyone else in my life, and I want to keep you – keep you close," she stumbled.

"No, yeah, you're r-right," Sutton's voice was thick with tears as she hiccupped. She stepped back as she wiped over her eyes with her sleeve. "I . . . I have to go. I – you – I'll see you."

Even though it was something she'd known would have to happen, now that the moment was here she was gripped by a sharp, frantic anxiety about Sutton leaving. "Sutton, please." She swallowed again to hold everything back that wanted to spill out. "We . . . you don't have to go."

"I do." She quickly turned from Charlotte. Which meant she had a perfect view of how her shoulders shuddered with her tears, and the burrowing ache in Charlotte's chest felt like it was widening into a chasm. "I have plans."

She followed her to the door, wanting to beg her to stay because a whole new fear had taken root with every step Sutton took. The fear that this was the last time she was going to see Sutton was alive and well as her ears echoed with the sound of her quiet, muffled tears.

"Don't; not like this. I know you need some time," her own words broke as she quickly wiped at her eyes, wiping harshly at the tears that gathered. "Can I order you a car?" She reached out for Sutton, then hesitated.

"I'll be f-fine." Sutton's shoulders heaved again and everything inside her felt absolutely wrecked. "I just – I need to go. I, um." She paused at the door, her hand on the knob, holding so tightly Charlotte could see her knuckles turn white. "Bye?"

The door slammed shut behind her and she was left in deafening silence.

It wasn't the last time she would see Sutton. It couldn't be . . . But the worry didn't go away in the least. In fact, it only burrowed in deeper, harder.

We were never going to be able to be anything real, she reminded herself, desperately. Ending it now saved them pain in the long run. Ultimately it was better for the both of them. It was the *only* thing that would save their friendship.

Her throat was so tight she could barely breathe, and she didn't even have it in her to panic even though she'd never felt like this before.

Her hands clenched hard, trying to help contain everything inside that wanted desperately to break open, as she turned to walk back into the kitchen. She couldn't look at the door and think about Sutton leaving and worry about how permanent it was.

She just had to get herself together. She just . . . she just . . . Sutton would realize that this was for the best. They would work through it. She just needed to wait out the storm. To wait out Sutton. To wait out this crushing feeling in herself.

She could do it. She –

Came to a dead stop when she actually looked at the kitchen table for the first time since arriving home. The same table where just this morning Sutton

523

had sat, wearing her glasses and drinking from the mug she'd claimed as her favorite.

Roses lay out on the table, a vibrant, yellow and red bouquet, nearly bursting out of the paper. Her hands shook when she reached out for the card on top, written in familiar, delicate writing:

Charlotte – I snuck back in with your key after I finished my paper. Even if we won't be seeing each other tonight, I wanted you to know that I had no doubts about how amazing you would be, and that I've been thinking of you and wishing you unnecessary luck all day.

Love, Sutton

She barely registered her knees giving out, sliding down the wall until she hit the floor. Her fingers curling into the card so tightly, as if it could serve as a connection to Sutton herself.

Chapter 21

The letter from the Roman Archives sat in Sutton's hands, welcoming her to the program with all of the necessary details. Despite having only gotten it the day before, it was already worn from the amount of times she'd read it then folded it up again.

She wanted to feel excited about this, and some small part of her did. But on the much larger scale, everything was such a mess and she felt utterly exhausted. Worn down and hollow.

It was one of the most prestigious internships she possibly could have applied for; something that she hadn't really believed she'd be capable of getting accepted to. And more than that, it was hers.

Something she'd done, for once in her life, without consulting her family and Regan first. Regan should have been the person she'd talked to about this, given that if she did go, she'd be leaving her alone in their apartment, her share of the bills unpaid. Instead, she'd only talked about it with Charlotte, and thinking about her soft smile when she'd encouraged Sutton to apply just hurt now.

Blowing out a deep breath, Sutton stared blankly down at the letter.

The thing she could admit to herself now was that she'd never expected to get to a point where this internship was a reality. She'd put this incredible but *far away* future on hold in her mind with the hope that before this would even be on the horizon, Charlotte would have confessed having feelings for her.

That she was in love with her in this painful, wonderful, heart-aching, wanting kind of way that Sutton loved her. That things would then slot into place, and she would just stay here, with Charlotte, and everything would work out.

But when it came to love, she always seemed to be wrong. With both Kyle and Joshua, her only two actual relationships, she'd constantly been guessing, misunderstanding, and easily taken advantage of. She'd just thought that things with Charlotte had been different.

"You're so damn *stupid*," she murmured. Her stomach clenched so painfully she lifted a hand to it and rubbed as if this was a physical ache she could make go away.

"I think that letter you've been smoothing out the nonexistent wrinkles from proves that you are far from stupid," Emma's voice came from behind her.

Sutton jumped, quickly rubbing at her eyes as discreetly as she could, before she turned to look over the back of the couch at her friend. Who had emerged from her room, dressed for the day, her messenger bag that she brought to campus every day slung over her shoulder.

She managed a pathetic excuse for a smile. "Hey." She flickered her eyes back to the internship letter. "I – no, I wasn't talking about *this*."

It was everywhere except for academics that Sutton felt like she was flailing.

Despite Emma's typical candid frank demeanor, she gave Sutton a quietly sympathetic look. "So, if we aren't talking about your amazing internship, does this mean you finally want to talk about the night that shall not be named?"

Sutton ducked her head. Embarrassed and miserable, exactly how she'd felt ever since she'd showed up here at Emma's apartment a few nights ago. After she'd left Charlotte's apartment, her heart shattered, barely able to see through her tears. She'd roamed the street until she'd felt fairly numb, before finally getting herself together enough to hop on the subway and get out of the frigid February weather.

It was almost a surprise to herself that she'd ended up at Emma's. But going home, facing Regan, felt next to impossible. Like if she went home, the cocooning numbness she'd taken refuge in would disappear.

She'd never been so well-acquainted with a friend's couch as she now was.

"No. Thanks, um, for offering. Again."

Emma offered a lopsided smile. "My couch might not be the most comfortable, but it's yours for as long as you want it." A look of disdain crossed her face. "Unless Regan comes hounding the TA office for you again; then I'll be forced to give up your location."

She couldn't even really muster up an appropriate scoff, instead giving an appreciative smile. "Thanks." Her fingers traced over the edges of the letter.

"I have to get going, or I'll be late for class." After a beat, she sighed. "Look, I know I'm not always the most . . . sensitive person. You can talk to me, though."

That really did garner a real smile, and it felt like she hadn't done that in days.

"I know."

"Good. And, uh, you're welcome to hide out here as long as you need. But sometimes it's better to rip off the band-aid from . . . whatever is going on." She nodded as if pushing out the words had been stressful. "Okay. Well. See you later."

Sutton got in a wave before the door creaked shut behind Emma and she found herself in the silent apartment. Taking a deep breath, she put down the letter and instead picked up the phone she'd been avoiding.

She knew she had messages on there from her family and from Regan, but she *knew* instinctively that the second she spoke to her mom or to her friend, that was it. There would be no more bubble to try to hide from the world.

Drawing her knees up to her chest, she rested her cheek against them and unlocked her phone.

She skimmed over the group chat with her siblings, where a long conversation had taken place involving the fact that Oliver and his groomsmen – including Lucas and Ethan – had completed the dance that he was going to be performing as a surprise at the wedding. Oliver had told her about it a couple of months ago, jokingly blaming her because, "She never would be teasing me about my dance skills if you hadn't told her I practiced all your ballroom dancing lessons with you when we were kids!"

That feeling of warmth faded when she scrolled a bit lower to Regan's messages.

Regan – 10:44PM
Am I gonna see you when I get home from work? I know you said you were working on a project with Emma, but the project will still be there in the morning, after a good night's sleep in your own bed!

Regan – 11:21PM
Okay, coming home during the day while I was at work and leaving me a note there about not coming home again tonight was sneaky

Regan – 11:40PM
I know it's only been a couple of days but I'm lonely without you :'(

Regan – 11:44PM
You're not mad at me, right? I returned the boots I borrowed from youuuu

Regan – 11:46PM
No, you'd have told me

Regan – 11:48PM
Goodnight, princess!

Regan – 9:01AM
Praise jesus, I have the day off! And I
did your laundry with mine & cleaned your
room. I hope you're coming home today, I
miss your beautiful face

The knots in her stomach coiled so tightly she thought she was going to be sick. This was precisely why she hadn't looked at Regan's messages when she'd gotten them last night.

She already felt guilty about avoiding Regan for the last few days just because . . . God, she didn't want to hear everything Regan would say about Charlotte. She didn't want to hear that Regan had known all along what Sutton had refused to believe.

That was without even touching on the topic of the internship.

How was she supposed to tell Regan? Who missed her enough after two days to do her laundry for her, a chore she detested. Who trusted that no matter what was going on, Sutton would have already told her.

When she hadn't told her that she'd applied for a program that would mean she would be moving out of their apartment for months. Moving to another country, at that. And, why? Because she had wanted something for herself? Because she hadn't believed she would be getting in, so why even share it?

Pressing her forehead tightly against her knees, she bit at the inside of her cheek. Regardless of whatever Regan was going to say about Charlotte, she had to go home. And she definitely had to tell her about the internship.

It was quite possible she *deserved* to be told off, after all.

Sutton – 10:51AM
I'll be home today. I promise.

She couldn't put it off anymore. Heart in her throat, she pulled up the one message thread she had simultaneously wanted to avoid but had been unable to not look at in the last few nights.

From the first night, right after the not-breakup was:

Charlotte – 2:09AM
I still want to be your friend, Sutton. I care so
incredibly much about you. So much. So . . . much.
And I know there's still some more to talk about, if
you wanted to.

And the following night:

Charlotte – 2:54AM
Please let me know whenever you're ready to
talk. I'm sorry.

She'd tried to write back to that one, even as her throat felt like it was closing on her. Was she sorry for breaking Sutton's heart? Sorry for *"blurring their lines"* as she'd said that night? Sorry for not loving Sutton the way Sutton loved her? Sorry for thinking that Sutton could just so easily fall back into being only her friend when they were so much more?

I'm not ready to talk now, seeing you would break me.
Do you know I love you?
I don't want you to be sorry, I want you to want me.
She couldn't say any of that.

Her teeth dug in deep to her bottom lip as she tried to gather herself, staring at the messages.

Charlotte didn't want to be with her. It had been days and she hadn't come to her and said she'd made a mistake. She wasn't going to reassure Sutton that she wasn't alone in this.

And she had to face that.

Sutton – 11:02AM
Hey . . . ~~do you want~~
~~Hi Charlotte, what~~
~~I'm sorry I've been avoiding~~
Can we talk?

She was *nervous*. She was nervous, about texting Charlotte, when only three days ago, it was just second nature.

Charlotte – 11:03AM
Where and when?

***

Two hours later she walked into The Grind. It was nowhere near as good as Topped Off, but it wasn't near Sutton's apartment or college, and that was why she'd chosen it.

She hadn't wanted to see Charlotte anywhere that it would be just the two of them. Sutton was hoping that she would be able to keep it together, but she knew if they met privately – if Charlotte could just *be Charlotte* and do something like reach out and stroke her cheek – Sutton would have no chance of not being a sobbing mess.

There weren't even good odds that she would be able to keep herself together now.

But The Grind also didn't hit peak traffic until the evening, after the businesses nearby closed for the day. It was the *only* relief she had as she stepped into the café, seeing that there were only two occupied tables and that they were both near one another at the front of the shop.

Her shoulders were so tense, she could barely roll them to try to relax, and she couldn't remember the last time she'd been dreading something so much.

She was prepared to hear Charlotte list everything that was truly wrong with her – in a nice way, because she still couldn't fathom Charlotte being cruelly unkind – or for Charlotte to confront the fact that Sutton was invested in them for real. To hear Charlotte say that no, in spite of all of Sutton's thoughts that they were on the same page, she never did have more than friend feelings and an attraction back. That she never would.

But she thought maybe she had to hear those things to have any chance of letting this go.

She was at least glad that she'd gotten here before Charlotte. It gave her time to settle in and –

"Sutton?"

She spun around and didn't know *why* she was surprised to see Alia, wavy hair falling down her back, to-go cup in hand. After all, the only time she'd been here, the only reason she knew it existed, was because they'd come here the first time they'd hung out.

"Long time, no see." Alia's smile was bright as she reached out to squeeze Sutton's hand.

She flushed; she'd last seen Alia right before going home for the holidays, and despite having been back for a month, hadn't texted her since. "I – yeah, I'm sorry."

Alia waved her off. "Don't be silly. We've both been busy. The real question is, what are you doing here? You were all, 'Topped Off has better tea selections.'"

"It *does*! But I –" wanted to have a devastating kind-of breakup talk in public to avoid less of an emotional breakdown? "Wanted something different today."

She attempted to grin, but even she knew it was more like a grimace.

Alia's eyes narrowed. "Don't take this the wrong way, but are you okay? You don't look. . . great."

Ugh, God. Now she felt herself blush and she ducked her head, pointedly looking at the floor for a moment. She hadn't slept all that well in the last few nights, and she knew that despite wearing her glasses to try to cover up the bags under her eyes, they were still alarmingly present. Plus, she hadn't stomached food all that well, either, and – well, she knew she wasn't looking anywhere near her best.

Or even anywhere near her mediocre.

"I'm fine." She could hear how weak her own assurance was; if she couldn't even lie to a new friend like Alia, it confirmed that her avoiding Regan and her family for the last few days had been for the best.

"Is it because of Charlotte, and what happened a few days ago?"

She choked on air, eyes wide as she looked around reflexively. "I – what? No? Why would you think it has anything to do with Charlotte?"

She'd never mentioned Charlotte's name to Alia; she was positive of that much. Not in any capacity that would out Charlotte or reveal that she was the one Sutton was sleeping with.

Alia slanted an incredulous eyebrow. "Sutton, please. I'm not *blind*. And I watched the debate last week when she straight up denied being romantically involved with anyone." She grimaced, "I was going to text you but . . . I didn't know what to say about it. I just figure, you know, having your girlfriend deny your whole relationship on television like that had to hurt."

She spoke softly, her tone sensitive, and Sutton still couldn't quell her anxiety.

"No."

She'd forgotten about that. Hadn't even registered it at the time. It was exactly the response she had known Charlotte would give. She knew about her worries when it came to coming out. But it was painful now. To think that it wasn't just a rejection or fear of coming out, but also a rejection of *her*. An outright statement that she did not have feelings for her.

She closed her eyes against these stupid tears that stung her eyes again, wanting so badly to fall. To think about how stupid she'd been when the signs were all there in front of her face, and she had still been hopeful that things were changing.

"No. We aren't . . ." Well, they weren't much of anything now. She took a deep breath. "We aren't girlfriends. We never have been."

The truth of it *hurt*, another notch on the vice that had been wrapped around her heart. But more than that, she felt an urgency to make sure Alia believed her.

It didn't work, that much was clear, as there was skepticism written all over her face. "But you were something."

She knew that this underlying panic she was feeling was entirely for Charlotte's sake, and despite this utter distress she'd been feeling in the last few days, she couldn't shake it.

"No," she denied, firmly, straightening her shoulders in a way she'd seen Charlotte do in the past that always seemed to make her look in control. "We're just friends."

"Sutton. I know the truth. I know Charlotte was the friend you had something going on with."

She *wanted* to deny it more, but she also wanted to know how exactly Alia knew, and what she'd done to give it away. "How?"

Alia looked sympathetic and she reached out again, her free hand cupping Sutton's warmly. "I'm not going to out her or anything. I wouldn't do that."

Both the touch and the words soothed newly frayed nerves. She wasn't sure how much more she could take today and Charlotte wasn't even there yet.

"And, just so you know, you weren't the one who gave it away," Alia murmured, holding eye contact as she sipped at her coffee, her other hand still lightly holding Sutton's.

She couldn't help but squeeze it now, glancing around again as if anyone was even near them, let alone interested in what they would be saying. "I wasn't? Who was?"

Dark eyes blinked at her slowly, seeming surprised. "Well, I sort of put it together a while ago. I saw Charlotte coming up to your place when I was leaving once." She sighed. "Then I started following along a bit in the election. And, if you know what to look for, it was kind of obvious."

Obvious?

They were obvious? How were they obvious? She hadn't even thought of that. Then again, she didn't know that anyone would even be looking into her and Charlotte's relationship.

She had to swallow back the thousand questions that she had, though. Alia wasn't the person who could give her the answers.

"Um, whatever you thought you knew. . ." That she and Charlotte were *girlfriends.* "We're not, anymore."

Alia gave her a sad smile. "Sorry." Another hand squeeze. "You have my number."

"I'm, uh, I don't think I'm ready for –"

"Not like *that*," Alia laughed, her smile reassuring. "Just, don't be a stranger. We haven't hung out in a while and I'd like to. Plus, if anyone in your life, as far as I know, can relate to not being with the woman you want to be with, it's me."

Taking a moment to let the offer sink in, she found herself nodding. She definitely didn't think she'd be able to try to date anyone yet, but it could be nice. Having another friend – just a friend this time – who could relate to this side of her.

"That sounds good." Blowing out a deep breath, Sutton's gaze darted to the clock on the wall behind the counter, and her nerves jangled just knowing that Charlotte was going to be there any second. "I'm, um, I don't mean to be rude, but I'm meeting –"

She cut herself off, hardly managing to stop herself from yelping before standing completely frozen. Alia used the hold she had on Sutton's hand to pull herself in close and tug Sutton in, her breath washing over Sutton's skin. She pressed her lips to Sutton's cheek, close enough to just barely miss brushing her lips.

She stood ramrod straight as she gave Alia a look of utter confusion from the corner of her eye. Perhaps cheek kisses weren't unnatural, but they'd never exchanged them. And the last time she'd had someone so deliberately kiss her on the cheek like that, it had been Charlotte.

The feeling was painfully not the same.

Alia smirked. "Trust me, you'll see." With a stroke of her thumb over the back of Sutton's hand, she let go. "Text me, Sutton Spencer. And who knows? Maybe eventually it can be like *that*."

Utterly thrown by the abrupt change in their encounter, she turned to watch Alia go as she walked by her . . . only for her eyes to land on Charlotte.

Well. She got it now.

Alia didn't pause, just walked right by Charlotte, who stood just a step inside the café.

It had only been a few days since she'd seen her, but it felt like a lifetime.

How did it feel like simultaneously she was breathless with the same feeling she always got when she saw her – that *Charlotte is so incredibly beautiful* breathless – and with that feeling like she was being kicked in the stomach all over again?

She was wearing her white jacket, that fell mid-thigh, leaving only a few inches of her dress for the day uncovered, her hair was as perfectly styled as always, and she looked perfect.

She turned sharply away when she felt the tears well up.

She felt more than saw Charlotte approach – slowly, hesitantly, and so very un-Charlotte-like. But at least she'd walked over, because Sutton didn't think she could have bridged the gap.

Blinking quickly to clear her tears, she forced herself to take in a deep breath through her nose. She could do this. She *had* to do this.

"Hi."

Charlotte stared straight ahead, eyes on the menu behind the counter, and her face was carefully blank. It was a look Sutton had seen before, but never toward her. It hurt.

"Hi," Charlotte echoed, her voice soft, and she turned just enough to look at Sutton again.

That's when she realized, knowing she was staring at Charlotte and unable to stop, that she was *trying* to make her face carefully blank but wasn't quite succeeding.

Just there, at the edges of her lips, her face was drawn tighter – but it was the way she'd looked that time at her grandmother's party. When she'd been jealous.

She didn't comment on Alia at all, though. She would have commented on it, before. Maybe not even necessarily saying she was jealous, but she would have said or done something.

She *hated* knowing that now.

Blue eyes drew up from where they'd settled on Charlotte's lips. Lips that she knew. Their softness, their firmness, their taste, the way they felt moving down her body – up to her eyes.

Those wondrously big, doe eyes that could be softer than a marshmallow or hard as stone. Sutton didn't know what Charlotte wanted them to be like right now, but she knew that she'd never seen Charlotte look so . . . wanting.

It wasn't sexy-wanting, but something entirely different. The way Sutton thought they might look at three in the morning when Charlotte was sending apology texts.

But if she was going to look at Sutton like that, then just *why*?

"I'm going to grab a table." As though there weren't twenty open tables compared to the two taken ones.

She felt Charlotte's eyes on her the whole time she walked to the back corner of the café but didn't let herself turn around. How was she supposed to look at Charlotte when she was giving her that look? How was Sutton supposed to do anything but love her?

She didn't know.

She didn't know anything, clearly, which was why she was here in this mess.

It felt like she'd barely had a second to try to gather herself before Charlotte sat across from her, sliding a cup across the table. "It's chamomile. I thought you'd want it . . . unless you already had a cup before I got here."

"I didn't."

Her hands were already wrapping around the warm mug as her stomach dipped. Of course Charlotte got her the tea she drank when she was stressed or hadn't been sleeping.

Neither of them took a sip and she felt fidgety. She wished she could touch Charlotte's hand and take some comfort in one of the simple touches that they'd always had between them, even before sleeping together.

After a few long moments of staring, Sutton realized that no, Charlotte didn't look perfect. Despite what she'd originally thought, she could see how she was wearing more makeup than was typical, the bags under her eyes barely concealed as she looked down at her coffee.

But it didn't make her feel any better. In fact, it just made her ache a bit more, knowing that everything between them was making her miserable too.

Charlotte took a sip of her coffee. "Well, it's not as good as Topped Off." Her eyes slid to Sutton's above her cup. "But I haven't been there in a few days."

538

The wrath of Regan was unspoken between them.

"Yeah. Regan doesn't know. About anything. I haven't been home much."

Charlotte was giving her a look of such consternation that Sutton couldn't tell exactly what she wanted to say, only that there were many things on her mind.

The last thing she wanted right now was for Charlotte to apologize. She didn't want Charlotte to feel pity. She wanted Charlotte to explain why she kept giving her that look – the same one she wore when she cupped Sutton's jaw and stroked her cheek like she was something to be cherished – if she wanted their intimacy to be over with.

The tea burned in her throat as she gathered all of her courage to push out the words. "I need to know. Was it because of our – were we too . . . obvious?"

It wasn't something she'd thought of until only minutes ago with Alia, but it was the only thing that made sense.

"Sutton –"

"You said there was more to talk about," she pushed, and it was surprisingly easy to do. Because she'd just had all of these questions for days, haunting her.

"There is." She hedged, her jaw set in a hard line. "But I just don't . . ." She pinched the bridge of her nose for a moment, before she looked up and trailed her eyes over the entire café, seeming on edge. "Nothing I say is going to make it easier, Sutton."

There was a pleading tone in her voice that nearly broke her. It was just so *not Charlotte* to sound like that.

"The truth." She couldn't care to hide her desperation. "I just want you to tell me the truth. You said it wasn't me, wasn't my fault –"

"It's *not*," her voice was like steel as she cut Sutton off.

"Then why? Why end what's between us if I didn't do anything?"

Charlotte took another deep breath, rolling her tense shoulders. "Because you were right. We were becoming too obvious."

She didn't know why she had expected that to make her feel better. Because she was proud to have Charlotte next to her, in any capacity. As her friend, as a lover, and everything in between. But the way Charlotte said it, like it was shameful or vile that they were obviously important to one another – it stung.

She tried to wipe at her eyes as surreptitiously as she could.

Charlotte's shoulders fell, as if holding the weight of the world. "And because after my debate, I found out that Naomi also thinks we were being too obvious. Because she knows that we're –" She took a sharp breath. "That we *were* more than friends, and threatened to out us. She isn't making idle threats; she has pictures of us together. Nothing indecent," she quickly assured, as Sutton's heart leapt into her throat at the implication. "She might not have anything now, but she is right that one day she would."

It was so strange to hear the defeat in her voice, to note how Charlotte resolutely didn't make eye contact, as she stared intently at the table between them and Sutton stared at her.

It made her skin crawl a little bit, just imagining the threat, and her mind reeled for a few seconds as she sagged back into her chair.

Her hand twitched, wanting to reach for her. She wanted so badly to reach across the table now and just hold Charlotte's hand. For her to know that Sutton realized how scared she must have been in that moment, for her to know that she *wasn't* alone.

As nauseous as it made her to think about the fact that Naomi Young had *pictures* of her – of her and Charlotte, together – she realized just how much more scared and furious and sickened it would make Charlotte feel.

Charlotte finally lifted her gaze to meet Sutton's, eyes big and pleading. "I want you to know, please *know*, that this isn't easy for me. But I'm doing what's best. For both of us."

The hand she'd been bringing toward Charlotte's fell abruptly to the table, her stomach clenching painfully. And for the first time in days, it wasn't from sadness or dejection but in sheer anger.

"You don't get to decide what's best for me."

Sutton may be patient to a fault and she knew that about herself, but she'd had her choices made for her in relationships too much to ever let that happen again. She'd always assumed Charlotte understood that. Charlotte had at least acted like she did.

"You don't get to decide what is best for me, because you don't know what's best for me." If she did, she would have known that being left wondering what was wrong with her that made it so easy for someone to not reciprocate her feelings, was *not* what was best. "Don't you remember the rules?"

Because she remembered explicitly adding onto them not to make assumptions.

"Don't *you* remember the rules?" Charlotte shot back, and whatever façade she'd been managing to keep up fell completely away in that moment. For the first time, Sutton could see all of the pain she was feeling was mirrored right back.

It was raw and real and it stole whatever response she had right from her.

"You wrote them! You came to *me*, this was your idea, and you left me with this piece of paper with the agreements that I've been staring at for days hoping that you really meant what you said. You're the one who wrote on there that we were *friends*. That we put that first," Charlotte's palm slammed onto the table, the same fire in her words, before she curled it into a tight fist. "And I've been terrified that I'm losing you for good. I need to know that we really are friends, Sutton. That I'm not going to lose you."

Her voice wavered, her typically so-controlled Southern accent slipping to prominence, and it was that vulnerability that cracked through her anger. That wrapped right around her heart, squeezing so tight, leaving her speechless.

Because Charlotte was right. This had been Sutton's idea. She had come up with the rules. She had propositioned Charlotte, and insisted that they be friends first and foremost.

And the sudden guilt she felt, about how she *couldn't* tell Charlotte that they would come out of this as friends sank like a pit in her stomach. It scared her and she stared at Charlotte, unable to speak even as Charlotte's anxious expression begged for the guarantee she couldn't give.

"Why weren't you just honest with me?" She asked instead, her voice a hoarse whisper. "Why didn't you just tell me it was because of Naomi and the pictures?"

Charlotte's face crumpled at her deflection and she looked away. "Would it have made a difference? The end result is the same."

"What if it didn't have to be?" Now *she* was pleading, but she couldn't help it. Her hands wrapped tightly around her still almost full-mug. "We could have kept going the same way. Instead of both of us being unhappy, we could have figured –"

"You keep saying I can't choose what's right for you, but Sutton, please listen to yourself!" Charlotte swiftly looked back at her and Sutton nearly jumped back at the intensity. She wasn't angry, she realized, but her voice was *begging*. "How would it have worked? I win this election and we completely dial back every public interaction we ever have?"

"For now, yes. It would have worked. Instead of just choosing to – to end everything at the drop of a hat. And I've never asked you for anything in public."

It wasn't *ideal*, of course, but their private moments, the ones with just them, were enough. They had been more than enough for Sutton. For the most part.

"It wasn't going to keep working, though." Her tone was gentler now as she leaned in, staring into Sutton's eyes. "Is that really what you want? To be my secret sex friend? Until when? When does that end? Were we just supposed to keep it going until everything blew up?"

There was this hopelessness about her, reflecting in those beautiful eyes that was so unfamiliar to see that it was unsettling.

It's blowing up right now! Her mind yelled, and she could feel the backs of her eyes burn with tears that demanded to be shed. She didn't realize they'd started falling until she looked down at the table and saw them land on her sleeve.

How did Charlotte not realize? How did she not see that no, Sutton didn't want to be her secret sex friend forever? That she didn't want to be her secret sex friend right now, but that there was more here. That there was so much between them, that Sutton would be willing to wait out the storm.

"Please," Charlotte's voice was desperate, and Sutton could see her knuckles turn white with her grip around her coffee cup. She instinctively knew that Charlotte wanted to reach out to her and was holding herself back. "Tell me what to do. Tell me what you want. We can take some time apart and get things under control or –"

"I want you." She couldn't stop herself from saying the words even if she wanted to, and in that moment everything in the world stopped.

Because she hadn't admitted that out loud to Charlotte. Never before had she crossed that line so explicitly, but there it was. "I don't want to take time apart. I just want *you*."

She bit so hard at her lip she was worried she might break through the skin as she wiped at her eyes with her hands, but she didn't stop looking at Charlotte. Couldn't stop looking at her, while her heart thundered in her chest.

Charlotte was frozen. Giving Sutton a look that was so . . . full. That was the only way to describe it. That there was so much going on in one single look, it could have filled a novel.

"I . . ." Charlotte's hands shook from where they were on the table, before she dropped them into her lap and clasped them together tightly. As if that would give Charlotte the control Sutton knew she always wanted.

Despite this burning rejection, there was a new strength inside her from the release of those words. It was freeing, to finally stop herself from holding back that truth.

"You know what I want. What do *you* want, Charlotte? Because I really just don't know."

Charlotte looked almost offended. Her voice shook, "You *know* what I want. I wanted to end our arrangement before it crashed and burned too far for us to come out of it with a friendship intact." She drew both of her hands, still shaking, through her hair, tension rolling off of her in waves so apparent she was surprised the café didn't tumble down with them.

Her eyes darted around the café, seeming unsure of where exactly to look, before landing on Sutton again, and they glittered with tears. "I want you to be in my life, because my life is better with you in it."

For one moment, everything else fell away to the background. Charlotte wanted her, too. And she was admitting it, and Sutton felt like she had that one shining pocket of hope shining brighter than she'd allowed it to in days.

 Before Charlotte hastily wiped at her eyes. "I want *you*, too, Sutton. But I just can't . . . do it in the same way you want me."

"You can't or you won't," she challenged, not bothering to wipe at the tear tracks she could feel on her cheeks. That small hope was dashed. She stared at Charlotte, needing the answer.

"I'm not the same as you are," Charlotte inhaled deeply, her breath trembling and Sutton hated that she wanted to comfort her even now. "I'm not – I don't have this natural romantic side who wants those things you want. I'm not this person who just has *feelings* for someone. And I'm certainly not someone who wants to lead on someone that I care about or make any of those promises. I'm not that person."

Sutton could only stare.

How did Charlotte not see that she already was that person? She thought she wasn't, but she was. All of those times they were together where Charlotte *was* romantic. Where she would stroke her fingertips over Sutton's back or jaw or skim them through her hair and just watch her. Where she would encourage Sutton to do everything, where she was so thoughtful even without trying?

How did Charlotte not see the way she'd made implicit promises with touches and looks and comments?

"You could be that person," she stressed, this utter *need* inside of her demanding that Charlotte just see the way things could be, and how easy it could be. How easy it already was.

Charlotte seemed, for once, completely and utterly out of her depth. "I can't be," she emphasized, staring back for long, searching moments. Her posture slowly corrected, her hands gripping at her thighs. "I'm not ready for that, Sutton. And neither is my career."

God, Sutton remembered the first time they had ever made plans to hang out in person. The way Charlotte had described her ambitions and what she was willing to do to make them come true. And it had seemed lonely to her then, but it seemed impossible to her now.

"So, your career is just *everything*, then?" She could hear her own disbelief, but – but she couldn't understand it.

Careers were important, life goals were important. Her parents, her siblings, they had goals and dedication, and she understood that. But . . .

"You knew that about me before we ever even met face to face," Charlotte shot back, eyes narrowed, as if she couldn't believe what she was hearing. "I've never hidden who I am or what I want. Not from you."

"And nothing has ever made you question yourself? *Nothing* has ever been worth a little risk?" Her throat felt like it was on fire with the question, her nerves jumping with anticipation of the answer.

Not even me? sat unspoken between them. Did Charlotte give any thought to her in this? Did she even contemplate for a second that she was breaking both of their hearts? Did she think at all about the fact that Sutton wouldn't ever demand her to come out before she was ready, that she wanted to just be there for her through it all?

Did she give any thought that maybe Sutton, maybe *they*, could be worth it?

"Nothing has ever been worth that risk," Charlotte confirmed. The words were little more than a whisper but they were absolute.

All she could do was stare at Charlotte as blood rushed in her ears. She wasn't worth the risk, and it *burned*. As though everything inside her was going up in flames.

"I just want everything to go back to the way it was," Charlotte cradled her head in her hands, her voice anguished.

She could still only stare.

How could Charlotte expect them to be friends, now? After *everything*.

"I don't think it can." Her words even stung herself.

Because, God, she didn't want to say goodbye to Charlotte either. She wanted to hold on, to cling, desperately.

It seemed that whatever had been holding Charlotte together fell completely away. Her eyes filled with tears and spilled over, as she sniffled – a sound Sutton would never have imagined hearing from Charlotte, let alone in public.

"Maybe not right now," Charlotte asserted, her voice was thin and reedy, "But in . . . a couple of months. We can go back to being friends."

She sounded so hopeful, as if the idea alone helped soothe her pain. Which was baffling to Sutton, because that idea just made her hurt even more.

"How can we? I don't think we were ever friends." The realization fell over her, and she felt like suddenly she was seeing the light. Because if the basis of *this* was friendship, Sutton wouldn't be feeling like this was killing her.

Charlotte whipped her head up, looking poleaxed, sounding wounded, "How could you even say that? You're the closest friend I've ever had. Even before – everything."

Sutton scrubbed her hands over her face, seeing their entire relationship with new eyes. "How were we ever just friends? We met on a dating app!" She laughed, an incredulous, hollow sound that she didn't even recognize. "There was this attraction the whole time between us, you said it yourself. And there were feelings in the beginning, too."

546

Charlotte didn't say anything to that. Instead, she just stared at Sutton, blinking slowly, as if she was still trying to wrap her head around Sutton declaring that they were never just friends.

When she continued to be silent, the pain dug even deeper into her chest – just one more thing she was alone in, then. "Fine, then, I guess it was only me who had feelings in the beginning. Great," she scoffed, before it caught on a sob, and she didn't know if she had ever felt so utterly angry and miserable in equal measure. "But I know I have them now."

She set both of her hands on the table in front of her, and she knew, she could feel in her stomach this certainty that this was it. That it was now or never, and the words felt so heavy they scraped her throat as they fell from her lips. "I can't be your friend, because I'm in love with you."

A dead silence fell between them for a few moments and Sutton had never before known what it really meant to hang yourself out to dry but now she did.

Charlotte stared at her, eyes wide. "Sutton," her voice just above a breath, so full of pain and warmth, and it was the warmth that broke her.

But she wasn't worth any risk to Charlotte's career, because apparently nothing was, not even this connection they'd built, and she couldn't do it anymore.

She couldn't sit here, so full of this painful *love* for Charlotte, who was still just staring at her.

She stood up, entire body shaking as she stared down at Charlotte. "I'm in love with you and that's not just going to go away because we aren't sleeping together. I think . . . I think maybe you love me, too. Or you could, and you're just too scared to do anything about it."

Everything inside of her demanded she get out of there as fast as she could, because even saying those words, confessing it felt like too much. But she waited for long, torturous moments, staring at Charlotte and begging her to just say yes. To say that Sutton wasn't wrong.

Charlotte took a deep, shuddering breath, and looked away.

That was the answer, then.

She didn't let herself look back at Charlotte, not once, no matter how much the voice inside of her wanted so badly for Charlotte to get up and chase her. She wanted it, but unlike a few days ago, she no longer had any hope. The band-aid was completely gone.

And she was *angry*.

The slightly chilly air whipped around her, and did nothing to soothe the way her blood pounded through her veins or how she couldn't hear anything over the rushing in her ears.

It was the anger that carried her home, blind to nearly anything else going on around her.

She was angry with Charlotte. So *angry* with Charlotte, for ending something that she knew would have been so beautiful. Something that already was beautiful.

Angry at her for not giving them a chance, and not having any faith.

She was angry with Charlotte for agreeing to this in the first place, when apparently, she thought it was always only going to end in disaster.

She yanked the door to her apartment open, her hand shaking and stomach rolling so harshly she thought she was going to be sick in the hallway.

Because mostly, she was angry with herself.

For starting this whole thing. Because Charlotte was right. It had been her who initiated this. It had been her who wanted this in the first place, who went to Charlotte's and insisted that they sleep together. It had been her who had suggested they be *friends* with benefits, despite the disastrous way their first time together had gone.

It had been her who was so disgustingly naïve, who thought this could work out just because she was in love, in spite of everything she knew about Charlotte. In spite of the fact that she *respected* Charlotte's drive, and she – what? Expected that she should just throw it away, for her? For Sutton?

She was so angry with herself. For being an idiot this whole time and deluding herself that Charlotte felt the same way and that something good would come of this.

She felt like she was burning and alive as she shut the door behind her. Still so wound up that it didn't hit her about why she'd been avoiding this for the last few days right away.

Not even as Regan shouted out, "Sutton? Are you home? I've missed you. I even brought you home a whole lemon cake from the café last night."

She barely registered anything until she stood in the doorway of the living room, breathing heavy and eyes stinging, as she saw Regan on the couch.

Her best friend had the remote in hand, grinning from ear to ear. "I'm so excited! We should order in and watch –"

Sutton didn't know what it was about that exact moment.

Maybe it was because everything with Charlotte – how raw it all felt, her admitting that she was in love with her, and how it was definitely *so* over – tore away any semblance of numbness and hope.

Maybe it was because hearing Regan and seeing her sitting on their couch, talking to her like she always did, reminded her so strongly of why she'd been avoiding her since this all happened.

Because this was *home* and she was safe here, and suddenly there was no more anger.

It was so fast she felt her knees go weak, because it felt like everything inside of her was breaking open. Every last thread she'd been holding onto snapped and she swayed in place.

"Sutton? What's wrong?" The urgency in Regan's voice, the utter concern, was the final straw.

Her arms fell uselessly at her sides, as all of the tears she'd been trying to keep at bay for *days* broke through. She felt like she could barely even breathe through it.

She couldn't see through her tears, but she heard and felt Regan jump off the couch, rushing to her. "What? What is it? Is everyone okay?"

Her friend's arms wrapped around her tightly, and Sutton leaned into her, sobs wracking her body. She should have told Regan everything from the beginning. She should have – God, she was the worst and everything was falling apart, and she shook her head.

"I'm s-sorry. I'm so sorry," was all she managed to get out on a broken whisper, hiccupping as Regan's arms just banded even tighter around her, keeping them both up.

She could feel her whole body shaking as she sank into her best friend, into the comfort here. "I – I applied for an internship in Rome. Months ago. And I never told you. And I got in." She wanted to pull away, to look Regan in the eye when she said it, but didn't feel like she could. "I'm sorry. I won't even go, I shouldn't go."

But Regan only held on to her tighter. "We'll figure it out! It's okay," she tried to soothe her, but with the warm way she rubbed circles into her back, Sutton could only cry harder.

"And you were right. Charlotte d-doesn't want to be with me. I'm in love with her and she doesn't want to be with me and it's over and I just didn't want to tell you. And I love her so much, I really do." She buried her face into Regan's neck, shaking, as she managed to whisper, "Please don't say you told me so. Please."

She couldn't handle it. She just couldn't.

Regan stroked her hair. "Never."

Chapter 22

When Charlotte opened the top drawer of her work desk, she was greeted with a Post-it that read *if you're reading this, it means you've stayed at the office too long! Go home!* in Caleb's handwriting.

She crumpled the note and tossed it in the trash.

"Nothing but net," she muttered under her breath as she pulled out the file she'd been searching for.

Under the file was another note from her brother: *seriously, woman? GO HOME!*

Tired eyes rolled hard as the second note joined the first. Rather than heed the advice, she tapped on her mouse to wake up her computer. Maybe it was Saturday morning and, yes, maybe she didn't typically work Saturday mornings.

But as of two and a half weeks ago, she'd been at work basically through every waking moment. It was crunch time; the election was in less than a month, and in addition to any last-minute campaigning, she also had to keep up with her day-to-day responsibilities. She still had an interview to do – two weeks from now, so it would come out right before the election – and she'd only just done her final, informal debate with Naomi a couple days ago.

It had thankfully gone smoother than the one before it. She had to figure that of course Naomi would keep trying to make a few digs into her love life, but during that debate it hadn't filled Charlotte with fear again.

There was nothing to find out anymore.

She hadn't seen Sutton in weeks.

Hadn't heard a word from her. Had gotten no long, rambling messages about her day. Hadn't had any warm and sleepy *good nights* whispered just before falling asleep.

It was her choice, she reminded herself; it had to be done.

Maybe she hadn't been entirely prepared for their entire friendship and communication to end. And maybe she hadn't been ready for the giant chasm she'd feel in the aftermath.

She certainly hadn't been ready for Sutton to sit across from her, heartbroken and angry, saying that she was *in love with her*.

It made her want to cry just thinking about it, for many jumbled reasons, and that was utterly ridiculous.

Sutton *loved* her. Was in love with her. It was the strangest, most wonderful, most painful feeling to hear Sutton say. Where her heart skipped a beat, and then her chest had seemed to feel so warm.

Before the reality of it all came crashing down with the realization: that was it. All of her potential hopes about friendship and somehow maintaining having Sutton in her life were gone with those words.

She'd seen it, written all over Sutton's achingly beautiful face in that moment. That there really was no going back to whatever friendship she'd thought they'd had.

Sutton was in love with her. And Charlotte had no idea how to be in love, let alone how to be in love with Sutton and have her best odds at accomplishing her dreams.

It felt like she'd been robbed of something, now. Something precious.

The remains of the world they'd built between the two of them came crashing down in a matter of minutes and she hadn't been able to manage to think of any words to say to make it better. Not when Sutton had declared that they'd never even been friends.

She'd done exactly as she'd set out *not* to do, and had broken Sutton's heart. It ate at her, taking away her appetite while her stomach felt tangled in knots. She wouldn't be hearing from her. Ever again. And that made her ache in ways she didn't want to think about.

Ways she couldn't think about. She wouldn't.

During her last debate she'd been filled with this same hollowed feeling that had taken up residence in her chest. It had been almost alarmingly simple to fall into the façade of that mask.

Unlike winning her first two debates though, there was no feeling of triumph and sheer happiness. She just felt tired.

Proud, of course. Successful, yes. The smile on her face that was featured on the news segment afterwards had been genuine. But also, exhausted. The very last thing she'd wanted that night was to go out with Caleb and Dean or even to have a late dinner with her grandmother; instead, she'd gone home, poured herself a drink, and promptly gone to bed.

Clearing her throat, Charlotte straightened her back and narrowed her eyes at her computer screen.

"My God, with that level of concentration, I'm shocked you haven't not only conquered the entire country, but also laser vision." Dean's voice jarred her and she managed to just stop herself from jolting in surprise, looking up just in time to see him fully walk into her area of the office.

"With that kind of comedy, I'm shocked you haven't made it in stand-up." She rolled her eyes, before glancing up at the clock. "What are you doing here?"

"*I* have a few reports to send in for the beginning of the month. The real question is what are *you* doing here?" He leaned his hip against her desk, putting his hand deliberately on top of her file, as if she was going to attempt to get any work done at this exact moment.

"I'm just finishing up some paperwork myself." She hedged, knowing that the second he looked at what she'd been about to work on, he would know the truth.

Only a moment later, his eyes flickered to her desk. Busted.

"This isn't even due to be finished for over a week. And it's a Saturday morning." He leveled her with a look.

Which she challenged with her own as she changed the subject. "When did you let my brother break into my desk and vandalize my things with Post-its?"

"I left my jacket here last night and we stopped on our way back from dinner. To be entirely honest, we were both shocked you'd gone home by then," he teased, but there was an edge of seriousness there as his eyes searched hers.

"Please. You two take so long to finish a dinner date, you probably didn't swing by here until nine or ten."

"And don't think I don't know how late you've been staying lately." He drummed his fingers on her desk, lifting a playful eyebrow. "It might come as a shock to you, but most people who work here actually don't need to be convinced by their boss to go home by five. And to *not* come in on weekends."

"Shut up."

To her surprise, he did. Only because he picked up the report on her desk and put it back in the file. "You aren't going to sit here all day and write up this report. It's the weekend. Go home. Visit your grandmother. Come out with me and Caleb for dinner. Walk around Central Park. Go visit a pet store. But you're not going to spend the day here and don't you dare come around tomorrow, either. And now that I have you here? You're actually going to take the day off on Monday, too."

He crossed his arms, as if daring her to argue.

Instead, she laughed, leaning back in her chair. "Oh, right, yes. I'll take Monday off. Sure."

Dean scowled. "I'm not joking, Charlotte. You're taking the day off. *And* the weekend, don't forget about that."

Charlotte rolled her eyes. "And why would I do that?" She had a whole laundry list of things she should get done this weekend. And taking a day off? She couldn't remember the last time she did that.

"Because I told you to." There were only a handful of times he'd used that dead-serious tone with her.

Her eyebrows lifted, incredulous. "I have work to do."

Dean let out a bark of laughter. "All of the work you could possibly have to do here for the next *two weeks* is already essentially done!" Shaking his head, he sobered and leaned forward to hold eye contact with her, interrupting before she could argue with him. "Charlotte, you've been here before seven in the morning every day for the last few weeks. You've been staying until well past six every night, on top of juggling your campaign duties. You've been coming in on the weekends." He gestured at her now, having caught her in the act. "As your boss, I'm telling you that you aren't going to show your face here until Tuesday at the earliest."

"As my boss, shouldn't you be glad that you have such a dedicated employee?" She shot back.

"Maybe," he conceded, before dropping his head to hold her gaze. "But as your *friend*, I'm worried about you. You've always been dedicated and that's a part of what has made you so incredible to work with. But . . . you need a break."

They stared at one another for a few moments and she *wanted* to argue with him. She had to actively hold herself back from arguing with him. To revolt against his abject ordering her around. There was always more that could be done and she narrowed her eyes.

"You know I'm right."

Damningly, she did. She was entirely caught up on her work – alarmingly so, for someone in her position.

But Charlotte didn't even know how to begin to explain that the very last thing she needed right now was a break.

That she'd been spending every waking moment in the last couple of weeks trying to keep as busy as possible – at work and on her campaign, wherever she could – because whenever she had downtime, she thought of Sutton.

Having free time made her *feel* everything she was desperately trying to put up a wall against.

How did she explain to him that free time led her to nights like last night, where she'd been unable to fall asleep and instead had broken down and looked at Sutton's Instagram? That she'd been avoiding looking at any social media that could possibly tempt her to snap her control and check up on how Sutton was doing?

How did she explain that she spent time at home cleaning everything to rid every trace of Sutton, only to prove to herself how embedded Sutton had become in her life? That she knew Sutton's birthday was next week and she couldn't bring herself to throw out the jacket she'd purchased for her over a month ago that was wrapped and now hidden in her closet?

How could she possibly put into words that she was waking up by five without an alarm? That constantly keeping busy throughout the day made it easier for her to drop into sleep at night without having time to let herself think about the way everything inside of her *felt*?

How did she even begin to describe to Dean that Charlotte needed to be here, taking meetings and checking on developments and working on her campaign, because she couldn't be alone with her own thoughts right now?

How could she explain that to anyone, when she'd spent her entire life priding herself on not being this kind of person?

She'd spent her entire adult life honing her control, creating boundaries, and carefully evading every situation where she would end up as this person. Now here she was anyway.

"I don't need a break." She finally settled on, quietly but firmly, steadfastly holding Dean's eye.

His mouth fell open. "Charlotte, if you've gotten more than five hours of sleep in a single night in the last few weeks, I'm a monkey's uncle."

"Kind of rude to talk about your niece like that."

"Shut up. You need a break and you're taking it starting today."

Charlotte pulled her hair back and out of the way as she let out an exasperated sigh. "I think you're being a little dramatic, *boss*."

Instead of giving her another talking-to in his stern voice and the look she was used to going with it, where his forehead was all scrunched up, Dean was quiet. He tilted his head to look up at the ceiling, deep in thought for a few long moments, before looking back at her with that same thoughtful look.

She stared back, lifting an eyebrow in question.

Dean shook his head before reaching out and placing his fingertips on the notepad in front of her, tapping lightly. "You know, a couple of years ago, I wasn't even thirty-five and I'd just become the mayor of this city."

Charlotte lifted a brow. "I'm aware . . ."

He continued, unfazed, looking over her shoulder at his closed office door. "There I was, wanting to prove myself, when a position opened up and a resumé landed on my desk." He looked back at her. "A young woman, a few years out of college, working for the governor, with an entire page of internships and jobs in D.C. already under her belt – but impressive as it was, I saw the last name and thought – did I really want this young and idealistic, likely headstrong and opinionated woman, the granddaughter of a fucking President, to be the first one I personally hired?"

"Probably not," she acknowledged. She'd never heard this before and honestly, she was grateful for the distraction.

God only knew she could use a good distraction lately.

"Probably not," he agreed and linked his fingers over his knee. "But you had the education, some experience, and glowing recommendations, so an interview was guaranteed."

She narrowed her eyes at him, but remained silent as Dean's grin grew at the memory.

"I was *convinced* that I wasn't going to hire you. Then was even more convinced when it was three minutes past the interview time and you weren't yet in my office. And that was when I looked out from my office and saw that you *were* here –"

"Oh, god," she groaned, shaking her head at her past self. Then again, it made her smirk, because she still wouldn't do anything differently.

Dean laughed. "And I saw that you'd walked right into a team meeting and instead of just walking by them and into your interview, you stopped. You asked what they were stuck on and you jumped in. In twenty minutes, you had helped members of this department delve into the groundwork for a new proposal and you weren't even employed yet."

After a moment, Dean sighed and his smile faded a bit as he nodded slowly. "I knew in that moment that, regardless of my doubts and worries, if I didn't hire you, you'd get another job in a heartbeat and I would miss out."

When he paused, she leaned forward, reaching for his hand. This was something she hadn't known she needed to hear. "Dean –"

But he held his hand up, stopping her. "I knew that day that you had a spark. That you had the intelligence and the drive, but also that extra . . . *thing* about you. But I didn't know that you'd so easily become my right hand here, that you'd become a friend."

No, she hadn't had any idea about that either. That Dean would be important in her life in any way beyond professional, and now, he was essentially her in-law.

"And I definitely didn't know then that you were going to be not only the youngest congresswoman ever elected, but that you're going to be the youngest lesbian, too." He put his hand down over hers. "I didn't know how much you were going to change the world, Charlotte, but I do now. And I want you to know that in these last few years, it's been an honor to have worked with you."

Damn it. She felt this welling of gratefulness inside of her, so strong it was almost overwhelming. No, it *was* overwhelming and she tried to laugh it off. "An honor, sure. I *am* idealistic and headstrong and opinionated, so you were right on that front."

"An *honor*," his tone offered no room for argument as he squeezed her hand. He met her eyes with his own and she knew he was as serious as he could be.

It broke a piece inside of her that had been holding tenuously on and her eyes filled with tears. "You absolute sap." She chuckled, but it was shamefully watery.

She pulled back and brought both of her hands up to wipe her eyes as carefully as she could with her thumbs, trying to maintain her makeup covering the bags under her eyes.

His hand landed on her shoulder and rubbed in comfort. She took in a tremulous breath, forcefully closing her eyes and willing the tears to stop. *Needing* for them to stop, before it got out of control.

"I'm sorry, for this. Lately I'm so –" She cut herself off, unwilling – no, un*able* to admit aloud how close these tears were to the surface in the last few weeks.

"There's no shame in having feelings," he spoke softly, handing her a tissue from the desk next to hers.

Charlotte rolled her eyes, using her phone to assure that her makeup hadn't run, even though her eyes were still glassy and her stomach was still in knots. "Come on."

"There's not. Especially when you have so many high-stress situations going on. With the election closing in and . . ."

A mirthless chuckle escaped her, even as her heart lurched painfully in her chest. "Yeah."

"For what it's worth, I truly do admire you and how damn strong you are."

She accepted it with a small nod, closing her eyes tightly for a moment. His words were a double-edged sword, this admission of admiration. She needed to hear that far more than she'd realized.

Because she sure as hell didn't feel very strong right now. When she would only let herself admit in the dead of night, how much she was hurting herself.

She just had to keep this in mind. This is all for a reason. Chin up, shoulders back. Pain was always temporary and she had a future that was put on hold for no one. Things would all line back on track, she just had to remember that.

She supposed there was no way she could change the world without experiencing some damn painful heartache herself, first.

"I'm going to do my paperwork as fast as humanly possible and then you and I are both leaving here. Your brother and I will take your mind off of work."

She acquiesced, only because she knew there was no talking him out of it. Besides, she allowed, her mind wasn't going to be really on work one way or the other.

Chapter 23

Sutton had always loved weddings.

She loved what they meant, what they symbolized. From the very first one she had ever attended – for a cousin, when she'd been four – she'd been mesmerized. From the beautiful clothes, to the ceremony, to the way someone's eyes looked when they looked at their new spouse, to the way everyone celebrated afterward.

The idea of forever with someone else . . . it was such a beautiful thought.

Before she could stop herself, a sigh escaped her as she slid her glasses off and rubbed her fingers over her eyes as a headache brewed just behind them.

Oliver's wedding to Jane was happening in a week and by staying at her parents' house for the time being, she was wrapped up in the wedding madness. Morning, noon, and night there were people in and out of the house – caterers, florists, bakers, photographers, and maybe even the Pope himself, for all she knew. For the first time since she'd returned home last week, there was silence where she'd cocooned herself in the kitchen with a cup of tea. It was also nearly one in the morning and everyone involved in the wedding had left over an hour ago, thankfully.

Their ceremony itself was going to be small, held at one their parents' estates. Followed by a very large reception at one of the grandest event halls Sutton had ever seen.

And Sutton was loving being a bridesmaid; she really was. Oliver was probably the happiest he had ever been and she enjoyed getting to be an up-close part of it.

It just also hurt.

Seeing Oliver and Jane together was sweet. Then there was Lucas and his longtime girlfriend Isla, Alex was bringing Chris despite refusing to call him her boyfriend, and even Ethan – Ethan! Her brother who had barely turned fifteen, had a date with someone from school for the wedding.

She was happy for all of her siblings. She wanted them all to not be lonely, to have someone to share private laughs with, to have someone to dance with, to have someone to join them at these events.

But it made her heart ache, because she wanted for once to join in on that. To have someone to bring to the weddings, to the holidays, to the parties. Instead of feeling the pockets of loneliness.

At this exact moment it was worse than it had been in the past, where she wished to have *someone* to be with during these times. Where her romantic side could bemoan not having someone, but she could sigh a bit and turn her attention to Regan and her other friends.

This time, though, she wished that she had *Charlotte* here experiencing the wedding chaos with her.

It was harder, now, knowing exactly what she was missing out on. She knew exactly how it felt to have someone be on the same page as her, to make eye contact and share a moment. How it felt to want to lean closer only to feel that connection.

She knew what she could have if things were different. If coming out wouldn't mean Charlotte was risking everything. If Charlotte cared about what was between them to feel like the risk was worth it.

It made it more difficult seeing other people have *that*, now that she knew exactly what *that* feeling was.

Shaking her head, she brought her fingers to her temples and rubbed hard to ward off the headache. She *hated* that she still felt this way. That it had been almost a month since she'd had any contact with Charlotte and it still hurt like this.

Blearily, she blinked her eyes open to stare blankly down at the paper in front of her. Lucas had sheepishly asked her if she would write and orate the Best Man speech, because words were far easier for her than they were for him.

As was public speaking. He'd made a heartfelt plea, citing that he wanted the best speech possible for their brother and that she would be the person for the job, and she agreed with enthusiasm.

It was only now when she really needed to buckle down and get it written, that she was unexpectedly struggling. She hadn't realized how hard it was to immerse herself in pretty words about love while her own heart was still tender and hurting.

As much as she wished there would be a magical way to snap her fingers to feel better and not miss Charlotte . . . Well, it was a slow process. But she was trying.

Besides, it wasn't like Charlotte would have even been here at the wedding with her even if she hadn't put an end to their arrangement last month. She never would have been her date to a wedding while she wasn't publicly out, which, she guessed, was precisely what she'd been getting at when she begged Sutton to look at things from her point of view.

It was an odd thing, she'd decided in the last few weeks, feeling both sympathetic to Charlotte because she *understood*, but also feeling stupid – so stupid. Caught between understanding what Charlotte could lose by coming out, but also wishing and hoping so hard for Charlotte to have done anything when she'd told her that she was in love with her.

For Charlotte to have run after her when she'd left the café that day. Stopped her and told her that there really was something here between them. That it was important and that she didn't want it to end, either, even if there would be consequences.

"God. Write," she commanded herself, tapping her pen against the table and blowing out a deep breath. "Ignore your own pathetic love life and find something nice to say about Oliver's."

"Sutton? What are you doing up?" Her mother's voice made her jump and she turned just in time to see her mom flick on the lights to illuminate the entire room. "Why are you sitting in the dark, honey?"

"I wasn't," she replied, teasing, as she used her pen to point up at the light directly above the kitchen table that she was sitting at.

Katherine rolled her eyes as a tired smile tugged at her lips. "You know what I meant."

Rolling the pen between her fingers, she watched as her mother made herself a cup of tea. In her silk robe, with her auburn hair pulled up into a quick but effortlessly beautiful chignon, Sutton felt acutely why she'd always idolized her.

"I was trying to make the least amount of noise and distraction as possible," she answered honestly. "You're such a light sleeper and you've been so busy, I didn't want to take any chances."

Her mother's eyes were warm as she walked over to the table and slid into the nook to sit beside her. "How's the speech coming?"

The sigh escaped her before she could stop it. Then she coughed as if she could cover it up. "It's – it's fine. I just, there's some fine . . . tuning . . ." she slowly trailed off as she watched her mom lift an eyebrow and reach over to spread all of the papers out over the table.

The papers that were either blank or were covered in scribbles.

She helplessly stared at the papers, searching for the words to explain to her mother. But how did she explain that every time she started writing, she got wrapped up in writing about her own thoughts on love. How that *hurt* so badly because every route of talking about love made her think about Charlotte, when she hadn't told her mother in specific terms about what had happened with her.

Even though she'd known they were sleeping together, telling her mom about all of the details – the whirlwind of feelings and how she finally understood what it meant to be in love. The subsequent heartbreak – still felt like a betrayal to Charlotte somehow. And made her feel like an absolute idiot.

"What are you doing up?" She was well aware that it was obvious that she was changing the subject but she didn't care.

"I was . . . I have a lot on my mind." Katherine's voice was introspective, as was the look on her face.

"With the wedding."

Her mom hummed, looking into her mug of tea.

"Oliver . . . he's happy." She noted as she studied Sutton.

"He definitely seems it."

Katherine took a large sip of her tea, staring across the kitchen for a long moment. "I was so reserved about Jane when Oliver first brought her home."

Sutton snorted. "Um, I remember."

She especially remembered because the first time Jane had come home with Oliver for a long weekend she'd been extremely shy. Beyond that, their mother's reputation had proceeded her, which meant Jane had spent the majority of the weekend nervously avoiding spending one-on-one time with her.

Katherine gave her a look, even though there was a smile edging along the corners of her mouth. "She was so quiet, the very definition of the opposite of Oliver – and of the girls he typically liked to date."

Sutton couldn't help but laugh, leaning her shoulder into her mom's. "You are *always* reserved about whoever anyone brings home, no matter what!"

Now her mom's grin emerged full-stop, not an ounce of denial in her eyes. "I eventually came around to Jane because I realized that she truly did love your brother. I could see it. And I wanted the best for him." Her voice took on that soft, contemplative tone that Sutton couldn't quite figure out. "You know I just want the best for all of you."

Sutton was about to nod when she realized her mother was not only just saying that as a fact, but that she was waiting for Sutton's response. "I know that. We all do."

That considering look fell away after a few seconds and Katherine leaned forward, kissing Sutton's forehead. It wasn't something that happened often anymore, but it had been something her mom would do when they were all

565

younger. A soft comfort that still worked so well, even when Sutton didn't know exactly what she was thinking.

"I'm proud of the beautiful, caring, smart woman you are. And everyone who is worth a second of your time will see all of that and love it, too," she murmured as she leaned back.

"Yeah, right." The words left her before she could stop them.

Squeezing her eyes closed, she took in a deep breath even as her throat felt tight.

She felt her mom's hand land on hers, squeezing, as her voice was quiet but direct. "Sutton, honey, why did you come home early? I know you said it's because you're just very excited about the wedding, but I know you. I didn't want to pressure you, but I'd very much like to hear about it."

"I . . ." When would she learn that lying to her mom was useless? She'd almost hoped that she was too distracted by everything going on to notice Sutton's turmoil.

The plan had been for Sutton to return for the wedding five days prior to the event, when her spring break started. The tickets had been booked for months.

Then her birthday had happened.

She'd gone out at Regan's insistence, despite the fact that she hadn't really been in the *going out* kind of mood. Regan had really pulled out all of the stops, though.

She'd made Sutton breakfast before she'd left to go to work, and had returned home with a full tray of her favorite lemon cakes, a pair of brand new boots that Sutton loved, and a card. However, she'd had Sutton open the card last, because it had been a part of the gift itself.

Sutton, my lovely ginger sunflower –

I know you still feel like you shouldn't go and leave me without half of the rent, but that is craziness. You're so smart and this is ROME! You're going to ROME and that is so fucking EXCITING! You're not allowed to feel guilty about your share of the bills here.

566

Because Emma – yes, your uptight and kinda bitchy friend Emma who can't stand anything about me, apparently, for no reason whatsoever – is going to live in your vacated room. She's been trying to get out of her shitty apartment with her vampiric roommate(s?) that's basically a subway cubicle for months and has agreed that despite her (insane) dislike of me, our apartment is a perfect place for her to live for the next few months.

It makes up the rent that I won't be able to afford and it gives her time to search for a viable option while not living in a miserable shithole. Plus it's apparently way closer to her new job or whatever. We have all of the details figured out. For all of her irritating aspects, her best feature by far is that she cares about you.

We have that in common.

Pack your bags, babe, because you are not going to miss out on showing off to the world how amazing you are. I took the liberty of filling out your acceptance form :) you just gotta send it in.

Happy birthday best friend!

It had made her tear up – in the good way. And Regan had surprised her by inviting over Emma and Alia. Regan had pulled out Sutton's favorite go-to outfit for when she went out and had sent Sutton to get changed with a firm pat on her ass and a shout, "It's your birthday and if you think any of us are going to let you sit inside and wallow, you are dead wrong!"

They'd gone out to dinner and then to a couple of clubs. They drank a little and laughed a lot. She'd even danced with a few other women and it had been . . . nice. She'd been very focused on not thinking about Charlotte at all and with everything going on, it was easy to push her to the back of her mind. Because Regan was right; even if it had only been three weeks post-break up, she did deserve to go out and have a good time.

It'd been fun. They walked home together, a unit, even as they stopped for McDonald's French fries. They blended in with many of the other people who were out at two in the morning, flushed and buzzed and laughing, and then – there was Charlotte.

Well, kind of.

On one of the giant electronic billboards they projected Charlotte's face, along with snippets on the bottom from her most recent interview. She looked dignified, gorgeous, and like she wasn't suffering nearly as much as Sutton was without her.

She'd come to a stumbling stop, laughter at one of Emma's stories dying on her lips.

She'd spent the weeks before her birthday walking a fine line between dealing with her feelings – like trying to accept the fact that Charlotte didn't want to be with her, trying to forget the way she'd looked when Sutton had walked away from her – without wallowing in self-pity too much.

Which meant avoiding most news about the upcoming election as much as she could help it, focusing on getting all of her midterms and TA grading done. Getting ready for the wedding.

All right, and some occasional nights in her bed with her sad songs playing because she just *needed* it. Distancing herself from the news was necessary, because it was so confusing with how much she wanted Charlotte to win compared with how much it hurt to see her at all.

That projection of Charlotte on a giant screen literally washing over her, she just – she felt so dumb, but it popped the bubble of the evening.

More than that, it had made her realize exactly how goddamn hard it was to truly get distance, when the woman who broke her heart was quite literally at the focal point of the city she was living in. She was everywhere.

So she'd finished the very last of the work she'd had to do before spring break, faked the flu to her professors for the first time in her life, and hopped on a flight home a week earlier than planned.

Her forehead furrowed as she bit her lip and tried to tamp down on the tears that threatened to break as she felt her mom's gaze on her. When she felt her mom's warm, comforting touch rubbing her back, it was useless.

"I can't escape her. Charlotte. She's – she was everywhere. Out in the world and in here." She tapped her fingers at her chest before using her sleeve to wipe at her eyes. "I told her I love her and she told me she – she can't risk her career. And I just thought," she took in a shuddering breath. "I thought she loved me, too. But I was so wrong. It's never hurt so badly being wrong."

"Honey." Her mom shifted closer to wrap her arm around Sutton.

She buried her head in her hands. "She's in my head all the time. It's so distracting, I can't even write this Best Man speech. A speech about love! I can't write about *love* for the first time because all I do is draw on my own experience and I . . ."

Sutton trailed off, uselessly wiping at her cheeks, as she stared miserably down at the papers in front of her. She managed to resist leaning into her mom for all of three seconds before she melted into her, against the comfort she offered.

She didn't know how long they stayed like that, with her mom's fingers combing through her hair, not offering any platitudes. She just knew that she finally – finally – felt like everything was totally in the open and it was a weight from her shoulders.

"Don't shy away from writing about it." Katherine pushed the pen toward Sutton. "You love to write and you are so good at it so now you can experience this: writing through the pain can make some of the most beautiful of words."

Chapter 24

Charlotte had come out to her grandmother the summer she'd turned seventeen.

She'd gotten her first internship in D.C. and had subsequently spent the summer living with her grandmother, and even though she'd been busy as hell, it had made her so hungry for more.

And, for the first time since she'd determined what she wanted to do with her life, worried.

It'd been easy for her to accept her own sexuality; even as a teenager, she'd had enough confidence in herself to feel no shame in her attraction to women. It was less easy to swallow when she was in the thick of things, able to see how underhanded everyone could be, and how much gossip there was.

Her grandmother had taken her confession in with a few moments of thoughtful silence, giving Charlotte an inscrutable look that she loved. It just proved to her that unlike almost everyone else in her life, her grandmother took her seriously. She never pulled punches. She never treated her like a child.

She'd said, "I'm not going to lie to you. You're right to think this will make the future more complicated." She lifted an eyebrow at her, before holding her gaze, "And you'll already have to be fighting harder for what you want than all of the men here, regardless of who you're attracted to."

Her grandmother held her gaze, her eyes alight with what Charlotte believed was all of the wisdom in the world, as she'd told her, "The world wants to sell the lie, especially to beautiful young women like you, that love is the pinnacle of what you should aspire to. But know, my dear, that there's so much more for you to look forward to than that. In the grand scheme of this life, you have all the power to control your fate if you make the smart choices."

She'd been thinking about that conversation with her grandmother a lot lately. The words, the advice, had stuck with her for years and had given her strength, especially in the past whenever she'd ever had fleeting moments of doubt.

She'd tried to draw strength from them in the last three and a half weeks.

Especially now, as she sat in her office after hours, across from her grandmother, having a light lunch before her final interview.

In ten days, she'd either be taking a step forward or a step backward from her future.

Her grandmother triumphantly put her phone down after having been furiously typing. "Perfect. That journalist –"

"Imani?"

"Of course." She waved a hand. "Are you expecting another one this evening?"

It was easy, thankfully, to curb the emotional spiral she'd been potentially falling down with her grandmother's frank attitude. "Obviously not."

"That journalist is getting her photographer and intern through security downstairs, so we don't have much time to discuss the matter, but I've just gotten word of the final pre-polling numbers." She cast her eyes around Charlotte's office, as if someone could possibly be hiding there.

Her heart pounded as she tried to discern whether the intensity was good or bad. "And?"

"And, my dear girl, you're leading the poll at an outstanding twenty-two percent." The gleam in Elizabeth's eyes wasn't one that many were privy to see. "Four points down from the poll a couple of months ago, but that's hardly more than an error margin."

God, but Charlotte almost wanted to collapse with the relief that coursed through her. Her legs suddenly didn't feel as strong and she let her head fall back as a weight left her shoulders.

Of course, she knew that there was still over a week left and that numbers could change on a dime – she'd be a fool to ever let herself believe otherwise and become complacent. But still.

She blew out a deep breath, her hand reaching for and squeezing her grandmother's without thought. She took comfort in her grandmother's strong grip squeezing back.

"I had no doubt, naturally, but with all of the things Naomi Young wants to try to spread around, the reassurance is always necessary," her voice was strong, almost terse in her annoyance, and she found comfort in that as well.

Rolling out her shoulders, Charlotte shook her head, "This is really good news to start my interview off with." She sighed before giving her grandmother's hands one more squeeze and then let go.

When she opened her eyes, she expected to be met with that same determined smile on her grandmother's face that she'd been wearing a minute ago. Instead, she was met with a speculative frown.

"Why are you looking at me like that?"

Elizabeth scoffed. "That's all you have to say? Christ, I had this expedited to my office before the numbers break on tonight's news, running on my elderly bones down to your department –"

She couldn't have rolled her eyes any harder. "Don't try to make it sound like you don't power walk every morning for an hour."

Her grandmother ignored her. "And your response to leading a poll at twenty-two percent is that it's great news to start your interview off with?"

Charlotte stared at her for a beat wondering if there was more forthcoming before repeating, "It *is* a great way to start my profile."

Elizabeth's eyes narrowed at her and with the close look, Charlotte very nearly wilted. She maintained her posture though, wondering what exactly it was that her grandmother was trying to read from her. Or, was reading from her; Elizabeth Thompson's perception was never a *trying* game.

"Yes, it is," her grandmother's tone was clipped and dismissive and comforting in how typical it was. Then it softened, "But you aren't happy."

Pulling back in surprise, Charlotte let out a disbelieving laugh. "What? Of course I'm happy."

The polling numbers did make her happy and she lifted her eyebrows in question at her grandmother.

Who huffed out an impatient breath. "There's a difference between being happy *about something* and being *happy*. One of them is fleeting."

The words weren't said sharply but she felt them as if they were, panging in her chest.

Elizabeth pursed her lips, observing her. "You make it sound as if I wouldn't recognize when my own granddaughter is happy. If I had told you that you would have this lead on Naomi at the very beginning of this election, your eyes would have lit up. You'd have had trouble hiding exactly how damn happy you'd have been and don't even try to deny it to me."

She . . . was right. Charlotte couldn't deny it, not to the woman who saw it all.

Her grandmother took a step forward, her eyes critical and as always, watching. "And don't try to deny that you've been spending less time with me in the last few weeks, either. Do you think my memory is going or did you believe I wouldn't have noticed that you canceled our Sunday plans for two weeks in a row?"

"As if your memory will ever go." She side-stepped, biting her cheek against the guilt.

Because of course her grandmother was right; she had canceled on her for two weeks in a row. She'd made sure to stop in and see her grandmother several times throughout the week, as was normal. They'd talked and had tea and touched base. But always – *always* – for short periods of time.

It was easier that way, for now. Just until she was over this heartache and was back to normal. Where there would be nothing for her astute grandmother to notice about her emotional state.

In all honesty, Charlotte wasn't sure exactly how much she could handle her grandmother, of all people, noticing just how much pain she was feeling right now.

Elizabeth crossed her arms. "You've been off for weeks, and I thought at first it was because of election stress."

Charlotte sighed, not letting herself reach up and rub her temples at the headache that seemed to be brewing nonstop. If she allowed herself that, she might not be able to stop herself from dropping her head into her hands and hiding there. For just a few moments.

"But it's not the election at all. It's the Spencer girl; you miss her."

At her grandmother's frank assessment Charlotte's head snapped up, eyes wide.

That was about as much as she'd heard anyone in her life mention Sutton in the last few weeks. Which was probably for the best, she knew. Because she certainly hadn't wanted to talk about her. Wasn't even sure if she could.

About how Sutton had crashed through every rule. How she had been so *brave* and reckless and beautiful and damning, denouncing their friendship and their rules and declaring her feelings before walking away from her.

About how Charlotte hadn't known just how long her heart could ache like this.

She felt caught, somehow, with her grandmother's knowing eyes on hers, knowing she could read everything Charlotte was feeling. Everything she'd been pulling a curtain over for the last few weeks and trying to get over.

And this time she had to break the eye contact, taking in a sharp breath as she stared just over Elizabeth's shoulder.

Those irritating tears, the ones that she'd been swallowing back every day, burned at the back of her eyes as she shrugged. "Well. That's neither here nor there, is it?"

It *hurt* to admit, but living that truth silently wasn't helping her in the least. It wasn't making her miss Sutton any less.

They sat in deafening silence for a few seconds while Charlotte knit back her composure inch by inch. This place, her work, was no place for – all of this.

Yet she couldn't help but rub her hands over her thighs, watching her own hands intently, as she murmured, "Don't worry. I'm doing the smartest thing for both of us."

Her words sounded hoarse and vulnerable even to herself, because they were. But it was the truth, she reminded herself. This was the smartest course of action and if anything, her grandmother would appreciate that.

After all, how many times in her life had she heard her grandmother talk about how glad she was that Charlotte wasn't just like the other young people – idiots – who went looking for love when there was so much *more* out there? How proud she was of Charlotte for having such a level head?

Instead of responding though, telling her how proud she was of her, she just looked at her for a few long moments. Before delivering some of her least used words. "I'm sorry."

Charlotte snorted in derision, a sound that surprised them both. "Please don't pretend that you even liked her, Grandmother. I know you didn't." It made her chest ache to even think back to that night. She rubbed at her throat for a moment, wishing her voice wasn't going so hoarse. "You only met her the one time and you barely spoke to her for ten minutes."

She wasn't even necessarily upset about that. She knew Sutton had so much more to offer than her grandmother could see in her initial assessment, that her grandmother was critical of her children and grandchildren, of their spouses, of trusted coworkers, of heads of state. She didn't begrudge her grandmother that.

But it didn't mean she wanted to hear it right now.

She took a deep breath, as deep as she could when her throat was feeling so tight, and the words came out before she thought them all the way through. "She's in love with me."

Saying it . . . hearing herself acknowledge it aloud hurt more than she'd thought it would. She blinked a few times, shaking her head as if it would shake away any possible tears.

"Or she *was*, at least."

It had been almost a month since Charlotte had just *stared* at her in silence and let her walk away from her, after all.

Her hand clenched into a fist and it felt good to have her nails digging into her palm. It gave her enough strength to clear her throat and allow herself to shrug. "It's probably for the best if she's realized she isn't in love with me or if that's all stopped now because she realized who I've been all along." The thoughts she'd had during those moments where she was utterly alone with herself and nothing to occupy her mind rushed to the forefront of her mind. "Too career-oriented or too driven, too ambitious. And maybe just a bit too selfish for her to be in love with."

She made herself straighten her spine, even as she couldn't stop the words from pouring out.

"I know you're disappointed in me. It wasn't what I planned." She tipped her head back to look up at the ceiling and blinked away her tears. "It all . . . got so out of control without my even realizing it."

Which Charlotte hated admitting. She hated knowing that she had a feeling that this entire friends with benefits thing would spiral out of control from the start and against her better judgment she did it anyway.

And it cost her much more than she'd expected.

Her breath came out trembling as she felt her grandmother's fingertips under her chin, tilting her head back to look at her. "First of all, my girl, your head should always be held high," she tapped her fingers lightly at Charlotte's chin as if it was a command, and Charlotte's lips twitched even as she had to reach up to wipe under her eyes.

One of the last things she wanted was to be judged by her grandmother for being in this situation; it was already hard enough.

Elizabeth's eyes held hers as she let out a long sigh and leaned back against Charlotte's desk. "I was never in love with your grandfather."

Surprised – and curious – it took Charlotte a moment to catch up to the non sequitur. "What?"

She shrugged, looking pensive as she repeated, "I was never in love with your grandfather. He was a kind man. Good-looking," she mused with a small, conspiratorial grin. "Not *un*intelligent. He quite enjoyed getting lost in his own world and was just fine with letting me take the lead in our relationship, in our family, and in public. Which, as you know, was not commonly the case fifty years ago. I saw my chance to marry a man that would let me be independent and I knew that would be to my biggest advantage, so I took it."

Charlotte nodded slowly, absorbing everything. It wasn't often that her grandmother spoke candidly about her grandfather; she hardly spoke of him at all. Not in a way like she wished to forget about him, but in the way that . . . well, it was clear that he simply wasn't on her mind all that often. Especially not now, not when he'd been gone for twenty years.

But whenever she mentioned him in public statements or even to Charlotte's father – to her memory, in any case – it was never so *honest*.

"I never regretted that decision. I never wished I got lost in all of that nonsense. I was never wishing I found someone I fell in love with. I was in love with my career, with navigating this journey, difficult as it was. And I've always been proud to have you following in my footsteps," she continued.

Charlotte's stomach lurched because the very last thing she could handle right now was her grandmother telling her that she was no longer proud of her for making this misstep. "Grandmother –"

Elizabeth cut her off with a look. "But I've never been proud because of you choosing to be like me, Charlotte. I've been proud because of who you are and what you want. And right now, I've never seen you so unhappy in all your life. You might think I'm disappointed in you for this development but what I want for you the most is for you to be happy."

A tangled web of gratefulness, love, and hopelessness hit her hard. "But what else can I do without losing . . . everything?"

Her grandmother sighed after a beat. "I wish I had all of the answers for you. But you know I'm not one to lie; we both know there could be serious consequences in this world for living your truth. As much as I wish I could always guide you, you're the only one who can determine what exactly the right path is in this case."

It shook her, more than a bit, to even hear that she should possibly think of deviating from this plan. From this life she'd cultivated for years, to take a chance at all with the high stakes she was playing with. It was nerve-wracking and unsettling and . . .

Charlotte slowly blew out a deep breath, viscerally feeling the heavy weight on her shoulders. "I've never been so conflicted in my life."

"I understand more than anyone this pull you have inside of you, for this life we're in." Her expression turned softer, in the rare way it did for Charlotte only, as she pushed away from the desk and reached for her hand. Charlotte gave it instantly, finding comfort and strength in her the touch. "But remember that even amidst serving the public, you don't owe them your personal life. You owe the world for you to be responsible and to be able to defend your professional and ethical choices ad nauseum. But your *life* is yours. And if there is anyone I've ever known in this game who I trust will know what to do when the time is right, my girl, it's you."

She didn't know at this given moment if she deserved that trust, because she'd been feeling at such a loss lately.

She squeezed her hands and Charlotte squeezed back, trying to soak in as much of her grandmother's knowledge and comfort as she could.

"Thank you," she murmured. She didn't know if the words could make her feel entirely better; she didn't think there was anything that could do that.

But it felt nice to hear, still.

Her grandmother squeezed her hands once more before dropping the hold and narrowing her eyes. "Now, hand me your cosmetic bag before that journalist and her team finally get past security. You can't look like this for your final interview before the election. There's going to be a cameraman in here for God's sake."

They had just enough time for her grandmother to – in her own words – fix Charlotte's face as she muttered about how Charlotte needed to take better care of herself, heartache or not. Then for her to slip out the side exit of the office to avoid any run-in with Imani before the woman in question knocked on the door, poking her head in with a little smile.

"Sorry it took a bit of time, we got held up in security with Greg's camera cases." Imani gave her a polite but warm grin.

"No problem at all, come in." Charlotte took a deep breath, shaking her head to get into the right mindset, before fixing on a well-practiced smile. "I thought we could sit at my desk, why don't you all come in?"

Something she appreciated about Imani and the reason why she'd requested whenever possible thus far in the election for her to be the journalist who covered her stories so often, was that she was always prepared. Even though she was warm and personable, she didn't waste time.

Within minutes, her intern was scribbling notes and holding the recording device in their direction, while her cameraman efficiently snapped photos – of her office and herself. Imani was poised in the chair next to Charlotte's desk, her own notepad in front of her.

"Why don't we start with what's most important – your politics. Even before this election, you've done quite a bit of work that would suggest you are fairly socially liberal. In your own words, would you agree or disagree with that?"

Charlotte nodded and took a breath as she leaned in; it was showtime.

They spoke extensively about her social views –

"I would say I'm socially liberal. There are certain things that are not up for debate, in my mind. Access to health care, to education, to housing, to food – these are basic human needs, and it's the role of the government to make sure its people have access to their basic human needs."

To delving more into her past projects –

"Yes, I've always been very involved in the group homes here in New York. The number of children who need homes and better services here are astronomical, even compared to many other major cities. It's one of the reasons I sought out this career in the first place."

To future initiatives –

"I'm currently working on two initiatives that I intend to keep a hand in moving forward, one involving housing projects and assistance for the homeless population, and the others involving a clean energy conservation in the city. I have consults from several senators and representatives working as a team already."

She damningly stumbled when Imani finished chuckling at one of her anecdotes about her grandmother from her adolescence and asked, "Speaking of your grandmother, one of the biggest landmark changes that has impacted our country under her leadership is, of course, the legalization of same-sex marriage throughout the nation seven years ago. Am I to assume that you have the same approval for the matter as she does? After all, it is very personal to you."

For a moment, she thought the world truly stopped spinning and all she heard was a ringing in her ears because *what did she mean by that* –

"Given that your brother, Caleb, is openly gay," Imani finished.

580

Charlotte had to control everything inside of herself that wanted to absolutely melt with relief. She had to deliberately make her smile warmer because she *knew* she was close to looking as panicked as she'd felt in that moment. "Oh, yes. He is, and my grandmother and our entire family has always been very supportive."

In that moment, as Imani nodded and she heard the shutter of a camera taking a picture of her smile, it was the first time she'd even felt like she was truly *hiding* something. It made her stomach churn and she wanted to fidget, but instead she slightly tightened the hold her fingers had hooked over her knee.

She cleared her throat and changed the subject to share a story about herself and Caleb in their college years that she knew would easily lead into a conversation about education.

After over an hour, Imani gave her an apologetic smile. "Everything you've given me so far is wonderful, Charlotte. Touching both on professional and personal . . . but something that I've been pressed to ask about for this full profile is a bit more personal."

She maintained her grin even as she steeled herself; she was ready for anything about her personal life. She had to be. "Of course."

"As has been spoken about by your competitor in this election, you have quite the sparse dating life, at least from the view from the public eye. As someone who is young, attractive, intelligent – well, it does read as a bit peculiar. Is there anything you'd like to comment on, officially, about that?"

Yes, she could do this, and it was hardly a lie. "I do, admittedly, have a sparse dating life. I'm afraid that there isn't much to comment on, because the truth of the matter is that I've always been far more focused on my career than on dating."

Imani sent her another smile, still apologetic though, and Charlotte could tell she actually meant it. "That's admirable, and not always an easy feat. In the effort to keep this as brief as possible, as we've been going on for an hour already, but to appease all curiosities and comments that have ticked up regarding the election . . ."

She paused and gestured to her intern, who quickly reached into his bag and pulled something out, handing it to Imani.

They were pictures, she realized, with a feeling of dread. A cold and heavy feeling weighing in her stomach even as she kept her expression neutral – interested, even.

"Aside from pictures with your family and coworkers, these have been the only ones our own photographers have captured during the election." She flipped the pictures over onto Charlotte's desk, laying them out for her.

It took everything inside of her to not react outwardly, even as her stomach clenched. It had been *weeks* since she'd allowed herself to look at anything with herself and Sutton together.

The saving grace was that the pictures were innocent – the two of them exiting Topped Off, the two of them walking down the sidewalk. And of course, the picture of them outside of her grandmother's party. The one that had been featured in the newspaper already.

"It's been no secret that your opponent has been making implications about you and the woman featured in the photos," Imani continued, with somewhat of an exasperated tone in her voice. "It's been widely received by many following the debate that this is a reach made by Ms. Young. But for our feature, I would love to have a definitive clarification."

Charlotte managed to tear her eyes off of the photographs, swallowing before she nodded and forced a smile. "Of course." She took a deep breath. "Yes, the woman in the photos was a friend."

Was. She had to snap her mouth shut in order to maintain her smile against the way that word and the pain that went with it made her want to grimace.

As much as she told herself not to, she couldn't help but look down again. It was like she *craved* seeing Sutton's face, even though she knew it was stupid. Even though she knew it would hurt her.

She looked down anyway and could barely breathe.

The pictures were all at least a month old now, and after a jarring moment, she realized that they felt like they were taunting her.

Because she wasn't even staring at Sutton; she was staring at herself. At her own face, as she stood and walked alongside Sutton, there was this *lightness* there. A happiness that she was completely and utterly devoid of right now. That she desperately missed.

That she wanted back and wasn't sure how to get to it, because . . .

She wasn't sure that she'd ever had that feeling before Sutton.

It was like the flip of a switch, just a *moment* that hit her so fast and she couldn't do anything but stare at the pictures.

What if Sutton had been right?

What if they really hadn't ever been just friends? What if it was true that this feeling of strictly friendship that Charlotte wanted to desperately go back to wasn't even real? That – that Sutton had done *that* to her, had somehow lit up something inside of her from the beginning and she hadn't even realized it was happening.

It felt like her heart was being squeezed so tightly and she could barely keep up with her thoughts as they raced. Her stomach turned so strongly she felt like she might be sick.

What if everything with Sutton had felt so new and different and *good* right from the start because of the fact that they'd never been just friends?

God, before Sutton living like she had been, without that feeling of levity, it had been fine. Fine, because she hadn't had any clue that she was missing anything. And now. . . now it was so fucking hard.

She never thought that she would be like this – could be feeling like this but –

You could be that person, Sutton's voice, insistent and so *believing* in her rang in her ears.

The only thing that had gotten her through the last few weeks, aside from keeping as busy as possible, was by reassuring herself that pain didn't last forever.

She was in pain now and she knew that time healed all wounds. That one day, she would be able to look at pictures like these ones and not feel like her breath was stolen right from her chest.

But.

God, she wished she had more time to process, because everything was happening so quickly. She shook her head softly to try to clear it. So, this feeling of pain would pass one day and then, what?

She looked up and felt caught in Imani's slightly confused but expectant look.

This was a can of worms that had already been opened, she realized, as her heart thundered in her chest so hard she felt off balance. Everything inside of her seemed to go numb and she could feel her hands shake as she clasped them in her lap. Naomi had opened this can of worms and Charlotte had made it easy for her to do so, but it was too late now.

Because it had been weeks, and she was still being asked about her and Sutton. Because her personal life was already a topic of interest and she could only imagine that now that it already was, it still would be in the future.

Was she supposed to always be looking over her shoulder, wondering if her opponents or the media or anyone with a god damn camera would be watching her, waiting for the next time she would slip up?

It was too late to follow her original plan, she realized with a terrifying certainty.

I truly do admire you – Dean had said to her. But how could he admire her like this? When she was hiding? When, for the first time in forever, she couldn't even admire herself? Before all of this, when her plan had been to wait at least ten years and come out – simply, quietly, after being an established member of the Senate, with a high approval rating, and already on track for the presidency, it had seemed so right.

But that wasn't the case anymore.

"Actually," she forced out, unable to maintain the smile that had been so easy to keep on her face. Not when everything inside of her felt like it was trembling from all of these nerves and anxiety.

Imani paused, lifting an eyebrow at her.

Charlotte's mouth went dry, her nervous system feeling like someone had slammed the emergency brake. The main voice inside of her head that had always seemed to be the logical reasoning part of her was screaming in alarm about trying to continue to stay the course, to not say anything.

She always listened to that voice. To the voice telling her to make a quip, to go back, to quell this sense of panic.

"I wanted to take advantage of this full profile, with a journalist I trust, to say. . ."

The words caught in her throat.

If there is anyone I've ever known in this game who I trust will know what to do when the time is right, it's you.

But she didn't know – God, how could she know for sure? Who knew that for sure?

The only thing she knew for sure right now, in this moment, with the evidence staring her in the face, was that things couldn't always stay the way they were forever. And sometimes there was no going back, only forward.

I can't be your friend, because I'm in love with you.

It played on a loop in her head, mixing with her grandmother's words and she couldn't stop it. She couldn't and maybe the most terrifying thing right now was that she could finally admit to herself that she didn't want to stop it.

She stared back at the picture with her heart in her throat, barely able to catch a deep breath.

I'm so in love with you.

585

Charlotte swallowed hard, forcing her spine up straight and clasping her hands together tighter to make them stop shaking. "That I'm a lesbian."

As the blood rushed in her ears, Charlotte felt like everything inside of her was imploding. The shutter of the camera stopped. The intern's scribbling of notes paused.

And Imani froze, staring at her with wide eyes.

She'd never known how saying those words would feel. She couldn't have fathomed it in the least, and honestly . . . she hadn't wanted to. But she hadn't known it would feel like this.

This sheer, uncomfortable and uncharacteristic terror, gripping her, like she could see everything falling apart right before her eyes.

Mixed with it, though, right under it, the tiniest kernel of relief. She bit all of it back.

"You – you know we are on the record?" Imani finally recovered a moment later.

"I know, yes," her words came out on a whisper and she cleared her throat. It was so dry it hurt.

Imani quickly reached for her pen, her eyebrows coming together in question as she flipped back through her notes for a moment. "As far as I'm aware, there have only been a small handful of openly LGBT members elected to the House."

"Yes." Her heart was pounding so loudly in her ears, and it was all she could hear. "That's entirely correct."

She could only go forward, she reminded herself. She sat up as straight as possible and stared Imani in the eye, even though she wanted to curl in on herself for just a few moments.

"So, the woman in the pictures is more than a friend then? That inference is actually true?" Charlotte could hear the tinge of surprise in her voice. As though she couldn't believe this actually happened.

Charlotte couldn't either and she somewhat felt like this was an entirely surreal experience, as she shook her head, "She's more than that. She's . . ." Swallowing hard, she dropped her eyes again, tracing them over the way Sutton was laughing so openly and boldly in those pictures. The sight gave her the slightest comfort, something to hold onto in this storm. "She's so much more than that."

Imani watched her closely. "We're ostensibly at the end of the campaign. Why come out now?"

For a moment, all Charlotte could do was stare at her. Why?

Because she was in love? Because she was miserable right now, and exhausted? Because after years of being just fine with her sexuality being a quiet truth, it only now felt like she was keeping a secret? Because how could she accept someone like Dean saying he admired her, when she couldn't admire herself?

"Because I owed it to myself." It was only as the words came out that she realized they were the truth.

She owed it to herself to win . . . or lose being open and honest. She had to do this, even though it was terrifying and she may very well live to regret it.

She owed it to herself to see what the big *deal* about this was. To really understand the songs and the movies and the things she'd long written off. She just hoped Sutton still felt she deserved it as well.

Chapter 25

Sutton picked up her knife, clinked it lightly against her glass, and was relieved when it actually worked to bring a halt to the wedding fun. The music playing in the background immediately lowered, conversation hushed, and she didn't have time to be worried about making her big speech because everyone was already turning to look at her.

"Hi, I'm Oliver's sister, Sutton. I'm going to be delivering the Best Man speech. As everyone might be able to tell, I'm not the Best Man."

The smattering of laughter boosted her confidence. "But if anyone knows the Best Man, they know that Lucas is a man of very few words, so I received a quiet plea and a dessert bribe to step in.

"In his plea, Lucas informed me that he was asking me because I've always loved . . . love," she admitted with a self-deprecating smile. "When we were younger, I was the one who had so many ideas about what it meant to be in love. I mean, as a child, I even had a list of qualities to look for in a partner.

"What Lucas doesn't know is that Oliver called me when he first started dating Jane, for the same reason Lucas did – to talk about love. Because he knew in the beginning that he'd never felt that exact way for anyone else."

God, it was just as hard as she'd expected it to be. To deliver a speech about love, while being in love but also heartbroken about it was so damn hard. Even as she tried so hard not to think about Charlotte.

Even if it was impossible not to.

After all, she'd been the inspiration for her words.

"I've learned that love is about finding someone who pulls you to them even when reason might tell you otherwise. Someone who pushes you out of your comfort zone, not because of them doing or saying anything, necessarily, but because they make you *want* to try new things. They make you want to be daring, because maybe something new and scary doesn't feel quite as scary by their side."

She thought about the support Charlotte had given to her about applying for her internship. The nights where Charlotte had encouraged her to talk to her about the writing she'd done both with her mother and alone, even when Sutton was initially embarrassed. The intent face she always had on her face whenever Sutton spoke, like she took to heart what she was talking about.

"Someone you see all of. Strengths and flaws, even the ones they aren't aware of." The times she'd seen not only how clever and passionate and ambitious Charlotte was – both in impressive ways and in detrimental ones.

But also the times she was able to see how beautifully vulnerable she could be, too. How loyal, how sympathetic. In ways she knew Charlotte didn't see herself in.

"Someone who sees you for everything you are, too." She bit her lip. "Someone who sees all of it and chooses you, anyway."

She had to break off for a moment, pulling the microphone away for a moment as her breath caught in her throat.

Her voice was a little weaker, scratching at the back of her throat as she pushed through it. "And the only thing that could ever be better than feeling this way about that person is that they feel it back."

Tears stung at the backs of her eyes, the silence in the room paying her rapt attention somehow reminding her of Charlotte's ringing silence after she'd confessed her love.

Then she forced a smile and turned toward her brother.

"What many of you *don't* know, and what Oliver probably doesn't want me to share, is that he had a crush on Jane very quickly after they met in college. She assisted him at the student health center for a sprained ankle. When he finally asked her out, she said no, and it wasn't until a couple of years later that Jane realized that Oliver checked those items on her list, too. But Oliver knew – right away – that he felt all of those things, for her.

"Growing up, Oliver was always the person to go to whenever you needed something. He's the kind of brother who would take dancing lessons with you because you didn't have a partner, for a completely random example." She paused, catching his eye and grinning as the room laughed.

"He's the kind of brother who deserves nothing but the best. The most ideal kind of love you can imagine. All of us in this room can see that you two make each other so happy and it's really an honor to be able to take part in your wedding."

She lifted her glass toward them and blew out a sigh of relief at the applause, as she turned the microphone off.

She managed to keep that smile on, holding on as hard as she could to the happy feeling as she went to hug Oliver and Jane.

The speech was the hard part, she reminded herself. Well – that and the dancing that was to come. She knew she wouldn't want to miss Oliver and Jane's first dance or even miss out on her siblings partaking with their respective partners.

It was the loneliness she was dreading. The thinking about Charlotte and the dances they'd never actually shared.

But she could do it, because she had to.

Step one of her plan for the night – find out where the hell Regan went. Step two, go and find more champagne. And step three, consume it all with her best friend.

Before she could put that plan into motion she stumbled over her own feet, almost rolling her ankle with her heels on, as she bumped into her dad. "God! Sorry."

After reaching out to steady her, he shoved his hands into his pockets in a way that screamed discomfort. "No need to apologize, honey, that was my fault. Just, uh, walking into your way." He scratched at the back of his neck. "I wanted to say something."

"Is something wrong?" It was hard to imagine, since everyone they really knew was already here.

"No! No." The denial was so vehement it made them both jump. "Ah, I don't want to do this the wrong way, because all of the internet websites said to not bring it up before you were ready."

"Internet websites. Dad, they're just called websi –" She sighed. "What are you talking about?"

He looked so uncharacteristically nervous it was making *her* nervous. "I don't want you to ever feel like you have to have to lie about who you are, Sutton. Not from me, not from anyone here, or anyone I associate with."

That certainly hadn't been what she'd been expecting. "What?"

"Damn. This miscommunication is one of the things the pamphlets talked about trying to avoid, but I just – I want you to know that I support you. Always." He nodded at her, decisively. "I know I'm not the best at times with showing my emotions, certainly not like your mother. But I don't want you to feel like . . . you can't bring your girlfriend to your brother's wedding as your date."

Sutton was so glad she wasn't holding onto the microphone anymore because she knew it would have slipped out of her hands in shock.

"What?"

"I know I'm not the most hip with recent technology and trends but in case it's ever been lost in translation, I'm a liberal man. And I'm sorry if you've felt like you couldn't tell me about who you are or like you had to hide your girlfriend in the hallway."

She felt dizzy with the realization of what exactly he was talking about and she had to close her eyes for a moment to gather herself. Especially when the tears pricked at them again.

"Dad, you don't have to apologize for anything."

Jack shook his head again. "No, I do. All of the pamphlets talked about parental attitudes and I didn't want to push you, either, but –"

"What pamphlets are you even talking about?"

"The ones from the groups on the internet, about how to support your child when they come out," he explained. The absurdity of it made her laugh through the tears that slipped out.

She pulled him into a hug, finding comfort in the way he gently patted at her back. "You are good at expressing your emotions. A lot better than you think. And I love you."

She drew back slowly. "I am bisexual. But I don't have a girlfriend."

He narrowed his eyes. "But –" He looked over his shoulder and then slowly back at her. "At the New Year's Eve party, with that woman? Charlotte?"

Her cheeks burned at the memory. How she'd kissed her on the balcony at midnight and it had been so worth every wanting glance.

"And the speech you gave seemed so personal."

Her stomach churned even more; she hoped to god that not everyone felt the same way. That not everyone who had listened to her could tell she was hopelessly in love with someone.

She tangled her fingers together in front of her, pressing them against the soft fabric of her dress. As if it could ward away the sinking feeling settling there. "No, we . . . we're not girlfriends."

"But, she –" He sighed in confusion and shrugged. "What do I know, I guess. But if you ever want to talk to me, I'm here."

"Thanks, dad."

Her father reached out to squeeze lightly at her arm, before making his way toward Oliver and Jane. Sutton stood there for another moment trying to wrap her mind around everything.

Like that her dad had assumed for the last three months that she'd been in a relationship, an actual relationship, with Charlotte Thompson. That he'd been able to tell that those moments in her speech had been drawn from her experiences with her.

What a day and it wasn't even over.

She braced her hand on Regan's shoulder as she sat at their table, still feeling a bit dazed.

With a deep breath, she turned to look at her friend, who was giving her a curious look.

"I'll tell you about it later."

She rubbed her hand over her face before she held her chin in her hand to look at her best friend. "Where were you? You've been gone for half an hour."

Regan gave her a guileless smile. "I was back just in time to hear your speech. My little writer."

"Shut up."

"No, seriously, though. It was really good. Makes me know I'm doing the right thing by being willing to live with *Emma* for half a year while you go off to Rome to feed your creative soul."

She rolled her eyes even as she couldn't help but grin. "You really are the best friend I've could ask for, you know."

"I know." Regan winked. "But it's not like I would be such a good friend for just anyone. Only you." Her teasing smile faded into a genuine one. "You're my best friend, Sutton. You know when I can be pushy or when I give you crap, I do really just want you to be happy."

Wondering where the hell this came from, she nodded. "I know that."

Regan quirked her lips to the side as she reached for her purse. "Like. I want you to be happy so much that I'm going to move in with Emma, who already sent me an email about 'guidelines' for living together."

She snorted. "Yes, you're a saint."

"I know it. Just know that I want you to have every chance you can at having whatever happiness you want."

"Okay . . . cryptic, much?"

Instead of elaborating, Regan pulled out her phone from her purse and put it on the –

Wait.

"That's *my* phone!" She snatched it, indignantly. "When did you even take my phone, thief?"

"When you were making your speech, obviously."

"I changed my password the last time you stole it." She cradled it against her chest.

Regan laughed, eyes glinting in mischief. "Like I don't know you well enough to guess your lock code three times over." She heaved a sigh, pushing herself up as she reached out to tap her finger against Sutton's screen. "Don't forget. I'm the best friend you'll ever have."

"I said the best friend I could ask for!" She scowled at her back before looking down at her phone. "Clearly, I could have asked for better," she murmured as she unlocked it.

God only knew what Regan was getting up to.

Her forehead wrinkled in confusion as she searched. Everything seemed the same as . . . oh.

The very sight of the SapphicSpark logo made her nauseous and she stared down at it before whipping her head up to try to find Regan again.

Because just – *how dare she*?

After everything that had happened? After the last month that she'd spent seeing how absolutely broken up Sutton was over Charlotte?

She only realized how tight the grip she had on her phone was when it vibrated in her hand.

It took her a conscious moment to *relax*, gritting her teeth and then untensing her shoulders, before she unlocked her phone.

Then very nearly dropped it.

Charlotte has sent you a message!

For a few moments, the music playing completely disappeared and everything just centered on her phone as her stomach bottomed out.

Her hand shook as she tapped on the notification, nerves alight, because – what?

Charlotte, 28, Boston
Likes: beautiful redheads who believe in second chances

Her phone slipped from her hand and into her lap as she stared. The picture was certainly Charlotte. And it wasn't even the one she'd used in the past, the first time she'd seen her on here.

It was the two of them. The one that had made the front page from the night of Charlotte's grandmother's party. The one where Charlotte's arm was around her waist and their faces were so close. Where Charlotte in the picture was looking at Sutton with a look that seemed so adoring.

But she'd been wrong about all of the thoughts this picture had caused her to have before.

Charlotte, 6:04PM
I was wondering if you could help me. I'm looking for a very particular someone.

In a flash, she had her phone back in her hand, the other balling up so tightly in her lap, trying to hold back everything that wanted to come spilling out even as she struggled to figure out what to actually say.

Sutton, 6:06PM
I'm... so confused.

Charlotte, 6:06PM
I'm interested in a woman who looks incredibly stunning in a blue dress.

Charlotte, 6:06PM
A woman who writes tear-inducing speeches about love that she truly believes in.

Charlotte, 6:07PM
And I'm very interested in a woman who can make even the biggest nonbeliever, believe in love.

Charlotte, 6:07PM
Do you know where I can find her?

The blue dress and the speech. Her dad looking so confused that she and Charlotte weren't together and him commenting about her feeling *like she had to hide her girlfriend.*

Charlotte was here.

She stood in an instant, feeling dizzy from confusion and the wonder of it all. She looked around unable to totally calm her nerves. Damn it, why did they have to have so many people at this wedding?

There were five entrances into the large, opulent venue that had been rented for the event, but Sutton felt like she could possibly search them all in lightning speed with the energy that was buzzing through her.

She ignored the looks she got as she hurried to the open archway on the far wall, nervously biting at her lip. As she walked, she hit send on the message she'd typed out back at the table.

After all, didn't have anything else to lose.

Sutton, 6:09PM
Um, I don't know if I should respond to your message.

My lesbian guru once told me that someone who has such specific wants on their profile is someone who isn't over her ex.

With a deep breath she walked through the archway. She peered down the long hall that appeared to be empty, save for the security guard at the very end.

"Your lesbian guru was right."

Even though she'd *known* Charlotte had to be here, surprise still rushed through her.

Charlotte pushed off from one of the pillars she'd just ran through and Sutton felt – she didn't even know what she felt.

Because Charlotte was here, right in front of her, in a green dress that draped over her body in such a beautiful, snug fit, fitted just for her. Her hair was just a bit longer than it had been the last time they'd been together in person, swept up on one side with a gold comb. Her big brown eyes seeming like they held a thousand questions and answers both.

Sutton was frozen in place, staring as her heart beat against her ribs. "What – what are you doing here?"

She just couldn't stop looking at her, like the image could be fake, as she had to swallow once, then twice, to get over the lump in her throat.

"I needed to see you." It took her a second to realize exactly how hesitant Charlotte looked. So very un-Charlotte.

"It's been a month." She had to close her eyes tightly, trying to ward off tears that wanted to escape. "A month."

A month of loneliness and crying and anger; the worst month she'd ever had and it was that thought that allowed her to tamp down any of the warmth or excitement that wanted to peek out.

"I told you I loved you." She hastily wiped away an errant tear with the back of her hand. "I told you a month ago and you didn't say anything, and you . . . why do you need to see me, now?"

597

Charlotte took another step closer, so close that Sutton could smell her light perfume. God, she'd *missed* it so much. "Because you were right."

"About what?"

"You were right," Charlotte repeated and took a step closer. A tentative step, her eyes closely watching Sutton. "We were never just friends, even when I convinced myself that we were."

She could barely breathe at the words. "But you said – " She rubbed hard at her eyes, trying to wipe away the tears and with them the confusion and the pain. "You let me go and you didn't say anything, and I thought – I thought I was wrong."

It was everything she'd thought and everything she'd wanted to hear weeks ago. She'd spent so much time telling herself that she had been dumb to say it, even more upset with herself for thinking it was true.

Charlotte shook her head, so firmly her hair swung over her shoulder, her face setting into a determined look. One that Sutton recognized only from times where Charlotte was practicing for a debate or talking about her career; it was so familiar it made her ache.

She loved that look.

"Sutton, I . . ." She took a deep breath, gaze falling to the floor. "From the very beginning, you were so refreshing. This whole world I'm in," she lifted her hands and gestured in a circle, before she pressed her fingertips together in front of her. "Is full of people who play games and lie and omit the truth and manipulate – and I'm a part of all of it, too. Then there's you. And you're so refreshing and honest and genuine, and I was so drawn to that." Her eyes snapped back to Sutton's, captivating her. "To you."

Her heart was beating so hard, she felt like it might just beat out of her chest. She was at a loss for words as her eyes searched Charlotte's, seeing nothing but honesty.

It couldn't be this easy, not after everything. Right? "But what are you doing *here*? What about the election? Your career?"

598

Sutton couldn't help but look around. No one was in the hall except security guards down at the entrances. But any one of the hundreds of people – of the politicians – merely feet away, could step out. Could see Charlotte, could hear them, and she lowered her voice, "Aren't you worried?"

Charlotte's throat bobbed with how hard she swallowed, her bottom lip trembling for a moment before she pursed them.

"I'm terrified," she confessed, looking more vulnerable than Sutton had ever seen her.

Regardless of the last month, despite the pain – despite everything – she wanted so badly to reach out to her. This lack of any mask made her itch to want to be there for her.

Before she could decide if she should take a step forward, Charlotte made her freeze. "Besides, they'll all know tomorrow, anyway."

"What?"

"I . . ." She trailed off, her jaw working against itself.

Charlotte broke their eye contact and looked down. She pulled her phone from her clutch and unlocked it, handing it to Sutton. Their fingertips brushed as she took it and for a moment her whole world lurched.

Then Charlotte's hand fell away from hers. Looking both defiant and scared, she gestured for Sutton to look at her phone.

From: M.Diop@nytimes.com
To: Charlotte_thompson@gmail.com
Subject: Interview – Advanced Copy
Date: March 26, 7:02AM

Charlotte – I figured you'd want to see this before it hits the literal and digital shelves tomorrow. Thank you for trusting me with this; I did my best to frame your courage and honesty in the admirable light you deserve for this step.

We both know something like this could kill your career. For what it's worth, I very much hope it doesn't.

She peered back up at Charlotte, stomach knotting in anticipation.

Because this seemed like . . . but there was no way. . .

Charlotte rocked back on her heels. "I've spent my entire adolescent and adult life with these goals and plans. And I want them, I do. I want to climb the ladder," there was a fire in her voice. "But I think I spent so much time focusing on what my grandmother did, paving the way for women as a whole, that I didn't ever think about what I should be doing. For people like me and you."

Charlotte Thompson, leading candidate in the House of Representatives election, gets candid in this personal and bold interview with Imani Diop.

"No," Sutton heard herself whisper as her stomach dipped.

She quickly scrolled down, until she landed on the text near the end – highlighted, bolded, enlarged to stand out in the article:

I'm a lesbian.

This was more shocking than anything else. More shocking than Charlotte being here, more than . . . god, Sutton felt like her breath was knocked out of her. "Charlotte."

"I want my career," Charlotte repeated, her voice firm but edging into a peculiar tone. The one that someone else wouldn't recognize, but Sutton knew that it only sounded so firm because Charlotte didn't want it to tremble. "But I don't want to lose who I am doing it. And it took losing you for me to see that."

Despite the month of pain between them, despite the fact that she'd spent that time thinking she'd been so wrong in her assertions about knowing the way Charlotte felt – she *knew* her.

And if *she* was feeling like the entire world was flipping on its axis, if *her* stomach was clenched so tightly that she could barely breathe, she couldn't even imagine what Charlotte was feeling.

Her watery eyes searched Charlotte's face. Her stunning face that was so open and nervous, as she watched Sutton.

There was no more voice in the back of her mind reminding her of what she'd been feeling and dealing with for the last month. She couldn't hear it, not when everything else seemed to slide into place, and more than anything else she needed . . .

She took the final two steps that she'd been edging on taking, both unable and unwilling to not bridge the gap between them. They'd had enough distance.

Her arms wrapped tightly, securely, around Charlotte.

Who was already stepping into her embrace as Sutton's arms wrapped around her waist. She felt her warmth and the softness of her cheek rubbing against her own as Charlotte's arms wrapped around her and held.

She knew she was right to do it, not just because she needed it. But because Charlotte melted into her.

She could feel it in an instant, the way Charlotte took in a deep breath against her and the tension that was so tightly coiled in her leaked away. The tears she'd blinked back so many times returned and she couldn't stop them now from falling.

It was so much. It was all so much with Charlotte in her arms solid and warm, pressing so close as if she couldn't be close enough.

Sutton held tighter when she realized that the rough breathing coming from Charlotte was crying, as she felt hot tears land on her collarbone.

"I can't believe you did that," she murmured, rubbing her hands up and down Charlotte's back. "You are so brave."

So maybe she could believe it. Because Charlotte was extraordinary and she'd always known it. But somehow, someway, she managed to surprise her.

A laugh puffed against her throat before Charlotte took a shuddering breath. "I can't believe I did it, either." Her breath caught as she pulled back, her hands landing on Sutton's waist in a tentative hold. As if she was expecting Sutton to want to pull away. "I'm sorry, Sutton. For everything."

Sutton shook her head but Charlotte continued anyway.

"Please believe that I didn't mean to out you in the article. I wasn't thinking, for once in my life, and I would take that part back if I could." Sincerity was etched into her features, as those doe eyes stared into her own. "I came here to tell you one very particular thing, but even if you don't want to hear that," she hesitated, and Sutton felt her fingers toy with the fabric of her dress before she caught herself. "I had to tell you in person about the article. About my talking about you in it."

Sutton had completely overlooked that aspect and it took her one jarring moment to realize that when the article hit tomorrow not only would Charlotte be outing herself, but that Sutton was mentioned as more than a friend.

"I don't care."

The words left her before she could deliberate over them but as soon as it happened, she realized it was true.

Charlotte quirked an eyebrow in a disbelieving look. "Sutton, please. We've spent much of . . . this not talking in whole truths about our feelings. If you're upset I need you to tell me."

"I don't care," she repeated, firmly. "My family, they all know. And so do my friends. Everyone who matters to me knows. And nothing matters more than this."

The hands on her waist flexed before Charlotte lifted one to her jaw. She couldn't help but close her eyes at the touch, living for the way Charlotte's hands felt on her skin. At the familiar way she cupped Sutton's jaw, like there had been no time since she'd done it at all.

The anticipation inside of her made time feel slower, her heart starting to pound again, as Charlotte leaned in closer.

Her breath washed over Sutton's jaw and her lips tingled as her eyes slid shut. Her hands that had both come to rest over Charlotte's shoulders slid into her hair, tangling into the soft strands as everything inside of her was pushed to the precipice.

Charlotte turned Sutton's head slightly and she brushed her lips against her cheek. Just the slightest contact, soft and warm, pressing in the gentlest kiss.

"What –" her voice broke as her stomach free-fell. "What is the one thing in particular you came here to tell me?"

She needed to hear it. She needed so much to hear exactly how Charlotte felt about her.

"You were right," Charlotte repeated, her voice falling into a whisper. She stayed exactly where she was, with her lips brushing Sutton's cheek. For a dizzying moment, she was thrown back to *months* ago, when she'd first realized that she'd had a crush on Charlotte. The first time she'd kissed her cheek as if it was the smoothest thing to do.

This moment felt like that, only a thousand times more nerve-wracking. Like she had everything on the line.

Charlotte pressed her forehead against Sutton's temple. "A month ago, you said that I was just too scared. And you were right. I'm so many things, Sutton. And many of them are not quite so simple to love, I imagine. But *you* are."

Sutton felt like her heart was going to give out with how hard it was beating. She let out a shuddering breath, waiting to hear the words.

"But I'm here because I would rather be terrified and openly myself and," she drew in a sharp breath, giving Sutton goosebumps. "And with you, than closeted and feeling like I'm hiding myself away."

She pulled back a bit, using the hand still holding Sutton's jaw to gently turn her face, and her eyes fluttered open. Her eyelids felt heavy, almost intoxicated, but she needed to look at Charlotte.

Who looked miraculously *not* afraid, as she stroked her thumb along Sutton's jaw. "I'm in love with you, Sutton. Terrifyingly, irreversibly, life-alteringly in love with you."

She hadn't been delusional. She hadn't imagined all of the times Charlotte touched her and held her like she was precious.

"I very much hope I'm not too late." Uncertainty clipped into her tone. "Because I know how much I hurt you and a month went by that must have been agonizing. And you deserve everything you want, Sutton. More than anyone else I've ever met, *you* deserve all of the goodness in the world." Sutton could feel the slightest way the hands shook. "I don't want to miss my opportunity to be with you."

It was almost laughable, really.

The idea that Sutton was *over* her. That this – all of this – wasn't out of her wildest, most unbelievable dreams.

She couldn't help but laugh with the thought as she shook her head. "How – how could I be over you?"

Brilliant and ambitious and caring and strong and soft Charlotte Thompson who was going to rule the world, was *in love with her.*

"You aren't the easiest person to get over," she confessed as if it were a secret.

Charlotte's smile was devastating. That beautiful, enthralling energy in her charmingly lopsided smile. God, Sutton had missed that more than she'd realized and seeing it aimed at her felt like she was staring at the sun.

"I was hoping you'd feel that way." Charlotte's eyes fell to Sutton's mouth and she didn't know who moved first.

She only knew that Charlotte's mouth was *finally* on hers after missing it for so long and it felt like salvation. The hands she had in Charlotte's hair tightened and Charlotte released a sharp breath against her lips that had her stomach dipping.

In her late night fantasies about this, there had been so many kisses that they would share in this moment.

But nothing she'd thought about could even feel nearly as good as it felt in reality.

There was no soft build up to the kiss. Just hunger and want and need. She slid one of her hands down to Charlotte's collarbone, stroking her soft skin, just wanting to feel more of her.

Charlotte scratched her hand down her neck and she shivered. Then whimpered as Charlotte nipped lightly at her tongue and chased it with her own. Her other hand slid down Sutton's back, her movements slow and making this hunger inside of Sutton grow the farther down she went.

Sutton gripped at Charlotte's waist, walking until Charlotte's back hit the wall. She exhaled on a groan into Sutton's mouth, her nails digging into the back of Sutton's neck as she pulled her even closer.

Everything she'd wanted for weeks poured into the kiss. A desperate, low moan came from the back of her throat as Charlotte stroked her tongue up the roof of her mouth, before tugging her top lip between her own.

Sutton didn't know if she'd ever been weaker in the knees as their kiss gentled. Like they were both finally on the same page and something shifted.

Charlotte's hands cupped her jaw, both of her thumbs stroking softly. As if savoring the feeling of her.

Charlotte ducked to press kiss swollen lips to both corners of Sutton's mouth. Then right at the seam of her bottom lip before the softest series of kisses to Sutton's mouth, ever so slowly lingering.

She shuddered at the touch, her voice just barely audible above their breathing, "How? How is this happening?"

Charlotte tilted her head back against the wall, her breathing just as ragged as Sutton's. Her pupils were blown and she was absolutely stunning. "It's been quite the past few days." She gently brushed Sutton's hair back over her shoulders. "After my interview on Thursday, I went to find you. To tell you – all of this. It turned out, clearly, that you weren't there."

"And Regan was." Jesus.

Charlotte gave her a wry smile. "Yes. It was . . . an interesting conversation. Regan isn't exactly my biggest fan, of course, and I know there is still a bit of understanding we have to reach between us, but – after I told her everything, she told me where you were. And as long as I promised I wouldn't hurt you, she agreed to help me with –" she gestured around them. "All of this."

"She really is the best friend I could have." Sutton was unable to stop grinning.

Charlotte's just looked at her for a long moment, eyes soft, before she quirked her eyebrow. "I knew I needed to see you before tomorrow, and I –" She rolled her eyes at herself. "I didn't want you lonely at your brother's wedding; I wanted you to have something special."

She couldn't resist leaning back in to press a kiss to Charlotte's lips. The slightest pressure, and only lingering for a few moments, before pulling back. But she could *do that now*. There were no rules.

Charlotte smiled slowly up at her. "And then, in order to make it onto the guest list and past security, Regan put me in touch with your mother."

"What? My *mom*?"

"Yes. I truly didn't know if she was even going to let me in. I, well, I'd gotten into contact with her last night but she isn't, apparently, as easily won over as Regan. So I . . ." she trailed off, rolling her eyes at herself. "I was standing outside, but she and Regan came to escort me in just in time to hear the majority of your speech."

She still couldn't believe it, her eyes searching Charlotte's. "I can't believe you convinced both my mom and Regan to help you with your plan."

They were very possibly the two staunchest protectors she could imagine.

That confident and proud smirk tugged at Charlotte's mouth. "I'm very persuasive."

"I love you."

It was all she could say in response. Because she'd never in her wildest dreams imagined Charlotte – anyone, really, but *Charlotte* – would do all of this

606

for her. She felt like she was in a dream, almost. Like that was the only way everything could fall into place so perfec–

Her internship.

The thought struck her so quickly and powerfully and she abruptly pulled back, staring at Charlotte, her stomach in knots.

"I'm, um, I got in." She ducked her head to look at the floor. "To my internship. In Rome. I got in."

Charlotte gave her a soft, accepting smile, instead of looking even remotely as stricken as Sutton felt. "I know. Both Regan and your mother told me."

Sutton shook her head. "No, but, I accepted. I'm – I'm supposed to be going to Rome in a month. Halfway around the world. For months."

Right when they'd just worked this out. Just as Charlotte had just come out and was in one of the hardest places she'd ever been in – Sutton should be there for that. She *wanted* to be there for that. For the beginning of this.

Conflicted, she pressed her hand to her stomach. "It's probably not too late to cancel it."

"No," Charlotte pressed, reaching out to take Sutton's hand and clasping it firmly with her own. "I'm *proud* of you. So proud." She brought her other hand up to stroke Sutton's hair behind her ear.

"There are other internships." It probably wasn't too late to find one in Manhattan and she knew Dr. Martin would still support her.

"Hey," her voice was gentle but her eyes had that firm set to them. "Do you *want* this internship at the Archives?"

"I . . . do," she admitted, because it really had been the one thing in the last month that had been truly good. Researching everything she could do and see while she was there, getting in touch with the internship coordinator and knowing that she'd been selected for a once in a lifetime opportunity; it had all been not only her biggest bright spot in the past weeks, but also genuinely *thrilling*. "But –"

But she just got Charlotte and she didn't want to give her up.

Charlotte shook her head. "I want you to go."

It felt like a small rejection in and of itself. "You do?"

"You are so much more than you give yourself credit for. You *deserve* that internship and you want it. So you'll go to Rome."

"But, you're here." And she knew that no matter what the outcome of the election was, it wasn't as though Charlotte could just come to Rome with her. "And I don't want to lose this. You." Anxiety nagged at her. "You want me to go?"

"I don't want to not be with you," Charlotte's voice was tender but honest. "Having you here and *with me* would be everything." She offered a self-deprecating smile. "And I can be selfish. But I'm not that selfish to want you to give this up."

Her fingers tightened around the ones they were tangled with. "What does that mean, for us?"

Charlotte used that hold to tug her forward again. "It means that I'll be here when you get back."

"Yeah?"

"I'll be here," she promised with utter certainty. "I've only just gotten you, Sutton Spencer; I'm letting you go, but I'm not *letting you go*."

Charlotte was in love with her. Enough to put much of the beginning of their official relationship on hold while she went to Rome.

"We'll talk about it more," Charlotte murmured, "We have a month to figure everything out. But I'm not going anywhere."

Now, she was the one to melt into Charlotte. She slid her arms around her once more, pulling her so close, and Charlotte easily moved with her.

She was at Oliver's wedding. Charlotte was in love with her and they could make it work. She was delirious with it as she slid her lips along Charlotte's. They were still sensitive from before and her stomach dipped with the feeling.

It was so heady she felt a little lightheaded as she pulled back.

608

She didn't open her eyes right away, instead she kept them resolutely closed to take in everything that had happened. They only opened when Charlotte's hands fell to her hips and gently started swaying along with the fall of music that came from inside.

She moved with her easily for a few moments, before she couldn't help but ask, "What would you have done? If I said it was too late?"

A few seconds beat by before Charlotte hummed against her ear. "I would have left. For now. But I am remarkably dedicated to achieving my goals, you know, and I plan for the long haul."

"So I would have been a goal, then? You'd have waited for me?" She let out a disbelieving laugh, and she didn't think she should be as utterly charmed by that as she was, but, here they were.

"Darling," Charlotte pulled back, a slow smile spreading over her face. "Haven't you ever heard that good things come to those who wait?"

Epilogue

Sutton wanted to marry Charlotte Thompson. She couldn't pinpoint the exact moment in the four years that they'd been together that this truth had become evident, but she didn't have a shadow of a doubt.

Maybe it was the night Charlotte had won her seat in the House of Representatives against Naomi Young. When their official relationship had still been fresh, Charlotte had still been anxious, but she'd nevertheless walked hand-in-hand with Sutton all night. When her victory had been announced, she'd turned to Sutton with the brightest grin on her face even before she'd sought out her grandmother or her brother or anyone else.

Maybe it was two years ago, when she'd so casually mentioned Sutton moving in over breakfast. When the words *well, after you move in* had been tiredly uttered without a second thought – and then she'd given her the widest-eyed look when she'd realized what she'd said.

Maybe it was last year, when Charlotte started making a habit of sneaking into the back of the courses Sutton had gotten a job as an English professor at Hunter College. She'd excused her sneaking in to witness Sutton teach with a sweet smile and the statement, "I just like seeing you in your element."

Maybe it was all of the times she'd witnessed Charlotte try to win over her mother and the fact that she never gave up. Maybe it was all of the times she'd marveled at her girlfriend's grace under pressure in the increasingly higher stakes career she was in.

She didn't know when it happened – she just knew it was a fact.

So, she'd set out to accomplish just that.

If she was going to marry the most prepared woman in the country, who always had a plan, then she had to have a perfect plan. After all, she was dating the woman who would very well become President one day. She wanted to give her a perfect proposal story.

In the last few months, while Charlotte had been in the tail end of campaigning for governor, Sutton was in the final stages of planning her proposal. It had seemed perfect. Like fate, almost:

On the night where Charlotte would win her election, they would be in her campaign office and celebrate with everyone else.

Then Sutton would take her back home, where she'd had Regan slip out of the celebration to go set up a garden – truly an indoor garden with Charlotte's favorite flowers – that lead right up to the balcony.

And on the table on the balcony, would be her favorite wine, with the open ring box.

At precisely that moment, the moment where Charlotte would see the box, Sutton had timed it all so that Alia would have gotten the go-ahead to manually send a message directly from the SapphicSpark server – as Sutton couldn't actually make a profile, not without stirring very unwanted and unnecessary rumors about their relationship status – asking, if the newly minted Governor wanted to take yet another leap forward, as Sutton's wife.

She very much wanted it to be one of the happiest nights in Charlotte's life.

Only . . . Charlotte hadn't won.

While watching it all happen on the screens set up in their office, surrounded by their friends, family, and everyone who they'd worked so hard with for months, Sutton's beautifully perfectly planned night turned into a nightmare.

Charlotte herself hadn't seemed shocked. Merely disappointed, but had conceded to her opponent with a gracious phone call. She'd turned to Sutton for a comforting hug before she'd pulled back to put on a brave face to thank everyone in the campaign office for their support and hard work.

Sutton – once the surprise wore off – realized that she hadn't planned for *that*.

A surprise proposal on the night that was very possibly one of the worst nights of her girlfriend's career was probably a terrible, awful idea. Why the hell would Charlotte want to commemorate the night she'd lost an election for the first time?

She'd had to frantically message Regan and Alia to tell them that the proposal was postponed and to get rid of every trace of it by the time they got home – receiving a message back from Regan that was just as frantic and panicked.

Regan – 10:54PM
Are you kidding me?! I just spent three
hours setting the most romantic scene
of my lifetime and now I have to ruin it!

Regan – 10:55PM
I need at least a half hour!!!!

It seemed to definitely be the right choice when, upon arriving home an hour ago, Charlotte walked out to the doors overlooking the balcony. She'd stared out at the balcony and that's when her composure crumbled.

Sutton didn't think she'd ever seen her look so forlorn and she felt helpless.

More than helpless, she felt responsible. Anxious.

She'd changed into pajama shorts and a tank top and was nervously waiting for Charlotte to emerge from the bathroom. Where she'd disappeared into forty-five minutes ago, closing the door behind her with a pinched look between her eyebrows that Sutton recognized as Charlotte trying to hold an expression back.

Which meant she was hiding it from Sutton, as she was the only one in their home.

"Fuck, this is a nightmare." She buried her head in her hands and refused to look at her phone. At the many articles she would find that would attribute Charlotte's loss in this election to her sexuality. To her openly gay relationship.

She'd be an idiot to pretend that didn't contribute to the loss, if it wasn't the entire reason. After all, she'd only lost by less than five percent of the votes and when it came just down to her politics, Charlotte was very well-received and well-respected.

It was one of her nightmares that their relationship would factor negatively into Charlotte's career. It hadn't caused any ripples for them in years, but what if after tonight . . .?

She was relieved when Charlotte emerged from their bedroom, even if she still looked more distraught than anything. If only so she could stop spiraling down this rabbit hole of what-ifs in her mind.

The ones that were causing her to second guess the entire idea of proposing at all.

She appreciatively ran her eyes over Charlotte's form. She knew her girlfriend took pride in her appearance, in being well put-together generally every time she left their home. It was true that they never knew exactly when someone would pop up to capture a picture, how far a picture would circulate. Charlotte looked so perfect, every day. With the way she styled her hair, with her skirts and dresses and blazers and tailored pants.

But she looked just as incredible just like this. Her face scrubbed free from makeup, her hair messily thrown into a bun, wearing the silky robe she favored around the house.

Charlotte crossed her arms in front of herself, walking back to the balcony doors and staring out of them. The frown on her face was so deep, Sutton ached with the pain she saw in her girlfriend's expression.

"Are you okay?" *Are you okay?* Was she an *idiot*? She grimaced at herself.

"Mm," Charlotte hummed thoughtfully, before she looked down.

Pushing herself off of the couch, she walked to stand next to Charlotte. Staring at their reflections in the balcony doors. It was only then that she noticed the rose in Charlotte's hand. The long-stemmed rose that had to have come from one of the arrangements she'd had Regan set up.

Her heart hammered as she absolutely froze, eyes glued to it. Regan must have left it after leaving the apartment in such a hurry. *Christ –*

"Do you want to get married?"

Sutton gaped.

The crinkle between Charlotte's eyebrows was back now as she stared intently at Sutton. She lifted the flower, holding it between them. "Isn't that where this came from? There's a whole arrangement in the bedroom."

"I – I don't mean… um. I'm – I mean." God, this wasn't how it was supposed to be! She was supposed to do it in a way that swept Charlotte off of her feet! "This isn't me – proposing."

Charlotte's eyes narrowed, her voice flat. "It's not?"

The blood rushed in her ears and she didn't know the last time she was so nervous talking about *anything* with Charlotte but it hadn't been in years. She brought her hands up, dragging them through her hair. "I . . ."

Swallowing hard, she thought of a handful of ways to reason away the flowers. But, really, it was too late. It was already out and all she could hear was her mind yelling *please! Marry me! I want to be your wife!*

"I know that the election didn't go the way we'd planned, and I know that…" She had to bite her lip, hard, trying to quell the guilt and anxiety. "That it's at least partially because of me – us. I know that you're disappointed, no matter how much you insisted back at the office that you're fine. You even managed to seem pretty normal until we got home. But as soon as we got here, I could see that you aren't okay at all.

"All I know for sure is that I'll be there for every election in the future, that you aren't alone.

She stepped even closer to Charlotte, sliding her hand down to hold her girlfriend's empty one. "I'll be by your side every single day and I'll try even harder. I'll make everyone, the public, love me, too. You losing an election, it'll never be because of me, again. I won't let it."

It was such an odd sensation, because this wasn't a secret; ever since truly being *together*, they'd never hit even a rough patch where breaking up was an option. It all felt simultaneously like none of this should be scary, because they were – them. They were Sutton and Charlotte, and she couldn't even imagine what could possibly drive them apart, but still this seemed overwhelmingly large.

"I never knew love was like this, until you. I didn't know everything I wanted as a little girl with my head in the clouds was real, until you. There's no one like you in all of the world, Charlotte Thompson, and I know that for a fact," the conviction – the truth – in her words seemed to burn her throat. "You're a force of nature, and who you are amazes me every day. And I just want to spend the rest of my life with you, supporting you and loving you."

She pressed her hand to her stomach, standing only inches from Charlotte before she slowly looked into her eyes.

Charlotte was still so *quiet*, though.

"And – and you deserve so much more than this." She looked around them, shaking her head with a watery laugh. "Than my asking you for the biggest commitment ever, asking you to spend your life with me even though I know there's so much on the line, still, for the future. This isn't how I intended for this to go –"

"I know," Charlotte interrupted, her hand squeezing Sutton's. "I know exactly how you intended this to go."

"No, you . . . you did?"

"Darling," her voice was so warm. "You sent the entire schematic, including a map of our apartment, to Regan, on one of the computers at the campaign office. The flower arrangements, the wine, your speech."

Amusement sparking in her eyes.

Sutton wanted to slap herself. "You knew?"

Charlotte's trademark half-grin fell, her expression growing a bit sheepish. "I did." Her eyes tightly closed. "I knew it was coming tonight. And it scared me," she whispered. "The idea of marriage, scared me. I have no intentions of not being with you, but I know you've wanted to get married. And I've been putting off thinking about it. Talking about it."

"Oh." In that moment, everything went numb. Her proposal *scared* Charlotte? "You didn't say anything."

"I didn't know what to say." She blew out a breathless laugh before she looked down. "I didn't know what I wanted to say so I just tried to focus on the election, and then I . . . lost. Clearly. And you're right. Everything didn't hit me until we got home."

Charlotte shook her head, her hand letting Sutton's go to slide up and cup Sutton's jaw. "But you're wrong in thinking it's about the election. I knew from the beginning that an election now was going to be improbable; I'm not even thirty-five, and no matter what my high approval is right now, I am a lesbian. In a public and deeply, passionate love affair with a beautiful woman." Her smile was sharp and teasing. "This election was good experience and publicity. And when I run for Senator in two years, I'll be more prepared."

Charlotte's eyebrows drew together in a clear sign of confusion as she slowly shook her head.

"Of course I was disappointed with the loss, but it was palatable. I'd already accepted it, even before tonight. I – I was upset because you didn't propose. It didn't even hit me until we were walking through the door. That I had *butterflies*. That the election wasn't the biggest thing to happen tonight."

Charlotte slowly dropped her hands to her sides, as her gaze searching Sutton's in question. "But nothing was here. No flowers, no message, no ring. And I realized when I stared out at the empty balcony that I was nervous but it was because I *wanted* it."

"You wanted me to propose?" She could hear the surprise in her own voice but after hearing that the prospect apparently had *scared* Charlotte, she'd expected the worst.

"I did. I do," the disbelief in Charlotte's own tone was clear, but her lips quirked into a smile before she laughed. She dragged her hands through her hair. "You push me, Sutton, in ways that no one else ever could. You push my boundaries in all of your beautiful, gentle ways without even trying to, and my ideas of what I thought I wanted, and I . . ."

She broke off, pausing even as her words were gaining momentum that had Sutton holding her breath.

"I want to marry you, Sutton Spencer," she admitted. "Winning or losing an election doesn't mean anything if you aren't by my side for it."

Her arms wrapped around Charlotte's waist, quick and hard enough that she knew she'd tugged Charlotte right to her tiptoes and then some above the ground. But it didn't matter when Charlotte's arms banded around her just as tightly with a laugh.

"You want to marry me," she murmured into the crook of Charlotte's neck.

"I've been so *off* tonight because I realized when the proposal didn't happen that I wanted it so much," Charlotte whispered back, raw honesty in her voice.

"I didn't, because I just – I wanted you to be happy, and I . . ." She couldn't even find the words but for once didn't feel like they mattered.

She pressed her mouth to Charlotte's neck, pausing there before she lifted her head, sliding her hands to Charlotte's back to support her more fully against her. She pressed a light, soft kiss against the corner of her girlfriend – fiancée's? – mouth, right where her gorgeous smirk would quirk typically.

Her mind was still reeling, she leaned into the touch as Charlotte's fingers stroked through her hair. As she realized –

The *ring*.

The intricately delicate yet ornate rose gold, diamond studded engagement ring that she'd searched to find for *months*, that was both ostentatious but

617

elegant in a way that she knew Charlotte would love, that was nestled safely in the pocket of her suitcase.

The image of it in her mind made her pull back with a gasp. "I need to – I have the ring I bought for you in the bedroom, I need to go get it."

Charlotte's hold on her tightened as she pressed her forehead to Sutton's. "It can wait."

Sutton didn't need that much convincing because she didn't want to relinquish her hold on Charlotte in the least.

Besides, the grin on Charlotte's face turned sharp and nearly made Sutton's knees weak. "It'll wait until the moment you bring me to bed, that is. I want your ring on my finger." She leaned in, her lips pressing a kiss just under Sutton's ear. "And you'll have to wait for the one I have for you until tomorrow. It's in my work desk."

"You got me one, too?"

"I think, even though I was nervous, I always knew it would be a yes," Charlotte held her gaze as the words sunk right into Sutton's heart. Her eyes glinted. "Isn't that always the case with you?"

She could only smile in response.

Charlotte's smirk was wide, and already turning into an adorable smile, as she lifted up the rose between them. "Accept this, in lieu of my ring for now."

"*You* keep it. I got them for you. Because I'm asking you. I *asked* you," she amended.

Charlotte shook her head as she teased, "Did you? I distinctly remember you saying your initial question wasn't a proposal . . ."

She leaned back just a bit, the smile fading a bit but still tugging at her mouth. "Charlotte Thompson, will you marry me?"

The smile on her face was both playful and so sincerely happy in a way that she didn't think anyone but Charlotte could accomplish. "Try to stop me."

∗∗∗

If you enjoyed this journey with Sutton and Charlotte, don't forget to read the continuation of their journey in the sequel novella *Forever and A Day*.

Forever and A Day excerpt:

||*Huffpost*||
Feature: How Charlotte Thompson is Becoming the New Face of Politics
March 22, 2020

Thompson nabbed the House of Representatives seat vacated eight months ago by the late John Kelvin in a close race last Tuesday. After leading Naomi Young in polls by at least twenty percent for the duration of the election, Thompson's lead fell to less than ten percent as she came out as a lesbian only ten days prior.

Thompson, 28, is now the youngest openly gay member of Congress and she's here to make a mark.

When questioned about her opponent, Naomi Young, Thompson spoke candidly.

"I haven't gotten into this life to mince words, like many of my peers have. Naomi Young made a point to threaten revealing my sexuality throughout this election. People like that have no business working in the government, where they would continue to work in the favor of oppression. I am a lesbian. And I'm not ashamed. And I'm going to fight for what's right as long as I'm in a position to do so."

Part 1

Since coming out as a lesbian so early in her career had never been *the plan*, Charlotte hadn't really known much of what to expect. Ever since the interview came out six months ago, she'd been on a learning curve.

Luckily, she'd always been a fast learner.

The fact that she'd still beat Naomi – even with her polling numbers taking a disheartening but unsurprising dip – had been shocking and elating, and it allowed her enough breathing room to have hope that she still could have her future intact.

One of the biggest changes was the publicity.

Going from a relatively faceless rising name in the New York City's Mayoral office to the House of Representatives would have been a decent shift into the public light no matter what. But since she'd done it while being an out lesbian, her media exposure was easily triple what most others experienced.

It wasn't as though paparazzi were chasing her through the streets – thankfully – but the publicity was extreme. Her face and name remained on news headlines longer than was typical, she was featured in handfuls gossip magazines even, but she'd done her best to take that in stride.

At the end of the day, she'd achieved what she'd set out to do. Doing more interviews and photoshoots and getting her name out there more wasn't necessarily a bad thing.

She just had to make the best of it.

The backlash, with her dropping polling numbers and the critical pieces that cropped up against her, were . . . unpleasant. To say the least. Anxiety-inducing to say the most, but she didn't let herself get that far. At times she couldn't quite let it all go as easily as she wished she could, but at the very least it was all entirely predictable.

She'd expected a backlash.

Opposite of that, however, had been the positive side that she hadn't quite ever let herself consider. The new allies and connections she'd gotten in her own world, and especially the people who'd reached out to her and used words like inspiring, powerful, moving. The people who'd thanked her for being the next step forward. The people who, in their words, she represented.

The influx of followers on all of her social medias alone was – overwhelmingly supportive. Almost alarmingly so.

She tried to not delve into those, either.

All in all, though, she didn't regret it. How could she? No, it wasn't her plan, but plans sometimes had to change.

The last six months had been an adjustment. A nerve-wracking, relatively public adjustment that at first had been terrifying but luckily Charlotte had always managed to be adaptable.

And in the place of not being *adaptable* at every turn, she was able to save face.

Everything was turning out to be *okay* as the dust had finally started to settle. That alone was better than she'd ever imagined.

The biggest change of all though, was being with Sutton.

Sutton, her official girlfriend.

Sutton, who had officially been in Rome for one hundred and thirty-three days – and counting, now that she'd gotten the offer to extend her internship for the additional three months.

Never in her life had she navigated this aspect of her life. Had to navigate being in a *relationship*, let alone juggling a relationship where her girlfriend was halfway around the world.

She'd also never made use of her vacation time since she'd worked in public office. Not once in over six years had she taken more than the mandated holidays off, and yet –

"I still can't believe you're here," Sutton breathed out, her voice just a bit hoarse and lazy still. Charlotte couldn't stop herself from smiling into Sutton's back as she continued planting slow kisses across the top of her back.

"Believe it," she murmured, tossing her hair over her shoulder and looking at the clock next to the bed. "At least for the next thirty-two hours."

She sat up on her knees taking in with a just barely sated hunger all of Sutton's soft skin on display, as she lay completely naked underneath her. All of that glorious long red hair was swept to the side, mussed and tangled from the night they'd spent in bed together after Charlotte had arrived.

Her lips quirked up a bit into a smirk and she brushed her fingers over the dark spot she'd sucked into the juncture where Sutton's neck and shoulder met, loving how she could see the way Sutton shivered at it.

The utterly self-indulgent satisfied feeling that slid through her with the fact that Sutton was *her girlfriend*, that they'd made it over those initial hurdles coupled with the fact that Sutton was still so completely responsive to her touch was on the precipice of familiar and novel. She reveled in it.

"I wish it was for longer." Sutton's voice was slightly muffled as she arched her back against Charlotte's hands.

She traced her fingers along the muscles there, biting her lip at the longing in Sutton's voice, because she felt it too. The want for more time together that was only hushed with the knowledge that this distance was temporary.

"I know, believe me. I'm sorry, darling, but these few days I have off have already killed my schedule," her voice was soft and full of remorse, because she *did* wish there was more time for them right now, to be together in the same place.

She was well aware that if her job and schedule weren't the way it was, taking a few more days off to stay in Rome wouldn't be out of the question. A

622

soft pang of guilt and the stresses she still carried about the future brought her slowly exploring hands to a pause.

She shook her head to push those thoughts away. Worries about the future would be normal in any relationship, she not only assured herself but had been assured by Sutton multiple times after sharing these feelings with her. They would just have to figure things out as they came and there were some things that couldn't be mapped out. She had to be okay with that.

She bent down, sliding her hands along Sutton's sides, to press her lips against the nape of her neck. The feeling of Sutton against her, the smell of her shampoo that lingered in her hair, was enough to help calm her ever-present thoughts about the future.

There was no way she was going to waste the precious little time she had here on that. Not when they were secluded in a room with just the two of them, away from everything and everyone.

She could *feel* Sutton melt even more into the mattress, even before she shook her head. "No, it's not – Charlotte, you have so much to do, and you took time off to come here. That's . . . you're so perfect." Her tone was dreamy.

It made Charlotte grin with the rush of pride, feeling the need to live up to that tone.

"Mm, I do try. You're no slouch in the busy department, either, over here making a name for yourself, and trying to squeeze those of us back home in when you can," she teased, stroking her fingers down, just over the sides of Sutton's chest, knowing the way she would shudder lightly from it.

Sutton scoffed, even as her heart skipped a beat that Charlotte could feel it from where her lips pressed against her shoulder blade.

"I've heard – *hmm* –" She broke off in a light hum as Charlotte pushed herself back up and stroked up her spine in a light massage.

She'd arrived at Sutton's apartment from the airport just in time for Sutton to get out of her internship and she hadn't been able to stop touching her since.

623

She'd mapped just about every inch of her body at this point, she thought, as she watched her own hands slide over Sutton's shoulders.

"I've heard," Sutton started again. "From a little bird, that you've even had dinner with Regan on her late nights at the café," her voice was a mixture between giggling and utter relaxation, before she turned her head enough to look at Charlotte over her shoulder, blue eyes sparkling in mirth. "You must *really* miss me back home if you and Regan are becoming dinner buddies."

Narrowing her eyes, she scratched down her spine, enjoying the way Sutton squealed at the change of motion. She tried to focus on that instead of the embarrassment that settled low in her stomach. "Don't mock; you've left us both in quite the lurch."

She and Regan *had* caught the occasional dinner together as of late. She wouldn't yet classify them as friends, but they were headed in that direction. Probably. It wasn't something she'd sought out to do but it was happening anyway, especially in light of both of them missing Sutton.

She pursed her lips and huffed out a breath. "Besides, I figure it's better if we resolve any remaining issues now. Get that all out of the way."

Not that they had many at this point. Her mortifying breakdown and declaration of loving Sutton, post her coming out interview when Regan had ultimately offered her help to get Charlotte into the wedding six months ago, had certainly helped them overcome most of their barriers.

"Yeah?" Sutton's head, that had previously been resting on the pillow while Charlotte had settled on top of her, popped up while a tentative, hopeful tone edged in her voice.

"Yes, well, you won't be here away from us forever." She reached out to push Sutton's hair over her shoulder as it had moved with her and splayed over her back, before she rose back up to her knees in preparation to push herself back into the spot next to Sutton on the mattress.

Who made a sound in the back of her throat in protest as Charlotte moved to shift off of her and she paused. Sutton instead maneuvered and flipped onto her back, looking up at her from the pillow.

Those blue eyes were tired but bright, the smile on her lips was lazy and sated, and she reached out to take Charlotte's hands with hers, their fingers easily threading together. She settled comfortably straddling Sutton's hips, flexing her fingers in the hands holding hers, and let her eyes drift closed for a moment.

Just to feel it all. She'd needed this.

They'd had barely a month together back home before Sutton had gone away for her internship, and that month had been so incredibly hectic. It had been Charlotte's busiest month of her career so far, tying up all loose ends and starting her new responsibilities and new –impossibly longer – hours.

Not to mention the media circus that she'd been trying to sidestep as much as she could.

Sutton had to finish all of her graduate school tasks and had spent another week and a half of that time with her family. They'd both agreed to not throw this – this warm, lovely, sparkling but incredibly *new* – relationship into the public fire that had only turned from simmer to boil as Sutton had left for Rome.

She had thought, apparently wildly incorrectly – and god knew how much she hated being wildly incorrect – that Sutton doing her internship wouldn't be the worst thing with the timing of it all.

She'd thought that she'd focus on her job and by the time Sutton came back from Rome she would have it and the newfound publicity well in hand. Not that she'd *wanted* Sutton to not be there with her, but she'd figured it wouldn't be terribly difficult to put the majority of her focus on other things while they were apart. That it would be a good time to regroup and fall more into a routine.

Loathe as she was to admit it, she'd been very wrong.

Of course, they video chatted regularly – every Saturday without fail, as it was Sutton's guaranteed day off even if her schedule got shifted around, and whenever else they could fit it in. They texted every day. They *communicated*, despite the six-hour time difference and both of their busy schedules, all of the time.

Logically, things should be easier without Sutton back in New York. She should have more time to focus on work and for their relationship to not be dragged into public speculation while she was also still dealing with the fallout of coming out.

But it wasn't easier at all.

Because in spite of still talking to Sutton every day, she *missed* her. She wished she could have their coffee dates or movie nights or even just come home to her. It was almost scary, how intense this want for Sutton was.

And because of a whole jumble of those feelings, she'd found herself booking a flight to Rome for a short trip. Just to reaffirm… all of this. For her to know that everything they had was still there and real.

They'd *reaffirmed* that this was most certainly still here and real six times in the last twelve hours; her body was still tingling with it.

"Should I always plan on you chasing me whenever I go away?" Sutton spoke softly, a teasing lilt in her voice to bring Charlotte out of her thoughts. But there was also a genuine wonder there, a soft insecurity.

"I think we've well established that I'm exceptional in seeking you out," she murmured. She could hear the affection in her voice mirroring what was lacing through her veins.

It should be mortifying, really, that she felt this deep, true affirmation inside of her – yes. She *would* chase after Sutton whenever she left, while they were together. Never in her life had she thought she would be someone who would take days off of work to fly literally across the world for matters of the heart. And yet –

The way Sutton's smile widened, brightened, her eyes crinkling with sheer happiness at her answer shredded any negative feelings she could have at that truth.

Charlotte quirked her head to the side, shifting her hips a bit to rock forward onto Sutton. "Should I always plan on you calling in sick when I arrive?"

"I – you – we were up all night!" Sutton's voice fell to a hush, as it had earlier when she'd called in faking sick to her supervisor. As though someone from her internship was going to pop up from the corner of the small rented apartment to catch her faking.

Charlotte found it equal parts adorable and hilarious, and she couldn't help but laugh even as she nodded. "We were. Perhaps you should have been the responsible person here and put a stop to it."

She let go of Sutton's hands and braced her own on the pillow on either side of Sutton's head as she ducked down. Her breath caught in her throat as her bare chest pressed against Sutton's, the arousal that hadn't fully been sated stirring again as she nuzzled Sutton's jaw, and felt her catch and hold a breath.

"I," she released it on a long shudder, her nipples hard and pressing into Charlotte's chest. "I don't think you're one to talk about res-responsibility," Sutton stuttered as she rocked her hips down against her and nipped at her neck.

It was so incredibly heady, this hunger for Sutton. She was still wet for her and wanting her all over again. And the fact that she could feel Sutton's pulse scrambling against her lips as she pressed a kiss to her neck just made it feel even headier.

"On the contrary; I'm very responsible," she whispered. "Or do you not know who you're talking to?" She scratched down Sutton's side, just enough to make her arch under her as she leaned back down. She sighed as she felt Sutton's hands move to grip her thighs.

And then she squealed as she was flipped onto her back, a rush going through her as it always did when Sutton surprised her in bed. Especially when Sutton surprised her and slid her hands down to Charlotte's wrists to hold them to the bed, with *that* glint in her eye.

"I know just who you are, Congresswoman Thompson," she whispered as she leaned down, stopping just a whisper before their mouths connected.

The wanting inside of her that was already so strong only got more intense as *Congresswoman Thompson* washed over her. She couldn't have stopped herself from leaning up and capturing Sutton's lips with hers even if she'd wanted to.

Sutton pressed her hips against Charlotte, grinding into her and she groaned low in her throat at the pressure, knowing Sutton could feel just how wet she was all over again.

She bit at Sutton's bottom lip, tugging it between her teeth as she brought her thighs up to wrap around Sutton's waist.

"God, I don't think you saying that will ever get old," she managed to get out, her breath already coming shorter as she rolled her hips up against Sutton.

She didn't think most things Sutton made her feel would ever get old and that alone was still a new, incredible feeling. It made something inside of her twist and dip low in her stomach, her heart skip a beat, and it was unfamiliar but *good*.

"We should probably make the most of that while you're here, then," Sutton panted into her mouth, her warm breath washing over Charlotte's jaw as she scratched her fingers lightly down Charlotte's sides, goosebumps popping up in their wake.

As Sutton's teeth nipped at the side of her breast, she groaned. "We definitely should."

One of her hands fisted into Sutton's hair as she continued her descent down her body; god, they had so much to take advantage of.

***

Other Books by Haley Cass:

When You Least Expect It

Caroline Parker knows three things to be true. First, she is going to be Boston's most sought after divorce attorney by thirty-five. Second, given how terrible her romantic track record is, falling in love isn't in the cards for her. And third, Christmas only brings her bad luck - being broken up with not once, not twice, but three times during the holidays is proof enough of that.

When she runs into Hannah Dalton on Christmas Eve, she has no reason to believe her luck will change. After all, though Hannah is probably the most gorgeous woman she's ever seen, she's also straight. And married to Caroline's work rival.

While being hired by Hannah throws her for a loop, winning a divorce case and sticking it to her ex-colleague should be enough of a thrill. But as the months slip by, bringing her closer to both Hannah and her adorable daughter Abbie, the lines between attorney and client begin to blur. And she could have never predicted just how much she wants them to.

In the Long Run

Free-spirited and easygoing Taylor Vandenberg left her hometown of Faircombe, Tennessee as soon as she could, and in the twenty-five years since, she has rarely looked back. She wouldn't change anything about how her life has turned out – having traveled to nearly every country, never staying anywhere long enough to feel stifled. Very few things can hold her attention back in Faircombe: her sister/best friend, her precocious niece, and perhaps the prospect of riling up Brooke Watson.

Brooke has known Taylor for her entire life, given that her best friend is Taylor's younger brother. And a lifelong knowledge of Taylor means that Brooke knows she's trouble: irresponsible, takes nothing seriously, and is irritatingly attractive. Unlike Taylor, Brooke loves their town so much that she's spent her adult life dedicated to making sure it doesn't get swept away like many of the other declining small cities of the American South. Faircombe means the world to her, and she's willing to do just about anything to make sure it flourishes.

Even if it means working with Taylor, whose path seems to continuously be crossing with Brooke's everywhere she turns...

Down to A Science

Ellie Beckett's life is simple and uncomplicated; she's on track to become a leading expert in biomedical engineering, she has a pub where she feels comfortable enough to hang out multiple times a week, and, so what if she doesn't have time for... people? She doesn't need or want them.

Until she meets Mia Sharpe.
As it turns out, maybe Ellie does want at least one person.

About the Author

Haley lives in Massachusetts, where she has a love/hate relationship with the weather extremities but would also hate to live somewhere without fall foliage. She spends most of her time watching too much television and thinking about the future. Oh, and writing.

Her mother likes to talk about the time she wrote her first story while sitting under the kitchen table for privacy. Twenty years later, she still likes to write but is slightly too tall to sit under the kitchen table.

Made in the USA
Middletown, DE
27 November 2024

65550441R10373